The Strange Case of Dr. Jekyll and Mr. Hyde

The Strange Case of
Dr. Jekyll and Mr. Hyde

by Robert Louis Stevenson
illustrations by François Place

Viking

Contents

Robert Lewis Balfour Stevenson was born in Edinburgh on November 13, 1850 and spent much of his childhood in 17 Heriot Row in Old Town Edinburgh (he later changed the spelling of his name to "Louis," perhaps because he considered it more exotic). He wrote *The Strange Case of Dr. Jekyll and Mr. Hyde* in 1885 while bedridden in the house of Skerryvore in Bournemouth on the south coast of England, which his father had recently given to his wife, Fanny Osborne. Like many of his stories, the work developed from a nightmare. Fanny woke him one night from a troubled sleep and he reproached her: "Why did you wake me? I was dreaming a fine bogey tale." Three scenes from his dream appear in the novel, which he wrote at top speed: "the scene at the window and the scene, afterward split in two, in which Hyde . . . took the powder and underwent the change in the presence of his pursuers." The first version he wrote was a straight adventure story. When his wife criticized it for not realizing the story's allegorical potential, he burned the manuscript in fury, but then wrote a new version in only a few days. *The Strange Case of Dr. Jekyll and Mr. Hyde* came out in January 1886 and was an instant success, with 40,000 copies sold in England in the first six months. It also met with great success in the United States, where it was often reproduced without permission. Although Stevenson had written several books before, *Dr. Jekyll and*

Stevenson and his mother in 1854. The medallion portrait is of his wife, Fanny Osborne.

Stevenson around 1885.

17 Heriot Row, Edinburgh, (left), and Skerryvore (right).

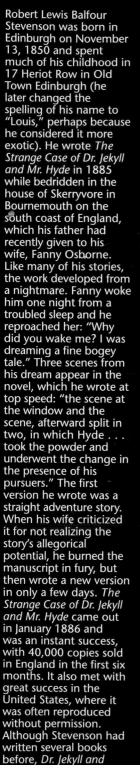

The execution of Deacon Brodie.

PUNCH'S ALMANACK FOR 1886.

The American writer Edgar Allan Poe.

Mr. Hyde established his reputation as an author. The novel's theme—the duality of personality and one man's struggle with good and evil—is drawn from several sources. Shortly before it was written, Stevenson had collaborated with W. E. Henley on a play entitled *Deacon Brodie*, based on the true story of William Brodie, a prominent Edinburgh businessman who led a double life as a burglar. Brodie's story had fascinated Stevenson since he was a child, and the play was based on an earlier version written in his teens. Stevenson's dark, melodramatic tone was strongly influenced by the American writer Edgar Allan Poe, who explored a similar theme in his short story "William Wilson." Stevenson's realistic description of a certain segment of Victorian society undoubtedly contributed to the book's lasting popularity. It has the brilliant narrative structure and suspense of a police thriller. It was written at a time when a fascination with psychology and the subconscious was blossoming. Although the book fell out of favor for many years after Stevenson's death, its theme remains timeless, and its multiple layers of meaning guarantee its enduring success. Only a few weeks after the novel's publication, a parody appeared in the satirical magazine *Punch*, showing how widely popular it had already become.

I

STORY OF THE DOOR

Mr. Utterson the lawyer was a man of a rugged countenance that was never lighted by a smile; cold, scanty and embarrassed in discourse; backward in sentiment; lean, long, dusty, dreary and yet somehow lovable. At friendly meetings, and when the wine was to his taste, something eminently human beaconed from his eye; something indeed which never found its way into his talk, but which spoke not only in these silent symbols of the after-dinner face, but more often and loudly in the acts of his life. He was austere with himself; drank gin when he was alone, to mortify a taste for vintages; and though he enjoyed the theater, had not crossed the doors of

66 Mr. Utterson the lawyer was a man of a rugged countenance that was never lighted by a smile.**99**

John O'Connor's 1881 painting of Saint Pancras Station and the London Town Hall evokes the haunted, hazy atmosphere of Stevenson's novel.

one for twenty years. But he had an approved tolerance for others; sometimes wondering, almost with envy, at the high pressure of spirits involved in their misdeeds; and in any extremity inclined to help rather than to reprove. "I incline to Cain's heresy," he used to say quaintly: "I let my brother go to the devil in his own way." In this character it was frequently his fortune to be the last reputable acquaintance and the last good influence in the lives of down-going men. And to such as these, so long as they came about his chambers, he never marked a shade of change in his demeanour.

No doubt the feat was easy to Mr. Utterson; for he was undemonstrative at the best, and even his friendships seemed to be founded in a similar catholicity of good-nature. It is the mark of a modest man to accept his friendly circle ready-made from the hands of opportunity; and that was the lawyer's way. His friends were those of his own blood, or those whom he had known the longest; his affections, like ivy, were the growth of time, they implied no aptness in the object. Hence, no doubt the bond that united him to Mr. Richard Enfield, his distant kinsman, the well-known man about town. It was a nut to crack for many, what these two could see in each other, or what subject they could find in common. It was reported by those who encountered them in their Sunday walks, that they said nothing, looked singularly dull and would hail with obvious relief the appearance of a friend. For all that, the two men put the greatest store by these excursions, counted them the chief jewel of each week, and not only set aside occasions of pleasure, but even resisted the calls of business, that they might enjoy them uninterrupted.

It chanced on one of these rambles that their way led them down a by-street in a busy quarter of London. The street was small and what is called quiet, but it drove a thriving trade on the weekdays. The inhabitants were all doing well, it seemed and all emulously hoping to do better still, and laying out the surplus of their grains in coquetry; so that the shop fronts stood along that thoroughfare with an air of invitation, like rows of smiling saleswomen. Even on Sunday, when it

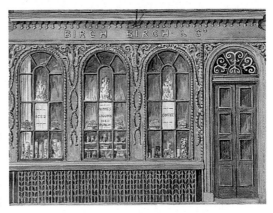

A typical London shop front near the Royal Exchange in 1871.

veiled its more florid charms and lay comparatively empty of passage, the street shone out in contrast to its dingy neighbourhood, like a fire in a forest; and with its freshly painted shutters, well-polished brasses, and general cleanliness and gaiety of note, instantly caught and pleased the eye of the passenger.

Two doors from one corner, on the left hand going east the line was broken by the entry of a court; and just at that point, a certain sinister block of building thrust forward its gable on the street. It was two storeys high; showed no window, nothing but a door on the lower storey and a blind forehead of discoloured wall on the upper; and bore in every feature the marks of prolonged and sordid negligence. The door, which was equipped with neither bell nor knocker, was blistered and distained. Tramps slouched into the recess and struck matches on the panels; children kept shop upon the steps; the schoolboy had tried his knife on the mouldings; and for close on a generation, no one had appeared to drive away these random visitors or to repair their ravages.

Mr. Enfield and the lawyer were on the other side of the by-street; but when they came abreast of the entry, the former lifted up his cane and pointed.

Sketch of Gough Square, London, in the late nineteenth century.

11

“Just at that point, a certain sinister block of building thrust forward its gable on the street.”

"Did you ever remark that door?" he asked; and when his companion had replied in the affirmative, "It is connected in my mind," added he, "with a very odd story."

"Indeed!" said Mr. Utterson, with a slight change of voice, "and what was that?"

"Well, it was this way," returned Mr. Enfield: "I was coming home from some place at the end of the world, about three o'clock of a black winter morning, and my way lay through a part of town where there was literally nothing to be seen but lamps. Street after street and all the folks asleep—street after street, all lighted up as if for a procession and all as empty as a church—till at last I got into that state of mind when a man listens and listens and begins to long for the sight of a policeman. All at once, I saw two figures: one a little man who was stumping along eastward at a good walk, and the other a girl of maybe eight or ten who was running as hard as she was able down a cross-street. Well, sir, the two ran into one another naturally enough at the corner; and then came the horrible part of the thing; for the man trampled calmly over the child's body and left her screaming on the ground. It sounds nothing to hear, but it was hellish to see. It wasn't like a man; it was like some damned Juggernaut. I gave a view halloa, took to my heels, collared my gentleman, and brought him back to where there was already quite a group about the screaming child. He was perfectly cool and made no resistance, but gave me one look, so ugly that it brought out the sweat on me like running. The people who had turned out were the girl's own family; and pretty soon, the doctor, for whom she had been sent, put in his appearance. Well, the child was not much the worse, more frightened, according to the Sawbones; and there

An alleyway near Golden Square, London. This engraving suggests how difficult living conditions were in the poorer London neighborhoods described in Stevenson's novel.

66 Well, the child was not much the worse, more frightened. 99

Although the novel takes place in London (above), many critics have noted that the city Stevenson describes resembles the Edinburgh of his childhood (far right). He sets some scenes in specific districts of the English capital but is vague about where many others take place. Stevenson had ambivalent feelings about Edinburgh even though it significantly influenced his book. Describing passengers leaving by train, he wrote: "Happy the passengers who shake off the dust of Edinburgh. . ."

you might have supposed would be an end to it. But there was one curious circumstance. I had taken a loathing to my gentleman at first sight. So had the child's family, which was only natural. But the doctor's case was what struck me. He was the usual cut-and-dry apothecary, of no particular age and colour, with a strong Edinburgh accent, and about as emotional as a bagpipe. Well, sir, he was like the rest of us: every time he looked at my prisoner, I saw that Sawbones turned sick and white with desire to kill him. I knew what was in his mind, just as he knew what was in mine; and killing being out of the question, we did the next best. We told the man we could and would make such a scandal out of this, as should make his name stink from one end of London to the other. If he had any friends or any credit, we undertook that he should lose them. And all the time, as we were pitching it in red hot, we were keeping the women off him as best we could, for they were as wild as harpies. I never saw a circle of such hateful faces; and there was the man in the middle, with a kind of black sneering coolness— frightened too, I could see that—but carrying it off, sir, really like Satan. 'If you choose to make capital out of this

66 I never saw a circle of such hateful faces. **99**

accident,' said he, 'I am naturally helpless. No gentleman but wishes to avoid a scene,' says he. 'Name your figure.' Well, we screwed him up to a hundred pounds for the child's family; he would have clearly liked to stick out; but there was something about the lot of us that meant mischief, and at last he struck. The next thing was to get the money; and where do you think he carried us but to that place with the door?—whipped out a key, went in, and presently came back with the matter of ten pounds in gold and a cheque for the balance on Coutts's, drawn payable to bearer and signed with a name that I can't mention, though it's one of the points of my story, but it was a name at least very well known and often printed. The figure was stiff; but the signature was good for more than that if it was only genuine. I took the liberty of pointing out

... and have heard for the last time the cry of the east wind among her chimney-tops! And yet the place establishes an interest in people's hearts; go where they will, they find no city of the same distinction; go where they will, they take a pride in their old home."

to my gentleman that the whole business looked apocryphal; and that a man does not, in real life, walk into a cellar door at four in the morning and come out with another man's cheque for close upon a hundred pounds. But he was quite easy and sneering. 'Set your mind at rest,' says he; 'I will stay with you till the banks open and cash the cheque myself.' So we all set off, the doctor, and the child's father, and our friend and myself, and passed the rest of the night in my chambers; and next day, when we had breakfasted, went in a body to the bank. I gave in the cheque myself, and said I had every reason to believe it was a forgery. Not a bit of it. The cheque was genuine."

"Tut-tut!" said Mr. Utterson.

This watercolor of the main room of Coutts Bank on the Strand was painted in 1900. Since the bank had only one branch in 1885, it was in this room that Hyde's check would have been cashed.

15

"I see you feel as I do," said Mr. Enfield. "Yes, it's a bad story. For my man was a fellow that nobody could have to do with, a really damnable man; and the person that drew the cheque is the very pink of the proprieties, celebrated too, and (what makes it worse) one of your fellows who do what they call good. Blackmail, I suppose; an honest man paying through the nose for some of the capers of his youth. Black-mail House is what I call the place with the door, in consequence. Though even that, you know, is far from explaining all," he added; and with the words fell into a vein of musing.

From this he was recalled by Mr. Utterson asking rather suddenly: "And you don't know if the drawer of the cheque lives there?"

"A likely place, isn't it?" returned Mr. Enfield. "But I happen to have noticed his address; he lives in some square or other."

"And you never asked about—the place with the door?" said Mr. Utterson.

"No, sir: I had a delicacy," was the reply. "I feel very strongly about putting questions; it partakes too much of the style of the day of judgment. You start a question, and it's like starting a stone. You sit quietly on the top of a hill; and away the stone goes, starting others; and presently some bland old bird (the last you would have thought of) is knocked on the head in his own back garden, and the family have to change their name. No sir, I make it a rule of mine: the more it looks like Queer Street, the less I ask."

"A very good rule, too," said the lawyer.

"But I have studied the place for myself," continued Mr. Enfield. "It seems scarcely a house. There is no other door, and nobody goes in or out of that one, but, once in a great while, the gentleman of my adventure. There are three windows looking on the court on the first floor; none below; the windows are always shut, but they're clean. And then there is a chimney, which is generally smoking; so somebody must live there. And yet it's not so sure; for the buildings are so packed together about the court, that it's hard to say where one ends and another begins."

The pair walked on again for a while in silence; and then— "Enfield," said Mr. Utterson, "that's a good rule of yours."

"Yes, I think it is," returned Enfield.

"But for all that," continued the lawyer, "there's one

Portraits illustrating a study of madness that was published in Stevenson's day.

More portraits of madness. Many pseudoscientific studies of the time associated physical deformities with abnormal character traits. Stevenson's description of Hyde reflects this popular notion. Hyde's appearance inspires an instinctive loathing.

point I want to ask: I want to ask the name of that man who walked over the child."

"Well," said Mr. Enfield, "I can't see what harm it would do. It was a man of the name of Hyde."

"Hm," said Mr. Utterson. "What sort of a man is he to see?"

"He is not easy to describe. There is something wrong with his appearance; something displeasing, something downright detestable. I never saw a man I so disliked, and yet I scarce know why. He must be deformed somewhere; he gives a strong feeling of deformity, although I couldn't specify the point. He's an extraordinary-looking man, and yet I really can name nothing out of the way. No, sir; I can make no hand of it; I can't describe him. And it's not want of memory; for I declare I can see him this moment."

Mr. Utterson again walked some way in silence, and obviously under a weight of consideration. "You are sure he used a key?" he inquired at last.

"My dear sir . . ." began Enfield, surprised out of himself.

"Yes, I know," said Utterson; "I know it must seem strange. The fact is, if I do not ask you the name of the other party, it is because I know it already. You see, Richard, your tale has gone home. If you have been inexact in any point you had better correct it."

"I think you might have warned me," returned the other with a touch of sullenness. "But I have been pedantically exact, as you call it. The fellow had a key; and what's more, he has it still. I saw him use it not a week ago."

Mr. Utterson sighed deeply, but said never a word; and the young man presently resumed. "Here is another lesson to say nothing," said he. "I am ashamed of my long tongue. Let us make a bargain never to refer to this again."

"With all my heart," said the lawyer. "I shake hands on that, Richard."

II

SEARCH FOR MR. HYDE

That evening Mr. Utterson came home to his bachelor house in sombre spirits and sat down to dinner without relish. It was his custom of a Sunday, when this meal was over, to sit close by the fire, a volume of some dry divinity on his reading-desk, until the clock of the neighbouring church rang out the hour of twelve, when he would go soberly and gratefully to bed. On this night, however, as soon as the cloth was taken away, he took up a candle and went into his business room. There he opened his safe, took from the most private part of it a document endorsed on the envelope as Dr. Jekyll's Will and sat down with a clouded brow to study its contents. The will was holograph; for Mr. Utterson, though he took charge of it now that it was made, had refused to lend the least assistance in the making of it; it provided not only that, in case of the decease of Henry Jekyll, M.D., D.C.L., LL.D., F.R.S., &C. all his possessions were to pass into the hands of his "friend and benefactor Edward Hyde"; but that in case of Dr. Jekyll's "disappearance or unexplained absence for any period exceeding three calendar months," the said Edward Hyde should step into the said Henry Jekyll's shoes without further delay and free from any burthen or obligation beyond the

> **❝** He took up a candle and went into his business room. There he opened his safe, and took from the most private part of it a document. **❞**

Cavendish Square was constructed in the early eighteenth century for Edward Harley, the second Earl of Oxford. Many notable Londoners lived in Cavendish Square, and its development continued throughout the century. Harley Street, which bordered its west side, was the most popular address in London for fashionable doctors.

A butler stands near his master's table in this 1883 painting. The dark décor exemplifies Victorian tastes of the time.

payment of a few small sums to the members of the doctor's household. This document had long been the lawyer's eyesore. It offended him both as a lawyer and as a lover of the sane and customary sides of life, to whom the fanciful was the immodest. And hitherto it was his ignorance of Mr. Hyde that had swelled his indignation; now, by a sudden turn, it was his knowledge. It was already bad enough when the name was but a name of which he could learn no more. It was worse when it began to be clothed upon with detestable attributes; and out of the shifting, insubstantial mists that had so long baffled his eye, there leaped up the sudden, definite presentment of a fiend.

"I thought it was madness," he said, as he replaced the obnoxious paper in the safe, "and now I begin to fear it is disgrace."

With that he blew out his candle, put on a great coat, and set forth in the direction of Cavendish Square, that citadel of medicine, where his friend, the great Dr. Lanyon, had his house and received his crowding patients. "If anyone knows, it will be Lanyon," he had thought.

The solemn butler knew and welcomed him; he was subjected to no stage of delay, but ushered direct from the door to the dining-room, where Dr. Lanyon sat alone over his wine. This was a hearty, healthy, dapper, red-faced gentleman, with a shock of hair prematurely white, and a boisterous and decided manner. At sight of Mr. Utterson, he sprang up from his chair and welcomed him with both hands. The geniality, as was the way of the man, was somewhat theatrical to the eye; but it reposed on genuine feeling. For these two were old friends, old mates both at school and college, both thorough respecters of themselves and of each other, and, what does not always follow, men who thoroughly enjoyed each other's company.

After a little rambling talk, the lawyer led up to the subject which so disagreeably preoccupied his mind.

"I suppose, Lanyon," said he, "you and I must be the two oldest friends that Henry Jekyll has?"

"I wish the friends were younger," chuckled Dr. Lanyon. "But I suppose we are. And what of that? I see little of him now."

"Indeed!" said Utterson. "I thought you had a bond of common interest."

This eighteenth-century vestibule of a home in Cavendish Square is typical of a prosperous Harley Street doctor's house.

"We had," was his reply. "But it is more than ten years since Henry Jekyll became too fanciful for me. He began to go wrong, wrong in mind; and though, of course, I continue to take an interest in him for old sake's sake as they say, I see and I have seen devilish little of the man. Such unscientific balderdash," added the doctor, flushing suddenly purple, "would have estranged Damon and Pythias."

This little spirit of temper was somewhat of a relief to Mr. Utterson. "They have only differed on some point of science," he thought; and being a man of no scientific passions (except in the matter of conveyancing), he even added: "It is nothing worse than that!" He gave his friend a few seconds to recover his composure, and then approached the question he had come to put.

"Did you ever come across a *protégé* of his— one Hyde?" he asked.

"Hyde?" repeated

"Old Town Edinburgh" built in medieval times, later became known as a district of poor people and thieves.

Lanyon. "No. Never heard of him. Since my time."

That was the amount of information that the lawyer carried back with him to the great, dark bed on which he tossed to and fro until the small hours of the morning began to grow large. It was a night of little ease to his toiling mind, toiling in mere darkness and beseiged by questions.

Six o'clock struck on the bells of the church that was so conveniently near to Mr. Utterson's dwelling, and still he was digging at the problem. Hitherto it had touched him on the intellectual side alone; but now his imagination also was engaged, or rather enslaved; and as he lay and tossed in the gross darkness of the night and the curtained room, Mr. Enfield's tale went by before his mind in a scroll of lighted pictures. He would be aware of the great field of lamps of a nocturnal city; then of the figure of a man walking swiftly; then of a child running from the doctor's; and then these met, and that human Juggernaut trod the child down and passed on regardless of her screams. Or else he would see a room in a rich house, where his friend lay asleep, dreaming and smiling at his dreams; and then the door of that room would be opened, the curtains of the bed plucked apart, the sleeper recalled, and, lo! there would stand by his side a figure to whom power was given, and even at that dead hour, he must rise and do its bidding. The figure in these two phases haunted the lawyer all night; and if at any time he dozed over, it was but to see it glide more stealthily through sleeping houses, or move the more swiftly, and still the more swiftly, even to dizziness, through wider labyrinths of lamp-lighted city, and at every street corner crush a child and leave her screaming. And still the figure had no face by which he might know it; even in his dreams it had no face, or one that baffled him and melted before his eyes; and thus it was that there sprang up and grew apace in the lawyer's mind a singularly strong, almost an inordinate, curiosity to behold the features of the real Mr. Hyde. If he could but once set eyes on him, he thought the mystery would lighten and perhaps roll altogether away, as was the habit of mysterious things when well examined. He might see a reason for his friend's strange preference or bondage (call it which you please) and even for the startling clauses of the will. And at least it would be a face worth seeing: the face of a man who was without bowels of mercy: a face which had but to show itself to raise up, in the mind of the unimpressionable Enfield, a spirit of enduring hatred.

From that time forward, Mr. Utterson began to haunt the door in the by street of shops. In the morning before office hours, at noon when business was plenty and time scarce, at night under the face of the fogged city moon, by all lights and at all hours of solitude or concourse, the lawyer was to be found on his chosen post.

"If he be Mr. Hyde," he had thought, "I shall be Mr. Seek."

And at last his patience was rewarded. It was a fine dry night; frost in the air; the streets as clean as a ball-room floor; the lamps, unshaken by any wind, drawing a regular pattern of light and shadow. By ten o'clock, when the shops were closed, the by street was very solitary, and, in spite of the low growl of London from all round, very silent. Small sounds carried far; domestic sounds out of the houses were clearly audible on either side of the roadway; and the rumour of the approach of any passenger preceded him by a long time. Mr. Utterson had been some minutes at his post when he was aware of an odd light footstep drawing near. In the course of his nightly patrols he had long grown accustomed to the quaint effect with which the footfalls of a single person, while he is still a great way off, suddenly spring out distinct from the vast hum and clatter of the city. Yet his attention had never before been so sharply and decisively arrested; and it was with a strong, superstitious prevision of success that he withdrew into the entry of the court.

New Town Edinburgh, built in the eighteenth century, is a much more elegant district. The front of Dr. Jekyll's house reflects the calm refinement of New Town, whereas the sordid back entrance to the house that Hyde used evokes the decay of Old Town. The symbolism was clearly intentional on Stevenson's part.

The steps drew swiftly nearer, and swelled out suddenly louder as they turned the end of the street. The lawyer, looking forth from the entry, could soon see what manner of man he had to deal with. He was small, and very plainly dressed; and the look of him, even at that distance, went somehow strongly against the watcher's inclination. But he made straight for the door, crossing the roadway to save time; and as he came, he drew a key from his pocket like one approaching home.

Mr. Utterson stepped out and touched him on the shoulder as he passed. "Mr. Hyde, I think?"

Mr. Hyde shrank back with a hissing intake of the breath. But his fear was only momentary; and though he did not look the lawyer in the face, he answered coolly enough: "That is my name. What do you want?"

"I see you are going in," returned the lawyer. "I am an old friend of Dr. Jekyll's—Mr. Utterson of Gaunt Street—you must have heard my name; and meeting you so conveniently, I thought you might admit me."

"You will not find Dr. Jekyll; he is from home," replied Mr. Hyde, blowing in the key. And then suddenly, but still without looking up, "How did you know me?" he asked.

66 Mr. Hyde appeared to hesitate; and then, as if upon some sudden reflection, fronted about with an air of defiance. 99

Soho Square in 1812, when it was home to many aristocratic families. By the end of the nineteenth century, Soho's reputation had been sullied somewhat. Hyde's residence in this formerly respectable address reflects Jekyll's moral decline.

"On your side," said Mr. Utterson "will you do me a favour?"

"With pleasure," replied the other. "What shall it be?"

"Will you let me see your face?" asked the lawyer.

Mr. Hyde appeared to hesitate, and then, as if upon some sudden reflection, fronted about with an air of defiance; and the pair stared at each other pretty fixedly for a few seconds. "Now I shall know you again," said Mr. Utterson. "It may be useful."

"Yes," returned Mr. Hyde, "it is as well we have met; and á propos, you should have my address." And he gave a number of a street in Soho.

"Good God!" thought Mr. Utterson, "can he, too, have been thinking of the will?" But he kept his feelings to himself and only grunted in acknowledgment of the address.

"And now," said the other, "how did you know me?"

"By description," was the reply.

"Whose description?"

"We have common friends," said Mr. Utterson.

"Common friends!" echoed Mr. Hyde, a little hoarsely. "Who are they?"

"Jekyll, for instance," said the lawyer.

"He never told you," cried Mr. Hyde, with a flush of anger. "I did not think you would have lied."

"Come," said Mr. Utterson, "that is not fitting language."

The other snarled aloud into a savage laugh; and the next moment, with extraordinary quickness, he had unlocked the door and disappeared into the house.

The lawyer stood awhile when Mr. Hyde had left him, the picture of disquietude. Then he began slowly to mount the street, pausing every step or two, and putting his hand to his brow like a man in mental perplexity. The problem he was thus debating as he walked was one of a class that is rarely solved. Mr. Hyde was pale and dwarfish; he gave an impression of deformity without any nameable malformation, he had a displeasing smile, he had borne himself to the lawyer with a sort of murderous mixture of timidity

The *Origin of Species*, published in 1859 by Charles Darwin (below), offered scientific evidence that humans and apes share a common ancestor. This idea created upheaval in scientific and religious circles, and was parodied in cartoons like the one above. Stevenson often ascribes simian traits to Hyde as if to underscore his primitive, unevolved nature. In calling Hyde a troglodyte, Utterson compares him to a caveman.

and boldness, and he spoke with a husky whispering and somewhat broken voice,—all these were points against him; but not all of these together could explain the hitherto unknown disgust, loathing and fear with which Mr. Utterson regarded him. "There must be something else," said the perplexed gentleman. "There *is* something more, if I could find a name for it. God bless me, the man seems hardly human! Something troglodytic, shall we say? or can it be the old story of Dr. Fell? or is it the mere radiance of a foul soul that thus transpires through, and transfigures, its clay continent? The last, I think; for, O my poor old Harry Jekyll, if ever I read Satan's signature upon a face, it is on that of your new friend!"

Round the corner from the by street there was a square of ancient, handsome houses, now for the most part decayed from their high estate and let in flats and chambers to all sorts of conditions of men: map-engravers, architects, shady lawyers and the agents of obscure enterprises. One house, however, second from the corner, was still occupied entire; and at the door of this, which wore a great air of wealth and comfort, though it was now plunged in darkness except for the fan-light, Mr. Utterson stopped and knocked. A well-dressed, elderly servant opened the door.

"Is Dr. Jekyll at home, Poole?" asked the lawyer.

"I will see, Mr. Utterson," said Poole, admitting the visitor, as he spoke, into a large, low-roofed, comfortable hall, paved with flags, warmed (after the fashion of a country house) by a bright, open fire, and furnished with costly cabinets of oak. "Will you wait here by the fire, sir? or shall I give you a light in the dining-room?"

"Here, thank you," said the lawyer; and he drew near and leaned on the tall fender. This hall, in which he was now left alone, was a pet fancy of his friend the doctor's; and Utterson himself was wont to speak of it as the pleasantest room in London. But to-night there was a shudder in his blood; the face of Hyde sat heavy on his memory; he felt (what was rare in him) a nausea and distaste of life; and in the gloom of his spirits, he seemed to read a menace in the flickering of the firelight on the polished cabinets and the uneasy starting of the shadow on the roof. He was ashamed of his relief when Poole presently returned to announce that Dr. Jekyll was gone out.

"I saw Mr. Hyde go in by the old dissecting-room door, Poole," he said. "Is that right, when Dr. Jekyll is from home?"

"Quite right, Mr. Utterson, sir," replied the servant. "Mr. Hyde has a key."

"Your master seems to repose a great deal of trust in that young man, Poole," resumed the other, musingly.

"Yes, sir, he do indeed," said Poole. "We have all orders to obey him."

"I do not think I ever met Mr. Hyde?" asked Utterson.

"O dear no, sir. He never *dines* here," replied the butler. "Indeed we see very little of him on this side of the house; he mostly comes and goes by the laboratory."

"Well, good-night, Poole."

"Good-night, Mr. Utterson."

66 'I will see, Mr. Utterson,' said Poole, admitting the visitor into a large, low-roofed, comfortable hall. 99

While Stevenson is vague about the location of Dr. Jekyll's home, he emphasizes that it is comfortable and in good taste, but located in a neighborhood in decline. His description is reminiscent of these eighteenth-century London townhouses.

The reception room of the Linley Sambourne House in Kensington has been preserved as it was in the late nineteenth century. The middle class of the time favored an elaborate décor.

And the lawyer set out homeward with a very heavy heart. "Poor Harry Jekyll," he thought, "my mind misgives me he is in deep waters! He was wild when he was young; a long while ago, to be sure; but in the law of God there is no statute of limitations. Ah, it must be that; the ghost of some old sin, the cancer of some concealed disgrace; punishment coming, *pede claudo*, years after memory has forgotten and self-love condoned the fault." And the lawyer, scared by the thought, brooded awhile on his own past, groping in all the corners of memory, lest by chance some Jack-in-the-Box of an old iniquity should leap to light there. His past was fairly blameless; few men could read the rolls of their life with less apprehension; yet he was humbled to the dust by the many ill things he had done, and raised up again into a sober and fearful gratitude by the many he had come so near to doing, yet avoided. And then by a return on his former subject, he conceived a spark of hope. "This Master Hyde, if he were studied," thought he, "must have secrets of his own: black secrets, by the look of him; secrets compared to which poor Jekyll's worst would be like sunshine. Things cannot continue as they are. It turns me cold to think of this creature stealing like a thief to Harry's bedside; poor Harry, what a wakening! And the danger of it! for if this Hyde suspects the existence of the will, he may grow impatient to inherit. Ay, I must put my shoulder to the wheel—if Jekyll will let me," he added, "if Jekyll will only let me." For once more he saw before his mind's eye, as clear as a transparency, the strange clauses of the will.

III

DR. JEKYLL WAS QUITE
AT EASE

A fortnight later, by excellent good fortune, the doctor gave one of his pleasant dinners to some five or six old cronies, all intelligent reputable men, and all judges of good wine; and Mr. Utterson so contrived that he remained behind after the others had departed. This was no new arrangement, but a thing that had befallen many scores of times. Where Utterson was liked, he was liked well. Hosts loved to detain the dry lawyer, when the light-hearted and the loose-tongued had already their foot on the threshold; they liked to sit awhile in

> 66 Mr. Utterson so contrived that he remained behind after the others had departed. 99

his unobtrusive company, practising for solitude, sobering their minds in the man's rich silence, after the expense and strain of gaiety. To this rule Dr. Jekyll was no exception; and as he now sat on the opposite side of the fire—a large, well-made, smooth-faced man of fifty, with something of a slyish cast perhaps, but every mark of capacity and kindness—you could see by his looks that he cherished for Mr. Utterson a sincere and warm affection.

"I have been wanting to speak to you, Jekyll," began the latter. "You know that will of yours?"

A close observer might have gathered that the topic was distasteful; but the doctor carried it off gaily.

"My poor Utterson," said he, "you are unfortunate in such a client. I never saw a man so distressed as you were by my will; unless it were that hide-bound pedant, Lanyon, at what he called my scientific heresies. O, I know he's a good fellow—you needn't frown—an excellent fellow, and I always mean to see more of him; but a hide-bound pedant for all that; an ignorant, blatant pedant. I was never more disappointed in any man than Lanyon."

> 66 As he now sat on the opposite side of the fire you could see by his looks that he cherished for Mr. Utterson a sincere and warm affection. 99

"You know I never approved of it," pursued Utterson, ruthlessly disregarding the fresh topic.

"My will? Yes, certainly, I know that," said the doctor, a trifle sharply. "You have told me so."

"Well, I tell you so again," continued the lawyer. "I have been learning something of young Hyde."

The large handsome face of Dr. Jekyll grew pale to the very lips, and there came a blackness about his eyes. "I do not care to hear more," said he. "This is a matter I thought we had agreed to drop."

"What I heard was abominable," said Utterson.

"It can make no change. You do not understand my position," returned the doctor, with a certain incoherency of manner. "I am painfully situated, Utterson; my position is a very strange—a very strange one. It is one of those affairs that cannot be mended by talking."

This engraving by R. W. Edis illustrated an 1881 publication on home décor.

"Jekyll," said Utterson, "you know me: I am a man to be trusted. Make a clean breast of this in confidence; and I make no doubt I can get you out of it."

"My good Utterson," said the doctor, "this is very good of you, this is downright good of you, and I cannot find words to thank you in. I believe you fully; I would trust you before any man alive, ay, before myself, if I could make the choice; but indeed it isn't what you fancy; it is not so bad as that; and just to put your good heart at rest, I will tell you one thing: the moment I choose, I can be rid of Mr. Hyde. I give you my hand upon that; and I thank you again and again; and I will just add one little word, Utterson, that I'm sure you'll take in good part: this is a private matter, and I beg of you to let it sleep."

A chemistry experiment is conducted in the amphitheater of the Royal Institution of Great Britain on Albemarle Street. Founded in 1799, the Royal Institution was dedicated to teaching applications of science in daily life.

Utterson reflected a little, looking in the fire.

"I have no doubt you are perfectly right," he said at last, getting to his feet.

"Well, but since we have touched upon this business, and for the last time, I hope," continued the doctor, "there is one point I should like you to understand. I have really a very great interest in poor Hyde. I know you have seen him; he told me so; and I fear he was rude. But I do sincerely take a great, a very great interest in that young man; and if I am taken away, Utterson, I wish you to promise me that you will bear with him and get his rights for him. I think you would, if you knew all; and it would be a weight off my mind if you would promise."

66 Hosts loved to detain the dry lawyer. To this rule Dr. Jekyll was no exception. 99

"I can't pretend that I shall ever like him," said the lawyer.

"I don't ask that," pleaded Jekyll, laying his hand upon the other's arm; "I only ask for justice; I only ask you to help him for my sake, when I am no longer here."

Utterson heaved an irrepressible sigh. "Well," said he, "I promise."

31

IV

THE CAREW MURDER CASE

Nearly a year later, in the month of October, 18—, London was startled by a crime of singular ferocity, and rendered all the more notable by the high position of the victim. The details were few and startling. A maid-servant living alone in a house not far from the river had gone upstairs to bed about eleven. Although a fog rolled over the city in the small hours, the early part of the night was cloudless, and the lane, which the maid's window overlooked, was brilliantly lit by the full moon. It seems she was romantically given; for she sat down upon her box, which stood immediately under the window, and fell into a dream of musing. Never (she used to say, with streaming tears, when she narrated that experience), never had she felt more at peace with all men or thought more kindly of the world. And as she so sat she became aware of an aged and beautiful gentleman with white hair drawing near along the lane; and advancing to meet him, another and very small gentleman, to whom at first she paid less attention. When they had come within speech (which was just under the maid's eyes) the older man bowed and accosted the other with a very pretty manner of politeness. It did not seem as if the subject of his address were of great importance; indeed, from his pointing, it sometimes appeared as if he were only inquiring his way; but the moon shone on his face as he spoke, and the girl was pleased to watch it, it seemed to breathe such an innocent and old-world kindness of disposition, yet with something high too, as of a well-founded self-content. Presently her eye wandered to the other, and she was surprised to recognise in him a certain Mr. Hyde, who had once visited her master and for whom she had conceived a dislike. He had in his hand a heavy cane, with which he was trifling; but he answered never a word, and seemed to listen with an ill-contained impatience. And then all of a sudden he broke out in a great flame of anger, stamping with his foot, brandishing the cane, and carrying on (as the maid described it) like a madman. The old gentleman took a step back, with the air of one very much surprised and a trifle hurt; and at that Mr. Hyde broke out of all bounds and clubbed him to the earth. And next moment, with ape-like fury, he was trampling his victim under foot, and hailing down a storm of blows, under which the bones were audibly shattered and the body jumped upon the roadway. At the horror of these sights and sounds, the maid fainted.

London maids wearing costumes typical of the end of the nineteenth century. Girls were hired as scullery maids at age thirteen or fourteen; later they might be promoted to chambermaid or cook.

It was two o'clock when she came to herself and called for the police. The murderer was gone long ago; but there lay his victim in the middle of the lane, incredibly mangled. The stick with which the deed had been done, although it was of some rare and very tough and heavy wood, had broken in the middle under the stress of this insensate cruelty; and one splintered half had rolled in the neighbouring gutter—the other, without doubt, had been carried away by the murderer. A purse and gold watch were found upon the victim; but, no cards or papers, except a sealed and stamped envelope, which he had been probably carrying to the post, and which bore the name and address of Mr. Utterson.

This was brought to the lawyer the next morning, before he

was out of bed; and he had no sooner seen it, and been told the circumstances, than he shot out a solemn lip. "I shall say nothing till I have seen the body," said he; "this may be very serious. Have the kindness to wait while I dress." And with the same grave countenance he hurried through his breakfast and drove to the police station, whither the body had been carried. As soon as he came into the cell, he nodded.

In 1829, when the London police force was founded, it was headquartered at Whitehall Place (above).

"Yes," said he, "I recognise him. I am sorry to say that this is Sir Danvers Carew."

"Good God, sir!" exclaimed the officer, "is it possible?" And the next moment his eye lighted up with professional ambition. "This will make a deal of noise," he said. "And perhaps you can help us to the man." And he briefly narrated what the maid had seen, and showed the broken stick.

Mr. Utterson had already quailed at the name of Hyde; but when the stick was laid before him, he could doubt no longer; broken and battered as it was, he recognised it for one that he had himself presented many years before to Henry Jekyll.

"Is this Mr. Hyde a person of small stature?" he inquired.

"Particularly small and particularly wicked-looking, is what the maid calls him," said the other.

Mr. Utterson reflected; and then, raising his head, "If you will come with me in my cab," he said, "I think I can take you to his house."

It was by this time about nine in the morning, and the first fog of the season. A great chocolate-coloured pall lowered over heaven, but the wind was continually charging and routing these embattled vapours; so that as the cab crawled from street to street, Mr. Utterson beheld a marvelous number of degrees and hues of twilight; for here it would be dark like the

Because the courtyard was the site of a residence owned by the kings of Scotland, the headquarters was called Scotland Yard.

The Scotland Yard station soon became overcrowded. When Stevenson was writing his novel, new headquarters for the London Metropolitan Police were under construction on the Thames Embankment. New Scotland Yard (above) was opened in 1890.

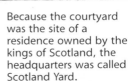

A London cab in 1884. Utterson's nightmarish cab journey through "chocolate-coloured" fog reflects Stevenson's nightmares in which he was haunted by "a certain hue of brown" that he "feared and loathed."

66 The dismal quarter of Soho seemed like a district of some city in a nightmare. 99

back-end of evening; and there would be a glow of a rich, lurid brown, like the light of some strange conflagration; and here, for a moment, the fog would be quite broken up, and a haggard shaft of daylight would glance in between the swirling wreaths. The dismal quarter of Soho seen under these changing glimpses, with its muddy ways, and slatternly passengers, and its lamps, which had never been extinguished or had been kindled afresh to combat this mournful reinvasion of darkness, seemed, in the lawyer's eyes, like a district of some city in a nightmare. The thoughts of his mind, besides, were of the gloomiest dye; and when he glanced at the companion of his drive, he was conscious of some touch of that terror of the law and the law's officers which may at times assail the most honest.

As the cab drew up before the address indicated, the fog lifted a little and showed him a dingy street, a gin palace, a low French eating-house, a shop for the retail of penny numbers and two-penny salads, many ragged children huddled in the doorways, and many women of many different nationalities passing out, key in hand, to have a morning glass; and the next moment the fog settled down again upon that part, as brown as umber, and cut him off from his blackguardly surroundings. This was the home of Henry Jekyll's favourite; of a man who was heir to a quarter of a million sterling.

An ivory-faced and silvery-haired old woman opened the door. She had an evil face, smoothed by hypocrisy; but her manners were excellent. Yes, she said, this was Mr. Hyde's, but he was not at home; he had been in that night very late, but he had gone away again in less than an hour: there was nothing strange in that; his habits were very irregular, and he was often absent; for instance, it was nearly two months since she had seen him till yesterday.

"Very well, then, we wish to see his rooms," said the lawyer; and when the woman began to declare it was impossible, "I had better tell you who this person is," he added. "This is Inspector Newcomen of Scotland Yard."

A flash of odious joy appeared upon the woman's face. "Ah!" said she, "he is in trouble! What has he done?"

Mr. Utterson and the inspector exchanged glances. "He don't seem a very popular character," observed the latter. "And now, my good woman, just let me and this gentleman have a look about us."

In the whole extent of the house, which but for the old woman remained otherwise empty, Mr. Hyde had only used a couple of rooms; but these were furnished with luxury and good taste. A closet was filled with wine; the plate was of silver, the napery elegant; a good picture hung upon the walls, a gift (as

A London bobby of the day assumes a classic pose. The nickname "bobby" for a police officer comes from Sir Robert Peel, who established the first police force in London.

The atmosphere of *Dr. Jekyll and Mr. Hyde* is all the more disturbing because most of the major scenes occur at night. The Victorian painter Atkinson Grimshaw specialized in nocturnal scenes of London. In this 1880 scene of a quay on the Thames near Parliament, he offers a more tranquil view of nighttime London than Stevenson's.

Utterson supposed) from Henry Jekyll, who was much of a connoisseur; and the carpets were of many plies and agreeable in colour. At this moment, however, the rooms bore every mark of having been recently and hurriedly ransacked; clothes lay about the floor, with their pockets inside out; lockfast drawers stood open; and on the hearth there lay a pile of grey ashes, as though many papers had been burned. From these embers the inspector disinterred the butt end of a green cheque book, which had resisted the action of the fire; the other half of the stick was found behind the door; and as this clinched his suspicions, the officer declared himself delighted. A visit to the bank, where several thousand pounds were found to be lying to the murderer's credit, completed his gratification.

"You may depend upon it, sir," he told Mr. Utterson: "I have him in my hand. He must have lost his head, or he never would have left the stick or, above all, burned the cheque book. Why, money's life to the man. We have nothing to do but wait for him at the bank, and get out the handbills."

This last, however, was not so easy of accomplishment; for Mr. Hyde had numbered few familiars—even the master of the servant-maid had only seen him twice; his family could nowhere be traced; he had never been photographed; and the few who could describe him differed widely, as common observers will. Only on one point were they agreed; and that was the haunting sense of unexpressed deformity with which the fugitive impressed his beholders.

66 Just let me and this gentleman have a look about us. 99

vineyards was ready to be set free and to disperse the fogs of London. Insensibly the lawyer melted. There was no man from whom he kept fewer secrets than Mr. Guest; and he was not always sure that he kept as many as he meant. Guest had often been on business to the doctor's; he knew Poole; he could scarce have failed to hear of Mr. Hyde's familiarity about the house; he might draw conclusions: was it not as well, then, that he should see a letter which put that mystery to rights? and above all, since Guest, being a great student and critic of handwriting, would consider the step natural and obliging? The clerk, besides, was a man of counsel; he would scarce read so strange a document without dropping a remark; and by that remark Mr. Utterson might shape his future course.

"This is a sad business about Sir Danvers," he said.

"Yes, sir, indeed. It has elicited a great deal of public feeling," returned Guest. "The man, of course, was mad."

"I should like to hear your views on that," replied Utterson. "I have a document here in his handwriting; it is between ourselves, for I scarce know what to do about it; it is an ugly business at the best. But there it is; quite in your way: a murderer's autograph."

Guest's eyes brightened, and he sat down at once and studied it with passion. "No sir," he said; "not mad; but it is an odd hand."

"And by all accounts a very odd writer," added the lawyer.

Just then the servant entered with a note.

"Is that from Dr. Jekyll, sir?" inquired the clerk. "I thought I knew the writing. Anything private, Mr. Utterson?

66 'No sir,' he said; 'not mad; but it is an odd hand.' 99

A London courtroom photographed in Stevenson's day.

A lawyer and a judge in their robes and wigs.

"Only an invitation to dinner. Why? Do you want to see it?"

"One moment. I thank you, sir"; and the clerk laid the two sheets of paper alongside and sedulously compared their contents. "Thank you, sir," he said at last, returning both; "it's a very interesting autograph."

There was a pause, during which Mr. Utterson struggled with himself. "Why did you compare them, Guest?" he inquired suddenly.

"Well, sir," returned the clerk, "there's a rather singular resemblance; the two hands are in many points identical: only differently sloped."

"Rather quaint," said Utterson.

"It is, as you say, rather quaint," returned Guest.

"I wouldn't speak of this note, you know," said the master.

"No, sir," said the clerk. "I understand."

But no sooner was Mr. Utterson alone that night than he locked the note into his safe, where it reposed from that time forward. "What!" he thought. "Henry Jekyll forge for a murderer!" And his blood ran cold in his veins.

66 'There's a rather singular resemblance; the two hands are in many points identical; only differently sloped.' 99

VI

REMARKABLE INCIDENT OF DR. LANYON

Time ran on; thousands of pounds were offered in reward, for the death of Sir Danvers was resented as a public injury; but Mr. Hyde had disappeared out of the ken of the police as though he had never existed. Much of his past was unearthed, indeed, and all disreputable: tales came out of the man's cruelty, at once so callous and violent, of his vile life, of his strange associates, of the hatred that seemed to have surrounded his career; but of his present whereabouts, not a whisper. From the time he had left the house in Soho on the morning of the murder, he was simply blotted out; and gradually, as time drew on, Mr. Utterson began to recover from the hotness of his alarm, and to grow more at quiet with himself. The death of Sir Danvers was, to his way of thinking, more than paid for by the disappearance of Mr. Hyde. Now that that evil influence had been withdrawn, a new life began for Dr. Jekyll. He came out of his seclusion, renewed relations with his friends, became once more their familiar guest and entertainer; and whilst he had always been known for charities, he was now no less distinguished for religion. He was busy, he was much in the open air, he did good; his face seemed to open and brighten, as if with an inward consciousness of

> ❝ A new life began for Dr. Jekyll. He came out of his seclusion, renewed relations with his friends, became once more their familiar guest and entertainer. ❞

service; and for more than two months the doctor was at peace.

On the 8th of January Utterson had dined at the doctor's with a small party; Lanyon had been there; and the face of the host had looked from one to the other as in the old days when the trio were inseparable friends. On the 12th, and again on the 14th, the door was shut against the lawyer. "The doctor was confined to the house," Poole said, "and saw no one." On the 15th he tried again, and was again refused; and having now been used for the last two months to see his friend almost daily, he found this return of solitude to weigh upon his spirits. The fifth night he had in Guest to dine with him; and the sixth he betook himself to Dr. Lanyon's.

There at least he was not denied admittance; but when he came in, he was shocked at the change which had taken place in the doctor's appearance. He had his death-warrant written legibly upon his face. The rosy man had grown pale; his flesh had fallen away; he was visibly balder and older; and yet it was not so much these tokens of a swift physical decay that arrested the lawyer's notice, as a look in the eye and quality of manner that seemed to testify to some deep-seated terror of the mind. It was unlikely that the doctor should fear death; and yet that was what Utterson was tempted to suspect. "Yes," he thought; "he is a doctor, he must know his own state and that his days are counted; and the knowledge is more than he can bear." And yet when Utterson remarked on his ill looks, it was with an air of great firmness that Lanyon declared himself a doomed man.

66 'I have had a shock,' he said, 'and I shall never recover.' 99

"I have had a shock," he said, "and I shall never recover. It is a question of weeks. Well, life has been pleasant; I liked it; yes, sir, I used to like it. I sometimes think if we knew all, we should be more glad to get away."

"Jekyll is ill, too," observed Utterson. "Have you seen him?"

But Lanyon's face changed, and he held up a

trembling hand. "I wish to see or hear no more of Dr. Jekyll," he said, in a loud, unsteady voice. "I am quite done with that person; and I beg that you will spare me any allusion to one whom I regard as dead."

"Tut, tut," said Mr. Utterson; and then, after a considerable pause, "Can't I do anything?" he inquired. "We are three very old friends, Lanyon; we shall not live to make others."

"Nothing can be done," returned Lanyon; "ask himself."

"He will not see me," said the lawyer.

"I am not surprised at that," was the reply. "Some day, Utterson, after I am dead, you may perhaps come to learn the right and wrong of this. I cannot tell you. And in the meantime, if you can sit and talk with me of other things, for God's sake, stay and do so; but if you cannot keep clear of this accursed topic, then, in God's name, go, for I cannot bear it."

As soon as he got home, Utterson sat down and wrote to Jekyll, complaining of his exclusion from the house, and asking the cause of this unhappy break with Lanyon; and the next day brought him a long answer, often very pathetically worded, and sometimes darkly mysterious in drift. The quarrel with Lanyon was incurable. "I do not blame our old friend," Jekyll wrote, "but I share his view that we must never meet. I mean from henceforth to lead a life of extreme seclusion; you must not be surprised, nor must you doubt my friendship, if my door is often shut even to you. You must suffer me to go my own dark way. I have brought on myself a punishment and a danger that I cannot name. If I am the chief of sinners, I am the chief of sufferers also. I could not think that this earth contained a place for sufferings and terrors so unmanning; and you can do but one thing, Utterson, to lighten this destiny, and that is to respect my silence." Utterson was amazed; the dark influence of Hyde had been withdrawn, the doctor had returned to his old tasks and amities; a week ago, the prospect had smiled with every promise of a cheerful and an honoured age; and now in a moment, friendship and peace of mind and the whole tenor of his life were wrecked. So great and unprepared a change pointed to madness; but in view of Lanyon's manner and words, there must lie for it some deeper ground.

A week afterwards Dr. Lanyon took to his bed, and in something less than a fortnight he was dead. The night after the funeral, at which he had been sadly affected, Utterson locked the door of his business room, and sitting there by the light of a melancholy candle, drew out and set before him an envelope addressed by the hand and sealed with the seal of his dead friend. "Private: for the hands of G. J. Utterson ALONE, and in case of his predecease *to be destroyed unread*," so it was emphatically superscribed; and the lawyer dreaded to behold the contents. "I have buried one friend to-day," he thought: "what if this should cost me another?" And then he condemned the fear as a disloyalty, and broke the seal. Within

A funeral procession in 1885. When church cemeteries in downtown London started to become overcrowded in the 1830s, large cemeteries were created outside the city. Because of the distance, the coffin was now driven to the tomb in a horse-drawn hearse instead of being carried on foot.

there was another enclosure, likewise sealed, and marked upon the cover as "not to be opened till the death or disappearance of Dr. Henry Jekyll." Utterson could not trust his eyes. Yes, it was disappearance; here again, as in the mad will which he had long ago restored to its author, here again were the idea of a disappearance and the name of Henry Jekyll bracketted. But in the will, that idea had sprung from the sinister suggestion of the man Hyde; it was set there with a purpose all too plain and horrible. Written by the hand of Lanyon, what should it mean? A great curiosity came to the trustee, to disregard the prohibition and dive at once to the bottom of these mysteries; but professional honour and faith to his dead friend were stringent obligations; and the packet slept in the inmost corner of his private safe.

It is one thing to mortify curiosity, another to conquer it; and it may be doubted if, from that day forth, Utterson desired the society of his surviving friend with the same eagerness. He thought of him kindly; but his thoughts were disquieted and fearful. He went to call indeed; but he was perhaps relieved to be denied admittance; perhaps, in his heart, he preferred to speak with Poole upon the doorstep, and surrounded by the air and sounds of the open city, rather than to be admitted into that house of voluntary bondage, and to sit and speak with its inscrutable recluse. Poole had, indeed, no very pleasant news to communicate. The doctor, it appeared, now more than ever confined himself to the cabinet over the laboratory, where he would sometimes even sleep; he was out of spirits, he had grown very silent, he did not read; it seemed as if he had something on his mind. Utterson became so used to the unvarying character of these reports, that he fell off little by little in the frequency of his visits.

Above, Scotland Yard's "Black Museum."

THE PENNY
ILLUSTRATED PAPER
AND ILLUSTRATED TIMES

Above, a criminal identification sheet. Below, old Scotland Yard.

SHERLOCK HOLMES" AT THE LYCEUM THEATRE

Sherlock and his would-be A

W.L. Abingdon — "Professor Moriarty" Henry M°Ardle — "Billy" Act II., Sc.II. William Gille... — "Sherlock H...

When *Dr. Jekyll and Mr. Hyde* was written, the detective novel as we know it did not exist. Most mystery stories were thrillers relying on melodrama, gore, and coincidences, rather than detection. Real-life crimes, such as the 1888 string of prostitute murders in London's East End by "Jack the Ripper," were reported with the same kind of sensationalism (center top). The complex construction and gradual introduction of clues in Stevenson's novel foreshadow the detective genre to come. With the first appearance of Sherlock Holmes the next year, the modern detective story was born. Arthur Conan Doyle, the creator of Sherlock Holmes and, like Stevenson, a native of Edinburgh, modeled his detective partly on Edgar Allan Poe's Auguste Dupin, and partly on an Edinburgh professor, Dr. Joseph Bell. In real life, also, the science of detection was in its infancy in the 1880s. In 1880, Scotland Yard established the "Black Museum" (top left) of relics of criminal evidence. The scientific classification and identification of criminals began with the work of a Frenchman, Alphonse Bertillon, who developed a system based on a series of precise measurements of the body. After the Englishman Francis Galton was able to prove that every person's fingerprints were unique, fingerprinting began to replace Bertillon's system at the turn of the century.

VII

INCIDENT AT THE WINDOW

It chanced on Sunday, when Mr. Utterson was on his usual walk with Mr. Enfield, that their way lay once again through the by street; and that when they came in front of the door, both stopped to gaze on it.

"Well," said Enfield, "that story's at an end, at least. We shall never see more of Mr. Hyde."

"I hope not," said Utterson. "Did I ever tell you that I once saw him, and shared your feeling of repulsion?"

"It was impossible to do the one without the other," returned Enfield. "And, by the way, what an ass you must have thought me, not to know that this was a back way to Dr. Jekyll's! It was partly your own fault that I found it out, even when I did."

"So you found it out, did you?" said Utterson. "But if that be so, we may step into the court and take a look at the windows. To tell you the truth, I am uneasy about poor Jekyll; and even outside, I feel as if the presence of a friend might do him good."

The court was very cool and a little damp, and full of premature twilight, although the sky, high up overhead, was still bright with sunset. The middle one of the three windows was half way open; and sitting close beside it, taking the air with an infinite sadness of mien, like some disconsolate prisoner, Utterson saw Dr. Jekyll.

"What! Jekyll!" he cried. "I trust you are better."

" The middle one of the three windows was half way open."

52

"I am very low, Utterson," replied the doctor drearily, "very low. It will not last long, thank God."

"You stay too much indoors," said the lawyer. "You should be out, whipping up the circulation like Mr. Enfield and me. (This is my cousin—Mr. Enfield—Dr. Jekyll.) Come, now; get your hat and take a quick turn with us."

"You are very good," sighed the other. "I should like to very much; but no, no, no, it is quite impossible; I dare not. But indeed, Utterson, I am very glad to see you; this is really a great pleasure; I would ask you and Mr. Enfield up, but the place is really not fit."

"Why, then," said the lawyer, good-naturedly, "the best thing we can do is to stay down here and speak with you from where we are."

"That is just what I was about to venture to propose," returned the doctor, with a smile. But the words were hardly uttered, before the smile was struck out of his face and succeeded by an expression of such abject terror and despair, as froze the very blood of the two gentlemen below. They saw it but for a glimpse, for the window was instantly thrust down; but that glimpse, had been sufficient, and they turned and left the court without a word. In silence, too, they traversed the by street; and it was not until they had come into a neighbouring thoroughfare, where even upon a Sunday there were still some stirrings of life, that Mr. Utterson at last turned and looked at his companion. They were both pale; and there was an answering horror in their eyes.

"God forgive us, God forgive us," said Mr. Utterson.

But Mr. Enfield only nodded his head very seriously, and walked on once more in silence.

❝ 'This is my cousin— Mr. Enfield—Dr. Jekyll.' ❞

VIII

THE LAST NIGHT

Mr. Utterson was sitting by his fireside one evening after dinner, when he was surprised to receive a visit from Poole.

"Bless me, Poole, what brings you here?" he cried; and then, taking a second look at him, "What ails you?" he added; is the doctor ill?"

"Mr. Utterson," said the man, "there is something wrong."

"Take a seat, and here is a glass of wine for you," said the lawyer. "Now, take your time, and tell me plainly what you want."

"You know the doctor's ways, sir," replied Poole, "and how he shuts himself up. Well, he's shut up again in the cabinet; and I don't like it, sir—I wish I may die if I like it. Mr. Utterson, sir, I'm afraid."

"Now, my good man," said the lawyer, "be explicit. What are you afraid of?"

"I've been afraid for about a week," returned Poole, doggedly disregarding the question, "and I can bear it no more."

The man's appearance amply bore out his words; his manner was altered for the worse; and except for the moment when he had first announced his terror, he had not once looked the lawyer in the face. Even now, he sat with the glass of wine untasted on his knee, and his eyes directed to a corner of the floor.

"I can bear it no more," he repeated.

"Come," said the lawyer, "I see you have some good reason, Poole; I see there is something seriously amiss. Try to tell me what it is."

"I think there's been foul play," said Poole, hoarsely.

"Foul play!" cried the lawyer, a good deal frightened and rather inclined to be irritated in consequence. "What foul play! What does the man mean?"

"I daren't say, sir," was the answer; "but will you come along with me and see for yourself?"

Mr. Utterson's only answer was to rise and get his hat and greatcoat; but he observed with wonder the greatness of the relief that appeared upon the butler's face, and perhaps with no less, that the wine was still untasted when he set it down to follow.

It was a wild, cold, seasonable night of March, with a pale moon, lying on her back as though the wind had tilted her, and flying wrack of the most diaphanous and lawny texture. The wind made talking difficult, and flecked the blood into the face. It seemed to have swept the streets unusually bare of passengers, besides; for Mr. Utterson thought he had never seen that part of London so deserted. He could have wished it otherwise; never in his life had he been conscious of so sharp a wish to see and touch his fellow-creatures; for, struggle as he might, there was borne in upon his mind a crushing anticipation of calamity. The square, when they got there, was

66 It was a wild, cold, seasonable night of March, with a pale moon, lying on her back. 99

The head butler in a rich household in the late nineteenth century. Butlers wore somber, dignified clothes, so it is surprising that Jekyll's butler, Poole, would carry anything as undignified as a red handkerchief.

all full of wind and dust, and the thin trees in the garden were lashing themselves along the railing. Poole, who had kept all the way a pace or two ahead, now pulled up in the middle of the pavement, and in spite of the biting weather, took off his hat and mopped his brow with a red pocket-handkerchief. But for all the hurry of his coming, these were not the dews of exertion that he wiped away, but the moisture of some strangling anguish; for his face was white, and his voice, when he spoke, harsh and broken.

A housekeeper and domestic servants in 1886. Domestic employees were organized in a strict hierarchy. The butler and housekeeper ran the household and gave orders to the maids and manservants. Most middle-class households employed at least five domestics. Even when a middle-class man like Jekyll was "alone," he was actually surrounded by a crowd.

"Well, sir," he said, "here we are, and God grant there be nothing wrong."

"Amen, Poole," said the lawyer.

Thereupon the servant knocked in a very guarded manner; the door was opened on the chain; and a voice asked from within, "Is that you, Poole?"

"It's all right," said Poole. "Open the door."

The hall, when they entered it, was brightly lighted up; the fire was built high; and about the hearth the whole of the servants, men and women, stood huddled together like a flock of sheep. At the sight of Mr. Utterson, the housemaid broke into hysterical whimpering; and the cook, crying out "Bless God! it's Mr. Utterson," ran forward as if to take him in her arms.

"What, what? Are you all here?" said the lawyer, peevishly. "Very irregular, very unseemly: your master would be far from pleased."

"They're all afraid," said Poole.

Blank silence followed, no one protesting; only the maid lifted her voice and now wept loudly.

"Hold your tongue!" Poole said to her, with a ferocity of accent that testified to his own jangled nerves; and indeed when the girl had so suddenly raised the note of her lamentation, they had all started and turned towards the inner door with faces of dreadful expectation. "And now," continued the butler, addressing the knife-boy, "reach me a candle, and we'll get this through hands at once." And then he begged Mr. Utterson to follow him, and led the way to the back garden.

"Now, sir," said he, "you come as gently as you can. I want you to hear, and I don't want you to be heard. And see here, sir, if by any chance he was to ask you in, don't go."

Mr. Utterson's nerves, at this unlooked-for termination, gave a jerk that nearly threw him from his balance; but he recollected his courage, and followed the butler into the laboratory building and through the surgical theatre, with its lumber of crates and bottles, to the foot of the stair. Here Poole motioned him to stand on one side and listen; while he himself, setting down the candle and making a great and obvious call on his resolution, mounted the steps, and knocked with a somewhat uncertain hand on the red baize of the cabinet door.

"Mr. Utterson, sir, asking to see you," he called; and even as he did so, once more violently signed to the lawyer to give ear.

❝ 'What, what? Are you all here? Your master would be far from pleased.'**❞**

" Mr. Utterson followed the butler into the surgical theatre, with its lumber of crates and bottles.**"**

A voice answered from within: "Tell him I cannot see any one," it said, complainingly.

"Thank you, sir," said Poole, with a note of something like triumph in his voice; and taking up his candle, he led Mr. Utterson back across the yard and into the great kitchen, where the fire was out and the beetles were leaping on the floor.

"Sir," he said, looking Mr. Utterson in the eyes, "Was that my master's voice?"

"It seems much changed," replied the lawyer, very pale, but giving look for look.

"Changed? Well, yes, I think so," said the butler. "Have I been twenty years in this man's house, to be deceived about his voice? No, sir; master's made away with; he was made away with eight days ago, when we heard him cry out upon the name of God; and *who's* in there instead of him, and *why* it stays there, is a thing that cries to Heaven, Mr. Utterson!"

"This is a very strange tale, Poole; this is rather a wild tale, my man," said Mr. Utterson, biting his finger. "Suppose it were as you suppose, supposing Dr. Jekyll to have been—well, murdered, what could induce the murderer to stay? That won't hold water; it doesn't commend itself to reason."

"Well, Mr. Utterson, you are a hard man to satisfy, but I'll do it yet," said Poole. "All this last week (you must know) him, or it, whatever it is that lives in that cabinet, has been crying night and day for some sort of medicine and cannot get it to his mind. It was sometimes his way—the master's, that is—to write his orders on a sheet of paper and throw it on the stair. We've had nothing else this week back; nothing but papers, and a closed door, and the very meals left there to be smuggled in when nobody was looking. Well, sir, every

❝ The very meals were left there to be smuggled in when nobody was looking.**❞**

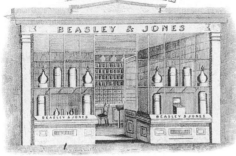

Apothecary jars displayed in a pharmacy window.

A pharmacist and his apprentices working in the laboratory at the back of the pharmacy.

An apprentice preparing a drug.

day, ay, and twice and thrice in the same day, there have been orders and complaints, and I have been sent flying to all the wholesale chemists in town. Every time I brought the stuff back, there would be another paper telling me to return it, because it was not pure, and another order to a different firm. This drug is wanted bitter bad, sir, whatever for."

"Have you any of these papers?" asked Mr. Utterson.

Poole felt in his pocket and handed out a crumpled note, which the lawyer, bending nearer to the candle, carefully examined. Its contents ran thus: "Dr. Jekyll presents his compliments to Messrs. Maw. He assures them that their last sample is impure and quite useless for his present purpose. In the year 18—, Dr. J. purchased a somewhat large quantity from Messrs. M. He now begs them to search with the most sedulous care, and should any of the same quality be left, to forward it to him at once. Expense is no consideration. The importance of this to Dr. J. can hardly be exaggerated." So far the letter had run composedly enough; but here, with a sudden splutter of the pen, the writer's emotion had broken loose. "For God's sake," he added, "find me some of the old."

"This is a strange note," said Mr. Utterson; and then sharply, "How do you come to have it open?"

"The man at Maw's was main angry, sir, and he threw it back to me like so much dirt," returned Poole.

"This is unquestionably the doctor's hand, do you know?" resumed the lawyer.

"I thought it looked like it," said the servant, rather sulkily; and then, with another voice, "But what matters hand of write?" he said. "I've seen him!"

"Seen him?" repeated Mr. Utterson. "Well?"

"That's it!" said Poole. "It was this way. I came suddenly into the theatre from the garden. It seems he had slipped out to look for this drug, or whatever it is; for the cabinet door was open, and there he was at the far end of the room digging among the crates. He looked up when I came in, gave a kind of cry, and whipped upstairs into the cabinet. It was but for one minute that I saw him, but the hair stood upon my head like quills. Sir, if that was my master, why had he a mask upon his face? If it was my master, why did he cry out like a rat and run from me? I have served him long enough. And then . . ." The man paused and passed his hand over his face.

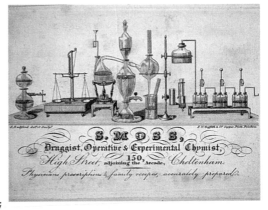

"These are all very strange circumstances," said Mr. Utterson, "but I think I begin to see daylight. Your master, Poole, is plainly seized with one of those maladies that both torture and deform the sufferer;

A pharmacist's calling card, illustrated with chemical equipment. The scales were used to weigh out precise amounts of powdered medicines.

hence, for aught I know, the alteration of his voice; hence the mask and his avoidance of his friends; hence his eagerness to find this drug, by means of which the poor soul retains some hope of ultimate recovery—God grant that he be not deceived! There is my explanation; it is sad enough, Poole, ay, and appalling to consider; but it is plain and natural, hangs well together, and delivers us from all exorbitant alarms."

"Sir," said the butler, turning to a sort of mottled pallor, "that thing was not my master, and there's the truth. My master"—here he looked round him and began to whisper— "is a tall, fine build of a man, and this was more of a dwarf." Utterson attempted to protest. "O, sir," cried Poole, "do you think I do not know my master after twenty years? Do you think I do not know where his head comes to in the cabinet door, where I saw him every morning of my life? No, sir, that thing in the mask was never Dr. Jekyll—God knows what it was, but it was never Dr. Jekyll; and it is the belief of my heart that there was murder done."

"Poole," replied the lawyer, "if you say that, it will become my duty to make certain. Much as I desire to

Illustration from Charles Delacre's *Pharmacie Anglaise* [English Pharmacy] (1889), showing a woman preparing a pharmaceutical mixture.

spare your master's feelings, much as I am puzzled by this note which seems to prove him to be still alive, I shall consider it my duty to break in that door."

"Ah, Mr. Utterson, that's talking!" cried the butler.

"And now comes the second question," resumed Utterson: "Who is going to do it?"

"Why, you and me, sir," was the undaunted reply.

"That is very well said," returned the lawyer; "and whatever comes of it, I shall make it my business to see you are no loser."

> 66 That masked thing like a monkey jumped up from among the chemicals and whipped into the cabinet. 99

"There is an axe in the theatre," continued Poole; "and you might take the kitchen poker for yourself."

The lawyer took that rude but weighty instrument into his hand, and balanced it. "Do you know, Poole," he said, looking up, "that you and I are about to place ourselves in a position of some peril?"

"You may say so, sir, indeed," returned the butler.

"It is well, then, that we should be frank," said the other. "We both think more than we have said; let us make a clean breast. This masked figure that you saw, did you recognize it?"

"Well, sir, it went so quick, and the creature was so doubled up, that I could hardly swear to that," was the answer. "But if you mean, was it Mr. Hyde?—why, yes, I think it was! You see, it was much of the same bigness; and it had the same quick light way with it; and then who else could have got in by the laboratory door? You have not forgot, sir, that at the time of the murder he had still the key with him? But that's not all. I don't know, Mr. Utterson, if ever you met this Mr. Hyde?"

"Yes," said the lawyer, "I once spoke with him."

"Then you must know, as well as the rest of us, that there was something queer about that gentleman—something that gave a man a turn—I don't know rightly how to say it, sir, beyond this: that you felt in your marrow—kind of cold and thin."

"I own I felt something of what you describe," said Mr. Utterson.

"Quite so, sir," returned Poole. "Well, when that masked thing like a monkey jumped from among the chemicals and whipped into the cabinet, it went down my spine like ice. O, I know it's not evidence, Mr. Utterson; I'm book-learned enough for that; but a man has his feelings, and I give you my bible-word it was Mr. Hyde!"

Victorian gentlemen did not wear wristwatches. The watch Utterson uses would have resembled

"Ay, ay," said the lawyer. "My fears incline to the same point. Evil, I fear, founded—evil was sure to come—of that connection. Ay, truly, I believe you; I believe poor Harry is killed; and I believe his murderer (for what purpose, God alone can tell) is still lurking in his victim's room. Well, let our name be vengeance. Call Bradshaw."

The footman came at the summons, very white and nervous.

"Pull yourself together, Bradshaw," said the lawyer. "This suspense, I know, is telling upon all of you; but it is now our intention to make an end of it. Poole, here, and I are going to force our way into the cabinet. If all is well, my shoulders are broad enough to bear the blame. Meanwhile, lest anything should really be amiss, or any malefactor seek to escape by the back, you and the boy must go round the corner with a pair of good sticks and take your post at the laboratory door. We give you ten minutes, to get to your stations."

the pocket watches shown above. They were attached to a loop in a small pocket by a chain that was often decorated with a charm.

As Bradshaw left, the lawyer looked at his watch. "And now, Poole, let us get to ours," he said; and taking the poker under his arm, he led the way into the yard. The scud had banked over the moon, and it was now quite dark. The wind, which only broke in puffs and draughts into that deep well of building, tossed the light of the candle to and fro about their steps, until they came into the shelter of the theatre, where they sat down silently to wait. London hummed solemnly all

around; but nearer at hand, the stillness was only broken by the sound of a footfall moving to and fro along the cabinet floor.

"So it will walk all day, sir," whispered Poole; "ay, and the better part of the night. Only when a new sample comes from the chemist, there's a bit of a break. Ah, it's an ill conscience that's such an enemy to rest! Ah, sir, there's blood foully shed in every step of it! But hark again, a little closer—put your heart in your ears Mr. Utterson, and tell me, is that the doctor's foot?"

The steps fell lightly and oddly, with a certain swing, for all they went so slowly; it was different indeed from the heavy creaking tread of Henry Jekyll. Utterson sighed. "Is there never anything else?" he asked.

Poole nodded. "Once," he said. "Once I heard it weeping!"

"Weeping? how that?" said the lawyer, conscious of a sudden chill of horror.

"Weeping like a woman or a lost soul," said the butler. "I came away with that upon my heart, that I could have wept too."

But now the ten minutes drew to an end. Poole disinterred the axe from under a stack of packing straw; the candle was set upon the nearest table to light them to the attack; and they drew near with bated breath to where that patient foot was still going up and down, up and down in the quiet of the night.

This pharmacy on Wigmore Street in London has been restored to the appearance it would have had in the early part of the century.

"Jekyll," cried Utterson, with a loud voice, "I demand to see you." He paused a moment, but there came no reply. "I give you fair warning, our suspicions are aroused, and I must and shall see you," he resumed; "if not by fair means, then by foul—if not of your consent, then by brute force!"

"Utterson," said the voice, "for God's sake, have mercy!"

"Ah, that's not Jekyll's voice—it's Hyde's!" cried Utterson. "Down with the door, Poole!"

Poole swung the axe over his shoulder; the blow shook the building, and the red baize door leaped against the lock and hinges. A dismal screech, as of mere animal terror, rang from the cabinet. Up went the axe again, and again the panels crashed and the frame bounded; four times the blow fell; but the wood was tough and the fittings were of excellent workmanship; and it was not until the fifth that the lock burst in sunder, and the wreck of the door fell inwards on the carpet.

The besiegers, appalled by their own riot and the stillness that had succeeded, stood back a little and peered in. There lay

❝ Right in the midst there lay the body of a man sorely contorted and still twitching. ❞

Tea has long been an integral part of the English image. When it was first introduced from China in the seventeenth century, it was considered a medicine—one advertisement claimed it could heal, "headache, dropsy, scurvy, sleepiness, loss of memory, looseness of the guts, heavy dreams, and collick proceeding from the wind" and "if you have had a surfeit it is just the thing to give you a gentle vomit." By Stevenson's time, afternoon tea had become a ritual, calling for a range of tea items such as those shown above. With their cozy associations with home and family, the tea things laid out in the cabinet are a clear symbol of the respectable Dr. Jekyll.

the cabinet before their eyes in the quiet lamplight, a good fire glowing and chattering on the hearth, the kettle singing its thin strain, a drawer or two open, papers neatly set forth on the business table, and nearer the fire, the things laid out for tea; the quietest room, you would have said, and, but for the glazed presses full of chemicals, the most commonplace that night in London.

Right in the midst there lay the body of a man sorely contorted and still twitching. They drew near on tiptoe, turned it on its back, and beheld the face of Edward Hyde. He was dressed in clothes far too large for him, clothes of the doctor's bigness; the cords of his face still moved with a semblance of life, but life was quite gone: and by the crushed phial in the hand and the strong smell of kernels that hung upon the air, Utterson knew that he was looking on the body of a self-destroyer.

"We have come too late," he said sternly, "whether to save or punish. Hyde is gone to his account; and it only remains for us to find the body of your master."

The far greater proportion of the building was occupied by the theatre, which filled almost the whole ground storey, and was lighted from above, and by the cabinet, which formed an upper storey at one end and looked upon the court. A corridor joined the theatre to the door on the by street; and with this, the cabinet communicated separately by a second flight of stairs. There were besides a few dark closets and a spacious cellar. All these they now thoroughly examined. Each closet needed but a glance, for all they were empty, and all, by the dust that fell from their doors, had stood long unopened. The cellar, indeed, was filled with crazy lumber, mostly dating from the times of the surgeon who was Jekyll's predecessor; but even as they opened the door they were advertised of the uselessness of further search, by the fall of a perfect mat of cobweb which had for years sealed up the entrance. Nowhere was there any trace of Henry Jekyll, dead or alive.

Poole stamped on the flags of the corridor. "He must be buried here," he said, hearkening to the sound.

"Or he may have fled," said Utterson, and he turned to examine the door in the by street. It was locked; and lying near by on the flags, they found the key, already stained with rust.

"This does not look like use," observed the lawyer.

"Use!" echoed Poole. "Do you not see, sir, it is broken? much as if a man had stamped on it."

"Ah," continued Utterson, "and the fractures, too, are rusty." The two men looked at each other with a scare. "This is beyond me, Poole," said the lawyer. "Let us go back to the cabinet."

66 Lying near by on the flags, they found the key, already stained with rust.**99**

They mounted the stair in silence, and still, with an occasional awestruck glance at the dead body, proceeded more thoroughly to examine the contents of the cabinet. At one table, there were traces of chemical work, various measured heaps of some white salt being laid on glass saucers, as though for an experiment in which the unhappy man had been prevented.

"That is the same drug that I was always bringing him," said Poole; and even as he spoke, the kettle with a startling noise boiled over.

This brought them to the fireside, where the easy chair was drawn cosily up, and the tea things stood ready to the sitter's elbow, the very sugar in the cup. There were several books on a shelf; one lay beside the tea things open, and Utterson was amazed to find it a copy of a pious work for which Jekyll had several times expressed a great esteem, annotated, in his own hand, with startling blasphemies.

Next, in the course of their review of the chamber, the searchers came to the cheval-glass, into whose depths they looked with an involuntary horror. But it was so turned as to show them nothing but the rosy glow playing on the roof, the fire sparkling in a hundred repetitions along the glazed front of the presses, and their own pale and fearful countenances stooping to look in.

"This glass has seen some strange things, sir," whispered Poole.

"And surely none stranger than itself," echoed the lawyer, in the same tone. "For what did Jekyll"—he caught himself up at the word with a start, and then conquering the weakness: "what could Jekyll want with it?" he said.

"You may say that!" said Poole.

Next they turned to the business table. On the desk, among the neat array of papers, a large envelope was uppermost, and bore, in the doctor's hand, the name of Mr. Utterson. The lawyer unsealed it, and several enclosures fell to the floor. The first was a will, drawn in the same eccentric terms as the one which he had returned six months before, to serve as a testament in case of death and as a deed of gift in case of disappearance; but in place of the name of Edward Hyde, the lawyer, with indescribable amazement, read the name of Gabriel John Utterson. He looked at Poole, and then back at the papers, and last of all at the dead malefactor stretched upon the carpet.

"My head goes round," he said. "He has been all these days in possession; he had no cause to like me; he must have raged to see himself displaced; and he has not destroyed this document."

He caught the next paper; it was a brief note in the doctor's hand and dated at the top. "O Poole!" the lawyer cried, "he was alive and here this day. He cannot have been disposed of in so short a space; he must be still alive, he must have fled! And then, why fled? and how? and in that case can we venture to declare this suicide? O, we must be careful. I foresee that we may yet involve your master in some dire catastrophe."

"Why don't you read it, sir?" asked Poole.

"Because I fear," replied the lawyer solemnly. "God grant I have no cause for it!" And with that he brought the paper to his eyes and read as follows:

> **The lawyer unsealed it, and several enclosures fell to the floor.**

MY DEAR UTTERSON,—When this shall fall into your hands, I shall have disappeared, under what circumstances I have not the penetration to foresee, but my instinct and all the circumstances of my nameless situation tell me that the end is sure and must be early. Go then, and first read the narrative which Lanyon warned me he was to place in your hands; and if you care to hear more, turn to the confession of

Your unworthy and unhappy friend,

HENRY JEKYLL.

"There was a third enclosure," asked Utterson.

"Here, sir," said Poole, and gave into his

hands a considerable packet sealed in several places.

The lawyer put it in his pocket. "I would say nothing of this paper. If your master has fled or is dead, we may at least save his credit. It is now ten; I must go home and read these documents in quiet; but I shall be back before midnight, when we shall send for the police."

They went out, locking the door of the theatre behind them; and Utterson, once more leaving the servants gathered about the fire in the hall, trudged back to his office to read the two narratives in which this mystery was now to be explained.

66 A considerable packet sealed in several places.**99**

IX

DR. LANYON'S NARRATIVE

On the ninth of January, now four days ago, I received by the evening delivery a registered envelope, addressed in the hand of my colleague and old school-companion, Henry Jekyll. I was a good deal surprised by this; for we were by no means in the habit of correspondence; I had seen the man, dined with him, indeed, the night before; and I could imagine nothing in our intercourse that should justify formality of registration. The contents increased my wonder; for this is how the letter ran:

A London mailman. Until the telegraph and telephone became more widely used toward the end of the century, people relied on written letters for basic daily transactions. Because letters were such a part of everyday life, novels composed entirely of letters were popular in the eighteenth and nineteenth centuries. The last half of *Dr. Jekyll and Mr. Hyde* is such an "epistolary novel."

> *10th December 18—.*
>
> DEAR LANYON,—You are one of my oldest friends; and although we may have differed at times on scientific questions, I cannot remember, at least on my side, any break in our affection. There was never a day when, if you had said to me, "Jekyll, my life, my honour, my reason, depend upon you," I would not have sacrificed my fortune or my left hand to help you. Lanyon my life, my honour, my reason, are all at your mercy; if you fail me to-night, I am lost. You might suppose, after this preface, that I am going to ask you for something dishonourable to grant. Judge for yourself.
>
> I want you to postpone all other engagements for to-night—ay, even if you were summoned to the bedside of an emperor; to take a cab, unless your carriage should be actually at the door; and, with this letter in your hand for consultation, to drive straight to my house. Poole, my butler, has his orders; you will find him waiting your arrival with a locksmith. The door of my cabinet is then to be forced; and you are to go in alone; to open the glazed

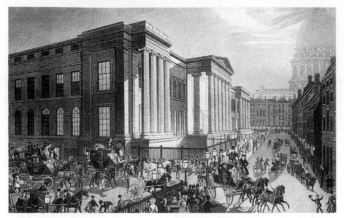

The General Post Office at St. Martin-le-Grand, with the dome of St. Paul's Cathedral rising in the background. Postal wagons left London at regular intervals to deliver mail all over the country. The General Post Office building was inaugurated in 1829 and demolished in 1912. Since mail was delivered several times a day in 1886, correspondents within the city could write a letter and receive a response in the same day. The London mail was so reliable that Jekyll could be fairly confident Lanyon would receive his letter the same day.

press (letter E) on the left hand, breaking the lock if it be shut; and to draw out, *with all its contents as they stand*, the fourth drawer from the top or (which is the same thing) the third from the bottom. In my extreme distress of mind, I have a morbid fear of misdirecting you; but even if I am in error, you may know the right drawer by its contents: some powders, a phial, and a paper book. This drawer I beg of you to carry back with you to Cavendish Square exactly as it stands.

That is the first part of the service: now for the second. You should be back, if you set out at once on the receipt of this, long before midnight; but I will leave you that amount of margin, not only in the fear of one of those obstacles that can neither be prevented nor foreseen, but because an hour when your servants are in bed is to be preferred for what will then remain to do. At midnight, then, I have to ask you to be alone in your consulting-room, to admit with your own hand into the house a man who will present himself in my name, and to place in his hands the drawer that you will have brought with you from my cabinet. Then you will have played your part and earned my gratitude completely. Five minutes afterwards, if you insist upon an explanation, you will have understood that these arrangements are of capital importance; and that by the neglect of one of them, fantastic as they must appear, you might have charged your conscience with my death or the shipwreck of my reason.

Confident as I am that you will not trifle with this appeal, my heart sinks and my hand trembles at the bare thought of such a possibility. Think of me at this hour, in a strange place, labouring under a blackness of distress that no fancy can exaggerate, and yet well aware that, if you will but punctually serve me, my troubles will roll away like a story that is told. Serve me, my dear Lanyon and save

Your friend,
H.J.

P.S.—I had already sealed this up when a fresh terror struck upon my soul. It is possible that the post-office may fail me, and this letter not come into your hands until to-morrow morning. In that case, dear Lanyon, do my errand when it shall be most convenient for you in the course of the day; and once more expect my messenger at midnight. It may then already be too late; and if that night passes without event, you will know that you have seen the last of Henry Jekyll.

Upon the reading of this letter, I made sure my colleague was insane; but till that was proved beyond the possibility of doubt, I felt bound to do as he requested. The less I understood of this farrago, the less I was in a position to judge of its importance; and an appeal so worded could not be set aside without a grave responsibility. I rose accordingly from table, got into a hansom, and drove straight to Jekyll's house. The butler was awaiting my arrival; he had received by the same post as mine a registered letter of instruction, and had sent at once for a locksmith and a carpenter. The tradesmen came while we were yet speaking; and we moved in a body to old Dr. Denman's surgical theatre, from which (as you are doubtless aware) Jekyll's private cabinet is most conveniently entered. The door was very strong, the lock excellent; the carpenter avowed he would have great trouble, and have to do much

❝ After two hours' work, the door stood open. **❞**

73

66 Here I proceeded to examine its contents. **99**

damage, if force were to be used; and the locksmith was near despair. But this last was a handy fellow, and after two hours' work, the door stood open. The press marked E was unlocked; and I took out the drawer, had it filled up with straw and tied in a sheet, and returned with it to Cavendish Square.

Here I proceeded to examine its contents. The powders were neatly enough made up, but not with the nicety of the dispensing chemist; so that it was plain they were of Jekyll's private manufacture; and when I opened one of the wrappers, I found what seemed to me a simple crystalline salt of a white colour. The phial, to which I next turned my attention, might have been about half-full of a blood-red liquor, which was highly pungent to the sense of smell, and seemed to me to contain phosphorus and some volatile ether. At the other ingredients I could make no guess. The book was an ordinary version book, and contained little but a series of dates.

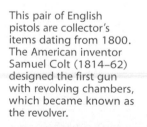

These covered a period of many years, but I observed that the entries ceased nearly a year ago and quite abruptly. Here and there a brief remark was appended to a date, usually no more than a single word: "double" occurring perhaps six times in a total of several hundred entries; and once very early in the list and followed by several marks of exclamation, "total failure!!!" All this, though it whetted my curiosity, told me little that was definite. Here were a phial of some tincture, a paper of some salt, and the record of a series of experiments that had led (like too many of Jekyll's investigations) to no end of practical usefulness. How could the presence of these articles in my house affect either the honour, the sanity, or the life of my flighty colleague? If his messenger could go to one place, why could he not go to another? And even granting

This pair of English pistols are collector's items dating from 1800. The American inventor Samuel Colt (1814–62) designed the first gun with revolving chambers, which became known as the revolver.

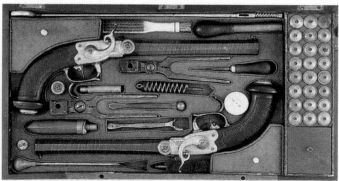

some impediment, why was this gentleman to be received by me in secret? The more I reflected, the more convinced I grew that I was dealing with a case of cerebral disease; and though I dismissed my servants to bed, I loaded an old revolver, that I might be found in some posture of self-defence.

Twelve o'clock had scarce rung out over London, ere the knocker sounded very gently on the door. I went myself at the summons, and found a small man crouching against the pillars of the portico.

"Are you come from Dr. Jekyll?" I asked.

He told me "yes" by a constrained gesture; and when I had bidden him enter, he did not obey me without a searching backward glance into the darkness of the square. There was a policeman not far off, advancing with his bull's eye open; and at the sight, I thought my visitor started and made greater haste.

These particulars struck me, I confess, disagreeably; and as I followed him into the bright light of the consulting-room, I kept my hand ready on my weapon. Here, at last, I had a chance of clearly seeing him. I had never set eyes on him before, so much was certain. He was small, as I have said; I was struck besides with the shocking expression of his face, with his remarkable combination of great muscular activity and great apparent debility of constitution, and—last but

not least—with the odd, subjective disturbance caused by his neighbourhood. This bore some resemblance to incipient rigour, and was accompanied by a marked sinking of the pulse. At the time, I set it down to some idiosyncratic, personal distaste, and merely wondered at the acuteness of the symptoms; but I have since had reason to believe the cause to lie much deeper in the nature of man, and to turn on some nobler hinge than the principle of hatred.

This person (who had thus, from the first moment of his

66 I went myself at the summons, and found a small man crouching against the pillars of the portico. 99

THE GUARDIANS OF THE NIGHT.

The cover of a dance score praising the police as "The Guardians of the Night," bears a picture of policemen patrolling Regent Street.

entrance, struck in me what I can only, describe as a disgustful curiosity) was dressed in a fashion that would have made an ordinary person laughable; his clothes, that is to say, although they were of rich and sober fabric, were enormously too large for him in every measurement—the trousers hanging on his legs and rolled up to keep them from the ground, the waist of the coat below his haunches, and the collar sprawling wide upon his shoulders. Strange to relate, this ludicrous accoutrement was far from moving me to laughter. Rather, as there was something abnormal and misbegotten in the very essence of the creature that now faced me—

something seizing, surprising and revolting—this fresh disparity seemed but to fit in with and to reinforce it; so that to my interest in the man's nature and character, there was added a curiosity as to his origin, his life, his fortune and status in the world.

These observations, though they have taken so great a space to be set down in, were yet the work of a few seconds. My visitor was, indeed, on fire with sombre excitement.

66 Twelve o'clock had scarce rung out over London, ere the knocker sounded very gently on the door. 99

Two styles of men's overcoats. Above, a velvet-collared coat from 1876. When Stevenson was a young man, he was nicknamed "velvet-coat." Below, an 1879 raincoat with tartan lining.

"Have you got it?" he cried. "Have you got it?" And so lively was his impatience that he even laid his hand upon my arm and sought to shake me.

I put him back, conscious at his touch of a certain icy pang along my blood. "Come, sir," said I. "You forget that I have not yet the pleasure of your acquaintance. Be seated, if you please." And I showed him an example, and sat down myself in my customary seat and with as fair an imitation of my ordinary manner to a patient, as the lateness of the hour, the nature of my preoccupations, and the horror I had of my visitor would suffer me to muster.

"I beg your pardon, Dr. Lanyon," he replied civilly enough. "What you say is very well founded; and my impatience has shown its heels to my politeness. I come here at the instance of your colleague, Dr. Henry Jekyll, on a piece of business of some moment; and I understood . . ." He paused and put his hand to his throat, and I could see, in spite of his collected manner, that he was wrestling against the approaches of the hysteria—"I understood, a drawer . . ."

But here I took pity on my visitor's suspense, and some perhaps on my own growing curiosity.

"There it is, sir," said I, pointing to the drawer, where it lay on the floor behind a table, and still covered with the sheet.

He sprang to it, and then paused, and laid his hand upon his heart; I could hear his teeth grate with the convulsive action of his jaws; and his face was so ghastly to see that I grew alarmed both for his life and reason.

"Compose yourself," said I.

He turned a dreadful smile to me, and, as if with the decision of despair, plucked away the sheet. At sight of the contents, he uttered one loud sob of such immense relief that I sat petrified. And the next moment, in a voice that was already fairly well under control, "Have you a graduated glass?" he asked.

I rose from my place with something of an effort and gave him what he asked.

He thanked me with a smiling nod, measured out a few minims of the red tincture and added one of the powders. The mixture, which was at first of a reddish hue, began, in proportion as the crystals melted, to brighten in colour, to effervesce audibly, and to throw off small fumes of vapour. Suddenly, and at the same moment, the ebullition ceased, and the compound changed to a dark purple, which faded again more slowly to a watery green. My visitor, who had watched these metamorphoses with a keen eye, smiled, set down the glass upon the table, and then turned and looked upon me with an air of scrutiny.

"And now," said he, "to settle what remains. Will you be wise? will you be guided? will you suffer me to take this glass in my hand and to go forth from your house without further parley? or has the greed of curiosity too much command of you? Think before you answer, for it shall be done as you decide. As you decide, you shall be left as you were before, and neither richer nor wiser, unless the sense of service rendered to a man in mortal distress may be counted as a kind of riches of the soul. Or, if you shall so prefer to choose, a new province of knowledge and new avenues to fame and power shall be laid open to you, here, in this room, upon the instant; and your sight shall be blasted by a prodigy to stagger the unbelief of Satan."

"Sir," said I, affecting a coolness that I was far from truly possessing, "you speak enigmas, and you will perhaps not wonder that I hear you with no very strong impression of belief. But I have gone too far in the way of inexplicable services to pause before I see the end."

"It is well," replied my visitor. "Lanyon, you remember your vows: what follows is under the seal of our

> 66 He measured out a few minims of the red tincture and added one of the powders. 99

W. Q. Orchardson, another citizen of Edinburgh, painted this scene of a late Victorian interior in 1886. The gentleman's austere attire and the fine furniture suggest the kind of well-to-do household that Dr. Lanyon would have had. As Stevenson does in *Dr. Jekyll and Mr. Hyde*, Orchardson often revealed the tensions that lay under the smooth surface of the English middle class life.

profession. And now, you who have so long been bound to the most narrow and material views, you who have denied the virtue of transcendental medicine, you who have derided your superiors—behold!"

He put the glass to his lips and drank at one gulp. A cry followed; he reeled, staggered, clutched at the table and held on, staring with infected eyes, gasping with open mouth; and as I looked, there came, I thought, a change—he seemed to swell—his face became suddenly black and the features seemed to melt and alter—and the next moment, I had sprung to my feet and leaped back against the wall, my arm raised to shield me from that prodigy, my mind submerged in terror.

"O God!" I screamed, and "O God!" again and again; for there before my eyes—pale and shaken, and half fainting, and groping before him with his hands, like a man restored from death—there stood Henry Jekyll!

What he told me in the next hour, I cannot bring my mind to set on paper. I saw what I saw, I heard what I heard, and my soul sickened at it; and yet, now when that sight has faded from my eyes, I ask myself if I believe it, and I cannot answer. My life is shaken to its roots; sleep has left me; the deadliest terror sits by me at all hours of the day and night; I feel that my days are numbered, and that I must die; and yet I shall die incredulous. As for the moral turpitude that man unveiled to me, even with tears of penitence, I cannot, even in memory, dwell on it without a start of horror. I will say but one thing, Utterson, and that (if you can bring your mind to credit it) will be more than enough. The creature who crept into my house that night was, on Jekyll's own confession, known by the name of Hyde and hunted for in every corner of the land as the murderer of Carew.

HASTIE LANYON

X

HENRY JEKYLL'S FULL STATEMENT OF THE CASE

I was born in the year 18— to a large fortune, endowed besides with excellent parts, inclined by nature to industry, fond of the respect of the wise and good among my fellow-men, and thus, as might have been supposed, with every guarantee of an honourable and distinguished future. And indeed, the worst of my faults was a certain impatient gaiety of disposition, such as has made the happiness of many, but such as I found it hard to reconcile with my imperious desire to carry my head high, and wear a more than commonly grave countenance before the public. Hence it came about that I concealed my pleasures;

An engraved portrait of Stevenson at work on his novel. Stevenson, like Jekyll, led a wild and frivolous life as a young man. At Edinburgh University, he recalled, "my acquaintance was of what would be called a very low order. . . . seamen, chimney sweeps, and thieves."

and that when I reached years of reflection, and began to look round me and take stock of my progress and position in the world, I stood already committed to a profound duplicity of life. Many a man would have even blazoned such irregularities as I was guilty of; but from the high views that I had set before me, I regarded and hid them with an almost morbid sense of shame. It was thus rather the exacting nature of my aspirations, than any particular degradation in my faults, that made me what I was and, with even a deeper trench than in the majority of men, severed in me those provinces of good and ill which divide and compound man's dual nature. In this case, I was driven to reflect deeply and inveterately on that hard law of life which lies at the root of religion and is one of the most plentiful springs of distress. Though so profound a double-dealer, I was in no sense a hypocrite; both sides of me were in dead earnest; I was no more myself when I laid aside restraint and plunged in

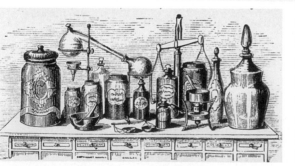

A doctor inspects a potion in *The Doctor*, painted by Dutch artist Gerard Dou in 1653. Medicine and alchemy were practiced in similar ways at that time. Alchemists were often suspected of having made a pact with the devil in order to gain knowledge. Stevenson's novel gives a modern psychological spin to this belief.

Tools of the apothecary's trade.

shame, than when I laboured, in the eye of day, at the furtherance of knowledge or the relief of sorrow and suffering. And it chanced that the direction of my scientific studies, which led wholly towards the mystic and the transcendental, reacted and shed a strong light on this consciousness of the perennial war among my members. With every day, and from both sides of my intelligence, the moral and the intellectual, I thus drew steadily nearer to that truth by whose partial discovery I have been doomed to such a dreadful shipwreck: that man is not truly one, but truly two. I say two, because the state of my own knowledge does not pass beyond that point. Others will follow, others will outstrip me on the same lines; and I hazard the guess that man will be ultimately known for a mere polity of multifarious, incongruous and independent denizens. I, for my part, from the nature of my life, advanced infallibly in one direction and in one direction only. It was on the moral side, and in my own person, that I learned to recognize the thorough and primitive duality of man; I saw that, of the two natures that contended in the field of my consciousness, even if I could rightly be said to be either, it was only because I was radically both; and from an early date, even before the course of my scientific discoveries had begun to suggest the most naked possibility of such a miracle, I had learned to dwell with pleasure, as a beloved daydream, on the thought of the separation of these elements. If each, I told myself, could but be housed in separate identities, life would be relieved of all that was unbearable; the unjust might go his way, delivered from the aspirations and remorse of his more upright twin; and the just could walk steadfastly and securely on his upward path, doing the good things in which he found his pleasure, and no longer exposed to disgrace and penitence by the hands of this extraneous evil. It was the curse of mankind that these incongruous faggots were thus bound together—that in the agonized womb of consciousness these polar twins should be continuously struggling. How, then, were they dissociated?

I was so far in my reflections when, as I have said, a side light began to shine upon the subject from the laboratory table. I began to perceive more deeply than it has ever yet been stated, the trembling immateriality, the mist-like transience, of this seemingly so solid body in which we walk attired. Certain agents I found to have the power to shake and pluck back that fleshly vestment, even as a wind might toss the curtains of a pavilion. For two good reasons I will not enter deeply into this scientific branch of my confession. First, because I have been made to learn that the doom and burthen of our life is bound for ever on man's shoulders; and when the attempt is made to cast it off, it but returns upon us with more unfamiliar and more awful pressure. Second, because, as my narrative will make, alas! too evident, my discoveries were incomplete. Enough, then, that I not only recognized my natural body for the mere aura and effulgence of certain of the powers that made up my spirit, but managed to compound a drug by which these powers should be dethroned from their supremacy, and a second form and countenance substituted, none the less natural to me because they were the expression, and bore the stamp, of lower elements in my soul.

I hesitated long before I put this theory to the test of practice. I knew well that I risked death; for any drug that so potently controlled and shook the very fortress of identity, might by the least scruple of an overdose or at the least inopportunity in the moment of exhibition, utterly blot out that immaterial tabernacle which I looked to it to change. But the temptation of a discovery so singular and profound at last overcame the suggestions of alarm. I had long since prepared my tincture; I purchased at once, from a firm of

A portrait of Sigmund Freud (1856–1939). Although the Viennese psychoanalyst had not yet published his theories on the unconscious mind and the divided nature of personality when *Dr. Jekyll and Mr. Hyde* was written, concepts of this sort already interested many scientists of the time. Stevenson's wife, Fanny Osborne, later said that her husband had drawn some of his inspiration from reading a French scientific journal article on the subconscious, which Hyde in some ways seems to represent. Stevenson himself referred to his subconscious as his Brownies, "who do one-half my work for me while I am fast asleep, and in all likelihood, do the rest for me as well, when I am wide awake and fondly suppose I do it for myself."

wholesale chemists, a large quantity of a particular salt, which I knew, from my experiments, to be the last ingredient required; and, late one accursed night, I compounded the elements, watched them boil and smoke together in the glass, and when the ebullition had subsided, with a strong glow of courage, drank off the potion.

The most racking pangs succeeded: a grinding in the bones, deadly nausea, and a horror of the spirit that cannot be exceeded at the hour of birth or death. Then these agonies began swiftly to subside, and I came to myself as if out of a great sickness. There was something strange in my sensations, something indescribably new and, from its very novelty, incredibly sweet. I felt younger, lighter, happier in body; within I was conscious of a heady recklessness, a current of disordered sensual images running like a mill race in my fancy, a solution of the bonds of obligation, an unknown but not an innocent freedom of the soul. I knew myself, at the first breath of this new life, to be more wicked, tenfold more wicked, sold a slave to my original evil; and the thought, in that moment, braced and delighted me like wine. I stretched out my hands, exulting in the freshness of these sensations; and in the act, I was suddenly aware that I had lost in stature.

There was no mirror, at that date, in my room; that which stands beside me as I write, was brought there later on and for the very purpose of those transformations. The night, however, was far gone into the morning—the morning, black as it was, was nearly ripe for the conception of the day—the inmates of my house were locked in the most rigorous hours of slumber; and I determined, flushed as I was with hope and triumph, to venture in my new shape as far as to my bedroom. I crossed the yard, wherein the constellations looked down upon me, I could have thought, with wonder, the first creature of that sort that their unsleeping vigilance had yet disclosed to them; I stole through the corridors, a stranger in my own house; and coming to my room, I saw for the first time the appearance of Edward Hyde.

I must here speak by theory alone, saying not that which I know, but that which I suppose to be most probable. The evil side of my nature, to which I had now transferred the stamping efficacy, was less robust and less developed than the good which I had just deposed. Again, in the course of my life, which had been, after all, nine-tenths a life of effort, virtue and control, it had been much less exercised and much less exhausted. And hence, as I think, it came about that Edward Hyde was so much smaller, slighter, and younger than Henry Jekyll. Even as good shone upon the countenance of the one, evil was written broadly and plainly on the face of the other. Evil besides (which I must still believe to be the lethal side of man) had left on that body an imprint of deformity and decay. And yet when I looked upon that ugly idol in the glass, I was conscious of no repugnance, rather of a leap of welcome. This, too, was myself. It seemed natural and human. In my eyes it bore a livelier image of the spirit, it seemed more express and single, than the imperfect and divided countenance I had been hitherto accustomed to call mine. And in so far I was doubtless right. I have observed that when I wore the semblance of Edward Hyde, none could come near to me at first without a visible misgiving of the flesh. This, as I take it, was because all

When Dr. Jekyll refers to "the prisonhouse of my disposition," he is echoing the theories of the German philosopher Friedrich Nietzsche (1844–1900). Nietzsche (below) claimed that societal laws, religion, and morality were designed to keep men of exceptional merit from rising above the masses. The Übermensch, or "superman," could not express his full potential unless he was freed of ordinary rules and constraints. However Stevenson's story provides a caution against this philosophy. When Jekyll is released from the bonds of morality, he does not rise above humanity, but sinks beneath it.

human beings, as we meet them, are commingled out of good and evil: and Edward Hyde, alone in the ranks of mankind, was pure evil.

I lingered but a moment at the mirror: the second and conclusive experiment had yet to be attempted; it yet remained to be seen if I had lost my identity beyond redemption and must flee before daylight from a house that was no longer mine; and hurrying back to my cabinet, I once more prepared and drank the cup, once more suffered the pangs of dissolution, and came to myself once more with the character, the stature, and the face of Henry Jekyll.

That night I had come to the fatal cross roads. Had I approached my discovery in a more noble spirit, had I risked the experiment while under the empire of generous or pious aspirations, all must have been otherwise, and from these agonies of death and birth I had come forth an angel instead of a fiend. The drug had no discriminating action; it was neither diabolical nor divine; it but shook the doors of the prisonhouse of my disposition; and, like the captives of Philippi, that which stood within ran forth. At that time my virtue slumbered; my evil, kept awake by ambition, was alert and swift to seize the occasion; and the thing that was projected was Edward Hyde. Hence, although I had now two characters as well as two appearances, one was wholly evil, and the other was still the old Henry Jekyll, that incongruous compound of whose reformation and improvement I had already learned to despair. The movement was thus wholly toward the worse.

66 Even as good shone upon the countenance of the one . . . **99**

Even at that time, I had not conquered my aversions to the dryness of a life of study. I would still be merrily disposed at times; and as my pleasures were (to say the least) undignified, and I was not only well known and highly considered, but growing towards the elderly man, this incoherency of my life was daily growing more unwelcome. It was on this side that my new power tempted me until I fell in slavery. I had but to drink the cup, to doff at once the body of the noted professor, and to assume, like a thick cloak, that of Edward Hyde. I smiled at the notion; it seemed to me at the time to be humourous; and I made my preparations with the most studious care. I took and furnished that house in Soho, to which Hyde was tracked by the police; and engaged as a housekeeper a creature whom I knew well to be silent and unscrupulous. On the other side, I announced to my servants that a Mr. Hyde (whom I described) was to have full liberty and power about my house

66 . . . evil was written broadly and plainly on the face of the other. **99**

in the square; and, to parry mishaps, I even called and made myself a familiar object in my second character. I next drew up that will to which you so much objected; so that if anything befell me in the person of Dr. Jekyll, I could enter on that of Edward Hyde without pecuniary loss. And thus fortified, as I supposed, on every side, I began to profit by the strange immunities of my position.

Men have before hired bravos to transact their crimes, while their own person and reputation sat under shelter. I was the first that ever did so for his pleasures. I was the first that could thus plod in the public eye with a load of genial respectability, and in a moment, like a schoolboy, strip off these lendings and spring headlong into the sea of liberty. But for me, in my impenetrable mantle, the safely was complete. Think of it—I did not even exist! Let me but escape into my laboratory door, give me but a second or two to mix and swallow the draught that I had always standing ready; and, whatever he had done, Edward Hyde would pass away like the stain of breath upon a mirror; and there in his stead, quietly at home, trimming the midnight lamp in his study, a man who could afford to laugh at suspicion, would be Henry Jekyll.

66 All human beings are commingled out of good and evil. 99

The pleasures which I made haste to seek in my disguise were, as I have said, undignified; I would scarce use a harder term. But in the hands of Edward Hyde, they soon began to turn toward the monstrous. When I would come back from these excursions, I was often plunged into a kind of wonder at my vicarious depravity. This familiar that I called out of my own soul, and sent forth alone to do his good pleasure, was a being inherently malign and villainous; his every act and thought centered on self; drinking pleasure with bestial avidity from any degree of torture to another; relentless like a man of stone. Henry Jekyll stood at times aghast before the acts of Edward Hyde; but the situation was apart from ordinary laws, and insidiously relaxed the grasp of conscience. It was Hyde, after all, and Hyde alone, that was guilty. Jekyll was no worse; he woke again to his good qualities seemingly unimpaired; he would even make haste, where it was possible, to undo the evil done by Hyde. And thus his conscience slumbered.

Into the details of the infamy at which I thus connived (for even now I can scarce grant that I committed it) I have no design of entering. I mean but to point out the warnings and the successive steps with which my chastisement approached. I met with one accident which, as it brought on no consequence, I shall no more than mention. An act of cruelty to a child aroused against me the anger of a passerby, whom I recognised the other day in the person of your kinsman; the doctor and the child's family joined him; there were moments when I feared for my life; and at last, in order to pacify their too just resentment, Edward Hyde had to bring them to the door, and pay them in a cheque drawn in the name of Henry Jekyll. But this danger was easily eliminated from the future by opening an account at another bank in the name of Edward Hyde himself; and when, by sloping my own hand backwards I had supplied my double with a signature, I thought I sat beyond the reach of fate.

Some two months before the murder of Sir Danvers, I had been out for one of my adventures, had returned at a late

66 The pleasures which I made haste to seek in my disguise were, as I have said, undignified.**99**

hour, and woke the next day in bed with somewhat odd sensations. It was in vain I looked about me; in vain I saw the decent furniture and tall proportions of my room in the square; in vain that I recognised the pattern of the bed curtains and the design of the mahogany frame; something still kept insisting that I was not where I was, that I had not wakened where I seemed to be, but in the little room in Soho where I was accustomed to sleep in the body of Edward Hyde. I smiled to myself, and, in my psychological way, began lazily to inquire into the elements of this illusion, occasionally, even as I did so, dropping back into a comfortable morning doze. I was still so engaged when, in one of my more wakeful moments, my eye fell upon my hand. Now, the hand of Henry Jekyll (as you have often remarked) was professional in shape and size; it was large, firm, white and comely. But the hand which I now saw, clearly enough, in the yellow light of a mid-London morning, lying half shut on the bed-clothes, was lean, corded, knuckly, of a dusky pallor, and thickly shaded with a swart growth of hair. It was the hand of Edward Hyde.

I must have stared upon it for near half a minute, sunk as I was in the mere stupidity of wonder, before terror woke up in my breast as sudden and startling as the crash of cymbals; and bounding from my bed, I rushed to the mirror. At the sight that met my eyes, my blood was changed into something exquisitely thin and icy. Yes, I had gone to bed Henry Jekyll, I had awakened Edward Hyde. How was this to be explained? I asked myself; and then, with another bound of terror—how was it to be remedied? It was well on in the morning; the servants were up; all my drugs were in the cabinet—a long journey, down two pairs of stairs, through the back passage, across the open court and through the anatomical

> 66 An act of cruelty to a child aroused against me the anger of a passer-by.99

> **❝** It was the hand of Edward Hyde. **❞**

theatre, from where I was then standing horror-struck. It might indeed be possible to cover my face; but of what use was that, when I was unable to conceal the alteration in my stature? And then, with an overpowering sweetness of relief, it came back upon my mind that the servants were already used to the coming and going of my second self. I had soon dressed, as well as I was able, in clothes of my own size; had soon passed through the house, where Bradshaw stared and drew back at seeing Mr. Hyde at such an hour and in such a strange array; and ten minutes later, Dr. Jekyll had returned to his own shape and was sitting down, with a darkened brow, to make a feint of breakfasting.

Small indeed was my appetite. This inexplicable incident, this reversal of my previous experience, seemed, like the Babylonian finger on the wall, to be spelling out the letters of my judgment; and I began to reflect more seriously than ever before on the issues and possibilities of my double existence. That part of me which I had the power of projecting had lately been much exercised and nourished; it

In May 1887, a Boston theater presented a stage adaptation of the novel with Richard Mansfield in the leading role. Mansfield continued to play the role until his death in 1907.

had seemed to me of late as though the body of Edward Hyde had grown in stature, as though (when I wore that form) I were conscious of a more generous tide of blood; and I began to spy a danger that, if this were much prolonged, the balance of my nature might be permanently overthrown, the power of voluntary change be forfeited, and the character of Edward Hyde become irrevocably mine. The power of the drug had not been always equally displayed. Once, very early in my career, it had totally failed me; since then I had been obliged on more than one occasion to double, and once, with infinite risk of death, to treble the amount; and these rare uncertainties had cast hitherto the sole shadow on my contentment. Now, however, and in the light of that morning's accident, I was led to remark that whereas, in the beginning, the difficulty had been to throw off the body of

Dr. Jekyll's reference to "the Babylonian finger on the wall" comes from the Book of Daniel in the bible. During a banquet, King Belshazzar of Babylon saw a mysterious hand writing illegible characters on the wall. When the king had the prophet Daniel interpret the signs for him, it turned out that they predicted the end of his reign. Rembrandt painted this scene of Belshazzar seeing the original "handwriting on the wall."

Jekyll, it had of late gradually but decidedly transferred itself to the other side. All things therefore seemed to point to this: that I was slowly losing hold of my original and better self, and becoming slowly incorporated with my second and worse.

Between these two I now felt I had to choose. My two natures had memory in common, but all other faculties were most unequally shared between them. Jekyll (who was a composite) now with the most sensitive apprehensions, now with a greedy gusto, projected and shared in the pleasures and adventures of Hyde; but Hyde was indifferent to Jekyll, or but remembered him as the mountain bandit remembers the cavern in which he conceals himself from pursuit. Jekyll had more than a father's interest; Hyde had more than a son's indifference. To cast in my lot with Jekyll was to die to those appetites which I had long secretly indulged and had of late begun to pamper. To cast it in with Hyde was to die to a thousand interests and aspirations, and to become, at a blow and for ever, despised and friendless. The bargain might appear unequal; but there was still another consideration in the scales; for while Jekyll would suffer smartingly in the fires of abstinence, Hyde would be not even conscious of all that he had lost. Strange as my circumstances were, the terms of this debate are as old and commonplace as man; much the same inducements and alarms cast the die for any tempted and trembling sinner; and it fell out with me, as it falls with so vast a majority of my fellows, that I chose the better part and was found wanting in the strength to keep to it.

Yes, I preferred the elderly and discontented doctor, surrounded by friends and cherishing honest hopes; and bade a resolute farewell to the liberty, the comparative youth, the light step, leaping pulses and secret pleasures, that I had enjoyed in the disguise of Hyde. I made this choice perhaps with some unconscious reservation, for I neither gave up the house in Soho, nor destroyed the clothes of Edward Hyde, which still lay ready in my cabinet. For two months, however, I was true to my determination; for two months I led a life of such severity as I had never before attained to, and enjoyed the compensations of an approving conscience. But time began at last to obliterate the freshness of my alarm; the praises of conscience began to grow into a thing of course; I began to be tortured with throes and longings, as of Hyde struggling after freedom; and at last, in an hour of moral weakness, I once again compounded and swallowed the transforming draught.

I do not suppose that, when a drunkard reasons with himself upon his vice, he is once out of five hundred times affected by the dangers that he runs through his brutish physical insensibility; neither had I, long as I had considered my position, made enough allowance for the complete moral insensibility and insensate readiness to evil which were the leading characters of Edward Hyde. Yet it was by these that I was punished. My devil had been long caged, he came out

Robert Louis Stevenson at sixteen, with his father, Thomas. Stevenson's father supported him for much of his adult life. As a young man, Stevenson argued often with his father, whose strong Calvinist principles clashed with his son's more liberal views. They had a temporary break, when Thomas responding to his son's profession of atheism, claimed, "I would ten times sooner see you lying in your grave than that you should be bringing ruin on other houses as you have brought it upon this." But there was also a strong affection between them.

roaring. I was conscious, even when I took the draught, of a more unbridled, a more furious propensity to ill. It must have been this, I suppose, that stirred in my soul that tempest of impatience with which I listened to the civilities of my unhappy victim; I declare at least, before God, no man morally sane could have been guilty of that crime upon so pitiful a provocation; and that I struck in no more reasonable spirit than that in which a sick child may break a plaything. But I had voluntarily stripped myself of all those balancing instincts by which even the worst of us continues to walk with some degree of steadiness among temptations; and in my case, to be tempted, however slightly, was to fall.

Instantly the spirit of hell awoke in me and raged. With a transport of glee, I mauled the unresisting body, tasting delight from every blow; and it was not till weariness had begun to succeed that I was suddenly, in the top fit of my delirium, struck through the heart by a cold thrill of terror. A mist dispersed; I saw my life to be forfeit; and fled from the scene of these excesses, at once glorying and trembling, my lust of evil gratified and stimulated, my love of life screwed to the topmost peg. I ran to the house in Soho, and (to make assurance doubly sure) destroyed my papers; thence I set out through the lamplit streets, in the same divided ecstasy of mind, gloating on my crime, light-headedly devising others in the future, and yet still hastening and still hearkening in my wake for the steps of the avenger. Hyde had a song upon his lips as he compounded the draught, and as he drank it pledged the dead man. The pangs of transformation had not done tearing him, before Henry Jekyll, with streaming tears of gratitude and remorse, had fallen upon his knees and lifted his clasped hands to God. The veil of self-indulgence was rent from head to foot, I saw my life as a whole: I followed it up from the days of childhood, when I had walked with my father's hand, and through the self-denying toils of my professional life, to arrive again and again, with the same sense of unreality, at the damned horrors of the evening. I could have screamed aloud; I sought with tears and prayers to smother down the crowd of hideous images and sounds with which my memory swarmed against me; and still, between the petitions, the ugly face of my iniquity stared into my soul. As the acuteness of this remorse began to die away, it was succeeded by a sense of joy. The problem of my conduct was solved. Hyde was henceforth impossible; whether I would or not, I was

66 With a transport of glee, I mauled the unresisting body, tasting delight from every blow.**99**

An 1878 edition of the popular magazine *The World* contained this illustration of a policeman discovering a body on a quay of the Thames. Stevenson borrowed many of the melodramatic elements of Sir Danvers's murder from the popular literature of the day.

" I destroyed my papers. "

now confined to the better part of my existence; and, oh, how I rejoiced to think it! with what willing humility I embraced anew the restrictions of natural life! with what sincere renunciation I locked the door by which I had so often gone and come, and ground the key under my heel!

The next day came the news that the murder had been overlooked, that the guilt of Hyde was patent to the world, and that the victim was a man high in public estimation. It was not only a crime, it had been a tragic folly. I think I was glad to know it; I think I was glad to have my better impulses thus buttressed and guarded by the terrors of the scaffold. Jekyll was now my city of refuge; but let Hyde peep out an instant, and the hands of all men would be raised to take and slay him.

I resolved in my future conduct to redeem the past; and I can say with honesty that my resolve was fruitful of some good. You know yourself how earnestly in the last months of last year I laboured to relieve suffering; you know that much was done for others, and that the days passed quietly, almost happily for myself. Nor can I truly say that I wearied of this beneficent and innocent life; I think instead that I daily enjoyed it more completely; but I was still cursed with my duality of purpose; and as the first edge of my penitence wore off, the lower side of me, so long indulged, so recently chained down, began to growl for licence. Not that I dreamed of resuscitating Hyde; the bare idea of that would startle me to frenzy: no, it was in my own person that I was once more tempted to trifle with my conscience; and it was as an ordinary secret sinner that I at last fell before the assaults of temptation.

There comes an end to all things; the most capacious measure is filled at last; and this brief condescension to my evil finally destroyed the balance of my soul. And yet I was not alarmed; the fall seemed natural, like a return to the old days before I had made my discovery. It was a fine, clear January day, wet under foot where the frost had melted, but cloudless overhead; and the Regent's Park was full of winter chirrupings and sweet with Spring odours. I sat in the sun on a bench; the animal within me licking the chops of memory; the spiritual side a little drowsed, promising subsequent penitence, but not yet moved to begin. After all, I reflected, I was like my neighbours; and then I smiled, comparing myself with other men, comparing my active goodwill with the lazy cruelty of their neglect. And at the very moment of that vain-glorious thought, a qualm came over me, a horrid nausea and the most deadly shud-dering. These passed away, and left me faint; and then as in its turn the faintness subsided, I began to be aware of a change in the temper of my thoughts, a greater boldness, a contempt of danger, a solution of the bonds of obligation. I looked down; my clothes hung formlessly on my shrunken limbs; the hand that lay on my knee was corded and hairy. I was once more Edward Hyde. A moment before I had been safe of all men's respect, wealthy, beloved—the cloth laying for me in the dining-room at home; and now I was the common quarry of mankind, hunted, houseless, a known murderer, thrall to the gallows.

> 66 The next day came the news that the murder had been overlooked. 99

My reason wavered, but it did not fail me utterly. I have more than once observed that, in my second character, my faculties seemed sharpened to a point and my spirits more tensely elastic; thus it came about that, where Jekyll perhaps might have succumbed, Hyde rose to the importance of the moment. My drugs were in one of the presses of my cabinet: how was I to reach them? That was the problem that (crushing my temples in my hands) I set myself to solve. The laboratory door I had closed. If I sought to enter by the house, my own servants would consign me to the gallows. I saw I must employ another hand, and thought of Lanyon. How was he to be reached? how persuaded? Supposing that I escaped capture in the streets, how was I to make my way into his presence? and how should I, an unknown and displeasing visitor, prevail on the famous physician to rifle the study of his colleague, Dr. Jekyll? Then I remembered that of my original character, one part remained to me: I could write my own hand; and once I had conceived that kindling spark, the way that I must follow became lighted up from end to end.

Thereupon, I arranged my clothes as best I could, and summoning a passing hansom, drove to an hotel in Portland Street, the name of which I chanced to remember. At my appearance (which was indeed comical enough, however tragic a fact these garments covered) the driver could not conceal his mirth. I gnashed my teeth upon him with a gust of devilish fury; and the smile withered from his face—happily for him—yet more happily for

> 66 At the inn, as I entered, I looked about me with so black a countenance as made the attendants tremble. 99

A hotel advertises its rates.

myself, for in another instant I had certainly dragged him from his perch. At the inn, as I entered, I looked about me with so black a countenance as made the attendants tremble; not a look did they exchange in my presence; but obsequiously took my orders, led me to a private room, and brought me wherewithal to write. Hyde in danger of his life was a creature new to me; shaken with inordinate anger, strung to the pitch of murder, lusting to inflict pain. Yet the creature was astute; mastered his fury with a great effort of the will; composed his two important letters, one to Lanyon and one to Poole; and, that he might receive actual evidence of their being posted, sent them out with directions that they should be registered.

A sheet of hotel stationery.

Thenceforward, he sat all day over the fire in the private room, gnawing his nails; there he dined, sitting alone with his fears, the waiter visibly quailing before his eye; and thence, when the night was fully come, he set forth in the corner of a closed cab, and was driven to and fro about the streets of the city. He, I say—I cannot say, I. That child of Hell had nothing human; nothing lived in him but fear and hatred. And when at last, thinking the driver had begun to grow suspicious, he discharged the cab and ventured on foot, attired in his misfitting clothes, an object marked out for observation, into the midst of the nocturnal passengers, these two base passions raged within him like a tempest. He walked fast, hunted by his fears, chattering to himself, skulking through the less frequented thoroughfares, counting the minutes that still divided him from midnight. Once a woman spoke to him, offering, I think, a box of lights. He smote her in the face, and she fled.

A match vendor. In towns all over England, children and adults tried to eke out a living by shining shoes or selling small items like boxes of matches, or "lights."

When I came to myself at Lanyon's, the horror of my old friend perhaps affected me somewhat: I do not know; it was at least but a drop in the sea to the abhorrence with which I looked back upon these hours. A change had come over me. It was no longer the fear of the gallows, it was the horror of being Hyde that racked me. I received Lanyon's condemnation partly in a dream; it was partly in a dream that I came home to my own house and got into bed. I slept after the prostration of the day, with a stringent and profound

Matchboxes of the time.

66 Above all, if I slept, or even dozed for a moment in my chair . . . 99

slumber which not even the nightmares that wrung me could avail to break. I awoke in the morning shaken, weakened, but refreshed. I still hated and feared the thought of the brute that slept within me, and I had not of course forgotten the appalling dangers of the day before; but I was once more at home, in my own house and close to my drugs; and gratitude for my escape shone so strong in my soul that it almost rivalled the brightness of hope.

I was stepping leisurely across the court after breakfast, drinking the chill of the air with pleasure, when I was seized again with those indescribable sensations that heralded the change; and I had but the time to gain the shelter of my cabinet, before I was once again raging and freezing with the passions of Hyde. It took on this occasion a double dose to recall me to myself; and alas, six hours after, as I sat looking sadly in the fire, the pangs returned, and the drug had to be re-administered. In short, from that day forth it seemed only by a great effort as of gymnastics, and only under the immediate stimulation of the drug, that I was able to wear the countenance of Jekyll. At all hours of the day and night, I would be taken with the premonitory shudder; above all, if I slept, or even dozed for a moment in my chair, it was always as Hyde that I awakened. Under the strain of this continually impending doom and by the sleeplessness to which I now condemned myself, ay, even beyond what I had thought possible to man, I became, in my own person, a creature eaten up and emptied by fever, languidly weak both in body and mind, and solely occupied by one thought: the horror of my other self. But when I slept, or when the virtue of the medicine wore off, I would leap almost without transition (for the pangs of transformation grew daily less marked) into the possession of a fancy brimming with images of terror, a soul boiling with causeless hatreds, and a body that seemed not strong enough to contain the raging energies of life. The powers of Hyde seemed to have grown with the sickliness of Jekyll. And certainly the hate that now divided them was equal on each side. With Jekyll, it was a thing of vital instinct. He had now seen the full deformity of that creature that shared with him some of the phenomena of consciousness, and was co-heir with him to death: and beyond these links of community, which in themselves made the most poignant part of his distress, he thought of Hyde, for all his energy of life, as of something not only hellish but inorganic. This was the shocking thing; that the slime of the pit seemed to utter cries and voices; that the amorphous dust gesticulated and sinned; that what was dead, and had no shape, should usurp the offices of life. And this again, that that insurgent horror was knit to him closer than a wife, closer than an eye; lay caged in his flesh, where he heard it mutter and felt it struggle to be born; and at every hour of weakness, and in the confidence of slumber, prevailed against him, and deposed him out of life. The hatred of Hyde for Jekyll was of a different order. His terror of the gallows drove him continually to commit temporary suicide, and return to his subordinate station of a part instead of a person; but he loathed the necessity, he loathed the despondency into which Jekyll was now fallen, and he resented the dislike with which he was himself regarded. Hence the ape-like tricks that he would play me, scrawling in my own hand blasphemies on the pages of my books, burning the letters and destroying the portrait of my father; and indeed, had it not been for his fear of death, he would long ago have ruined himself in order to involve me in the ruin. But

An 1879 watercolor of the rear view of apartment buildings near Holborn. This scene suggests the kind of back entrance Dr. Jekyll's house would have had.

66 . . . it was always as Hyde that I awakened. 99

The gallows at Newgate Prison. The last public execution at Newgate took place outside on the prison grounds in 1868. After that, convicts were hanged in this room of the prison.

his love of life is wonderful; I go further: I, who sicken and freeze at the mere thought of him, when I recall the abjection and passion of this attachment, and when I know how he fears my power to cut him off by suicide, I find it in my heart to pity him.

It is useless, and the time awfully fails me, to prolong this description: no one has ever suffered such torments, let that suffice; and yet even to these, habit brought—no, not alleviation—but a certain callousness of soul, a certain acquiescence of despair; and my punishment might have gone on for years, but for the last calamity which has now fallen, and which has finally severed me from my own face and nature. My provision of the salt, which had never been renewed since the date of the first experiment, began to run low. I sent out for a fresh supply, and mixed the draught; the ebullition followed, and the first change of colour, not the second; I drank it, and it was without efficiency. You will learn from Poole how I have had London ransacked; it was in vain; and I am now persuaded that my first supply was impure, and that it was that unknown impurity which lent efficacy to the draught.

About a week has passed, and I am now finishing this statement under the influence of the last of the old powders. This, then, is the last time, short of a miracle, that Henry Jekyll can think his own thoughts or see his own face (now how sadly altered!) in the glass. Nor must I delay too long to bring my writing to an end; for if my narrative has hitherto escaped destruction, it has been by a combination of great prudence and great good luck. Should the throes of change take me in the act of writing it, Hyde will tear it in pieces; but if some time shall have elapsed after I have laid it by, his wonderful selfishness and circumscription to the moment will probably save it once again from the action of his ape-like spite. And indeed the doom that is closing on us both

Birdcage Walk, the cemetery of Newgate Prison, where ninety-seven executed convicts are buried. The only record is their initials engraved in the wall.

has already changed and crushed him. Half an hour from now, when I shall again and forever reindue that hated personality, I know how I shall sit shuddering and weeping in my chair, or continue, with the most strained and fearstruck ecstasy of listening, to pace up and down this room (my last earthly refuge) and give ear to every sound of menace. Will Hyde die upon the scaffold? or will he find the courage to release himself at the last moment? God knows; I am careless; this is my true hour of death, and what is to follow concerns another than myself. Here then, as I lay down the pen, and proceed to seal up my confession, I bring the life of that unhappy Henry Jekyll to an end.

Death row at Newgate. Even though Newgate was no longer used as a long-term prison after 1881, the last hanging took place there in 1901, the year the building was destroyed.

At left, the Siamese twins Chang and Eng Bunker around the year 1860.

Below, Cain and Abel by the 15th century Flemish painter Frans Floris.

The Lie, by Salvador Rosa

Fredric March in his Oscar-winning role as Dr. Jekyll and Mr. Hyde, in the 1932 film by Rouben Mamoulian.

The theme of a dual or split personality is central to Stevenson's novel. This was not a new idea; in some ways, the monster created by Dr. Frankenstein in Mary Shelley's novel was a precursor to *Dr. Jekyll and Mr. Hyde*. Oscar Wilde, Kipling, and Poe had also experimented with the idea. The duality of human nature was a recurrent theme in nineteenth-century thought. The scientific community was fascinated by such phenomena as twins and Siamese twins. Freud and other psychoanalysts explored the concepts of split personality and multiple personality disorders; the light that Dr. Jekyll sheds on these issues is prophetic. The struggle between good and evil, as symbolized in the biblical story of Cain and Abel, is as old as the hills. In Stevenson's novel, the conflicting beings are one and the same person, who uses the mask of respectability to conceal a much more primitive being. Stevenson emphasizes in his letters that the evil in Jekyll/Hyde was not that he was addicted to vices but that he was "two-faced." He wore the mask of hypocrisy: "The Hypocrite let out the beast Hyde—who is no more sensual than another." Stevenson's story functions as a mystery novel and thriller while on a deeper level it confronts the reader with the dilemmas and complexity of the human soul.

PICTURE CREDITS

Éditions Gallimard

Director: Pierre Marchand
Editor: Marie Aubelle
Picture Research: Suzanne Bosman
Layout: Marilyn Gatepaille
Copyeditor: Simone Sentz

Viking

Editor: Jill Davis
Design: Nina Putignano
Production Editor: Janet Pascal

VIKING
Published by the Penguin Group
Penguin Putnam Books for Young Readers, 345 Hudson Street,
New York, New York 10014, U.S.A.
Penguin Books Ltd, 27 Wrights Lane, London W8 5TZ, England
Penguin Books Australia Ltd, Ringwood, Victoria, Australia
Penguin Books Canada Ltd, 10 Alcorn Avenue, Toronto, Ontario, Canada M4V 3B2
Penguin Books (N.Z.) Ltd, 182-190 Wairau Road, Auckland 10, New Zealand

Penguin Books Ltd, Registered Offices: Harmondsworth, Middlesex, England

This illustrated edition published in 1999 in France by Éditions Gallimard
Published in 2000 in the United States of America by Viking, a member of Penguin
Putnam Books for Young Readers
Simultaneously published in a paperback edition

1 3 5 7 9 10 8 6 4 2

Copyright © Éditions Gallimard Jeunesse, 1999
Illustrations by François Place
Notes by Suzanne Bosman
Note translation by Barbara Brister

All rights reserved

Library of Congress Catalog Card Number: 99-75659
ISBN 0-670-88865-6

Printed in Italy
Set in Trump Mediaeval

AMBER BROWN
WANTS EXTRA CREDIT

Paula Danziger

AMBER BROWN
WANTS EXTRA CREDIT

Illustrated by Tony Ross

G. P. PUTNAM'S SONS   NEW YORK

Acknowledgments

To everyone at the American School of
London—especially some of the most
terrific fourth graders ever (1994–95)

To Bruce Coville—for listening

To the Evans family—Gill, Greg, Dan, and Isobel

Text copyright © 1996 by Paula Danziger
Illustrations copyright © 1996 by Tony Ross
All rights reserved. This book, or parts thereof, may not be reproduced
in any form without permission in writing from the publisher.
G. P. Putnam's Sons, a division of The Putnam & Grosset Group,
200 Madison Avenue, New York, NY 10016.
G. P. Putnam's Sons, Reg. U.S. Pat. & Tm. Off.
Published simultaneously in Canada.
Printed in the United States of America
Book design by Donna Mark
Lettering by David Gatti. Text set in Bembo

Library of Congress Cataloging-in-Publication Data
Danziger, Paula, 1944– Amber Brown wants extra credit / by Paula Danziger;
illustrated by Tony Ross. p.　cm. Sequel to: Amber Brown goes fourth.
Summary: Unhappy over her parents' divorce and her mother's boyfriend Max,
nine-year-old Amber finds her schoolwork suffering.
[1. Divorce—Fiction.　2. Schools—Fiction.]　I. Ross, Tony, ill.　II. Title.
PZ7.D2394At 1996　[Fic]—dc20　95-586 CIP AC

ISBN 0-399-22900-0
1　3　5　7　9　10　8　6　4　2
First Impression

To Ben Danziger
Your book, with love from Aunt

AMBER BROWN
WANTS EXTRA CREDIT

Chapter One

★ ★ ★ ★ ★ ★ ★ ★ ★

AMBERINO CERTIFICATES

I, Amber Brown, being of sound mind and no money (I spent it all on a book, a computer game, and some junk food), do hereby give my mother five Amberino Certificates for her birthday.

Amberino Certificates allow The Mother (Sarah Thompson) to ask her beloved only child (Amber Brown) to grant her five wishes. . . . Just remember, these have to be wishes that I can actually do . . . . not stuff

like move the Empire State Building or eat
spinach or find the cure for dandruff (not
that you have it or anything). Just remember, I'm just a nine-year-old kid, so make
the wishes doable . . . but then you always
do!!!!!!!

HAPPY BIRTHDAY AND LOVE FROM

amber Brown

♡ ♡ ♡

★　★　★　★　★　★　★　★　★

Chapter Two

I, Amber Brown, am being held captive by a madwoman.

That madwoman is my mother, and she's very mad at me for having a messy room.

She's also very mad at me because my teacher, Mrs. Holt, sent home a note saying that I'm "not working up to the best of [my] ability."

My mother is very, very mad at me because of the note. Actually what she said is that what she's very angry about is the reason for the note . . . . me not doing my schoolwork the way I should.

Now I'm supposed to be a perfect little student.

And she's using one of the Amberino Certificates to make me clean up my room.

She says that I can't leave my room until it's "neat as a pin."

How can a room be neat as a pin? Does a pin have a bed in it—a dresser, curtains, a person living in it?

The words "neat as a pin" are the second-silliest thing I've ever heard.

The first-silliest thing is expecting me to have a neat room.

I wish I never gave her those Amberino Certificates for her birthday.

Doesn't she know that if my room is neat, I can't find anything?

It makes me nervous if everything is too organized.

She never used to mind that my room wasn't neat.

She never used the Amberinos to make me clean it up.

The telephone rings.

I rush out to answer it.

My mother gets to it first, picks it up, and listens.

Then she says, "Brandi, I'm sorry, Amber can't come to the phone. . . . ."

"I'm at the phone. . . . I don't have to come to the phone." I pull on my mother's sleeve.

My mother points her finger at my room. "Back, Amber . . . . I'm serious. You have to clean your room before you do anything else."

"But Mom . . . ."

"No 'But Mom's,' " she says. "CLEAN YOUR ROOM . . . . NOW."

She starts talking on the phone. "Brandi, she can call you back as soon as her room is clean. . . . . Yes, I'll remind her to bring her new game cartridge when she goes to your house tonight . . . if she gets her room organized by then, you will see her and the game. Otherwise, I'm not sure you'll see either."

I stomp into my room.

This isn't fair.

My room is a little messy, but I, Amber Brown, don't think she's really angry about my messy room.

I think that my mom is really angry because I don't want to meet her dumb boyfriend.

That's one of the big reasons why she's in such a bad mood.

Just because she wanted to use one of her Certificates to have me finally meet Max and go out to dinner with them . . . and just because I said, "No, I'm not ready yet, and you promised I don't have to until I'm ready. You promised that a long time ago . . . . so the Certificate can't make me go."

If I meet Max, I'll have to actually know that he's a real person . . . . a real person who is going out with my mom . . . . and if my mom is going out with him . . . . . that really means that there's less chance that she and my dad will get back together.

And what if I meet Max and actually like him? That wouldn't be fair to my dad, who's in Paris, France, which is so far away.

So, I'm not ready to meet Max, and I may never be ready.

I stomp some more and then I start throwing things into garbage bags . . . . . .

my dirty clothes, my clean clothes, the book report I've been working on for the last week.

And then I put the garbage bags in my closet.

Next, I put in all of the important things from the top shelf of my bookcase . . . the Dad Book that I keep so that I can look at pictures of my dad and talk to him sometimes . . . . the ball that Justin and I made from our used chewing gum . . . . the scrapbook that my aunt Pam and I made up of our trip to London. (It even has a chickenpox scab in it to remind me of how I got sick there.)

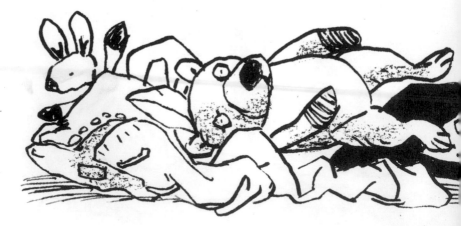

I open the top drawer of my dresser and shove everything on top into it.

I get into bed, and from under the covers, I start to make my bed, pulling up the sheets and then the blanket and then the bedspread . . . . then I get out and kind of smooth everything down . . . . the Amber Brown Way to Make a Bed.

Then I throw my stuffed animals on my bed.

I guess there's not only a madwoman in the house but a mad kid.

There's no madman in the house, though, because he, my father, and my

mother got so mad that they got divorced, and now he's in France because of his dumb job.

I, Amber Brown, wish things would go back to the way they were before . . . . before my dad left . . . . . before Justin, my first best friend, moved away . . . . . before my mother changed her last name back to the name she had before she got married so that we don't even have the same last name anymore . . . . before Max, the dumbhead boyfriend, met my mother . . . . before it was so important to get me to keep my room neat.

I wish.

Chapter Three

I'm escaping.

I'm out of the house.

My room passed inspection.

I'm really lucky that my mother didn't look in the closet or dresser drawers, or I would still be in my room instead of getting a ride to Brandi's sleepover.

My mother and I are in the car, not saying much of anything.

What she did say is that she is "really not happy with the way I've been acting."

Well, I'm really not happy with the way she's been acting.

I keep staring straight ahead.

Then I look over at my mother.

There are tears rolling down her face.

She hardly ever cries.

I've only seen her cry big time four times
. . . . . Once was when she got a call that
my grandfather, her father, had died . . . . .
and once was right after my father left. Even
though she'd said she wanted him to leave,
she still cried. And once I saw her cry when
I was about five and I ran out into traffic and
almost got hit by a car, but it stopped in
time. She yelled at me and then picked me

up, hugged me, and told me never to do that again. Then she told me how much she loved me and then she cried.

And now she's crying.

"Mom, what's wrong?" I touch her arm.

She pulls the car over by the sidewalk and looks at me. "Amber, it's so hard. I want to be a good mother."

"You are." I tell her that to make her stop crying and because even though I get mad at her, I know it's true.

She wipes her eyes. "And I want to be good to myself, too."

I sit quietly.

"You are making it very hard for me," she says.

I continue to say nothing.

"It's not all your fault," she says. "I've read all the books. Sometimes I'm even afraid that I'm beginning to sound like one of them. . . . . I understand that sometimes, many times, it's very hard for a child to accept the fact that parents divorce and then start dating other people. I understand . . . . . but I don't like it."

"I don't like it either," I tell her. "This isn't a book. This is my life. I can't help it if I want you and Daddy to stay together and for both of you to not go out with other people."

She sighs. "Your father is in France, doing whatever he wants to do, without your knowing, without your making it difficult for him."

14

I think about what she said.

Even though I don't want to admit it, she's right.

I say, "If I knew that he had a girlfriend, I'd tell him that I wouldn't want to meet her any more than I want to meet Max."

"But you don't even know, do you?" my mother says softly. "But you do know what I do because you live with me . . . . and, Amber, you know that I want you to live with me. . . . I'm not complaining or upset about that . . . I just want you to listen, to try to understand and to try to make things easier for me."

There are more tears rolling down her cheeks.

"I'll listen. I'll try." I hate to see her cry.

She continues. "We live with each other full-time. In some divorce families, children spend some time with each parent, and that allows the parents some time to themselves.

We're not, at present, a family that can do that. So you know a lot about what I do and who I spend my time with."

"So . . . ." I ask, "what do you want me to do?"

She takes a deep breath. "I want you to understand that I need to get on with my own life, to meet new people and include these new people in my life . . . . in our lives."

"New people . . . . you mean Max." I look at her.

She nods. "Especially Max. You know, Amber, it's not as if I'm asking you to meet an ax murderer. Max Turner is one of the nicest men I've ever met. He's a good man, funny and gentle and kind."

"Are you going to marry him? Are you going to expect me to call him Dad?" Now I feel like crying.

She shrugs. "I don't know if I'm going to marry him, but I do know that I like him a lot . . . and, no, I don't expect you to call him Dad. You already have a father. You can call him Max."

"Max," I say softly, thinking about how I once knew a Max, but he was a dog.

I wonder if I said, "Roll over and play dead" to Max the person, if he would do it.

I smile, thinking about making Max the person roll over and play dead.

My mother smiles back. "See, it's not so bad thinking about meeting him. You just smiled."

"I was thinking about the Hawkinses' dog, Max," I say in a mean voice, "and how they used to have him roll over and play dead."

My mother stops smiling and starts to cry again, just a little.

I really do hate it when she cries.

"Oh, okay," I sigh, and give in.

"Then you'll meet him? Promise?" She sounds happier.

"I promise to meet him. I don't promise to like him," I say, and think . . . . . *Okay, Max . . . . . roll over. Play dead.*

"It's a beginning." She smiles.

Chapter
Four

"I'm going to kill my brother." Tiffani Shroeder pretends to wring an invisible neck.

"There are laws against that." Brandi laughs.

"What did he do this time?" I ask, dipping my potato chip into the onion dip.

Tiffani grabs a potato chip, puts it in her mouth, and crunches.

While she swallows, I smile, thinking about how much I like her five-year-old brother, Howie. He's very cute and does stuff that makes me laugh.

Tiffani eats a few more potato chips, while we wait for her to tell us what happened.

I look at Tiffani.

She has potato chip crumbs sitting on her chest.

If potato chip crumbs dropped on my chest, they would end up on the floor.

Tiffani Shroeder is the first girl in our class to have to wear a bra.

Hannah Burton wore a bra first, but she really didn't need one.

Tiffani speaks. "You know my Barbie doll collection? Well, you know that I don't play with them anymore. I mean, that would just be too baby. But they are my Barbies."

I wonder if since Tiffani changed the spelling of her name from y to i, she's changed the spelling of Barbie to Barbi . . . . I guess that her whole collection of the dolls, though, would still be Barbies. (I, Amber Brown, am very good at the spelling of plurals.)

Tiffani continues. "Well, that little runt and his little runt friends were playing with their X-Men toys and they decided to declare war. . . . . I came home and found my Barbies strangled with my grandmother's yarn and strung across the living room. Prom Barbie. Business Barbie. Lifeguard Barbie. College Barbie . . . . and all of the others. It was Barbicide," Tiffani says.

"Yuck. That's weird." Naomi makes a face.

Tiffani nods. "They also strung up all of the little runt's G.I. Joes."

"An Equal Opportunity Massacre." I shake my head.

Everyone groans, and Brandi empties the last of the potato chip bag on my head.

The potato chip crumbs fall off my head, onto my sweatshirt, and onto the floor.

Tiffani says, "One of the little runts even accidentally stepped on my book report and ruined it. Now I have to spend most of tomorrow redoing it."

I think about how my own half-finished book report is in one of the garbage bags in my closet. I'll have to fix mine up, too.

But tonight, while my mother and Max the person are out on a date, I, Amber Brown, am at a pajama party, having fun with my friends.

As for the book report . . . . . . It's Saturday night. I'll think about it on Sunday. After all, tomorrow is another day.

Chapter
Five

"We must . . . . . we must . . . we must . . ." Naomi and Alicia scream out of the car as Naomi's mother drops me off at my house.

I can't stop laughing.

I also can't stop hoping that they won't finish the cheer, which is "We must . . . we must . . . we must improve our bust. . . . We better . . . we better . . . before we wear a sweater." It's a cheer that the sixth graders do.

Last night we did jumping jacks to that cheer.

As far as I can tell, nothing much has changed about my body except that it's very tired.

No one gets any sleep at a sleepover.

Tiffani tried, but we kept whispering in her ear, "Beware your little brother. Today a Barbie doll . . . tomorrow a big sister."

I look at the driveway to see if there are any strange cars in front of my house . . . . To see if Max is there.

No car . . . . . no Max . . . . . . He's not in the house, either. . . .

Just my mother, sitting in the kitchen, drinking a cup of coffee.

"Did you have fun last night?" She smiles at me.

"I did." I pour myself a glass of milk and sit down.

"Mrs. Colwin let us use some of her old makeup and try on her jewelry. Can I get my ears pierced? And then we played Truth or Dare . . . . and we all had to name the boys we want as boyfriends."

My mother laughs. "Slow down, honey . . . . I can see that you put makeup on . . . . When you get older and are allowed to wear makeup, might I suggest that you don't outline your lipstick in green? . . . It's just a suggestion, though. Don't think I'm being critical."

I laugh, too. "It was dark. It was late. I

thought it was lipliner. It was eyeliner."

She continues to smile. "Amber Brown, you know we decided that you could get your ears pierced when you are twelve."

"Mommmmmmmm," I beg, "everyone is getting it done."

My mother raises one eyebrow.

I know that is a definite no.

I squint my eyes closed and stick out my lower lip.

She knows that is a definite pout.

Changing the subject, she says, "Who did you choose as a boyfriend, did you take the dare?"

"The dare was that I would have to go up to Fredrich Allen in school on Monday and give him a kiss. He's the kid who picks his nose and chews it."

My mother makes a gagging sound and says, "Who did you say your boyfriend was?"

"I said it was Justin." I sigh, thinking about my best friend, who moved away at the end of the last school year.

"You really miss him, don't you." She ruffles my hair.

I nod.

It makes me sad to think that Justin is so far away and that he hardly ever writes to me.

It's not that he was really a boyfriend, he

was a boy friend . . . . but I said he was a boyfriend because I didn't want to kiss Fredrich Allen.

I do miss him.

He would understand why I don't want my mother to go out with Max, why I miss my father.

My dad used to take Justin and me to baseball games. He took us fishing. He took us to see the gory horror movies that my mother hates.

"Amber," my mother says softly.

"Yes?" I get nervous sometimes when my mother speaks very softly. . . . It's like she wants me to listen very carefully . . . . usually to something I don't want to hear.

"Amber . . . . remember yesterday when you said that you would be willing to meet Max? . . . Well, he's going to take us out to dinner tonight." She refills my glass of milk and then looks at me.

I have to figure out what I want to say, so I sit quietly for a minute.

"Mom . . . . . I said sometime . . . not immediately. . . . I have homework to do today. . . . . I have to think about it. . . . How about over Christmas vacation?"

"Amber." She shakes her head. "This is the beginning of October. We're not waiting until the end of December."

"My homework," I plead, knowing that she knows how important it is that I get it done.

She stares at me. "Do it now. You have all day to finish it . . . . and you know it better be done well. Max won't be here until around six o'clock. That gives you a lot of time. Now, Amber, you promised that you'd meet Max. I'll even use up two of the Amberino Certificates on this."

I stand up.

I know it's no use to argue.

And I started out having such a nice Sunday.

And then she ruined it.

Well, just wait till she sees what I'm going to do to hers.

Chapter Six

I stomp (all the way) up the stairs on the way to my room.

On the first step, I stomp because I have to meet Max. . . .

On the second, because I'm going to have to sit down at a table and eat dinner with him. . . .

On the third, because my mother is making me do this. . . .

On the fourth, because my father isn't here to see what's happening and get back together with my mother. . . . . .

I stomp with both of my feet on the fifth

step because my parents have changed my life without my permission. . . .

I stomp up the rest of the way because I know it will really annoy my mother and because my feet just want to stomp.

Then I slam my door.

My hands just want to slam.

I throw my knapsack on the bed and then I throw myself on the bed.

I lie on my bed and think about Max.

I just know I'm going to hate him.

I bet he looks like a gorillahead . . . or probably a gorillabutt.

I bet he's gross-looking, with hairs growing out of his nose and ears, and I bet that he smokes cigarettes and belches and blows his nose in the dinner napkin and then puts the napkin on the table . . . and I bet he hates nine-year-old girls.

I pretend one of my stuffed animals is Max. I choose the gorilla.

Pretending to be a ventriloquist, I put the

gorilla's face near mine. "So, Amber . . . I understand that you don't want me to take your mother out."

"That's right, banana breath." I stare at Maxgorilla.

The gorilla voice says, "Ha-ha, you lose. I'm a grown-up, and what I say goes."

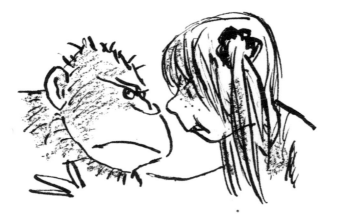

I glare at Maxgorilla. "Who says, you foul fur-face?"

"I says . . . . and so does your mother. After all, she did make you meet me," the gorilla tells me.

I throw Maxgorilla across the room.

He hits the wall and falls into the garbage can.

Trying to calm down, I count to ten.

That doesn't work.

I count to twenty, thirty, fifty, one hundred.

That doesn't work either.

I try to think about all of the stuff I have to do.

That definitely doesn't work. Who can think about homework at a time like this?

I just can't calm down.

I get up and take out my Dad Book. Opening it up, I talk to my favorite picture of my dad.

I tell him what's going on.

I beg him to come home and try to straighten things out.

I say, "What happens if Max isn't so bad and I actually like him?" Will my dad hate me for liking Max, for going places with him and Mom?

I wish that my father would speak to me
face-to-face, person-to-person, Dad-to-
Amber. Hearing his voice once a week on
the phone just isn't enough.

And it isn't easy for me to say some of this stuff into a phone.

I tell his picture this and ask him what he's going to do about what's happening.

But he's only a picture, so he doesn't answer; and I don't want to have to pretend to be a ventriloquist to make him say what I want to hear, so there's only silence.

It's so silent.

I'm screaming inside . . . . . and I don't know how to make anything come out.

Chapter Seven

I sit at the restaurant table, making a list of
things that I, Amber Brown, don't like.

1. I don't like eating at restaurants. It's so boring . . . . waiting to get a table . . . . waiting to order something to drink . . . . . waiting for the waiter or waitress to come and take the order . . . . waiting for the dinner to arrive . . . . . waiting to order dessert . . . . waiting for the check.

I personally think that not only the people who work at the restaurant should be called waiters, I think that the people who eat there should be called waiters, too.

Take me to a fast-food restaurant anytime. You stand in a short line, or you even get to go through in a car. Everything arrives at once in a nice little box with your own packets of ketchup and stuff. You don't have to say, "Please, pass the _____." It's all there, and sometimes you even get a toy or something with it. And then you eat it and you're done. You don't have to sit around gabbing all day.

2. I don't like having to sit in a restaurant with Max, who I don't like.

3. I don't like complaining all the time, but what's a kid to do when nothing is going the way she wants it to go?

"Amber, please pass the salt." Max smiles at me.

I pass him the salt.

He could have just as easily asked my mother to pass him the stupid salt, but, no, he has to ask me.

"Thanks."

"It's nothing."

My mother starts to talk. "You know . . . . the two of you have a lot in common.

You both like to tell jokes. You both like to eat the center part of the Oreos."

Great, I think, *that'll be another thing we have to share.*

"You like to read. You like to travel. You like to see horror movies." She babbles on.

I look at Max. "My dad takes me to horror movies. He'll be taking me to a lot of them when he moves back here."

"Amber," my mother says softly.

Max says, "Well, maybe we can just see a few of them until he comes back."

"He can take me to all of them." I glare.

"Amber," my mother says again.

Max looks at my mother and says, "Sarah, honey, relax."

How dare he call her honey. That's what my dad used to call her before they started fighting. That's what my mom calls me.

He puts his hand on top of hers, and they hold hands at the table.

I accidentally spill my drink on the table.

While we wait for the waiter to clean it up, my mother tries to sponge up the liquid with her napkin.

She's no longer holding Max's hand.

I don't want to like Gorillaface, not for one single moment.

And he's acting so nice. He does seem like my mom said he would be. I hate it that he's acting so nice. This would be much easier if my mom WAS dating an ax murderer. Then I could really hate him.

Max and my mother are hugging.

I look over at my mother.

She and Max are kissing.

That's so gross.

I say, "Mom, I hope that the fungus in your mouth is getting better."

And then I look at Max and smile. "The doctor says that in girls it's curable. Boys die from it."

"Amber," my mother says, "stop that."

Max laughs.

I hate it.

He really doesn't even look like a gorilla. He's got dark hair, brown eyes, and he smiles a lot.

My mother continues. "You both like to chew gum. You'll have to show Max your chewing gum ball sometime."

Max pretends to take out a stick of gum, put it in his mouth, blow a huge bubble, and pop it all over his face. He pretends to wipe it off.

I will not smile at Max.

I will not smile at Max.

I will not smile at Max.

I will not smile at Max.

I will not smile at Max.

Chapter Eight

Mrs. Holt collects all of the book reports
. . . . . all of them except for mine and Eric
Feinstein's.

Eric's not in school today because he
broke his arm over the weekend.

Some kids will do anything to get out of
doing their homework.

I know Eric didn't do it intentionally, but
he's lucky that he's got a real excuse . . . . .
and he's unlucky that he's got a broken arm.

I wonder if he broke the arm he writes
with.

I wonder if I should have made up a list

of excuses, or maybe I should have broken my arm, but I hate it when I even break my fingernail.

It's not really my fault that I didn't do my book report.

All Sunday I was too angry to work on my report.

When we got back from dinner, I told my mother that I had to go upstairs to finish my homework, but since Max didn't leave

right away, I had to sit silently and sneakily on the top of the steps, spying on them.

I thought I was doing a real good job of spying and listening until Max called out, "Do you want us to speak louder, Amber?"

Max thinks he's so funny.

So does my mother, because she laughed when he said that.

So I went into my stomp-and-slam routine, and then my mother came upstairs and told me that enough was enough, that she was trying to be patient with me but she'd had enough, and it was time for me to go to bed.

So I went to bed.

So it's really my mother's fault that I didn't get my homework done.

Mrs. Holt is calling out everyone in the class by name to take attendance and to have that person bring up the book report.

"Amber Brown." Mrs. Holt gets to my name.

Very softly, I say, "I'm here but my book report isn't. I'll bring it in tomorrow."

Someone goes, "Dun-di-dun-dun . . . . dun."

Someone else goes, "Not-done-di-done . . . . done."

Hannah Burton looks at me and smirks. "It figures."

I cross my eyes at Hannah Burton.

Mrs. Holt writes something in the marking book and calls out the next name.

It's just my luck that it's not a regular written-on-a-piece-of-paper report that can be passed up to the front without everyone knowing that you didn't do your work. But it's a book report that is supposed to be shaped to look like a cereal box.

I really did start mine. It was called *Anastasia Krupnik Krunchies* (it was about one of Lois Lowry's books). I'd already done the book summary that was supposed to go on the back, along with:

NUTRITION FACTS

Character Development   100%
Adventure   50%
Interest   100%
Personalities   100%
Dialogue   100%
Pictures   80%

*Anastasia Krupnik Krunchies
contains the ingredients found only in
the best food for thought.*

1 knew what I was going to do for the front cover . . . . . . draw a picture of Anastasia and show that inside the box would be an author trading card. I was going to make up one about Lois Lowry, with facts and a Xeroxed picture.

So I did have a lot done, but I scrunched it up when I was mad and then never finished the report.

I read the book and loved it.

I did most of the work.

It's only a book report.

So what's the big deal?

Chapter Nine

"I can't believe you didn't do your book report. Amber, what's going on? You've been acting so weird." Brandi puts a tuna fish sandwich on her tray.

I take a sandwich and a bowl of red Jell-O.

I, Amber Brown, love red Jell-O. I love the way it squishes through my teeth while I'm eating it.

I, however, don't feel good about having to talk about why I'm acting so weird.

I try to make a joke about it. "People have always said that I'm weird."

Putting my tray down on the counter, I grab my ponytails and pretend they are motorcycle handlebars, and make engine noises.

Usually this makes her laugh.

This time it doesn't.

She does smile, though, and says, "That kind of weird is what I like about you .... This is a different kind of weird."

We continue to go through the line.

"You're in a lousy mood sometimes, and you're not as much fun as you used to be ..... and you won't talk about what's bothering you."

I pretend to have trouble making up my mind about whether to choose chocolate milk or regular milk.

Brandi sighs.

We pay for our food and sit down.

At the table on the right, some of the sixth graders are blowing straw wrappers at one another.

At the table on the left, some of the third graders are having a competition to see if they can make milk come out of their noses.

I unwrap my peanut butter, jelly, and banana sandwich and add some potato chips to it.

Naomi and Alicia join us.

So does Hannah Burton.

Having to sit next to Hannah Burton is enough to make me lose my lunch . . . and I'm not talking about misplacing it.

She takes out her lunch, which she's brought from home.

It's Chinese food, probably leftovers.

I love Chinese food.

But I would never ask Hannah to share it.

Hannah takes out a pair of chopsticks and starts using them.

She's such a show-off.

I love Chinese food but I hate chopsticks.

The only way that I don't drop everything when I use them is if I spear the food.

"Nice work, Amber. I can't believe that you didn't do your book report. Couldn't you find a book to match your interests? Did the library lend out the last copy of *Where's Spot?*" She picks up some cold noodles with sesame sauce on them and chopsticks them into her mouth.

"Are you enjoying your lunch? Worms with worm doodoo, isn't it? Mmmmmmm, good."

Hannah puts the chopsticks down for a minute, and then she picks them up again. "You are just so immature, Amber. Late growing up . . . . . . late turning in your homework."

I wonder what Hannah Burton would look like with chopsticks up her nose.

Seeing Hannah with the chopsticks reminds me of last year when our class studied China, and Justin and I dueled with our chopsticks.

Why couldn't Hannah have moved to Alabama instead of Justin? Maybe she could have even moved to China.

Tiffani Shroeder joins us.

She opens up her lunch bag, looks inside, and says, "I'm going to kill that little goofball."

"What is it? What has Howie done this time?" I know who she is talking about. "Goofball" is one of the cleaner things that Tiffani calls her younger brother.

Tiffani pulls something out of her lunch bag.

It's a Barbie doll wrapped in a piece of bologna. One of its arms sticks out through the bologna. The other arm sticks out of the top.

"It's Lunch Meat Barbie." I giggle.

"I'm going to get that kid." Tiffani shakes her head. "I don't know what I'm going to do, but I'm going to get him."

"Is that your whole lunch? Want some of mine?" I offer her half of my sandwich.

She looks back into the bag. "No, thanks. The little creep put this on top of the lunch that my mom made for me."

The rest of her lunch looks absolutely normal.

I was hoping that Howie had done more . . . . . like included Barbie-Q chips or something . . . but for a five-year-old he does pretty well.

We continue to eat and talk.

Hannah Burton drops *moo goo gai pan* on her sweatshirt.

I like lunchtime.

It's a good time for me to forget my problems.

The first bell rings, and we take our garbage and throw it in the bins.

As I walk back to class, I hear Mrs. Holt call out, "Amber."

I walk over to her.

She's very nice, but I just know that she's mad at me.

She says, "Amber, I would like you to see me after school before you go to Elementary Extension."

I nod.

I, Amber Brown, am in deep trouble.

Chapter
Ten

The end-of-the-day bell rings.

Everyone else gets up to leave.

I just sit there.

"I'll see you in Elementary Extension," Brandi whispers. "Good luck."

Hannah Burton smirks at me.

Smirk. Smirk. Smirk. Hannah Burton is such a jerk is what I think.

Everyone else leaves.

It's me and Mrs. Holt, alone in the room.

My stomach hurts.

I, Amber Brown, never used to get in trouble in school . . . . . not for grades and

not for not doing my work . . . sometimes
for talking and giggling, but not for big stuff
. . . . I don't know what's going to happen.

I walk up to Mrs. Holt's desk and wait
until she's finished writing something in her
marking book.

I stand there and look at the clock, waiting.

Something must be wrong with the
clock. I feel like it's hours and I've only been
standing here for minutes.

Mrs. Holt looks up.

"I'll turn the book report in tomorrow,"
I promise.

"Amber, bring a chair over and sit down
here."

I get the chair and sit down by the side of
her desk.

Her desk is so big. Her chair is so much
higher than mine.

I look up, try to smile, and wait for her to
say something.

She waits, too.

There really must be something wrong with the clock. It's ticking loudly, very loudly.

I can't stand the quiet. "Mrs. Holt. I promise I'll bring the book report in tomorrow."

"Amber, what are we going to do?" She puts down her pen and looks at me. "I've

sent a note home. Do you want me to start sending home worksheets with your assignments on them so that your mother can see them and sign them? Is that what you want?"

"No." I bite my lip and try not to cry.

She looks at her marking book. "You're missing assignments . . . . not just the book report, but three math homeworks, two essays . . . . and you've gotten low grades on several tests. And it's only October."

"Are you sure?" I ask, even though I know she's right.

"I'm sure." She nods. "Amber, I know you can do the work. I've checked your records, spoken to your old teachers."

"They're not so old," I say, and then I put my hand over my mouth.

I can't believe that I said that. It just came into my brain and out of my mouth.

She looks at me for a minute.

It's another very long minute, and then she smiles.

Mrs. Holt has a very nice smile, for a person who is probably going to flunk me.

Amber Brown. Fourth Grade Failure.

"Amber," she says.

"I'm sorry," I say.

Amber Brown. Sorry Person.

"As I was saying, I've been speaking with some of your past teachers."

I think . . . *And they passed me. . . . Please pass me too* . . . . but I don't say it out loud.

"You know, Amber, when I spoke to Mr. Cohen, he told me what he'd written in your 'Passport to Fourth Grade' . . . . how he loved your sense of humor, your sense of exploration . . . how you're willing to try out new things even when they're hard. I've been able to see some of that, but I'd love to see more of it . . . . and more of your homework assignments."

We smile at each other.

"Amber, I know you can do the work. What's wrong? Is it anything I can help you with? Is it anything anyone at the school can help you with? I know that there have been some changes in your life, and I'll try to be understanding . . . . . but you must do your work."

"Everything's okay." I try not to cry. "I promise I'll do the work. Don't make me take one of those papers home."

She thinks for a minute.

I sit there very quietly.

"Okay. For now, I won't make you take the paper home, but I do want you to make up your back work and turn in your book report tomorrow. Each day, your grade will go down one mark from what it would have been if you had turned it in on time."

I bite my lip. "Can I do extra credit?"

She shakes her head. "In this case, you may not. Extra credit's reserved for people who have tried their best and need an extra boost, or for people who are already doing their best and want to do more. YOU are not in either one of those categories."

She closes her marking book. "You have a chance to bring up your grade. Just make sure that you turn in all of your missing work."

I take the list of missing assignments that she hands me.

She continues. "Tomorrow, the class will be given a major project. Do well on it. I can't emphasize this highly enough. It will help bring up your grade for the marking period and will show me that you're serious about doing well."

I nod.

I, Amber Brown, may not be serious about a lot of things, but I am serious about this.

Chapter
Eleven

"How-To" Assignment

YOUR ASSIGNMENT: Giving Directions

Be prepared to give directions
to the class. Be logical. Be concise.
You may show how to build, make,
or do something (for example, you
may show how to build a fort,
make a dress, do karate, play an
instrument). Your directions must
be clear.

In addition to giving directions,

create something original concerning what you are explaining (e.g., making a poster, a film, or a computer program).

Your presentation can take between five and fifteen minutes.

I look at the assignment.

I have no idea what to do.

"Think about it," Mrs. Holt tells the class. "Tomorrow, let me know what you will be doing."

"How-To" . . . . . What does she want from me? What can I do to get the best grade possible? What will impress Mrs. Holt?

How to do . . . . I look around the room to try to come up with ideas. . . .

How to redecorate the classroom . . . How to stop Fredrich Allen from picking his nose and chewing it . . . . . How to crochet those ugly dolls that cover toilet-

paper rolls . . . . How to keep
from having to get a list of daily assignments
signed by my mother . . . How to find time
to do this project while I'm still finishing my
makeup work . . . .
. . . . . . How to have a worry attack about
school . . . . How to not have a worry attack
about school . . . . How to come
up with a great idea for this project.

"Can we work together on the project?"
Naomi asks.

Mrs. Holt shakes her head no.

My brain hurts from trying to think up a
good project.

I start to doodle and write on my notebook.

I must, I must, I must improve
my grades.
I better, I better, before I have
to take home a letter.

Maybe I should just let Mrs. Holt write the letter and get my mother all upset.

It would serve her right for going out with Max.

And then she would have to tell my father and then he would get all upset.

It would serve him right for going off to France and spending so little time with me.

It would serve them both right for getting divorced.

Amber Brown . . . . School Failure.

Sarah Thompson and Phil Brown . . . . . My Parents . . . . . . Family Failures.

The lunch bell rings.

I grab my lunch and head out the door.

Brandi's already rushed out.

Some days she makes a fast dash to the girls' room.

She hates to ask for a pass in class.

One of the boys always says, "Hope everything comes out okay."

Mrs. Holt smiles at me. "Your book report was very good, Amber."

"Thanks. What'd I get?" I need to know.

"A C," she says. "It would have been a B if you'd turned it in on time."

Walking down the hall, I think about it . . . . A C. *Not a great grade, but not a bad one—"C" no evil.*

I laugh.

Sometimes I just make myself laugh.

Lunchroom.

Sit down with my friends.

"That little dirtbag." Tiffani opens her lunch.

This time, a Barbie arm is coming out of the lid of a yogurt.

"It's Cultured Barbie," I say.

"Maybe your project should be 'Things to Do with a Barbie Doll,'" Brandi suggests. "I bet that Howie could be a great help."

"I think . . ." Tiffani grins . . . . "it could be 'Things to Do to a Little Brother.' . . ."

"Brother Ka-Bobs," Bobby suggests. "Or what about . . . . . . Little Brother Sushi?"

"EW . . . . . . GROSS . . . . Stop it. I'm eating." Alicia makes gagging sounds.

Bobby can't stop . . . . "Microwave Brother . . . Brother McNuggets."

Bobby used to be an only child, just like me.

Then his mom got remarried and just had a baby boy.

I don't think he's overwhelmingly happy about not being an only child.

I, Amber Brown, can understand that.

"I know what I'm going to do for my project," Brandi says. "I'm going to show everyone how to do sign language."

"I know sign language," Bobby says.

"The only sign language you know could get you suspended." Jimmy starts to laugh.

They are so immature.

Brandi ignores them. "I'm going to teach some sign language and then show how a song we all know can be signed and interpreted. It's really beautiful."

"How do you know it?" I am surprised.

I thought I knew mostly everything about Brandi. I guess not.

When she moved here a year ago, Justin and I were still best friends, so we didn't really get to know each other until last month, and I guess it takes a while to learn everything.

She says, "Remember my cousin in California, the one who taught me to make the braids?"

I do remember. She made Brandi feel much better after she moved here and felt bad about not having any good, close friends.

"Well," Brandi continues, "her best friend is deaf, and they taught me to sign. I'm really good at it."

She moves her hands and signs something.

"What did you say?" I want to know.

She smiles. "I said, 'Do you want to share my brownie?' "

Licking my lips, I nod.

She makes a sign. "Yes."

I repeat the sign.

She hands me half her brownie.

"What's the sign for thank you?" I ask.

She shows me.

I make it and then start eating the brownie.

School brownies are not great.

My mom and I make really great ones.

And then I get an idea.

Chapter Twelve

AMBER BROWNies.

Sitting on my bed, I start taking notes.

How to make AMBER BROWNies.

That's it.

I'm going to show how to make brownies.

Brownies . . . . . cakelike chocolate squares that are brown.

Not the Girl Scout kind of Brownies.

I know just making brownies is not going to be enough to get an A . . . . but I, Amber Brown, will do the best brownie project ever.

I'll explain . . . . the best explanation ever.

I'll experiment . . . . brownies with marshmallows, candy bits, fudge, tuna fish, to name a few ingredients.

I'll create an AMBER BROWNie cookbook.

I'll write to famous people and ask them for their recipes for brownies and I'll ask them to tell me brownie stories, memories.

I'll prepare a brownie questionnaire.

I'll create computer pictures of brownies.

I'll design Brownie Barf Bags for people who have eaten too many tuna brownies.

I'll make up a character and tell stories about him or her. . . . I don't know yet who it will be . . . . maybe Santa Brownie or the Easter Brownie or who knows.

I'll write a brownie song.

I'll get an *A*.

I'll also probably gain a zillion pounds and get brownie pimples from all of the research that I'm going to have to do.

But who cares . . . . . . I, Amber Brown, just have to get a great grade on this project.

Putting down my pen, I get up and rush downstairs.

"Mom!" I yell.

"Amber!" she yells back. "Stop the yelling."

I rush into the kitchen. "Mom, we've got to go shopping."

I stop rushing.

My mother is sitting with Max at the kitchen table.

He's not only sitting at the table, he's sitting in the chair where my dad used to sit.

"Hi, Amber." Max smiles at me.

"What are you doing here? I didn't know you were coming," I say.

"Amber." My mother does not look pleased. "You are being very rude."

"I didn't mean to be rude," I say. "I didn't know he was going to be here."

"Your mother didn't either. I was just

passing by and decided to drop in." He smiles at my mother.

I look at the flowers that are on the table that weren't there when I went upstairs about half an hour ago. Next to the vase is an envelope that says, *Sarah.*

Yeah, sure, I think . . . . . *Max was just passing by.*

"I lied about the just passing by," Max says.

"I figured." I grin at him.

It's hard not to grin at Max.

But I try.

I don't want this guy to think that he can drop in whenever he wants to.

"Mom." I turn to her. "I need to go shopping. It's for school. I've got to go to the grocery store."

"Amber, why didn't you tell me this morning when I went to the store? I have to do some work this afternoon." She shakes her head.

"But Mom . . . . . it's for school. I have to explain how to do something for school. I'm going to explain brownies. I NEED to go to the store. You don't want me to fail, do you?" I plead.

"No, I don't want you to fail." She sighs. "Explain what you need and when."

I tell them all of my ideas. "And I need to do the baking this weekend . . . either today or tomorrow . . . to test everything out, to make sure that it will work when I actually have to do it for the class. Please, oh please, oh please . . . . I just have to do a great job on this project. You have no idea how important this is to me. Please, oh please, oh please."

And I NEVER want my mother to find out just how important this really is to me, how I need to do well to make up for all the bad work and no work that I've been doing . . . . or not doing.

"Sarah, I can take Amber to the store

now. . . . . You can do some of your work while we're gone, and then I'll take you both out for pizza tonight." He turns from her to look at me. "Not brownie pizza, though."

Brownie pizza, I think. *It's possible.*

My mother looks at him. "Max Turner, I told you that I had to work tonight . . . . that we would spend tomorrow together. You're very sneaky."

I agree. Max is very sneaky.

I bet he's offering to help me just so that he gets to spend more time with my mother.

"Tomorrow," he says, "we can all bake the brownies."

"Are you still going to be here tomorrow?" I want to know.

My mother looks at me.

Then she looks at Max.

Then she looks back at me.

And then at Max. . . . .

Max looks at my mother.

And then he looks at me. "I would like to have pizza with you and your mom, and then I know she has work to do so I will leave right after dinner."

My mother smiles at him.

He smiles back.

There is too much smiling, much too much smiling going on around here.

He continues. "Since the plan was for Sarah and me to spend some time together tomorrow, I think we should use that time to help you with your project."

I wish he would stop being so nice . . . . . One of these days, I'm going to have to do something terrible to him to make him lose his temper.

But not today. . . . . I need to go shopping.

Chapter Thirteen

"Wagons Ho," I say, putting on my seatbelt.

"Wagons Ho" is something my aunt Pam always says when we go someplace. It's become kind of a family thing to say at the beginning of some journeys.

I can't believe I've said it to Max, who is definitely not family. I wish I could take it back . . . but can't figure out how to do that . . . . so I think about taking it . . . . . . backward . . . that would be . . . . . . Oh Snogaw.

"Oh Snogaw," I say softly.

"What?" Max asks as he backs out of the driveway.

"Never mind." I shrug.

This is the first time I've been alone with Max . . . . and I've got a lot to tell him . . . . and a lot to ask.

I change the subject. "Do you have any kids? Have you ever been married? Do you want to marry my mom? Do you know that even though my mom and dad are divorced, there is a very good chance that they're going to get back together . . . . . that they're just taking a break from each other . . . . kind of like recess?"

Max keeps driving, without saying a word.

It makes me nervous that he's not saying anything.

I've never had to meet anyone that my mother was dating . . . mostly because she didn't go out on dates for a long time after my dad left . . . and then because she said I didn't have to meet anyone unless it was serious, and now she's made me meet Max, so I know this must be serious.

So I continue. "Do you know that my mom and I have been very happy just living together by ourselves? We like it that way . . . . . until my dad moves back from France. Then we're going to all live together again . . . . my mom . . . . my dad . . . and me."

I wait for him to say something.

Just before we get to the supermarket, Max pulls into the Dairy Queen, my favorite ice cream place.

"You can't bribe me," I say.

The car stops, and Max says, "I know. I just think that we should talk, and when I talk with friends, we often discuss things over a cup of coffee. I didn't think that we should have coffee."

"I don't drink coffee," I tell him. "I don't know a lot of nine-year-olds who do. . . .

My friend Justin used to like coffee ice cream, though."

We get out of the car and order ice cream.

I get two scoops in a dish, chocolate chip mint and vanilla fudge.

He gets coffee ice cream.

We sit down.

I mush up my ice cream and wait for the answers.

Chocolate chip mint and vanilla fudge mushed together looks pretty gross.

Max starts. "I've never been married. I don't have any kids. My niece, my sister's daughter, Jade, and I are very close. Jade's father left before she was born, so I've been like a father to her. She's six."

"My dad would never do anything like that," I say.

Max looks at me and nods. "I know. Your mom has told me how much he loves you."

"He does," I say, and then ask, "Do you want to marry my mom?"

Max looks at me. "Amber, your mother and I have only been dating since this summer . . . a few months. We're not talking about getting married . . . but when WE do talk about it, I'm sure that your mother will talk to you."

"You said WHEN, not IF." I let my ice cream drip down my chin.

He looks surprised. "I guess I did. . . . . . That's very interesting."

"My dad will be back soon," I remind him.

"Your mother said that he was going to try to move back. But Amber, I think you should talk to your mother about this . . . . . . about whether or not they're going to get back together."

I stand up. "We better go shopping now."

He stands up too, picks up a napkin, and

wipes the dripping ice cream off my face.

"Are you being nice to me because you want me to like you?" I ask.

"I'm being nice to you because I'm basically nice." He grins. "And, yes, I do want you to like me. But I'm not going to like it if you do stuff to try to mess things up between your mother and me . . . . but I will try to understand . . . . and to remember how rotten I was to the man who eventually became my stepfather."

Stepfather. I don't like that word.

"Would you tell me some of the things that you did to him?" I want to know because that information might be useful someday.

He laughs. "Not on your life. . . . Why should I tell you? So that you can use them on me? Do you think I'm nuts?"

I just smile at him.

"Don't answer that." He smiles back.

"You can tell me. Come on. I thought

87

you said you're a nice guy. it would be nice to tell me."

"I'm not that nice." He shakes his head.

One of these days, I'm going to get him to tell me . . . . and then I'm going to do the same thing to him . . . . . whatever it was . . . . I don't want to make all of this too easy for Max.

I'm beginning to like him . . . but I don't want to like him too much. . . . After all, what if he decides to stick around . . . or what if I like him a lot and then he decides to leave?

We get into the car, go to the supermarket, and get a cart.

The shopping begins.

We play supermarket basketball, lobbing all of the ingredients, except for the eggs and oil, into the cart. We get more points the farther we throw the items.

We also get strange looks from some of the other shoppers.

Then we play Guess the Weight.

Max picks up an item. Then he hands it to me and we both guess how much it weighs.

Then he takes it over to the fruit-weighing machine and we see who wins.

I'm ahead, fifteen to seven.

"Two points!" I yell as I throw a bag of marshmallows into the cart.

Max pretends to guard it, but it goes in.

There's loud cheering. It's the Nicholson brothers, Danny, Ryan, and Kyle. Danny, who's in third grade, gives Max a high five and says to me, "Amber, your dad is so much fun. . . . . ."

Max smiles.

I yell, "He's not my dad!" Danny looks really surprised that I yelled like that.

Max looks sad.

I look at both of them and then I say to Danny, "He's my mother's friend."

And then I add, "And he's my friend too."

Max looks happy again.

And I feel good that I've said that he's my friend.

I also feel a little guilty.

I'm not sure that my father would like it if he knew about Max and if he knew that I said that he's my friend.

Max throws a bag of jelly beans into the cart. "Two points."

By the time we get to the checkout counter, we have a tie score.

No one wins.

No one loses.

Chapter
Fourteen

It's Brownie Baking Day, and Max is back
again.

The ingredients that I put in the refrigera-
tor yesterday are on the table, and I'm emp-
tying the rest of the stuff out of the bag.

"I don't believe you two." My mother
shakes her head.

"Believe us." Max comes up behind her
and puts his arms around her waist.

She doesn't move away or anything.

I continue to put the ingredients on the
table.

"When you two came back last night, I

should have looked through the shopping bags." She shakes her head again.

Sprinkles . . . . M&M's . . . . Reese's Pieces . . . . . marshmallows . . . . gumdrops . . . . slivered almonds . . . walnuts . . . a can of tuna fish . . . a Mars bar . . . a bag of potato chips . . . . . Cheez Doodles . . . Gummi

worms, a bar of white chocolate . . . Good
& Plenty . . . . candy false teeth . . . . . candy
corn . . . strawberry Twizzlers . . . .
Cheerios . . . peanut butter . . . . . grape jelly
. . . . plus all of the regular stuff that goes into
plain brownies. . . . . . .

"This is disgusting." My mother shakes
her head . . . again.

"I know." I grin. "It's great."

"I'm never sending the two of you out
shopping together, never again." My
mother just keeps shaking her head.

She's beginning to look like one of those
bobbing dolls that some people have in the
back window of their cars.

Her head would probably be falling off if
she knew *how* Max and I shopped.

Max.

He's put one hand over my mother's eyes
and is feeding her some of the ingredients
and making her guess what they are.

Marshmallows are easy for her.

So are the nuts, candy corn, and Twizzlers.

Max puts an M&M in my mother's mouth.

"This one's a piece of cake," my mother says.

"No. Wrong. It's an M&M." Max takes his hand away from my mother's eyes and gives her a kiss.

I, Amber Brown, could have told him that "a piece of cake" in my mother's language means that it's super easy . . . but something tells me that Max already knows that.

I, Amber Brown, can also tell him that I'm not too sure about how I feel about him kissing my mom.

My mother starts to laugh, and then she looks over at me.

She looks a little guilty, sort of like she knows that I am not crazy about them kissing each other.

I clap my hands. "Come on, everyone, let's turn on the oven and do some preheating."

My mother and Max both laugh.

I don't get it.

"What's so funny?" I want to know.

"Nothing." My mother moves away from Max and puts the oven on.

Max puts out the cupcake papers, which we're using instead of baking pans so that we can make individual brownies with different stuff in them.

"What's so funny?" I repeat.

"Nothing," my mother repeats.

I make a face.

"It was a private joke," my mother tells me.

I don't think that Max and my mother should be having private jokes, not so soon.

I hate it when adults laugh in front of you and then say that it's a private joke.

It's kind of like when you're real little and

grown-ups spell in front of you.

And it's not fair.

Parents always make kids tell when the kids have a private joke.

And teachers always say things like, "Amber, would you like to share that with the rest of the class?"

And then if you say, "No, I really wouldn't," they make you do it anyway or they give you detention.

"The oven's heating up." My mother smiles. "Let's get this show on the road."

We get started.

Max pretends to be a French chef . . . "And now for zee eggs . . . ."

My mother starts singing, "Hi-ho, hi-ho . . . . . it's off to work we go," and she pretends to be one of the Seven Dwarfs . . . . Dopey, I think.

Max says that he's the eighth dwarf, Hun-gry.

I pretend to be the grown-up, lecturing

them on taking the job seriously and telling them not to eat so much of the batter (which I keep doing).

Our faces are covered with chocolate.

Max has just made a tuna–jelly-bean brownie.

My mother looks at his brownie and makes retching noises.

She's decorated her marshmallow brownie with sprinkles.

I'm filling my brownie with Gummi worms crawling through it and over it.

The phone rings.

It's my father.

Chapter Fifteen

"Hi, honey." My dad sounds like he's practically next door, not all the way in Paris, France. "How are you?"

"Fine," I say.

"What are you doing?"

I don't want to mention the good time that Max, Mom, and I are having, so I say, "Not much."

"I miss you so much. Do you miss me?"

"Yes, Daddy, I miss you bunches."

I sit in the living room, talking on the phone.

My mother and Max are in the kitchen.

"I miss you," I repeat.

"How much?" He's smiling . . . I can tell by his voice.

"This much." I spread my arms as far as I can while holding the phone between my shoulder and my ear.

"And how much is that?" he says, playing the I-love-you-this-much game we've always played with each other.

"To the next universe," I tell him.

"To the farthest galaxy," he tells me. "I love you and miss you that much."

I try to imagine what he's looking like at the other end.

I haven't seen my father for a couple of months, not since last summer when my aunt Pam took me to London, England.

I was supposed to visit him in Paris for a week but then I got the stupid chicken pox and he came to London instead.

We only got to spend a couple of days together.

And even though we talk on the phone every week, it's not the same.

Just before I start to tell him some stuff about me, he starts talking about what he's been doing, how he went to Euro Disney with a friend of his from work . . . . and with her little boy.

I was supposed to go to Euro Disney with him last summer.

The stupid chicken pox.

All I have is a Euro Disney sweatshirt that my dad sent me before I even went to England.

"Who is your friend, the one with the little boy?" I twirl the phone wire. "Did her husband go too?"

There's a pause for a minute, and then my dad says, "They're divorced. You know, Amber, you'd really like Judith and her son, Todd. He's the cutest little six-year-old. I've been spending a lot of time with them lately."

I think, *Here we go again.*

I'm just getting used to Max. Now I have to find out about Judith and Todd.

I say nothing for a minute, and then, "Cuter than when I was six?"

"No one was cuter than my Amber," he says.

My stomach starts to hurt.

I wonder if I've been eating too much brownie batter.

My father continues. "Maybe you can come over here during Christmas vacation and meet them. . . . . I'm sure that you'll really like them . . . and we'll finally be able to spend some time together."

There's so much to think about.

I'm getting a headache.

A headache . . . . . a stomachache . . . . maybe it's the attack of a killer flu that suddenly attacks nine-year-old girls who have eaten too much brownie batter. Maybe it's a telephone virus.

I don't want to meet this stupid Judith person and her stupid little dweeb son, who get to spend time with my father in Euro Disney when I hardly ever get to see him.

Why did my father even have to mention them?

This is my phone call, my time with him.

"Amber, I really miss you so much. Tell me what you've been doing. I feel like I'm missing so much."

"You could move back," I tell him.

"I can't, not yet." He sighs. "We've been through this already. It's my job . . . . and I need to earn money. I've got a lot of extra expenses."

"Maybe you'd have more money if you weren't taking strangers to Euro Disney."

"Amber, don't be silly," he says.

I hate to be told that I'm being silly when I tell him how I feel.

"Look. I've got to be going now. Mom and I are in the middle of making brownies with her friend Max. He took me shopping yesterday. We're all having so much fun."

There's silence at the other end.

I continue. "In a couple of weeks, there's going to be a carnival at school. I'm probably going to be very busy going to that with Mom and Max. You'll probably be very busy doing something with Judith and her little dweeb . . . . so if you don't call, it'll be okay."

"Amber." He raises his voice. "Stop this. Stop it right now. Don't be angry. Be reasonable. I only mentioned Judith because I want you to know about my life . . . so that we can stay close. I'm sorry if I've done this the wrong way."

"You could have asked about my schoolwork," I say. "Actually, I've been getting into trouble at school, not doing my schoolwork."

There's silence at the other end for a minute, and then he says, "Why didn't your mother call me to talk about this?"

"She's handling it," I lie. "She didn't have to spend her money on a long-distance phone call. And anyway, she talks to Max about stuff like that now."

"Amber, when we've finished talking, I want to speak to your mother."

"She and Max are watching that the brownies don't burn. And I've got to go back now and help them. Well, it's been nice talking to you."

I hang up the phone.

I hang up the phone before we even have our kissing contest, which we always have at the end of a call. That's where we make kissing sounds into the phone until one of us gets tired and quits and the other one wins.

No kissing contest this time . . . . . no winners.

I can feel myself start to cry.

The phone rings.

I run upstairs.

Chapter
Sixteen

My Dad Book . . . .

I open the top drawer of my dresser, take it out, and sit down on my bed to think about the best ways to destroy it.

I could feed it into the garbage disposal.

I could take each picture out of the book and rip it into tiny, tiny, minuscule pieces.

I could take a picture of him and add drawings to it of what I think Judith and the little dweeb look like . . . and then I can rip it into tiny, tiny, minuscule pieces.

I could blow my nose on some of the

pictures . . . . put a little snot across my father's face.

I could . . . . but I can't.

I don't want to destroy my Dad Book.

Opening it, I look at some of the pictures . . . . . . the time my dad and I won the father-daughter race at my school. I wonder who's going to win it this year.

Maybe they'll have a mother's boyfriend–daughter race this year and Max and I can win it.

Max.

I don't know what to think about Max either.

I don't know why everything had to become so complicated.

There's a knock on the door.

It's my mother.

I know.

Now's the time for the mother-daughter talk . . . how it's not easy for any of us

. . . . . how my parents have to make new lives . . . how we all have to try to be flexible and understanding . . . . how while they don't love each other, they'll always love me.

I don't say anything.

There's another knock on the door, and then my mother walks in and sits down with me on my bed.

"I know . . . . . . you love me . . . . you have to make a new life . . . . . Max is a wonderful person . . . . . . you and Dad may hate each other's guts but you'll always love me." I look at her.

"Well, I guess that's it." My mother stands up.

She sits down again. "No. Actually, there is more. Do you want to say it . . . or should I say the rest of things that need to be said . . . . . and need to be done?"

"I think I said everything." I shrug.

She picks up the Dad Book and opens it.
The page she has turned to is a picture of
my dad, with me sitting on Santa's knees.
She smiles at it and then looks at me.

"Amber, your dad is very upset that you hung up on him like that."

"What do you care? You hate his guts." I make a face.

She thinks for a minute. "Some of his guts I hate . . . . but, Amber, I don't hate all of his guts."

I laugh. "Just how many of his guts do you hate?"

She shakes her head. "Don't try to make me laugh. . . . This is serious. . . . Don't make a joke out of this. I know you're upset. Your father told me what's upsetting you. . . . Amber, you have a right to your feelings . . . . but you know that you have to be open to changes."

"They're not *my* changes. They're yours . . . . yours and Dad's. . . ." I am not laughing.

"You're making changes too. . . . You're getting older. . . . . You like different things

. . . . You even look different. Your dad and I have to get used to your changes too."

"But I'm a kid. I *have* to grow and change and be different."

"So do we." My mother is trying to be

calm. "Everyone in the world has to grow and change in some ways."

"But everyone doesn't have to like the changes." I pout. "You don't like everything I do."

She pretends to pout. "And you don't like everything *I* do."

I pout more. "I'm sick of having to hear this all the time."

"And I'm sick of having to say it all the time." She makes a super pouting face and then she smiles. "Amber Brown, you have to get used to change."

We both are quiet for a minute, and then she says, "And what's this about you're still not doing your schoolwork? Did you mean what you told your father?"

Great. I try to work really hard so that she doesn't find out and then I tell on myself.

I tell her what's going on.

I explain about how Mrs. Holt won't give me extra credit.

"She's right, you know." My mother pats me on the head.

It makes me nuts when she pats me on the head.

"But I want extra credit. . . . . I want a gold star for all the stuff I'm going through."

"It's called living. . . . Everyone goes through real stuff. . . . No one gets a gold star for doing what they should be doing."

"This is one of those great truths." I look at her. "One of those mother-daughter moments I'm always going to remember. . . . . ."

"And cherish . . . . ." my mother says, and then she laughs. "And then someday you will be saying the same things to *your* daughter."

"If I ever get married and have a kid, I'll never get divorced."

"I hope you never have to." My mother looks at me and then gives me a hug.

I hug back.

Then we look at each other.

"Mom." I hold her hand. "If I can't have a gold star . . . . can I at least have a brownie?"

She squeezes my hand and nods. "Let's go down and get some before Max eats them all."

"I bet he's not eating the tuna-fish-and-marshmallow brownie."

"I bet he's not," she agrees. "And I bet you don't either."

We get up and go downstairs.

On the way, I think of a slogan to use on my project.

With AMBER BROWNies, You Get Your Just Desserts.

Chapter
Seventeen

Progress Report

After some initial problems,
Amber is doing quite well at school
in her subject areas. She is turning
in good work on time. Amber still
needs to work very hard in math,
but I can tell that she is trying.

Her attitude is much better . . .
and her AMBER BROWNie report
was a delight . . . . and quite
tasteful!

Amber deserves credit for doing her best.

I look forward to watching her progress for the rest of the year.

A Soldier
of the
Great War

A SOLDIER
OF THE
GREAT WAR

MARK HELPRIN

A HARVEST BOOK | HARCOURT, INC.

Orlando Austin New York San Diego Toronto London

www.HarcourtBooks.com

The Library of Congress has cataloged the hardcover edition as follows:
Helprin, Mark.
A soldier of the great war/Mark Helprin.—1st ed.
p.   cm.
I. Title.
PS3558.E4775S65   1990   90-45987
813'.54—dc20
ISBN 0-15-183600-0
ISBN-13: 978-0156-03113-4 (pbk.)   ISBN-10: 0-15-603113-2 (pbk.)

Text set in Adobe Garamond
Designed by Liz Demeter

Printed in the United States of America
First Harvest edition 2005

E G I K J H F

FOR ALEXANDRA AND OLIVIA

❧ CONTENTS ❧

A Soldier
of the
Great War

ROME, AUGUST

ON THE ninth of August, 1964, Rome lay asleep in afternoon light as the sun swirled in a blinding pinwheel above its roofs, its low hills, and its gilded domes. The city was quiet and all was still except the crowns of a few slightly swaying pines, one lost and tentative cloud, and an old man who rushed through the Villa Borghese, alone. Limping along paths of crushed stone and tapping his cane as he took each step, he raced across intricacies of sunlight and shadow spread before him on the dark garden floor like golden lace.

Alessandro Giuliani was tall and unbent, and his buoyant white hair fell and floated about his head like the white water in the curl of a wave. Perhaps because he had been without his family, solitary for so long, the deer in deer preserves and even in the wild sometimes allowed him to stroke their cloud-spotted flanks and touch their faces. And on the hot terra cotta floors of roof gardens and in other, less likely places, though it may have been accidental, doves had flown into his hands. Most of the time they held in place and stared at him with their round gray eyes until they sailed away with a feminine flutter of wings that he found beautiful not only for its delicacy and grace, but because the sound echoed through what then became an exquisite silence.

As he hurried along the Villa Borghese he felt his blood rushing and his eyes sharpening with sweat. In advance of his approach through long tunnels of dark greenery the birds caught fire in song but were perfectly quiet as he passed directly underneath, so that he propelled and drew their hypnotic chatter before and after him like an ocean wave pushing through an estuary. With his white hair and thick white mustache, Alessandro Giuliani might have seemed English were it not for his cream-colored suit of distinctly Roman cut and a thin bamboo cane entirely inappropriate for an Englishman. Still trotting, breathless, and tapping, he emerged from the Villa Borghese onto a long wide road that went up a hill and was flanked on either side by a row of tranquil buildings with tile roofs from which the light reflected as if it were a waterfall cascading onto broken rock.

Had he looked up he might have seen angels of light dancing above the throbbing bright squares—in whirlwinds, will-o'-the-wisps, and golden eddies—but he didn't look up, for he was intent on getting to the end of the long road, to a place where he had to catch a streetcar that, by evening, would take him far into the countryside. He would have said, anyway, that it was better to get to the end of the road than to see angels, for he had seen angels many times before. Their faces shone from paintings; their voices rode the long and lovely notes of arias; they descended to capture the bodies and souls of young children; they sang and perched in the trees; they were in the surf and the streams; they inspired dancing; and they were the right and holy combination of words in poetry. As he climbed the hill he thought not of angels and their conveyances, but of a motorized trolley. It was the last to leave Rome on Sunday, and he did not want to miss it.

THE ROAD traveled relatively straight to the top of the hill, but descended the opposite side in switchbacks that, unlike their mountain counterparts, cupped fountains in the turns. Stairs cut through its shuttling, and Alessandro Giuliani took them fast and painfully. He tapped his cane at each step, partly in commemoration, partly in retaliation, and partly to make it a metronome, for he had discovered long before that to defeat pain he had to separate it from time, its most useful ally. As he went down, the walking became easier, and a short distance from the crossroads where he would board the streetcar he found himself on ten flights of gradual stairs and landings in a thick green defile. Through a confessional grille of tangled trees in a long dark gallery penetrated at intervals by the blinding sun, he saw the pale circle of light that marked his destination.

Drawing closer, he knew from the open blue awning that— unlike everything else in Rome that day—the cafe that seemed to exist solely for people who awaited the rarest streetcar in Italy had not shut its doors. He had neglected to buy presents for his granddaughter and her family, and now he knew that he would be able to take something to them. Though his great-granddaughter would not be pleased by gifts of food, she would be asleep when he arrived, and in the morning he would walk with her to the village to get a toy. Meanwhile, he would buy some prosciutto, chocolate, and dried fruit, hoping that these would be appreciated as much as his more elaborate presents. Once, he brought an expensive English shotgun to his granddaughter's husband, and at other times he arrived with the kinds of things that were to be expected from a man who had many years previously outrun any possible use for his money.

The tables and chairs on the terrace of the cafe were crowded with people and bundles. The overhead wires neither vibrated nor sizzled, which meant that Alessandro Giuliani could walk slowly, buy provisions, and have something to drink. On this line the cables always began to sing ten minutes before the tram arrived, because of the way it gripped them as it rounded the hill.

Walking through the thicket of chairs, he glanced at people who would ride with him on the way to Monte Prato, though most would leave the streetcar in advance of the last stop, and some even before it lowered its whip-like antennae, switched to diesel, and ran far beyond the grid of electrical wires from which it took its sustenance on the streets of the city. It had rubber tires and a pantograph, and, because it was a cross between a trolley and a bus, the drivers called it a mule.

A construction worker who had made for himself a hat of folded newspaper thrust his right hand into a bucket to encourage a listless squid that Alessandro knew would have to die within the hour from lack of oxygen. The headline running along the rim of the hat said, inexplicably, "Greeks Make Bridges of Gold for the Rest of 1964." Perhaps it was related to the Cyprus Crisis, but, then again, Alessandro thought, it might have had something to do with sports, a subject of which he was entirely ignorant. Two Danes, a boy and a girl in blue-and-white student hats, were at one corner of the terrace, seated next to German army rucksacks almost as big as they were. Their shorts were as tight as surgeons' gloves, and they were so severely and brazenly entangled in one another that it was impossible to tell his smooth and hairless limbs from hers.

Several poor women of Rome, perhaps sweepers or cafeteria workers, sat together over glasses of iced tea and were overcome now and then with the hysterical giggling born of fatigue and hard work. Sometimes they were free for a few days to go back into the country, where they had once been sylph-like little girls completely different from the obedient cardigan-covered barrels they had become. As Alessandro went past they lowered their voices, for although he was courtly and deferential, his age, bearing, and unusual self-possession awakened their memories of another time. They looked down at their hands, remembering the discipline not of the factory, but of childhood.

At another table were five strong men in the prime of life. They were truck drivers, and they wore sun glasses, striped shirts, and faded army clothing. Their arms and wrists were as thick as armor; they had huge families; they worked impossibly hard; and they thought they were worldly because they had driven over the high

Alpine passes and spent time with blonde women in German bordellos. Without thinking, Alessandro formed them into a squad of soldiers in a war that had long been over and would soon be forgotten, but then, catching himself, he disbanded them.

"It hasn't arrived yet, has it?" he asked the proprietor of the cafe.

"No, not yet," the proprietor answered, leaning over the copper bar to glance at the wires, for he could read their vibrations as if they were a schedule. "It's nowhere near; it won't come for at least ten minutes.

"You're late, you know," he continued. "When I didn't see you coming, I thought you had finally given in and bought a car."

"I hate cars," Alessandro said, without the slightest energy. "Would never buy one. They're ugly and they're small. I'd rather ride in something airy and open, or walk, because to be in a car gives me a headache. Their motion frequently makes me want to vomit, although I don't. And they're so cheaply made I don't even like to look at them." He made a gesture in imitation of spitting. He was too refined to have done this in normal circumstances, but here he was speaking the language of the man behind the counter, who, like Alessandro, was a veteran of the Alpine War.

"These *automobiles*," Alessandro said, as if he were conceding the existence of a new word, "are everywhere, like pigeon shit. I haven't seen a naked piazza in ten years. They put them all over the place, so that you can't even move. Someday I'll come home and find automobiles in my kitchen, in all the closets, and in the bathtub.

"Rome was not meant to move, but to be beautiful. The wind was supposed to be the fastest thing here, and the trees, bending and swaying, to slow it down. Now it's like Milan. Now the slimmest swiftest cats are killed because they aren't agile enough to cross streets where once—and I remember it—a cow could nap all afternoon. It wasn't like this, so frantic and tense, everybody walking, talking, eating, and fucking all the time. Nobody sits still anymore, except me."

He looked up at a row of medals displayed in a glass case above a battalion of liquor bottles. Alessandro had medals, too. He kept them in a brown Morocco-leather folder in the credenza in his study. He hadn't opened the folder in many years. He knew exactly what they looked like, for what they had been awarded, and the order in which he had earned them, but he did not wish to see them. Each one, tarnished or bright, would push him back to a time that he found both too painful and too beautiful to remember, and he had never wanted to be one of the many old men who, like absinthe drinkers, are lost in dreams. Had he owned a cafe he probably would have put his medals in a case above the bar, because it would have been good for business, but for as long as he could, until the last, he would keep certain memories locked away.

"Let me offer you something," said the proprietor, "compliments of the house."

"Thank you," Alessandro answered. "I'll take a glass of red wine." He had always associated the expression 'compliments of the house,' with some giant establishment twenty or fifty times the size of the one he was in—perhaps an enormous casino, or a resort on an island bulging with Germans in tiny bathing suits.

As the proprietor's hand grasped the bottle, he asked, "Anything to eat? Bread? Cheese?"

"Yes, but I'll pay for them," Alessandro told him.

This was answered by a quick gesture that said, remarkably, 'I offered, at least, but I'm glad you want to pay, because although things are not impossible, lately they've been kind of slow.' Then, as his customer was eating, the proprietor edged closer and spoke in a camouflaged voice.

"Do you see those two?" he asked in reference to the lascivious Danes. "Look at them. All they can do is eat and fuck."

"I wish I could."

The proprietor looked puzzled. He saw that Alessandro was taking alternating and vigorous bites of bread and cheese. "What are you doing now?"

Alessandro swallowed, and looked the proprietor in the eye. "I can tell you what I'm not doing," he said.

"Yes, but that's *all* they can do."

"How do you know?"

"Because if I carried on the way they do, I wouldn't be able to do anything else, would I?"

"If you carried on the way they do, I wouldn't be able to do anything else, would I?"

"If you carried on the way they do," Alessandro said, with complete assurance, "you'd be dead. You know what they do? I'll tell you what they do. They eat dinner and then they go back to their hotel, and for twelve hours they strain like gymnasts to pressure-weld themselves together, to fill every socket. By day, they sleep on buses and beaches. At night they're Paolo and Francesca."

"It's disgusting."

"No it isn't. You're jealous of their bliss because in our day such things were hardly possible."

"Yes, but at their age I drove mules, real mules!"

Alessandro awaited the connection.

"I pushed mule trains over the passes in the middle of winter. The animals were so heavily laden and the ice so hard and smooth that we would lose them. They would vanish from us and fall great distances, always silently, but we went on. The snow was blinding and the ice-clad walls of rock towered over us, streaming mist for a thousand meters."

"What has that to do with them?" Alessandro asked, glancing at the Danes.

"They don't know such things, and I resent it. I envy them, yes, but I'm proud."

"If you were one of the mule drivers," Alessandro said, "I may have seen you. I may have spoken to you, half a century ago."

They let the subject drop, but certainly they had been in the same places: the front line in the north had stretched for only several hundred kilometers. Doubtless they would have been able to reconstruct in conversation a little of what it had been like, but they knew that to do so in a few idle words while waiting for a trolley would not be right.

"Someday we'll talk," the proprietor said, "but..." He hesitated. "I don't know. These things are like the things of the Church."

"I understand. I never speak of them either. I want to buy some food before the trolley comes. Can you get it for me?"

The proprietor shuffled back and forth between the cases and counters, and as the wires began to sing and the people outside touched their luggage to make sure that it hadn't walked away on its own or been taken by short or invisible thieves, Alessandro Giuliani was presented with half a dozen neat packages, which he slipped into his small leather briefcase.

The wires were singing like afternoon locusts. Every now and then one of them would be drawn down so tightly that it would begin to shriek like the worst soprano in the hottest town in Italy.

"How much?" Alessandro asked. He was anxious because he knew he would have difficulty mounting the high step of the streetcar, and would have to fumble for money while supporting himself with his cane and balancing the briefcase and wallet as the car lurched from side to side.

The proprietor didn't answer. The streetcar was grinding around the bend. It sounded like a traveling machine shop. "How much?" Alessandro asked once again. The people outside had arisen and were waiting by the side of the tracks.

The proprietor held up his right hand as if to stop traffic.

"What? Again?" Alessandro asked.

The proprietor shook his head back and forth.

"We're no longer soldiers," Alessandro said quietly. "That was a lifetime ago. Everything has changed."

"Yes," said the proprietor, "but once, a lifetime ago, we were, and sometimes it all comes back, and moves my heart."

THE FARE to Monte Prato had risen from 1900 lire to 2200, which meant that Alessandro could not merely give over two 1,000-lire notes, pocket the change, and walk away in balance, as he had planned. Instead, he found himself holding on to many things at once while the airy streetcar swayed violently and the sun flashed through the trees. Trying to withdraw a 500-lire note from his wallet was difficult, but it would have been worse had not the young Dane separated himself for a moment from his sunburnt and beautiful lover to hold Alessandro's briefcase and take his arm as a son might have done for a father.

Alessandro thanked the boy, pleased that lack of decorum did not necessarily imply lack of courtesy.

The best seat was next to the man with the newspaper hat and the squid. "Good day," Alessandro said, addressing both man and squid. Sensing mischief, the construction worker looked away sullenly.

A few minutes later he peered into the bucket and poked the squid with his finger. Then he lifted his eyes and stared at Alessandro as if Alessandro were to blame. "Dead," he said, accusingly.

Alessandro shrugged his shoulders. "Not enough oxygen in the water."

"How do you mean?"

"He needed oxygenated water to breathe."

"That's crazy. Fish don't breathe. They live under water."

"But they do, they do. There's oxygen in the water, and they extract it with their gills."

"So why didn't this one?"

"He did, until there was no more left, and then he passed away."

The construction worker preferred to believe otherwise. "The bastards at Civitavecchia sold me a bad squid."

"As you wish."

The construction worker thought for a moment. "Would he have lived if I had blown into the water with a straw?"

"Probably not, since you would have been blowing in more carbon dioxide than oxygen. How far are you going?"

"Monte Prato."

"Impossible," Alessandro said, briefly shutting his eyes for emphasis. "It's far too warm. The bucket should have been half full of ice."

"How do you know these things? I think you're wrong."

"I know them because they're obvious."

"Do you have a fish market?"

"No."

The construction worker was tremendously suspicious. "If you don't have a fish market, what do you do?"

"I'm a professor."

"Of fish?"

"Of chicken," Alessandro answered.

"Then you don't know enough to talk."

"Ah," said Alessandro, holding up his finger. "A squid is not a fish."

"It isn't?"

"No."

"What is it?"

"It's a type of chicken, a water chicken."

The construction worker looked abject. Feeling sorry for him, Alessandro said, "I'm not a professor of chicken, and as far as I know, there is no such thing, but the part about the oxygen is true. I regret that your squid died. He had already come all the way from

Civitavecchia, and before that he had been pulled from the sea, which was his home, and he suffered many hours in the hold of a fishing boat as it worked its way back to land in the August heat. The journey was too much."

The construction worker nodded. "But of what are you a professor?"

"Aesthetics."

"What are aesthetics?"

"The study of beauty."

"Beauty? What for?"

"Beauty. Why not."

"Why do you have to study it?"

"You don't. It's everywhere, in great profusion, and always will be. Were I to cease studying it, it would not go away, if that's what you mean."

"Then why do you?"

"It entrances me, it always has, so it's what I do—despite occasional ridicule."

"I'm not ridiculing you."

"I know you're not, but others say that mine is an effeminate or a useless calling. Well, for some it is. Not for me."

"Don't get me wrong; I don't think you look effeminate." The construction worker drew back to study him. "You're a tough old bastard, I think. You remind me of my father."

"Thank you," Alessandro replied, slightly alarmed.

Now the way to Monte Prato was clear. He had only to fall into the pleasant hypnosis of travel; to watch the long ranks of trees as they passed; to view the mountains when they first rose over the fields; to observe the great round moon and its attendant bright stars shining through the streetcar's glassy walls; to match the whirring of the engines with the mad chorus of the cicadas; to be comfortable, and old, and content with small things. He assumed that the remaining hours would pass without incident, that he would rest, and that he would be alone—free of memories too great for the heart to hold.

BEFORE IT came to the edge of the city, where it would pick up speed, the trolley wound through many small streets not as congenial as the one on the side of the hill where Alessandro Giuliani had embarked. It crossed and recrossed the river Aniene, and rattled down desolate boulevards scored by the patterned shadows of iron fences and trees. At every church, the sweeper ladies crossed themselves, and now and then the squad of truck drivers noticed a new German truck, or a piece of construction machinery, and turned their heads to look at it while one of them told how much it cost or how many horsepower it had.

At each stop the driver looked up into his mirror to scan both the interior of the car and the street, to see if anyone would insult and delay him by wanting to get on or off. Though no one had a short ticket, people sometimes changed their minds about how far they wanted to go, and he had to be alert: but Rome hardly stirred, offering not a soul to slow his progress. The streetcar made excellent time, and when it reached the edge of the city it was running ahead of schedule. This delighted the driver. If he beat his fares to a stop he could hurl himself forward and arrive even earlier at the next stop, where he would be less likely to encounter someone else. In this way he was able to convert his viscous long-distance local into the most ethereal express. He hated deceleration and he hated to make change, but he did like to drive, and each stop that he could pass at speed was for him the partial satisfaction of his long-standing dream of riding in the steeplechase as a jockey or even as a horse.

At a place that was neither Rome nor the countryside, where fields of corn and wheat alternated with lumber yards and factory compounds, and where a distant highway was visible, sparkling like a stream as its traffic beat against the sunlight, they made an insincere lurch at an empty stop, and started off again as usual. Alessandro had begun to dream, but was pulled from his reverie by the insistent and conscientious action of the corner of his eye. Off to the right was a slightly sloping dirt road littered with potholes. A little way down this road, someone was running desperately, leaping the potholes and waving his arms.

A long moment passed during which Alessandro begged to remain at rest but was again overruled by the corner of his eye. He turned his head for a full view. Whoever it was, he wanted to get on the streetcar, and was screaming for it to stop. Although he could not be heard, what he said was apparent in the movement of his arms as they jolted slightly at each shout.

"There's someone," Alessandro said weakly. Then he cleared his throat. "There's a person!" he shouted. Because no one else had seen the runner no one knew what Alessandro meant. They were not surprised that an old man, even one as dignified as he, would blurt out something incoherent on a hot afternoon. Except for one sweeper woman, who smiled idiotically, their reaction was to hold still and not look at him. The car was on a straightaway, accelerating to the southeast.

Alessandro jumped to his feet. "Driver!" he screamed. "There's a person who wants to catch the streetcar!"

"Where?" the driver shouted, without taking his eyes from the road.

"Back there."

The driver turned his head. No one was visible. "You're mistaken," he said. They were far away now from the corner of the dirt road. "Besides," the driver continued, "I can't pick anyone up between stops."

Alessandro sat down. He looked back, and saw no one. It was not fair for the driver to race through the stops, especially because this was the last car of the day. Alessandro began to compose a letter of protest. It was short, but he rephrased it repeatedly. During this time the streetcar traveled a kilometer or two and was forced to slow down behind a huge truck that was hauling an arcane piece of electrical equipment almost as big as a house.

"Hey, look," the construction worker said to Alessandro.

Alessandro turned to see where the construction worker was pointing. Far behind them on the road, the slight figure from the dirt track was chasing them, after having run for two or three kilometers without flagging. No longer was he begging, and he had stopped waving his arms, as if he had decided that since the streetcar would give him nothing he would save his strength so he could get what he wanted himself.

"I'll tell the driver," Alessandro said to the construction worker. He rose and made his way to the front. "Signore," he implored the driver, "look in back of us. Someone is chasing."

The driver glanced up into his mirror. He saw the runner. "It's too late," he said. "The next stop is fifteen kilometers away. He'll never make it."

"Why don't you let him on?" Alessandro demanded, his voice rising.

"I told you. We don't pick up passengers between stops. Please sit down."

"You sped right by the last stop, early. That's why he's running."

"Please sit down."

"No," Alessandro said. "I want to get off."

"You get off in Monte Prato."

"I want to get off here instead."

"I can't do that."

"Why not?"

"Here? There's nothing here! We don't let people off here."

"These are my fields. All these fields are mine. I want to check the wheat."

The streetcar rolled to a stop and the doors were thrown open.

"Okay, then," the driver said, glancing at the mirror, "check the wheat."

"Just a minute," Alessandro answered. "I have to get my briefcase." He began to walk back to his seat, very slowly.

The driver was angry. "Come on!" he screamed. "You're holding us up."

"Just a moment, just a moment," Alessandro said, and, upon reaching his seat, he added, "I dropped something."

The driver closed the door and started up again, but the persistent runner was gaining. Alessandro looked back, and saw a boy of eighteen or nineteen sprinting behind the bus. He was wearing heavy leather work shoes, and he looked as if he were about to die from overexertion. His hair was plastered by sweat onto the sides of his forehead. He breathed hard through an open mouth. He was the color of a ripe pepper.

"He's here!" Alessandro shouted.

The driver looked stonily ahead, but the boy put on a final burst of speed and ran up to the door, where he hopped onto the step and held on. He was heaving, dripping sweat, and his head was bowed.

Alessandro, briefcase under his arm, tapped his way to the front of the streetcar and hit the roof with his cane. "Signore," he said in a surprisingly deep and powerful voice, "I believe you have a passenger." At this very moment the boy, who looked like someone from a wild valley in Sicily, began to beat furiously on the glass. The way he hung on the door and pounded with his fists reminded Alessandro of his own tenacity in other times, and he was filled with affection and pride, as if the boy had been his son.

The driver pressed hard on the brakes. Alessandro flew headlong into the windshield but was cushioned by his briefcase and his arms, and was able to stay in balance. The boy swung around and slammed against the streetcar in the fashion of a flexible whip, but he hung on.

When the door was opened, both Alessandro and the boy thought that they had won, but when the driver got up, they saw that he was a giant. Alessandro bent his head to look at him. "I didn't realize how..." he started to say. Then he looked at the driver's seat and saw that it had been lowered all the way to the floor.

As the driver descended, the boy backed away from the door. "If you touch this vehicle again...!" the driver said before he became voiceless with rage.

Alessandro walked down the steps and hopped to the ground. "If you don't let him ride, I won't ride either. I'm an old man. It might cost you your job."

"Crap on my job," the driver said, leaping back into the car. "I always wanted to be a jockey." He closed the door, and the street-car started up suddenly and began to pull away.

Alessandro was shocked to see the construction worker in the newspaper hat pressed up against the window behind which he himself, only a few minutes before, had been resting. The construction worker lifted his hands in a gesture of hopelessness. Then he changed his mind and rushed to the front, but whatever he did or said there, the car did not stop, and the faces of the truck drivers, the sweeper women, and the Danes looked back at the old man and the boy, like expressionless moons.

"Seventy kilometers to Monte Prato," Alessandro said under his breath as the streetcar disappeared down the long straight road.

"In a few hours the other car will pass on its way back to Rome," the boy declared, still breathing hard from his run. "Maybe less than that."

"I just came from Rome," the old man said. "What good would it do me to go back? I'm going to Monte Prato. And you?"

"To Sant' Angelo, ten kilometers before Monte Prato."

"I'm aware of that."

"To my sister. She lives in the convent there."

"She's a nun?"

"No. She washes for them. They're very clean, but they can't do it all themselves."

Alessandro looked back and saw that, in leaving most of the city behind, the road had become beautiful. To right and left were fields now golden in the declining sun, and the tall trees on either side sparkled and swayed as the wind rushed through them. "I'll tell you what," he proposed. "I'll go with you as far as Sant' Angelo, and then continue on my own to Monte Prato."

"I don't know if they'll give the two of us a ride," the boy replied. "There isn't any traffic anyway. There hardly ever is, on this road, and not today, not on a saint's day."

"Do you think I would stand on the road and beg for a ride?" Alessandro asked indignantly.

"I'll do it for you."

"No you won't. I've had legs for seventy-four years, and I know how to use them. In addition," he said, rapping his cane on the surface of the road, "I have this. It helps. It's as long as a rhinoceros's penis, and twice as stiff."

"But you can't walk seventy kilometers. Even I can't," the boy said.

"What's your name?"

"Nicolò."

"Nicolò, I once walked several hundred kilometers over glaciers and snowfields, with no rest, and if I had been discovered I would have been shot."

"That was in the war?"

"Of course it was in the war. I'm going to Monte Prato," Alessandro declared, cinching up his belt, straightening his jacket, and patting down his mustache. "If you like, I'll accompany you as far as Sant' Angelo."

"By the time I get there, if I walk," Nicolò said, "I'll have to turn around and go back."

"Would you let a little thing like that stop you?" Alessandro asked.

Contemplating the old lion in front of him, Nicolò said nothing.

"Well, would you?" Alessandro demanded, his face so tense and peculiar that Nicolò was frightened.

"No, of course not," the boy said. "Why would I?"

"THE FIRST thing you have to do," Alessandro told him, "is take inventory and make a plan."

"What inventory, what plan?" Nicolò asked dismissively. "We have nothing and we're going to Sant' Angelo."

The old man was silent. They walked about a hundred steps.

"What do you mean, inventory?" Nicolò wanted to know. When he received no answer, he looked straight ahead and decided that if the old man chose not to talk, he wouldn't talk either. That lasted, as Alessandro knew it would, for no more than ten steps.

"I thought inventory was what they did in a store."

"It is what they do in a store."

"Where's the store?" Nicolò asked.

"Merchants take inventory," Alessandro stated, "so that, knowing what they have, they can plan ahead. We can do the same. We can think in our brains of what we have, and what obstacles are in front of us to be overcome."

"What for?"

"Anticipation is the heart of wisdom. If you are going to cross a desert, you anticipate that you will be thirsty, and you take water."

"But this is the road to Monte Prato, and there are towns along the way. We don't need water."

"Did you ever walk seventy kilometers?"

"No."

"It may be difficult for you. It will be very difficult for me. I'm somewhat older than you, and, as you can see, I'm half lame. If I'm to succeed, it will be by a narrow margin, and, therefore, I must court precision. It's always been that way for me. What do you have with you?"

"I don't have anything."

"You have no food?"

"Food?" The boy jumped in the air and whirled around, turning a full circle to show that he wasn't concealing anything. "I don't carry around food. Do you?" he asked.

The old man went to one side of the road and sat on a rock. "Yes," he answered, opening his briefcase. "Bread, and a half kilo each of prosciutto, dried fruit, and semi-sweet chocolate. We'll need a lot of water. It's hot."

"In the towns," Nicolò volunteered.

"Only a few towns line the route, but between them are springs. As soon as it gets hilly, you'll see, we'll have plenty of water."

"We don't need food. When we get to a village, we can eat there."

"The next village is fifteen kilometers away," the old man said, "and I walk slowly. When we arrive the stars will be halfway across the sky and every window will be shut tight. Though we won't be able to eat in the towns, this food will see us through. You'd be surprised at how much you burn up on a march."

"Where will we sleep?" Nicolò asked.

"Sleep?" Alessandro repeated, with one bushy white eyebrow riding so far above the other that it looked for a moment as if he had been in an automobile accident and had not quite recovered.

"Aren't we going to sleep at night?"

"No."

"Why not?"

"On a march of seventy kilometers you don't need to sleep."

"Yes, you don't *need* to sleep," the boy said, "but why not sleep? Who says you shouldn't?"

"If you slept you wouldn't be properly intent. You'd be swept away by dreams, and miss the waking dreams. And you would insult the road."

"I don't understand."

"Look," Alessandro said, grabbing Nicolò's wrist. "If I decide that I'm going to Monte Prato, seventy kilometers or not, I go to Monte Prato. You don't do things by halves. If you love a woman, you love her entirely. You give everything. You don't spend your time in cafes; you don't make love to other women; you don't take her for granted. Do you understand?"

Nicolò shook his head back and forth to express that he did not. He expected that the old man might be more than he could handle and was perhaps an escapee from an asylum, or, worse, someone who had contrived to avoid asylums altogether.

"God gives gifts to all creatures," Alessandro continued, "no matter what their station or condition. He may give innocence to a lunatic, or heaven to a thief. Contrary to most theologians, I have always believed that even worms and weasels have souls, and that even they are capable of salvation.

"But one thing God does not give, something that must be earned, something that a lazy man can never know. Call it under-standing, grace, the elevation of the spirit—call it what you will. It comes only of work, sacrifice, and suffering.

"You must give everything you have. You must love unto ex-haustion, work unto exhaustion, and walk unto exhaustion.

"If I want to go to Monte Prato, I go to Monte Prato. I don't hang around like an ass with half a dozen trunks who has gone to take the waters at Montecatini. People like that continually expose their souls to mortal danger in imagining that they are free of it, when, indeed, the only mortal danger for the spirit is to remain too long without it. The world is made of fire."

Alessandro's homily was a success, and Nicolò was beginning to get fiery himself. Swept up remarkably fast in a storm of passion and dreams, within a minute or two he had decided his fate and declared that he would go to Sant' Angelo, to Monte Prato, twice the distance, three times the distance, without rest, driving himself until he came close to death. His face, with its dark, lateral, wolflike eyes, a crooked mouth, and a sharp and substantial nose, was tight with resolution.

Alessandro released his grip and held up one finger. "Of course," he said, "you must always rest." A cloud swept across the boy's face as he was knocked from his reverie. "There are times for sleep, for inactivity, dreaming, indiscipline, even lethargy. You'll know when you deserve these times. They come after you've been broken. I'm speaking of a helpless, tranquil state before the great excitement of dawn."

"Dawn . . ." Nicolò repeated, confused.

"Yes," said Alessandro, "dawn. Tell me, what kind of feet do you have."

"My feet?"

"Yes, your feet, the ones that are attached to your legs."

"I have human feet, Signore."

"Of course, but two kinds of feet exist. Every army knows this but won't admit it for fear of losing recruits.

"You may be tall, handsome, intelligent, graceful, and gifted, but if you have feet of despair you might just as well be a dwarf who shines shoes on the Via del Corso. Feet of despair are too tender, and can't fight back. Under prolonged assault they come apart. They bleed to death. They become infected and swollen in half an hour. I have seen men remove from their boots, after less than a day's march, feet that are nothing more than bloody sponges, soft shapeless things that look like skinned animals.

"On the other hand, if I may, are the feet of invincibility. In extreme cases such as those of South American mountain peasants it may appear that a man is wearing an old torn-up muddy pair of boots, when actually he is barefooted. Feet of invincibility are ugly, but they don't suffer, and they last forever—building defenses where they are attacked, turning color, reproportioning and repositioning themselves until they look like bulldogs. They do everything but bleed and feel pain.

"During your first days in the army you realize that despite all other differences mankind is divided into two classes. Well, what kind of feet do you have?"

"I don't know, Signore."

"Take off your shoes."

Nicolò sat on the ground and unlaced his shoes. When they and his socks were strewn on the stones beside him, he rolled onto his back and put his legs up into the air so that Alessandro could inspect his feet.

The old man first looked at the soles. Then he felt under the heel. He glanced at the toes. "Your feet are repugnant, objectionable, and invincible. Put your shoes back on."

"And what about your feet, Signore? Are they invincible?"

"Need you ask?"

Nicolò had not needed to ask, for he had observed that Alessandro had scars even on his palms.

Then Alessandro took inventory of his briefcase. The first objects did not please Nicolò entirely, for they were a set of webbing straps that attached to the case so that it could be carried like a knapsack. "Take it," Alessandro said matter-of-factly, "until Sant' Angelo. You're young." Next to emerge was a pocket knife, very sharp and very old, with a flint in the handle. "The flint pulls out, you see," Alessandro said, "and if you strike it against the top of the blade, you get a spark. When we rest, we may need a fire to keep us warm."

"In August?"

"The higher you go, the colder it gets, even in August."

After the packets of food came a map. Having the appropriate map at hand, Alessandro explained, was an obsession that he had had for a long time. He liked to know where he was in the world and what was around him. A map, he stated, was for him what a Bible was for a priest, a book for an intellectual, and so forth.

They discovered on their map, among mountains, rivers, empty plains, and settlements too small to have their names shown, four beacon-like towns strung along the road. Alessandro knew that at night these towns would sparkle and shine. Just their few lights in the slate-blue darkness would have, in their simplicity and purity, more of what made up light itself than the accumulated phosphorescence of whole ranks of great cities.

He indicated on the map that, here, if they were hungry or had not already eaten, they would halt for dinner. Here they would be able to see Rome far behind them, lower, and seething with lights. Here they would see no villages, Rome would be obscured, and they would have only stars—because the moon would rise that night, Alessandro said, late, but when the moon did rise it would be perfectly full. Here they would go off the road and traverse a set of rounded peaks that overlooked Sant' Angelo and, farther beyond, Monte Prato.

Alessandro said that they would walk through the night, the next day, the whole of another night, and the early part of the next morning. The weather would be good and the full moon would be their lantern.

Already Sant' Angelo and Monte Prato had become far more than just mountain villages on the line of the motorized trolley. They seemed far away, beautiful, and high. Before reaching them, Alessandro Giuliani and Nicolò would have much walking to do, and would have to pass through the towns of Acereto, Lanciata, and perhaps five or six others with beautiful names, equidistant over civilizing fields and groves of trees waving against the perfectly blue sky. At the start of their long walk, the road was deserted, and, perhaps because the world was silent, they were too.

ALESSANDRO GIULIANI believed that if all things went smoothly and well on a journey, the momentum and equanimity of walking or riding would overshadow whatever the traveler had left behind and whatever he was traveling to reach. Making good time on the road was in itself reason for elation.

Once, in a lecture, he had stated this in passing, only to be abruptly challenged by a student who had wanted to know if the respected professor thought that elation could come to a condemned man on his way to the gallows.

"I don't know," Alessandro had answered. "Usually, the way to the gallows is not long enough to be called a journey, but let us say, for example, that a condemned man must be transported from one extreme of a country to another, where he will be executed, and that his journey will take days or weeks."

"Is that realistic?" the student asked.

"Yes," Alessandro replied. "Yes, it is realistic. In such a case," he continued, "the man may know the greatest elation and the most savage despair—as if, in anticipation of eternity in heaven or in hell, he were previewing both."

"I don't understand. Elation in a man condemned to die?"

"Elation, mad elation, visions, euphoria." A long silence had followed, during which the lecture audience had been as motionless as if it had been under the gun, and the professor had been unable to resume the lecture, on account of memories that made him forget momentarily where he was and what he was doing.

Even a trip across the city provided minor joys and desperations that, although of a lesser order than those experienced on a journey of days or weeks, stood in relation to one another nonetheless in much the same way as those of a voyage around the world. The scale might change, but the patterns were the same. Alessandro guessed that Nicolò would expect the walk to be of one complexion. Why should it not be? Despite enough variation in the experience of a child by the age of fourteen to show him twenty times over that life is stupefying and complex, a single great force drove him forward and gave him both the momentum he would need for the rest of his life and the immediate resilience for surviving the blows he attracted with his adolescent stupidities and excesses. Nicolò would have chased the streetcar not only to Acereto, but, if he hadn't caught it there, to Lanciata and perhaps all the way to Sant' Angelo. He expected the world to be complected uniformly.

Nicolò would be bitterly disappointed by the slow and difficult, but Alessandro had learned to love these as much as or perhaps more than he loved the fast and easy. To him, they seemed not so far apart. It was almost as if, facing off invariably at odds, they conducted a secret liaison, with their hands enwrapped under the table.

Nicolò could not yet know this, and he would be troubled when the road grew dark and steep. For that reason, Alessandro was disappointed that they had set out with such glory all around them, everywhere—in the trees that swayed lightly, like ocean waves; in the rich colors of late afternoon as the retreating sun made the east a shadowless perfection of evenly throbbing light; in the slightly dusty haze that came with the approach of evening, dry and cool; in the wheat as the wind traveled through it as slowly as a boat in the thick of polar seas; and in all the memories summoned by these beauties to resonate and sing, until, in their ecstatic multiplication, they closed themselves off to mortal view by virtue of the light that is too bright to see.

Nicolò had no notion that everything was not well. He thought that the fine weather, the flat road, and the sun at their backs were all to be expected. He was surprised by Alessandro's silence, for he had assumed from the very beginning, because the old man had left the streetcar for Nicolò's sake, that the walk would be paved with his words. Did he not, in his first sentences, launch the explosive shell about his escape over the ice fields? Even if the old were inconsistent and cranky, they did sometimes tell good stories, and this fellow, with his shock of straight white hair, his finely tailored suit, the slim bamboo cane, and a noble bearing that Nicolò had seen only . . . well, had never seen . . . would undoubtedly have a lot to say.

He wanted Alessandro to talk endlessly in stories and regale him with things from an age before he was born. He would listen eagerly not because he had any hint of what the old man would elucidate, but, to the contrary, because he hadn't the vaguest idea of what had made the man who limped steadily alongside him on the road to Sant' Angelo and Monte Prato.

Nicolò also didn't understand that Alessandro knew exactly what a young man would expect, and (before Nicolò had given any indication whatsoever of such expectations) was offended by what were, in fact, the boy's assumptions.

After all, Alessandro Giuliani was paid more than decently to speak and to write. Why should this boy expect that, in walking, he would overflow with speech? And why should the boy assume that the old man, having seen what he had seen, having contended throughout his life with great and ineffable forces, having survived into old age, and having known, intimately and deeply, both natural and feminine beauty, would want to say anything at all? For kilometers and kilometers, they walked the straight road in absolute silence.

NICOLÒ FOUND it difficult to believe that Alessandro was not moving faster, for, perhaps because of the blurred-spokes effect caused by the movement of his legs and his active cane, and the unusual up-and-down motion of his limping gait, he looked as if he were going very fast. It seemed as if, had he been able to channel all the energy with which he moved and checked himself, he would have been swifter than a gazelle. But he was slow.

Nicolò, who moved smoothly and effortlessly, ached to run or climb. "What's that?" he asked, though not as a question, pointing to a mound of earth sitting in the middle of a field. Soon he was racing toward it, the briefcase bouncing against his back as he jumped irrigation ditches and ran among the furrows. Then he returned by way of a little dam over which water was pouring in a curve that looked like a leaping fish.

"What are these side trips?" Alessandro inquired.

Nicolò shrugged.

"You know, I once had a dog," the old man continued, "a big black English dog named Francesco. Every time I took him for a walk, he covered three times the distance I did."

"Why do you tell me this?" Nicolò asked.

"I don't know," Alessandro said, waving his arms in the air as if to indicate confusion. "It just came to me."

"Do you still have him?"

"No, that was a long time ago. He died when I was in Milan, but I think of him on occasion, and in teaching I often use him as an example."

"You're a teacher?" Nicolò asked, with noticeable discomfort, for he had never been to school, and he thought of teachers as a dangerous species of male nun.

Alessandro didn't answer. The sun was low now. Everything was warm and golden, and they were still ten kilometers from Acereto. Soon it would be dark. The old man did not want to waste energy, because he was beginning to warm up, to feel an oncoming sensation of strength and equanimity. If he didn't upset it, the equanimity would carry him forward in a trance.

They continued on in silence until Nicolò began to dance through his steps.

"You have so much energy you can't contain yourself, can you."

"I don't know."

"Marvelous. I, if I had your strength, could unite Europe in a week and a half."

"You were young," Nicolò challenged. "Did you unite Europe?"

"I was too busy thinking about girls and climbing mountains."

"What mountains?"

"The Alps."

"With ropes and things?"

"Yes."

"How do you do that? I saw a movie once where the guy fell. Do you throw the rope to catch on a rock, or what?"

"No. It's different, but if I have to explain, I won't have any breath."

"You're a teacher. Teachers should explain."

"Not when they're on long marches."

"What do you teach?"

"Aesthetics."

"Who are they?" Nicolò asked, thinking that they might be initiates in a hilltop religious order.

"You mean what are they. You're the second person to ask me that today," Alessandro said. "Are you sure you want me to answer? If I do, your squid may die."

Nicolò's suspicions about the old man's sanity resurfaced.

"He came all the way from Civitavecchia." Alessandro turned to the boy and looked into his eyes. "Marco . . . the water chicken."

"Don't tell me Marco the water chicken," Nicolò commanded. "What are aesthetics?"

"The philosophy and study of beauty."

"What?"

"What?" the old man echoed.

"They teach that?"

"I teach it."

"That's stupid."

"Why is it stupid?"

"For one, what is there to teach?"

"Are you asking or telling?"

"Asking."

"I'm not telling."

"Why not?"

"I've already answered you, in a book. Buy the book and leave me alone. Better yet, read Croce."

"You wrote a book?"

"Yes, many books."

"About what?"

"About aesthetics," Alessandro said, rolling his eyes upward.

"What's your name?"

"Alessandro Giuliani."

"I've never heard of you."

"I still exist. Who are you?"

"Nicolò Sambucca."

"What do you do, Mr. Sambucca?"

With some pain, in the way of self-deprecating beginners who are facing long apprenticeships, Nicolò said, "I make propellers."

Alessandro stopped to stare at Nicolò Sambucca. "Propellers," he said. "Naturally! I'm going to walk seventy kilometers with a kid who makes propellers."

"What's wrong with propellers?" Nicolò asked.

"Nothing's wrong with propellers," Alessandro answered. "They're necessary to drive airplanes. Where do you do this, if I may ask? Certainly not at home."

"At F.A.I. I don't really make them, I help. Next year I'll be an apprentice but now I'm a helper. I sweep the chips and the curlings, keep the tools in order, serve lunch, and push around the big frames that they make the propellers on. It takes a long time to make a propeller: it has to be tested. We have wind tunnels. Because of the union, I'm not allowed to touch the propellers yet. I can't even put my finger on one."

"Did you finish school?"

"I didn't start," the boy said. "When I was little, we moved here from Girifalco, in Calabria. When I was a kid, I sold cigarettes."

"What does your father do?"

"He puts up clotheslines, the kind that have the steel towers, you know, near the house."

"Those are very useful."

"I don't really understand you," Nicolò said.

"Good. We met only this afternoon, and we've said very little. I'm glad that I have retained an aura of mystery."

"Yeah, but you're a teacher."

"What's not to be understood?"

"It doesn't match."

"What doesn't match?"

"A lot of things, but teachers don't do that."

"Don't do what?"

"Walk over ice fields, hunted by armed soldiers."

"In the war a lot of people did things they weren't accustomed to doing."

"Did you fight the English?"

"Sometimes, but they were on our side."

"I thought we fought them and the Americans. Hey, we like the Americans, but they were on the other side," Nicolò said.

"That was in the *Second* World War. I was too old for it. All I did was sit on the ground while I was shelled and bombed. I knew how to do that because I had had a lot of practice in the previous war."

"There was another one?"

"Yes," Alessandro said, "there was another one."

"When? I never heard of it. Who did we fight? Are you sure?"

"Why do you think the Second World War is called the Second?"

"It makes sense. Maybe I'm stupid, but I didn't know about the first one. Was it big? Did it last long? What did you do? How old were you?"

"You have asked me many questions at once."

"Yeah."

"If I answer you, you'll be listening all the way to Sant' Angelo. I don't have the breath to walk that distance and explain these things. The hills are far too steep for me to give a treatise. There are numerous books about the First World War. I can give you a list, if you want."

"Is there a book about you in the war?"

"Of course not. Who would write a book about me in the war? Why would anyone want to, and who could ever know?" Alessandro looked askance at Nicolò. "Let me put it this way," he said. "I don't know myself well enough to write my autobiography, and if anyone else ever tried, I would say: Forget about me, tell the story of Paolo, Guariglia, and Ariane."

"Who were they?"

"Never mind."

"You talk to me, Signore, like this was the propeller shop. This isn't the propeller shop."

Alessandro looked at him, and smiled.

It was nearly dark, and as they walked down the road they could hardly see one another's faces. Having lapsed into silence once again, they listened to the click of Alessandro's cane and watched the brightening planets arise as vanguards for the more timid stars that would eventually blaze up from behind and smile upon the whole world.

They saw sparks from fires in the distance as field hands working on the harvest cooked their dinners. And the many shooting stars that fell in August, Alessandro stated, made up for the lack of rain.

Several kilometers from Acereto, when they still could not see its lights, Alessandro said, "We'll eat by the fountain in Acereto. Maybe if someplace is open we'll have hot tea, but I doubt it."

They walked on. "To understand the First War," he said, "you have to know a little of history. Do you?"

"No."

"Why did I ask? You're a tabula rasa."

"I'm a what?"

"There's no point."

They continued in silence for ten minutes or so. Again, Alessandro turned to Nicolò, as he had done after Nicolò's declaration about propellers. "Or maybe there is," he said. "Maybe I can summarize it succinctly."

"I don't care," Nicolò said. "I just hope we can get some tea or coffee in Acereto. Can I have a piece of chocolate now, to hold me until we eat?"

"First," Alessandro said, paying no attention to Nicolò, "first, you must understand that history arises as the interpretation and misinterpretation of passion. What do I mean by that? It's complicated, but perhaps you ought to listen."

"I'M NOT a historian. My colleagues would probably be greatly offended that a humanist crossed the windbreak into their field, and would bark like dogs until I crossed back."

"That's just like F.A.I.," Nicolò said. "There was an engineer named Guido Castiglione. He was the head of testing, so he tried to test things at all stages of production, in each department. That would have been the best way to do it, to catch mistakes where they started. But all the department heads—like Cortese in airframes, and my boss in propellers, Garaviglia—they plotted to shoot him down. You can't take someone's bread, that's what my father says. Anyway, now Guido Castiglione doesn't work at F.A.I. anymore. And it's the same way with the helpers. If one is supposed to sweep and he sees anyone else with a broom, say the last rites."

"We're like that, too," the old man said, "only the last rites are words and glances and things that people say about you when you aren't there.

"Historians have their method, just like anyone else, and they're jealous of it, but the *Iliad* shames any history of Greece, and Dante stands supreme above the world's collected medievalists. Of course, the medievalists don't know it, but everyone else does. As a way to arrive at the truth, exactitude and methodology are, in the end, far inferior to vision and apotheosis. I don't claim to have a patent on either, and history is not my profession, but I do have some ideas about the times that I have seen. Forgive me if I'm not as learned or subtle as I might be."

"What?" Nicolò asked.

"A preface to warn you that I'll be speaking outside my area of expertise."

"You're crazy. Stop apologizing," Nicolò said. "You didn't do anything wrong. Just tell me the story. I can see you ordering coffee and bread. You walk up to the guy and you say, 'Forgive me. I'm not a baker, and I've never been to Brazil. What's more, I don't work in a restaurant, but, though I didn't bring my microscope, please, can you give me a cappuccino and a roll?'"

Alessandro nodded. "You're right," he said. "The reason for my hesitation is not my academic manner. I never had much of an academic manner. It's because, once, these things hit me like a huge wave, an avalanche, and for a long time it was as if I were in a long and emotional dream where I could neither speak nor move, and the world was passing me by.

"But that's over. I'll tell you the elementary history of the war. I won't stray from the objective. There isn't a need for anything about me."

"Okay," Nicolò said. "Here I am. Anytime you're ready."

"Though Italy is flanked on three sides by the sea, and in the north by a mountain barrier," Alessandro began, "and though its early history is an illustration of the success of uniform administration and centralism, this country has exemplified division, contention, and atomization. Mind you, for art, for the development of the soul, nothing is better than a landscape of separate and impregnable towers. The variety, the sense of possibility, and the watchfulness that such an environment creates have given to us many honors unparalleled in the world. Politically, however, it's a different story."

Nicolò was following carefully, struggling to understand. No one had ever spoken to him like this.

"Paradoxically, countries with open and vulnerable borders—France, Germany, Poland, Russia, Hungary—and those with populations divided by language, race, and religion, found the strength and means to unify themselves and act as nations far earlier than did we. Perhaps it was because they were pushed into doing so by the very diversity they had to overcome. I don't know the causes, but I do know the results of the difference between them and us.

"We were, and are, politically weak. Whereas their policies toward other nations remained fairly consistent because of their elementary political harmony, we have always been like the family that must receive visitors, and quarrels bitterly until they are at the door. What if the visitors are predatory? How does such a family deal with the threat? If the visitors come with sword in hand, the family forgets its quarrels and fights as one. The nineteenth century, however, was the century of diplomacy. It was a splendid system—or would have been, had it not collapsed in nineteen fourteen—in which no one rushed in with swords. It was subtler than that.

"When they came to the door, they had their eyes on everything in the house, but they were more like jewel thieves than vandals. In an atmosphere of international civility, we were at a terrible disadvantage, because it wasn't threatening enough to distract us from our own struggles."

By this time, no matter how hard he tried to understand, Nicolò's eyes had begun to glaze, but Alessandro had no fear of bending green cane, because he knew it seldom broke.

"Remember this, then—even if you don't agree—for two reasons. First, factional paralysis made Italy weak on the international stage, and, second, it exaggerated inconsistency and volatility in internal matters.

"Are you with me?"

"Yes," Nicolò replied.

"Good. Much of the reason that the nineteenth century after the Congress of Vienna was as peaceful as it was, is that the European powers were absorbed in getting and running colonies. This cushioned many bursts of energy that otherwise might have led to war, and provided a margin of wealth and space that greatly relieved Europe of its tensions. Some little wars captured the public's imagination because of their exotic locations, but they weren't real wars. You know how when you get into a disagreement with your friend and it comes to a fight the first thing you do is start making rules about how the fight will be conducted? No punching in the face, no weapons, outside so you won't break up the furniture? That was the last century. The rules were clear, and Europe had an outside—the rest of the world—in which to carry on a fight without smashing its own crockery.

"Italy was left out of all this. We had our underdeveloped country right in our own south. And when we tried to imitate England, France, Germany, Holland, and even Spain, in seizing regions of the world, it was pathetic. It was comical. So, by the early part of this century Italy was crazy for making up lost ground. From the Nineties on, we had begun to look to Africa with a vengeance. We built naval bases at Augusta, Taranto, and Brindisi, and waited for a chance to redeem our prestige in Europe by seizing coconuts and diamonds. Why not? In ancient times, the whole of North Africa was ours.

"Our colonial failings made us feel as if we were always missing the boat. The next time, we wouldn't make '*il gran rifiuto.*' No, the next time, no matter how dangerous it looked, no matter how stupid, we would cast in our lot. The next time, we would avenge Custoza, Lissa, and Aduwa."

"What were those?" Nicolò asked.

Alessandro seemed resentful of humiliations so distant that Nicolò had not even heard of them.

"Those were battles in which we were made to look ridiculous—at Custoza, in the mountains, and at Lissa, on the sea, and at Aduwa, in Eritrea, by a bunch of Africans."

"I wish I had been there," Nicolò said.

"Really?" Alessandro asked. "We might have used you at Caporetto, too."

"Just tell me about the war."

"There's nothing to tell about a war unless you tell how it began."

"That's boring."

"Only for someone who doesn't know anything. When you get older, battles of any sort become far less interesting than what led to them and what they brought about. I know, I know. I have three hooves in the pasture and one already in the grave, but I have a few things more to tell before I get to the smoke and thunder.

"The Triplice, have you ever heard of it?"

"Of course not."

"It was an alliance with Austria-Hungary and Germany, in which we applied to the European balance of power what we had learned at home about a mobile, weak faction acting out of all proportion to its size. We balanced off our allies in the Triplice with France, Britain, and Russia, blowing hot and cold one way and then another, living in the cracks, as it were, the Italian tail wagging the big dogs of Europe. The lesson we might have learned from our own internal politics, from history, and from human nature, was not clear to us. If you play off one side against another, sooner or later you will either be crushed between the two or forced to join one of them. In the end, we lost interest in staying aloof, because we wanted the Alto Adige from the Austrians far more than we wanted Corsica from the French. What could we have done with Corsica? Sardinia is enough of a problem.

"The elements of instability might have been controllable if we had allowed our culture to buffer the shocks of bad politics. This was not too much to expect. After all, we are not Greenland. For millennia we have substituted culture for politics, and it has been a success.

"But in the years before nineteen fifteen, we were just like everyone else. The absence of a strong ethic suited to our age, the rise of the machine, the decadence of Romanticism as it ended a long and fruitful existence... who knows? Whatever the factors and in whatever combination, they led to the conviction that what we believed was no longer true, things had come apart, God had deserted us, and nothing in the whole world was left that could be called beautiful. Half a decade of dissonance, and philosophers in a never-ending stream mount the platform to keen that the light of the world has been extinguished forever.

"It passed me by, for when I was young I was sure of the good of the world, its beauty, and its ultimate justice. And even when I was broken the way one sometimes can be broken, and even though I had fallen, I found upon arising that I was stronger than before, that the glories, if I may call them that, which I had loved so much and that had been darkened in my fall, were shining ever brighter. And nearly every time subsequently that I have fallen and darkness has come over me, they have obstinately arisen, not as they were, but brighter.

"As if history were not the steady alternation of the dark and the light, people become resigned and pessimistic, and when the fields are left open, in rush the lunatics and idiots. Does it remind you of factional politics and the Triplice? It's the same. When greater forces are immobilized, the splinter factions run riot.

"As in other demoralized countries, we too had our madmen of station. A movement of 'Futurists' was led by a mental case named Marinetti. When, at age nineteen, I read his manifesto, even I was appalled. It's almost impossible to appall a boy of nineteen. Have you ever been appalled?"

Nicolò shook his head. "No."

"Parts of it have been with me ever since. I can quote from it: 'We sing the love of danger. Courage, rashness, and rebellion are the elements of our poetry.... We are for aggressive movement, febrile insomnia, mortal leaps, and blows with the fist.... Our praise is for the man at the wheel. There is no beauty now save in struggle, no masterpiece can be anything but aggressive, and hence we glorify war.'

"Febrile insomnia? Mortal leaps? It might have been funny but for their influence on the rest of the country. When people write violent absurdities on the walls of a city, the city becomes violent and absurd.

"You're probably not familiar with Folgore's odes to coal and electricity, and you needn't be. It is conceivable that one could write a decent ode to coal or electricity, but these were humorless, monomaniacal, terrifying exercises, matched rather well with the socialist realism on the other side of the political spectrum."

At this, Nicolò drew himself up, blushed, and announced in the manner of a police agent in a melodrama revealing himself to a group of saboteurs, "I am a Communist." Though he was proud, at the same time, he was mortified.

Alessandro took a few steps, wondering exactly why he had been interrupted, and looked at the boy, with the same gently mocking expression with which he had followed Nicolò's declaration about the lost battles where his presence might have helped Italy to prevail. "Good," he said, "is there anything you would like me to say, or may I continue?"

"No, but what you said about . . . whatever it was, was not nice. Please keep in mind that I am a Socialist."

"I thought you were a Communist."

"What's the difference?"

"Are you a member of a party?"

"I don't think so."

"A youth organization?"

"The soccer team at the factory."

"Then why do you say you are a Socialist, or a Communist?"

"I don't know, I just am."

"How did you vote?"

"I'm too young."

"How will you vote?"

"I'll stand in line, they'll give me a piece of paper. Then I take it to a little place where I can..."

"I don't mean that. I mean for whom will you vote, for which party."

"How am I supposed to know?"

"Then how do you know what you are?"

"I told you, I just am."

"So what?" the old man demanded indignantly, suddenly angry at having been interrupted.

"Are *you* a Communist?" Nicolò asked, hoping, for no reason that he could fathom, that Alessandro was not a Communist but, rather, a Christian Democrat.

"No."

"What are you?"

"Who cares? Would it make any difference to you what I am? No. So let me continue. There were others, too. They multiplied like rabbits. Papini, that son of a bitch, wanted every library and museum to be put to the torch. He maintained that the profoundest philosophy was that of a moron, and he could only have been led to that conclusion by self-adulation.

"Combine this with Marinetti's campaign against spaghetti, De Felice's wish that every child be taught to slaughter animals, and the various odes and symphonies to coal, drill presses, daggers, and stick pins, and you have a school. Combine it with D'Annunzio, and you have a movement."

"D'Annunzio who?"

"D'Annunzio—*who*?" Alessandro repeated.

"It sounds familiar."

"I can't explain the whole world to you. I should have known that. How can I expect you to understand the theory when you don't know the story. It was a mistake to start out from such a high point. Let me begin as simply as possible.

"There was a great, devastating war. It was fought in Europe from nineteen fourteen to nineteen eighteen. Italy stayed out until the spring of nineteen fifteen. Then, mainly because we had designs on the Südtirol, the Alto Adige, we went to war against Austria-Hungary, and almost a million men died."

"That was the war you were in?"

"That was the war I was in."

"Tell me what it was like."

"No," Alessandro said. "Among other things, I simply do not have the strength."

They passed through the few outlying streets of Acereto. Even at ten o'clock, the town was asleep, the windows shuttered. In the center of the village was a piazza, and in the center of the piazza, a fountain. They sat down at its edge.

NOT A single light burned, and the moon had not risen, but the piazza and the buildings surrounding it were of a pale color that amplified the starlight enough to outline shapes and give away anything that moved across fields of varying contrast. Water rose from the fountain's spire in a thick steady stream that waved back and forth, collapsing gently upon itself as it fell into the cold pool below. Sometimes spray from colliding masses of falling water would sweep lightly across Alessandro Giuliani and Nicolò Sambucca.

Alessandro's hands were folded on top of his cane. In daylight he might have been taken for a landowner, the mayor, or a doctor resting by the fountain after having attended a very sick patient. He felt pain in his right leg, in the thigh and just above the knee.

It was one of the wounds that grew worse over time, but he welcomed the pain. Pain was inevitable, and he knew that in his struggle with it he would eventually be the master. When he had returned from the war, in winter, to the sullen and demoralized city of Rome, he had often missed the fighting that he had longed so deeply to leave. So with the pain.

Perhaps because of the age of his traveling companion, Alessandro himself felt as if he were young, in a different time, and he dreaded the prospect of once again thinking through his youth. Some of his colleagues and a few of his students claimed to have been moved so by a book that they had read it again and again. Who were they? Of what were they made? Were they dissembling? Perhaps he was a fool, but he thought that if a work were truly great you would only have to read it once and you would be stolen from yourself, desperately moved, changed forever. It would become part of you and never leave, and you would love the characters as if they were your own. Who would want to plow over ground that has been perfectly plowed? Would it not be, like living one's life over again, infinitely painful and dissonant? In his work he had to read over, and he often found it to be an operation of despoliation and agony.

He looked at Nicolò, who was lying on his side, his right ear pressed against the stone rim of the fountain, shirt sleeve rolled up, arm fully extended into the water, straining to grasp a submerged coin with the tip of his fingers.

"Do you think it's worth it?" Alessandro asked.

Wanting to answer by holding up a glistening 100-lire piece, Nicolò didn't reply.

After he retrieved the coin he straightened himself with relief and took a box of matches from his pocket, one of which he lit with his left hand, which was dry. "What's this?" he asked Alessandro, who saw in flickering match light that the boy's arm had been whitened by its submersion in the cold water.

"Let me see."

Nicolò struck another match.

"It's Greek," Alessandro told him.

"How much is it worth?" Nicolò asked with the particular tension common to people who find a foreign coin that they suspect may be many times more valuable than they fear it really is.

"About a lira, or less," he was informed.

"A lira? One?"

Alessandro nodded affirmatively before the match went out. "How can that be?"

"What did you expect? Do you think people throw away gold? The only time it's profitable to pull money from a fountain is if it's crowded with coins. I used to do it myself."

"But you were rich."

"So? I was a kid. We used to get money for ice cream by dipping in the fountains."

"Didn't your father give you money?"

"Not for ice cream."

"Why not?"

"He knew I got my ice cream money from the fountains."

"He was smart."

"That was the least of it," Alessandro said. "How old are you, Nicolò? You look about eighteen."

"Seventeen."

"Nicolò, in nineteen hundred and eight, more than half a century ago, I was a student just starting in the university. One day I passed a fountain that was choked with silver. I knew it wasn't quite right for me to take off my jacket, roll up my sleeve, and struggle to get the money from the bottom. Though I wasn't sure why, it seemed to have something to do with dignity. Then a policeman arrived and intimated, in the forceful way in which they often intimate, that I should return the coins to the water. He told me that it wasn't proper for me to be doing what I was doing, that I should leave it for the children.

"It had nothing to do with dignity. One shouldn't ever do anything to protect one's dignity. You either have it or you don't. It was a matter, it seems, of fairness. And by recognizing that it was a matter of fairness, I advanced the idea of dignity instead of trying to make it advance me. You see what I mean?"

"But it's Greek, Signore," Nicolò protested.

"Wouldn't that be exciting for a little boy?" the old man asked.

Nicolò bent back his arm, about to throw the coin into the middle of the fountain.

"Ah!" Alessandro said, bringing him up short. "How's he going to get it? Do you want him to drown?"

"Let him swim," Nicolò said.

"No," he was answered. "It's for a little child."

Nicolò dropped the coin and rolled up his sleeve. He didn't like the idea of throwing away even one lira. "This whole stupid town is closed up," he said. "Imagine, not a single light, not one..."

"I saw a light when we came in, at the crossroads."

"But not in the town itself. I can't believe it. It's only ten o'clock. Right now on the Via Veneto things are just beginning to heat up," he stated, as if he went there every night.

"Do you frequent the Via Veneto?" Alessandro asked.

"Sometimes."

"What do you do there?"

"I look for women," Nicolò answered, blushing so deeply that, even in the dark, Alessandro muttered, *"Pomodoro."*

"It's a good place to look for women," Alessandro said. "Lots of them go there, but do you find them?"

"Not really..." was the answer, in a sort of hoarse whisper.

"Have you ever slept with a woman?"

"Not yet," Nicolò confessed, ashamed.

"Don't worry," Alessandro told him. "You will. You probably don't even know that women want to sleep with you as much as you want to sleep with them."

"They do?"

"It's true, but I know you won't believe me. *I* wouldn't have believed me. Anyway, it's something that you should never come to accept fully. If you do, it's tragic, because it means you've become a peacock. You don't even begin to get an inkling of it until you're much older than you are now.

"You should be confident. You're young, you're serious, and you have a good job. I would think that women would be strongly attracted to someone who makes propellers."

"You think so?"

"Yes. It's honorable, unusual, interesting, with the possibility of advancement. Admittedly, it's not like being a doctor or a lawyer, but who's to say that you won't work hard, become an engineer, and maybe, someday, become the head of F.A.I."

"Of F.A.I.?" Nicolò asked skeptically, in the way that people of suppressed dreams often preclude their own possibilities. "Me? Never. A hundred and twenty thousand people work for F.A.I."

Alessandro did not indulge Nicolò's lack of belief in himself. "Look, stupid," he said, turning Nicolò from red to white. "It'll be hard enough for you to rise. Fate, circumstances, and other men will at times be almost overwhelmingly against you. You'll be able to beat them only if you don't join them, only if you don't condemn yourself from the start. If you have no faith in yourself, who will? I won't. I wouldn't waste my time, and neither will anyone else. Do you understand? You can be the head of F.A.I. You're still young enough to be the Pope."

"The Pope? They'd never have a pope as young as me."

Alessandro sighed hopelessly. "You're still young enough to *become* the Pope."

"Would I have to be a priest first?"

"I think that is the minimal qualification, yes."

"I don't want to be the Pope."

"I'm not suggesting that you become the Pope, you little idiot! I'm only saying that you're still young enough to try."

"Why would I want to?"

"You wouldn't, necessarily, but your youth is a magical instrument with which you can accomplish anything."

"Every two seconds you say I'm an idiot. Why?"

"Because every two seconds you are. You're wasting what you have."

"You sound like the soccer coach, and we lose to everybody. We always lose to Olivetti. We even lose to the Musicians Union. Fabrica Aeronautica Italiana, maker of war planes, loses to bald-headed guys who play the violin."

"I don't want to walk all the way to Sant' Angelo with a . . . with someone who defeats himself before he's begun," Alessandro said. "I'm going to tell you something that you may or may not understand, and I want you to memorize it and say it to yourself now and then, until, someday, you do understand."

"Is it long?"

"No."

"Go ahead."

"Nicolò," Alessandro said.

"Nicolò," Nicolò repeated.

"The spark of life is not gain."

"The spark of life is not gain."

"Nor is it luxury."

"Nor is it luxury."

"The spark of life is movement."

"Movement."

"Color."

"Color."

"Love."

"Love."

"And furthermore . . ."

"And furthermore . . ."

"If you really want to enjoy life, you must work quietly and humbly to realize your delusions of grandeur."

"But I don't have them."

"Start to have them."

Nicolò shook his head affirmatively. "I understand, Signore, I understand what you're saying. I do. I think I do."

Alessandro grunted.

Neither of them spoke while Alessandro carefully laid out a meal of prosciutto, fruit, and chocolate, after which he and Nicolò began to eat, leaning down now and then to dip a cupped hand into the numbingly cold water for a drink.

"You eat like an animal," Alessandro said matter-of-factly. Nicolò stopped for a moment, shocked again, with his mouth and cheeks full of a difficult sheet of prosciutto. He couldn't answer, and he half suspected that the old man had timed his criticism accordingly. Cheeks puffed like a squirrel's, he listened. "You mustn't hum when you eat—not that animals do—for it connotes a certain primitive idiocy. No one is going to snatch the food away from you, so you can cut it or tear it apart before you put it in your mouth. Don't breathe so intently—it sounds as if you're going to expire. And don't make so much noise when you chew.

"Cafes on the Via Veneto are full of people who follow the rules I just stated. Believe me, well dressed women don't look twice at someone who eats like a jackal on the Serengeti. Another thing: don't keep shifting your eyes from side to side as you eat. That's half the battle right there."

"I never heard of the Serengeti," Nicolò said, after swallowing from shame a mass of food that might have stuck in his throat and killed him. "Is it a street or a piazza?"

"It's a place half the size of Italy, filled with lions, zebras, gazelles, and elephants."

"In Africa?"

"Yes."

"I would like to go to Africa," Nicolò said, putting another huge pile of prosciutto into his mouth.

"There are better places to go than Africa," Alessandro stated. "Much better places."

"Where?"

"There," the old man said, pointing north-northeast to the great mountains he knew were rearing up far away in the dark, to the Alto Adige, the Carnic Alps, the Julians, and the Tyrol.

Nicolò turned to look in the direction his guide had indicated, and he saw a lightened mass of buildings that, even in the darkness, conveyed a reassuring and uniquely Italian sense of dilapidation.

"What's so great over there?" Nicolò asked. "There aren't even any lights on."

"I don't mean there," Alessandro said, thinking of snow-capped mountains and the electrifying past. "I mean far beyond; if you flew into the night as if in a dream, and rose, the wind tight against your face, the stars drawing you to them, the landscape beneath you blue-black. I have suddenly vaulted into the mountains," he said, "after never having gone back, ever, for fear of encountering my lost self."

"There aren't any people up there anymore, fighting wars. Once things happen, they pass, and that's it."

"No," Alessandro said. "If they happen once, they stay forever. I never spoke of them, because I have faith that they are everlasting, with or without me. I'm not afraid to die, because I know that what I have seen will not fade, and will someday spring full blown from someone not yet born, who did not know me, or my time, or what I loved. I know for sure."

"How?"

"Because that is the soul, and whether you are a soldier, a scholar, a cook, or an apprentice in a factory, your life and your work will eventually teach you that it exists. The difference between your flesh and the animate power within, which can feel, understand, and love, in that very ascending order, will be clear to you in ten thousand ways, ten thousand times over."

"Have you ever seen a spirit?" Nicolò asked.

"By the million," came the answer, surprising even Alessandro, who was now not entirely in control of himself. "By the million, in troops of the glowing dead, walking upward on a beam of light.

"Now you listen!" he said to the boy, leaning forward and slamming his palm with his fist. "If you were to go to every museum in the world to look at the paintings in which such a beam of light connects heaven and earth, do you know what you would find? You would find that in whatever time, in whatever country, painter to painter, the angle of light is more or less the same. An accident?"

"I'd have to see. I'd have to measure. I don't know."

"Measure?"

"With a protractor."

"You can measure such things solely with your eyes, and besides, when the last judgment comes, even Marxists won't have protractors."

"I will. I always carry one in my pocket. Look," Nicolò said, pulling out a little red plastic box in which were neatly placed a six-scaled rule, a protractor, a small contour rule, calipers, and precision calipers, nesting there as if they had been prepared for Alessandro Giuliani to see. "You don't know. When you work with machines and you shape things you always have to measure and remeasure to get it right. The machine doesn't tolerate mistakes or excuses. It has nothing to do with what you want or what you hope. You have to get things right or it won't work." As he made this declaration he was so innocent and so exact that he forced the old man into silence. "What?" Nicolò asked, to get Alessandro to talk.

"Your argument is beautiful and surprising, Nicolò," Alessandro said. "In short, you are correct. You must measure and remeasure, to get things right. And because I have not measured all those beams of light, I am ashamed."

"Signore, what happened to you there?"

At this, perhaps because he was exhausted and strained by the walk, the old man bowed his head onto his loosely clenched left fist.

Nicolò leaned forward in a complicated, unfathomable gesture that showed he would become a wise and compassionate man. He did not apologize for having led Alessandro on, for Alessandro had led himself, but, still, Nicolò was moved, and he felt affection for the old man who, though lame, was teaching him how to walk.

THEY PICKED up the pace outside of Acereto. Perhaps because they had eaten and rested, Alessandro found strength. "God compensates perfectly," he said to his companion. "You cannot fall and expect not to rise. Call it the wheel, the lesson of Antaeus, what you will, but strength floods in after a fall.

"And then again," he said cheerily, "it may be just that the moon is about to rise, or it may be the chocolate, or a second wind. Tell me if you want to walk more slowly."

"I think I can keep up with you," Nicolò answered sarcastically.

For the next hour or two, keeping up with Alessandro would be a task that would set the boy to breathing hard and make him think that something might be wrong with his heart, because he found it difficult to stay even with an old man who carried a cane and whose every step was a cross between an uncontrolled pivot and a barely arrested fall.

They were walking up. The road from Acereto to Lanciata was steep in places, ascending to the ridge line of the low mountains that from the rooftops of Rome looked like the Alps, and then twisting dizzily into sheltered valleys where herds of sheep glowed in the moonlight like patches of snow.

They passed drop-offs where the milk-white shoulder of the road became a luminous ramp into an attractive void of weightlessness and rapture. In making the turns, Alessandro came perilously close to the abyss, and at times the edge of the cake would crumble away noiselessly after his foot had left it. He seemed not to notice or care, but to be protected by their almost supernatural momentum, which Nicolò interpreted as a friendly race to see who could rise faster to the topmost ridge, where the moon would hang voluminously over a noiseless world.

Nicolò stayed away from the edge, and Alessandro was amused. "Of the many excellent things about mountaineering," he said as much to the night, the cliffs, and the air as to the boy taking quick steps beside him, "one of the finest is to become unafraid of heights. When I was a boy, and would climb with my father and the mountain guides he knew or hired, I abhorred the vacuum of an abyss, and my fists were white from clutching the rock. Meanwhile, the guides would sit with legs dangling over an infinite precipice; they would stand on tiny pinnacles, smoking their pipes, coiling ropes, and sorting the climbing hardware; and they would run up and down goat trails sometimes no less vertical and no more contoured than Trajan's Column.

"After a few days in the mountains my father hardly paid attention to the drop underneath the overhanging walls upon which he would stand with his heels on the rock and the rest of his boots projecting out into space.

"I don't remember when I lost my fear, but, perhaps because I'd been afraid for so long, when finally I did it never returned. I haven't been in the mountains since the war, but I don't fear heights. Over the years—along the cliffs of Capri, atop Saint Peter's, climbing onto the roof to straighten a crooked tile—I've found that this part of me, at least, has remained young."

He was in as fine a heat as a youthful runner on a good day. "Do you want me to slow down?" he asked Nicolò.

"No," Nicolò answered, breathlessly, "but perhaps you should, since we are, after all, going up."

"Don't slow on my account," Alessandro warned. "I'll be devastated by morning no matter what I do, so I might as well push hard while I can. Nicolò, the world is full of tart little surprises. Here I am, seventy-four years of age, racing up a mountain, putting you to shame because you are a boy of seventeen and you're breathing like a nonagenarian. Don't worry. In a few hours you'll probably have to carry me, but, for now, indulge me, sweat a little, follow along in the race."

"What if you keep on like this all the way past Sant' Angelo?" Nicolò asked desperately.

"Then you'll have lots of time to spend with your sister, and they'll bury me in Monte Prato. Better to be buried there than in one of those marble filing cabinets in Rome."

"Aren't you afraid to die?"

"No."

"I am."

"You're not tired."

"I'm not brave, either."

"It has nothing to do with bravery. Bravery is for other things."

"Yes, but you miss people."

"I know that."

"So there's nothing you can do about it, is there."

"You keep them alive."

"You do?"

"Yes."

"Come on!"

"You keep them alive not by skill, not by art, not by memory, but by love. When you understand that, you won't be afraid to die. But that doesn't mean you'll go to your death like a clown. Death, Nicolò, is emotional."

"So is life."

"One hopes."

"Look, Signore, you'd better not die on the road, especially if I'm not there to tell, and you'd better not die especially if I am there, you know what I mean?"

"My granddaughter will know to move me next to my wife. And she and I have a bond strong enough that it hardly matters where we are put, for we have never really parted."

"Oh," Nicolò said, unable to say more, because he was too busy breathing.

"It's true. Anyway, death awakens lawyers. They'll get busy when I go. I've left precise, typewritten instructions. I even say what to do with my suits, my papers, and the little things I have in my desk.

"Almost everything is to be burned. You live on not by virtue of the things you have amassed, or the work you have done, but through your spirit, in ways and by means that you can neither control nor foresee. All my possessions and all my papers will be burned in the pine grove behind my house.

"There I have a metal cage to prevent the flight of cinders large enough to set other things on fire. It's against the municipal code to burn refuse in the center of Rome, but I've taken care of that. I have an envelope addressed to the local inspector and one for his supervisor. I have written a carefully composed ode, in perfect *terza rima,* begging a single indulgence. When I realized that they might not care for my poetry, I thought to enclose twenty-five thousand lire for the inspector, and forty thousand for the supervisor."

"Ten thousand would have done it. Why so much?"

"Because inflation is not unknown in this country, and I may live longer than I expect. Though why I would want to is a mystery. I'm so cautious and conscientious that I feel entirely free to die. If I die on this road, just keep walking. They'll find me. Everything will be taken care of properly."

"You think you're going to die?" Nicolò blurted out between breaths. "I think *I'm* going to die."

"Don't worry," Alessandro said, infuriating him. "I'm still quite fit. I think you probably misinterpreted my gait. Since the war, I've slowed down a bit, and lately I've had to use this," he said, knocking the cane on the road, "but I've rowed on the Tiber, except when it has been bone dry or in flood, for forty years. I row in the heat and in the rain. I've been rammed by motorboats and attacked by swans. I've seen conquering armies march in on the bridges above me, and then, some years later, march out. I've even been on the river in the snow, and seen it hissing onto the water next to me as my oars swept past, as if I had been not in Rome, but in England. I try not to overdo it, but I'm not feeble like many men my age."

"I can see that," Nicolò responded, sweat glistening on his forehead. "You give another impression," he continued. "The way you dress . . . it makes you look like a sugar cake."

"What do you mean?" Alessandro asked, looking down at his clothes.

"It's all white. And your hair's white. You look like a priest in summer, or an ice cream man."

"An ice cream man!"

"Well, that's what you look like. You look so delicate I thought you were about ninety or a hundred."

"A hundred?!" Alessandro was not pleased by such flattery. "In twenty-six years, maybe, when you're forty-three, I'll be a hundred. And the suit isn't white. It's a light cream color. You see?"

"Looks white to me."

"It's hard to make distinctions in starlight. Wait till the full moon rises."

"How do you know it's going to be full?"

"Among other things, it was full yesterday except for a tiny splinter. Tonight, it will be perfectly round. That's why I'm walking so fast."

"You walk fast when the moon is full?"

"Just outside Acereto is a high ridge. Over there," he said, pointing ahead and to the right, to a dark hill that rose higher than the others around it. "There, in the evening, when I don't get thrown off the bus, I can see the sun set over the sea—though at this distance the sea is a line as thin and blue as a tentative stroke in a watercolor. And you can see Rome as it lights up, faintly at first, but then like a city that's burning. To the east are half a hundred mountain ridges. In the dusk their undulations make them look more like the sea than the sea itself.

"If we can move fast enough we can be there when the moon rises. First it will be orange and amber, like Rome on the opposite side, glowing like the remnant of a bonfire.

"For a moment the amber moon to the east and the amber city to the west will seem to be mirror images, and from the height of the ridge we'll watch them face one another as if they were two cats on either side of a fence. Then, as the moon comes up in ten thousand colors, we can have a drink and eat some chocolate—it's better than watching a movie."

"Is there water up there?" Nicolò asked. "Even now, I'm thirsty. It's because you walk so fast."

"No, there isn't any water up there. It's too high, but I filled a wine bottle that I found. At the top of the ridge, we can drink the cold water of Acereto. We'll need it because we will have worked so hard."

"Where is it?"

"In the briefcase on your back. Part of the reason you're breathing so hard."

"You found a bottle with a cork?"

"I found a bottle, but it has no cork."

"How do you know the water hasn't spilled?"

"I have observed you carefully," Alessandro said. "Since we left Acereto you have not been upside down for a moment. Don't walk on your hands."

"All right," Nicolò promised. He was known among his friends, and at the factory, for being able to walk on his hands.

"Remarkable thing," Alessandro said, "the moon rising. Especially when it's full. It's so gentle, so round, and so light. Every time I see the full moon rise, I think of my wife. Her face was bright and beautiful, and if it had any imperfection it was that it seemed too perfect, especially when she was young.

"I walk fast because I want to see the moon rise. And I want to see the moon rise because . . . I've already told you. Come, it won't wait for us, but it will be there."

They walked on steadily. Nicolò found his breath. He tucked his shirt carefully into his pants and brushed his hair back from his eyes as if he were going to be introduced to someone. And as they walked, he reminded himself now and then that he was not to walk on his hands.

"N O T A single cloud," Alessandro said as they sat down on a flat rock at the summit of the ridge toward which they had been walking. "For three hundred and sixty degrees, and all the way to the top of the sky, it's as if clouds had never been invented."

The darkness spread away from them on all sides. Even the whitened road curved into a little bow on the summit and then was hidden as it continued down along the ridge. They had left the road and climbed for a minute or two to reach a ledge at the very top of a hill around which the world had been draped like a swirling fluid that has suddenly frozen.

"There's Rome," Alessandro announced, "the color of an ember, but sparkling like a diamond. The dark ribbon you see is the Tiber cutting through the light, and those white flakes, like mica, are the large *piazze.*

"If you look west you'll see a tranquil line just beyond the hills. That's the Mediterranean. You can tell it from the sky, for, although they are the same color, in the narrow band of the sea are no stars. The distinction is faint, because the atmosphere dims the stars as they approach the horizon, but if you look hard you'll see."

"I don't see," Nicolò declared. "I don't see stars out there, only above." He strained and squinted, moving his head to and fro.

Happy to have beaten the moon to the top of the hill, and to have a lovely lair from which to capture it as it rose, Alessandro might have ignored Nicolò's inability to see the stars near the horizon, but half a century of explanation and elucidation would not let him. "Look straight up," he commanded.

"Where?"

"There." He pointed toward Rigel, his favorite star. "Count the stars that you can see in a space the size of a coin."

"I can't."

"Why not?"

"They stand on top of each other."

"What do you mean, 'they stand on top of each other'?"

"They're too blurry."

"They don't look like pinpoints?"

"No, they look like someone spilled paint."

The old man pulled from one of his jacket pockets a rigid leather case that he snapped open in a well practiced movement of his left hand. "Try looking through these. They may make things sharper."

Nicolò took a pair of gold-framed spectacles from the bed of velvet upon which they had been resting, and put them on. He turned his head back to Rigel, and, for the first time, he saw the stars.

"And those must be all wrong for you," Alessandro said. "Yet, an improvement?"

"Yes! The stars are deep in the sky, and I can see them one by one."

"Have you never had spectacles?"

"Never. I don't need them." He paused. "I do need them."

"Was it because they were too expensive?"

"No. In the clinic I could have gotten them for free. They make things sharper, but girls don't like them."

"Who said?"

"Everybody."

"I've found it to be just the opposite, and as for the opinion that girls are less pretty if they wear glasses, that's only for apes. Many times, the thick spectacles of a young girl have been the barb of the hook she sinks into my heart. Even these days, I'm entranced by the nearsighted ones who sit in the front row and stare at me through concentric rings of sparkling crystal. And when they're slightly cross-eyed, it's that much better."

"You're crazy."

"A marvelous invention, entirely compatible with physical beauty."

"They were invented?"

"Do you think they grow in the wild?"

"Who invented them?"

"A Florentine, Alessandro di Spina. Spectacles even have a patron saint, Saint Jerome, because in Ghirlandaio's portrait of him they hang from the edge of a table as if they were the commonest things in the world. It was Raphael, however, who made them famous, in his painting of Pope Leo the Tenth, the four-eyed son of Lorenzo de Medici, the one who expelled Martin Luther."

"I don't know any of those guys," Nicolò said.

"That's all right. I don't either."

"Except Saint Jerome. I know the saints."

"That's good. Whose day is it today?"

"I don't know."

"I thought you did."

"Not like that I don't. You think the Pope knows?"

"I'd bet on it."

"So what saint?"

"I'm not the Pope, but today is the ninth of August. Saint Romanus, I believe. He was a Byzantine."

Nicolò, who had never heard the word *Byzantine,* said, "That's too bad."

"Where's the water?" Alessandro asked. "And the chocolate."

"My father says that if you eat too much chocolate, you turn black."

"That's undoubtedly true," Alessandro answered. "After all, chocolate comes from Africa, and Africans are black. But what about Switzerland? A lot of chocolate comes from Switzerland."

"So?"

"Are the Swiss black?"

"They're not?"

"Well what do you think?"

"I don't know," Nicolò offered, obviously confused. Taking the water bottle from Alessandro's briefcase and placing it carefully on the flat slab, he asked, "Is Switziland in Africa?"

"You mean *Swaziland*?"

"*Switziland*," Nicolò insisted.

Alessandro felt his heart pounding against his chest. His breath came slowly. "What did you say?" he asked.

Nicolò struggled to envision the world. "Which is the one that has an ocean, Africa or Peru?"

"Let's start closer to home," Alessandro said. "First, name the countries of Europe."

"What are they?"

"I'm asking you."

"Asking me what?"

"What are the countries of Europe?"

"They're countries," Nicolò said.

"Name them."

"Italy, of course..."

"Excellent."

"France."

"Yes."

"Germany, Spain, Ireland, and Mahogany."

"Mahogany?"

"It's a country, isn't it? It's in Brazil."

"It isn't, but keep going."

"Is Germany a country?"

"Yes, but you've said it already."

"There are more?"

Alessandro nodded.

"Is there one called Great Dane?"

"When you get back to Rome," Alessandro said gravely, "you must look at a map. Haven't you ever seen a map of the world?"

"Yes I have, but I don't know what it says. I can't read."

"You can't read at all?"

"No, not even my own name. I told you, I never went to school."

"You have to learn to read. They'll teach you at the factory."

"They say I have to read before I become an apprentice, and they say they'll teach me. I'm supposed to go to a place in Monte Sacro. It's okay. I can do numbers. I can do numbers very well. Look! The moon."

Alessandro turned to the east. His cane clattered down upon the rock as he caught sight of a tiny orange dome, rising coolly, unlike the molten sunrise, from behind the farthest line of hills.

The arc rapidly turned into a silent half circle, spying upon them with its old and tired face. It had about it the air of being intensely busy, as if its occupation with the task of floating in perfect orbits had made it justly self-absorbed.

"The whole world stops as this stunning dancer rises," Alessandro said, "and its beauty puts to shame all our doubts."

It *is* like a dancer, Nicolò thought, as the perfectly round moon began to float airily above the silhouetted hills it had begun to illumine. "So smooth," he said.

"Without saying anything, it says so much," Alessandro continued. "In that sense, it's better than the sun, which is always holding forth, and butting at you like a ram."

Because of Alessandro's spectacles, Nicolò was able to see that the moon had mountains and seas. His sudden apprehension of the moon, so close and full, riding over them like a huge airship, endeared it to him forever. For perhaps the first time in his life he was lifted entirely outside himself and separated from his wants. As he contemplated the huge smoldering disc he was easily able to suspend time and the sensation of gravity, and a sort of internal electricity overflowed within him. It came in waves, and grew stronger and stronger as the moon glided from orange and amber to pearl and white. And then, after only a few minutes, the soul that had taken flight returned to a body in which the heart was pounding like the heart of a bird that has just alighted from a long fast flight.

"What happened to me?" he asked, with a convulsive shudder.

"When I was your age," Alessandro said, "I had already learned to compress what you just experienced into bolts of pure lightning."

Nicolò didn't know what to think, so he stared ahead.

"When a great sight comes to sweep you down, fight it. It will take you, for sure, but keep your eyes open, and you can beat it, like molten steel, into beams of light.

"I used to take long walks in the city, and when I was able to immerse myself in a cross-fire of beautiful images I would ignite just as you did. It has many names, and is one of the prime forces of history, and yet it keeps itself hidden, as if it were shy.

"A favorite trick of mine, that I have since abandoned, was to concentrate the overflow upon the horses of the *carabinieri* to make them rear up on their hind legs and whinny. They're very sensitive to human feelings, and when they know that you are greatly moved they will often react in sympathetic fashion."

"How did you do that?"

"It wasn't hard. I had to be all worked up, but when I was young I was like a perpetual lightning storm. I would concentrate upon the horse as if he were the emblem and paradigm of every horse that ever was or ever will be, and then throw the current across the gap.

"The horse would turn his head to me and draw it back, widening his eyes. Then he'd shudder as if a sudden chill had come over him. At that point I'd open the gates to let the power sweep out all at once, and he'd rear and cry out the way horses do, with a sound that seems able to pierce through all things.

"I'll never forget the surprise of the *carabinieri,* the fall of their coats, and the banging of their swords as they stood rigidly in the stirrups so as not to be thrown. They were never angry. After the horses had expressed themselves so completely, they and their riders always seemed to regard each other with awe. More often than not, as I passed I would hear the rider saying to his agitated mount, 'What got into you? What has moved you?' You could see them patting the horses' necks to calm them down.

"I don't do it anymore. I'm not sure I could.

"But the moon, what a lovely thing. To see it makes me very happy. My wife's face, especially when she was young, would have been perfect—in the sense that she could have been a star in films—had her eyes not been so full of love. When she smiled," he said, indicating the cool glow that had begun to climb steeply into the sky, "it was as lovely as that."

"This is how you've never left her," Nicolò said.

Alessandro made a curt bow, closing his eyes for an instant. "In this and in many other ways, but they are not enough. My symbols, my parallels, my discoveries, cannot even begin to do her justice and cannot bring her back. The most I can do is to make the memory of her shine. So I touch lightly, ever so lightly, seeking after gentle things, for she was gentle.

"Now look at the apposition," he said, drawing himself up from what might have made him falter, "of the moon on one hand, and the city of Rome on the other.

"Rome still looks like catacombs of fire, and will remain this shattered and amber color throughout the night, although as morning comes the whiter lights will leave the field more and more to the strings of amber streetlights. But the moon, as it moves, has already run through a number of scenes. First it was a farmer's fire, almost dead in the field, ruby red. Then it ripened through a thousand shades of orange, amber, and yellow. As it gets lighter it sheds its mass, until somewhere between cream and pearl, halfway to its apogee, it will seem like a burst of smoke that wants to run away on the wind. Then do you know what happens?"

Nicolò moved his head back and forth.

"It gets as white and hard as glacial ice. It dazzles so that you can barely look at it—and all the weight comes back until it seems like one of those huge chandeliers that, at the opera or in palaces of state, in being so high, sharp, and heavy, tend to discourage people from standing underneath them.

"With the city off to one side and the moon directly above, I hope I don't walk crookedly, like a Dutch milkmaid with one bucket at the end of her yoke and the other balanced on her head.

"In the darkness you will see two large bodies of light—one fixed and the other moving in a sure arc. Only in the morning, when the sun comes up, will you see three, and, as the sun rises, the other two will fade away."

"Not true," Nicolò said. "Look. Here's the third. It's making noise."

Alessandro turned, and saw lights winding along an erratic path. The perfect apposition of the moon and the city of Rome was broken by the unexpected arrival of a convoy of cars and trucks. One of the trucks, strung with lights that sparkled across the valley, was carrying a brass band.

"That's why Acereto was deserted," Alessandro speculated. "They must have been helping out in Lanciata. It's higher and colder there. They probably pool resources to take in the crop at Lanciata first. And they bring along a band."

"They're going to pass by," Nicolò declared.

"Of course. This is the road."

"What shall we do?"

"What would you wish to do?"

"Should we just sit here?"

"Unless for some reason you want to stop them," Alessandro answered.

"They won't even see us."

"So what. We'll see them."

"We'll be in the dark. They'll go right by."

"What's wrong with that?"

"I don't know. It'll be as if we don't exist, as if we're dead."

Alessandro nodded.

"I would have run out to greet them."

"You can if you wish."

"I don't want to be a pair of eyes in the darkness."

"Struggle as you may," Alessandro said, "that is what you will someday be. Tell me, a minute ago was Rome any the less, was the moon any the less, because you could not run out to greet them?"

Nicolò was already resigned to watching the lights as they passed in the dark. "No," he said. "They weren't less."

"If anything," Alessandro continued, "the distance is to our advantage. I'm perfectly content to watch the celebrants from here in the dark. Let them go by. We'll lose nothing. To the contrary, and may God forgive us, as they go past and we remain, we'll take from them everything they have."

PARTS OF a song floated up to them on the wind, and were interrupted like a telephone conversation on a faulty line, but as the band truck and the convoy it led came closer, the music was welded together and its stammerings vanished. Riding on the truck was a village orchestra with old instruments, not enough time to practice, and a little too much wine. Every musician, however, was a virtuoso who followed an independent line. Though the conductor made dramatic, elegant, sweeping gestures, the meaning of which he had never learned, even had he known what they meant his musicians would not have.

Still, the music was enchanting, if only because of accidental harmonies in its collective dissonance. The clarinet and the glockenspiel, unknowingly, would for a moment or two engage in an apparently random duet that could have put the musicians of La Scala to shame, and then go their separate ludicrous ways. Sound upon sound, reinforcing and combining outside the poorly followed plan, sometimes lit up the amateur orchestra with a kind of glory that transfixed the old man, who knew that this was how brass bands have packed village squares from time immemorial.

On rows of improvised benches built into hay trucks were scores of exhausted farmers and their wives. One truck pulled a trailer stacked with tools that glimmered in the moonlight. As the convoy passed Alessandro and Nicolò in the shadows, they saw a figure rise to its feet in one truck and lean against the slatted railing. "You get me up on time tomorrow, Bernardo, or you can walk home, you son of a bitch."

From the other truck came the reply. "What can I do? The full moon throws off the clocks!"

"Hey, what's that?" the first man asked, pointing at the ledge where Alessandro Giuliani and Nicolò Sambucca sat in the moonlight. Word was passed from vehicle to vehicle, the convoy halted, and the band stopped playing. The only sound was from the knocking of diesel rocker arms.

"No matter what they say, don't answer," Alessandro told Nicolò under his breath, "and don't move."

"Why? What for?" Nicolò protested.

"To enrich their folklore."

"You're crazy!"

"Shut up."

"Hello!" someone screamed from a truck. "Hello there!"

When no answer came, everyone pressed against the rails on one side, and the trucks tilted.

For a time the farmers were as still as the objects of their curiosity. Then one of them jumped to the ground and scrambled up the rock. He approached Alessandro and Nicolò more gingerly than he would have approached an angry bull. Though for every step forward it seemed that he took two steps back, he magically advanced to within five paces of them. "What do you want?" he asked, as if they had insulted him.

Since neither of them wanted anything, it was easy not to answer.

The farmer stared at them for a while, mumbled something, and ran away. When he reached the road, he said, "It's an old man, all dressed up, and a boy. They say nothing! They're like stone!" This caused much buzzing.

"Shine a light on them!" someone shouted.

A truck backed up and maneuvered itself so that its headlights shone on the two mysterious figures. They stared into the lights and were absolutely still.

"You see! I told you. I said it, didn't I? Just like I said."

"Hey you," someone yelled. "Who are you? What are you, spirits or something?"

One of the women began to wail. Soon it was a chorus. The truck that had left the line quickly returned, and the farmers drove away, crossing themselves.

"In a thousand years," Alessandro said, "this incident will be remembered. By then, of course, we will have become angels, devils, or a dragon that breathes fire—but we have given this rock a story that will be passed on."

"What good is that?"

"It isn't to our advantage, if that's what you mean. However, it's pleasurable to cast a line into the future, no matter how tenuously. You never know, the line may be unbroken all the way to the last judgment.

"Which is better, you see, than just living and dying, and being buried in a filing cabinet near a chemical factory. Or do you want merely to tread the mill until you drop off? Nicolò, mischief is important. But why should I be telling this to you? At your age, you should have it in your bones, even if you don't know why you should. It's because we don't know everything. Therefore, it sometimes makes sense to break the plan and go where we are not supposed to go.

"Besides, it was none of their business. I didn't feel like being interrogated in the night. This is our journey, not theirs."

The band started up again. "They've recovered," Alessandro said, "but they're going to make me pay."

"Pay? How can they make you pay?"

"Their music." Alessandro seemed weak. He closed his eyes.

"What can I do? Do you want water?" Nicolò asked.

"No," the old man said, waving him away, "I'll be all right. Leave me alone for a while, and then we'll start walking again."

Nicolò moved to another part of the ledge. He heard Alessandro sigh, and then saw him rest his head in his hands. He was the strangest man Nicolò had ever seen. His behavior was at times inexplicable, but though Nicolò didn't understand Alessandro, he knew that whatever was happening to him was proceeding on its own schedule, independently of events on the road even if they lent themselves to its expression.

Alessandro was drawn back in time. As if it were really in front of him, he saw a metal wheel silhouetted against a perfectly clear sky, turning steadily as it pulled-in steel cable and paid it out. He bent his head and covered his eyes as the sun flashed through the spokes. The wheel was the upper terminus of a freight trolley that ran over a vast abyss.

IN THE South Tyrol, in July of 1899, surrounded by belled cows and flat farmland, the small settlement of Völs stood alone on a plateau at the foot of forests and meadows that climbed up a steep mountainside to the point where it became vertical rock. Two kilometers above it, often higher than the clouds, on a fortress plateau where the wind was icy even in summer and trees could not grow, was the Schlernhaus. Most buildings of the several European alpine clubs were called *Hütten,* and rightly so, but not this, for it was tremendous. To haul the stone, timbers, and slate of which it had been built, and to keep it supplied thereafter, mountaineers had pulled up line after line of increasingly heavier rope until at the end of the last one (winched to them by a steam engine they had carried in many pieces on their backs) came a shiny steel cable.

The wheel upon which the cable turned had been revolving smoothly in three-quarter time for more than a decade when the Roman lawyer Giuliani first brought his son to the mountains, and the boy, at age nine, had run across a rocky meadow to the machinery outlined against a sky that rivaled the maritime blues of Venice.

The four-spoked wheel seemed as light as air. As if it had a will of its own, it pulled at times against its torsion brake, or held back, it slowed down or sped up, or sometimes stopped dead and then started again, full of purpose and resolve. Alessandro was amazed to realize that on the delicate lines of the cableway and through the graceful spinning of its wheel the massive Schlernhaus had been built and was maintained.

"Sandro!" his father called, and watched as his son returned to him over the meadow, jumping from rock to rock like a little goat.

It wasn't enough for Alessandro to measure the proportions of a room with his eyes; he had to touch every wall and agitate from boundary to boundary as if he were a torrent settling into a pool, and in their tiny wooden-walled bedroom he bounced back and forth like a cannonball. The beds were so high that he had to use pegs in the wall to climb into them, and he jumped from one to the other, sailing over the narrow chasm between. Though the window was small, it gave out upon a scene of silver-and-white mountains that challenged the eye to follow them into the distance. Before dinner the first night, Alessandro climbed up on the ledge to open the window. He undid the latch, and the wind came in so violently that at first it tumbled him backward onto the bed. When the attorney Giuliani returned from shaving, a china bowl in his hands, he saw his son, all bundled up in wool, crouching on the sill like a cat. As air howled through every crack in the walls, the young Alessandro stared into the wind as if he had discovered it.

In the daylight hours they visited the peaks, with Alessandro roped to his father like a dog on a leash when they scrambled across rock faces and over glaring snowfields. They ascended the Schlern itself, the Roterd Spitze (which they called the Cima Rossa) and the Mittagskofl. They descended into the Seiser Alpe, gently sloping meadows that had no apparent limits and seemed to be a world unto themselves. They went as far east along the mountain line as the Cresta Nera, where they saw only two other climbers but a dozen shaggy milk-white goats standing on ledges that could only have been miraculously attained. Wandering in the many hours of light, the attorney Giuliani and his son learned to crave the cold wind so that the more they were in it, the richer they felt. Their eyes followed the omnipresent distances, and as the mountains acted upon them and their spirits were calmed and enlarged, they saw the difference between what they once had been and what they had become. After a day's or two days' absence from Rome, they never would have been able to sit in the center of a snowfield, feeding upon the silence and the sun, but after a week they could, and they trudged to snowfields, cliffs, and empty valleys, where they passed the time as quietly as goatherds.

One evening they approached the Schlernhaus in the dark. Its glowing windows, shining through patches of frozen cloud, were like lighthouse beacons. Inside, sullen cadets in blue aprons and rounded blue-and-white army caps worked feverishly in a huge kitchen as humid and warm as a steam bath, and peeked into the dining room as often as they could to see if they could see a woman.

It was high summer, so only the cookstoves were lit, and not the huge tiled heaters in the main areas. After twelve or fourteen hours on the snowfields and in the wind, many diners shuddered with chill.

Alessandro found it difficult to come from the outside, where it was below freezing, and sit down to drink hot soup in a room little warmer than the rime-covered meadows they had just left. Every day at dusk he was overcome by great sadness, and he longed for his mother, his house, and the summer in Rome. His father, too, was unusually quiet at this time, and often spoke of cutting a few days from the trip, but one evening they returned to the Schlern-haus and didn't think about such things even for a moment.

Two soldiers of the *Leibregiment,* the Hapsburg royal guard, were stationed at the main door. Like elite soldiers the world over, they looked as if they would be delighted to stay outside all night, and their heavy fur cloaks suggested that perhaps they would. The huge spaces of the Schlernhaus, even the warren-like upper floors, were warm and dry. A fire burned in every stove, flags were draped from the rafters, and one of the floors was roped off. Behind the rope were another two soldiers even larger than the set downstairs.

Alessandro changed, and descended to the uncharacteristically warm dining room. The attorney Giuliani leaned toward a table at which were seated half a dozen Viennese, and inquired in his best German about the sudden heat, the guards, and why the cadets in the kitchen were buttoned up, polished, and overwhelmed by trays of cakes, oven-fired casseroles, and roasting game.

The Austrians consulted among themselves by eye. The attorney Giuliani was Italian, and Italy had designs upon the very mountains where they, the Austrians, had to respond to questions posed by Italians who had had the gall to come there in the first place. Nonetheless, they answered him, coldly and briefly, in two words: *"Eine Fürstin."* That was enough, in 1899, in the Südtirol, to explain everything.

Alessandro was rapidly learning German, but his teachers had omitted this word. "What is it? What is it?" he chattered, shifting around in his seat, his legs hanging far off the floor, but his father was asking a passing waiter why no bread was on the table.

"No one eats until she comes down," the waiter said, "but in return for waiting, you get to have what they have—venison, pheasant, cakes, things I have never even seen. They brought two chefs, and the cable was busy all day with provisions, one entire gondola just for baking supplies."

"What did he say? What did he say?" Alessandro asked, jumping out of his skin. "What's *'eine Fürstin'*?"

As if his language were ugly and prohibited, the attorney Giuliani leaned over and said, *"Eine Fürstin è una principessa... Eine Fürstin* is 'a princess.'"

Alessandro froze. The very word *principessa* had shut him up immediately, and he was now in a daze, eyes glassy, mouth open. He had read about princes and princesses far beyond whatever can be expressed by the term *ad nauseam,* and here were a castle on top of a mountain, soldiers in fur cloaks, and a real princess herself. Suddenly, in the normally frigid room where they had their soup and cutlets, all the elements of his dreams had combined to hit him in the face like an ermine glove.

Alarmed at the strange, twisted expression on his son's face, the attorney Giuliani took hold of Alessandro's shoulder and shook him.

Then they heard the ringing of a little silver bell, and a real, professional flunkey in a powdered wig swept into the room and screamed, "All rise!"

Everyone did, even the attorney Giuliani, egalitarian and republican, perhaps because he knew that old cats and dying empires viciously insist upon decorum.

Still forgetting to breathe, Alessandro mounted his chair, napkin in hand. From a distance he looked like a tall man with a very small head. As a group of people clomped down the stairs, Alessandro was so excited that he feared he would fall off the chair. Then, exactly as he had expected, a girl of about eleven entered the room as if she had lived there all her life. She was what adults call a slip of a girl, slim and delicate, with perfect, glowing features, blond hair, and red cheeks. She was dressed in a flowered dirndl that departed from the standard in that it had been made from sable-like black velvet and embroidery thread of real gold.

Alessandro's heart burst, broke, swelled, heaved, froze, stuck, stopped, and surrendered all at the same time. He bowed deeply, sweeping the checkered napkin across the table. Fortunately for him, no one saw this, for they were waiting for the princess to enter the room and she was still on her way. The little girl was the child of someone in the royal entourage.

The princess entered slowly, supporting herself on two ebony canes. Two retainers walked beside her so that she might not fall. She was attired in black, and a heavy veil obscured her face. She was so frail that it was not out of the question to think that the soldiers of the *Leibregiment* had carried her up the mountain, for it had to have been either that or a ride in the open freight gondola.

She faced the climbers and hikers, who bowed or curtsied with tremendous satisfaction. She was their mirror. In bowing to her they merely were paying respect to themselves, honoring the world they had made, and confirming that all was right within it. Whether or not this was true, they believed that no better shield of tranquillity existed than an empire on land. For centuries and centuries the Hapsburgs had ruled and protected quiet unvisited valleys, plains thundering with horsemen, and chains of godly and indomitable mountains—all with a fullness and peace that warred with the illogic of their vast untenable domain.

When the princess sat down, everyone did. The little girl, whose hair was braided and piled in the local style, was at the end of the royal table. Her legs dangled, too, but not quite as far off the floor as Alessandro's. She nervously played with her knife, which led the attorney Giuliani to note that when people play with silverware it is usually with the knife.

The waiters charged from the kitchen to serve the princess first, but she waved away practically everything. Though in the end her plate held nine or ten peas, a lettuce leaf, and a piece of meat the size of a minnow, her wine glass was properly filled and she drained it in one swoop. It was immediately taken away and another put in its place. The second had champagne, or beer—it was hard to tell—and this she sipped slowly.

As the waiters carved up sides of venison and served vegetables and roasted potatoes from copper salvers, the village orchestra of Völs trooped into the room and took up position in front of a glowing tile stove as high as the ceiling. Of the eight musicians, six were remarkably corpulent, and they had all walked up the mountain not long before. To make the room itself a perfect temperature, the stove was stoked up and burning like a forge. Standing next to it was absolutely unbearable, especially in a wet goat-hair cloak. The trumpet player lit up like a brand. His face could have served the railroad as a signal light for stop. Still, when the orchestra started to play, he followed. Some people nodded, because they recognized the first selection as the regimental hymn of the *Landesschützen,* and they wanted everyone to know that they knew. Nothing seemed amiss until, at the end of the second song, *"Die lautlose Bergziege"* ("The Noiseless Mountain Goat"), the trumpeter was taken ill.

He had great trouble breathing, and, to conceal his agony, he smiled until he seriously distorted his embouchure. Then he keeled over, spinning as he fell, and landed flat on his back against the floor amidst the crashing and clattering of instruments.

The princess exhibited her concern by laying her fork upon her plate. The hut master ran from the kitchen with the officer of the guard. They loosened the trumpeter's clothing and carried him out, after which the hut master returned immediately and tapped his baton on one of the overhanging beams. "Is a doctor present?" he asked. "Is a doctor in any of the parties now registered?" No doctors were present. Nonetheless, the hut master, one of the most famous mountaineers in the world, surveyed his clientele with the willful and acquisitive efficiency of a climber seeking a hold. It was as if the doctors were merely hiding, and he had determined to smoke them out. His gaze settled on Alessandro.

"Me?" Alessandro asked in soundless pantomime, pointing to his chest with his thumb. The hut master continued to stare. Alessandro looked to his father to assure him that he was not a physician or a nurse. The attorney Giuliani squinted at the hut master, trying to fathom his motives. It was clear. The famous guide, who was known to be sane, and who desperately sought a physician, had fixed his eyes on Alessandro.

"He's only nine years old," Alessandro's father said.

The hut master turned on his heels and left. Alessandro breathed in relief. Next, the princess looked his way and smiled. He smiled back as best he could, and she laughed because he had been mistaken for a physician. Then she speared a pea and put it into her mouth, at which point everyone in the vast dining room picked up his fork and started to eat, and the musicians began to play a second, trumpet-free version of *"Die lautlose Bergziege."*

Soon the music absorbed even the music makers, and seemed to convince them that all would be well with their comrade. The climb from Völs had been difficult, then the waiting outside in the cold, then the hot stove and the gravity of playing for a princess. He was undoubtedly in the kitchen, a cloth on his head, sipping whiskey. As thoughts of their friend's sudden collapse faded, they played with more energy. The fires in the stove and in the fireplaces leapt in time to the music. Alessandro started his attack on a sizzling slab of venison that had been placed before him by a sweating cadet who had also ladled out an enormous amount of roasted potatoes and vegetables. A pitcher of beer was on the table. Neither the attorney nor his son would have any part of it.

Alessandro almost asked his father to cut the meat for him, but decided that this could not be done in the presence of the blonde girl he had thought to be the princess. After several minutes he managed to separate a small piece from the rest and was about to eat it, when the hut master re-entered and strode across the floor.

The princess was interested in both of them, her entourage was interested in what she was interested in, and the hall grew quiet.

Alessandro dropped his cutlery on the plate.

"We need the boy," the hut master said to the attorney Giuliani, in Italian.

"For what?" was the answer.

"I'll tell you outside."

They went into the kitchen. Under a huge copper hood, a whole side of venison was turning above a fire that begged and devoured its drippings. Cauldrons bubbled over with boiling things that surfaced as if to scream, and then were pulled under before they could express themselves. The cadets worked at tables, handling crusts and dessert plates and refilling tureens. In the center of the floor, a stretcher holding the stricken bandsman lay catercornered between a pastry table and a bin of onions. One of the soldiers, bent over the sick man, was kneading his chest as if he were preparing dough.

Alessandro knew he was not a doctor. What if they expected him to cure the man? The sole remedy with which he was familiar was hot tea, lemon, and honey, and when he was sick his mother baked chocolate cookies and sat by the bedside, watching him for hours and hours. These were the only medical procedures in his experience.

"I think he had a heart attack," the hut master declared, "but he's still alive, and he may survive if we can get him to a lower altitude and to the doctor in Völs. When I say 'doctor,' I speak loosely, but he will have to do."

"Perhaps," the attorney Giuliani said, "but what do I have to do with all of this?"

"Not you, him," the hut master said, pointing at Alessandro. "He's the only one who can save him."

Alessandro felt horribly inadequate.

"The victim's heart must be massaged, or it will stop. The gondola has no room for two grown men."

"Absolutely not!" Alessandro heard his father say. "Are you out of your mind? You want him to ride on that thing, that, that thing, with a dying man?"

"It's perfectly safe. We'll rope him in. It will be impossible for him to fall off. Even if he did, he wouldn't go anywhere."

"I won't even consider it. The cableway was not made for the transportation of human beings," the attorney Giuliani said, in a sentence perhaps more at home in Italian than in any other language.

"Exactly!" the hut master replied. "It's made to carry loads of stone and slate, plinths of a thousand kilos—ten times their combined weights. The cable is inspected every week. It's five centimeters in diameter. It could hold a fully loaded wagon with ease, a railroad car...."

"The Baths of Caracalla?"

"Yes, one stone at a time. I've ridden it for years. When my daughter was sick, we sent her down on it." He took the elder Giuliani aside and whispered. "Don't tell anyone, but today the princess came up in the gondola. She was quite comfortable."

"If my son is willing, and you'll stake your life on the outcome. When he's on the gondola, I'll hold a rifle on you. If anything happens to him..."

For a moment, the turning of the spit and the boiling of water were the only sounds other than that of the brass band in the dining room. "What rifle?"

"Ask one of the soldiers. I insist. It's the only way to make sure you're telling the truth. I'm not bluffing. I'll kill you if anything happens to him."

"All right."

"And only if he agrees."

"Of course."

The attorney Giuliani took Alessandro aside. "Sandro, if you don't want to do this, you don't have to. The hut master is a great mountaineer. People entrust their lives to him every day. Each time we ride in a train, or stand on a balcony, we are exhibiting the same kind of trust. What do you say?"

"Can we go home tomorrow if I do it?"

"We can do anything you want, even if you don't do it."

"I will. Why shouldn't I?"

"Get a heavy sheepskin," the hut master commanded a cadet, "and fill a vacuum flask with hot tea."

After Alessandro and his father had gone to get warm clothing they and a dozen men went out into the night, with the bandsman on the stretcher. As they made their way through the mist to the cable terminus, the soldier continued to knead the trumpeter's chest, announcing periodically to those in train that the trumpeter was still alive.

The hut master tied Alessandro securely to the steel bracket with which the wooden gondola was hung from the cable. He and the attorney Giuliani checked and rechecked the climbing harness and the knots. "Even if you fall from the gondola," the hut master told Alessandro, "you'll just hang off the side. You're tied in doubly. I've taken people up the Marmolada with far less than what you have here. Nothing to worry about."

Alessandro's father took a rifle from one of the soldiers. Embarrassed by his mistrust of the famous mountaineer, and by what he knew the Germans would consider his overly Italianesque response, he understood that he had to make good on his stated conditions. Though he didn't train the weapon on the hut master, he loaded it, and the hut master heard the unmistakable sounds of a rifle bolt opening, a cartridge rising, the cartridge rammed into the barrel, and the locking of the bolt.

Alessandro buttoned up his loden coat.

"Do you want the hood?" his father asked.

"No, I want to see what's around me."

He was lifted up into the gondola and he positioned himself on the sheepskin that swaddled the trumpeter. They told him what to do, pinned a note on his back, and pulled a wooden lever that rang a bell in the terminal below.

"Don't stop until someone takes over," the hut master instructed. After a few minutes, the cable shuddered, and the gondola moved off into the dark.

"Why is this here?" Alessandro shouted upon noticing the tea flask tucked between the sheepskin and the sideboard of the gondola.

"Against the cold. Drink it on the way back," they screamed over the wind, but he heard nothing after 'cold,' for he was already flying through a cloud that seemed as dense as cotton.

He pushed against the bandsman's thick chamois shirt just as the soldier had done. Though he could see nothing, he knew he was still riding across the plateau on the summit, and that the gondola would soon carry him backward over the edge.

He could feel the presence of the abyss the way a blind man feels the presence of the sea beyond a beach. Then he passed over, and he felt a weightless chill when he recognized the irresponsive silence of great height. Because the cable was steeply inclined, he had to lean forward to stay upright. Though his restraints might have saved him had he tumbled over the side, they didn't hold him in place: he accomplished that with his knees and by pressing his feet against the walls of the gondola.

In less than a minute they left the envelope of cloud that covered the mountain and were in the free air. The stars were everywhere, even below, swaying in grand nausea. From the dark outline
of peaks and valleys, Alessandro saw that he was a thousand meters
above the ground, with not even a ledge nearby. No matter where
he might reach out, he would find nothing, and all he could hear
was the sound of wheels on the cable.

Suddenly the body under him stirred. Still, he kept pushing as
he had been told. "Marie!" the bandsman shouted in painful confusion. Alessandro hoped that the subject of his efforts would understand what was happening.

"Marie!" the trumpeter shouted once again, with disturbing
power, as Alessandro realized that he was on a horse without a
saddle.

"What are you doing?" the trumpeter asked in German of the
local dialect, his eyes as wide as those of an enraged eel.

Alessandro didn't understand the dialect, and guessed that the
man had asked for the time. "It's night," he said, not knowing the
hour exactly. He felt obliged to make conversation. "No moon, no
nightingales, but all is well, and the badger is in his hole."

The thin Italian voice, the heavy odor of sheepskin, the cradle-
like rocking of the gondola, the hiss of the air, the darkness, and his
own pain and distress were too much for the simple bandsman of
Völs. He panicked. This was a nightmare, and all his life, whenever
he had had a nightmare, he had thrashed. Now his main object was
to rid himself of the little gargoyle that sat upon him with its wings
folded like a bat, and continually butted his chest. These devilish
creatures, they knew, and they were terribly cruel, because the
heart was the place that hurt the most.

"*Waldteufel!*" he screamed. "Forest devil!" He lifted his bulk
from the waist up and latched on to Alessandro. Both hands, big
fat things like rows of kielbasa, grabbed the boy's fragile neck and
locked into rigor mortis, though the bandsman remained very
much alive and, apparently, healthy.

As Alessandro felt the blood collecting in his head he remembered what had happened to the mercury thermometer he had put in the kitchen oven. Had he had the reach, he would have pulled the trumpeter's ears, shoved a fist into his mouth, and ripped at his nostrils, but his hands did all this in the air in front of the assailant's face.

"Filthy bat! Hideous creature! Ahhh! Horrible! Horrible!" the trumpeter trumpeted.

Casting about for a weapon, Alessandro found the vacuum flask. He passed it around his back from his left hand to his right. Then he clubbed his tormentor. After a bang and a muffled smashing of glass, nothing changed except that the strangle hold grew tighter.

Knowing that he could not last much longer, Alessandro struggled to unscrew the cap on the vacuum flask. The cadet who prepared it had not taken into account that it was to be opened by a boy of nine. With all the force he could muster, Alessandro turned it. He thought he pulled every muscle in his body, and the cap sailed into the abyss. Steam rose and burned his hands.

"Let go of me," he thought more than said, for he had no air left in his lungs. When the huge bandsman responded to Alessandro's pathetic gurgle by tightening his fists until Alessandro thought his neck was about to snap, the boy bared his teeth and jerked the open flask toward the face of the strangler.

A stunted rainbow of boiling tea and broken glass shot directly into the target. The trumpeter screamed, dropped his hands, and fell against the wooden floor, knocking himself unconscious. Forgetting where he was, Alessandro leapt to the side and tumbled into empty space, but, as the hut master had said, he was securely tied in, and he found himself dangling from the harness, a short distance from the gondola.

"Mama!" he cried, almost in tears, but then he felt stupid, because, obviously, no one was there except him, and he himself had to do whatever had to be done.

Though he was scared even to look up, much less down, he raised his hands and caught the side of the gondola. With a stream of curse words known principally to the fourth class of the Accademia San Pietro in Rome, he pulled himself back.

The trumpeter lay on the sheepskin in perfect quiet. Perhaps he was dead, but, dead or not, Alessandro had to massage his heart. He started pushing against the chest. In between strokes, he tossed the flask overboard, and then deftly did the same for each shard of glass.

The trumpeter was still alive. He stirred. The wind had ceased and now, as they floated through the tops of the pines, Alessandro could hear the cable engine puffing not far below.

On the way back, Alessandro reclined on the sheepskin. Warm, secure, and disgusted, he marveled that the trumpeter had been able to jump up and run from the cable car station. Still, Alessandro would be a hero when he got back. He wouldn't be able to avoid it. They would carry him in and cheer for half an hour while he finished his dinner. After dismissing them he would ascend not to his room but to the room of the blonde girl in the velvet dress. She would take him into her bed, where they would spend the entire night alone in the dark, pressed together, motionless. This would mix their hearts forever, and thereafter they would be married. The problem was where to live—in Rome or in Vienna. Perhaps Paris, as a compromise. He decided that her name was Patrizia.

He did hear cheering as he came over the lip, now clear of clouds, but it was not the sustained hysteria that he had expected. No matter, the big part would come in the dining hall, with an orchestra, lights, flags, and warm fires.

The attorney Giuliani passed the rifle to a soldier and watched the hut master undo the harness. Dinner had ended, Alessandro was told, but they would cook for him anything he wanted, and serve it in the kitchen. He wanted only dessert. Though he was as thin as a switch, he imagined that if he were to eat that night, he would be too fat to lie with Patrizia.

The dining hall in the Schlernhaus was dark. Everyone had gone upstairs except some soldiers and mountain guides who sat around a grate of glowing coals in the guides' room, talking about war. The sound of a zither came softly from the upper floors—for the princess.

No one cheered. The guides stared at him because he walked so pompously, and the kitchen cadet who had to stay late to serve the food was anxious to go to bed, because he had to rise at four A.M.

"Tell me about it," the attorney Giuliani asked, "what it was like. Why was the tea spilled? The note they sent back with you said that Herr Willgis ran all the way to his house. That amazes me...."

"All right," his father said, "I can understand why you might not want to talk. I'm going to bed now. If you like, we can go home tomorrow."

Alessandro nodded.

The cadet put a piece of Sacher torte on the table, took off his blue apron, and stumbled dizzily out the kitchen door toward the cadet barracks, saying, "Just put the dishes in the sink, so the rats don't jump on the table." Alone in the kitchen, his courage beginning to ebb, Alessandro thought to seek out Patrizia before he was too afraid to do so. He was tempted just to go to bed, but the image of the beautiful, shy, blonde girl made him rise. He trembled so much as he put the dishes in the sink that the fork clattered against the plate and the cup against the saucer like palsied old men. Then, with the weighted heartbreaking tread of someone on his way to be hanged, he walked toward the stairs. He wanted to hold her, to kiss her, to breathe—in her breath, and he bumped against the stairs in the dark and started to ascend to the upper floors and their dizzying, intimate warrens.

During the day the soldiers of the *Leibregiment* stayed rigidly by the doorposts of the royal compartments, and nothing in the world, not even a tiny July gnat, could get past them, but, inexplicably, at night they paced back and forth like bears in a shooting gallery, taking long trips down the hall at precisely timed intervals when it was easy for a small boy treading softly on alpaca socks to glide into the forbidden wing and have his choice of twenty doors in two facing rows.

His chances of finding her before he himself was discovered were not good: he could tell nothing from the doors themselves; it was quite dark; and his time was limited because someone would undoubtedly come out into the hall.

Choosing a middle door at random, he was about to put his hand on the latch but was deterred by a raspy voice from within. Someone was talking to himself. "... to Gisella! But Hermann will be exposed for what he is within a week. In a year's time, I'll be the favorite in court, and the monkey will jump on the nut. On the other hand, no one ever got rich by putting octopus ink in a drinking glass, and the emperor likes Von Schafthausen—mistakenly, of course. . . ." Clearly this man was going to stay up all night, and he was not Patrizia.

Alessandro moved to a door at the end of the hall. Slowly, quietly, he lifted the latch and looked within. There, in the flashing, cloud-scudding moonlight, lay a huge beached whale of a woman, with exceedingly spacious gaps in her teeth, enormous fleshy lips, a porcine nose, and ears shaped like powder horns. Who was she? She had been too ugly to come to dinner. Perhaps she was a maid, or an unfortunate royal relative forever hiding on the upper floors of palaces and inns.

After shutting that door, Alessandro despaired of finding Patrizia, but after his eyes adjusted to the darkness he saw that neatly placed in front of each door was a pair of shoes or boots. Ordinarily, no one was permitted to wear boots in the Schlernhaus, and they were kept on racks under the stairs, but royal shoes and boots were allowed to sleep near their masters and mistresses.

Some were huge, others womanly, and the shoes of the servants had telltale buckles. The door with no shoes in front of it must have been the princess's, since she was probably allowed to wear them even to bed. One pair of slippers was unmistakably petite and had not been left neatly, but thrown down in front of the door as if its owner had had to rush across the cold floor to a warm bed. Alessandro approached these shoes as if they were saintly relics. They were sprawled in front of the last door near the window at the end of the hall, across from the monster, in the moonlight. He was entranced by the casual angle at which she had left them, the way the straps fell, and the way they looked in the white light that machine-gunned across them through rapidly driven clouds, and he wondered if he would be able to love Patrizia herself as much as he could love the poignant and accidental traces of her.

Then a soldier began to stride down the hall. Presented with a choice between love and death, the young Alessandro lifted the latch, pivoted inside, and closed the door silently behind him.

Patrizia lay under a silver satin coverlet illuminated by the light of the moon. She looked different with her braids undone and her golden hair splayed across the pillow. She opened her eyes when he came in, and they followed him as he approached. She herself remained motionless, unafraid.

He put his fingers to his lips. Her hand appeared from under the covers and she did the same. It was a game, but it was more than a game.

"Can you talk Italian?" he whispered.

"Yes," she answered, also in a whisper. "We go to Italy each spring."

"Do you remember me?"

"From Italy?"

"No, from tonight."

"No," she said, lying.

"Oh," he answered, downcast. "I saw you in the dining room."

"What's your name?" she asked.

"Alessandro Garibaldi," he replied.

"Are you related to Garibaldi?" Most of the people she knew were related to other people of whom everyone else had heard.

"I'm his youngest son."

"But didn't he die a long time ago?"

"Yes. Pay it no mind. He was my brother's father, and the uncle of his half wife was my cousin's grandmother's sister. She married my uncle's brother, who was him, and by her he had me. Who is the strange woman in the room across the hall?"

"Did you enter each room?" the girl asked, surprised, and, to Alessandro's delight, jealous.

"It was an accident."

"That's Lorna. She's my cousin. She hides, because she's so ugly. It's very sad, but she's nice, and I love her. She reads to me."

"Look at what the clouds do when they interrupt the moon," Alessandro said. "It makes me dizzy."

"Are you cold?" she asked in a way that would have been un-mistakable to anyone but a nine-year-old desperate to do exactly what she wanted him to do.

"No," he answered, shivering not from chill but from the pos-sibility of rejection and the terror of acceptance, both.

"You can come in here with me," she offered, although it was difficult for her to say. "If you want..." She lifted the covers, and he jumped in.

It was warm. It was more than warm. What with the feather bed, her flannel nightgown, the thick down cover, and his woolen clothing and alpaca socks, it was like a Dutch oven.

Alessandro didn't know what to do. When she leaned her head against his chest, gales of wonder and emotion swept over him. He kissed her hair. Never in his life had he smelled anything so sweet or touched anything so soft.

But this moment of utter perfection was as vulnerable to dis-ruption as the mirror-smooth surface of a lake at dawn. Suddenly, and against his strongest wishes, he was disturbed and unhappy because his father didn't know where he was. Perhaps the attorney Giuliani had gone downstairs to look, and, finding the kitchen empty, had stepped outside to ask the cadets what had happened to Alessandro, only to become lost in the fog and chill. Alessandro winced when he thought of his father wandering blindly over the meadow, close to the high cliffs. Or perhaps he was just lying in his bed, thinking and remembering, in a way that always seemed to Alessandro to be very sad.

Alessandro had no choice but to go back. As wonderful and light as things now were—and he felt as if he had been born to slip into Patrizia's bed—he had to leave her and go back to his father, far less angelic a form, with his goat-like Roman lawyer's beard, his thick hands, and the smell of pipe tobacco that had settled into him forever. As powerful a figure as this man was, still, he was more vulnerable than the slight little girl next to Alessandro. Even Alessandro knew, even at this moment, that the world had worn down the attorney Giuliani in ways that his son simply could not understand. The little ones, the delicate ones of nine or eleven, had all the strength, really.

Alessandro's reflections were immediately banished by the metallic sound of a door latch that had been lifted by someone who did not feel obliged to sneak around in alpaca socks.

He dived under the covers. Whatever the danger, the sudden arrival of a third party was a blessing. When he was deep down in the satin, Patrizia held him tenderly and protectively. That she did so in secret was the most intimate gesture Alessandro had ever experienced. The pressure of her hands, their steadiness while she dealt with the interloper, were what he had dreamed of when he had thought that they would mix their hearts.

Just inside the doorway, Lorna stood almost on tiptoe, her arms folded across her breast and her face upturned to the inrush of moonlight, in the most pathetic, awkward, and repulsive stance that can be imagined. And yet, she was a good soul, tormented immeasurably and destined to suffer forever in a body that was a fortress against love, an impregnable glacis. She stood in her cousin's room, in tortured ecstasy, poised like one of the three little pigs in prayer, drinking-in the moonlight with her gloomy cow eyes.

"I had the most marvelous dream!" she exclaimed. "*Ich träumte, ich tanzte mit einem Schwan! Er hatte die wunderbarsten flauschigen Polster an dem Füssen, und er war auf einem Mondstrahl in mein Zimmer gekommen*—I dreamed I was dancing with a swan! He had the most marvelous little puffy white feet, and he came into my room on a moonbeam."

"Dear God," Patrizia said softly, for she knew that when Lorna had one of her truly wonderful dreams, her custom was to get into her cousin's bed to tell her of it in great detail. "Lorna, dearest one, do you think that perhaps you could tell me in the morning? Tomorrow we rise early to descend to the Seiser Alpe, and I'm so tired!"

"Certainly not!" Lorna said with maddening insensitivity. "You know that if I wait until morning I'll forget the details, and it's the details you love."

"But Lorna..."

"He was a thin swan, he had a beak that was as orange as the orange in the rainbow, and he loved me. I asked him how he traveled on a moonbeam, and he told me by singing a golden song.... Move over." She half lifted the quilt, and hopped into bed in one quick graceless leap—all of her. The Schlernhaus quivered.

Patrizia, whose name, of course, was not Patrizia, was alarmed. She had lost Alessandro, who was underneath Lorna, completely subsumed. She wondered if he could breathe, or if he were screaming.

"The golden song was like a warbling horn. Once, I heard a bird singing like that, at Grandfather's estate in Klagenfurt.... What is this? Is this your leg?"

As if to answer in the negative, Alessandro, who for the second time in a matter of hours found himself unable to move and without air, bit Lorna fiercely in one of her huge buttocks.

The cry that escaped from the massive young woman made the rare golden song of her imagined swan as common as a streetcorner ditty. It had the force and power of a great railroad horn. It sounded so terrible that the entire Schlernhaus awoke. Each and every mountaineer, the cadets in their barracks in the fog, the attorney Giuliani, the royal party, and everyone else sat bolt upright in their beds as if they had been struck by lightning. Even little Patrizia began to scream.

"*Was ist es! Mach es tot! Mach et tot!*—What is it? Kill it! Kill it!" Lorna cried, and resumed her mad howling.

Never before had the lamps of the Schlernhaus been lit simultaneously or so fast. The light that flashed against the fog suggested the work of either a photographer or a cannon. Four soldiers in heavy boots charged through the hallway, bayonets unsheathed. They were so excited that rather than lift the latch they kicked down the door. When it hit the floor it sounded like a bomb. Members of the royal party, born and bred on assassination, gave out a collective moan.

Alessandro sought refuge by wrapping himself up in a ball in the quilt. Patrizia was weeping. Lorna, backed up against the bedposts, was completely silent. Her outstretched finger pointed accusingly at the bundle on the bed.

"What is it? Is it an animal?" asked the officer of the guard, drawing his saber.

"It has *horrible fangs!*" Lorna shouted.

Alessandro peeped from behind a mass of satin. The soldiers were temporarily stunned as he extricated himself from it, stepped off the bed, and started to walk away, intending to return to his room. He was not sure, however, that he was going to be able to do this.

Two sergeants took hold of his ears and dragged him down the hall. He vaguely understood that they had been humiliated, that he had affronted the holiness of order, and that at this moment it was distinctly disadvantageous to be Italian. "Papa!... Papa!... Papa!" he screamed rhythmically, afraid that he was going to be killed. As the whole world collapsed, his tears flowed silently. He was no longer Patrizia's lover or Garibaldi's son, but the chief criminal of the Hapsburg Empire, an assassin, an animal with fangs.

"What are you doing!" the attorney Giuliani shouted at the armed soldiers, even though he was in his dressing gown and they seemed to be twice his height. "Let him go!"

Alessandro saw in his father all the light of the world, but the soldiers still held him.

"Are you mad?" the attorney from Rome asked the officer of the guard. "Is this how you treat children?"

"Our children are decent, clean, and well behaved," the officer shouted in a voice so full of hate and rage that the senior Giuliani and his son were silenced. The officer then proceeded to narrate to the assembled onlookers his version of what had happened. Even though he understood little of this, Alessandro trembled.

The princess appeared, scowling in anger, a palsied hand dancing upon her hip. "This child tried to violate my granddaughter," she announced. And then, shaking feebly, she added, "In other times, I would have had him shot."

The attorney Giuliani whitened. He was afraid for Alessandro's life, and he had to take the initiative.

"Sandro," he asked, "is this true?"

Alessandro, who had not understood the accusations, had nonetheless understood their tone, and he knew that his embrace of Patrizia had been the finest and purest thing in the world. "No," he said.

Still, his father raised his hand, and brought it down against Alessandro's face. The sound was heard throughout the hallways as Alessandro collapsed onto the floor.

Then the attorney Giuliani picked up his son. "We're leaving in the morning," he said, and carried the boy back to their room.

Once inside, he lifted Alessandro into bed, and covered him. They were obliged to whisper.

"I'm all right," Alessandro said.

"It wasn't my hand," his father told him. "I was terrified of what they might do. They're not like us."

"I know," Alessandro answered.

"You have to understand," his father begged. "I've never hurt you before, and I'll never hurt you again. The soldiers were armed. Their bayonets had been unsheathed. These people punish their children severely. I didn't want to hit you...."

"I know," Alessandro said, touching his father's face, as his father often touched his. Though he was staring at the attorney Giuliani, he saw the wheel steadily turning in the sunlight, almost with a will of its own.

"Papa? When we go home tomorrow, the wheel will be turning, won't it."

"What wheel?"

"The cable wheel."

"Yes, it turns all the time."

"Even when we don't see it? Even if we're not there?"

"Of course. It has nothing to do with us."

"Even if we're dead?"

"Yes."

"Then, Papa," Alessandro announced, "I'm not afraid to die."

"ARE YOU all right?" Nicolò asked. "We've been here for hours. The moon is headed down. Maybe we should go on, unless you want to sleep."

"Help me up and we'll go," the old man said.

As they took to the road, Nicolò asked, "What were you thinking? I could see that you weren't asleep."

"I wasn't asleep. I was thinking of something that happened a long time ago."

"What?"

"The way history, geography, and politics influence love. And the way it, in turn, influences them."

"That doesn't sound like much. I mean, you could make up a hundred stories to show that, couldn't you."

"You could."

"And that's not very imaginative—making things up—is it."

Alessandro closed one eye and lowered his head almost like a bull. "I suppose not," he said, "Mr. Sambucca."

"What was the real story? I ask you what you were thinking, and you tell me history, geography, politics, love. All I wanted to know was what happened to who. Isn't that enough?"

"It's enough when you're seventeen and most of it is ahead of you, but when most of it has passed, you try to make sense of it. Sometimes you do, and sometimes you don't. I was just thinking of my father. I should have comforted him more than I did. Once, he had to hit me in front of some Austrian soldiers, and it made him unhappy out of all proportion; not only at the time, but for the rest of his life. He believed that he had betrayed me, and I could never convince him that it wasn't so."

"Did they make him do it?"

"In a way."

"You should have killed them."

"I did. And not too much later, either."

"How did you do it?"

"How did I do what?"

"Kill them."

"I shot them with a rifle, and, at close range, I used a bayonet."

"Jesus!" Nicolò said, his eyes wide. "How did you do it? I mean, how exactly do you do that?"

"I'm afraid I'm not going to satisfy your curiosity."

"Why not? You weren't the only one ever to be in a war."

"I know, but I survived. That puts me on a lower plane."

"A *lower* plane?"

"Lower than the one of those who perished. It was their war, not mine. I was able to walk out of it, leave it behind. Though God preserved me, the best stories were theirs, and these were cut short. The real story of a war is no story at all—blackness, sadness, silence. The stories they tell of comradeship and valor are all to make up for what they lacked. When I was in the army I was always surrounded by thousands of men, and yet I was almost always alone. Whenever I made friends, they were killed.

"If I describe what I saw of the war, you'll know it from the point of view of the living, and that is the smallest part of the truth. The truth itself is what was finally apprehended by those who didn't come back."

"Then tell me the smallest part of the truth," Nicolò said, "for how else can I know?"

"There isn't enough time between here and Sant' Angelo for even the smallest part of the truth," was Alessandro Giuliani's reply.

They were walking down into a long valley. The moon was low and full. As it rested on the jagged horizon below them it seemed miraculously close, as if they had risen to it or it had dipped down to earth to take a look. It seemed to be in league with the dawn, glowing pearly and blue at one and the same time.

Though the moon soon disappeared beyond the ridge behind them, most of the world remained in its light, even as they themselves were walking in shadow. Alessandro had begun to shake with fatigue. How stupid, he thought, to have set out on such an expedition. He simply did not have the strength that once he had had, and now Nicolò was setting a fast pace without realizing how difficult it was for the lame old man to keep up. And yet, because the world beyond was illumined in a softening white glow, he kept on, hoping that, even if he did not deserve it, strength would find him as it had so many times before.

If it did, he thought, and by some grace he were to be lifted from his fatigue and pain, he would tell Nicolò what Nicolò had asked to hear. They hadn't far to go until they parted, and in the time they had he would tell a simple tale in which he would skirt the danger of a lost or broken heart, though he knew that recollection could be more powerful and more perilous than experience itself. What vanity had moved him to think he could walk over the mountains again, pushing forward day and night, like a young soldier?

And then he answered the question he had put to himself. Throughout his life he had suffered periods of despair only to be lifted from them and to rise at the speed of falling. It had happened in footraces, when he had sometimes been slapped awake like a newborn and had burst into the lead effortlessly and without warning. It had happened in climbing, when he was suddenly transformed from a frightened novice into someone who could dance up the cliffs. And it had happened in his doctoral examinations, when the young Alessandro, trembling and afraid, had become the examiner of his examiners.

"Do you want to rest?" Nicolò asked just before dawn, as they began to walk southward through the cultivated valley twenty or thirty kilometers in length. "It's almost morning. We've been making good time, but now you're going very slowly. I think that if we rest again we can better our pace. I know you can walk fast; you almost left me behind going up the mountain. As you said, it was the going down in the morning that was difficult."

"My heart feels bad," Alessandro said. "It's hard for me to breathe. I'm afraid that if I stop I'll get so stiff and tired I won't be able to get going again. Walk slowly, if you can bear with me until I recover. This time of night is always the most difficult. If I can get through it into the daylight..."

A delicate white mist had risen from the irrigation ditches. It covered the fields and tried unsuccessfully to arch over the embankments on either side of the road. The sky had grown light enough to obscure the stars and planets. As night became morning, it seemed that all the birds of central Italy began to sing and dance in a mounting ecstasy that soon covered the countryside with sound. The trees were as busy as hives, with hopping or swooping birds and dislodged leaves that spiraled down through the still air.

With the swelling light came swelling sound, a swelling breeze, and the rattling and rustling of leaves. Finally beaten down, melted, and conquered by wind, heat, and light, the mist was swept from the fields. Rich colors bloomed in midair from what had been tentative vanishing grays. When the wind roared over the road and lifted the dust, Alessandro knew that something was happening. He shuddered as he saw the inanimate and lifeless world moving, and the dead things, dancing.

The sun rose on the left and turned the glossy leaves of the poplars into a blinding haze of light too bright to behold until the wind coursed through the trees and they began to bend and sway, softening the glare.

Alessandro felt the world take fire. His heart repaired to the past and he barely touched the ground as he walked between trees that now were shimmering in the dawn. No matter that distant thunder is muted and slow, it comes through the air more clearly. After half a century and more, he was going to take one last look. He no longer cared what it might do to him. He just wanted to go back. And he did.

RACE TO THE SEA

THE GARDEN of the attorney Giuliani's house was divided into quarters, and long after Alessandro left home he knew their every attribute by heart. The first quarter was given to an orchard the gardeners seemed never able to leave well enough alone; they were always cutting back, grafting, and lifting the soil around the thriving trees. Year after year, forty trees produced fruit for the Giulianis' table and for the wicker baskets that the gardeners carried home on their shoulders or balanced on the handlebars of their bicycles. The second quarter was tilled as a vegetable garden that produced crops appropriate to a small farm, and that even in January provided half a dozen kinds of greens for the cook to harvest every day, and little white daisies that the gardeners chose to overlook in their weeding because they were the only flowers of winter. In the third quarter a flower garden bloomed in so many colors that it seemed to be coolly on fire, and in the fourth a grape arbor produced much of the Giulianis' wine.

Dividing the vegetable garden and the orchard, on one side, from the flowers and the arbor on the other was a crushed stone path flanked by hedges high enough so that Alessandro, at twenty, could leap them only with difficulty. Green lawns were laid down like enameled intarsia between the quarters, and rows of pines and date palms at its edge made the garden seem like a clearing in the forest. Though the palms were so tall they could be seen from the Villa Borghese as they crested the Gianicolo near the Villa Aurelia, they were sterile. The fruit that hung from them in massive bunches never ripened, and in autumn it blazed up in wasted yellow untouched by swarms of birds that alighted in their crowns.

Though some of the Giulianis' modest wealth was not of Alessandro's father's making, he had had to squeeze the rest from stones. Many whose wherewithal had been solely a matter of birth looked down upon the industrious lawyer for having worked, some who had become rich entirely from their own labor resented that he had had an inheritance, and those who had done and received neither were bitter that he had either. But the Giulianis hardly cared, and Alessandro, at twenty, hardly knew. They had their house and they had their garden.

The garden stretched in the direction of Ostia and the sea. Though they could not see very far in that direction, their front windows gave them all of Rome from high enough to glance down upon its present as if it were history. An eastern view of the city and the Tiber was so deeply engraved in Alessandro's memory that he was able to summon it at will. Even when he was in the maze of streets below, he knew exactly where he was, and could see everything as if he were looking down from one of the pale clouds that so often and so stubbornly hold their place in the Roman sky.

The aerial perspective extended far beyond Rome, to the Apennines. In summer they were chalk white at the summits and along the ridges, and in the setting sun the huge and roughly shaped half spindle of the Gran Sasso gleamed across space until its light was captured weakly in the glass of a framed picture on the west wall of Alessandro's room. The picture was of the Matterhorn, but the silky image, half lost in the glass and far more engaging, was the uninvited presence of the Gran Sasso impudently asserting that life itself was better even than its best remembrance.

ONE MORNING, in April, before going down to breakfast, Alessandro stood near a hall window, buttoning his shirt. He had returned for a short time from his studies in the north, and was happy to be home. The morning sun illuminated the western portion of the garden so brightly that Alessandro was able to see its every detail. In the middle of what once had been solid masonry at the far end was an iron gate through which he could see the windows of a house on the other side of the wall.

Someone had breached the wall and could now see into the Giulianis' private park, into the Giulianis' windows themselves. They might even have seen Alessandro buttoning his shirt.

He ran downstairs to the kitchen, where his father was blindly attending to his breakfast as he read the newspaper. The attorney Giuliani hardly noticed his son. Alessandro's younger sister, Luciana, was standing in a corner, in a white apron. She had been about to leave the room, and her hands were poised on the apron's bow, but her brother's excitement made her refrain from pulling it apart.

"What's that thing in the wall in the garden?" Alessandro demanded in a tone suggesting that he believed his father might simply deny anything was there, and that, in fact, when Alessandro looked again, nothing would be there.

"What thing?" his father asked, unable to look up from a dispatch about the perpetual instability of Morocco.

"The gap in the wall, and the gate."

"What about it?"

"What's it doing there?"

"I don't know," his father answered, wanting to finish the dispatch. He had always been mesmerized by newspapers.

"What do you mean you don't know!" Alessandro asked.

"It's a gate so that the other people can get into the garden." The attorney Giuliani finished reading and took a bite of toast.

"Other people? What other people? Who?"

"The people who live on the far side of the gate. Their name is Bellati."

"Why would they want to come into our garden?" Alessandro asked.

"It isn't our garden. It's their garden."

Alessandro looked like someone who'd been shot.

"I sold it to them, but we have a twenty-year lease. During that time, everything will remain the same, except that they can use the garden just as we do. They'll pay half for the gardeners, we'll divide the produce equally, they'll let us know when they have a party, we'll let them know, et cetera, et cetera. It's an advantageous arrangement."

"What are we going to do in twenty years?"

"We'll cross that bridge when we come to it."

"They can build a house there, or a public building. A hundred families might be living right on top of us!" the boy screamed.

"Alessandro," the attorney Giuliani said, "the use of the land is controlled by law, and I have it in the agreement as a condition of sale that, even if the law changes, the garden must remain undeveloped for fifty years. That's nineteen hundred and sixty, Alessandro. By that time they will have built giant floating cities in the sea, Europe will be united into one state, and you will be seventy years old. Don't worry about it now."

"But why did you do it?" Alessandro asked in a voice so puzzled and forlorn that his father folded the newspaper and pushed aside his tea and toast.

"It's very simple," the attorney Giuliani said in the tone he used when he was about to reveal something excellent. "Do you know the Via Ludovisi?"

"No."

"Nobody knows it. It's a small street near the Villa Medici."

"What about it?"

"A little triangle of land sits between the Villa Medici, the Borghese, and the Via Ludovisi itself, which is the base. In the triangle are fields, paths, and some buildings. Now I'll tell you what I was thinking. This is what I was thinking."

Alessandro was influenced by his father's enthusiasm as surely as the many magistrates before whom his father appeared in earning his living.

"Rome is a city of ruins. It's very quiet, as befits an ancient city. The economy has problems, as does the system of transport, and the rest. The English tourists come here to look at stones, and they want Rome to be rusticated."

"So?"

"It isn't going to stay that way forever. The days are numbered when flocks of sheep are driven through the Piazza Navona, and, as things change, Rome will become more and more like Paris, London, and Berlin. The city will grow: it has to, it already is growing."

The elder Giuliani shook his finger at his son as if to say, behind this finger is your father. "The question is, how will it grow?"

"And you know."

"I made a good guess. I've been to every major city in Europe, and I've noticed one thing about all of them, something obvious. The fashionable neighborhoods, the districts of wealth, are all near parks—Passy, the Bois de Boulogne, Hyde Park and Mayfair, the Belvedere in Vienna. This is where the land is always most valuable. So it will be, eventually, with the Villa Borghese. Rome will build itself around the Villa Borghese, and the choicest section will be just to the south, leading down the hill to the center of the city. In anticipation of that I have bought one and seven-tenths hectares of land in the triangle that I described—enough land for scores of buildings. Long after I'm dead, your mother, perhaps, but certainly you and Luciana, and all your children, will benefit. It may make you very comfortable someday."

"I don't care about being comfortable," Alessandro protested.

"Neither did I, at your age. I know what you care about now, I'm paying for it. And I was much the same as you, but everything changed, and everything changes, even if you don't yet know it. I sold the garden out from underneath you so that in half a century, in a century, the Giulianis may be free to do what they wish, or perhaps just to survive.

"It's a gamble, and we now have nothing in reserve. I borrowed against the house and I sold the garden to Bellati, who either has the same ideas I have and hasn't been to Paris, or is simply fond enough of nature to put forward a substantial fortune to acquire it."

BELLATI HELPED to run the Bank of Italy. His son, ten years older than Alessandro, was a captain in the army, and wore a sword. When the King of Italy wanted to talk about money, he invited Bellati to court. Never had the two men spoken to one another of anything other than interest rates, the relative values of currencies, or the merits of a particular venture. The King of Italy didn't want to be heard in conversation about as vulgar a thing as money, so he would walk with Bellati to a quiet place out of earshot but in full view, and there confer with him as others looked on in envy. Bellati made a fortune from what people assumed, and was much in demand as a guest at dinner parties, where he never ever mentioned the king, which made everyone absolutely sure that he and the king were as close as a wheel and an axle.

The Bellatis were as social and gregarious as the Giulianis were not. The attorney Giuliani relied upon his skill in court rather than upon his connections, and he went his own way, preferring to the social life of the capital the risk of climbing mountains. He and his family stayed at home, and their lights burned throughout the evening.

The lights of the house newly visible through the wall usually blazed until eight, and were then extinguished until one or two in the morning, when they came on just long enough to see the inhabitants to the upper floors and into their beds.

A student of aesthetics and philosophy, in training to see the patterns in which one thing was differentiated from another,

Alessandro noticed this immediately. And in the ten days or so that he was home he also noticed and was thankful for the fact that these people had never made an appearance. Alessandro began once again to think of the garden as his own, and once again, as he walked in it, his thoughts were able to wander and he could talk to himself in the feverish way of lunatics or university students overburdened by many sure beauties and contradictory truths.

And he did, pacing back and forth one evening at dusk, until his intellect was overpowered by his stomach, and he decided to abandon meditation on the aesthetic in favor of grilled veal chops. He was about to turn around when he noticed that one of the gardeners had left a spade leaning against a hedge. He picked it up, leapt the hedge, and began to walk toward the shed. Though it was now almost entirely dark, the sky was still a bright and decadent color that resembled the warm pink silk that often lined the interiors of ancient carriages.

The Bellatis were preparing to attend a dinner across the Tiber, as they did almost every night. Their son was at that moment with a detachment of soldiers on a warship steaming in the Adriatic, and their daughter had gone to the garden to get the flowers that they would take to their hosts. She had spent too much time in dressing, and now it was dark, but her father had told her of a lantern, in the garden shed, that was new, and that she could handle without fear of carbon black.

As Alessandro approached the shed, shovel in hand, he decided that one of the gardeners might have left it out for a reason, and that the best thing to do would be to lean it against the door.

Inside, in total darkness, Lia Bellati took from the pocket of her velvet cape a box of Finnish matches. She pushed open the tense little drawer, took out a match, and struck it. She looked about. A brand new lantern hung from a beam. Even though she was perfectly proportioned, she was short, and sometimes she jumped to reach things, but only after ascertaining that no one would see. At the age of twenty-two, and yet unmarried, she could not afford to appear ridiculous, and one never knew who was about to come into the kitchen or the library, and who, therefore, might see her body stretch like a cat as she leapt at what she wanted.

The garden shed was high at the peak and the gardeners were a tall race of men, at least compared with Lia Bellati. They had held the lantern by its base and hooked the wire handle around a nail. The match was half burnt-through as Lia looked about for something on which she could stand. A cement mixer was in the corner, far too heavy to move. Ladders for use in pruning the trees were stacked along a wall. The shortest was taller than the highest part of the shed. The match burned out.

Alessandro leaned the shovel against the door. The sound it made frightened the young woman inside, but she concluded that it must have been the wind, and she struck another match.

Just as he was turning away, Alessandro saw light flare through the cracks between the boards. He had seen the gardeners leave much earlier. Perhaps this was an escaped thief, or a thief who had not escaped. The ladders were of ancient oiled hardwood, their fittings brass. The cement mixer was a prize, maybe, if it could be spirited through the streets. He peered through a space between the boards.

In the middle of the shed an elegantly dressed young girl was holding a burning match in her left hand as she repeatedly leapt into the air. She had been at it long enough to lay her cape across the ladders. It, like her skirt, was a very fine black velvet, and in the lapel was a brooch that sparkled like a diamond because, even if Alessandro thought it was too big to be a diamond, it was a diamond. Her hair, although not quite blond, was sun-bleached enough to catch the light of the match, and it gleamed in places as if it had been bound in gold cords. Again the match went out.

Alessandro continued to peer into the darkness, wondering if he had imagined the dance he had seen, and hoping that it would resume. It did. Another match flared. She stared to heaven, breathing heavily and muttering. Then she leapt high into the air. It startled Alessandro so much that he banged his nose against the shed, but he retained enough presence of mind not to cry out.

Though she was a small woman, she was lithe, and, as she demonstrated with such arresting oddity, athletic. Though from some rare angles the side of her face seemed almost crooked, it was magnificent in the frontal view. As she turned in her jumping, Alessandro found the alternation of contrasts unbearably exciting. In addition, her silken cream-colored blouse was fitted tightly around a body that would have been highly desirable even had it been as still as a marble in the Villa Doria Pamphili; but she was moving strenuously and, as she jumped, Alessandro observed not dispassionately that her breasts were friendlier to gravity than the rest of her on the way up, and more reluctant to descend on the way down. Heredity and perhaps a devotion to gymnastics and swimming had made her figure both very pretty and very full.

Alessandro didn't understand that she was trying to reach the lantern. All he knew was that she was leaping in the air and talking to herself in the garden shed. The match went out again.

The next time, with another flame, she walked over to the cement mixer and, to see if it could move, shook it violently. Alessandro opened the door. She turned and held up the match. He still had not seen the lantern, but the advantage was his. "Are you trying to go someplace?" he inquired.

She turned so deeply red that the blood and heat rushing to her face sent her perfume billowing through the room. Had Alessandro known her only from this, he might have fallen in love. Still, he asked, "What were you doing?"

"None of your business," she said, bitterly.

Alessandro smiled, which embarrassed her more.

She seized her cape and rushed past him.

He thought he would never see her again, but as she passed

him she put the Finnish matches into his hands and commanded him to follow her.

He did. When she reached the hedge she threw the cape over it and walked into the flower garden. Alessandro went after her, overcome by her perfume and that of the flowers. He was late for dinner, but he didn't care. "Light the matches," she said.

"All at once?"

"Of course not, idiot. One by one."

When he lit a match and held it up, she looked at him for the first time, staring at him until the match burned down.

By the time Alessandro lit another match she was bent over the flowers. She hadn't been able to turn from him until the match was extinguished, because he struck her as the kind of man she might marry. Men with fortunes, men ten or fifteen years her senior, had wanted to marry her, and she had declined. Too much reading of the *Dolce Stil Nuovo,* her father had said, too much Petrarca, too much independence. "What will you marry?" he had asked. "A tennis instructor? A shepherd?" Every time her father spoke like this, two dozen bankers and industrialists died in her heart. She would marry whomever she pleased.

"You must be from over there," Alessandro said, gesturing toward her father's house.

She had gathered an armful of flowers, and now she stood facing him. "I am."

"What's your name?"

"Lia Bellati. You are a Giuliani."

"Alessandro."

She held out her hand for the matches, and he gave them to her. Then she went to the hedge and retrieved her cape. "Let me take you to the gate," he offered. "I know the garden well enough to find my way in the dark."

She took his arm. Though she did it stiffly, he felt the heat rising from her, and he breathed deeply just because they were touching.

"How old are you?" he asked as they reached the gate.

"Old enough not to be asked such a question," she replied. It stung him, as she had intended.

"I have a horse," he said as she passed through the gate.

"That's nice."

"Do you ride? I know that you jump."

"I do ride," she answered, "but so what." Then, without looking back, she went toward her house.

Alessandro turned to walk down the path that led through the carefully apportioned quarters of the garden. His hands still smelled of perfume and sulfur from holding the matchbox. He tried to think of a way to see her. If she would not ride with him, he would have to meet her in another fashion, but he was inept at such things, and terrified of parties and receptions, where he was all legs.

ALESSANDRO WOULD sit by his window waiting for Lia to appear. Every minute, sometimes more frequently, he would look up from what he was reading to see if she had come into the garden. He had walked for hours in Monteverdi and in the Villa Doria, hoping to encounter her, and after a week in which he had had no success he began the first of many letters that ended up in the fire. Most of these were single sheets of paper with only one or two lines, because his longing for her and his strange agitation had given birth to sentences like, "My heart is crushed, my soul black, I cannot move."

As if to compensate for the shame of being thus overboiled, he would become one of Lermontov's young officers, the kind who would drink a glass of fruit brandy, put their revolvers to their heads, smile, and pull the triggers just to show that they were the sort of fellows to whom nothing meant anything. Having read Lermontov and other Russians, and having stayed up until four in the morning, Alessandro found himself making declarations such as,

"All I desire is one night with you, after which I will quickly cause myself to be disemboweled."

One clear morning when the sky was wildly blue and the sun was hot from the instant it cleared the mountains, Alessandro went out early, hoping to see Lia in the street or in the Villa Doria. He had just passed the stable near the Porta San Pancrazio when he looked back and saw her coming toward him from the garden. She was wearing riding boots and the strange pants that women wore when they rode: out of the saddle, they appeared to be a dress. He thought they were called *cotillons,* but, to be safe, he called them *mezzi pallonetti,* or "half balloonlets." She held a leather crop in her left hand.

"You're going riding," he said accusingly.

She looked at her dress, looked up, and said, "Isaac Newton."

"Would it weigh upon you too heavily were I to accompany you?"

She smiled as she resumed her walk to the stable.

"Even though I have to change, I'll catch up," he said as he ran down the hill to his house.

He threw open the front door with such violence that everyone in the house ran into the hallways in expectation of a terrible event. He was up the stairs in a second. In another second he had thrown off his clothes. On went the summer riding pants, a polo shirt, and (with much cursing) a pair of cavalry boots. He pulled his wallet from a desk drawer, grabbed the money, and dropped the rest. In an instant he rinsed his mouth with dental salts and brushed his hair, one stroke. He shot out the door. He shot back in to seize his riding crop. He shot back out and made a tremendous racket in his heavy boots as he descended the stairs.

"You look very handsome," his mother called out as he disappeared beyond the front door.

He ran up the hill. Lia was gone. Her horse had probably been saddled and waiting.

Though she might have fifteen or twenty minutes' head start, he could catch her. He was a fierce rider and he had a great horse. His father had provided the animal, tack, and board, because he wanted Alessandro to see the country not from a speeding train but slowly and in detail, as he himself had seen it.

"You'll learn more in your journeys to and from Bologna, if you make them on horseback, than from all your professors combined," the attorney Giuliani had said, and he had almost been right. Just for this visit home Alessandro had ridden from Bologna by way of Florence and Sienna, and it had taken eight days. He did it with a compass, and was off the road much of the time, especially in the treeless plains by the lakes north of Rome. The horse was the best hunt horse, young but not inexperienced, the color of an expensive gun-stock and built almost like a racing thoroughbred, except that his legs were thicker and stronger. He could run all day, he could jump high walls, and at times he was astonishingly fast. He was good at swimming rivers, and if the surf were gentle he would canter into the sea.

Though Alessandro had run up the hill and arrived at the stable in a sweat, he entered calmly and put a saddle on the horse as if he were going to exercise him in the park. It was a hunt saddle, and the horse, whose name was Enrico, became edgy.

"Did Lia Bellati leave here a little while ago?" Alessandro asked the stableman as he cinched the saddle and elevated the stirrups as if for racing.

"Half an hour ago," the stableman said imprecisely. "She went to the sea, on the Laurentina."

"I'll catch her," Alessandro said as he put the bridle on Enrico.

"I don't think so," the stableman said.

"Why not? You know Enrico. You know how I can ride."

"The Signorina Bellati rides extremely well. Her brother is a cavalryman and she's on his horse."

"I thought he was in the navy."

"I don't think so. He has a sword."

"They all have swords."

"He has the long kind, the kind, you know, that can reach all the way to the ground even when a man is sitting in the saddle. The kind that's like a scythe, that can cut you in half."

"To hell with his sword. You can judge horses. Which is better?"

The stableman was silent.

"I see," Alessandro said. "I'll catch her anyway. Enrico can take fences like a bird. I'll catch her in the forest just before she comes to the sea."

"Tell me if it's so," the stableman said as he led the horse from the stall.

When the horse came into the light he pranced and waved his head. Alessandro jumped into the saddle, and on his way up he was blinded by the bright sun.

"Don't go too fast in the city," the stableman cautioned. "The *carabinieri* will chase you."

"I have to go fast. She left me no choice," Alessandro replied. Then he spurred Enrico and galloped him recklessly down the hill.

They crossed the Tiber on the Ponte Aventino early enough in the morning for the fishermen to be on the bridge, lowering their square nets from complicated little derricks. The river was beginning to run low, but in April it was still clear and it smelled fresh. The grass on the banks was green, and the walkways had been swept clean by the March floods.

Alessandro looked to the sides and ahead for mounted *carabinieri*. They would not be out in force, because mounted police detested the morning. That he knew this enabled him to ride through the city much faster than he was sure Lia had dared, and he guessed that he would cut her lead by five minutes.

A man with white mustaches and a white suit did not like the way Alessandro sped past his carriage: "Monkey! Cretin! Fool! Who gave you permission to ride so fast?"

Alessandro turned in the saddle. He was twenty years of age, and insults were fast and automatic. "A cheese like you has no right to talk," he screamed. "Cannibal, suck-worm, lecher, penis-head, fungus."

The streets grew broader and the spaces more open. Alessandro let Enrico gallop, because it seemed safe that no mounted *carabinieri* would be stirring in the less populated sections of Rome. He pressured Enrico's strong sides with the heels of his boots. Though no fox or rabbit was ahead of him, Enrico elongated his strides, and horse and rider rounded a wide corner, oblivious of everything except their speed and the blue sky opening up ahead over the countryside.

Two mounted *carabinieri* riding precisely in tandem on high-spirited, chestnut-colored horses were heading toward the city. They were tall in the saddle, dressed immaculately in blue uniforms and long black boots. Their buttons gleamed, and broad white sashes crossed their chests, the slings for their cavalry swords. Both men had shiny holsters that closed upon oversized wooden pistol-handles, and their saddles were fitted with scabbards from which projected the oiled stocks and gleaming bolts of standard military rifles. They carried ammunition in neat little leather pouches that hung from their belts and saddles. Their caps had heavy insignia propped against a striking red band. They even wore white gloves.

Alessandro had often wondered if, in fact, a man in a tailored dress uniform, loaded down with straps, buckles, sashes, pouches, a hat, a sword, a pistol, white gloves, a huge rifle, and, perhaps most importantly, his dignity, could really ride and fight.

He guessed, from having been a boy and from having climbed mountains, that if one were not comfortable, could not bend, or were restricted and weighted down with equipment, fighting would be most difficult.

Even if the *carabinieri* were merely symbols who rode through the streets and parks to commemorate the real work they did in more rugged places and more rugged dress, would not their pride, training, and experience cause them to forget that they were mounted peacocks, and make them ride like hell? Washerwomen and seamstresses who worked within their closely guarded fortresses must have been ready to correct rents in their uniforms and starch them silly. Still, weighted down like that, how would they and their horses enjoy the action? He had never been able to win a race without enjoying it. Could they?

Enrico took the corner with huge strides, running almost like a cat, bending his whole body.

They ran right into the *carabinieri,* whose mounts parted and reared. You could gallop past these gentlemen at your own risk, but never, never, could you go between them. They would prefer to be shot.

Alessandro had not intended to part them or to panic their horses, but now he had five seconds in which to decide what to do.

Were he to capitulate, rein Enrico in, and swear that his horse had been stung by a hornet or frightened by a train whistle, his fine and sentence might not be unbearable. On the other hand, if he slapped Enrico's heated buttocks with the crop, bent into the wind, and raced for his freedom, he might escape embarrassment, fines, and imprisonment, he would have an answer to his question about how the *carabinieri* rode and fought, and he would be almost certain of overtaking Lia Bellati. In this case, if he were caught, the penalties would be more severe. In fact, the *carabinieri* might dismount, pull their rifles, and shoot him.

They would not do it easily. For all they knew, he was a novice on a runaway horse, a lunatic, or a retarded boy who worked in a stable. Even if they decided to bring him down, he thought, they would not stand much chance of doing it unless they were right on him with their pistols, for even in open country with a clear shot, by the time they dismounted, secured their horses, got their rifles, dropped to the ground, took aim, and fired, neither he nor Enrico, moving at high speed over an uneven track that caused them to bob and sway, would be good targets. And not only that, he was already moving quite fast in the direction in which he wanted to go and he doubted that the handsome horses of the *carabinieri* could take a fence or dodge the trees and bushes the way Enrico could. The *carabinieri*'s pouches and swords would be jangling and bouncing all over them, and Alessandro was dressed to slip through the wind. Besides, he was already elated with the chasing. How just that he should be chased. He would be not only pulled ahead, but pushed. Fear, delight, and being twenty were made for each other: he whipped Enrico's flanks and bent forward. Enrico, who was never whipped and who was very intelligent, received the message and ignited like a rocket.

The *carabinieri* were trained soldiers. They neither said anything nor looked at one another. They merely pulled their caps down tight, inhaled, reconciled themselves to ruining their uniforms, and dug their spurs into their horses' sides. Perhaps Alessandro's decision would have been different had he known that their weapons and pouches were designed and secured for fast pursuit on a horse, and that these men who were so heavily encumbered had been trained to ride and fight in fancy clothes.

He was on a straightaway parallel to a ruined aqueduct. Its arches flew past him as if they were the spaces between cars in a train speeding the other way. The road was clear, flat, and dry, he had at least a kilometer's lead, and, although he didn't look back, he felt that he was enlarging it. He was riding so fast that everyone he passed turned to look after him, but the horses of the *carabinieri* were somewhat better on a straightaway than Enrico, whose legs were as thick and strong as those of a steeplechase horse.

After five minutes running, Alessandro heard two pistol shots. He looked back. The *carabinieri* were uncomfortably close. Their pistols were held in the air. He could even see the silver badges set in the red bands of the caps.

His throat tightened as they gained, but he chanced that they would tire sooner than Enrico, if only because they outweighed him and their saddles were heavy and elaborate. The road veered to the right, went through one of the aqueduct's arches, and then veered around to the left again, parallel to a railway. On the left side of the road was a ditch filled with cream-colored water, beyond which was a field sectioned by chest-high barbed wire. The road and the railroad resumed their parallel course on the other side of it. Here was the kind of oxbow that he had planned to cross so that he might catch up to Lia. He reasoned that if he could use such a thing to draw even with a beautiful girl who had a twenty-minute lead, he might also use it to escape the *carabinieri,* so, instead of veering toward the arches, he kept Enrico straight in the curve and closed on the ditch.

Enrico loved to jump. He cleared the stream with a wide margin, and he went too high, merely from exuberance. The *carabinieri* knew their horses could not take the fences. They kept to the road and disappeared through the arches of the aqueduct. Enrico jumped the wire, leaving a great deal of space between it and his lean belly, and Alessandro didn't look back until they had cleared the third and last fence.

When he saw no one behind him, he knew they had taken the road, and after Enrico leapt over a green bank back onto the track, Alessandro saw them two kilometers behind, at the bend. It was so hot that waves of heat rising off the fields made the mounted soldiers look like a single black carriage lifted from the road and traveling on air.

Alessandro heard half a dozen pistol shots. He knew that his fate now depended not upon the principles or training of the *carabinieri* but upon the degree of their frustration, and he realized that because of the *carabinieri* he would have to avoid the Laurentina for a year, and that, to return to Rome in the evening, he would have to swim his horse across the Tiber near Ostia, where it was wide and deep, and approach the city from the north. But these thoughts were premature, for he looked back and saw the riders still in pursuit, still raised above the road and jiggling hypnotically as if they were a flying machine or an automobile. When would their horses give out? It had to be soon, because of the weight they carried, but it hardly mattered. Soon he would lead them into enormous tracts of forest crossed at random with ravines, gullies, stone walls, and cattle fences, where a horse had to dodge like a boxer, and a rider had to be subtle and quick to avoid hanging limbs and sharp brambles as thick as anacondas.

If Enrico could hold his lead on another few kilometers of straightaway, he would lose them forever in the forest. They would dismount for some listless rifle shots before their quarry vanished into the city-sized green thickets. Then, safe from the *carabinieri,* Alessandro would speed through the foliage, enchanted by the dark leaves and the wind in the pines until he emerged from the forest at the coast, onto an empty white beach with the sound of the waves obliterating his hard breathing and the wind cooling his sweat-drenched horse.

Alessandro's image of the waves and the wind on the sea made him narrow his eyes and sent cool sparkling bolts of electricity coursing through him. Enrico followed suit and shuddered even as he ran, starting ahead as if he had been stung.

As he was thinking about his marvelous advantage and comfortable long lead, Alessandro was knocked forward by a huge blast from behind. He turned in the saddle, and he saw a great light suspended high in the air. He was so shocked that it took him a second or two to realize that it was the headlamp of a locomotive running on the track next to the road. Gradually the locomotive pulled up even. The blur of its rods and wheels, the steam that issued from steel, the distance chased down and beaten by fire, the ten thousand sounds, and the complex and contradictory movements that combined to push it forward along the two silky rails that lay before it, were like a dream.

Two men in the cab and one on the coal car were smiling at him and waving their arms. They knew neither that he was chasing

Lia Bellati nor fleeing the *carabinieri*. They were lighthearted in the fine weather. They were proud of their engine. They wanted to race.

Why not? Alessandro looked through heat that bent the light, and raised his right hand, his thumb pointed up. The black locomotive churned the air and clattered over the silver rails. The fireman began to shovel coal into the firebox, and the engineers stopped smiling. As their speed increased, the concoction of hysterical pistons and spokes moved into a frenzy that drew Alessandro to it as if it were the magnetic black water under a bridge: he had to fight not to lean in its direction.

Now and then he passed astonished people on the road. Had two carts blocked the way he would have jumped them. He didn't think he could beat the train, and had the race lasted longer he would not have, but they approached the forest, and the horse, who could smell it, stretched forward as if carried on the thundering engine's invisible bow waves.

When the race was over they rose into the green. The forest took them as Alessandro had thought it would, lightly and gently. They ran through it, disappearing into its shadows, and gradually they slowed. Enrico was dancing as smoothly through the brush as a swallow that maneuvers through a tangle of trees.

HAD LIA taken the Laurentina, Alessandro thought, she probably would have broken off toward the sea on a particular road that followed the course of a clear stream. This was the most direct route, and the prettiest, and, after swimming in the sea, one had merely to push from the waves into the stream's pulsating plume, traveling up the transparent shallows to emerge free of salt and chill, for even in early spring the currents could be as warm as bath water.

That she intended to swim alone, and had ridden alone to such a deserted place, puzzled him. Though the countryside around

Rome was neither Sicily nor Calabria, it was not safe for an unaccompanied woman, it never had been, and it never would be. He turned almost blue with the thought that she might have—indeed, must have—met a lover on the road, in which case his triple race would have been for nothing, and his shame would drive him to emigrate to Argentina. He began to think about Argentina, and it was not unpleasant, but before he left he would stand by the stream that flowed into the sea and watch as Lia and her lover emerged from the dunes. What an exquisite look he would give them. His expression would be that of a spurned horseman on foot in a Budapest cafe, who, about to shoot himself in the head, would glance at the woman he loved, and smile. All was forgiven, if only because everything was so magnificently bittersweet. Even at twenty, Alessandro knew that he had been dazzled by the greatness of Pushkin, and that, despite the pronouncements of opera, Italians were far more practical in these matters than were the Central Europeans who wore epaulets and bearskin helmets and killed themselves in cafes or jumped out of windows with playing cards in their hands. Nonetheless, many Italians, including Garibaldi, had gone to Argentina and come away better, far-seeing men with white mustaches, wrinkled faces, and eyes that had grown wise in the Andes, so to speak.

While Enrico lapped the warm river water and Alessandro was planning the layout of a hacienda on the Pampas, Lia rode over the crest of the dunes. She was struck by the fact that Enrico had stretched out his long neck and carefully spread his forelegs so he could drink, and that Alessandro, after having done the impossible, was lost in thought. He might have been strutting back and forth on his horse, amazed that he had beaten her overwhelming head start, but he seemed almost to be unhappy, and she liked that more even than she knew.

As her cavalry mount, his head held high for balance, quietly slid down the cool sand, Alessandro turned in surprise.

"You must have flown," she said. "I pushed my horse all the way.

"We cut through the forest." He looked down at Enrico. "He thinks it's his duty to jump fences and walls, to go through the bushes and the trees like a rabbit, and to cover great distances without tiring—and I never told him it wasn't."

"They used to ride like that in Argentina," she said.

"Argentina?" Alessandro asked, in amazement.

"My father was overseeing the construction of a rail line from Bahía Blanca to Buenos Aires."

"I thought your father was a banker."

"Who do you think provides the money to construct railroads?"

"How long were you there?"

"A few years. The beaches there are more beautiful," she said, looking out at the sea. Her hair was kept in motion rhythmically by the breeze that came off the waves. "There weren't any people for tens of kilometers. I used to swim in the sea with nothing, not even a ring."

She reddened across her face and neck, and, although he could not see it, her chest and shoulders. The heat began to travel even down her back, but the wind ballooned her clothing and cooled her.

"Was it dangerous?" Alessandro asked. They had begun to walk their horses, south of the stream, toward Anzio.

"The waves were high, but the currents were gentle," she answered.

"I mean without clothes."

"I wasn't alone."

Alessandro felt like a rock that is thrown into an unfathomably deep sector of the sea. In imagination of yet another of her lovers, he knew oblivion.

"I had a horse."

"What if someone had come along?"

"Who?"

"Someone of horrendous intentions."

"There wasn't anyone for as far as you could see."

Alessandro nodded. Still, he could not help but feel irritation at the scandalous behavior that, were he to marry her, would reflect badly upon him. Something was wrong if a beautiful and delicate young woman were so careless with herself. "What if someone did come?" he asked. "What if a man had been hiding in the dunes? No one was around to help, except your horse."

"My horse would have been enough."

"Was it trained to bite?" Alessandro asked sarcastically.

"No, it was trained not to flee, and to carry my saddlebags, in which I kept this," she said, reaching into one of a small set of balanced saddle pouches that looked, if not Argentine, at least un-Italian. She drew a heavy revolver and held it expertly in her right hand, with the barrel pointing straight up. "It's British," she said, "a Webley and Scott."

For half an hour they walked their horses down the beach, talking about Argentina, ballistics, and the sea. Though it was not quite warm enough to swim, Alessandro couldn't rid himself of the image of Lia swimming. When he saw them spinning together in the waves, scandal was of no consequence.

Any thoughts Alessandro may have had in this regard were chased from him when he became aware that a storm over the Tyrrhenian had risen as if from nowhere and was speeding directly toward them. They heard faraway rolling thunder that began on the sea and tracked toward Rome in masses of black like the clouds of swallows that nest by the Tiber and sometimes obliterate the November sky.

Soon the solid wall of the storm stretched from the cape at Anzio to the horizon. Small yellow serpentines of lightning weaving amidst the coils of charcoal cloud lit the sea and made it as green as emerald. The storm was sailing on the wind, tossing distant waves into white crests, running for the coast, turning the light above it to gray, purple, and gold.

Lia turned to Alessandro.

"I can beat it to Rome," he said.

"Of course you can't."

"I can."

"That's foolish," she told him.

"No it isn't. I know my chances. I've always known when they're good, and they're good right now." He rested his hand on Enrico's taut neck.

"I'd like to see it. Tell me if you get through."

"Why don't you come with me?"

"I have no intention either of fighting storms or outrunning them, and I have no intention of accompanying anyone who tries. It doesn't work. It never did, and it never will."

HAD ALESSANDRO known that Lia went into the garden early in the morning he would have arisen each day at five and been there to have met her accidentally. It was the end of April and he hadn't seen her for weeks. Nor had he heard from her. Nor had he known how to approach her. Lacking the social graces, he was unable to ask her to the theater or the opera, and he was not likely to meet her at a dinner party, never having been to one. He solved the problem by lying in bed.

Early one morning, before the sun struck the picture of the Matterhorn, his father came into his room and shook him.

"I want to sleep."

"You can't."

"What do you mean, I can't?" Alessandro asked.

"I need you today. Umberto is sick and hasn't been in for three days, we have a tremendous backlog, and Orfeo told me yesterday that, if I didn't get a substitute, he wouldn't work. You know what Orfeo is like. Shave and dress. We're late."

"Can't you hire a scribe?" Alessandro asked indignantly.

"Scribes are not fireflies," his father said. "They're cautious and slow. I've never been able to hire one for less than three months, or find one in less than two."

"There's something wrong with my hand," Alessandro stated. "After just a little bit of writing, it freezes up hot. I think I must have a paralysis, or the beginnings of a terrible disease...."

"Probably the gold has worn off the point of your pen. Bring it. Orfeo will take a look: he's an expert."

"But today I wanted to ride to Bracciano to swim in the lake."

"Today you must replace Umberto."

"I prefer not to."

"You have no choice."

"Still, I prefer not to."

His father left the room.

"'You have no choice! You have no choice,'" Alessandro repeated. Though at first he put his pants on backwards, in five minutes he had shaved and bathed, and he appeared downstairs dressed like a lawyer, in suit, tie, and vest.

"Breakfast!" he cried as his father pulled him out the door.

"In the office," the attorney Giuliani said.

They descended the Gianicolo on winding paths, streets, and stairs. Soon they were at the edge of Trastevere, where they went down a series of steep and crumbling steps that had been the death of old men and that on slick January mornings had even dispatched into the next world so cautious and agile a creature as a cat.

Going down the hill made Alessandro and his father walk fast, and, listening to the cadence of their steps against the cobbles, they cut through the level parts of Trastevere almost at a run. Taking a bridge across the Tiber, they joined a stream of other men intently on their way to work as if the morning light on all the marble palaces, advancing through the gardens, and filling the perfectly proportioned squares, were nothing.

"When you walk through the city in the morning, what do you think about?" Alessandro asked his father.

"Many things."

"Do you think of the city itself?"

"No. I used to, but I've had a profession for a number of years, and it has mastered me. A profession is like a great snake that wraps itself around you. Once you are enwrapped, you are in a slow fight for the rest of your life, and the lightness of youth leaves you. You don't have time, for example, to think about the city even as you are walking through it."

"Unless you make it your profession."

"Then you're an architect, and you're always thinking of how to get clients."

"But what if you were to choose the profession of looking at things to see their beauty, to see what they meant, to find in the world as much of the truth as you could find?"

"For that you need to be independently wealthy."

"What about a professorship?"

"Of what?"

"Aesthetics."

"Aesthetics?" the father asked. "That's ridiculous. You'll live like a slave for twenty-five years. Better to go into the Church."

"I would rather die than live without women," Alessandro said.

"What about the army?" Alessandro's father inquired. "In my view, universities are like the army. The only difference is that the officers don't wear their ranks on their uniforms: they write them after their names and announce them in the degree to which their speech is pompous, mellifluous, and monotonous."

"The army?" Alessandro asked. "The army kills people!"

The attorney Giuliani looked at his son with a pointed expression. "Have there been reforms of which I have not heard? Don't you know that the only people the army kills are the people who eat its food? Our army, of late, is composed of saints and martyrs. They march into battle and don't come back, and the enemy holds his ground. To fault them for killing people is truly a slander."

"Lia's brother is in the army. He seems capable."

"Lia..." his father said.

"Lia Bellati?"

"I see. How old is she?"

"My age, more or less."

"How old is her brother?"

"Thirty."

"What rank has he?"

"Captain."

"Impressive," the attorney Giuliani said. "He carries a sword, and has a magnificent uniform." He stopped in the middle of a street, and, as carriages passed on either side of them, looked his son straight in the eye. "Respect him for what he is, but picture the uniform covered with blood, and the man inside it blue with death, lying abandoned on a field. For what? Usually, for nothing. Whatever you do, don't join the army. Is that clear?"

"I have no intention of joining the army! You're the one who said the army is better than a university."

"It is."

"What shall I do, then, become a lawyer?"

"Wouldn't you like to be a successful attorney?"

"Wouldn't *you*?" Alessandro shot back, instantly. That his father was successful was irrelevant. Alessandro had meant to hurt him, and he had, but his father forgave him immediately because he knew that Alessandro might never forgive himself.

At the law offices they walked up many sets of stairs squared off about an enormous atrium. They climbed in silence, but the attorney's heart was light, because his son had brought up, even if obliquely, the very thing about which the attorney had always dreamed.

They turned the handle on an enormous wooden door the color of Enrico. The floor inside was of marble so highly polished that they walked across as carefully as if they had been on ice. The spacious offices of this firm, in which the attorney Giuliani was the principal partner, looked over Rome as if to govern it, and they were remarkably serene, except for the office of the scribes, where pens scratched across paper in a sound that approximated that of a granary invaded by mice, or a coop of a hundred scratching chickens.

Before Alessandro sat numbly with the scribes he wanted breakfast. A beautiful wooden table stood by the windows in the principal partner's office. They sat down at it, and a waiter in a white jacket appeared. The attorney Giuliani held up a finger: this meant no variation, which, in turn, meant a brioche and a cappuccino. The waiter turned to Alessandro.

"Four hot chocolates, five brioches, and five *cornetti.*"

"That's all?" Alessandro's father asked, wincing.

"I'm not hungry," Alessandro said.

They heard the waiter on the stairs, descending to a *pasticceria* to get more supplies. Ten minutes later, Alessandro poured a cup of chocolate as thick and hot as lava: the thickness, it seemed, held the heat. It even looked like lava, because it was filled with sluggish bubbles and sharp, scalloped, sponge-like depressions. He began to slice and butter the brioches and *cornetti.* On some he put jam.

"You're not going to butter and jam every one of those, are you?"

"Why not?" Alessandro asked, noticing that as people passed by the open doors of his father's office they paused to look in. The waiter had made him a legend.

"Let me ask you something," the attorney said.

"What?"

"This Lia . . ."

"Yes?"

"Do you know her?"

"Of course I know her."

"You know her well?"

"Yes and no."

"What do you mean, 'yes and no'?"

"Why are you excited?"

"Do you, have you, does she... She's supposed to be wild, but perhaps she has a sister. Someone implied that she was amoral."

"He was probably in love with her, and she not with him," Alessandro said confidently. The *cornetti* were gone.

"I warn you sternly..." the father began.

"You warn me sternly? What kind of syntax is that?"

"You don't know where such behavior can lead. It can be disastrous."

"What behavior? I've said nothing."

"I trust this will nip it in the bud."

"Nip *what* in the bud?"

"The production of miniature human beings!" his father screamed.

"I don't plan to produce miniature human beings," Alessandro said.

The attorney Giuliani leaned forward with both hands on the table. "Just don't do anything stupid."

"I won't," Alessandro answered, backing out of the room.

"Be sure to act sensibly."

"Have I ever not acted sensibly?"

The attorney Giuliani had the expression of a man who has just lit a fuse.

"Papa," Alessandro said, his eyes closing. "She swims nude in the sea. She carries a pistol. And she wears perfume that makes me dizzy. Sometimes I go to the garden gate and smell the handle, because, when she touches it, the perfume stays."

The attorney Giuliani was frozen still. "Be disciplined," he urged.

"Were you?"

"Not enough. That's how I know."

ALESSANDRO WAS received by Orfeo, the chief mouse of the granary, the commander of the scratching chickens, who brought him to a desk near his own. Both shared a magnificent view of

Rome. "It's sunny today," Orfeo said. "How nice to be indoors in the shade."

Alessandro peered at the deeply seductive blue, closed his eyes, and saw a huge white wave sparkling in the sun. Flying within its airy circular crest were he and Lia Bellati, without a stitch of clothing, without gravity, tumbling, all limbs, glistening, wet, careening in the foam.

"Think of all those devils out there in the heat," Orfeo went on, "with heavy loads on their backs, sweating like mules." Orfeo was an old man who had begun work as a scribe not long after the nineteenth century had passed its midpoint, and who still had not a single speck of gray. Perhaps he dyed his always gleaming hair with coal tar or some other intensely black substance. His height and his posture had been the cause of many thousands of fleeting internal debates as people who passed him on the street tried to decide whether or not he was a dwarf and whether or not he was a hunchback. In fact, though he was short and stooped, he was neither a hunchback nor a dwarf, but could look the part of both, depending upon his state of agitation and the energy of his resentment. He had the face of a far taller man who had been compacted in an olive press. It was all there, but very little space existed between it. "Much better to be a gentleman, out of the glare!" he said, hoping to please the son of the *padrone*.

Alessandro smiled in pain for being in the shade, but Orfeo took his expression to be that of anger and embarrassment. Orfeo should not have implied that he and the attorney Giuliani's son were gentlemen of the same standing. Had the boy been a year younger, perhaps, yes, but Alessandro had crossed an imperceptible line, and had no doubt long since stopped eating with the servants, no matter how much he may have loved them. Orfeo, however, did not think that this was a threatening predicament. It had, rather, a thousand exits, and he chose one almost at random, speaking in rapid fire.

"All kinds of gentlemen exist. There are gentlemen such as your father, and you, who are of exalted status. Perhaps not the most exalted status: God and the angels, and His holy blessed Son, bless him, are certainly the most exalted, but as there is the sun and Saturn, so are there the moons that circle in rich profundity. And then there are the other ranks, far below the exalted ones, which are to the moons of the planets as the mountains of the moon are to the moon itself. They ride upon his back, though they are upright and uncongealed, and perhaps if you and your gracious father are moons that sail and dip in the rainbow lines of Saturn's rings, I am but a true, but a proud tree, on the mountain of the moon, standing upright in the cool light of the blessed protector, whose cloak of silk like a luminous mantle is draped across the stars, and from the dog that rides in the godly sea of space, this exaltedness runs in train, trying to lap its blessed luminous sap."

One of the other scribes, a young man with a mustache, caught Alessandro's eye. The index finger of his left hand was pointed to his head, and as he wrote with his right hand the left twirled in a circle.

Orfeo had begun to describe in spectacular detail the "gracious luminous sap that falls like the blood of the Cross from the tree in the valley of the bone-white mountains that circle the moon," when Alessandro produced from his vest pocket the beautiful fountain pen with which he wrote anything and everything—his essays on aesthetics, his departmental examinations, letters declaring love to married women in Bologna who dared not answer, summaries of account, instructions for feeding his horse, epistles (also never answered) to the prime minister of Italy. It was the most precious of all the instruments he possessed, including his penis, though, admittedly, the pen was irreplaceable.

"My father said to ask you about this," he told Orfeo. "I find that when I write for ten minutes or more I lose control of my hand, which pains me, and shakes. It's also very hot. And yet nothing is wrong with the rest of me, I think."

"Let me see, sir." Orfeo took the pen, seized a magnifying glass, and examined the point. "You idiot!" he said. "You don't hold it correctly, sir! The left side is worn down completely, no gold at all left on it. It's like a knife now. A good penman glides over the page. You, my boy, cut. That's no way. This needs a new point. Put it back in your coat. Come. I'll give you a new pen."

Alessandro followed meekly to a captain's chest that stood near the window. Orfeo pulled out an enormously wide and deep drawer that floated to them as if across bearings of silk, with not the slightest sound. The north light illuminated dozens, scores, and hundreds of pens. "This wealth, this treasure," Orfeo said, "belongs to your father, but is entrusted to me. I'll give you the best one of the lot. Most are ebony. Not this. Look."

He held up a perfectly smooth, matte-black pen. The heavy point was dazzling even in north light. "Your father let me order it from England. It's ceramic—Wedgwood. You must not drop it. It's perfect—smooth, flawless, cool to the touch, and the point is so massive that it's as flexible as a whip. I'll fill it for you. I'll use treaty ink that costs twice as much for a little bottle than what we pay for a liter of the standard." He filled the pen and wiped its point on a clean linen towel suspended from a hook on the captain's chest.

"Now we'll copy," he said after they had taken their seats. "Here's the third section of the Portuguese contract. You'll be working on a copy for the records. It isn't a presentation copy, and it doesn't have to be fancy, but it does have to be clear. Work hard. In two hours, the singers will come, and the work will seem easier."

"What singers?" Alessandro asked.

"Singers come an hour before noon," the mustachioed scribe answered, still working. "They sing until we go home for lunch."

"Are they good?"

"They're *angels,*" Orfeo said, looking at the ceiling. "Two women, and a man with a voice that echoes in the piazza."

"If they're so good," Alessandro asked, "why do they sing in the piazza? And who pays them?"

"That's simple. They're from Africa, so that's why they sing in the piazza, and that's why no one pays them even though they sing like angels and they should be in La Scala. Of course, they can't be. They've been here for a month. They must have come from Africa because of the rainy season, or because their goats died. I hope they never go back. After each song, the piazza is beaten by a hailstorm of silver. You'll see. From every window, every office."

Waiting for the singers, they settled down to work. In copying the Portuguese contract, Alessandro found that it was as if the massive gold point on the Wedgwood pen had a mind of its own. When ink was needed, out it flowed. If Alessandro were to hesitate, the ink would hold itself back rather than blot the page. The result was an effortless glide, like skating with the wind at your back, with virgin ice mirroring the easy strides across its surface. Apart from the fact that it was in Portuguese, the Portuguese contract itself was not all that forbidding, being mainly a set of ground rules for currency arbitrage in the purchase of cattle, salt fish, and oil.

Now and then Orfeo would lean over to check his transient apprentice. "A gentleman's hand. Look at all that flying and skating!"

"You fly and skate, too," Alessandro said.

"Yes, but, notice, always in exactly the same way. That is the mark of an old order scribe—consistency. Each letter is always the same. Gentlemen gallop their horses across the fields and leap fences as they choose. Scribes must follow the streetcar tracks; still, the discipline affords satisfaction. It's like the moon that circles the planets of the outer reach, and the dance of the flatulent animals on the surface of the desiccated brook. . . ."

"Tell me, if scribes value consistency so much," Alessandro interrupted, to stanch the monologue before Orfeo got on to the luminous sap, "then why not get one of those new machines, typewriters, and every letter will be exactly the same?"

Orfeo stopped writing. "Let me explain something to you, sir," he said urgently. "We in this office are very advanced. We make use of the miracles that God has chosen to give us—little bird-like machines, fountain pens, bottles with caps that screw on, chairs that adjust up and down. We are at the forefront. If this typewriter of which you speak were a plausible invention, we would not hesitate to use it." He leaned back with a satisfied, amused smile.

"It isn't a plausible invention?"

Barely able to restrain his laughter, Orfeo shook his head. "Of course not! All the establishments that are buying these machines are doomed! They'll never be used in offices, *never!* I can give you my word. They're too impersonal. You can tell nothing of what is behind the words. And everything will have to be written at first by hand anyway. I've been a scribe for fifty years. I would lay my life down immediately if what I say is not true. These machines will not come into general use. They're entirely impractical. I pity the inventor. I pity the users. I pity the seller."

"I don't know," Alessandro said. "When they're improved . . ."

"How could you possibly improve them!" Orfeo shouted.

"Let's say you could put a motor in them."

"A motor?" Orfeo broke into laughter. "What, a steam engine?"

"No, an electric motor to strike the impressions."

"Impossible! Every time you touched it . . . you'd get killed! And if they found a safe way for you to touch it—a rubber suit perhaps, or ivory plugs so the fingers would be like stilts, or sitting on a rubber throne—then the electricity still wouldn't know what to do. How could electricity know what to do? Human fingers! Human fingers! They were designed to make beautiful curves, not to hit keys."

"What about a piano?"

"What about it?"

"The music of a piano comes out in beautiful curves, and you get it by striking keys."

"A German, yes, but not us."

"Italians don't play the piano?"

"There are degrees of sympathy, and degrees of sympathy," Orfeo said in a kind of panic, his face and body twitching. "What if they swept down here speaking that ugly language that sounds like a monkey choking on an orange. Sometimes I dream that a German is laughing at me because I'm short. He looks at me and points, and his mouth curves like a scroll. 'You're so short!' he says. 'What *are* you, a meter tall?'

"But I have it completely under control. I simply pay no attention. I am the master of the situation. I have this dream every night. Those people are tall but they're crazy. That's why they speak like they're undergoing surgery without anaesthetic."

"I don't think the language is ugly," Alessandro said. "It's as beautiful as ours, almost."

"Don't cede Venice to those garglers."

"I didn't say I would."

Orfeo cocked his arm and made a fist. "Will you fight?"

"Fight whom?"

"The Germans, that's whom!"

"There isn't a war."

"Does there have to be a war?"

"Yes! There aren't any Germans here except tourists!"

"People like you..." Orfeo said, with unconcealable disgust, "are the ruin of Rome. It's been like that for thousands of years."

"Why? Because I don't kill tourists?"

"No, because of the elephants."

"Elephants."

"They thought they were safe, because the elephants were across the sea, but Hannibal was smarter than them. He fed the elephants grapes and honey until they were as fat as couches, and he coaxed them into the water off Ceuta, saying, *Let's just go for a little swim,* and the currents carried them to Spain, where they climbed up on the beach." He turned to the mustachioed scribe. "Is this not true?"

"I don't know, I wasn't there," said the scribe.

"Ah! Two cowards," Orfeo said, "and, for two cowards, two

things. They'd conquered most of Italy already—Milano, Venezia, Firenze, Bologna, Genova. It was a close call, and the people who beat them were the people who had been training and willing to fight all along, like the geese that honked in the night."

"That's three things," said the other scribe.

"So what! Who are you to carp at numbers? I can't even read your fives: they look like sixes."

This quickly became an argument among the scribes. Alessandro returned to the Portuguese contract, thinking about fat elephants climbing from the sea on the southern coast of Spain. The Austrians, of course, had battle cruisers in that sea, and had only to sweep down from the Tyrol, elephantless, but it was a time of peace, and he did not need to think of fighting, and he would not have to die young. This was history's gift to him, he was grateful for it, and he refused to demean it by imagining a war that did not exist. He was free, and he knew it.

At eleven, the singers came. They weren't Africans. Nor were they angels, but they were very good, and the time until lunch went as smoothly as if all the scribes had been drifting down a river. At one, when the female singer finished her last aria, the doors and windows that faced the piazza were filled with a hundred clerks who made their silver coins into a short and violent hailstorm.

ALESSANDRO HAD lived all his life in the bosom of his family, and for him a social gathering of any type was an ordeal. He thought that conversations repeatedly nipped in the bud, microscopic chatter, people who stood talking to each other with their eyes scanning the room like hunters looking for birds, and the overwhelming weight of hierarchy, propriety, and manners necessary for an evening without unpleasant incident, were as exhausting and terrifying as a battle. Although he had never been in a battle, he knew nonetheless that he preferred it to a situation in which he was forced to hang himself with collar and tie, dance with ugly women, and get powdered sugar all over his pants.

When the invitation arrived, it was sealed with wax and tied with the kind of cord that, in a thicker incarnation, was used in draperies in the dining rooms of expensive hotels. The paper looked like white leather, and the card within was printed in raised black, gold, and red letters, and embossed with the Hapsburg crest. Signora Giuliani had spent the day trying not to open it.

"What's that?" Alessandro asked.

"Open it," his mother commanded.

"Later," Alessandro said, since part of his business was to be contrary.

"It's probably for your father. If you don't open it, I will. It may be important."

"I'll open it later, if I may," Alessandro said. "I've been copying all day—a thirty-six-page contract in Portuguese—and I'm tired. It can wait until morning. Undoubtedly, it's trivial."

He walked to his room, calmly shut the door, and ripped open the envelope as if it contained the last bit of breathable oxygen left on Mars. His Excellency the Baron Zoltán Károly, Minister Plenipotentiary, Extraordinary Legate of the Austrian Emperor, was requesting Alessandro's presence at dinner a week later at the Palazzo Venezia, the embassy of Austria-Hungary.

Why him?

Why not? In fact, it was perfect. For years Alessandro had been reading Cicero and English parliamentary debates, with no outlet for his oratory except impatient fellow students who did not appreciate the worth of the great cadences Alessandro now had by heart. Of late he had been reading the newspapers as if with a jeweler's eye, and had yearned for the opportunity to engage what he imagined might be nascent political talent. Of course, not every one of the hundreds of guests at an embassy reception had the opportunity to give a speech, but Alessandro didn't need anything more, really, than fifteen minutes' barking time at a Belgian second secretary, and of this, or something like it, he was confident.

It took him two days to buy fancy stationery, compose the fruity language in which to say yes, and get Orfeo to write it out with as many as possible of the curlicues and flounces that Alessandro usually tried to avoid. Alessandro put the envelope in a leather bag, jumped on Enrico, and rode to the Palazzo Venezia. At the gate were two grenadiers, private soldiers so elaborately dressed that they put to shame those Brazilian birds in the zoo who died each winter in droves because for them Rome was as cold as the Arctic.

The soldiers wore skintight patent leather boots, white pantaloons, green swallow-tailed jackets with gold braid, red ribbons, insignia, piping that ran all over them like rodents frolicking on the carcass of a dead horse, white sword-belts, bearskin helmets, feather plumes, high red collars, sashes, medals, leather pouches, and swords entangled in rustling tassels. It was a wonder that they could move. It was a wonder that they could stand. *"Kurier für den Botschafter,"* Alessandro said, handing his letter to one of the soldiers.

"Grazie," the soldier answered.

As Alessandro rode away he thought of the moment when he would stand in the embassy courtyard, alone in a world he did not understand. He blinked twice that week, once to get fitted in evening clothes, and the second time to polish Enrico's bridle and saddle, and then, barely breathing, he dismounted in the courtyard of the Palazzo Venezia, where a lackey dressed like a monkey took his horse.

With trembling legs, he walked to the front door. The lights of palaces and embassies are unlike lights anywhere else, and they sparkle as if someone had learned how to capture winter stars. The sound of a full orchestra poured out the doors, and Alessandro could see white flashes as gowns waltzed by, led or pursued by slim black suits with sashes that ran from shoulder to thigh. A hundred people were waltzing in a huge circle in a cavernous white hall that looked like an inside-out wedding cake, as others milled slowly about the edges, so that eventually everyone would get a chance to talk to everyone else.

Alessandro was the only man with neither sash nor medal. The servants had bright cummerbunds that tied off into sashes, little girls in white gowns and red shoes sported regal-looking ribbons, and the women were dizzying concoctions of cloth, flesh, and jewels. The way they moved in the waltz, like windblown waves, added greatly to their appeal, especially when they were contrasted to the strange, skinny, humpbacked dowagers who wore diamond tiaras, moved with great stiffness, and whose pale flesh was slightly gray with disease.

The music swelled into a delirium as an ecstatic percussionist overplayed the little instruments that imitated the sounds of trilling songbirds. The more birds, the better. Their song, even if the product of a demented musician twisting wooden screws, was beautiful. The lights on the chandeliers and candelabra multiplied and danced a thousandfold in happy crystal icicles that made the room of white columns sparkle like a mountain village in the snow.

Alessandro was faced with someone he took to be a military attaché—a man in polished boots, scarlet pants, a white jacket with a gold collar, and a red-and-white sash. He had a lot of medals.

"I'm sorry, I don't think we've met," the attaché said.

"Giuliani, Alessandro."

"Ah!" said the military man, for whom Alessandro was as much a surprise as if he had sprung from the head of Zeus. "We're so delighted you could come. Please enjoy yourself. And why shouldn't you? You're the youngest man here." After saying this he tried to wink. "Many unattached women are about, and if you get them dancing fast enough you can outrun their chaperons, who stand on the sidelines, heads bobbing and eyes blinking, like owls. Do a lot of spinning. It dizzies them. Then you can go with the young woman into the garden."

Alessandro was happy to have found in such a place a man to whom he could speak frankly. Obviously it was because he was a soldier. And because Alessandro knew no one among the guests, he grabbed the attaché by the elbow and pulled him to the side.

"Look," he confided, "I've never been to something like this. I'd much rather be on my horse. What shall I do?"

"When?"

"In general."

The attaché pondered the question. "You're nervous?" Alessandro shook his head. Now that he had a friend, he was not as nervous as he had been before, but he was still extremely uncomfortable. "You needn't worry. I'll watch out for you."

"May I sit next to you at dinner?"

"One is seated according to protocol."

Alessandro looked disappointed.

"But don't worry. All you have to do is walk into the crowd, take a glass of champagne, and look for someone whose face you like. Time and events will do the rest."

"And if I meet the ambassador do I call him Excellency, Your Highness, Baron?"

"No."

"What do I call him?"

"You don't call him anything."

"What if I have to address him?" Alessandro was now more at ease, if only because ten minutes had passed and he was functioning quite well. In fact, though he thought that he was imagining it, it seemed that all eyes were upon him.

"If you have to address him, call him Zoltán. That's his name."

"They'd throw me out."

"Are you sure? He's just a man. He has a son your age. He, too, was once a student. Call him Zoltán."

Alessandro bent close to his friend's ear. "*Zoltán* is such a strange name. In Italian it sounds ridiculous, like the name of a Persian god, or a company that makes electric motors."

"I know, I know. Now why don't you just go in and find a pretty girl. I have to greet people. I'll see you later on."

Alessandro moved confidently toward the circle of delirious dancers, deftly snatching a glass of champagne from a silver tray on the upraised hand of a speeding waiter. The instant he grasped the thin crystal stem he was surrounded by a single gigantic woman in a sparkling dress. She was at least a head taller, with a jaw that had been copied from the bow of a trireme. And yet she had beautiful hazel eyes, a long straight nose, and strong white teeth. Furthermore, although she was large, she was well proportioned. Her breasts were three-quarters exposed, and her décolleté made them taut enough for an observer to monitor not just her breathing, but her heartbeat. She had had two bottles of champagne.

"Let me guess your nationality," she said, backing him against a table of hors d'oeuvres as if she were going to arrest him. Her rapidly rising and falling bosom was right in his face. He felt like someone who goes to an ocean promontory on a stormy day and stands with his feet in jeopardy of the sea. "You're Czech!"

Alessandro shook his head.

"British!"

Again, he had to shake his head.

"You can't hide from me. I've spotted you," she said, pressing her lower body upon his as if she were a construction worker fitting something to a wall. "I'm not a little chicken, but you've conquered me completely. You, like me, are Bulgarian."

"I'm Italian."

She blinked.

"Is it true," she asked, as if she were talking about politics, "that young Italian men do not make love to women until marriage?"

"They do, but only upside down."

Her puzzlement gave way to a sort of growl, and she thrust her face toward his. "A woman twice your age," she said in such a way as to numb him, "might want to keep you in her bed for several days on end." She looked coyly at the ceiling. "I usually get up at one or two."

"In the afternoon?"

"My husband is in Trieste, and I am at Via Massimo, one forty."

The next he knew, she was gone. Encountering a group of people she had undoubtedly seen a dozen times in the previous week, she greeted them as if she and they had met by accident at the North Pole.

Alessandro thought that he was not doing so badly, since he had already survived for half an hour and made two friends. He turned to face the table over which he had leaned so far backward.

Many glasses of champagne, fifty shrimp, and a score petits fours later, he left to find a face that he liked. He now understood how one could tolerate conversations atomized into measly little snuppins and snidgets, how men could dance with crane-like dowagers, and women with men who were as fat as barrels of Turkish olive oil.

He eavesdropped along the perimeter of the dancing. People spoke of places to which he had never been, things that he could not afford, figures of whom he had not heard, and accomplishments that he found hard to believe. The duchesses and diplomats fabricated as much as laborers in a tavern. Alessandro remembered that his father had said, "Of all people on earth, only merchants tell the truth, but only when they are talking to each other, and sometimes not even then."

A bewigged servant made his way through the crowd, ringing a silver bell. The orchestra stopped and a long line of guests began to move toward the dining room.

Though the musicians rested, the percussionist who worked the bird machines was unable to stop, and the guests filed ahead like the huntsmen in one of Uccello's dark green forests. Two servants on each side of the door held engraved leather seating boards—diagrams of the long table, with name cards matched to the seats.

An ancient Neapolitan couple came to the sign. "De Felice," the man declared.

"Onorevole Dottore Fabio De Felice," one of the servants said, indicating a position fairly close to the ambassador's wife, who was at one end of the table, *"e la signora."* He held his hand over a place across the table exactly as far away from the ambassador as the husband was from the ambassador's wife.

"Giuliani," Alessandro said, not quite believing they would have remembered his name and place.

"Il Signor Alessandro Giuliani," the servant intoned, and pointed to a card solidly in the middle of the long table.

"That says, *De Sanctis, Maria,*" Alessandro stated.

The servant peered over the board to scan the cards, reading upside down. He pronounced the names in a panic that resembled the recitations of an embezzler trying to cover his tracks.

"Er war eine Veränderung," another servant instructed, pointing to the card that represented Alessandro. *"Pardon."*

Alessandro was to be seated at the left side of the ambassador, across from the ambassador of France. "It's a mistake," he said.

The servants checked their cards. "No, sir," one ventured. "The baroness herself moved the card."

"It's impossible," Alessandro declared.

The right eye of one of them started to wink involuntarily while the left side of his mouth collapsed inward.

As Alessandro walked toward the end of the table he was not so surprised to see that the ambassador was the kindly military fellow with the gold collar and white jacket.

Seated directly on Alessandro's left was Lia Bellati. Her hair was up, she wore an emerald necklace, and her gown was so blue that Alessandro thought of the Atlantic. He believed that the world was not constructed this way, and that, if it were, his luck was sure to turn. "Zoltán!" he said in a voice that was pleasant, authoritative, unwavering, and deep, and that was so difficult to summon that he nearly fell off his chair as he sat down.

The ambassador shook Alessandro's hand. "Good to see you, Alessandro," he said. "The last time we met, everything was different."

Then he introduced Alessandro to the French ambassador, who was deeply disturbed that he did not know the identity of the young man opposite him, undoubtedly a prince or a musical prodigy. The French ambassador racked his brain so hard to figure out who Alessandro was that he began to resemble a beehive.

Alessandro turned to Lia and found that he had to do all he could do to restrain himself from kissing her. Her eyes sparkled, and the ocean-blue dress and emerald necklace framed her young face so beautifully that he ignored the representatives of the great powers.

"How did you do it?" Alessandro asked.

"My brother," she answered, glancing diagonally across the table at a young man in the military uniform of Italy. His face was kind, and stronger than Alessandro's in every detail, perhaps because he had been tested as Alessandro had not been. One could tell merely by looking at him that he was not only an excellent shot, but one of those people who in war are usually untouched. "He arranged the invitations," Lia said, "but we had no idea that you already knew the ambassador, who just told me that, despite protocol, his wife never once has failed to put you directly on his left."

"Who cares about him?" Alessandro asked.

A servant in livery removed the gold-rimmed plate that had been holding Alessandro's name card, and put one exactly like it in its place. Alessandro wondered why he hadn't simply removed the card.

"These cards can have filthy edges," Lia said as she watched his expression during the substitution.

The cutlery and china arrayed in front of Alessandro made a small city, behind which was a toy mountain range of crystal—five forks, three knives, half a dozen spoons, three napkins, four wine glasses, a champagne glass, and a water goblet. Each place had before it three decanters—for red wine, white wine, and water. This, it seemed, was the custom of the imperial family.

As the soup was brought in, the orchestra (which had relocated in an aerial bower in back of the baroness) began to play the various Viennese bird delirium waltzes that had encouraged Alessandro to eat his hors d'oeuvres rhythmically. He began to sway, but then, when he realized that the musicians were soft-pedaling the music, he soft-pedaled too, wanting to avoid disastrous mistakes. His confidence was growing, and the relief that he felt for having survived so rigorous a social test brought him not just ease, but rapture.

"What's the soup?" he asked the ambassador point-blank. "It's the best soup I've ever tasted."

"It has a special ingredient," the ambassador answered.

"What is that?"

"All the champagne you've been drinking in the past hour." He leaned over and whispered so that neither the French ambassador nor anyone else could hear. "I don't drink anything, so that I can talk politics and keep secrets, and from my position of sobriety I don't think the soup is so good. I've had better soup in the army during maneuvers, and everyone knows that in the army they cook with horse piss."

Alessandro choked on his soup.

"Say to me this funny," the French ambassador called out from across the table.

"No."

"Why not?"

"I don't want to provoke an incident."

"Zoltán," the French ambassador answered, harking back to their previous conversation, "the only incidents we have to fear are those between your friends the Germans, and the Italians."

"How do you mean?" asked Alessandro, in his capacity as the highest-ranking Italian in the conversation.

"The poor Germans," the French ambassador declared with perfect Gallic sarcasm, "are really heartsick for colonies. We've seen them trying to establish a foothold in North Africa: we've seen them fail. And they'll continue to fail, because they lack naval bases in the Mediterranean, and probably would not choose war in Europe for the sake of acquiring colonies. For that very reason they won't best us and they have no chance against the British. They have a chance only against *you*."

"Me?"

"Italy."

"How?"

"In Cyrenaica and Tripolitania."

"No, I don't think so," the Baron Károly offered. "The Germans have no interest in that wasteland. Besides, it would displease us enormously."

"They may have no interest now, but as they probe along the coast and we stand our ground in Morocco, Algeria, and Tunisia, and as the British hold fast in Egypt, where will they go?"

"But they're not probing."

"German gunboats passed Gibraltar yesterday," the French ambassador said. "Of course, they may only be trying to get some sun."

"By whom was this reported?"

"The British. It hasn't appeared yet in the press. It will. We would have spotted them ourselves, eventually. I meant to ask you, tonight, if you knew anything about it, since they're *your* friends."

"It's the first I've heard."

"They're not scheduled for port calls in Trieste or Dubrovnik?"

The ambassador of Austria-Hungary shook his head. "I would know."

Astounded to have been included in just the conversation that he had wanted, Alessandro said, "This sounds to me like an incident between Germany and Austria, not Germany and Italy."

"No," the French ambassador replied. "Italy will react, fearing for Cyrenaica and Tripolitania—the weak spot on the North African coast. It may provoke a war between Italy and Turkey."

Though outside the conversation, Lia nodded.

"Turkey?" Alessandro asked.

"Italy will have to pre-empt in Libya," the Baron Károly stated, "to protect its interests. My guess is that before the year is up you will declare war on the Sultan."

"Not if I have anything to say about it," Alessandro said.

Perhaps because they were so used to listening to conversations between potentates, the ambassadors felt reflexively that Alessandro was speaking on behalf of Italy. Rather than saying, "But you don't," the French ambassador asked, "Why not?"

"Nothing in Libya is worth a war," Alessandro said. Finally, his command of rhetoric, coupled with the power of his voice, silenced a dinner table in an embassy.

Lia's brother spoke up. "That's not so," he said. "Italy has developed Libya over the years. There are mineral deposits of great value, and the agricultural potential allows the surplus population of the south somewhere to go. And what about our honor, not to mention the right to a colony in Africa, our history there, the problem of access to the canal, and the complete inacceptability of a German naval base off our shores."

Alessandro answered, spurred on because so many people were listening to him.

"Captain," he said, respectfully, "Libya is Ottoman territory. We are there as guests, and all the effort we have expended in the last ten years is not equal to half the new construction on the Via del Corso alone. Although you say that the mineral deposits are of great value, you might better have said that they have great skill, for they hide so well under the ground that no one has yet been able to find them.

"As for Libya's agricultural potential—something that is severely prejudiced by the fact that nothing grows there—when the day comes that an Italian of the South will leave his dry and rocky soil for sand, then perhaps it will be wise to war against the Sultan. These people are going to America, where they will continue to go whether or not we fight Turkey, in that respect making our fight with Turkey rather pointless.

"And our history is such that were we to follow it in making policy we should declare war not only on our former possessions in Libya, but on Britain, Spain, Germany, France, Austria, and Carthage. Perhaps we can prevent the establishment of a German naval base to the south not by declaring war on Turkey, which seems rather a roundabout way of doing it, but by informing the Germans that it would be *casus belli*. And as for our honor, honor is a complex and important matter best served by doing the right thing."

"Better to go to war with Germany later than with Turkey now?" Lia's brother asked.

"Better to go to war with neither."

"Better to *risk* war with Germany, later, than to win a war against Turkey now?" the captain pressed.

"Who said we would win?"

"I assure you, we would win, and I am not able to offer such assurances regarding Germany."

"As far as I can see," Alessandro said, "it would be far more sensible to let the Germans build a naval base in Libya, if that's what they want, and build three naval bases in the boot of Italy to overwhelm it. That way we'd have nothing to worry about, we'd be stronger, and we'd avoid wasting blood and money in a war."

"Maneuver," the captain said, "is far more important than mass or balance. You've neglected maneuver for the sake of equation. In war and in the competition between states, position is everything."

"Ah yes," said an Englishman, in superb German. "Give me a proper platform, and I will move the world!"

Because no one could tell precisely when the English chose to be sarcastic, those who sided with Alessandro assumed that the Englishman was mocking what Lia's brother had said, and those who sided with Lia's brother believed that he was in agreement.

The baroness took advantage of this and started half a dozen conversations on half a dozen subjects all at once. Leaving the Mediterranean, the two ambassadors began to talk about Russia.

Alessandro sat back in his chair and turned the color of a plum. Overcome with pride and embarrassment, he was too young to know that the question was still open: he thought that he had settled it.

Then he went on to discover that diplomatic dinners have many courses, and that he was mistaken not to have imitated the ambassadors and Lia, who merely tasted each serving. Instead, spurred by triumph, he ate almost everything that was served to him, and after fourteen courses and three desserts he felt so heavy that he was not sure Enrico would be able to bear his weight.

That and the champagne forced him to sit in a chair, like an old man, and watch Lia glide about the floor in waltzes that seemed to last forever. The trick, it seemed, was not to eat so much that you couldn't work it off in dancing immediately thereafter. Lia was waltzing with a soldier. Alessandro would dance with her later. Now he had the privilege of apprehending her beauty from afar, and though he had very little experience to tell him so, he felt that this was better because it was more likely to last into time. She moved like a cloud.

LIA AND her brother left the Palazzo Venezia at eleven-thirty. As Alessandro stood on the cobbles and watched them get into a carriage, he wondered if he would marry her. She was exquisite, and he feared that he was blinded to everything else, that he was drawn to her by weakness, that his passion for her was incomplete. Knowing all too well the deeply religious love of the Italian poets for women they had merely seen on the street, he feared that his infatuation for Lia could never be compared to the elemental union that can occur between men and women when God is present and light surrounds them.

He knew very well that love could be like the most beautiful singing, that it could make death inconsequential, that it existed in forms so pure and strong that it was capable of reordering the universe. He knew this, and that he lacked it, and yet as he stood in the courtyard of the Palazzo Venezia, watching diplomats file quietly out the gate, he was content, for he suspected that to command the profoundest love might in the end be far less beautiful a thing than to suffer its absence.

Once, high in the Julian Alps, he and his father had watched a flock of birds scatter in the presence of an eagle. As the eagle moved with uncanny slowness, like a great battleship confidently steaming far offshore, and the birds scattered to bait the eagle away from their young, Alessandro's father said, "Their souls, at this moment, are full, and the eagle is nothing. God is with them for what they lack."

His reverie interrupted by the return of his horse, who was happy to be brought up from unfamiliar stables, he mounted, and Enrico cantered out the gate into the warm spring night.

It was a Wednesday. Rome was quiet. They went on the Via del Corso all the way to the Piazza del Popolo, but instead of turning to cross the Tiber and make their way home they galloped into the Viale del Muro Torto and through the Porta Pinciana to the small triangle of land for which the attorney Giuliani had traded the garden. Looking over the empty lots and undistinguished buildings, Alessandro suddenly realized that if he married Lia he could keep the garden. If the union would put to right the question of a garden on the Gianicolo, then perhaps other balances, too, would be set to right.

As they rode homeward along the Villa Medici in the cool night air, under stars brighter than in any city of Europe, Alessandro heard an orchestra. Even hours earlier, this would have been a shock, an orchestra playing in the open air, and as he drew closer he heard singing. In the garden of the French Academy, a full orchestra accompanied singers in the *"Ma di'..."* from *Norma.* Alessandro tied Enrico to an iron window grate embedded in the wall, and used it as a ladder to get over the top.

Though it was almost midnight, neither the singers nor the musicians showed any signs of exhaustion, and by the time Alessandro dropped into the garden, perfectly camouflaged in his formal clothes, they had finished the aria and started up again. If the Austrians could impale themselves ecstatically upon Strauss, the French were equally capable of a delirium spurred by *Norma,* even if in both cases the singers and musicians were Italian. They left *Norma* and jumped to *Ernani* and then to *"Ecco la barca,"* from *La Gioconda,* and all the while, hundreds of people wandered through the gardens. Perhaps because this was the French Academy, scores of them were attractive women. In respect to this, the embassy in the Palazzo Venezia (apart from Lia) was hopeless. Alessandro wondered why he hadn't come here rather than to the dinner. The music was better, the atmosphere less formal, the fellows of the academy and their guests not too much older than he. As the singers led the orchestra in *"Già nella notte densa..."* Alessandro felt every atom of the cool night air.

Though the wide paths in the garden of the Villa Medici were lit by wavering torches, the fountain was illuminated by half a dozen electric lights. Somewhere beyond the residence, unseen, an engine turned a generator in unfailing circles to make the current that made the light. During pauses in the music, if one listened carefully, one could hear its steady optimistic sound.

Whereas the waltzes of the Austrian embassy were wonderfully pleasurable, the singing in the garden of the Villa Medici had led him deep into speculation. He walked slowly amid the guests of the French Academy, seeking anchors for his racing thought—a dark waving branch with waxen leaves, a sight of the stars through a cut in the trees, a girl throwing back her hair to the irresistible rhythm of the song, a concordance of colors compressed in a torchlit line of sight, the stirrings of women in their silken clothing.

Not far from the fountain, out of Alessandro's sight, were three girls who looked like they might have been models for Fragonard, one of the academy's previous residents, in that they seemed not only to reflect light, but, somehow, to hold and perhaps even to generate it.

Younger than the youngest of the fellows, they did not know quite what to do. They talked for show even when too far from anyone to be overheard, because they accurately sensed that, however awkwardly, they were beginning to play a part.

First in line as they paused to watch the reflections in the water was Jeannette, the youngest daughter of one of the residents. Second was Isabelle, the daughter of a second secretary in the French embassy. And last was Ariane, the daughter of an Italian doctor and a Frenchwoman. She could turn from French to Italian as fast as a swallow could change directions, and she had studied Latin, Greek, and English enough to navigate in them largely without mistakes.

She was the youngest, but she stood out among the other girls because of her beauty. When she was a child the physical characteristics that would later make her very beautiful were so striking that she seemed to have been almost homely. Only someone of long experience might have seen breathtaking beauty awkwardly sleeping in what appeared to have been catastrophically misaligned features—the broad expanses of her cheeks and her forehead, the independent energy of her eyes, the painfully beautiful arch of her brows, the smile that, even at a distance, even in memory, filled anyone who had seen it with love and paralyzing pleasure.

Throughout her childhood she had thought that she was ugly, and though all the evidence would later militate against her earliest conclusions, she could never abandon them, and she, more beautiful than any woman Alessandro had ever seen in life, in painting, in photographs, lived with the conviction that she was less than plain, and went about with the discomfort of someone who is embarrassed to be seen. She never quite believed, even later, when she had heard many protestations to the contrary, that when people stared at her it was not because they thought she was hideous, and this made her beautiful almost beyond belief.

Jeannette, Isabelle, and Ariane circled the fountain, walking as slowly as they could without halting at each step, and talking as enthusiastically as if everyone were listening to them as they moved upon a lighted stage. They spoke about Aix-en-Provence. To hear them you would have thought that Aix-en-Provence was not only the capital of France and perhaps even Europe (or at least the Holy Roman Empire), but a French Valhalla.

Young girls in Paris spoke this way about Deauville, Biarritz, or Nice, and young girls elsewhere spoke this way about Paris, but these three, not knowing Paris, had to settle for Aix. They sounded both conspiratorial and blasé, to convince themselves and others that they were on to something. They alternated experimentally between the two states, trying to find the proper voice.

When Jeannette described an afternoon by a waterfall, she did so with erotic luxury. The girls and boys had been captivated with the idea of catching speckled trout that hovered in the waist-deep pools, and had gone in, in their clothing, at first only up to the knee, but then up to the waist, and eventually, slowly, they were diving under the water in pursuit of the fish, and emerging with their hair matted down and fresh cold water running from it, sparkling in the sun. The girls' summer dresses clung to them, showing their breasts and nipples. The boys had taken off their shirts. They lost their sense of time, which, Jeannette said, is what happens in the water, and soon began to embrace and waltz together in the cold stream, holding on for love and warmth. It would have been even more scandalous, Jeannette declared, had someone not caught a trout now and then, and, in doing so, broken the spell.

"Were you on the bank watching this?" Ariane asked, for Jeannette had been the youngest.

"No," Jeannette answered, as if confessing that her life had been ruined by indiscretion. "I was in the water," she said, lying, "I was in someone's arms."

"Whose?" Isabelle asked, burning with curiosity. Jeannette would not and could not tell.

Perhaps because she was too tall and had a spray of freckles, Isabelle expected to be eventually like her mother, the mistress more of a house than to a man. She had her eye on a farmhouse on a hill, with orchards and vineyards. Someday, she said, she would redo it, and she described rooms and new fabrics as if her heart were breaking in slow motion from the thought of substituting such things for love, although the house would be next to a river, her children would swim there, and perhaps their lives would be ideal.

When Isabelle and Jeannette had twice remembered the bakery, and three times the cafe where they sat with their friends and drank wine, they turned to Ariane to bring in something new, to show why Aix was the superior place that made them fascinating because they had been there.

Though she tried, Ariane couldn't do it. "I love the light in Aix," she said, but, even though she did, her heart was not in it. "And the fields. My father and I walked through the fields every day last summer, almost every day."

One refrained from mentioning parents unless it was to lie about their youthful characteristics that one presumed would soon be handed down, or to drop offhandedly a hint about their wealth, or whom they knew.

"What did you talk about?" Jeannette asked, almost cruelly.

"Everything," Ariane said. She was only sixteen, and though she understood everything Alessandro understood, she had not formulated it. She was in no way glib, except when coasting on the seas of her many languages.

"Like what?" Isabelle asked.

"My mother," Ariane answered.

Knowing that Ariane had lost her mother, Jeanette and Isabelle realized that they had come to a dead end.

They kept walking, all three desperately trying to think of another line to follow, not least Ariane. Her love for her mother had welled up, as it often did, and made her conversation that evening, her walk around the fountain, her gown, her aspirations, ambitions, and all that she wanted in life, a betrayal. In an accidental test of loyalty, she was filled with love and blinded to everything around her.

She felt the world fall away, as she knew someday it would entirely, and she felt nothing but love for the woman who had died when Ariane was twelve years old, for the woman who, in dying, was broken and tortured because she was leaving her family forever, but happy that it was she who was dying and neither her husband nor daughter.

Alessandro had been pacing at exactly the speed of Isabelle, Jeannette, and Ariane, hidden from them by the plume of the fountain as perfectly as the speculative planet on the other side of the sun, the twin to earth, that cannot be seen. But then, as the songs of the three singers met in the air to create a fourth, more beautiful even than the others, arising as if by magic, he had turned on his heels and begun to walk counterclockwise.

He looked up. Standing before him was a young girl, in tears.

IN JANUARY of 1911, in the library in Bologna where Alessandro did most of his work, it was often cold enough to see breath turn white. One afternoon, an hour or so before darkness, only a few scholars were in the reading room, which was so enormous that a large woodstove heated only a shallow layer of air near the ceiling. With his legs pressed together to conserve heat, and his collar buttoned up around his neck, Alessandro was bent over half a dozen volumes spread out on a long table. He often read six books at once, not because he enjoyed it, but to check one against the other and to compare arguments and accounts. The truth was often great enough to cover in its self-contradictory expanse at least six points of view, and where one was weak or incomplete the others continued the narrative. Alessandro examined the books as if they were witnesses, and despite having to turn pages back and forth almost continuously to bring various incidents into alignment, he employed this technique to considerable advantage, for the compilation of accounts seemed to yield a product rather than a sum.

But to read six books at once he had to study very hard, and no time was left for social affairs. He had few friends, and, when not forgotten, he was considered eccentric. In fact, he was always at the brink of being asked to leave the university. Never had he hesitated to challenge a professor, for he believed that the only authority was what was right. "The best chance you have, if you want to rise," his father had said, "is to give yourself up to loneliness, fear nothing, and work hard."

"Are you Giuliani?" someone asked from across the ancient table where Alessandro was working, but he had whispered so softly that Alessandro hadn't heard.

"Giuliani?"

Alessandro looked up. Sitting across from him was someone who looked English but who spoke in unaccented Italian.

"Yes?"

"Do you know Lia Bellati?"

"Yes."

"It's more than that."

"More than what?"

"Never mind what I already know. In Bologna, someone with whom her family is acquainted is in trouble. Will you help? He has very few friends, and he could use one now."

"I don't have many friends, either," Alessandro said.

"That's perfect."

"I don't know who he is, and I don't know who you are."

"I came to see you because I heard that you once fought two *carabinieri.*"

Alessandro put down his pen. "They chased me."

"They fired, and you kept going?"

"Do you see that as an accomplishment?"

"Most people would have stopped dead."

Alessandro turned up his hands. "What do you want from me?"

"You have here quite a few students who are monarchists."

"Of course we do. They don't study—they march, put up posters, and fight duels. I confess that I don't understand them, given that we already have a king."

"They want to make him into a god."

"He's too short."

"That won't stop them."

"Maybe not, but because of all that interbreeding, I think, he looks like a Calabrian hill dwarf. They have their work cut out for them."

"And they'll make a lot of trouble on the way."

"So?"

"They have a fencing club. The twenty in the club have found a Jew in the Faculty of Law."

"Considering how many Jews are in the Faculty of Law, that isn't very impressive, is it."

"They talk about killing him."

"Why?"

"He's from Venice. His mother is German. They think he's disloyal."

"To what?"

"To Italy."

"That's almost impossible. Is he?"

"No. He's apolitical, and if he were political he would probably be quite unexceptional."

"Why don't *you* help him?"

"If one Jew comes to the aid of another, it won't matter."

Alessandro was puzzled. The cloud of his breath died in the air.

"They can always outnumber us, and they know it, but a Christian . . . My friend lives on the Via Piave, number sixteen, top floor. Tonight they're going to push him out on the street and beat him."

"What about the police?"

"I went to them. They knew about it already, and they didn't care."

"How is Lia connected to this? You know her, and he knows her, and you all seem to know each other. . . . She's a Jewess?"

"Yes. Our friend's name is Raffaello Foa. They think that his father is a banker in league with the Austrians."

"Is he?" Alessandro asked, closing his six books two at a time.

"He's a butcher."

"So why doesn't this Rafi tell that to the monarchists?"

The other student smiled with a bitterness that Alessandro had never seen in someone so young. "It would make no difference," he said.

The park was silent but for the slow burn of gently falling snow. Not far from where he lived was a gunsmith's shop, and Alessandro had often stared at the pistols, shotguns, and hunting equipment in the window, and he had once seen the gunsmith draw a pistol through the protective iron bars without troubling to unlock them.

In the dark, the streets were deserted and the shutters were shut. The snow had driven everyone inside, and wood fires from a hundred chimneys made the air sweet with the smell of soft-woods from Finland and Russia.

Alessandro was too scared to take much in. His peripheral vision had fled and his heart was running away with him when he raised his leg and kicked the glass with the heel of his boot. The window collapsed with a sound that Alessandro thought would be heard in Naples. He pulled a pistol through the bars and put it in his coat.

"Walk calmly," he whispered to himself. No one came.

As he vanished into the park he was still frightened, but now he knew he had a good chance of protecting Raffaello Foa, who should have either gotten his own gun or stayed in Venice. It would soon be over, and then, if he were lucky, Alessandro would go home and bury himself under his down quilt for at least fourteen hours. The next day, the sun would have melted the snow and would be evaporating the small streams that trickled over the cobblestones.

Number 16 Via Piave was a dark building with not a single light visible through its shuttered windows. As Alessandro stood silently before it he heard a distant thunderstorm. Thunder hardly ever came in snow, and the thought of lightning bolts striking blindly through cold gray air made Alessandro look up. The sky held no flashes, but only the rumble of thunder, and everything rattled. Alessandro felt his chest vibrate with each concussion, and though he would hear them many times again, lashing out from hidden places in the snow-choked air as if they were calling him and his generation to things so stunning and unexpected that no one had even begun to imagine them, the concussions were so far away and so unworldly that they seemed not to be real.

He felt his way to the stairs, and as he walked up the four flights cracks of thunder shook the skylight. The higher he rose, the lighter it got, and at the top the whitened glass, brushed by snow and vibrating like a snare drum, lit everything in its glow.

The door was answered by a tall young man of Alessandro's age, whose cheekbones were so high and eyes so slanted that it made Alessandro think of Tamerlane. The very height of the man (he had to bend his head in the doorway) and his expression made Alessandro wonder why he, Alessandro, had presumed to protect him, for he looked the match of all the monarchists and anarchists in Italy.

"Are you Italian?" Alessandro asked.

"Yes, I'm Italian. Are you?"

"You look like one of the Golden Horde," Alessandro told him.

"Magyar," Rafi Foa answered, "and some German, and some Russian, and all Jew, if that's what you're driving at, or even if it isn't."

"I wasn't driving at it."

In Rafi's room a wood fire burned in a small terra cotta stove. Books and notebooks were spread out between two kerosene lamps on a tremendous library table. A bed was in one corner. Apart from a bookshelf and a chair, the room held nothing else.

"You can sit in the chair," Rafi said after they had introduced themselves.

Rafi had heard nothing of the monarchists, and though he took note of what Alessandro said he was neither frightened nor surprised.

"Do you know him?" Alessandro asked, referring to the go-between. "He had blue eyes, straight brown hair, and a red face. He looked English."

"I don't know him. Perhaps he's a monarchist."

"How do you know Lia?"

"I met her brother a few years ago, when he was stationed near Venice. We included him in our *minyan*—prayers. I stayed with the Bellatis in Rome, once when he was there and the other time when he was in Sardinia. These military people get around."

They heard the sound of people coming up the stairs.

"What are you going to do?" Alessandro asked. "I have this." From his coat he withdrew a hunting pistol with a long barrel and a heavy handle. "It isn't loaded, but they won't know."

"Unless they happen to have one, too," Rafi said. "Take it with you. Go to the stairs that lead to the roof."

"What about you?"

"God will protect me."

"God?" Alessandro asked in amazement. Whoever was on the stairs had almost reached the top floor, too close now for Alessandro to escape unseen. "They think your father is in league with the Austrians."

"My father?"

"Yes. They think he's a banker."

From a drawer in the library table Rafi took a prayer shawl that he threw over his shoulders. Except in engravings, Alessandro had never seen a Jew at prayer. For him it was as startling as the approach of the monarchists.

"My father is a butcher," Rafi said, "in league with the housewives of Venice."

"Aren't you going to fight?" Alessandro asked.

Rafi opened a prayer book, stood to his full height, and kissed it. Just as they banged on the door, he began to pray, and as he started to sway back and forth Alessandro stepped behind the curtain that served as the door of the closet.

Shattering the cast-iron latch, five young men broke into the room. Flanked by the flickering kerosene lamps, uttering his prayers, looming over them, Rafi frightened them more than they frightened him, but they had come with a plan, and would overcome their fear, seize him, and strike him down. "Are you Raffaello Foa?" they asked, as if his confirmation would justify what they were going to do. Continuing in his strange prayer, he refused to answer.

Alessandro knew that they would attack the material before they would touch the flesh. They would strip him of his prayer shawl and cap, and when he was like them and they were no longer afraid, punish him for having made them fear.

They scattered the books and tore them in pieces. Before this was over, someone had grabbed the shawl and ripped it away. Rafi refused to look at them even when they began to hit him. They held their breath and punched him as hard as they could. They battered his chest, his arms, and his head.

He remained standing, repeating one phrase over and over. Propped against the table, he refused to go down. His face was covered with blood, and when they hit him the blood flew off him and spattered against the walls. They hit him in the back, the kidneys, in his ribs, his genitals. They kicked his legs. But he refused to go down.

"Jewish bankers run this country!" one of them shouted. "But no more, no more."

Rafi was still muttering, his eyes closed, when one of the students who were beating him took from his coat a sheathed saber and began to strike him with it as if he were hitting a canvas bag hung from a beam in a fencing atelier. Rafi twirled, spitting his own blood, and fell over the table, where he lay between the lamps, still moving and still muttering.

As the student with the saber grasped it with both hands and slowly raised it, Alessandro emerged from behind and hit him on the back of the head with a sideways stroke of the pistol, opening his scalp and knocking him to the floor.

With the pistol in both hands, Alessandro backed around the table. When he cocked the hammer, the click echoed from the walls and ceiling.

He thought they would leave, but one of them slowly opened his coat, put his hand inside, and took out his own pistol. Alessandro didn't know what to do. The thunder was barely audible and the wind had come up just enough to shriek a little in the cracks of the windows. He held.

"The Jews are allied with the . . ."

"Shut up!" Alessandro shouted, tensing so that he looked as if he were about to fire. "The problem with the Jews, isn't it, is that they aren't allied with *anyone.*"

The thunder persisted. Alessandro had no idea that thunder, muffled in wild snow, sounded exactly like artillery. He held his position because it was all he could do, and the monarchists backed down.

YOUNG SINGERS of little experience and old ones of poor voice often found themselves in Bologna in a theater that was supported by huge trusses and timbers arrayed against its bulging outer walls. The architectural decorations on the façade of this doomed opera house had been so worn down by wind and water that the devils were toothless, the gargoyles faceless, and the cornices round, but Italy had always been full of buildings that seemed just about to fall down, and this one, in its timber girdle, waited until Alessandro had left the city.

Three times a week, Rossini and Verdi marshaled sufficient force and beauty to shut the students up and bring them to the kind of rapt attention that the singers of La Scala thought the natural state of mankind. When one singer questioned another about a run in this theater, the query was, "For how long did you clear the air?" meaning for how many minutes in his aria was he able to rid the sky of the paper airplanes that crossed and collided over the orchestra in a traffic unlike any that had ever been seen on earth. They were sometimes ten and twenty layers deep, they would meander in circles, or zigzag, a hundred or more sailing about unimpeded.

Everyone kept his eye on his own craft or on a favorite. As the planes darted through the huge empty space, the singers looked out not only upon the missiles themselves but upon a thousand boys whose heads, as if in a completely anarchic tennis match, moved back and forth in many different directions—and not only back and forth, but slowly and gradually down. Singing there was like performing in a hospital for nervous diseases.

On occasion, one or more students who knew the lyrics and were gifted with powerful voices stood in their seats and competed with whatever wretch was unlucky enough to be onstage. Whether it was done as a compliment or in derision was immaterial. The result was the same. Worse, perhaps, was the unfolding of several hundred newspapers, signaling an insulting neutrality. Bombardment by eggs and vegetables, shouted insults, and the occasional shoe that landed next to a terrified soprano, were, of course, unambiguous.

But should a young singer with the heart and courage to face these things and keep on singing, sing well, a thousand boys as unruly as animals and as jumpy as unbroken horses or caffeinated bulls on a festival day, would suddenly become still. The house electrified, beyond the footlights a thousand faces would show expressions of sadness, longing, and desire, and some would sparkle back at the lights, in tracks that ran down the cheeks from bright eyes that caught the light. And when the aria ended, after a few seconds of silence the students would erupt into a roar of appreciation that put the audiences of major opera houses to shame.

After a lively overture with an orchestral signature attributable mainly to the fact that theatrical impresarios have known for ages that adolescents can be quieted by hunting horns, the curtain rose, crushing several paper gliders in its folds. An extraordinary painted backdrop glowed in the light. Giotto's blues and Caravaggio's shadows had been united to portray a tranquil forest in neither night nor day but, rather, in a condition of the spirit. In combination with the overture, the weak and dream-like blue, the clouds of dark green that marked the tops of the trees, and the motile and confusing shadows, several forms of art kept the students as quiet as the dead.

But not long after a group of obese 'hunters' had stepped from the trees and begun to sing, Alessandro noticed that the white objects had begun to glide down from the highest balconies. In the orchestra, with contempt for the fire laws, two students had set up a brazier and were grilling small cubes of meat. Alessandro leaned against what had once been the velvet-covered rail of the middle balcony, and smiled. He was thinking of the girl in the Villa Medici. Although she was too young, she was French, he didn't know her name, she had been surrounded by protective companions, and their encounter had been like a dream, she was more familiar to him than someone he had known all his life. When their eyes met he had felt immense gravity, as if fifty years had been compressed into ten seconds. He wasn't infatuated with her, but instead he loved her so quietly that he thought he would soon forget her, although when he considered the prospect of forgetting her his love for her grew, and this made him remember that heavy blizzards start as gentle and persistent snow.

In her absence, and in the absence of anyone like her, he was drawn to many things that, in being beautiful, were her allies— the blue of the stage-set in the floodlights, the grace of a cat as it turned its small lion-like face to question a human movement, a fire that blazed from within the dark of a blacksmith's shop or a baker's and caught his eye as he passed, a single tone arising from a cathedral choir to shock a jaded congregation with its unworldly beauty, the mountaintops as snow was lashed from them by blue winds, the perfect and uncontrived smile of a child. Upon such observations, because they came so thick and full, he had begun to build an arsenal of uncoordinated aesthetic principles. Though the system that was forming was not well in order, he trusted that as things progressed he would watch the images run together.

At the end of their song the hunters went offstage in disappointment, and then came several scenes that had not been composed for an audience that rocked back and forth in its seats like stir-crazed leopards in a zoo.

Alessandro leaned forward, eyes fixed upon the illuminated painting. As the air passed over the candles in the footlights and their flames struggled against it, differing light was thrown upon the rich forest.

"I've been tapping your shoulder for at least a minute," Rafi said to Alessandro.

Alessandro turned to squint into the darkness.

"You look rather dumb when you listen to music."

"You're well now?" Alessandro asked.

"Yes. I even played tennis. Can we talk here?" Rafi asked, as if it were a regular theater.

"We could fight a duel and no one would notice," Alessandro answered, "but let's go outside."

When they were sitting on a long flight of white marble steps from which they could see far out over the countryside surrounding Bologna, Alessandro asked, "Why didn't you fight?"

In the last year of his legal studies, Rafi could do anything he pleased with either a question or an answer. "I did fight," he said. "I fought as hard as I could, and I carry the wounds from it."

"*They* don't."

"That isn't my concern."

"A strange way of fighting."

"It binds me to what I seek."

"I suppose it does," Alessandro told him, "and if I hadn't been there with a pistol that I stole by smashing a store window, you would have been bound so close to what you seek that to see anything you would have had to look out."

"True," Rafi said, infuriatingly.

"Why haven't you learned to strike back?"

"As you may know," Rafi said, "the streets of Venice are made of water. Fights there tend to be very short, because after a few moments one of the combatants usually ends up in the canal. When I was young I was thrown off bridges and embankments a number of times."

"Look," said Alessandro, who had never been in a real fight in his life, "I can show you how to acquit yourself properly in physical combat." He considered the object of conversion. "You're tremendous, but you're probably not very strong. Size itself is unimportant: you have to exercise. Why are you smiling?"

"I'm rather strong, you see."

"Oh, I doubt it," the smaller of the two said pompously.

"For six months of the year I study law, but in the other six I work for my father."

"Slicing cutlets doesn't make a Hercules."

"My father doesn't have a butcher shop with a glass window and a display case. He's a wholesaler. His warehouse is the size of the Arsenal and he has a hundred and fifty employees. Most are cutters. Since cutting demands great skill and I was supposed to be a lawyer, there never was any reason for me to learn how to cut, so I carry and hang meat."

"How much?"

"Quarters."

"What do they weigh?"

"A hundred kilograms or more. You wear a blue coat with a hood. Before you carry, you flip the hood so your hair doesn't get bloody. You take the quarter off the hook, mount it on your back, and walk. If it's in the hold of an oceangoing ship you may walk for ten minutes before you get to the warehouse. Then you flip the carcass over your shoulder, hold it steady, and hang it. The meat can also come stacked. In that case you have to pick it up from the ground and hoist it onto your shoulders."

"So why didn't you pick up the monarchists and throw them down the stairs?"

"I've never done that sort of thing."

"Let me show you."

"All right," Rafi said, "show me."

"On the weekend," Alessandro answered, "if the weather is good."

They shook hands.

BECAUSE HE hadn't had the slightest notion of how to do it, Alessandro spent the next few days figuring out how to toughen up Rafi Foa, and on Sunday morning the two of them stood by the railroad tracks as a train approached from out of the winter sun. Not wanting to be seen by the engineers, they hid in the brush.

"What are we going to do?" Rafi asked.

"First we jump the train," Alessandro replied. "We climb onto the roof and run down to the caboose."

"Why?"

"So the men in the caboose will chase us over the roofs of the cars while the train is in motion."

"What if they catch us?"

"They won't: that's the purpose of the exercise."

"On a moving train, where can we possibly go to get away from them?"

"Ten kilometers out, a railroad bridge goes over the river. Imagine how surprised they'll be when we jump!"

"Imagine how surprised *I'll* be when we jump. It's January."

"Just do exactly as I do."

"Have you ever done this before?" Rafi asked apprehensively as the train rumbled forward, the sound of its engine shaking everything around them and penetrating their chests so that their voices vibrated.

"Of course," Alessandro said.

They ran alongside and caught on to a cattle car. "Climb up, as if it were a ladder," Alessandro yelled over the noise of the wheels.

They went straight up the open boards until they found themselves at the beginning of a rounded, slippery roof on which handholds were nonexistent.

"Now what?" Rafi screamed.

"Work your way to the corner," Alessandro said, improvising. They moved to the corner. "Keep your hands on the edges of the roof and go up while you walk on the cross beam."

"How can you put your feet there?" Rafi shouted as they were tossed around above the tracks. "It's not big enough and it's too high."

"It's big enough. You have to bend." Alessandro began to move across the end of the car. His hands were cut on the edges of the filthy metal roof, and it took every muscle in his body to keep from being thrown into the maw between cars. Rafi followed.

The noise was tremendous—thunderous booms when empty cars passed over uneven spots in the rail, steel grinding against steel as wheels strained against the track, the bedlamite rattling of unsprung empty boxcars moving at a rapid clip.

Smoke and cinders swept along the top of the train. Half the time Alessandro and Rafi had to shut their eyes, and the other half they spent in irritating tears. They could hardly breathe. If they had fallen between the cars, the dragging and cutting would have made them unrecognizable.

Alessandro looked at Rafi, whose face showed some strain. "Hoist yourself up," he said.

"I don't have enough of a hold," Rafi said desperately. "It's too high. I'll fall."

Alessandro didn't know if he could do it. His hands were slippery from sweat and blood. "You can do it. Put your hands over the top, like this," he said as he began to pull himself up.

His hands slipped, but when they slid back he clawed forward like a cat and pulled himself onto the roof. Then he grabbed Rafi's wrist and helped him through the same frantic motions until they both lay face down on the roof, breathing hard, sweating, filthy with soot, and covered with blood from their lacerated hands. The smoke sometimes covered them in nauseating black clouds.

"You do this all the time?" Rafi asked.

"When I can," Alessandro said, spitting out cinders and grease.

"You're crazy!" Rafi screamed.

"I know."

"What about tunnels?"

"Keep a sharp eye out for tunnels," Alessandro said, grateful to have been reminded. "At the first sign of a tunnel you have to hang between the cars. Otherwise, of course, you get scraped off the roof. There probably aren't any tunnels nearby, I would imagine." He stood up on the moving train. The wind, smoke, and sideways jolts of the freight car conspired to throw him off, but they couldn't accomplish the maneuver.

Rafi stood as Alessandro prepared to jump to the car behind them. "What happens if you fall off?" Rafi yelled.

"You don't!" Alessandro shouted before he made a running start and, with 'no apparent hesitation, sailed into the air. He came down on his right foot, on the roof of the next car, and didn't look back, assuming that Rafi was right behind, for in this operation Alessandro had no way to guide him other than by example.

As he gained speed in running along the tops of the cars it became progressively easier to clear the gaps. He would land with a feeling of joy that he would never forget. After the first five or ten times, he lost his fear and sprinted through the rushing air and smoke. Burning cinders hit the back of his neck. He heard the sound of Rafi's footsteps following.

They went forty cars, flying through the jumps with arms spread like wings to catch the steady and stabilizing air. The longer they were airborne, the happier they felt, and when they reached the caboose they began to pound the roof with their heels.

Three men raced onto the platform in the back of the caboose.

One was carrying a bottle of wine, and another a sandwich. When they saw two boys with crazed expressions and bloody clothes they began to shout and gesticulate, and the one with the bottle of wine waved it around in the wind as if it were a pistol.

"Is this the train to Rome?" Alessandro screamed through cupped hands. "Where's the dining salon? May I bring my poodle aboard if I put a cork in his ass?"

As Alessandro and Rafi laughed, the trainman with the wine bottle threw it, but it missed and smashed against an abutment. Another one tossed a sandwich at him as hard as he could, but it burst apart in the wind, and the ham wrinkled itself up at Rafi's feet. As Rafi tried to explain to the stunned railwaymen, in pantomime, that he was Jewish and didn't eat ham (the first part of the pantomime was to convey that he was circumcised) Alessandro grabbed him by the shoulder. "The bridge!" he shouted.

The bridge was as far above the water as twice the height of the train itself, and the river was running full and deep. The trainmen's jaws dropped when first Alessandro and then Rafi leapt off the roof, sailed through the air for a miraculously long time, and smashed into the water like stones.

The shock of the cold water was electric. It stanched their wounds and washed them clean of blood, sweat, and filth. When they surfaced, their throats were full of choking ice water and it was difficult to see, but the current carried them swiftly to a bend in the river and they swam to a sandy beach, where they climbed out.

As they trotted through the fields to keep from freezing to death, they felt that they could do anything. Alessandro said, "Most people don't do this, but it's what saves you. It tests you in the right way."

"Only for war," Rafi added.

"We'll almost certainly never have to go to war. It's unlikely that a war will break out in Europe, and even if it did it's less likely that Italy would be included, but I want to be prepared. And this is not just for war, you see, it's for everything."

ONE EVENING when Alessandro returned to his rooms he found a letter. It was written on the finest paper, in an authoritative and elegant hand. After removing his wet jacket, he lit the lamps and the fire. This was the kind of letter, he thought, that brings a new turn in life. As the room started to warm, he opened the envelope.

"Most Excellent Sir:" the letter began. "My life as a man upon the tiger world is rapidly drawing to a close. In seventy years of pain, I have been pushed about by one thing or another in the struggle to earn my livelihood, support my family, and continue the course upon which I have been thrown.

"As a young man I believed that with patience I would eventually become something like a king. I was convinced that I would sleep in a bedchamber five storeys high and fifty meters wide, that I would lead armies, that fate would elevate me to those high places from which life appears to be fast and beautiful.

"But my luck has been poor. The highest position I have attained has been that of chief of the old order scribes in your father's law office. The other old order scribes render me their obeisance, but this is far from what I expected, especially since they never obey me.

"This week I suffered the ultimate indignity. On Tuesday, your father brought into the office a machine that I believe is referred to as a 'typewriter.' Within a day, Antonio, a young man with a spastic and inelegant hand, had betrayed his profession and was pecking at this monstrosity, like a cross-eyed chicken, making contracts of prime importance. He can do two pages an hour! This miraculous speed has rendered me impotent.

"Not only are first-quality documents to be written on this and perhaps another machine, but the devil who brought them into the office arrived on Thursday with a ream of filthy black paper that, when inserted in alternating layers between pieces of bond, renders up to *five copies* of an original document.

"Though the results are hideous, everything goes much faster now, and we have work for only three scribes and three machines. Your father plans to retain one old order scribe such as myself to record minutes, take letters, and accompany him to court. My hand is no longer fast enough for that kind of work. As you know, it is not easy.

"I will have to retire, but I cannot afford to retire. I have spent all my money on the sap.

"As you have expressed the same view that I hold of these writing machines, I now beg your assistance. Help me to make my one last leap.

"I must become a professor of theology and astronomy at the university you now attend. I have been studying and formulating for many years ideas and theories that will make clear the mysteries of this painful life. I do not ask for much money, but only an amount equivalent to the annualization of what I have spent upon the sap.

"You must arrange this position for me. If it is already filled I will assist the present honorable occupant in his duties, if required, for nothing, as I will shortly begin to receive a small pension. In fact, if necessary, I will contribute to the maintenance and upkeep of the professorship whatever sum is necessary to sustain my participation.

"I arrive in the middle of next week to make my last leap. With regards, and etc., Orfeo Quatta."

The next day, Orfeo was waiting in the doorway when Alessandro returned from his last lecture.

"What is that?" Alessandro asked, pointing at a huge, round, plug-like, hide case bound with straps.

"That's my suitcase," Orfeo replied, as if Alessandro were very stupid.

"Yes, but it has hair on it. I've never seen a suitcase with hair on it."

"Untanned hides are the strongest," Orfeo replied. "These are the kind of suitcases Americans carry, but Americans leave the heads and tails on."

"What animal was it?"

"A cow."

Alessandro invited Orfeo to stay with him, so that he might dissuade him from leaping and send him back to Rome with a letter that Alessandro would write to his father, explaining the humanitarian necessity of rehiring the scribe on his own terms.

But Orfeo was not easy to dissuade.

"Orfeo," Alessandro found himself saying as they sat in front of a comfortable fire, "there isn't any way in the world that they would make you a professor or even let you assist. Not for a day, not for a minute, not for a second. If you return to Rome with the letter I'll write, all will revert to its original state."

"Adam and Eve."

"Whatever."

"The water gardens of Babylonia."

"I don't know, whatever you wish, Orfeo."

"No," Orfeo said with a confident smile. "If they hear of the blessed sap that I have discovered in all fonts, they surely will invite me to be on their faculty."

"I don't think so."

"Oh, but they will. I know they will. I have all the theories here," he said, putting his finger to his temple, "gravity, time, purpose, free will, you name it. The pain of the world is worked out."

"All right, then. I'll take you to the appropriate official, and you can tell him yourself."

"Not quite!" Orfeo declared. "That would never work."

Alessandro drew a blank.

"I have no degrees. They don't know me. It takes years to become a professor."

"That's exactly what I've been saying."

"And these men may not know of the dog-like, howling pain of the universe, or the gracious sap."

"I assure you that even if they do they won't admit it."

"We have to outsmart them. Open my case."

Alessandro gingerly unstrapped the hairy barrel that he had carried up the stairs and pulled out the most extraordinary academic robes and hat that he had ever seen. They were trimmed with purple bands and fur. A red-fox rosette was stuck on the breast, and a vermeil chain looped about the shoulder. The hat looked like a fourteenth-century warship that had been reincarnated as a purple pillow.

"What is it?" Alessandro asked.

"The robe of the president of the University of Trondheim: that is, Trondheim, Norway. No one has ever heard of him, and, besides, he's dead."

"Did you rob his grave?"

"Everyone knows that my brother-in-law is a tailor in Hamburg. Years ago, when the president of the University of Trondheim was in that city, he gave the robe to my brother-in-law to let out. He had to deliver a speech, and had put on weight—probably from eating too many of the Norwegian pancakes called *jopkeys*. But he died, and his wife told my brother-in-law to keep the robe. My brother-in-law, who has long known of my ambition to leap, sent it to me."

"How do you plan to use it?"

"Isn't that obvious? I, the president of the University of Trondheim, am passing through Bologna, where I will give an important lecture."

"But you don't speak Norwegian."

"No one speaks Norwegian. And I speak such perfect Italian that even if someone did, why would he bother?"

"What about another Norwegian?"

"I tell him that I'm a Hungarian on my way to Trondheim to take up the post, and that if he wants to speak to me it should be in either Hungarian, Latin, or Italian. Which one do you think he'll choose? Ha!"

"I hope you have in mind a name that can be taken as both Norwegian and Hungarian, if there is such a thing."

"Orflas Torvos," Orfeo said without missing a beat.

Alessandro's eyes bounced back and forth, seeking escape.

"All you have to do," Orfeo said, "is find out when the most important lecture place is empty, and help me put up the posters."

"What posters?"

Orfeo reached into the hairy barrel. "These." He had dozens of beautifully printed posters announcing his lecture on "Astronomy, Theology, and the Blessed Sap That Binds the Universe." Blank spaces for the place, date, and time awaited his superb penmanship. He was determined to leap.

Early in the evening of one of the last days in January, as sparkling gas-fired chandeliers blazed in the cavernous Teatro Barbarossa, and an express train of cold air had descended from Switzerland to freeze Italians in their beds, Orfeo made his leap. As often happens in moments of destiny, the man who takes his chances—in this case, Orflas Torvos—was perfectly calm and collected.

ALONE ON the high stage, he trod back and forth in his magnificent robes and purple hat, an astounding counterfeit. He wanted to affect the bored, irritated, arrogant expression common to academic lecturers who are pompous and cruel enough to try to humiliate several hundred people at once.

For a few seconds, Orfeo communed with his pocket watch. Then he closed it, and waited. As the very last of the thousand or so who had come to hear him took their seats in the back of the ancient gas-lit lecture hall, he cleared his throat and stepped to the podium.

He looked into the vast interior of the Teatro Barbarossa and nearly reeled from fright and sadness. The fright arose from the sight of a thousand people looking up at him like babies who want to be lifted into the air, and the sadness from remembering that his mother and father had spent their lives in front of audiences, lit by undulating footlights and spiraling torches. They had died almost three-quarters of a century before, and had been left somewhere on the road, in simple graves. The last their four-year-old son had seen of the wood markers had been from the top of one of the circus wagons as it pulled toward the next show.

Before Orfeo was ten years of age the president of the circus called him over by an apple tree and said, "Orfeo, you must leave us. You aren't sufficiently deformed, and you've grown far too tall."

"Where are my parents buried?" he had asked.

"I don't recall. I think it was somewhere in Rumania."

"Where?"

"By the side of the road."

"I know, but where?"

The president of the circus shook his head. "It wasn't anywhere near the Black Sea, or I would have remembered."

"Thank you."

The next ten years had been spent with a group of Gypsies, live-stock traders, who employed him as their scribe. When he reached marriageable age, because he was not one of them, they had left him in Trieste. From there he had made his way to Rome, where for half a century he had been a legal scribe, as the first office to which he had come near the railway station had been that of an attorney.

Now it was he who was illuminated by footlights and spiraling torches, and it seemed just, that the world made such circles, for a circle was the only means he had to get back to the lost place where his heart had been broken. He had always believed that he earned a credit for every letter well formed, for every page without a blot. The whole world was a task of waiting that one had to fulfill.

"I miss my home in Trondheim," he said in an astoundingly authoritative, quasi-governmental, contra-basso. "I miss the way the arctic winds push the icicles from the eaves, and how they shatter as they fall, like a bomb exploding in a city of glass."

The audience came to attention in its seats. What it didn't know was that as Orfeo spoke in his deep contra-basso his soul was swaying to the music of the circus.

"You don't know anything about the sap," he said. "You haven't the vaguest idea of the blessed sap, the most gracious sap that fills the bone-white valley of the moon."

His listeners pulled themselves up ramrod straight, their brows knit, trying to accommodate his pronouncements.

"You little snot-noses, baboons. You look like the monkeys on the Rock of Gibraltar."

Their hearts thudded, they could feel the blood massing in their aortas, and they were as tense as crickets. He went on, growing more and more relaxed, his ease the inverse function of their tightening stomachs.

"All my life I've suffered this deformity while you sat in your parents' well appointed kitchens stuffing zabaglione into your gorgeous bodies—the girls, sunburnt and green-eyed, with thick tresses of blond hair braided in lascivious basket weave that fell across their strong backs. . . .

"The boys, stupid granite-jawed idiots twice my height, intoxicated with their handsomeness, simply arrived in the afternoon, played tennis, ate, and coasted into delicious nudity with those beautiful, perfectly formed women.

"I knew even before I had desire that it would be gnarled and knotted, black and hard, a tree that would never bear fruit, a fish that would never jump, a cat that would never meow. All my life, bitterness and regret, bitterness, and regret.

"And yet," he said, briefly closing his eyes, "I was able to imagine the softness and sweetness of love, for a time." He rested his head upon his right hand, in a gesture worthy of a classical actor, and everyone in the Teatro Barbarossa heard his breathing.

He looked up, and then he began to speak gravely, almost in a monotone. "The frozenness of the blessed sap, the exalted gracious sap, will unfreeze, and the world will catch fire. In the degrees of exaltation the first is the stoppage of all motion in the profoundest of movements. The gracious one looks upon the whiteness of the poles. The second degree is the slow-moving sap that falls like lava from the edge of the outer reach, and so on and so on, until the blessed sap of the tenth degree, physically indistinguishable from what has been called," and here he paused, as if in pain, "... *gas* ... is the true sap, the very gracious sap, that constitutes the major part of it.

"You can jump on, and you can jump off. It's like jumping on a bird feather, or the dance of flatulent animals upon a desiccated brook. Take a throne, for example, that sits in a grove of trees. The oxygen of the stark white valley of the boneless silent moon turns you upside down. You close your eyes. You listen to the crickets that sing in the night. Your mother strokes your head as the wagon rolls. No matter that she is half a meter tall, no matter. She loves you. The love of a mother and child is enough, even for bent people who are only half a meter tall, because the babies don't know it. They love, and can be loved.

"What is the tragedy? The tragedy is this, but what would you know?" he asked, "you bunch of ignorant little snot-noses. Before your *fathers* were born my hand guided the streams of blessed sap across white oceans of vellum that—had my masters only had the vision and the courage—could have changed the world as if my hand had held a hundred kings.

"As rivers of white passed through my pen, I put down the opposite image of the gracious sap in forms that paralyzed my heart.

We had the proper seals, or I could have gotten them. The orders I have written, all together, have had the power to lift whole mountain ranges. My will sang the proper song, but the sap was black, like blood.

"I began to study the effects of opposites, so that in understanding them I could call down the gracious one and change the path of his cloak across the vellum. After many years I had meticulously regurgitated the ten degrees of holy blessed sap, and mixed it in every conceivable formulation. I was on the verge of discovering how to transpose the degrees and flip the sap back to strike the vellum and char it black, which would have turned the gracious sap from black to white and back to black.

"My orders would for a time have glowed white, and luminously reformed the world. But this boy's father," he thundered, without, to Alessandro's eternal gratitude, indicating anyone in particular, "bolted during the last few seconds and robbed from me my mastery of the sap. He destroyed the entire system that I had so carefully built to lure the sap to the chopping point.

"Do you know what he did? I'll tell you what he did," Orfeo said, abandoning the podium to glare at the front rows until no one dared breathe.

"He brought in machines for writing, the so-called 'typewriter,' which is noisier than a flush toilet, as ugly a thing as you can imagine, and writes in individual letters that are all the same, exactly the same, dead. Machines have no grace. It cannot make a flourish, vary the thickness of a line, or tantalize the reader with a lapse into an indecipherable but lovely style. A good penman can make rivers that race to the sea, rivers as wild and dizzy as a flume in the Alps, as choppy as the Isarco, as wide and smooth as the Tiber at Ostia, or as deep as the Po where it rolls into the Adriatic.

"But the so-called 'typewriter'? It has attacked the holy blessed sap that binds all things. It is mine own executioner. Mechanized and quick, as dead as steel, like those guns that shoot a hundred bullets at a time, it has killed my life, it has broken the beautiful lines, it has bullied and beaten time. The old world is dead, and now, you know, they'll put motors in them, and you'll have to sit on a rubber throne or wear a rubber suit so they won't electrocute you.

"And they'll attach your hands to the keys, and you'll just sit there, in the electric light that hurts your eyes, on your rubber chair, with nothing left of this life. Can't you see? Nothing whatsoever."

He was finished. He walked in silence up the center aisle. Heads turned as he passed, but no one rose to follow. When he had left the Teatro Barbarossa, a huge collective sigh escaped from a thousand souls, but not a single person spoke as the audience filed out into the cold night air. Several graduates of the University of Trondheim disappeared down the narrow streets, anxiously wondering what the morrow would bring.

When Alessandro reached home he found neither Orfeo nor the round suitcase. He ran to the station, where the last train to Rome was just about to leave. Rushing up and down the platform to look for Orfeo, he didn't see him at first, because Orfeo was in the water cabinet, afraid to flush the toilet before the train left the station. Finally, Orfeo gave up and went back to his compartment, where Alessandro saw him putting his strange suitcase up onto one of the luggage racks.

Alessandro stood outside, recovering his breath. Orfeo opened the door so they could talk.

"What are you going to do now?" Alessandro asked.

"Go back to Rome and die," said the old scribe.

"I'll talk to my father. I'll make him get rid of the machines, or at least keep you on for as long as you like. You'll be able to do the contracts in the old way, as if nothing had changed."

"No use," Orfeo said. "I was fooling myself. Those machines are ubiquitous. Everyone uses them now. They began to use them ten years ago, but I just wouldn't admit it. When the pamphlets arrived in our office, telling about what these machines could do, I threw them away." He shook his head. "It's all over."

"I'll write to my father," Alessandro said, walking with the train, which had begun to move and was picking up speed.

Orfeo shook his head once more. "Thank you," he said. "It's over."

He leaned out to pull the door closed, and as he glanced at the boy now running alongside the train, his face showed intense pity. When the door slammed shut and the train pulled from the station into the winter night, Alessandro remembered Orfeo poking him in the chest and saying, "If the world is not held together by the holy blessed sap, then what does hold it together?"

FOR SEVERAL weeks in June of 1911 it was hot enough for the cats in the Giulianis' garden to lie like tigers in the trees. The minute the sun flashed over the Apennines the city began to bake, even at the top of the Gianicolo, where a breeze swept through the dense pines.

Alessandro and Lia were in the garden. The grass had been bleached white, with touches of silver and gold, by a sun that beat down upon it day after day from a cloudless sky, and by a hot dry wind that seemed to come from all directions, but the heat was dry enough and golden enough never to be unpleasant. In the early part of the month, with the memory of the winter rains and the damp, it was as welcome as it would be unwelcome in August.

When Lia was deep in thought her face was darkened just enough to suggest a sharpshooter concentrating on a difficult target. When she laughed she did so not only with her face and voice but with a slight motion of her shoulders and arms, in a subdued and euphoric whiplash that ended always in a slight curving and relaxing of her fingers.

Alessandro desired her intensely. Sometimes he fixed upon one of her physical attributes, something minor of which she might not even have been aware, such as the curves of her neck as it swept into her shoulders, or the microscopic geography of her lips, and brought her into surprised and pleasant stupefaction. She might be talking to him, her head slightly turned, and then she would notice that he was staring at the slope of her upper lip. At first she would attempt to escape, but short of turning away completely evasion was impossible. She would slowly become intoxicated as she felt the upper lip go slightly numb, and then the rest of her, and this was better than a kiss, for it could last as long and longer, and did not waste its power in fulfillment.

That he could, even in complete silence, bring Lia to a state of sexual distraction and turn her almost as scarlet as a poppy in the Villa Doria was a triumph for the academics that the attorney Giuliani loved to disdain, for they had taught Alessandro a thing or two about how to see.

A hawk dropped from the empty sky into the topmost branches of a tall pine. Lia quickly looked up, shading her eyes from the sun, and at that moment Rafi Foa emerged from the Giulianis' house, dressed in a full business suit and carrying a leather briefcase. Having just walked up the hill, he looked like a soldier on maneuvers in the desert, but he would neither loosen his tie nor take off his jacket, because the suit had a logic of its own, and as he had chosen to wear it, he did not want to contradict it.

"This one is complicated," Alessandro said as Rafi approached. "He's made great strides, but he still wears a suit on a day like today."

Rafi sat down on the blond grass and threw the briefcase in front of him. He had finished his studies with great distinction and was making the rounds of palaces and ministries in hope of starting near the top, but because of the way the government operated, and because his heart was not in it, he hadn't found a place. Even the guards and doormen sensed his hesitation, and judges and

deputy ministers knew immediately that he was pulled by something far above the law, by something holy and alive.

"I went to see the chief of protocol for the Supreme Court,"
Rafi said, soaking in sweat. "He's old enough to be thinking about
a successor. He was impressed by my record, and asked about my
French. I said it was adequate, and he began to shout in the dialect
of the Savoyards—Aostian Italian, we used to call it at school—
and he spoke with such insanity and with such a squeaky voice that
I couldn't help laughing."

"You shouldn't have laughed," Alessandro said. He was proud
of Rafi and wanted him to get as high a position as possible.

"I couldn't help it. He asked a lot of questions that I only half
understood, and he didn't hesitate between them. I think his object
was to prove that, even though I said I knew French, I didn't.

"What did you do?"

"I told him that."

"You did?" Lia asked.

Rafi nodded. "And I told him . . . I said, 'You may think you're
speaking French, but you sound like a village idiot.' He got red and
he started to make strange noises."

"What happened?"

"What happened? I left his office. Perhaps I'm not cut out for
the law."

THE FIRST thing Signora Giuliani had done after Alessandro and
Rafi had arrived from Bologna, after a week's ride, was to give Rafi
a little room that overlooked the garden. When she showed him
the bathroom, she had tiptoed in and put her finger to her lips.

"You have to be very quiet," she whispered, "or you'll wake Luciana. She's leaving tomorrow with her classmates for an end-of-
the-year trip to Naples. She'll be gone by the time you get up."

"Who's Luciana?"

"My younger sister," Alessandro answered.

"You never mentioned her."

Alessandro shrugged.

Signora Giuliani carefully and silently closed the latch on the door that led to Luciana's room, and began to let the water into a huge bathtub that stood on Egyptian legs. "There's plenty of hot water now," she said.

Alone in the bathroom, Rafi quietly removed his dirty clothes and lowered himself into the voluminous tub. After submerging himself, he broke the surface with a splash, but after that he took pains to be quiet. When he was finished, just before he turned off the light and allowed the bathtub to sing to itself as it emptied in the dark, he noticed a cup on a shelf. Taped around it was a piece of paper with a note in a feminine hand that said, "For an article of clothing." The cup was half full of small coins. The handwriting was neither free enough of the rules of penmanship to have been that of an adult nor sufficiently innocent to have been that of a child.

He slept deeply, and when he awakened the next morning Luciana was halfway to Naples. For several days at dinner he sat in her place. The attorney Giuliani often referred to his daughter as Lucianella. Rafi asked nothing about her. She was a schoolgirl, a child, but every night when he came home from his rounds of the palaces and ministries he approached the little cup with the hand-lettered sign, and carefully studied the writing.

THE ASSISTANT to the minister of justice was a better man to meet than the minister himself, the attorney Giuliani had told him, because the assistant did the hiring.

"Don't tell Giuliani," Lia's father told Rafi, "but see the minister first. If he likes you he'll walk you into the office of the subordinate to be confirmed and processed—depending."

"Depending on what?"

"On the specific situation at that moment in the Turkish bee-hive that we call the Ministry of Justice. The minister's subordinates may control his every move. If he's a fool, he'll rely upon them too much and too often, and they'll usurp his power until, should he be lucky, they'll squander it in fighting among themselves."

"What is the situation at the Ministry of Justice?"

"I don't know."

"The attorney is a friend of the assistant."

"Then you've got to decide the approach. If you wish, I can get you an appointment with the minister directly. Just tell me. My wife says that the brother of his mistress is married to a Veneziana. It's up to you."

The night Luciana returned from Naples, Rafi, Alessandro, Lia, and Lia's brother had gone to hear an orchestra from Budapest. Rafi was astounded not to be able to hear the music over a dozen furiously whispered debates on the diplomacy of Austria-Hungary, for in Venice the music was drowned out by talk of sex and money.

In the debate that followed, in a restaurant in Trastevere, Rafi was, like most lawyers who consider politics, uninteresting. Alessandro had contrary and volatile opinions and did a good job of justifying them even when they were totally absurd. He continued to read diplomacy and to devour the several newspapers that arrived with the dawn. He combined his burgeoning knowledge with logic, enthusiasm, and rhetoric, and he made a little go a long way.

They had returned at midnight, and Rafi had noticed that Luciana's cup was gone, and the latch in a different position. The next morning he had an appointment with an official who, as the cocks were crowing in the gardens on the hill in back of his ministry, would speak expansively about the demands he made of his staff. Before setting out to meet him, Rafi had pulled on his pants and shoes, and, with his suspenders hanging down, shirtless, gone to shave. When one half of his face had emerged from the drifts and the other was still covered, the door to Luciana's room opened. With his hand still on the razor, and the razor about to glide from the top of his cheek downward, he turned.

Having forgotten that someone was staying in the house, Luciana had come into her bathroom after awakening, and she stood before him, in a short nightgown, absolutely immobile and hardly breathing. He was almost as startled as she, not by her entrance but, rather, by her beguiling appearance. She was taller than her brother, with a shock of golden hair that had yet to be combed that day. Her legs and arms were so long and slender that it was hard to draw conclusions about her age, just as it had been hard to deduce anything from her handwriting save contradictions that, if he had been of a mind to read them, would have told him her age exactly.

She was too tall to be a child. Twice as high as Lia Bellati, it seemed, she already had authority, and she would grow no more. On the other hand, she was too slight to be a woman. The delicacy of her limbs testified that they had not existed long enough for much to gravitate to them.

Rafi knew little about women, but he was a good observer. Because she focused her eyes at him in a way that exaggerated her look of surprise and made her seem like someone who has never seen another human being, he knew immediately that she wore glasses. He guessed that she kept them off whenever she could, for reasons of vanity, and although he didn't know exactly why, he liked that.

She and her classmates had done a lot of swimming off Capri, and because of this she was sunburned and her hair wildly blond. The brevity of the nightgown gave Rafi a pleasant shock, but he couldn't take his eyes off her face.

For her part, she seemed as fragile as a reed, frozen in place in the presence of the huge man who was stripped to the waist and bent over her washbasin. The table in which the sink was set came up to the middle of his thighs, and the top of the mirror showed his shoulders and throat. To shave, he had to lean down. Had he been fully dressed, his black hair and sparkling Kirghiz eyes would have stopped her heart, but to see in addition to this the lean frame that years of heavy work had coaxed and changed into something that looked as solid and powerful as a marble statue, was for her an embarrassing pleasure. Only after several minutes had passed, as the steam billowed from the tap, had she said, "Oh, I guess I'd better back up." The memory of this would keep Rafi awake for many hours in the nights thereafter.

At dinner she had been unable to look at him except in quick glances. She was in her schoolgirl's uniform, and she stumbled over her words and left the table as soon as she could. He was a model of composure.

He could have gone back to Venice, but he stayed.

ALESSANDRO HEARD a ringing in his ears as he and Rafi alighted from their train onto a flinty rail bed near the station at Barrenmatt. The air at two thousand meters was so thin and tranquil that it seemed to be only a gloss of the light. Sound carried differently, and was not so urgent. The body's forced economy of movement translated into a gift of grace, and the August sunshine was less warm than clear. They took their packs from the doorway of the single baggage car, piled them beside the track, and sat down on their rolled-up tent.

At noon, hardly a cloud was in the sky. To the left, on an outcropping, was the village. Of its five buildings, including the station, the largest was the hotel, which had four storeys and an attic. Every window in the town was framed by shutters and by flower boxes in which were unrelieved ranks of geraniums. The only street led up the hill and doubled back toward the station, and the rest of Barrenmatt was rock, track, building, road, or field. The fields were empty now because the cows had migrated to a higher altitude, where they nervously and continually rang their tin or copper bells. Such bells are heard mainly from afar, and the habit is strong, so they sound far away even when they are close.

The train pulled a few meters down the track and stopped so some women with parasols could delicately descend the outboard steps. The space between these women and the two young men and their climbing equipment was the distance between the freight and passenger terminals, but it might as well have been an ocean. The train itself was a mountain train, its engine a muscular little plug of cylinders and rods. It had pulled only two cars, each smaller than a normal railway carriage, each made of aromatic wood that creaked at every bend in the tracks. The windows in the passenger car were actually made of crystal, which was heavy, clear, and thick, with a barely perceptible tinge of purple, and the rock faces that could be seen through it came out sharp and in bright detail. Steam shot lazily to the ground and then disappeared near the feet of a railroad worker tightening bolts as the ladies descended from his beautifully made toy.

Had these things been in Rome they would have been surrounded by other such things, their attributes bled into chaotic illusion. In Rome they would have seemed larger, but at two thousand meters in the open air they were as inconsequential as the cows in the upper pastures, rendered invisible by the distance. Both the train and the little houses were compressed by standing alone in the midst of vast openness. Their colors seemed intense and friendly, their masses solid and dense. Like many man-made objects that originate in the mountains, they seemed to have been perfectly realized within well defined limits. The beauty of the Swiss watch lay in its precision, and its precision had sprung from modesty. It did not have to be an orrery or a tower clock any more than a yodeler has to sing in symphonies, and this friendliness to restriction had left the designers within easy reach of perfection.

According to Alessandro this was simply because people who lived in the mountains knew that all the truly great things had already been accomplished. They did not need to imagine ladders that would lead to heaven, or things of massive size that would astound the heart, because they had them in such profusion that it was difficult to get from town to town, and because of them the sun itself often was denied a chance to shine, or forced to break in gold through opaque ridges of ice and snow whiter than physics would allow.

At noon the scale of the landscape was shockingly apparent, and everything but the mountains seemed freakishly small. The very sky had relinquished a third of its volume to the thrones of rock and ice, and though the massif was half a day in the distance, it rose so high that Alessandro and Rafi felt as if they were standing within arm's reach of a tall garden wall.

No end was apparent to the silvery creases glinting amid folds of ox-blood-colored rock, to the shattered glaciers that poured from between spires and sheer walls, and to the meadows large enough to hold a city. Engraved upon the electrifying height and mass of the rock were inverse wells, steeples, and gleaming towers that echoed thunder and spun lightning like wool.

Alessandro and Rafi leaned back against their equipment, hands shading their eyes, heads tilted. After the train left, the sun went behind a mountain, and though they themselves were soon covered in cold shadow, the cathedrals ahead still shone.

THE FOLLOWING day they made two trips to their campsite at the top of a wide meadow, next to a wall of pines. On the first trip they carried their equipment, and on the second, ten days of provisions. They ate in the hotel restaurant before setting out in the afternoon. Ascending with their heavy frame packs was agony, and by the time they reached their camp it was dark. They left the packs leaning against a tree, and slept as if they had died.

The tent was big enough to stand up in, and they hung their climbing equipment from the ridge poles—ropes, slings, iron pins and chocks to drive into cracks in the rock, carabiners, ice axes, crampons, smoked glasses. Alessandro held aloft a sack of pitons and jangled them. "Many more people in the world hunt whales or train elephants than know how to use these," he said.

"So?" Rafi asked.

"More people are freaks in sideshows than know how to use these."

Rafi stared at him blankly.

"More people," Alessandro continued, undeterred, "have eaten dinner with the King of England."

"But the King of England has dinners for hundreds of people."

"That's true. However, he's been king for only a short time."

"What are you saying?"

"I'm saying that we are more or less alone, and that the places we're going to are often places where no human being has ever been—ever, since the beginning of time. You'll feel it when you're there. It's different from anything you've ever felt."

The left side of the tent was Rafi's, the right Alessandro's. Provisions and clothing were piled in a ridge down the center. They made a kitchen in the space in front of the tent, building a stone firebox and a table, and arranging sectioned logs as chairs. They got their water from a waterfall that was ejected horizontally from the mountain wall before it fell fifty meters into a rock cauldron perpetually filled with spray. The jet of water, as thick as a train, was so fast and powerful that they could stand next to it and see their reflections in its smooth wall. Not a drop left the confines of the ice-cold beam. To get water, they merely touched it with their fingers and bled a stream into their buckets.

"It's wasteful not to turn off the faucet when you're done," Rafi said as a million tons of water passed by.

The first night, they boiled dried beef, potatoes, mushrooms, and various greens, in the purest water of the world. They had carried up four bottles of beer, and these they drank with their soup as they looked at the lights of Barrenmatt. Except as suggested by a vague pink glow in the western sky, above a distant town, no other lights were visible. The stars were not yet out, the air was warm, and they were slightly drunk on the beer and the altitude. That day Alessandro had spent ten hours going over the equipment and its use.

"I can talk all I want," he said, swaying slightly in the dark. "We can sit for days, with you memorizing knots, technique, and rope handling, but in the first hour of climbing you'll learn more than anyone can tell you in a month—because your life will depend on the knots, the way you place a piton, and how you run the rope."

"Sometimes, Alessandro, you sound like a rabbi."

"I've never heard one. Do they sing?"

"Others sing."

"Aren't you afraid? Most people are terrified the night before they climb, although they call their fear anxiety. I breathe hard as I'm walking through the pastures to the base of the wall, but as soon as I cease to think of anything but the rock and the route up, I lose my fear."

"I'm not afraid," Rafi said.

"Why not?"

"If I die tomorrow it will have been useless to have been afraid today."

By ten o'clock they could hardly keep their eyes open. After boiling their pots and utensils clean, they stumbled into the tent and fell on their blankets.

Alessandro tried to lift his head to see the moonlight on the mountains that shone in the distance over the meadows and the great spaces of blank air, but he couldn't move. When his eyes closed, he forced them to open, but in two breaths they were closed again, and in another he was deep asleep.

THE NEXT day they climbed a hundred-meter wall. The base wasn't far from the waterfall, and they heard the roar of water below them and the sound of the wind whistling over the top of the rock far above. Rafi asked why they were going to carry oilskins. It would be hard enough to pull oneself up the face of the rock while bearing the weight of rope and iron.

"What if it rains?" Alessandro asked in turn. "What if the temperature drops, and a wind rises? You might be seventy-five meters up, with twenty-five to go. You can't afford to be too cold or too wet."

"But look at the sky!"

Alessandro studied the sky. A few matronly clouds were gliding across a field of blue, their origins beyond the cliff top unseen. "A huge thundercloud might be just beyond the rim," he said, still looking up. "Ten seconds from now we could be in a rain and lightning storm the likes of which you've never seen.

"What we're going to do is relatively simple," Alessandro said as he uncoiled one of the climbing-ropes. "I'll start to climb while you belay me from the ground. As I go up, I'll bang in a pin here and there, or set a chock in a crack. Then I put a runner on it, and clip a carabiner onto the runner. I pass the rope through the gate of the carabiner. Now the rope is anchored to the rock at that point, so, if I fall, I fall past it and the rope doubles over the carabiner: you would feel an upward pull. You'd let the rope slide around your body and through your hands, and you'd stop it gradually to break my fall.

"You see those ledges and trees? The first is about forty meters up, and the second about thirty more."

Two tiny splays of vegetation projected from what seemed to be sheer overhanging rock. Rafi looked dubious. "Trees?"

"Dwarf pines. The trunks are probably three times as thick as your arm, and can support the weight of fifty men. The roots are strong enough to split granite, and they penetrate far into the rock. The pine itself is sinewy and dense. These are the belay points we'll use today. They're easier than just using the rock. When I get to the first belay, I'll tie myself in and bring you up.

"As you ascend, you remove the pins I've driven and knock out the chocks. Unclip the carabiners and loop the runners over your head. Should you fall, you won't fall. I'll be holding you on a taut rope all the way up. When you join me at the belay ledge, you tie in to the tree, give me the stuff you've collected on your way, and off I go, repeating what we've just done. The space between belays is called a pitch. Three pitches, here," he said, looking up and shielding his eyes, "and we're at the top."

"What happens if *you* fall?"

"I can only fall twice the distance of the length of the rope between my last setting of protection and the point where I start to fall. If the holds are poor, I'll be putting in protection frequently, so if I do fall, it won't be far. Then I gather my wits and begin to climb again, like a spider."

"And if you're injured or unconscious?"

"Lower me."

"The first tree is forty meters..."

Alessandro stepped back to re-estimate. It seemed that in the mountains his head was always bent back and he was always squinting. "More or less."

"The rope is fifty meters long. How am I going to lower you down to me? I would need forty more, or you'd be hanging in the air and I'd have no rope to play out."

"That's one of the reasons the second man carries another rope, the other being that the first man, by the time he gets to the belay point, may already be carrying the entire weight of the rope that's tied to him. Why make him carry two, especially when he's more exposed to falling because he isn't top-roped like the second man?"

"I would tie them together, then."

"In a fisherman's knot, a double fisherman's knot, if you please, *before* you take the first rope from around your waist, of course."

"It's an ingenious system," Rafi stated.

"It's a beautiful system," Alessandro said. "The refinements are even better. For example, I don't tie the rope around my waist.

Instead, I use some runners and attach myself to the rope with a figure-eight knot and a carabiner. And wait until you see how we rappel down. It's like flying."

"I hope this doesn't turn out to be like the cathedral, Alessandro."

"There were practically no holds at the cathedral. I couldn't drive any pins, and we had to climb in the dark."

"I know."

"And here no priests are going to run out to scream at us, because the Church didn't build these mountains, God did. I'm going to climb. Don't pull on the rope, or you'll pull me off the rock. Watch me. If I fall you'll see it before you feel it on the rope. You can be prepared for the uptake."

Rafi looked very serious.

"I'll see you up at the first tree." Alessandro stepped to the base of the wall and pushed a rack of carabiners and pitons around to his back. A wide crack went almost all the way to the first belay point. Halfway up, it disappeared at a series of ledges that looked like they might offer good holds. Then it resumed, tapering off a meter or so below the tree. The rock there was completely smooth. Rafi didn't know how Alessandro was going to get past it.

Alessandro started smoothly and slowly. At first he breathed hard and was conscious of the ground. Then, as he rose, he forgot about the ground, forgot about his breathing, and forgot about everything in the world except the route and his strategy for climbing it.

He stopped only to hammer in a piton after he had gone about ten meters. The crack was both wide and deep, it had many good handholds around the edges, and his momentum had carried him quickly and far.

"I'm putting in a pin here," he shouted as he hammered it into a narrow crack paralleling the larger one, "because the crack's getting more difficult and I'm high enough to want insurance." When the singing of the alpine hammer against the iron reached a very high pitch, Alessandro holstered it and clipped a carabiner through the hole in the piton. "I'm not using a runner here," he called down. "The crack is relatively straight, so even without a runner the rope will follow a vertical line. That's what you want: if it zigzags from place to place you get a lot of friction at the angles, which translates into weight as you pull the rope up after you. When your protection or the route itself goes to the left or right, you use a runner to stretch out to a center line where the rope can run unimpeded. Understand?"

"Yes!" Rafi called up.

Alessandro clipped the rope into the carabiner. "If I fall I can only fall twice the distance that I go from this piton. Climbing!" he shouted, and continued up after leaning out and tilting his head to see where he was going to go and what he was going to do to get there. The handholds became footholds, and, as he rose, everything ahead and above was a promise fulfilled.

Alessandro had been following a fissure into which he was able, when he wanted, to insert half his body from head to toe, after which he had simply to bend his knee and sit back, and he was completely wedged in, free to drive a piton, rest, or survey the route above. As the crack narrowed he had to turn his feet sideways, and he found himself searching the rock face alongside for handholds for his left hand as the right worked the main fissure. Even then, he could rest simply by letting his body lean to one side and torquing his feet solidly into the crack. He did this to put in a piton and, subsequently, five meters above it, while setting a chock in the narrow crack itself.

A chock was an iron bolt into which several holes had been drilled to make it lighter for a climber's use. Where the crack was narrow, or where he could slip it into a little hole and turn it so it was blocked, he could put a runner through it, attach a carabiner, and clip the carabiner around the rope. When the crack began to fade as he was coming up to the ledges, he set a chock and told Rafi what he had done.

Then he moved over the ledges, as if they were a ladder, to the beginning of the next crack. He put in a piton relatively early, and soon found himself almost at the top, about a meter below the tree.

The tree was very obliging. As little trees on rock walls often do, it dipped down in a U shape before it rose again, as if it were attempting to meet him. He was still an arm's length short of it.

The rock between Alessandro and the tree was completely smooth. From the ground, he had thought that the chances were good that he might find a handhold visible only from up close. It did not need to be too solid, as he required only that it help him pivot upward in one cavalier motion and leap for the tree.

The rock looked polished. "I'm a meter under the tree," he called down, "and the rock is as smooth as glass. I'm going to do something that's really out of order, but I have no choice. I hadn't planned to show you artificial climbing today. Now you'll get to see it."

He jammed his feet into the crack, held on with his left hand—thirty-five meters above the ground—and removed a piton from the rack. "I'm going to drive in a pin as high as I can." He moved his left hand up the crack until it no longer fit, and put the piton over it with his right hand, pushing it in until the tip held, and balancing it on his left hand's upturned index finger.

He delicately unholstered his hammer and tapped the head of the piton until he was able to drop his left hand to a more solid hold and swing hard at the piton, which went in and stopped at its neck, with the characteristic singing noise.

"It's solid," he said, testing it by hitting it sideways with the hammer. He holstered the hammer, removed a carabiner from the rack, clipped it through the eye of the piton, and attached the rope. "Now I'm protected, but I still have to get up, so I'll take another carabiner and clip it through." Then he took two runners and

looped them together into what the French call an *étrier,* and affixed one end to the carabiner.

Grasping the piton, he climbed the two-step ladder until he
was standing on the higher step, bending over in a bowed position
so as to keep hold of the piton, which was now only a short distance from his left foot. He was so badly balanced that he didn't
dare look up. Rafi held his breath.

In slow motion, Alessandro raised his right arm as high as he
could, but it was still two hand-lengths away from the curve in the
trunk of the tree. He turned his head upward just as slowly, stopped,
and lifted his eyes to the top of their sockets so that, without further
endangering his stance, he could see how far he had to go.

Then he simply stood up straight, as if he were standing on
the floor of a cafe in Trastevere, and caught the tree like a trapeze
artist. In two seconds he was sitting on the ledge, fussing with his
equipment.

When he had tied himself to the tree, pulled up the slack in the
rope, and passed the rope around his body into the belay position,
he called out to Rafi: "Climb!"

The minute Rafi's hands touched the rock, he knew that everything had changed. The sun had come around the cliff now and
the air was warmer, even hot. He could smell pine resin on the updrafts that brought the sound of the steadily thundering waterfall.
The world and the blue sky were behind him, and he walked up
the crack as if it had been a ladder. A shock ran through him and
he feared to trust what he felt so strongly. He had not been born,
it seemed, to be either a butcher or a lawyer, but to do this. The
length of his arms and legs, the strength of his hands and fingers,
and his extraordinary and newly discovered balance saw him up
the first pitch.

When he wedged himself in to knock out Alessandro's well
placed pins he did not shiver or shake the way new climbers often
do, and he was happy all the way up. He didn't ask for advice, he

needed no tension on the rope, he climbed twice as fast as Alessandro had expected, and at the stretch below the tree he absolutely astounded his teacher.

Instead of using the *étrier* and abandoning it on the piton, he knocked out the piton, racked it, and looked up.

"Now what are you going to do?" Alessandro asked. "I'll have to pull you up."

"No," Rafi said as he began to climb, using an almost imperceptible handhold. When his hands had moved as high as they could inside the narrow crack, he began to bring up his feet. Soon he had formed himself into a bow, with his hands and feet sharing the same nearly impossible hold. "No tension," he said as Alessandro looked on in amazement. Then, just as Alessandro had done, Rafi stood up, but in the inhospitable crack rather than in a solidly anchored *étrier.*

He began to fall, but as he did he caught the bent tree with his fingertips, and soon thereafter he, too, was sitting on the ledge.

IN TEN days the pupil had begun to outdistance the teacher and was leading the most difficult and precipitous pitches, the ones that had to be climbed artificially because they offered not a single hold. These were the walls upon which climbers developed their immense strength, driving fifty bolts into the rock in an afternoon.

Five hundred meters in the air, with nothing beneath him, Rafi felt entirely at ease and would peg his way up an impossible hairline crack, never seeming to tire.

They rappelled off many a spire, almost flying, spending a whole day's hard climb in one joyous hour. They climbed ice and snow and reached the top of peaks where the light was doubled by reflection. They accomplished several extraordinary glissades, skiing without skis for kilometers and kilometers down couloirs of untouched powder.

Though they ate prodigiously, they lost weight as the altitude and exercise whittled them down. They were asleep before dark and up before the light. Just as the sun was beginning to set and they had come in from a climb, they would wash, devour a few packets of biscuits, cheese, and dried meat, and surrender to oblivion. They slept without dreams, and jumped up every morning, when the moon was sinking into Switzerland, full of energy, stronger than they had ever been, able to run up the steep meadows in the half light and push themselves eagerly into the vertical world where, by midday, hawks glided in dizzying circles below them.

As Rafi grew more competent, his passion for climbing and Alessandro's diverged. He was interested in passing beyond his limits, in doing what neither he nor anyone else had done, and because the limit was, by definition, danger itself, he was always courting risk.

He enjoyed standing at the very edge of a cliff, sometimes with only his heels on the rock, like a mountain guide impressing clients, or staring into an abyss so profound that, had he fallen, Alessandro would not, without a telescope, have been able to have seen where he had come to rest, and would not, without a microscope, have been able to have found him where he had fallen. They dropped boulders from these heights, and many seconds later, if they were looking in the right place, they would see a soundless puff of smoke.

Rafi said that the iron he pounded into the rock, and the ropes that were lithe and beautiful as they flew from a rappel point, were far better than indexes and citations, and Alessandro understood, for he knew that the beauty of climbing is that at times the failure of things to go exactly right subjects even ordinary men to saintly tests that elevate them far beyond what they have expected, and that a climber's return to camp can sometimes be like the footless gliding of the angels who cross the pits of hell.

Rafi was suited perfectly to the mountains, for when he was tested and worn down to practically nothing, his soul was unencumbered, and it rose, drawing him closer to where he wanted to be. He cared little for safety, and noticed less and less the small things that were for Alessandro the most important reasons for climbing. Alessandro loved the smell of the plants that grew on the vertical rock. As they were crushed by a boot or the horizontal motion of the rope they gave off a sweet and resinous perfume that took to one's clothes, and when Alessandro made a fire, the fragrant smoke worked its way into everything he possessed and was with him pleasantly all day. The morning sun glinting off huge lacquered agglomerations of rock far above, where clouds and mist scudded and sparkled, was a divine explosion that rushed through the eyes to capture the heart. And best of all was the thunder.

On their last climb they had set out at three in the morning for the base of a vertical spire a thousand meters high and so creased and battered that there seemed to be a hundred thousand ways to scale it, but as often is the case, the higher they went the more difficult things became, and the last spire was no exception.

Far below the summit the ledges stopped, the cracks narrowed to nothing, and overhangs appeared more frequently while the ways around them became less and less apparent.

At four in the afternoon, exhausted from a full day of artificial climbing, they were a long way from the top. With only a few hours until dark, they decided to rappel down. To descend would take longer than usual, because their belays had been pitons driven into the rock, not trees or boulders. They would have to rappel from the pins they had just driven, so they would have to reset them with care.

Time was running out and the weather was worsening. Had they any doubt about the merits of retreat, it vanished with the gathering clouds. They made their decision as they both stood in *étriers* clipped into a heavy piton. They were tied onto it by their waists, and they rested by leaning out over seven hundred meters of empty air.

They were very careful in setting up the rappel. To unclip the wrong carabiner would mean falling silently to one's death. Their lives depended upon the ropes, the carabiners, and the heavy piton that Rafi had driven into the cliff. He had taken five minutes to hammer it in, and as he worked his sweat had vanished in the brightening wind.

Laden with iron that he had collected on the way up, as second, Alessandro was about to descend to set the next piton, when the wind pushed a huge volume of black cloud over the top of the spire and shrieked through the empty spaces as the sky was about to break.

The dark clouds came tumbling at the two climbers, slowly unfurling and rolling over, pushing ahead of them a mass of agitated and conflicting winds so violent that they pressed back Rafi's beard and made him look like a goat. In one gust of wind they were hit with rain, snow, and hail, one rapidly following the other, and then dried by cold air blasting through their clothes until everything they wore ballooned out from them as if to tear away.

They struggled into oilskins as the first lightning bolt snaked down the precipice and raised their hair on end. Everything went white and they were thrown against the rock like fishing floats. Instant thunder rattled their skulls and reverberated out toward other mountain ranges for a minute or more. Even as it ceased, their ears were ringing and they could not see.

When their vision returned they saw dark clouds rising into the same sort of obliging curves in the pine trees on the ledges. The high front rushed west and made a wonderful, terrifying, obedient dip right above the two climbers as it crested and abandoned the spire, like a snake that takes a wall.

It left an army of thunderbolt throwers to castigate the mountains for slowing it down, but the punishment was beautiful. Eyes opened wide, breathing deeply, shaken by concussions raging about them, Alessandro and Rafi dangled in the air, stupefied. The thunder was so deep, the lightning so bright, and the wind so strong that they wondered why they were surviving. Perhaps they were too small for the explosions that passed over them. Had they been as big as mountains they might have felt pain, but they were immune. Even when the sharp flashes were so close and common that it was as if Rafi and Alessandro were dangling at the mouth of a cannon firing point-blank, they were untouched.

AT THE beginning of winter, Alessandro published an essay arguing against the war with Turkey that had begun in October of 1911. Though he had spoken of the subject many times, in the silence of his room he added the kind of powerful phrasing that would not have occurred to him as he spoke, because its origins were in the collaboration of hand and pen.

The essay saw light in a newspaper in Rome after Alessandro had been forced to rewrite it twenty times, depriving it of at least half its original power. He was deluged with letters, some of which were from monarchists, Garibaldini, and military officers who questioned his patriotism. A few were from simple people who wrote to express their disapproval or their agreement. Most, however, were from workers within an invisible political web entirely of their own making, something not quite real that they hoped to bring suddenly to life. They wanted to use Alessandro for their own purposes, advancing the goal of ending the war with Turkey as merely a first step. In fact, they didn't care about war, Turkey, or much of anything else, for they had hidden agenda that overrode everything.

Three-quarters of these people made Orfeo Quatta seem by comparison a paragon of stability. They hated Italy, the military, the government, capitalism, horses, swords, and encyclopedias.

They hated encyclopedias because they perceived conspiracies within them, conspiracies that were not only different from their own, but subversive. They disliked capitalism and swords: that was not surprising, but Alessandro could not understand why they hated horses.

Rigorously trained in several philosophical schools, he had realized early in his university career that, however admirable any one of them, none was sufficient to explain life in the world. In fact, even when combined, they were miserably inadequate. He had no patience with Marxism, Julianism, socialism, and the other economic faiths that endeavored not merely to explain everything but to reorder and replace that which had come into being in spite of a thousand philosophies, ten thousand theories, and uncountable millennia of nature, necessity, and chance.

He hated neither Italy, swords, horses, nor encyclopedias, and he didn't see the war in Libya as the logical result of but, rather, as a deviation from the way things were, and yet he received entreaties from strange Italians infatuated with the Turkish Empire. Even some Romans, who lived nearby, moved in a dream world, in crowded tasseled rooms of soft crushed velvet walls and Moorish decoration. Having taught themselves once to look through Islamic eyes, they could not return to the West, and were like young captives, deep in the enemy's country, who must rearrange their souls.

On a cold day in January when millions of swallows had taken possession of the trees along the Tiber and flown in mad black clouds that blocked the sky, Alessandro had watched from his father's office as thousands of people had passed through the winding streets below on their way to the Campidoglio. Holding banners strung between poles, they chanted in and out of unison, demanding the end of the war and protesting the way the war was going. Their strongest ally was the stalemate in the Libyan desert, where cholera and typhoid were leveling the Italian expeditionary force.

The protesters filled the rain-slicked streets as if they were the cobblestones. Apart from what they were saying, the chanting itself brought Alessandro to a high peak of excitement, and he wanted to join them.

"Go ahead," his father said, not looking up from his desk. "It can't hurt. It might even help."

As Alessandro started for the door, his father added, "Let me caution you, however."

"Against the swords of the *carabinieri*?"

"I know that you're quick enough to stay out of their way, and that you'll march silently and skeptically at the edge of the crowd."

"Then, what?"

"You imagine that you will make a speech."

"No I don't."

"Yes you do. I can see it in you. At the Campidoglio you'll step forward and, suddenly, Cicero. But Alessandro, they won't let you, and even if they did, you would be speaking to a thousand different conceptions. Everyone has a self-made pass for travel through the terror and sadness of the world, and because, in the end, nothing is sufficient, everyone wants to share his own method, hoping for strength in numbers.

"When I was a child, my father told me the story of a troop in Napoleon's army in Russia. They were ten thousand men, and they could not imagine that with their mass they could succumb to something as prosaic as the cold. Ten thousand souls are, after all, a city, and cities don't freeze to death. They were too busy, they were too many, they felt safe in each other's company—but they did freeze to death, because they were lost in the snow.

"Mortality is like the cold. It cannot be altered by human conceit or solidarity, and at the end you will be on your knees, in shock and amazement, and then you'll have only one sword, one shield, one great thing to carry you through."

Alessandro waited to hear what that was, but his father would not say. "If you don't discover it yourself, it will be nothing more than an exhortation from me."

A fight erupted in the crowd below. Anarchists were using the poles of their black banners to flail the crowd, and mounted *carabinieri* were sidling upon their horses to herd them into a maze of meandering side streets.

"You see," the attorney Giuliani said, "not only is there no comfort in unanimity, but they cannot even achieve it."

"I could unify them."

"That's silly, Alessandro. If they supported you, or even listened, it would be because you flattened yourself and your ideas until everything that once was steep and noble was gone."

"What if I speak my mind, forcibly, and carry them along with me?"

"That would make you a demagogue, a windbag. Why do you think great leaders and great orations are coincident with wars, revolutions, and the founding or ending of governments and states? Common interests then are so clear that speeches are effortlessly drawn, but at present neither the facts nor the consequences are sufficiently clear to make oratory legitimate. This is the kind of war that will wind on and make fools of its partisans and opponents both."

The crowd was thinning. "And one thing more," the attorney said, still at work at his desk, scratching out some legal document as he spoke, confident that the crowd's diminishing solidarity had made it less attractive to his son. "You know how the sheep are driven through Rome in the fall and spring? They go at uniform speed, they have their shepherds and their bell-wethers, and they bleat for change, but all they do is go back and forth from one pasture to another, and everything stays the same.

"You have much more to offer than wool and lamb chops. Don't go into crowds unless you can lead them, and don't try to lead them until they need you."

"What am I supposed to do in the meantime?"

The attorney looked up. "Isn't there enough in the world to occupy you?"

"Yes, certainly, but I mean to bring about a withdrawal from Libya."

"Write another essay."

"I've already said what I had to say."

"If you think you've said everything you have to say," his father told him, "talk to the opposition."

AT FIRST Lia thought she had vanquished Alessandro, as if action were vindication, as if the declaration of war were proof of her argument, or, rather, her brother's argument, that a war was necessary. Alessandro, however, did not concede his points merely because some officials had judged wrongly. In the first round neither he nor Lia had to contend with anything unpleasant. With the fighting not started, nothing was proved and everything in a state of uncertainty. Elio, Lia's brother, had written from the north of Italy, where he was stationed with a cavalry detachment, that it seemed the war would be won with a quick bombardment and he would not see Africa.

The more Alessandro argued with Lia the more he was drawn to her. As they debated, he forgot about what he was saying and grew dizzy with many variations of desire—some base, some ordinary, and some ethereal. At times, even when they were not alone, he would grasp Lia's hand in making a point, and all their contention would vanish. Sometimes they teased, and sometimes they were serious—harrying one another with history, reason, and statistics, but as the war was not yet bitter, neither were they, and in October, after the declaration and after their arguments had spawned cool fire, they began to kiss.

They had made forty circuits of the garden, looking up to see the swallows and sparrows maneuvering in the cool gray clouds. In the dusk the lights of their houses were comforting and serenely yellow. At the gate, Lia said, "I'm sorry, Alessandro, that we disagree."

Covered by darkness and sheltered by distance and the wall, he pulled her toward him and they touched with no more pressure than would have been appropriate at an embassy dance, but then he lowered his left hand along her velvet cape, to the small of her back, and held tight. She returned the embrace, and for the first time they felt one another from top to toe, hard enough so that they could feel the blood rushing. He kissed her mouth, her perfume rose, her breasts swelled against him, and for half an hour they leaned against the wall. When they parted, they were hot, numb, and pleasantly short of breath. Politics and war seemed easy to forget.

In November the fields were dry and empty. It was easy, just a short distance from the Aventino, to find a pine grove with a soft floor, or a place where the hay was down. Though the horses would have given warning had a peasant or a hunter happened by, no one even came close to seeing the exceptional scenes they played out in the trees and against sheaves of whitened hay.

But the little war refused to leave them alone. Elio had been moved to Venice, where he and his brigade of cavalry were secretly taken aboard ship at dawn. His family had not known that he had been in Libya, until the tenth of December, after he had been there nearly a month.

Just thirty days there taught him that, rather than his own abilities, it was chance that kept him alive. He sounded as if he were writing from prison knowing that his jailer would read the letter—and yet he was full of hope.

They wondered what he had seen, and they began to find out. The papers revealed constantly revised predictions of victory, calls for volunteers, the existence of a ship of the Knights of Malta that took on hundreds of cholera victims and rushed back to Naples, staying only a day to resupply, the black-bordered death announcements, and the panicked rumors from those in power.

The Italian troops were hugging the coast, barely able to cope with the disease that coursed through their ranks. They had underestimated the enemy's strength, assuming that Libyans would side with Italy against their Turkish overlords, but the Libyans took to the desert, and did not fight like gentlemen. When an Italian detachment was overrun, the soldiers could expect to die as they were slowly dismembered. Winter closed in, and few in Rome knew how difficult it was.

RAFI'S CONVERSATIONS with Luciana had always been cautious and polite. Though sometimes she laughed as he told her of his efforts to find a place in ministries swollen with bureaucrats, her laughter had ended sadly, and in the fraction of a second between these states they would search one another with their eyes. Neither of them knew the other was aware, but, once, when she had come to answer the front door, their eyes had locked in surprise, and from that moment they had known.

In the courtyard of the Spanish Synagogue in Venice was a little garden that did not get much sun. An old man with a white beard was using a narrow hoe to make an intricate set of shallow irrigation canals around the base of several date palms. His shirt was soaked with sweat, and he talked to himself as he worked.

Rafi stepped out from the palms, bound in jacket and tie. The rabbi looked up. "A funeral or a wedding?" he asked.

Rafi shook his head.

"Why are you dressed like that? Is it your nature?"

"It's a habit that I picked up in going from office to office. Is the rabbi in?"

The rabbi looked at the open sky. "It depends what you mean by in."

"You're the rabbi."

"You're looking for a job."

"May I speak with you?"

"Why ask permission for something you are doing already?"

"As a courtesy."

"Courtesy thrives at beginnings, and this is the middle. I'm not a Gypsy or a seer. If you want to talk to me, you have to do it in words."

"It's difficult," Rafi said.

"People confuse the meanings of time and difficulty."

"I'm in love with a young girl."

"What's wrong with that?"

"Too young."

"How young?"

"Not quite a woman."

"How do you love her?"

"How?"

"Yes. Do you love her physically, materially?"

"No."

"Why?"

"She isn't ready for it."

"Do you love her like a daughter?"

"No, she's too old for that, and I'm too young."

"What, what's all this? What is there, a year's difference in your ages?"

"Eight."

"I guess that's something, but not that much. Do you love her like a sister?"

"No."

"Why?"

"I love her too much."

"Thus far," the rabbi said, pushing his hoe, "everything is going very well, which is why you feel what you call difficulty. Without difficulty, you and she would be in terrible trouble. I can tell from the way you talk that you love her deeply, in perhaps the best way a man can love a woman. You love her well enough to come to see me.

"You want to know what to do. You're not the first man to ask me such a question, nor even, I might add, the first woman. The first one to ask was me, and even I knew the answer, a long time ago, when I hardly knew a thing—and you know the answer now."

"I didn't ask a question," the young attorney said.

"It depends upon what you mean by *ask*. According to me, you asked. You're as red as a persimmon. Your eyes are wide, you're breathing slowly, and you're as still as a deer. To my mind that's asking. I know the right answer, and so do you: *wait*."

"How long?"

"Three years."

"Three years?"

"By then she won't be awed by you, and she'll have had the opportunity to reject you. You will have had time to prove that you love her not only for what she is now but for what she will be then, and for what she will become. What do you do for a living?"

"I'm a lawyer."

"In that case it will be easy to keep yourself busy for three years."

"Can I see her?"

"Of course you can see her. You have to see her. And you can let her know, but you must wait. It may be difficult. Learn to love the difficulty.

"I assume she loves you? We'll have to start all over again if she doesn't. She does, doesn't she. Ah, yes, I can tell by your expression. Perfect! You look like a Christian Beatitude." The rabbi had forgotten to ask if she were Jewish. Perhaps he had assumed that she would be, or perhaps he sensed that it did not matter.

ONE AFTERNOON late in August, Rafi was playing chess with Luciana in the garden. Everyone else was in the shade or in the house, sleeping, going mad with the *scirocco,* or, in Alessandro's case, buoyantly reading in a tub of cool water.

Oblivious of the heat, Rafi and Luciana sat on canvas chairs in the middle of the orchard, the chess set between them on an up-ended fruit box. Luciana's hair was by now the color of white gold, and her smooth sunburned skin was a perfect, even color, suggesting the shades of many of the buildings in Rome, but her eyes, in contrast, were polar blue.

Mainly for her sake, they didn't use a chess clock. She took five or ten minutes to make each move, and was easily flustered. As soon as she moved, Rafi would follow, without pause. Never once did he ponder, always setting his position to right immediately. He calculated everything far in advance, kept several strategies alive simultaneously, and stared at her as she scowled at the board. He loved to watch her wintry eyes skip and slew in perfect symmetry across the field of battle on top of the fruit box. She was beautiful all the time, but she was most beautiful when she did not know she was being watched.

"What do you have in mind for yourself, Luciana?" Rafi asked. "When I was your age I had decided to study law. It was tragic."

"I don't want to study law," she said with the same tone as if she had been saying, *I don't want to turn into a cockroach.*

"Having a family is the most important thing," said Rafi, "but it gets somewhat less interesting and somewhat more uniform if it's done well. I wondered if perhaps you might be thinking of something else, or something in addition."

"Like what?"

"I don't know. Playing the piano? Running away to the South Seas?"

"No, but I don't dream of marriage, either, perhaps because I don't know who my husband will be." Even in the bright sunshine, she blushed and was forced to look down. "How can I think about marriage when I don't know what form it will take."

"Then what do you have in mind?"

"I've never told anyone," she said, as she looked around the garden at the cats sleeping soundly on the lower branches of the fruit trees, "but I'm not going to live in Rome. I'm not ambitious and I don't want an ambitious husband who will waste his life working for position. And I don't care about money."

Rafi didn't know whether it had sprung from the mother, the father, or both, but the Giulianis were maddeningly the same.

"I'm going to go north," she said, "to the mountains."

Rafi fell back in his chair.

"I haven't thought it out, but I'll just go there. It may be difficult at first—I'll settle in. It isn't that far, and we've always gone to the Alps in the summer."

"Would you be content," he asked, "to marry a mountain guide, or a forester, or a local petty official—someone who, in comparison to a resident of the capital, would have little power, someone, as it were, offstage?"

"I have another point of view. I've always thought that the most wonderful thing would be to live on a mountain farm, with sheep, goats, and vines. That would mean, wouldn't it, marrying a farmer, offstage or not. I think that the closer you are to power, the less you understand of what it is to be alive."

RAFI FOUND a place to stay on the top floor of a building in Trastevere. Because the room was small and required the stamina of an alpinist to reach, it rented for next to nothing. Whereas someone in his situation might have squandered his money in restaurants and in the theater, and on clothing, cabs, and useless talismans like walking sticks and fancy watches, Rafi ate with the railroad workers, dressed modestly, and walked every place he went.

The money he saved was for a house on a hill above an Alpine town. His windows gave out on the Gianicolo, where he could see the lights of the Giuliani house, and once a week or so he went there for dinner.

Time passed, war was declared, the leaves vanished noisily and, then, after Christmas, it snowed. One day he brought a friend to dinner, a Milanese, and the Milanese provided a carriage that took them up the hill and would take them down again. After they had left the house and climbed back into the carriage, Rafi looked back and saw Luciana at the window of Alessandro's room.

"Wait a minute," he said to the Milanese. "I've forgotten something."

He ran into the house and up the steps. By the time he got to Alessandro's room he was out of breath. Though Luciana turned to him, she remained at the window, and he remained at the door.

"Luciana," he said. "I don't know how to say this. Your parents are downstairs and they must think I'm crazy. Luciana, I love you."

Her answer was expressed first in her face and then in her breathing. "Will you wait for me?" she asked.

"We'll only have to wait two years," Rafi told her. "That should be enough."

Luciana moved her head from side to side, as if she were admonishing him, and then she raised her right index finger. "One," she said. "What anyone else thinks, what anyone else says, doesn't matter."

IN FEBRUARY of 1912, plague ships called at Naples overnight with the wounded, the sick, and the dying, and an incessant gray rain fell on Rome. In thunderstorms and barrages of lightning it gradually became clear that those who had left in the previous bright October had reached a coast of hell. One could, if one knew to do it, measure the suffering and the pain indirectly in the accounts of bravery. It was easy to mark the journalists who had actually been there, as opposed to those who stayed on the ships and used binoculars, for the ones who had actually been there were transfixed by detail. One man seemed to think a particular water bucket was the saddest thing in the world after no one was left to drink from it. Another was moved by the electric lights on the ships that carried the wounded: as the ships made their way through storms in the Mediterranean the propellers would sometimes lift out of a trough in the waves and the lights would flare briefly as if in a divine signal for those whose last moments were to be on the winter sea.

Alone in his room in Bologna, with a fire in the stove and a world of slate-colored clouds mounting in the sky, Alessandro was especially haunted by a journalist's account of artillery: *Once you have heard it, whether from afar or close by, you will believe forever in things that you may never have known in a comfortable life. No thunder was ever as deep or as threatening, for thunder comes from above and is preceded by light. Though artillery sometimes shows a broad white flash that turns night to day, it seems to have escaped from a fissure in the ground, and its deep and terrible sound has no relation to the aerial tantrums with which we associate it. No, the sound of artillery comes from below, and though its occasional rumbles and booms are as casual as rolling waves, it sets the soul afloat in a world of darkness.*

At the beginning of the new year, the name Alessandro Giuliani had appeared under articles in several of the most important newspapers in the country. Although he was neither the best, the best known, nor the most effective critic of the war, he held a special place because his prose had extraordinary power and not the slightest trace of bitterness. The opposition often sounded so much like warriors that no one believed them when they professed to be against war. Alessandro, on the other hand, was all strength, and uninterested in fault-finding, punishment, guilt, or accusation. He wanted only to do what was right—not for some vague notion of humanity, or for the sake of the Turks, or for socialism, but for

Italy. This discipline and appearance of balance brought him a following, and his readers assumed that he was a man at least twice his age. Throughout January, he strengthened, his arguments grew clearer, he learned not to fear repeating them, and he enjoyed the newfound power with which he could move the country—even if only a little—while sitting in his chair, pen in hand, trying to touch upon the truth.

Toward the end of the month, when clouds of swallows were still in perpetual motion above the tree-lined boulevards, he came home from Bologna, bringing with him reprints of his articles in several newspapers and journals. He knew that his father and mother would be proud, and he hoped that Lia would be impressed even if she did not agree.

He arrived at his house just as Rome was beginning to get dark. His father had returned early, and before Alessandro had even removed his coat he dumped the reprints on the dining room table. The attorney Giuliani was now an old man. It had happened without anyone's knowledge, as if no one had been paying him the proper attention. He took out his reading glasses, switched on a light, and began to read.

"Will Rafi come tonight?" Alessandro asked.

"Rafi's in Paris," Luciana answered.

"What's he doing there?"

"For the firm," Alessandro's father answered, looking up briefly. "An Italian collier was hit in the harbor at Cherbourg. We're suing the French owners of the ship that rammed it."

Alessandro's mother looked at him with the kind of expression that he thought signified something that only she could take seriously, such as, was he going to appear before his professors in a torn shirt? "Didn't you get my letter?" she asked.

"I didn't get it," he answered, with the peculiar satisfaction of someone who has genuinely failed to receive a letter.

"Then you don't know."

"Don't know what?" Alessandro felt a shock of fear, as if he were looking over a great height. Luciana's eyes got teary, and his father looked up from the editorial that he had been set to read, as if he didn't intend to finish it.

"What is it?" Alessandro asked, rising from his chair. He wanted to know immediately. "Did someone die? Who died?"

Signora Giuliani closed her eyes and dipped her head.

"Who?" he asked, now weakly.

"Elio Bellati."

Luciana was weeping, and Alessandro couldn't understand why. She was shaking as if she had seen it with her own eyes.

As her mother went to comfort her, her father stood up, removed his glasses, and faced his son. "Alessandro, they tore the body to pieces. . . ."

Alessandro dropped into his chair. "How do you know?"

"It was reported. He wasn't the only one. There were many."

"What about Lia? Have you seen her since?"

"I think you'd better get used to doing without her, Alessandro."

"Why?"

"Because that's the way things work."

Later, Alessandro walked through the garden, which was covered with wet and rotting leaves. Though only a few lights were burning in the Bellatis' house, he opened the iron gate. A servant whom he had never seen came to the door, an old man who appeared as if he specialized in temporary work in houses of mourning. His manner was a buffer for every emotion and every request. If asked to bring the paper, he would have said, "Just a moment. I'll go to see if perhaps one has arrived."

Alessandro announced himself. The servant went away, and returned. "Perhaps you can leave your card."

"I don't have a card," Alessandro told him. "I live across the garden."

The servant gently shook his head. "They won't see you," he said.

HIS PORTRAIT WHEN HE WAS YOUNG

IN OCTOBER of 1914 Alessandro went on horseback from Bologna to Rome. He was young, the weather was beautiful, and Europe was at war. Though Italy had remained neutral, Alessandro was sure that the newly unified country would find the test of combat irresistible, and that he would be forced to take his place in the front lines. During the mad days of August, the attorney Giuliani had expressed the sudden desire that his only son should go to America, but Alessandro rebuffed all efforts to remove him from danger, protesting that only a few months remained before the confirmation of his doctorate, and that he had to be present for the final examinations.

"You can come back," his father had said.

"Why leave if I'll come back?" Alessandro had asked, and then had quoted Horace. "'New skies the exile finds, but the heart is still the same.'"

His thoughts had been not merely of practicalities and not merely of Latin poetry but of the girl in the Villa Medici. Had he known her name, or that he had been close to her on the street half a dozen times without realizing it, or that from his window he could see her house far away across the Tiber, his life might have been different. More than once he had seen her lamp light amidst the ten thousand lamps of evening, so distant that it flickered like a star.

Now he had been riding since early morning, when it was cold and the moon had refused to abdicate, hanging delicately over a pine-covered hill, as bashful as a doe, and as still. At the highest point of a ridge that seemed to run diagonally across all of Tuscany, he dismounted, quieted Enrico, and looped the reins around a pine bough sticky with resin. A few steps took him out of the shade and into the clear, close to a cliff that dropped away until the land rose up again in a line of mountains far to the north.

He tilted his head slightly and looked at the light over the horizon. To the north the air was tortured and quick, undulating like the air above a fire and bending the light into untrustworthy contortions. Somewhere along the line of sight, under the canopy of pale blue, was France and the war. Rooted in the stillness, Alessandro was like a farmer watching a blaze consume the forest at the edge of his fields.

The world was going to be torn to pieces. In the driving apart of so many families, every family would be driven apart; in the death of so many husbands and sons, every husband and son would die; in the anarchy and gravity of suffering, God's laws would emerge in all their color, hardness, and injustice. Were Alessandro to survive he would have to start anew, but he wondered if, left with nothing familiar and no sign of anyone he loved, he would be able even to think of starting over.

Alessandro took in the grace of the surrounding landscape like a blind man whose vision is suddenly restored not in a small room in a clinic but on a high and windy promontory overlooking half the world. Before him were rounded green hills, floating clouds, a river, pines, and a distant line of mountains. Though the only noise in the forest was the chatter of birds, he was able to hear music that he took from memory and fused with the sound of wind in the trees. From the fullness of the clouds, the arc of a swallow, and the sparkling of the sun upon a shattered river, came sonatas, symphonies, and songs.

Safe in the greenery, under a canopy of blue, Alessandro watched the birds flit by in momentary ribbons of blurred color, but over the horizon the action that bent the suffering air shook him awake as if from a dream. Though he could feel the end approaching—the end of the familiar, the rearrangement of the elements of beauty, the death of his family, and his own death—he believed that as night pressed its ever-expanding claim, the things in which he placed his faith would assume their brightest mantles and come most alive. Even the silent things would sing, and fight their undoing by rising up before it to their full and greatest height. After suffering must come redemption. Of this he had no doubt.

A WEEK on the road had made Enrico lean and half wild. When they crossed the Tiber Alessandro had difficulty holding him back, for the horse knew the road and strengthened with each familiar turn. Knowing that his stable at the Porta San Pancrazio was just at the top of the Gianicolo, where he had been born and where the air was perfectly familiar, Enrico bolted forward and took Alessandro to the top of the second-highest hill in Rome as if he were a bird rising out of control in a storm.

Once, Alessandro had come home after having ridden for weeks on hot dusty roads, and had announced his arrival by firing a pistol in the air as he came up the hill to his house. Now he merely knocked at the door.

When his mother greeted him she did not have her customary energy, and she pulled him into the reception room and closed the door behind them.

"Why are you home?" she whispered.

"What's wrong?" he asked. "Am I not supposed to be home?"

"Your father isn't well. He mustn't be upset. Have you been expelled?"

"How could I be expelled?" Alessandro asked, never failing to be astonished that his mother, who had had no formal education, did not understand that getting rid of doctoral candidates was a process equivalent to starving a plant rather than obliterating it, and that it never took less than five or ten years. "What's the matter with him?" he asked.

"His heart isn't well," his mother said, clutching her own heart. "He has to rest for a month, and not climb stairs."

"Can he go back to work?"

"Yes."

"How will he climb all the stairs at the office?"

"The doctor said that when he gets better he can do it slowly."

"How serious is this?"

"He'll be all right. He's even resumed overseeing the firm. Every day at five-thirty Orfeo comes to note your father's directions and take letters."

"Orfeo!"

"Yes."

"I thought he wouldn't come back."

"Your father will tell you what happened, but I want to know why you came home early."

"The university is in recess because of the war," Alessandro said, lying.

"We're not in the war," his mother protested.

"Half the students are French and German, as are many of the professors, and a lot of Italians are enlisting in the armies anyway. The war has touched everything, everywhere."

He had neglected to mention that he himself had joined the navy.

His mother's and father's room took up most of the second floor, with half a dozen windows that overlooked Rome, and a fireplace at each end. From the bed one could see the Apennines bathed in evening light, and the city spread out beneath, with palms rising now and then from masses of walls and roofs that looked like lakes of ochre and gold. A large desk was at the north end, opposite a couch surrounded by tables and bookshelves.

The door had been left half open to let in heat. Alessandro entered and stood just inside. His father was sleeping, hands decorously clasped on his middle.

"Papa," Alessandro whispered. The old man's eyes opened.

"Alessandro."

"Why aren't you under the covers?" Alessandro asked when he noticed that his father had been sleeping on a made bed, with a heavy woolen blanket drawn over him.

"I'm only taking a nap. I'm dressed." He wore a shirt, collar, tie, pants, braces, and his suit vest.

"Why are you dressed?"

"I'm not sick, I'm just resting. I hate to stay in bed all day. Orfeo's coming this afternoon so I can dictate letters and instructions, because I'm still working on cases. When he comes I put on my jacket. I don't want him to see me without my jacket."

"For thirty years he's seen you when you take off your jacket."

"Not in my bedroom."

"Is that why all the books are straightened, the papers stacked, the pencils upright in the pencil cups?"

"No. That was from before, in case I died. I was very sick. I collapsed, and they brought me home in an ambulance."

Alessandro stared at his father, unwilling to imagine him so weak.

"I wanted to get the little things out of the way. I'd like the last thing I see to be the golden light on Rome, or snow on the mountains, or a great thunderstorm—not a pencil cup. Take them out of the room."

"You're recovering."

"I don't care. Get them out of here."

Alessandro gathered the pencil cups. "This one isn't so nice, the red one," he said, holding it up, "but the black one is beautiful: it's like the Wedgwood pen in the office." He moved them to the hall, and returned.

"I know," his father said. "The black ones were a set. I bought them in Paris in seventy-four. Bring it back and put it on the desk."

Alessandro did. "That looks good. I broke the set because . . . I don't know why, but it wasn't much good as a set. You don't keep a pen in a pencil cup, or the point dries out."

"What about the others? They're still in the hall."

"They were choking the room. Why are you home?"

Alessandro told the lie about the university being in recess.

"That's a lie," his father said.

"I was told not to upset you."

"Lying upsets me."

"I enlisted in the navy."

"In the what!" his father screamed.

"The navy."

"The navy? Since when did you enlist in the navy?"

"Since last week."

The attorney Giuliani pulled himself up on the pillows and gathered the blanket.

"You stupid! Why?"

"It's a gamble, but it makes sense."

"To give up a professorship to enlist in the navy when Italy may soon be at war!" his father shouted. "That makes sense?"

"Let me finish. First of all, the professorship is purely hypothetical. I start as a lecturer, detested by the department because I don't see things as they do. . . ."

"Why did they take you?"

"So they can drop me later."

"Alessandro, you don't enlist before a war, not unless you want to die. Wasn't Elio Bellati enough?"

"Papa," Alessandro said, holding up his index finger in exclamation, hesitatingly. "I treasure my life. I'm not like the men who fly into the flame of war for no reason other than to perish. I'm not doing that."

"No?"

"Of course not. You're thinking of small wars, like the last. This one is different. You've read of the battles, the need for men, the way they use them up so quickly. France and Germany have conscription, and Asquith will fall if he should fail to institute it in England. If Italy enters the war, we, too, will have mass conscription. At my age and in my condition I'll go right into the trenches, where the death rate is tremendous.

"The navy is different. In the navy, the targets are the weapons themselves, whereas on land the target is the man who carries the weapon. You see? And if Italy doesn't enter the war, I will have been in the navy during a time of peace. I think, though, that we will go to war. I've taken a chance that everyone I know is afraid to take. They prefer to hope for the best, but if things go badly they'll be in a disastrous position.

"Precisely because I don't want to die in a senseless war, I have, for the first time in my life, calculated. I have retained all my passions, but I've changed. Perhaps for the sake of keeping my passions alive."

"When do they take you?" the attorney Giuliani asked.

"The first of January."

"That's not as soon as it might be," his father said, now resigned.

"I know. I came home to get things in order—just like you."

"Livorno?"

"Venice, officer training, but before I go in I'm going to Munich."

"Why Munich?"

"To see a painting while I still can."

Alessandro and his father turned at the sound of three sharp raps upon the door. Standing before them as stiff and short as a penguin, with a briefcase in one hand and a pencil cup in the other (he had knocked with his head), was the president of the University of Trondheim.

LUCIANA FOLLOWED Orfeo, slipping into the room so quietly that her brother would not immediately have noticed had it not been for the striking picture she now presented, in that she was no longer thin, and what had been lost in delicacy had been returned in grace and composure. She wore a yellow dress, and her hair, which was tied with a yellow ribbon, looked as if it itself were the source of the light that played upon it, like strong sunlight shining in a stream.

"Sir," Orfeo said, bowing slightly before the attorney Giuliani and acknowledging Alessandro with his eyes. "As I rose upon the Gianicolo in harmony with the blessed afternoon sap that filters through the universe and lands in the palms, I thought of the one whose cloak, *deliciae humani generis,* sweeps across the vale of the moon. Neither Artemis nor Aphrodite, overwhelmed with the sense of the gracious sap..."

"Please, Orfeo," the attorney Giuliani interrupted. "We agreed that because of my condition we would refrain from speaking of the exalted one and the blessed sap."

"Forgive me," Orfeo asked, waving his hands around his face in a totally unfathomable gesture, and then looking toward the ceiling, transfixed. "The chariots of the exalted one are so near! They sweep across the sky in golden flares. I am hard pressed not to sing, but, I know, the heart. The heart is a wheel that exultation can spin so fast that it can break apart. At our age," he added, "we must be cautious, lest we be overwhelmed with the blessed sap and die before we receive it."

"That's right," the attorney Giuliani said, thinking that Orfeo was now ready to work. "Are you ready to work now?"

"Yes, I'm ready to work now."

"Are you calm?"

"Yes, I'm calm," he answered. "But the glory!" he shouted, his body tensed and trembling, waves of joy and madness vibrating through every muscle. "The glory and the joy of the blessed sap and the exalted one! The light! The light!"

"Orfeo. Orfeo," his former employer entreated. "The heart. The fragile heart!"

"Oh yes," Orfeo said, trying to take control of his trembling body. "Sir," he continued, nearly under his breath, "the realms I sometimes see!"

"Let's talk about the earth," the attorney Giuliani said.

Orfeo nodded.

"Good. Small things, Orfeo, small things, like oil on the waters. Quiet pleasures, good things."

Orfeo closed his eyes.

"A tree in the shade," the attorney went on, attempting to pacify the scribe. "A nice cup of minestrone. A quiet violin. A bird. A rabbit..."

Orfeo, now calm, opened his briefcase and presented the attorney with papers that were to be signed and those with written questions necessary for the guidance of the firm. As the invalid slowly read, Orfeo turned on both heels, penguin-like, to Alessandro.

"I do this from magnificence," he said. "I am no longer employed by your father."

Alessandro looked puzzled.

"I'll tell you," Orfeo continued, stepping closer and lowering his voice so as not to disturb the attorney. He beckoned to Luciana to join in. "I have made the incredible leap"—he made an arc with his left hand, following it with his eyes—"and vaulted above the deathly animal that is going to eat the century.

"You know that there was no more for me to do in your father's office. The so-called typewriter..." He turned and made several gestures, the last of which was to pretend to spit.

"In throwing myself to the wind, I saved myself, though unwittingly. Your father offered me continued employment, but I refused his kind charity. Several weeks passed, and I returned home, ready to clutch the sap.

"Surprise of surprises, a carriage came to my door. Your father had thought about my situation, and, together with Signor Bellati, had found a place for me.

"While my trade was vanishing, and found no demand in the

legal profession, a need was growing elsewhere. I, a scribe of the old order, have been put in charge of a hundred new order scribes and a thousand of those disgusting things that are called 'typewriters.'"

"Where?" Alessandro asked, thinking that perhaps Orfeo was describing a dream.

"The Ministry of War. With the build-up of the armies they need scribes to write proclamations, commissions, and fancy communications. They needed a scribe of the old order to direct the scribes of the new order."

Alessandro's father looked up from his papers. "Soon, he'll move his pen and the earth will shake."

"I'm going into the navy in January," Alessandro told Orfeo.

"The navy! I do everything for the navy. I make admirals, I launch ships, I establish new bases. What would you like? Just say."

"Make me an admiral," Alessandro said, smiling.

"All right," Orfeo said. "I'll bring the papers tomorrow." He was serious.

"Orfeo, you can't do that," Luciana insisted.

"Yes I can. I'll use one of the royal seals, and instruct the minister of war to make him an admiral. I'll write a directive from the minister to the navy, and then I'll write up the commissions, back enter them on all the books, et cetera, et cetera. It will take about three or four hours, but once it's done he'll be an admiral."

"Some things would tend to give him away, Orfeo," Alessandro's father said, "such as his age."

"I'm not responsible for anything other than creating him. Then I walk away. It's happened before."

"What about something less ambitious," Alessandro asked, warming to the idea.

"The less ambitious the faster it can be done. Would you like to command a ship?"

"I don't know how, but I'll tell you what. After I finish the officer's course, I'd like a squadron of small boats in the Adriatic."

"How many boats would you like?"

"Twenty."

"Would you like your own base? I could give you a small island somewhere, maybe in the water."

"What about one of the Isole Tremiti?"

"I'll see to the details. I have to advance you in rank, but I'll give you the kind of order that will let you take what you need in men and supplies. Tell me the date that you'll graduate from your course, and leave the rest to me. I'll put so much wax and ribbon on it that you'll need a wheelbarrow to carry it."

"No," the attorney Giuliani said. "You will not do this, Orfeo. Both you and he," he said severely, pointing to his son, "could be shot. I forbid it. Drive it from your thoughts."

"As you wish," Orfeo answered.

Though deeply disappointed, Alessandro was also relieved.

"Did you count the steps?" the attorney Giuliani asked Orfeo.

"Yes," Orfeo answered. "Seven flights of stairs, or fourteen if you count the landings as divisions. Twenty steps on each flight. Thus, a hundred and forty steps. I counted them one at a time, both going up and coming down. It was the same number."

"I'm not surprised," the attorney Giuliani said, taking out of his vest a gold pocket watch that showed phases of the moon against a star-dotted indigo sky. "If I take one step every five seconds, which will be easy to do, because the watch is marked to suit, that will be seven hundred seconds, or about twelve minutes."

While his father dictated to Orfeo, and Luciana left to help with dinner, Alessandro sat in the window-seat. As the sun disappeared behind the Gianicolo its light filtered through the palms and pines that stood upon the crest, and part of Rome, though gold and ochre, was tinged with a green color that suggested a city of the East.

Orfeo worked for an hour or so and then capped his pen. The attorney Giuliani instructed him once more not to elevate Alessandro, and Orfeo agreed. As he left, he turned in the darkness in the hall and looked at Alessandro, who was sitting motionlessly at the window. Alessandro had fallen asleep, but in the shadows where he sat he looked awake, because his head was propped on his hand as if he were lost in thought. Orfeo checked to see that the attorney was absorbed in his papers. Then he looked once again at Alessandro, and, thinking that Alessandro was looking back, he winked.

For the next fifteen minutes a number of servants in the kitchens of houses on various levels of the hillside looked up from their dough and their saucepans as a bat-like figure in a dark cloak fled down the many flights of stone stairs, laughing out loud as he went, and intoning what seemed to be some sort of incantation. No one understood the words, but everyone heard them quite clearly: "Cumbrinal the Oxitan, Oxitan the Loxitan, Loxitan the Oxitan."

DINNER WAS served on the second floor, where Alessandro's father was confined. The food, dishes, and cutlery were carried upstairs to a sitting room with a small fireplace. At this time of year the Giulianis normally would have eaten in the garden, but, now, even had the attorney not suffered maladies of the heart, they would have been driven indoors by an unusually frigid and surprisingly windy October. The cafe tables and chairs had already been stacked or removed, the streets had emptied, and leaves had begun to litter the roads on the Gianicolo. Though November might yet be like summer, October was almost like winter. Anyone walking in the dark little streets near the Piazza Navona would see orange suns blazing inside the shops and restaurants, as fragrant apple wood and oak burned in terra cotta stoves.

"Who wants to go to Germany?" Alessandro asked everyone at once in the middle of the soup course. His mother, his father, Luciana, and Rafi, who had just come in from the cold, continued eating their soup without looking up. "Who wants to go to Germany?" Alessandro asked again, as if he had not been heard.

Finally, Rafi looked up and said, "No one." Then he took more soup.

"Why not?" Alessandro asked, with characteristic tenacity.

"No one wants to go to Germany most of the time, Alessandro," Rafi assured him, "especially Italians. You must know that. And in the winter even more people don't want to go to Germany. Add to that the fact that Germany is at war."

Luciana gurgled with delight.

"I'm not suggesting that we go as tourists," Alessandro said, irritated that his best friend was now the slave of his little sister.

"What do you suggest, then, that we invade?" Rafi asked.

"We may soon do that," Alessandro said, "but that's not what I mean. I'm going to Germany and I thought that maybe you'd like to come with me, but since I seem to be talking to hermits, I'll go myself."

"Alessandro, be careful," his mother urged. He didn't hear her, because she said the same thing whenever he went anywhere or did anything.

"It's a good idea," Rafi said.

"What is?" the attorney Giuliani wanted to know.

"To invade Germany."

"All we have to do," Luciana asserted, "is send Orfeo."

"There's no sense in beating a mad horse," her father told her. "He's lived a quiet life, and suffered incomparably."

"Why is he mad, Papa?" Luciana asked.

"I don't know."

"Alessandro," Luciana continued, "why *are* you going to Germany?"

"To see Raphael's portrait of Bindo Altoviti."

"All the way to Germany just to see a painting?" Rafi asked.

"All the way to Antwerp?" Alessandro shot back, "to argue about a dent in a ship?"

"We get paid for it."

"That may be so," Alessandro said, "but remember one thing."

"What?"

"A dent is a dent."

THOUGH ALESSANDRO had a second-class Wagons-Lits ticket, he was informed at the station that the second-class sleeping car had been withdrawn from service.

"What am I supposed to do?" he asked. "I don't want to sit up all day and all night and arrive in Munich indistinguishable from a laundry bag. I paid for a bed. I have a reservation."

"There's nothing *I* can do, sir," the ticket agent said. "I would like to put you in first class...."

Alessandro lifted his eyes in anticipation.

"But first class is packed."

Alessandro gave up, and then was revived as if by a million volts of electricity.

"The only open space is one which, I am afraid, you would have to share with a passenger of the opposite sex."

"You mean a woman?" Alessandro asked, his pulse banging against his wrists.

"Yes," the ticket agent replied, scanning his lists. "The compartment is for two. It will be open until Venice, and then it is booked for one, and that is a woman. I can't put you in with a woman."

"I'll just have to suffer," Alessandro said, hoping that the female entraining at Venice would not be a bash-faced Albanian widow with three types of skin disease and a vomiting dog.

"I can't assign you to a compartment with a passenger of the opposite sex," the agent protested.

"Why not? Everyone needs to sleep—men, women, everyone."

"I'd get in trouble."

"Not now you wouldn't," Alessandro proclaimed in a voice suitable for his occasional performances on the lecture platform in the Teatro Barbarossa. "This train terminates in Munich. Munich is in Germany. Germany is at war with France, Britain, and Russia. Hundreds of thousands of men have died, and millions may follow. Do you think that when the train arrives in Munich some authority will know from the empty air inside it that a railway agent in Rome mixed the sexes? Do you think that anyone will care?"

"We're talking about rules," the agent asserted, "and we're talking about Germans."

"But the entire nation is at war!" Alessandro pleaded. Behind him stood a Calabrian family in transit to the north. Two of the three sons held wooden cages stuffed with chickens—strange, clay-colored, sleek, muscular chickens. These were Catanzaro fighting hens. The pressure was building upon the ticket agent.

"I would like to know, sir, if you are truly concerned with your comfort or merely attracted to the idea of enforced and coincidental intimacy?" the ticket agent asked, bursting with indignation, but with the Calabrian family growing more and more anxious, Alessandro had him in a stranglehold. Still, he answered truthfully, because the words *enforced and coincidental intimacy* had caused him to feel a pleasant sensation throughout his entire body.

"To be honest," he said, "the idea of being alone with a woman for sixteen hours in a small cubicle with a bed enchants me. . . ."

"*Ca Caw!*" said the chicken.

"All right," the agent interrupted, "but, remember, I didn't give these to you. I gave them to a woman who came in your place. Track four."

Whenever Alessandro set out on horseback his senses sharpened exhaustingly, but a train journey threw him into a Tibetan trance. Riding on Enrico, he continually made judgments and choices and moved like a dancer as he dodged the brush, but on a train he was in suspended animation, all eyes, as the landscape passed by like a short history of the world. Even as he walked through the great hall of the station, its iron gates similar to the elaborate grillework of some Spanish churches, he began to experience the elevated state that is the true purpose of railroads.

The station was like a vase of luxuriant flowers. In the golden light of a slightly humid late October morning the colors were astonishingly rich, and beams of sunlight shone as if with keen attention upon dust particles floating under the vaulted roof. A line of tired soldiers about to be slain by the beam of sunlight that animated the dust lay upon their packs and duffels, rifles and bayonets protruding from their midst like stakes in a vineyard. Their uniforms under the light became a golden cross between yellow and red, as bright as tulips, and when the soldiers bent their heads in fatigue and held their hats in their hands, they moved even hurried passersby.

The stores and restaurants that lined the concourse were full of people who bought something and ran with it, or lifted glasses and cups while closing their eyes. Porters with jaded and resentful expressions pulled creaking wagons that were mainly empty, and one cut a straight path along the side of the concourse, drawing after him an enormous cart of wood and steel, upon which rested a single wicker-covered jug of wine.

Alessandro bought half a dozen rolls and two bottles of fruit juice before crossing the vital stream of traffic on the concourse. After his ticket was punched and he passed through the barrier he began to walk next to a long line of lacquered railway cars. He was early. The few people boarding the train went down the platform and then suddenly disappeared as if they had been flies snatched by feeding fish. Almost everyone walked on the right side, near the train, but by an empty track on the left an old man in a white suit took a few steps forward and then stopped to rest on a cane. He looked up, first at the light pouring into the train shed from outside, then at the soot-blackened roof, and then at the train itself. After staring at the pavement for a moment, he started off again.

The old man had great difficulty with a small suitcase that he carried in his left hand. Alessandro offered to carry it for him.

"You'll have to spend ten minutes waiting for me," the old man said, "when you can probably just skip down there and jump up the steps."

"I don't mind walking slowly," Alessandro replied, taking the suitcase.

"Do you know why you walk slowly when you're old?"

"No."

"Because with age you receive the gift of friction. The less time you have, the more you suffer, the more you feel, the more you observe, and the more slowly time moves even as it races ahead."

"I don't understand."

"You will."

"The less time, the more friction, difficulty, and viscosity. Time expands. Is that correct?"

"Yes."

"At the end, when no time is left, it will pass so slowly that it will not pass at all."

"Correct."

"Then, at death, time stops?"

"What did you think death is?" the old man asked, taking a few more steps. "In death, time *unifies*. Old men on their deathbeds call for their fathers not because they are afraid, but because they have seen time bend back upon itself."

"How do you know this?" Alessandro asked politely.

"I don't know for sure. When I was your age I was skeptical and quick. I made fast work of the myths of heaven and hell and of the vastly deficient idea of nothingness. As I've grown older I've seen that the world is made of perfect balances and exact compensations. The heavier the burden and the closer you get to the end, the more viscous time becomes, and you see, in slow motion, intimations of eternity."

"Such as?"

"Beams of light, birds springing up."

"Birds springing up?"

The old man stopped. "It sounds crazy," he said, "but when you see birds rising, as if they're startled, their graceful flight becomes motionless. Their startled song, too, which should be so quick and crisp, freezes into one long note before the hunter fires. I've seen it many times now. They fly in arcs. The arc stops still, forever.

"If there are pigeons in this shed," he said, looking up, "and if a train blows its whistle and they scatter, you'll see, if you concentrate at the moment of the whistle blast."

The old man looked back at Alessandro. "You think I'm crazy," he said.

"I don't."

"You do. Come on, help me up the steps."

They crossed the platform and Alessandro gave him a boost into the train.

"What's for lunch?" the old man asked.

"In the dining car?"

"Yes."

"I don't know."

"Why not?"

"I don't work for the railroad."

"Since when?"

"I never did."

"Oh," the old man said, not so much embarrassed as confused.

"But I can find out, if you'd like."

"No no. It's not necessary. I get confused sometimes." He began to laugh at himself. "And I sometimes forget where I am. But that's all right, young man, because, sometimes, to forget where you are makes you feel very light and free."

IN MID-MORNING, as the train panted in the light-filled station in Bologna, Alessandro bought a bottle of mineral water that he placed on the table near the window. He leaned out as he departed, flying by the tiled roofs of the city that had for so long been his home, and as the train accelerated and began to run north, the yellows and golds of fields just harvested, or just about to be, disappeared into the blue. A lariat-line of smoke was pulled after the train, and then, in the silence just before the afternoon crickets resumed their song, it rose effortlessly into the open sky.

Rushing across the lowlands of the Po and the Adige, Alessandro never took his eyes off the October countryside. Relative to the points toward which his eye was drawn, he was moving at three-quarter time, more or less, and the motion of the train became a kind of music superimposed upon the landscape. Once again, music was arising from the inanimate, the elemental, and the dead, as if to bring them alive. The landscape itself appeared in repetitive volleys of deep color, stopped now and then at a whitened rapids or a dark chasm.

As they rolled over the marshes before Venice, he fell back in his seat, windburnt and exhausted, and noticed that the bottle of water, but for its slight and elegant blue tint, was the smoothest, clearest, and most transparent thing he had ever seen. All that was reflected in it was sharp, subdued, and calm. The fields outside, beyond the reeds; the reeds themselves, waving green and yellow; the water, shockingly blue in north light, were clarified, compressed, and preserved within the lens. And if bottles of mineral water could pacify the light of mountains, fields, and the sea, to what painful mysteries would the lens of beauty be opaque? Even death, Alessandro thought, would yield to beauty—if not in fact then in explanation—for the likeness of every great question could be found in forms as simple as songs, and there, if not explicable, they were at least perfectly apprehensible.

The train slowed to cross the bridge over the lagoon of Venice. Arch after arch, Alessandro's thoughts arose and took their places, as in the building of a cathedral, and by the time he had crossed half the bridge he had stumbled upon something that would be confirmed only after a lifetime of verification.

He straightened the bottle, adjusted his tie, tucked in his shirt, and waited. On the platform, conductors in dark blue uniforms walked back and forth with a quail-like gait that had never failed to signal the departure of a train. The engine released clouds of steam to rest forever in the vaguely green light, and startled pigeons took flight, forced by glass and steel into maneuvers tighter and more agile than in the open air. Venice seemed buoyant, as in a dream, and gave Alessandro the uncanny feeling that were he to leave the train he might defeat time by reaching out to grasp the opposite part of the loop upon which time was about to billow. But even if that had been literally true, if by breaking his ticket and making an early unplanned exit he could confound time, he would not have done it, for the attractions ahead were too bright to skip, and he had the notion that the harder and better he seized every dazzling particular, the greater would be the light in the end.

THE PANELED door of the first-class compartment opened and closed faster than the shutter of a camera, and suddenly a tall woman with a small suitcase in her hand was standing directly in front of him.

"Seven-C?" she asked.

Alessandro shrugged. He never remembered the number of his compartment after he had found it, and was always eager to throw away his ticket as soon as he could. She put down her suitcase, unfolded her ticket, and pulled the door into the compartment so she could read the number on the outside. "Seven-C," she said, closing the door, and then, to Alessandro, while she hoisted her valise up onto the rack, "Perhaps you have the wrong accommodations."

She sat down across from him, looked him in the eye, and said, "I think you are in the wrong compartment." She smiled a forced, deliberately insincere smile that seemed to say, "You *idiot*."

Alessandro shook his head slowly from side to side, and then looked out the window at the sandwich carts racing down the platform. She was a striking, unusual woman. She was as tall as an Englishwoman could get without difficulty in finding a marriage partner, and as slender and lean as if she were tied up in corsets. But the way her black-and-red silk dress fit her indicated that she had no corsetry and that her flesh was as hard as that of a country woman. The way she dressed signified neither wealth nor ease, but an unfamiliarity with both. Her fingernails were carefully painted and glazed, and her hands, though long and powerful, were delicate nonetheless.

"Well?" she asked.

Still trying to assimilate her appearance, he did not answer, but he did return her gaze. Masses of red hair fell about her face, which was almost ablaze with equal masses of freckles. This is not an Italian trait, and he had begun to conclude from her accent that she was Irish.

"Criminy," she said to herself. "Can you talk?"

He continued staring. Now her mouth was partially open as she awaited his answer. The skin on her face was stretched so tightly, and her white teeth were arrayed in such a way, as to give her a permanent look of irony, or even savagery. He had not yet seen her smile soften the Northern gauntness and rage into heart-stopping feminine beauty.

"Not only a man," she said to herself as she shuffled through her tickets, "but a deaf mute."

"My friends say I can talk snails into orgasm," Alessandro said.

At first she was dumbstruck, but then she said, in flawless Irish-accented Italian, "Well, then, as one snail said to another, I've been taking this train for the past ten years. I believe you have been placed, or have simply walked into, the wrong compartment. Sleeping compartment. You are a man. I am a woman. Sleeping compartment."

He unfolded his ticket and passed it to her. She took it and went over it very carefully. "Seven-C," she said. "Clerical error."

"Yes," he told her, leaning forward. "That's what happens when you buy your railroad tickets in a monastery."

The train had begun to move and half of it was already in the sunlight.

"I didn't buy my tickets in a monastery, thank you very much," she said.

"You're welcome. I did," he answered. "Monks never cheat."

"I'm a travel agent," she said. "I've never heard of this."

"Have you ever been to Rome?"

"Naturally."

"Do you know the Palazzo San Rafaello?"

"No."

"Fifty-five thousand monks live there. They have barber shops, bakeries, watchmakers, stationery stores, everything. And they have a railway agency. Why wouldn't they? They're always on the move."

"That may be so," she said, but then she just stopped talking and looked at him.

"What kind of travel agent are you?" he asked.

"I'm a booking agent for Nederland-Lloyd," was her reply. "I've sent tens of thousands of English and Scandinavian tourists to the Levant. They go there to see the ruins, and they stop off in Greece to look at the light. It hypnotizes them, one and all, and they come back ready to endure another season of darkness."

"Tell me something," he said.

"Yes?"

"Let us say that you were in your office—where is it?"

"On the Piazza San Marco, behind the columns. We're in the shade, and must have electric light even on summer days."

"You've been living in Venice for ten years?"

"Six. I was in Athens first."

"Do you speak Greek?"

"Yes."

"As well as you speak Italian?"

"No. It's harder."

"But there you are, in your office, and a woman comes in to buy a ticket to..."

"Alexandretta."

"She sits down across from you."

"I stand behind a counter."

"She faces you. She has booked a cabin, but you tell her there aren't any left."

"Yes?" The train was now picking up speed, moving across the bridge over which Alessandro had only half an hour before passed in rapt seriousness.

"That she must ride to Alexandretta in steerage."

"We would never do that."

"A hypothesis."

"Go on."

"She protests."

"Of course."

"*I won't ride in steerage. I'm entitled to a cabin.* But you have only a cabin with a man in it. What would you do?"

"I would *not* put them together."

"Even if she looked to you like a woman who was tense, and lovely, and virtuous—a woman who loved, a woman whose life was one of restraint, but for whom a mixed-up trip to Alexandretta would be, perhaps, the kind of thing that makes restraint worth bearing, justifies it? What would you do for one of your sisters in that position?"

Now the train was running across the marsh. The Irishwoman, whose name was Janet McCafrey, did not answer Alessandro directly, but her savage, red, tight, and beautifully crooked face composed itself into an alluring and patient smile.

"The monks are practiced in precisely this kind of distinction," he added.

"What did I do," she asked no one, "to get this man in my compartment?"

"We have two beds," he noted, observing that her dress was tighter around her body than would be required to make her constantly aware of the idea or memory of an embrace. "And in regard to your guilt," he added, "in my profession, as in agriculture, neither guilt nor innocence has a place."

The train was racing across golden fields once again. The bottle of mineral water knocked against the window now and then. It was sunny outside, and cool in their shaded compartment.

"Nor, might I add, in mine. And let me say that I know we have two beds."

"I understand," Alessandro said. He envisioned the long, slow, exciting ritual of their undressing for bed. He would endeavor to close his eyes or stare out the window, and she would disrobe within a foot of him, knowing that the very sound of her clothing would be more powerful than a hundred voluptuous nudes. Somehow, he would manage to get into bed, in the dark, and then he would lean over to speak to her, and she would have let her nightgown fall just, ever-so-slightly, a bit too much. And there they would be, parallel, rushing through the dark, caught in between the sheets, looking at one another's faces, aching to touch.

THE TRAIN was long: two locomotives, two coal cars, four sleepers, eight passenger cars, two dining cars, a mail car, and the private carriage of an unknown aristocrat, bringing up the rear with a little platform upon which he was sitting in a maroon smoking-jacket. When the train rounded bends, one could see the locomotives, as busy as ever at the front, the shuttlecocks of Europe, rushing about here and there like crazed cats crisscrossing a garden in pursuit of voles.

Now they had attained the steady speed that makes the landscape a thing of perfection and elevates the thoughts of someone observing it, but Alessandro was held closely to earth by the presence of Janet McCafrey, and thought of nothing but her. In railroad compartments, she mostly met fat-men who thought she was freakish because of her un-Italian, bird-like, Anglo-Irish gauntness, but Alessandro loved this sharp quality. He intended to put her off balance at first, to see her admirable intensity intensify. As the train sped along he leaned forward and said, "Tell me then, now that we seem to be sharing the same compartment, why Bucharest?"

She clutched her chest with her right hand, paled, and became immobile. She stood up, as if to pull some sort of cord, and sank back in despair, for she had intended to go to Munich from Venice, and now she thought that she was rushing at seventy kilometers per hour toward Bucharest. "Bucharest?" she asked meekly. "Bucharest?"

"Did I say Bucharest?" he replied. "That was a foolish mistake. Sorry."

She closed her eyes and passed her left hand across her brow, sighing in relief.

"I meant *Budapest!*"

"Oh God!" she said, giving up hope.

"Don't worry," Alessandro assured her, "we're on the track to Munich."

She was not angry, but wary. She wondered who he was, and she knew that he liked her. "I suppose," she offered, "that precision is not one of your strong points," and then she gave him the same smile that she had used in accusing him of being a deaf mute—so challenging, so impudent, so inviting.

"Perhaps not," he conceded, with a touch of feigned distress. "It's all the same to me—Budapest, Bucharest, Munich, Prague, Barcelona. I'm constantly on the move. All cities get to look alike, especially since my mission in each is the same."

He became deliberately silent, and looked out the window. Eventually, she had to ask, and she did, delicately and with caution, "What is your mission?"

"I'm a toothbrush salesman," he said, rifling through his haversack. While she sank back yet again in disappointment, he ignited. "We have a revolutionary dental cleaning instrument of a very elegant character that has been used primarily by the heads of the royal houses and that has yet to be brought to the general public. This instrument, while relatively expensive, is made of the best materials, will last a lifetime, applies the dentifrice in the gentlest and most effective manner, will not disturb the tooth enamel, and is comfortable to use." His hand settled inside the haversack on Enrico's tail brush, a duplicate of which he intended to find in Munich. It was a Viennese contraption twice as long as a man's hand and surrounded over half its long handle by bristles as thick as spaghetti projecting stiffly from it as far as a finger. Hanging from the end was a collection of vicious-looking scythe-like bladed hooks that, pulled gently through Enrico's tail, gave it a mesmerizing curl. At the base of the bristles was a broad serrated knife. The bristles themselves were covered with glistening black horse lanolin to which many kinds of things had clung.

"I go from pharmacy to pharmacy," he said. "It's hard. Some people are put off by the modern design, they distrust modernity, but then I tell them that it is this that whitens the teeth of the King of England."

He smiled proudly and pulled out the tail brush.

She looked at it for a while and her eyes leapt from it, to him, to the door. Then she leaned forward. "Tell me something," she asked earnestly. "When did you escape, and what do you want?" Leaning back, she added, as dryly as could only an Irishwoman who has spent ten years issuing steamship tickets to impatient English aristocrats, "You can call me Nurse Janet."

This made Alessandro laugh, and she joined him. The people in the next compartment rapped on the wall, and their muffled command came through the veneer in severe Plattdeutsch, "Laugh not in time of war!"

"You know," she said, "I've never heard an Italian man laugh at himself. Are you sure you're Italian? What has happened to your pride?"

"My pride," Alessandro said. "My pride. Let's see. I never had too much to start—I was too busy. Too much to see, too many fine things that have nothing to do with me." He hesitated. "Of late, I've deliberately taken whatever pride I had and led it to slaughter."

Her eyes were green, and so animate now that it seemed that she was dancing. "Why?"

"My father asked the same thing."

She nodded, waiting for him to go on.

"The war," he said. "Like an animal compelled by the seasons to engage in a course of behavior that it cannot understand, I feel directed to shed my skin, to dance, to burrow in the dirt, to behave like a fool. I don't know why, but something says to me, *Abandon your pride, drop it, sink it, leave it, be foolish, be indiscreet, shame yourself.* I really don't understand this, but the impulse is over-whelming and I'm going to honor it."

"You're going to *survive*," she said.

"I may not be able to avoid the trenches, but I'm going to change myself in whatever way is necessary so that I may walk out of them. That's what I intend."

She sat back to observe her accidental companion. She would not have cared had she been on her way to Bucharest, and neither would have he. "What's your name?" she asked.

"Alessandro Giuliani," he replied, just before a long blast of the steam whistle.

THE TRAIN passed great and small cities and pushed on toward the mountains. The harvest, the sun, and the October light had made Italy a chain mail of fields, their richness and tranquillity shattered only by the railway, and even then, after the trains had passed through, contentment would close-in the way cold blue water fills the trough made by an oar.

The Italian conductor would be replaced in Bolzano by an Austrian *Schlafwagenmeister*. He therefore felt keenly his vanishing prestige, and he eyed Alessandro and Janet with eyes that could not have been shiftier or more wary had they been given to a weasel. His peaked hat and waxed mustache exaggerated the effect. Here were a man and a woman of sexual age, together in connubial quarters, unmarried, and perhaps even unacquainted.

"Does anyone wish to exercise the right of complaint?" he asked.

They stared at him blankly.

"It is within my competence to adjust malfeasance and to see to the comfort and dignity of the passengers, for example, while the train is in the field of maneuver at Bolzano."

When they made no requests, he punched their tickets, made a nervous bow, and backed out the door, knocking a fat Austrian woman against the windows.

"What do you do when you're not selling toothbrushes or making geography mistakes?" Janet asked as they knifed through a village where the bells were ringing and the birds flying around the steeples to wait them out.

"I will have been delayed by military service, but I was about to take a position as a lecturer at the university in Bologna. I'm supposed to explain to undergraduates, while in the process of discovery myself, what is beautiful and why. Of course, neither I nor anyone else can do it, but I can try, and to do so I have to know the theories of beauty from Aristotle's forward, and before I die I'm supposed to come up with one of my own."

"Well," she said, "it's a nice toothbrush."

"Thank you. I could cite one of the many laws of contexts and contrasts. For example, associated with a cavalryman's saddle, rifle, bayonet, and curry combs, let us say, pictured in brown and golden tones hanging haphazardly on a worn stable door, with the smooth lines of the horse itself vanishing off the canvas, and the cavalry-man, in his bright colors, standing to the center, it might in fact be beautiful, but if in association with, for example, your masses of red hair, your white teeth, your extraordinarily beautiful mouth, and your bare shoulders, it would, of course, be ugly.

"That's all in reference to me or to you. It might have a better chance if seen in another eye. An octopus is a hideous, baggy, slimy, thoroughly disgusting creature. Which is worse, its sharp beak hidden within folds of soft flesh, its pod-like eyes, its flaccid sack, or its bumpy tentacles? Some have cited it as proof that God did not create the universe, but, at a distance, swimming smoothly through the water, it's as graceful as a prima ballerina. Sectioned under a microscope, it presents patterns of inexhaustible brilliance. And to an octopus of the opposite sex, or even to an adolescent squid who needs someone after whom to model himself, it can be handsome or beautiful, as the case may be.

"Throw in some Latin and Greek; magnify, enlarge, draw back now and then to get your bearings; and show that, despite context, position, and point of apprehension, nothing, in fact, is relative, and all beauty is absolute; and you have the basis for a lecture.

"That's what I do."

"It's *totally* unnecessary," she said.

"No one knows better than I that it's all here, and need not be explained or interpreted—just seized. What we see from the window of the train as it slowly alters our perspective and speeds across different registers of color and form; the light in this bottle of water; the rhythm of the engines; the way the clouds are pushed on waves of wind; you yourself, Nurse Janet, your entire body, apprehended in toto, part by part, in the light, in the dark; your smile, the way you move your eyes and lean upon your arm; the coincidence of colors in your dress and in your hair; the very angles of your teeth; that they glisten with moisture; your long fingers as they rest in your palms, like the radians of a nautilus; the pace of your breathing; the sweetness, I presume, of your breath, and the taste of your mouth. Such things, and I have only brushed the surface, render my profession totally unnecessary, and I know it."

"Lock the door," she said.

He leaned over and flipped the lock.

As if it had been timed by nature, they both stood to make a quick leap to the other's bench, and collided forcefully, still standing, in the middle. The train swayed first one way and then the other as it rounded a turn. She was pushed into him initially, and then he was pushed into her, and when the force of the turn pressed them together they magnified it by clasping tighter.

They remained standing as the train climbed into the hills, kissing until they were stupefied. Then they sank down, touching only lightly, and they kissed for at least an hour. She surfaced as if from an undertow. "It's the war, isn't it?" she asked, and then he took her back under. They were on the high ridge that rises between war and peace, and, like alpinists, they were intoxicated by the magnitude of the country below.

They both lost track of time, but after the change of engines in Bolzano, where they pulled the curtain down, it began to get dark. To the north, in country that Alessandro knew well, the mountains were a rose-colored gold along the snow line, and the Dolomite rock spires, rising from darkened meadows, were red. As the train ascended into the ice world, Alessandro and Janet flushed with heat of their own making. Their eyes were glazed, their hair looked as if it had been disheveled in a hurricane, and they said things that were far different from words.

Before the moon came up, someone rapped on the door, but they hardly heard it. The Austrian sleeping-car master, who had boarded while they were semi-conscious in Bolzano, announced that dinner was ready.

When they entered the dining car, heads turned. They looked as if they had been in the sun for several hours, and they walked together and carried themselves unmistakably.

THE MENU offered only ten schnitzels.

"What am I supposed to do?" Janet asked. "I don't like eggs, I don't like bread crumbs, and I don't like veal."

"How have you survived in Venice for six years?" Alessandro asked.

The waiter arrived with a towel draped over his mallet-like forearm. "I'm sorry to announce," he said, "that, due to the war, we have not *Wiener Schnitzel, Salzburger Schnitzel, Heimlich Schnitzel, Schweizer Schnitzel, Fest Schnitzel, Schlange Schnitzel, Nelke Schnitzel, Unverwandt Schnitzel, Ganzlich Schnitzel,* and *Auberst Schnitzel.*"

"What do you have?"

"Chicken and potatoes."

"How do you cook the chicken?"

"Over a flame, sir," the waiter replied, frigidly.

"Directly?"

"No, sir. In a pot of *heisses Wasser.*"

"Boiled chicken?"

The waiter was rent by conflicting defiance, disgust, shame, and pride. "At the front, men are dying."

"I'm sorry," Alessandro said. "Bring us whatever there is. What comes with the boiled chicken?"

"Potatoes, as I have indicated..."

Janet held out her index finger and smiled viciously, but the waiter did not understand that he had not actually *indicated* any potatoes.

"A small *Salat.* Plenty of *Mineralwasser.* Dessert is your choice—rhubarb flan, or festival torte. Rhubarb flan speaks..."

He was taken by the shoulder as the dining car master walked by and whispered something to him, leaving Alessandro and Janet with his last words echoing in their ears: "Rhubarb flan speaks..."

"And the festival torte," he continued, with a sigh, "is sugar and flour with a dash of cocoa."

"We'll have the talking flan."

"Italian swine," he said under his breath.

Janet heard it. "I'm Irish," she stated.

After this aggression, Alessandro no longer felt guilty about wanting to eat while men were dying at the front. He remembered as well that he soon might be doing the same, or, at the very least, killing them. "Bring the festival torte," he commanded.

After the waiter left, Janet said, "If this were England, he'd pee in our soup."

"He's German and I'm Italian," Alessandro offered. "He already did."

"Thank God Ireland is neutral."

"On which side?"

"England's."

"Italy may not enter the war after all," Alessandro told her. "We have no real interest in it. Although we make noise, we always make noise, and seldom does anything come of it. If we do declare war, whether against the Central Powers or the Entente, it will be at the end, perhaps next spring. We might send a battle fleet to sea and fire a few shots before the armistice. That's the Italian ethos."

"It's not the English ethos," she said. "And it's certainly not the German ethos."

"Nor the Russian," he added, playing intently with his knife. "The many millions of them are capable of inflicting great damage, not least on themselves."

Outside Innsbruck the train slowed to a walk as it passed through an enormous barbed wire barricade and into a vast military area. Alessandro rose in his chair, surprised that a civilian train would be allowed in an armed camp. The cars were closely watched by guards in sandbagged enclosures all the way along the route, and electric lights were focused on the undercarriages, sending up a strange white glow that suggested not railway ties and a gravel trackbed but the entry to another world.

The slow pace of the train enabled Alessandro to observe carefully this encampment of the Imperial Army. For as far as he could see west toward the mountains that formed one wall of the valley of the Ruetzbach were lines of tents, rows of wagons and artillery pieces, and fires that stretched down the long alleys like flaming shrubbery.

Dozens of men were gathered around each blaze, at least a hundred fires ran down each row, and the rows did not stop appearing as the train filed past—twenty, thirty, forty, fifty; they kept on coming. Alessandro calculated that the encampment held a hundred thousand men or more.

He felt a chill when he saw this, as if he were looking through a window to the future. And just when the chill was over he turned in his seat to look out the opposite rank of windows. There, too, the casual diners had been stunned by the new world, for there, too, were yet another hundred thousand men in a city of tents and fires.

Most of the soldiers were boys only somewhat younger than he. Their hair was closely cropped, and their big, awkward, adolescent faces were appropriate for sawyers or guides in an Alpine village, or for the discontented sons of grocers in those cities big enough for churches and squares. The ones in the guard posts, who watched the train as it passed through their encampment, had the expression of miners looking out from the dark. It was not just that the floodlights reflected back by the shining undercarriage almost blinded them, but that they had been completely removed from the world they had known. In gray coats and high boots, burdened with rifles and ammunition, they appeared to be silent, fated, and strange.

The fires stretched so far into the distance that they seemed to be lapping at the base of the hills, and the earth seemed to have opened, and released a ghastly white light.

Then an army officer carrying a pistol walked through the dining car. Though he was inspecting the interior, his eyes were turned upward to follow the footsteps of someone who paced him, out of sight, on the roof.

They crossed the perimeter and rolled quietly into Innsbruck, where not a soldier was in sight.

MORE THAN a hundred years before, Raphael's portrait of Bindo Altoviti, "when he was young," had traveled by horse cart from Florence to Munich. During rainstorms in the valley of the Adige the dirty gray canvas that protected the cart had leaked in many places, but the wooden case that held the painting was watertight, having been caulked at the seams, and Bindo Altoviti stayed dry. In the Brenner Pass after a quick snowstorm one of the mules slipped on a sheet of ice and nearly pulled everything down the face of a steep cliff. Otherwise, the journey had been unremarkable—except that an important part of the soul of Italy had been moved north to reside in the Alte Pinakothek. That the Germans should consider its few pfennigs' worth of oxides and canvas among their proudest possessions, and that the Italians should feel relatively empty for their absence, said a great deal about the principles that Alessandro Giuliani continually struggled to understand and that Raphael had mastered completely.

Alessandro had wanted to go to Munich not only to study the painting but to look into the eyes of young Bindo Altoviti and see a man who had come through time propelled and pressured by the laws of art. He stood with Janet in a quiet gallery that smelled of freshly applied oils hundreds of years after the fact. How this came to be, they did not know, but the shadows, the great expanse of dark wooden flooring, and the snow-covered mountains that they could see through the windows seemed to conspire to lift and hold the paintings as if they were balanced atop columns of water or light. Had the paintings merely been tacked to the walls instead of resting atop the breaking surf of sunlight and shadow, they would not have been a tenth as arresting.

Janet stepped off to the left to examine a huge painting of a medieval battle. The horses were as rounded and swollen as balloons and had red martingales and bridles of gold. And the horses, pathetically rotund, frozen, floating in time, bared their teeth in the fight, like dogs, as their enemies and their allies ascended quietly into the place of the imagination where their motion evaporated and left them infinitely wise.

With neither apologies nor care, nor thought, nor credit given to the many contrary proofs, Alessandro believed that the portrait of Bindo Altoviti— *"il ritratto suo quando era giovane,"* his portrait when he was young—was as alive as any of the light that calibrates the time that says of us that we live. His eyes could see, his hand could touch, and he was breathing. The black silk that fell from his shoulder was new, and beyond the emerald wall behind him, Rome breathed in May.

Young Bindo Altoviti, looking out from time, made a perfect coalition with the mountains, the sky, and the tall redheaded woman who had bent over just slightly to examine a raging battle that was long over. Alessandro imagined that Bindo Altoviti was saying, half with longing, half with delight, "These are the things in which I was so helplessly caught up, the waves that took me, what I loved. When light filled my eyes and I was restless and could move, I knew not what all the color was about, but only that I had a passion to see. And now that I am still, I pass on to you my liveliness and my life, for you will be taken, as once I was, and although you must fight beyond your capacity to fight and feel beyond your capacity to feel, remember that it ends in perfect peace, and you will be as still and content as am I, for whom centuries are not even seconds."

The striking visage of Bindo Altoviti was of a type that had lasted and could be seen on the boys who worked in the cafes on the Via del Corso or drove tourists through the back streets, in carriages that hardly fit between the walls. If Bindo Altoviti could last through time not only to live in his portrait in a German cloister but to sweat in the bakeries of Rome, then perhaps Alessandro had to abandon his own short view of history in favor of the careful process of descent, the awesome repetitions, the inexplicable similarities and reappearances that made a unity of many generations of fathers and sons.

In the eyes of Bindo Altoviti, Alessandro saw wisdom and amusement, and he knew why the subjects of paintings and photographs seemed to look from the past as if with clairvoyance. Even brutal and impatient men, when frozen in time, assumed expressions of extraordinary compassion, as if they had reflected the essence of their redemption back into the photograph. In a sense they were still living. Bindo Altoviti, unknowingly, had become the young men, unknowing, on the streets of Rome. Had they been aware, they might have come to see his portrait, but it hardly mattered, for what they did would make no difference in the way time cracked and burst above their short lives like a thundering star shell. Except that now Alessandro had seen a benevolent diagram of passion and color in perfect balance, and he knew from Bindo Altoviti's brave and insolent expression that he was going to stay alive forever.

A DISTANT sound rattled the windows of the Alte Pinakothek. Though faint, it shook Alessandro's chest and reverberated in his lungs.

"What is that?" he asked an old museum guard.

"Nothing to worry about," the guard replied in Italian, even though the question had been posed in German. "It has happened every morning at eleven, without fail, since the war began. It's the testing of the field guns."

"Where is it done?" In the echoing rooms, Alessandro was unable to determine its direction.

"I don't know."

Alessandro and Janet went outside, and were able to tell that the firing was coming from the east. They hired a carriage and told the driver to take them to it.

After an hour of following quiet streets, crossing railroad tracks, and traveling roads that went through forests and fields, they came to an enormous parade ground.

Coils of barbed wire spilled into the dirt track, isolating the military encampment from walkers and picnickers. Cannon, caissons, and motorized trucks in tightly regimented equipment parks covered most of what had been green in the fields, and over and beyond them, on a low hill, were the guns, a hundred of them in a single unbroken line. The order of firing proceeded steadily down the long row almost like the ticking of a clock—except that clocks alternate, first ticking, then tocking, and this great machine expressed itself in a monotone.

"Ka-phoom!" it would say, immediately after one of its segments had convulsed, sprung back, and coughed out a burst of fire and smoke, and then, "Ka-phoom!" when, two seconds later, the next gun let loose.

Methodical as it was, neither the method nor the maddeningly exact timing was what held the carriage driver and his two passengers still, but, rather, the sound itself. Alessandro thought that no matter how many times he would hear it, he would never get used to it. He was wrong.

The signature of each blast was a deep concussion, alone for a tenth of a second and then joined by a sharp metallic rattling like that of the sheet metal used in the theater to mimic thunder. "Ka-phoom! Ka-phoom! Ka-phoom!" As the metallic effect was slightly out of phase with the initial concussion, beginning an instant later and ending an instant later, so with the soundless waves that followed upon each shot. They were felt through the entire body; mostly in the chest and throat, but also in the extremities, on the forehead, and, depending upon the position of the jaw and the tightness of the cheeks, within the mouth. Natural thunder was neither as deep nor as sharp as this, and though Alessandro had grown up in Rome, a city that is perhaps the best catcher of thunder in all the world, he had never heard it come on so evenly, for even thunder rests.

The horse was skittish. Just a little way over the fields, the snake of a hundred segments kept up its concussive bursts, and each report moved the carriage and made the wheels creak.

"It's beginning to make me shake," Janet announced, trembling not from emotion but from the charged air that shook her lips, her chest, and the muscles in her upper thighs and arms.

The sound of the air blasts rolled down the hillsides and over the fields. With never a pause, tiny figures in gray next to each gun quickly reloaded. Alessandro's infatuation with Janet was overwhelmed by the imperative of the guns, for they were deeper even than thunder. "Ka-phoom! Ka-phoom! Ka-phoom!" This was the sound that, on the Western Front, had begun to drown out the music of the world. It was clear to Alessandro, and easily understandable, that, for some, music would cease to exist. But not for him, not for him. The electricity rose up his spine and he trembled not from shock but because, over the sound of the guns, he was still able to hear sonatas, symphonies, and songs.

THE 19TH RIVER GUARD

SEPTEMBER, 1916 ... A dozen soldiers stood just inside the entrance to the tunnel, or squatted, leaning slightly forward, using their rifles for support. They loitered there to get out of the sun and to catch the continuous cool breeze that came from within. A lieutenant of infantry emerged from the grove of pale trees that protected the mouth of the shaft, walking briskly, with his left hand resting on his pistol belt and his right grasping a short stick. Following him was a stocky young naval cadet who struggled under the weight of a duffel bag, his rifle knocking against his side.

The men in the tunnel began to rise, but sank back down when the lieutenant motioned with his hand that they should ignore him. Nonetheless, the ones who were smoking removed the cigarettes from their lips and held them at a polite angle in front of their stomachs until the officer had passed.

"Is this a naval installation?" the cadet asked as they stepped into the tunnel, a hundred kilometers from the sea. "It has to be a mistake."

"Put your duffel and the rest here," the lieutenant said, having taken up position next to a wooden cart on tracks that ran through the tunnel.

The cadet had red hair and a chipped tooth in the front of his mouth. He gladly threw down his things. He followed the lieutenant into the shaft, pulling the cart after them. "I was on the sea," he said, as if to protest.

"If a supply train comes through in either direction we'll have to lift this off the tracks. We each take an end and move the cart to the other side. The supply trains move fast, but you can hear them from far away."

They had been walking for about ten minutes, passing beneath a seemingly endless chain of dim bulbs and wood beams, when the lieutenant answered the naval cadet's question. He didn't get right to the point, as if he didn't care, or could no longer concentrate. "Don't worry," he said. "It isn't really dangerous here anymore. At sea, you wouldn't be much safer."

"Safer? I was on the *Euridice*."

"The cruiser?"

"Yes, sir, the cruiser. I came aboard in the evening, the next morning at four we left Brindisi, at two in the afternoon we hit a mine, and at two-ten we began to sink. Almost everyone would have escaped, but a submarine was following us. It surfaced and motored around to take advantage of our list. On the starboard side, our guns wouldn't depress low enough to hit it. Our shells passed over the conning tower, and as we rolled more and more they got higher and higher.

"I saw their captain. He put three shots in our side point-blank. The first two shots made the ship shudder. The third hit the magazine and we blew apart in a dozen pieces. I had been in the signals room and I was blown through the door, over the sea. In mid air the wall passed by me and I went through the door again as it caught up with me and moved ahead. When I hit the water, I was thrown against the maps. They crumpled up and I slid into the sea. I smashed my face against something and swallowed brine, but I came to the surface and swam around until I grabbed a half-submerged chair."

"A chair?"

"I think it may have been the captain's chair, but I don't know. It wasn't the signals chair, it was too heavy. I sat in it and bled for an hour until I was picked up by one of our destroyers. I kept my head above water until the chair rolled over, and then I'd get up on it again and try to keep my balance. The wound was on my face, as you can see. I was lucky. If it had been lower down I would have bled into the sea until I died, the way a lot of us did.

"When the submarine passed through the debris, I thought the crew looked remorseful—because the wounded were giving up, letting go, and sinking—but when they passed me they laughed. The bastards."

"How many men were lost?"

"We had twelve hundred and forty-two when we went out. The destroyer pulled a hundred and fifty-seven from the water."

The lieutenant shook his head.

"I got a medal. I was on the ship for less than a day, and I never even saw the code book. I got a medal for keeping my balance in a floating chair."

"Every day," the lieutenant said, "shells land somewhere along this line with good effect, and soldiers sail through the air. They don't end up in floating chairs."

Now and then they passed groups of men on their way out. Few wounded were among them, and those who were wounded were walking.

"It's quiet now," the lieutenant told the naval cadet. "Very little has happened since the middle of August, which probably means that in the fall we're really going to get it."

"There are cycles?"

"Like the weather."

"We've been in this tunnel for a half an hour."

"It's four kilometers long. We'll emerge on the riverbank. It's the only way to go to and from the trenches, safe from artillery. We're descending not because we're going deeper into the earth but because the terrain slopes toward the river: we're always eight meters from the surface, unless we pass under a hill. The earth is soft here, no rock. The miners did this in less than a month."

"Sir, I'm in the navy," the naval cadet said, stopping as if to go no farther.

"So am I."

"You are?" The cadet was astonished. In his well broken-in green uniform and infantry belts the lieutenant was the paradigm of a seasoned soldier.

"Yes. Do you think you're going to wear that stupid uniform when you get up ahead? You'll exchange it for an army set within a day. It's too easy to be shot in blue. You stand out too clearly."

"They have commissaries in the trenches?"

"No, you pull it off a man who has been killed. He gets to be buried in your naval uniform, you wash his and sew up the holes, and you're both happy."

"I see. We're both happy. Why is the navy in the trenches, anyway?" the cadet asked. Despite his experience on the *Euridice*, he thought the sea might be safer, and he considered going back to it.

"We're the River Guard," the lieutenant answered. He stopped to take out a cigarette. The tunnel seemed infinite, and the cadet wondered if he were not dreaming or dead. "The river's water, isn't it? At the beginning of the war they didn't know things were going to go this way up here—so badly, so slow—and they apportioned too much to the navy."

"Not when I went in."

"You went in late. Before that, it was different. All kinds of clever asses joined the navy to keep out of the trenches, and ended up here."

"Yes, but what is it that we *do* here?"

"The North is always in danger of an Austrian wheeling movement, but, here, because we're near the mountains, we have few attempts at maneuver. The real infantry stays to the south, and we hold the water line. Someone thought it would assuage the pride of the navy, if we had to fight on land, to call us river guards."

They started walking again. "The river runs like this," the lieutenant said, motioning with a stick, "from the mountains. Ten kilometers to the north, on steep limestone cliffs, the Alpini take over. Nothing big can come through in a place as vertical as that.

"We're deployed on the western bank of the Isonzo, from the cliffs to a point about ten kilometers south of where we are now. The river does most of our work for us, but you have to watch it closely.

"They're not Jesus Christs, you see. They can't walk on water, so they can't make a massed attack, because we can deal with boats, swimmers, and bridges. When they try that kind of stuff they get killed: volunteers—Czechs? Hungarians? How the hell do I know. I think they aren't told. They get in the boats, or they swim. Even at night, most of them die before they get to this side.

"The only ones who make it into our trenches are the ones who swim on moonless nights, like Indians, and suddenly they jump down from nowhere and kill you with a bayonet."

"That's happened?"

"It happens every week. It's for morale. It's supposed to make them feel good and us feel bad. I know it makes us feel bad, but I really can't see how it makes them feel good. To begin with, they seldom get back to their lines. I told you. Volunteers. Idiots. Suicides. The same with us."

"Us?"

"We're supposed to reply in kind."

"Am I going to have to do it?" the cadet asked, his voice cracking.

"How many times do I have to tell you? It's all volunteers—the strange ones, the ones who think they're Indians, the ones who decide it's time to die."

A white pinhole of light appeared ahead. As they moved toward it, they could hear the muted sound of machine-gun fire.

"It's quiet," the officer said, "but we've got a problem."

"What's that?"

"No rain. The river's drying up. Another two weeks and you'll be able to run across."

"Oh God."

"Well, yes, they've been moving up lots of men. In the last month, their cooking fires doubled. I don't know what they eat, but it smells like shit."

"We do the same, don't we?"

"Eat badly?"

"No. Move up reinforcements."

"We've been screaming for reinforcements, and they finally sent them."

"How many men?"

"So far, only you."

They had reached the exit, where a group of soldiers stood, as at the entrance, to escape the heat.

"You're kind of short," the lieutenant went on, "but you'll take care of us, I know."

The cadet had never heard machine-gun fire, and had never been in a trench.

"Okay," the lieutenant said, "I'm taking you out to the Nineteenth." Now he was tense. He bent forward. He had his pistol in his hand. "Keep your head down." They began to walk through a maze of trenches that were as hot as hell and filled with light that was far too bright.

Without a cart for his baggage the cadet began to breathe heavily and sweat. The footing was often difficult. Though they had been dry for months, the trenches had been built with the rain in mind. Uneven and rashly constructed plank walks lined their floors, and one had to jump gaps, step over upright pieces, and avoid feet that protruded from places of burial in the trench walls where the sand had fallen away and either no one could put it back or no one cared.

In places where the sides of the trench wanted to collapse and were reinforced with timbers, the cadet had to vault the timbers or bend under them. He could not round a bend, he discovered, without banging either the duffel, his rifle, his elbow, or his head into things that projected from the walls. In some stretches the lieutenant motioned for him to crouch down low, or to run very fast, or even to do both. Sweat stung his eyes and he was so exhausted that he felt as if he were coming apart. Even the lieutenant, who carried nothing but his pistol and short stick, was breathing hard, and had dark wet patches on his uniform.

"Where are our soldiers?" the cadet asked. "We've gone several kilometers in the open and I haven't seen anyone except the few who passed us going the other way."

"These are the communications trenches," the lieutenant said, without stopping. "When we get to the lines at the top of the T, it'll be crowded. Enjoy the space while you can."

They continued on until they reached the crossing of the T, where a wider trench ran for several score meters on both sides before a gradual bend cut off the view. Fifty men, more or less, were sitting against the trench wall, standing on the fire-step and peering out slits at the top, or looking through telescopic periscopes to see what lay above and beyond.

The trench had no shadows, the sun was blinding, and the cadet asked for permission to drink.

"When we get to the Nineteenth."

"How far?"

"Not as far as we've come. You want to see something?"

The cadet didn't answer, but he was grateful for a chance to rest.

"You're in the line," the lieutenant said, "so let me acquaint you with the facts. Give me your helmet and your rifle."

The cadet opened his kit bag and passed the iron helmet to the officer, and then his rifle.

"All right," the lieutenant said as he put the helmet on top of the sheathed bayonet, "watch this."

He raised the helmet above ground level and took it down, all in a second. As it descended, shots rang out and earth was scattered into the trench. "They were slewing their guns that time. They didn't even come close. Watch now."

He pushed up the helmet and wiggled it. Following dozens of machine-gun and rifle bursts, the sky darkened momentarily as sand and earth were kicked over the top of the trench. When the helmet came down, it had two graze marks on it.

"The Austrians are better at that than we are," the lieutenant said. "They have more discipline, and they care. You must keep your head down at all times, except at night. You'll see the river at night. It's beautiful, especially when the moon is reflected off the surface. Even during a full moon, they can't see you. Some lunatics in the Nineteenth swim at night. They claim it's safe if you stay close to our side. They can claim anything they want."

"They must be crazy," the cadet asserted.

"Yes," the lieutenant said, his pistol now holstered, his shoulders bent forward as he set out again toward the Nineteenth. "Can you imagine being up to your neck in ice-cold water, naked, with ten thousand guns on the opposite shore?"

"I don't swim without a chair," the cadet said, showing the chipped tooth as he smiled at his own witticism.

"Don't stand so straight, you idiot. You're on a platform, you'll get your head shot off. And put the helmet on."

They moved through the forward trench, passing hundreds of men, dozens of machine-gun emplacements, and the slightly wider circular excavations, reached through a thin zigzagging sub-trench, where the trench mortars and their shells were kept. The hope was that if these were hit by counter-battery fire the force of the explosion would be absorbed in the baffles of the sub-trench, but when an enemy shell found its target and the magazines had been newly stocked, the explosion was so great that the baffles didn't seem to matter and the concussion would slay men up and down the trench for twenty-five meters and knock to the ground soldiers who were standing much farther away.

Rotting camouflage nets were draped along the earthen walls. "Why don't you use that stuff to make some shade?" the cadet asked.

"We did, once," the lieutenant answered, "but it showed them where to aim."

"Then why not cover everything?"

"Not enough netting, and when you jump up to fire you get tangled in it."

After the lieutenant stopped several times to talk to soldiers in their redoubts, they came to a branch in the system, extending northeast at a thirty-degree angle from the main trench.

The lieutenant said, "This leads out to your post, which projects ahead of the lines about a hundred meters onto a bluff above the river. We call it the Bell Tower, because of the view. You see these?" he asked, kicking two insulated wires fastened to one side of the trench. "They're telephone wires. One goes to battalion headquarters, which is just on the other side of the T where we came in, and the other goes to divisional headquarters and the brigade office. So when you talk on that telephone you never know if Cadorna himself will be listening, and you have to be correct."

"I'm going to be talking to Cadorna?"

"Fuck Cadorna. You're going to be calling in reports, when you get the hang of it, and I've given you proper warning. Another thing you should know is that nobody stays in the communications trench between here and the Bell Tower." Firing erupted down the line—machine guns, rifles, some small mortars.

"What's that?" the cadet asked nervously.

"What's what?" he was asked in return.

"That gunfire."

"I don't know," he said. "It's nothing. No one stays in this trench—it's too exposed and shallow, and the angle's no good. As you can see, it won't protect against incoming shells. You have to know the password at both ends, or you'll get shot. In the daytime they usually look to see who it is before they open fire, but don't count on it. At night they shoot right away. You have to say the password loudly enough so that it can be heard, but not so loudly that it will carry across the water."

"What is it?"

"It used to be *oil can,* but now it's *Vittorio Emanuele, Re d'Italia,* but that's too much, so we say, you know, *Verdi.*"

"What if I forget?"

"You won't."

"What if I do? Words can be knocked out of your head."

"Tell them who you are, speak Italian as fast as you can, and pray."

They started up the communications trench that led to the Bell Tower. The lieutenant had cocked his pistol as if he expected the enemy to confront him somewhere ahead.

A few minutes later they arrived at the entrance of the Bell Tower and found themselves staring into the barrel of a machine gun.

"Password!" they heard before they could see who was saying it.

"Verdi!" they said, perhaps more clearly than any words they had ever spoken, and then they went inside.

You could hear the wind in the Bell Tower as if it had been, in fact, a bell tower—not in the city but, rather, on the seacoast, because the steady breezes that came down from the mountains whistled through the beams, the corrugated metal, and the firing slits. They whistled past the mouths of the guns, in turbulent eddies that turned the gun barrels into otherworldly flutes. Despite the wind, the Bell Tower was hot, because the cool air that came through the ports was not enough to relieve the pressure of the sun on the open areas or to refresh the hidden bunkers.

"I brought a new man," the lieutenant said to some soldiers at the entrance. Then he turned around and left without saying anything or looking at the cadet, who feared that the lieutenant had disliked him. The lieutenant had not even decocked his, pistol, and he sped through the trench like a strange kind of rabbit that was afraid to lift its head. Then he rounded the corner and disappeared.

"He's done his work for the day," one of the soldiers said. "Now he'll eat some *rostissana Piacenza,* and sleep until nightfall."

"So what? We'll go swimming," another soldier said. "Who is this?" he asked about the cadet.

The cadet felt short and overwhelmed, because he was short and overwhelmed, but he wanted to hold his own with soldiers who seemed inured to war, so he said, "I was on the *Euridice.*" Because they seldom saw newspapers they had never heard of the *Euridice,* and from then on they called him by that name, even though it was a woman's name, even after he died.

THE BELL Tower was a round concrete fortification about the size of the arena in a provincial bull ring. Around an open *cortile* eight meters in diameter were nine bunkers, each of the same size. The *cortile* was used mainly for taking the sun and air. Shells had fallen directly in the center and would have killed everyone had it not been for a heavy wall of sandbags in a concentric ring between the *cortile* and the bunkers. The Austrians seemed to have discovered this somehow, and had stopped aiming for direct hits.

The nine bunkers might have been of different sizes had the fortification been designed by those who were to use it. Twenty men lived in the Bell Tower, and with Euridice, twenty-one. The three rooms for sleeping were jammed with cots. Binoculars, coats, weapons, and haversacks hung from rifle-shell casings pegged into planks and beams. A lantern was on a table in the middle. Against the outside walls and under the firing ports were chairs, rifles, and boxes of ammunition. Seven men slept in each room. At least seven men were always on duty, peering through firing ports in the seven bunkers facing the Austrian line. At times fourteen men, at times all twenty-one, fired, loaded, and shifted from one side of the emplacement to another, desperately hauling their three machine guns. In the assault that they feared would come, their number was to be doubled, so that two soldiers would man each firing port, one to fire and one to load, or simply to take the place of the other if he were tired or if he fell. The maps and telephones were in one of the rooms, the kitchen in another, stored ammunition and food in three others. The Bell Tower had no hospital because it had no doctor: stretchers, medical instruments, and material for treating wounds were stockpiled in the map room. Of all the rooms, however, the most remarkable was the latrine.

This surely was the end of the world, these two rows of filthy planks suspended above overbrimming cesspools. One would almost rather die than either breathe, hear, or see in this place. No animal defecating in the open field, whether a horse whose tail lifted deftly on the run, or a solemn and indifferent cow, had less dignity than the two lines of grimacing, twisting, groaning creatures with shaved heads and bad teeth, who struggled not to fall into the horrible soup they strained to augment. Alessandro learned to survive there, but slowly. He took wet mortar flannels with him to clean the wooden bar upon which he had to balance on his thighs, feet precariously off the ground, leaning forward so as not to topple backward into the trench—a fate visited upon two Neapolitans who had been playing with one another's parts. He wrapped his head in a blanket so as not to see, hear, smell, or be seen. Soon, everyone followed suit. When Alessandro was suffering upon the bar, desperately keeping in balance, head turbaned-up in a mass of filthy wool, he dreamed of walking through the Villa Borghese on a cool clear day in the fall, in his finest clothes, with the leaves and the fresh air blowing by him like an express train. Some of the other soldiers sang, while others screamed in pain, muffled in the wool helmets that Alessandro had invented. Being blind in this place was desirable, but risky, for if one were involved in a vendetta one could easily and anonymously be flipped backward, like the Neapolitans.

Euridice put down his duffel on the cot next to Alessandro's. "What's the book?" Euridice asked, assuming that since he himself was a graduate of the *liceo* and had been a naval cadet, he was the only one on the river who really knew how to read. He looked closely. "It's Greek," he said, drawing back in wonder. Alessandro, after a year and a half on the line, was gaunt, muscular, and sunburned. To Euridice, he looked experienced, and besides that, he was six or seven years older. "Can you read Greek?"

Alessandro nodded.

"That's wonderful, really stupendous!" Euridice said, pointing to the open page. "In the *liceo* I learned only Latin and German, not Greek."

"I know," Alessandro said, and went back to his book.

"How do you know?" Euridice asked.

Alessandro looked up. "Because this is Arabic."

Euridice opened his duffel and started to unpack. "No one's fat," he said, having noticed that all the soldiers were lean.

"Except you," someone said, cruelly.

"No one's fat," Alessandro repeated without taking his eyes from the book.

"Why?"

Alessandro turned his head. "We're nervous."

"I look forward to losing weight. In the navy, the food was too delicious."

"Don't get bullet holes. You wouldn't be waterproof."

"Waterproof?"

"I keep my ammunition under your bed," Alessandro said, still not looking up. "When it rains it leaks there."

A cat slinked into the room, gliding along on its belly as flat as it could get. It took a look around, jumped onto Alessandro's cot, and began to lick itself.

"What's that?" Euridice asked, looking at the cat.

"That's a cat."

"Yes I know, but what's it wearing?" The cat was encased in leather and metal, in a harness that looked like a cross between a medical appliance and a military apparatus.

"She was hit by a shell fragment," Alessandro said. "It tore a big patch off her back. It took six months to heal, and without the harness she opens it with her teeth." At this, as if on command, the cat turned to try to lick her back. She couldn't get to it, and, instead, she licked the air.

"What's her name?"

"Serafina."

"What does she eat?"

"Macaroni and rats."

Alessandro put down his book and pulled the cat, a blur of brown, orange, and blond, into his arms. "What's sad about her," he said, "is not that she was wounded but that, if she wanted, she could bound out of here—you know how quick cats are, how fast they can run, and how high they can jump—and she could go anywhere she wanted, away from the battle. She could go to a little town in the Apennines and catch mice under an olive tree, and she'd never hear a gunshot again in all her life except when the farmers went out after birds." He looked at Euridice. "But she doesn't know. She stays with us."

TWO NIGHTS later, when the moon was hardly visible behind a thick blanket of hot gray cloud, they went swimming. The soldiers of the Bell Tower believed that although it was obviously dangerous to swim in the branch of the Isonzo that ran below them, it was perfectly all right, even rational, if the swimming party numbered no more and no less than three men.

No one had ever been killed on such an excursion, or even detected. The first time they crawled down the slope and through the mine fields they had been three, and in every subsequent three-man expedition nothing had gone awry. More than three men, it was said, would be too large a block. Their movement, whether simultaneous or serial, would attract the attention of that part of the eye that is irritated by sequences. Two men, or even just one, would not move 'scale-like' enough across the landscape. A tiny Ligurian had postulated that movement across nocturnal terrain occurred in three categories: points, scales, and plates. Plates, in being more than three men, were large enough to disturb the eye. Points, in being less than three men, were small enough to disturb the eye. Scales, however (and everyone knew that a scale comprised three men), were moderate and soothing, nearly invisible to sentries and observers, part of the landscape, and not so big that their apparent movement would appear unusual. Everyone believed this, even Alessandro, who didn't really believe it but refused to disbelieve it. The Ligurian, whom they called *Microscopico,* asserted that he had proof. He himself was a point, and when once he had had to crawl to the brink of the Austrian lines to retrieve a wounded comrade (Microscopico had been chosen on the assumption that his small size would allow him to go unnoticed) the night had failed to protect him, and a thousand shots had been fired in his direction. He had escaped only because a feral pig that had been feeding on the dead had been startled by the firing and had run through no-man's-land, usurping the Austrian aim while he himself dragged the dead body of his friend through the muddy depressions. The pig had been felled, because the pig, too, was a point, which all went to show that scales were the only way to move about between armies.

A soldier called the Guitarist, an affable Florentine who, with his classical songs, made the long nights tolerable, had refused to believe the scale theory. They ostracized him. When he entered the latrine, they would exit. When he spoke, they would pay him no heed. He tried to retaliate by putting his guitar up on the wall, but the absence of music hurt him more than it did anyone else, and in a week their tyranny had beaten him down and, allowing that the theory of scales was correct, he had resumed his playing.

Alessandro told him that, of course, the theory was nonsense, but that it held things together. Everything would be all right as long as everyone else believed it. Within a day or two, everyone, even Microscopico, had sought out the Guitarist and said precisely the same thing.

It was so hot that in the daytime the infantrymen doffed their shirts and rolled their pants up above the knee. Summer's fat and successful flies could hardly move: when they alighted on something they wanted it to be forever, and often died in the cause. The cat lay stretched on her back and didn't mind if she were wetted down with cold water. Even the machine guns seemed to fire much more slowly, though that was just an illusion.

After midnight, Alessandro, Euridice, and a Roman harness-maker named Guariglia set out for the river. They carried no weapons and wore only light khaki shorts. In that state of undress it was likely that if an enemy patrol discovered them they would be captured rather than killed, and as everyone knew, captivity was safe. Guariglia was tall, balding, dark, and heavily bearded. His eyebrows merged into a single moss-covered bough.

The three soldiers slid down the once-grassy slope that led from the Bell Tower to the river, freezing motionless or ducking behind boulders whenever the clouds brightened with the moon. A wide strip that ran from the fortification to the riverbank was open to Italian fire and had not been mined. They had exited by a small steel door at the base of the tower and rolled back three fronts of wire just enough to squeeze through: the wire at the riverbank had been washed away long before.

The ground was soft, with neither thorns nor nettles. Even pressing up against a boulder at the cue of the moon and clouds was a pleasant sensation, for the rock was cool, and the blue-green lichen on the north side smelled sweet when it was crushed. Their timing was keyed to the moon, the boulders, and gravity, and they descended as silently as if they were part of the hill itself.

The heavily armed enemy was dug in on the opposite bank, and the three naked soldiers in cloud-muffled moonlight were in range of five hundred rifles and half a dozen machine guns. Waiting for them as well were mortars, star shells, flame throwers, and grenades. Back from the line, the heavy guns were silent but ready, and would magnetize to whatever pre-set spot their observers directed.

This arsenal, however, was not the real danger, which was, rather, a keyed-up enemy infiltration party armed to kill in silence with tomahawks, bayonets, and maces. If the swimmers' nakedness did not disarm such an enemy, they would simply be lost.

Just as they reached the river's edge the Austrians sent up a flare a few hundred meters to the north. "Don't move," Alessandro whispered, and they froze and bent among the whitened rocks in the dry part of the riverbed so that even the mothers of the rocks would not have been able to tell them apart.

"Why do we have to whisper?" Euridice whispered. "The water is loud enough to drown out everything."

"For us," Alessandro answered. "We can't hear anything because we're next to it, but if you're far away, you can hear. One of their patrols made that very mistake, and we fired a bunch of flares in a flat trajectory onto the riverbed. The phosphorus exploded into daylight. Even though it was only a short burn, there were no shadows, and we hit every one of them."

The cool white light of the flare got brighter and closer as the wind carried its gay parachute south and the mass of the earth called it in. "Are they still here?" Euridice asked.

"Who?" Alessandro asked in return.

"The Austrian patrol."

"They're dead," Guariglia answered.

"But are they still here?"

"No," Alessandro whispered. "It was a while ago. The water rose and carried them away."

Euridice asked how many there were.

"Six that we got," Guariglia answered, "a plate." He spoke with maddening assurance. Then he said, "Shut up until the flare passes," and they waited among the rocks until it did.

EXCEPT PERHAPS in the sandy deltas that usher them into the Adriatic, the Isonzo and its spurs are seldom warm, especially in the north, where the water still carries a feeling for its origins in mountain snows, but September holds the heat of summer as surely as March preserves the ice on lakes. The great heat, a nearby shallow run, the time in the sun, and the pools and shoals where it had been trapped made the water warm.

In quiet pools and still water where they couldn't afford to break the surface, they swam silently and smoothly, as if in oil, in unexpectedly feminine breast strokes, or underwater in complete darkness. In what was left of the rapids, where the boulders fractured the water into surf, they swam vigorously, leaping, kicking, doing all they could just to stay in the same place and not be swept downriver.

After a while they came to a white log that had lodged in the rocks and become a spill over which the river poured in a perfect silver roll. They hung on to the smooth wood and placed their faces against the steady crest of the wave. It pushed them back until their muscles ached; the water thundered over them and gave them a scouring, and they could hardly breathe, but they stayed, staring at the moon and stars faintly wavering in the cool scroll that swept past them. Alessandro looked up. Apart from a few shards of cloud, the sky was open and still. The stars blazed.

"It cleared," he said to Euridice and Guariglia. "Look. It's clear."

"What are we going to do?" Guariglia asked.

"Maybe it'll cloud over again," Alessandro said, but the sky tended to the kind of clarity that rules the south of Italy in summer and for which the summer nights there are justly famous.

Guariglia moved his head from side to side. "No."

"I must have been insane to come down here," Euridice said.

"Why do you say that?"

"They'll see us," Euridice shouted angrily. "They'll kill us."

"So?" Guariglia asked. "Is death beneath you or something?"

"Oh Christ!" Euridice said, almost letting go of the log.

"Wait a minute," said Alessandro. "So what if there's a full moon? We're going to move in a scale. There are three of us. What's the problem?"

"Oh Christ!" Euridice said again, and kept on repeating it into the roll of silver water.

"You shut up, you fucking little tick," Guariglia told him.

"Wait," Alessandro whispered. "You're getting excited for nothing. They haven't seen us. Let's just go back. Until they start to shoot, there isn't any point in worrying."

"Tell me you're not nervous," Euridice commanded.

"He didn't say he wasn't nervous, did he," Guariglia asked. "He said he wasn't worried. That's different. We're always nervous, but we don't worry. . . ."

"That's right," Alessandro added.

"Until they start shooting. And don't be so scared of getting killed, you little asshole, or you'll get us all killed."

"Is that how it works?" Euridice asked, nasty and mocking.

"Yes!" Guariglia said. "You haven't been here for ten minutes, you goddamned fucking little chipped-tooth tick. You don't know a thing. I've been on the line a year." Guariglia's face tightened. "That's how it works."

"Nobody knows how it works," Alessandro said. "Come on."

They moved left in a graceful line against the current, swimming powerfully and with purpose. In the rapids they burst forth like athletes, making good progress against the white water as it churned around them, slapping it down with their strokes, moving always intently, surprised at their own strength. At a large stretch of black water that merely drifted and swirled, no one said anything, but they all knew they could not disturb it. With their arms and legs tight from the previous exertion, they submerged and swam underwater, surfacing with great control to take a deep breath, slowly sinking down, and starting off again. Alessandro led them silently through the darkness. They could follow him because in their utter weightlessness they could feel the turbulence of his strokes, and, sometimes, when they were near the surface, they could see the moonlight flash against his feet. Then they crawled up a shallow watercourse to the place in the dry river where they had come in.

"Why don't we just run?" Guariglia asked. "By the time they know what's happening we'll be halfway up the hill, and by the time they fire a star shell we'll be home."

"They don't have to fire a star shell. That's the point. Anyway, if we run they'll definitely see us. Maybe we can run the last half of the hill, but now let's go quietly."

"Are we going to crawl?" Euridice wanted to know.

"What for?" Alessandro asked. "They're looking down on us. It wouldn't make any difference. Move away from the rocks, all crouched down, as if you're a rock. Stay still most of the time. You know, pretend you're an Indian."

As soon as Alessandro said "Indian," they heard the launch of a mortar shell.

"Go!" Alessandro screamed, contradicting everything he had just said. They ran forward over the rocks, smashing their feet, listening to the whistle of the shell as it climbed. "Keep on until just after it bursts!" he yelled. "It blinds them at first."

Euridice did what he was told. The star shell burst into eerie daylight.

"Now!" Alessandro shouted. He and Guariglia found places behind boulders at the beginning of the slope. Euridice followed, but a little late. They heard gunfire to the north and south—unintelligible bursts that signified neither pattern nor event.

"They see us," Euridice exclaimed.

"No they don't."

Another mortar shell was launched, and another, and another, right toward them.

"They see us," Alessandro said.

"Why don't we just stay behind the rocks?" Euridice asked in a pathetic high voice. "We're protected."

"That's what you think, you goddamned little tick," Guariglia said so rapidly that it came out almost as one syllable. "If they drop an explosive round in front of us, that's it."

"Run," Alessandro said.

They started to sprint as the three mortar shells were still whistling above them. First one burst, then the next, and the next. The light was so blinding that for a moment they were slowed, but the four star shells burned so brilliantly that it was like daylight, and they could do nothing but regain their speed.

The soldiers in the Bell Tower refrained from firing, not wanting to alert or stimulate the Austrians into doing more than they were inclined to do, but the enemy had seen the figures on the exposed slope. Ten meters from the wire the hillside was raked by machine-gun fire. They had to stop. They hid behind rocks, but the rocks weren't big enough. Bullet fragments and boulder chips were flying everywhere.

Something hit Alessandro in the throat directly under his Adam's apple. He was bleeding, but he could still breathe. Euridice screamed.

"Don't scream, you're out of breath," Guariglia said, hardly able to get the words out.

Alessandro looked up and saw things flying over the Bell

Tower, tumbling through the air, blocking out the stars. At first he didn't know what they were, but then he recognized them.

"Genius!" he shouted. "Genius! They're going to be blinded with phosphorus. Get ready...."

From the Bell Tower twenty phosphorus grenades had sailed over the parapet. They tumbled in the air and exploded, blinding anyone looking in their direction. The Austrian machine-gunners were silenced for ten or fifteen seconds, and when once again they could see, the swimmers had passed the wire and gone into the Bell Tower.

Emerging from the narrow passage that led to the *cortile,* they found that Alessandro had been cut deeply in the throat. He bled profusely over his chest. Guariglia had a bullet hole in his calf. He feared that the bullet was still in him, and frantically examined his leg. When he saw a second hole on the other side, the expression on his face was like that of a man who has just won money in a horse race.

Euridice was proud of himself. "I didn't die," he declared. "I didn't die, again."

"Now they know we swim," Alessandro said as one of the many men crowding around them pressed a bandage to his throat.

"Maybe not," said Microscopico. "Maybe they think we walk around at night half naked."

"I hope they do," Guariglia said, doubled up in pain. "I hope they do think that, those fucking tick-assed Austrians."

"No more swimming," the Guitarist commanded.

"It doesn't matter," Alessandro announced. "It's getting too cold to swim."

IN DIRECT sunlight, out of the wind, it was hot, but in the shade the infantrymen wore their tunics. Though a half dozen men were sitting shirtless in the *cortile* taking in the last of the summer sun,

Alessandro, Euridice, and the Guitarist were in the map room, in wool sweaters. The shade was as cool as the dark purple in the distant mountains, which they could see as if through a block of clear crystal.

The map room faced north. Until a bend in the river, both banks were open to view for many more kilometers than the maximum range of Alessandro's captured Mauser 98, which was more accurate and better built than the Italian Martinis, with a bayonet that was shorter and more maneuverable. He had never used the bayonet, and hoped never to have to, but the order of the day was always to keep it fixed and sheathed, which made for a lot of trouble when moving around in the redoubt.

Though Alessandro would have preferred to have been in the sun, his duty was to observe the northern sector from six in the morning until several hours after dark. He sat on a cane chair near the center firing port, squinting outward. The bottom of the port was narrower than the top. Here his rifle rested, a round in the chamber, sights elevated for two hundred meters, the bayonet detached and leaning against the wall. A telescope on a tripod that straddled the rifle was set at eye level, its barrel, like that of the rifle, tilted down in the slope of the port. With twenty-power magnification and a spacious eighty-millimeter lens, this instrument from the naval stores gave Alessandro an unparalleled view of the mountains.

Far to the north was the pure white rim of the Tyrol, the heart of Austria. That even enemy country should be so pristine, beautiful, and high, frozen white through summers of heat and blood, seemed to Alessandro an unambiguous promise. Hardly a clear day passed when he did not go to the map room and sight this rim until he felt light and pure enough to float.

Euridice sat on the edge of a cot underneath the sector map. No one could peer through a telescope all day long. An alternate was necessary even if, as in the case of Euridice, he had not been on the line long enough to know exactly what he was seeing and became so entranced with the colorful terrain moving effortlessly in the sweep of the telescope that he forgot to concentrate on the enemy. It amazed Alessandro that the men of the Bell Tower were entrusted, without training, as spotters for a large portion of the Italian artillery in that section. An artilleryman arrived periodically to check coordinates, writing everything down in a book, explaining that his profession was now practiced mainly at night by men who didn't need to see for themselves but who took in numbers insatiably.

In the middle of the afternoon, the mountains were blinding across their white rim. The cook brought three mess tins of *pasta in brodo.* Although this time they had much *brodo* and very little *pasta,* at other times they had much *pasta* and very little *brodo.* The cat Serafina came in behind the cook, sat at attention, and looked earnestly at the three containers of food on the map table.

"Pasta in brodo," the cook said before he left, deeply offended that no one had turned to look at him, except the cat, for he was doing the best he could with what he was given.

Anxious, earnest, eager, proud, and pathetic all at the same time, the cat moved not a muscle, refrained from blinking, and sat as perfectly still as a diplomat transformed into an owl.

"Eat fast, Euridice," Alessandro said, scanning the northern Austrian trench line. "I'm hungry."

Euridice didn't have to be told to eat fast. Still plump, he took comfort in the little food he could get. As he and the Guitarist ate, occasionally feeding pieces of macaroni to the cat, Alessandro grew more and more intent.

"Put in a call," he said to the Guitarist. "I see a lot going on in the near trench at the border of three-sector." The Guitarist turned the crank on the telephone to raise the headquarters. "Brigade-sized unit pouring into first trench just south of three-sector," Alessandro reported. The Guitarist repeated it.

"Can you tell which units?" the Guitarist asked Alessandro for the officer on the other end of the line.

"Spiky helmets," Alessandro answered.

"Feathers?"

"I don't think so, but they're too far away to tell with certainty."

"Hold on...."

Alessandro watched occasional helmets bob up when a tall soldier or one who had a sprightly step rounded an elbow in the faraway trench, and he waited for the Italian comment. In about a minute and a half, he heard it. Thunder came from cannon behind the lines, and because it was a clear day with the light streaming down, Alessandro actually saw the shells as they descended. Huge blasts, tinny and bright, shook the earth on both sides of the trench.

Another two dozen shells came in, scattering the sandy soil. "Perfect aim," Alessandro reported, "but it didn't do anything."

The Guitarist relayed the message. "They say to continue observation and supply rifle fire when necessary."

Alessandro elevated the rear sight of his rifle, positioned himself, and fired a round at the corner of the trench where he had seen the helmets. As he ejected the first cartridge and moved the bolt to load and lock, his ears rang with the concussion of the last shot and he smelled burnt powder blown inward through the gun port. He placed five more shots in the same area and reloaded the rifle.

Hardly able to hear himself, trembling slightly from the concussions, he said, "Now they've got their rifle fire. I like to aerate the soil. It's like gardening."

"I don't understand," Euridice proclaimed as he ate. "Why don't the Austrians concentrate their artillery fire on this post and obliterate it?"

"That's what they'll do in the offensive," the Guitarist answered.

Euridice stopped eating. "Why?"

"How can you ask why, when you've just asked why not?"

"I also want to know why, that's why, and why is different from why not."

"In this case," the Guitarist said, "if you know why not, you also know why."

"How?" Euridice asked.

"Subtract the not," Alessandro added, still using the telescope, "and eat, will you?"

Euridice hurriedly finished his soup, depressing the cat. "You mean that in the offensive they'll level the Bell Tower?"

"They have to," the Guitarist said. "It's too good an observation point and firing position, even if it isn't supposed to hold in a full scale assault."

"What will we do?"

"When the bunkers are about to collapse, those of us who still can will run back to the line."

"And those who can't?"

"They'll stay."

"To die."

"Euridice, by the time the bunkers start to go, the communications trench will already have been filled in. We'll have to go back on the surface, over our own mines, in the open. Probably both sides will be firing at us. What's the difference?"

"Everyone is going to die," Euridice said, realizing it for the first time.

"That's right," Alessandro confirmed, turning from the gun port.

"Let me ask one question," Euridice continued.

"Soon you're going to have to pay us," the Guitarist said.

"When's the offensive?"

"When the river gets shallow enough."

"And when is that?"

"A week, two weeks. It depends on the rain."

"There is no rain."

"Right."

"But we're not sure they'd mount an offensive even if the river dried up completely," Euridice stated.

"Why wouldn't they?"

"Pressing business in other places."

"What other places?"

"Herzegovina, Bosnia, Montenegro . . ."

"Euridice," the Guitarist said, "this is the place where they have pressing business. In the war between Italy and Austria, the Austrian army is over there, and here—you, me, him—is the Italian army."

"I'm in the navy."

"So are we."

"Why don't they send us back to sea?"

"Why don't you ask them?"

Euridice was discontent until evening. Then the sunset made the mountains pink and gold, and, as the others had done long before, he resigned himself to the fact that he was going to die.

THOUGH THE men of the Bell Tower considered the regular army a sub-species, they held them in awe for making suicidal attacks, as on the Western and Russian fronts, in which they climbed out of their trenches and into a wall of machine-gun fire. On occasion, along a stretch of less than a kilometer, five thousand men might go over the top, and within a few minutes suffer a thousand instantly dead, a thousand wounded who would die slowly on the ground, a thousand grievously wounded, a thousand lightly wounded, and a thousand who were physically untouched but spiritually shattered for the rest of their lives, which, in some cases, was merely a matter of weeks.

Only certain portions of the line had to undergo carnage in the French style, but knowledge of it was all-pervasive. Everything the 19th River Guard knew came from quiet meetings in the communications trenches, conversations with sleepless, bitter infantrymen who had been transferred up from the fiercer fighting in the south.

If some of the River Guard were on the edge, many of the regular infantry had gone over it long before. Especially disturbing to the naval contingent were reports from down below that Italian troops now were shot quite casually for disciplinary reasons, and that the Italian generals, like their French counterparts, were executing men in decimations for crimes they had not committed. Men with families were pulled from the ranks along with equally mystified adolescents and put to death for acts attributed to others whom they had never seen.

One very clear day, a major in the Medical Corps, a man with no military bearing whatsoever, arrived at the Bell Tower and spoke to the assembled troops, who thought it was going to be yet another useless lesson about venereal disease—they never had leave—but, instead, the major asked for volunteers.

Of course, no one dared, but Alessandro, who bet that the army would not execute volunteers, stepped forward almost without thinking. Guariglia followed, out of friendship and perhaps because he had had the same thoughts. "All I need is two," the doctor said, and off they went, not knowing where, as the other soldiers, who had had more time to project, made mosquito sounds to suggest that the two would be the subjects of a malaria experiment.

"Is there any danger of death?" Alessandro asked as the three men trotted through the communications trench.

"No, but there's cheese and tomatoes."

"Sir?"

"Lunch."

"It's a dietary experiment?"

"Who said anything about an experiment? Just follow me."

At the end of the tunnel they climbed into a truck that then drove toward the mountains. Two hours later, the twenty soldiers inside, all of whom had been anxious and silent, climbed out into a sunny mountain meadow covered with blue flowers. A cold breeze was blowing, but if you dropped close to the ground the temperature was perfect.

The doctor and the truck driver spread checkered table cloths and brought bread, cheese, bottles of wine, and chocolate from a cabinet on the side of the truck. When the food was laid out, the doctor told them to eat, but no one touched it for fear that it was poisoned.

So he took a little of everything from everywhere, and after they saw that he didn't die the soldiers began to put away vast amounts of it, their eyes shifting to and fro, wondering what was going to happen.

"They're going to shoot us and dissect our brains," said a Sicilian who wore a hair net.

"That isn't plausible," Alessandro stated.

"Why does it have to be plausible? What does plausible mean anyway? I suppose you think they just wanted us to go on a picnic."

"We'll find out what they want."

After lunch the doctor had them return their utensils and wine bottles. They shook out the table cloths, but then they laid them down again.

"You see this little blue flower," the doctor said, spinning a tiny flower between his right thumb and index finger. They nodded. They thought he was crazy. "For the next five hours, I want you to pick them, leaving the full stem, and pile them on the table cloths."

"They're going to shoot us," the Sicilian said.

"Shut up," Guariglia told him.

"Sir?" Alessandro asked. "May I ask why?"

"No. Just do as you're told."

For five hours, they picked flowers. Gradually, very gradually, the piles of petals and stems grew into fat humps, and the soldiers' anxiety vanished. The driver picked, too, while the doctor slept in the sun, a newspaper folded over his face, his head resting on a loaf of bread.

"Why?" they asked the driver.

"I don't know. We've done this every day since spring. We take volunteers all up and down the line."

"What happens to the flowers?"

"They're shipped in crates in boxcars, to Milano."

"The son of a bitch has a perfume factory!" the Sicilian exclaimed.

"I don't think so," Guariglia told him. "Smell them."

The Sicilian smelled the flowers in his hand, and recoiled. "These are stinky flowers!"

"Yeah," the driver said.

"Is it always the same flower?" he was asked.

"Always the same."

They spoke as they picked. The Sicilian, who worked in a dry goods store, told them his dream, which had consumed him so intensely that it had followed him from the store in Messina to a sunny meadow in the mountains where the air was fresh and the light clear. He spoke for two hours, ceaselessly repeating and enumerating the objects of his desire, as if that would reserve them for him in later life. His ambition was to own a villa overlooking the Tyrrhenian, a Bugatti automobile, a Caravaggio, a mahogany-and-teak yacht, and an apartment in Seville, Spain. The villa would be a thousand square meters, the Bugatti green, the Caravaggio a crucifixion scene, the yacht a ketch, and the apartment close to the cathedral. His further descriptions of every detail and statistic pertaining to those items were extremely irritating, because he intoned them like a parrot.

"So what?" Alessandro asked.

"If I could have these, if I could have them..."

"Yes?"

"They'll take all my life to get."

"And?"

"When I have them, I'll be happy."

"What if you had them now, and you went back to your unit and got killed," Alessandro speculated.

"I don't know, but I want them."

"You'll spend your whole life getting them, and it won't make any difference whatsoever."

"You're just jealous."

"I'm not jealous. You've turned to the material as comfort in the face of death, but the more you rely upon it the more you'll suffer."

"Oh go fuck yourself," the Sicilian said, tossing a handful of flowers onto one of the piles. "I'm not suffering. Are you? I'm fine. I'm perfectly fine. I know what I want. Life is simple. I don't think about death."

"Of course you don't."

"Why should I bother?"

"You'll see," Alessandro told him. "Your materialism will make you suffer terribly not only at the end but also on the way."

"Someday," the Sicilian told him, "I'll lie in my marble bathtub, looking up through the skylight, a pizza within reach, a real Victrola playing *Carmen,* and I'll think of you." Pleased with himself, he laughed.

"In a way," Alessandro said, "I do envy you," and then he went back to picking flowers.

They were never told what exactly they had been doing, and they would never forget that they had done it.

THE BEGINNING of October was cloudy, the sky looked like slate, and the air was dry and cool. Summer was over and they would have to learn once again to live in darkness. A heavy rainfall was necessary to stop the offensive, but the days passed without rain.

The mood of the infantry changed. Small irritations that had been burned away by the heat and light of summer now came to the fore. The ceilings of the bunkers seemed to be much lower. Aching teeth tormented their owners and only got worse, for all the dentists in the army were in places a half-day-pass away. An appointment could be had with three months' advance warning, but no one wanted to tempt fate with the arrogance of assuming that he would be able to keep it.

The food became unbearable even though few soldiers ever had enough. Laundry took longer to dry, a shower meant trembling for two hours afterward, and except when occasional sunshine broke through the clouds (which drove-in the fact that no rain had fallen), only the lice were happy.

During this time the army on the other side of the Isonzo was quiet. They fired hardly a shot, but wagons arrived at night with men and materiel. Though the Italians harassed the nocturnal re-supply and reinforcement with constant artillery fire, it neither stopped nor slackened.

Still, with each day that passed, hopes grew stronger that in being so meticulous about preparing the offensive the enemy was trading a chance to walk across the river for the delay that would accommodate one day's murderously heavy rain.

"It doesn't matter," Guariglia said. "The day that it rains is the day they'll attack. They're waiting until then; the river will be at its lowest and they will have brought up the greatest number of men."

"The artillery barrage will start immediately," Microscopico added from his cot, making a diagram with his hands. "For six hours, constant shelling. Then many thousands of men will appear from the trenches all at once. They'll start off slowly, but in a few seconds they'll be up on their feet and running. When they cross the river many will fall, but thousands will get to the hill. How many will get to our trenches is another story. Some will, however, and you'll meet them face to face. At that point they'll be rather overstimulated and a few will think they're God. They'll be firing as fast as hell and using their bayonets."

"Austrians are better with bayonets than we are," said Biondo, a taciturn machinist from Torino, who had enlisted in the navy be-cause of his belief that he would be most valuable in the engine rooms of stricken and damaged ships.

"Why is that?" Euridice asked meekly.

The explanation was obvious, but no one could put it into

words. Finally, someone said, "They're taller," and for a brief moment not a man among them did not feel seasick with foreboding.

At night, now, because of the cold wind that came down from alps marvelously clad in ice and snow, they had a fire in an oil drum stove. Though most of the wood they burned was what remained of the lumber used in constructing trenches and fortifications, a large pile of apple wood had somehow found its way to the Bell Tower, and two or three apple logs were put on every blaze.

It was a shame, for they could tell by its sprouts and shoots that the tree was still bearing fruit when it had been cut, and would have continued for another twenty years, and all they had now was the scent.

For a week before the offensive, Alessandro had the day watch and could sleep at night. The week before that, he had had night duty, and changing over exhausted him to the point where he feared his heart would give out. As time passed, however, he slowly regained his strength and was able to sleep properly and dream. He dreamed of Rome.

After dinner they would wash up, open the gun ports wide to let in the cold night air, throw some apple logs onto the fire, extinguish the lantern, and wrap themselves in their wool blankets. Sleep came easily as the wind whistled through the fortification and the fire crackled. Each man saw in the fire what he saw in his heart. For Alessandro the opening tableau was always the same, a perfect, hot blue day in the Villa Borghese, when the shadows among the trees were so dark that they had red in them. In a grove of hysterical cypress, where the leaves danced in the wind like sequins, the clash of so many beams of light against the dark made a continual phosphorescence. All through the shadows were glimpses of blue so rich that it could almost be breathed.

The water in the fountains of the Villa Borghese was bright and cold. It could take the sun blindingly, like the flash of a sword, collapse upon itself in surf-like white, float in a mist of rainbows, or rush from darkness to darkness, emerging momentarily over a bed of yellow pebbles as if to be proved clear by the sun.

His father, mother, and sister were on a bench in the shadows, and Alessandro was in a white suit, by the fountain, half blinded by the light, his hand shielding his eyes as he searched the darkness. Luciana dangled her legs from the bench and swung them back and forth, looking to her right for a child with whom to play. Alessandro's mother and father were dressed as he had seen them in nineteenth-century photographs in which, even in the stiff portrayal of their youth, they had seemed as unconcerned with mortality as if the year 1900 were to have been a cap against which the geyser of time would rise only to fall back in decorative plumes.

THE NEXT day, Alessandro sat with his back propped against the wall of the *cortile* in the Bell Tower. His rifle, bayonet fixed, was leaning against the same wall. Beyond the rim of the fortification, in the circular lake of sky visible to the soldiers in the *cortile,* dark clouds raced on high winds. Their undersides were black, the rest gray. Though sunshine broke through now and then and the soldiers strained their necks to look, shielding their eyes in a salute, most of the time they were in cool shade.

The urgency of the clouds hurrying down from the north was captivating even to those who did not know why. "It's because they come from the north," Alessandro said to the Guitarist. "They've flown over Vienna, rushed along the Danube, and floated above military camps and the Ministry of War. Now they've come to look at us. They want no part of any of this, and they speed toward the Adriatic. They'll cross the sea and float untouched into Africa like lost balloons. They hear nothing. They float over silent deserts and struggling armies as if the two were indistinguishable. I wish that I could do the same."

"Don't worry," said the Guitarist. "Someday you will."

"Do you really believe that?"

The Guitarist thought. "You mean, if there's something on the other side of the fence?"

"Yes."

"I don't know. All logic says no, but my wife just had a baby boy—I've never seen him. Where did he come from? Space? It isn't logical at all, so who cares about logic."

"It takes a lot of balls to risk the hope, doesn't it."

"It does. I have the feeling that I'm sure to be punished for the presumption, but I've already had the bad luck to have been a musician and a soldier, so maybe I'll get a break.

"Music," the Guitarist continued, with affection, "is the one thing that tells me time and time again that God exists and that He'll take care. Why do you think they have it in churches?"

"I know why they have it in churches," Alessandro replied.

"Music isn't rational," the Guitarist said. "It isn't *true*. What is it? Why do mechanical variations in rhythm and tone speak the language of the heart? How can a simple song be so beautiful? Why does it steel my resolution to believe—even if I can hardly make a living."

"And being a soldier?"

"The only halfway decent thing about this war, Alessandro, is that it teaches you the relation between risk and hope."

"You've learned to dare, and you dare to believe that someday you're going to float like a cloud."

"If it weren't for music," the Guitarist answered, "I would think that love is mortal. If I weren't a soldier, I might not have learned to stand against all odds." He took a deep breath. "Well, that's all very fine, but the truth is I just don't want to be killed before I see my son."

Euridice and Microscopico were kicking a soccer ball back and forth across the *cortile*. Always a little awkward, Euridice met the ball with his toe too low and raised his foot too high in compensation. The ball soared in the air. Everyone in the *cortile* watched it rise against the background of cloud, and hoped it would not go over the wall. It did, and was five meters out when it started to return as the wind pushed it toward the center of the *cortile*. It landed against the near wall, bounced, flew into the air in a low trajectory, and came to rest on the grassy rim that formed the roof of the Bell Tower.

They watched silently as it settled. Someone said, "That's a good ball." Half the soldiers who had been leaning against the walls stood to get a better view. Alessandro and the Guitarist remained sitting because they could see it from where they were.

"*I* kicked it," Euridice said, moving toward the wall.

"Don't go up there," Guariglia warned him as he was about to grip the handholds in the wall and climb up.

"Why not?" Euridice asked. He was still the new man.

"It's on the edge," Guariglia told him. "They have the edge sighted-in."

"But if I go quickly, stay low, and just grab it and fall back, they won't have time to shoot."

"I wouldn't do it," Biondo said.

"But we don't have another ball," Euridice insisted.

"Let Microscopico get it," the Guitarist called out.

"Fuck you," said Microscopico, who was sick of being a small target. "Why don't you get it?"

"I didn't kick it up there," the Guitarist answered, "and I'm not a midget."

"I told you what to do," Microscopico called out.

Euridice was already up on the grassy part of the roof. Guariglia shouted for him to wait. Alessandro and the Guitarist rose to their feet. "Come back," Guariglia called. "Leave it until nightfall. Not now. It's not worth it."

Flat on his stomach, Euridice crawled along the grass toward the ball. He stopped just short of the rim and looked back. "It's nice up here," he said. "All I have to do is reach out my hand."

Alessandro stepped forward and shouted in anger. "Euridice, don't be an idiot. Come down from there."

For a moment, Euridice didn't move. He twisted, and looked down the length of his body at everyone who was looking up at him. Now he was one of them. "All right," he said, "I'll get it later."

They sighed in relief, but then, for a reason that no one ever knew, perhaps because he felt he was so close, perhaps because everyone was watching, because no one had died since he had arrived, or because he forgot where he was and imagined that he was still in school, Euridice stretched out his hand to get the ball.

In so doing, he raised his head. The soldiers in the *cortile* froze where they stood, hoping that Euridice's impulsiveness would be his guardian, but just before his hand would have swept the ball back down the grassy slope, his head snapped back and he tumbled down the incline. The right arm punched the air, puffing the body with it. He went over the sandbag wall and fell into the *cortile,* on his side.

They knew by now how to recognize death, and they stood silently as a hundred clouds passed overhead, rushing south.

Dearest Mama and Papa, Alessandro wrote.

I have been writing infrequently because, although we don't do much here, it takes up all the time we have. My life is a little like that of a forest ranger, so you'd think I'd have some peace. I stare out into the hills and mountains for twelve hours, and then I'm free. Presumably, with all the time in the world to reflect, I could write brilliant essays and letters that you might read more than once, but I can't. It's too tense here, and everyone is too unhappy. In fact, if I ever get a short leave, I'm going to go to Venice and drink three bottles of wine.

Today I saw something miraculous. I was looking southward through a firing port, with a telescope. It was evening and the light was coming from the northwest. Over the trenches a black cloud appeared, changing direction and moving as rapidly as an airplane, but it was the size of a palace. It writhed, dropped, rose, and fell again, catching the light like chain mail or dulled sequins. It was a cloud of starlings or swallows that feed upon the corpses in the no-man's-lands between the lines. Guariglia, who has served farther down, says that they come out every evening and dance over the dead. I don't know what to make of it, as it is at once so beautiful and so grotesque.

We are continually expecting an Austrian 'tick-ass' to come from nowhere, throw a grenade, fire some shots, and bayonet a poor idiot coming out of the latrine. This kind of thing makes you tense twenty-four hours a day. So do the shells. On average, eight to ten a week hit the Bell Tower, and you never know when they're coming. When they do come, they knock you out of bed if you're sleeping, or knock you down if you're standing up, or get you up onto your feet if you're sitting down. These shells, they don't like the status quo. They reverse everything. Dirt comes down from the roof, the walls shake, objects fall to the ground.

We always have to look out for cannon drawn up close to our position. The enemy would like to fire point-blank, in an almost flat trajectory, at our gun ports. The shell would go through the steel plates and that would be the end of the Bell Tower, so the minute we see a cannon we all run to fire at it with rifles and machine guns, we pull the trench mortar into the cortile and drop shells into it, and we call up our own artillery. Even if we see some sort of optical device or wood frame, we assume that they're pre-sighting the gun ports so that they can move the cannon up at night, and we respond with the same great diligence. If someone were to put up a cross or try to make a laundry frame, he would draw all our fire and he probably would never know why.

I fire twenty or thirty rounds a day, which may account for my shaky handwriting. I don't hear very well anymore, either. I don't know if I'll ever be able to go to the opera again, because I could hardly hear it even before my right ear drum was ruined by my own rifle.

Another source of tension here is that we have no privacy. Most people have never had their own rooms, as I did, and because they were never alone they learned to live without reflection or contemplation. If

I'm in a room with Guariglia, for example, a Romano, a harness-maker, and I sink into thought, he'll feel it, it will make him uncomfortable, and he'll do his best to distract me or engage me in conversation. Physical privacy doesn't exist here. The best you can do is to go to one of the store rooms, where there might be only two other people, who are concentrating on observation and firing out the ports.

Although I don't write often, at least not as much as I used to, I have some things I'd like to clear up with you, or try to clear up, while I can. I feel that I've been living beyond my time, that we may never see each other again. It wasn't that way at first, but something has changed. Anyway, the passes that I get are not long enough to let me come home, and I don't have a way of alerting you so that you could meet me in Venice. Perhaps I'll get home this Christmas—I don't know. We're safe at present, more or less. The last one killed was a boy who, for the sake of retrieving a soccer ball, exposed himself to enemy fire rather than wait until dark. One never knows what will happen, and we're expecting an offensive now at any time.

I mean a local offensive, because it seems unlikely that the Austrians will move along the whole line, but even that is possible. It rained so little this summer that the river is very low. We used to go out at night to swim, and the last time we did we found that at its deepest it was only up to the middle of my chest. That was a few dry weeks ago, and since then the snow has stopped melting in the mountains. Now the river is shallow enough to walk through in a dozen places. In a few days they'll be able to walk across it anywhere. Even if it rains tonight, it's too late, which is why I write.

I promise several things. I'll fight well, I'll try to stay alive, and I'll concentrate on the former rather than on the latter, because the best way to stay alive is to be resolute and to risk. I don't care about our claims on the Alto Adige, so I'm fighting for nothing, but so is everyone and that's not the point. A nightmare has no justification, but you try your best to last through it, even if that means playing by the rules. I suppose a nightmare is having to play by rules that make no sense, for a purpose that is entirely alien, without control of either one's fate or even one's actions. To the extent that I do have control, I'll do what I can. Unfortunately, the war is ruled inordinately by chance, to the point almost where human action seems to have lost its meaning. They're executing soldiers not only for theft and desertion, but, sometimes, for nothing. I believe that after the war, for a long time, perhaps even for the rest of the century, the implications of this will reverberate through almost everything, but I'll save that kind of speculation for when I get home. We'll sit in the garden and talk about all these things, because if I get home I want to buy the garden back. I want to take out the weeds, thicken the grass, prune the trees, and make it what it once was. I have the energy, the will, and, for the first time in my life, the patience.

I want to tell you now how much I love you, all of you, and I've always neglected Luciana but now I'm so proud that she has become the beautiful and impressive woman that she has become. Don't worry about me, no matter what happens. We're nervous here, but not afraid. We have all looked into our souls, one way or another, and are content to die if need be. The only thing left to say is that I love you.

Alessandro

At the end of the month summer had been pushed back, winter was beginning to flood the Veneto with high clouds that had begun their relaxed flight to Africa, and the mountains were covered in white. When far to the north a blue lake in the clouds enlarged to the size of a principality and the sun came through, the Alps would glare in their entirety like flash powder, and the great white image would roll over the north of Italy, hanging in the azure air for all to see.

Thirty more men arrived in the Bell Tower, army conscripts who had been in the lower trenches taking the brunt of the fighting since the beginning. Cynical, violent, and mutinous, they completely destroyed the civilized equilibrium of the naval contingent, made a great deal of noise, fouled the latrine, and fought among themselves. They played cards, drank, vomited, and whacked at each other with sheathed bayonets.

The River Guard was at their mercy because they had brought a sergeant with them who rearranged everything and told everyone what to do. With their raucous laughter, their unshavenness, their skin diseases, their syphilis, and their apparent delight in killing, they seemed as overpowering as the war itself.

They sent out nightly patrols of men who could see in the dark and who brought back with them a boar, a feral pig, and once even a foolish buck that had followed the nearly dry riverbed far from his home in the mountains. Huge feasts of meat and wine followed each patrol, and even these did their part in setting everyone on edge and convincing the River Guard that they were doomed.

In a week the clouds broke apart in cool sunshine, and hopes were raised, but shortly after the sun reappeared so did thousands of enemy cavalry. They were visible in the rear of their lines, beyond artillery range, raising dust as they came into formation or deployed from one sector to another. It was possible to tell where they were even without a telescope. Wagons and caissons made dust clouds that looked like smoldering grass fires. Cavalry raised dust like a train. It moved evenly and smoothly across the landscape in an unmistakable indication of swift well fed warhorses.

"I wish I were in the cavalry," Alessandro said to Guariglia. "I was raised to it. I studied riding and swordsmanship all my life."

"Don't be crazy," Guariglia told him. "Our machine guns are waiting for those bastards and their poor horses. They won't last a minute."

The soldiers knew exactly what was coming, as if it had been in their blood. "They're here for the break," they said of the distant cavalry, "to make a hole in our lines in several places and then pour through like grain that spills from a torn sack. Horses are not like men. They don't have the patience to sit around waiting. They only bring up horses just before the attack. The river's low. They'll be knocking at our door in two or three days."

The whole line came alive and was packed with men, but not as much as the Austrian lines, which nearly burst with new uniforms and bobbing bayonets. So much ammunition was carried into the Bell Tower that each bunker was greatly reduced in size. The army men cut new firing ports, laid new mines, and put up new wire.

"You naval cocksuckers don't know how to landfight. Why don't you go back to the sea, where you came from?" asked an infantryman who had a disc-like scar in place of much of his chin.

"Give me a ticket," said Biondo.

They persecuted Microscopico until he told them why he was in the navy. He was conscripted to sweep chimneys and clean boilers. "Because I'm so small," he said, "I can crawl through the pipes. And don't tell me you're brave until you've crawled through the guts of a boiler and out the stack. If you get stuck, you're through. They don't dismantle warships on account of chimney sweeps, and you *can* get stuck. Keep the ticket, thanks: I'd much rather be here." It was totally a lie: he had been a baker's helper on a supply ship.

Huge rain clouds were visible over the mountains on the day when the artillery bombardment started. The clouds looked like wine-colored rock walls, and they moved slowly southward, feeling their way with tendrils of yellow and white lightning.

The Italian artillery had been active for weeks in harassing the Austrian build-up. Shells sped overhead several times a minute, and the Austrians compressed their answer into the period between dusk and dawn. They had no need of observation, because nothing failed to come under their fire.

When Alessandro had stood at the edge of the testing ground in Munich he was shaken and awed. Now the line of a hundred guns was ten deep, and it fired continuously, a hundred at a time, without let-up, allowing not a second for breathing at ease. When a shell actually hit the Bell Tower, which happened scores of times that night, everyone would be thrown to the floor, hoping that the roof would not collapse.

"I wonder if we're going to be ordered out on a charge," the army man between Alessandro and Guariglia kept saying. "I see no sign, but they may decide to send us on a charge." Then he would laugh. He did this all night. At four o'clock in the morning, when everyone was deaf and trembling from artillery, he came to Guariglia and said, "You won't tell them who I am, will you?"

"Who are you?"

With obvious pain and dread, the soldier replied, "The king's son."

"What are you doing here?" Guariglia asked.

"My father sent me here to die."

"Who's your father?" Alessandro asked, not having heard.

"The king."

"The king of what?"

"Of Italy."

"I want to talk to him after the war," Guariglia said. "I have a few things I'd like to say to him."

"Everyone says that," the soldier answered, "but when they come into his presence they find that they can hardly speak."

"You'll be there, won't you?"

The mad soldier shook his head from side to side. "I'll be dead."

"You have a point," Alessandro said. The prince was suffering so from fear that he turned to run for the latrine. "All right, all right," Alessandro called out after him. "You'll go to heaven. The king's son always goes to heaven."

At five o'clock, just before the light, the artillery stopped. Though as soon as the enemy formations rose from the trenches the Italian artillery would throw everything it could onto the advancing tide, it was quiet. For a while no one knew. Their senses had been so disrupted by exploding shells that it took them fifteen minutes to understand silence.

The rain had begun, and at night the river had risen because of storms in the mountains. The wind lashed the Bell Tower and droplets flew through the gun ports. Every few seconds bolts of lightning were followed by a deep forest of thunder, but after the barrage these thundercracks seemed gentle. The air was full with the smell of whiskey as the besieged 19th River Guard listened to the reassuring sound of rain pattering lightly against the roof, and they all were thinking of home.

THE GUITARIST was in the communications room, and at five-fifteen he screamed that his lines had been cut. An infiltrator was in the trench.

The River Guard looked anxiously at the infantry, who looked back with contempt. "It's not our redoubt," one of them said.

"Go ahead," another added nonchalantly. "Someone's knocking."

Everyone looked at Guariglia, who was the toughest, and the biggest, but it wasn't fair, and they knew it. They knew his children as if they had met them, and they understood the love that had moved him to describe them again and again. Besides that, he had done more than his share of difficult and dangerous things. Then they looked at the Guitarist, who had not done his share, but he was a musician, he was soft, he had a family, and he stared at the ground. Microscopico was too small. Biondo was at the gun port. The others were in other bunkers.

With his heart fluttering, Alessandro threw the sheath off his bayonet. It hit the wall and clattered to the floor. In an instant he had picked up the rifle and was running through the doorway, then across the *cortile,* then past the machine-gunner and into the communications trench.

When he started out he had been afraid, but with each step his anger rose, until, as he rounded the slight bends in the trench, he was ferocious and electrified. He flipped the safety catch on the rifle and steered the raised bayonet adroitly through the turns. He felt bodiless, as if he were only two strong arms, a well oiled rifle, and a flashing bayonet gliding through the trench at top speed. He wanted only to kill the interlopers who had dared cut the lines.

It would be too dangerous for them to go back. They would be there, waiting. They were.

As he came around a sharp corner a shot was fired at him. It missed and drove into the wall of the trench. The Austrian soldier who had fired it shrank back in panic and worked the bolt on his rifle.

Alessandro kept running. Just as the enemy soldier, a young boy with a delicate face, a stranger, had expressed another round into the chamber and was about to raise his rifle, Alessandro plunged the bayonet into his chest, doubling him up as if his body were a clenched fist, killing him. Two shots sounded from ahead.

The two companions of the boy Alessandro had just killed were firing at him. One shot missed. The other struck Alessandro at the top of his shoulder, throwing him backward into the sandy wall of the trench. He hadn't let go of his rifle, and it pulled out of the dead soldier and righted itself in his hands.

The Austrians dropped to their knees and worked their bolts. Alessandro was in no condition to aim. He pointed the rifle in their direction and fired. One of them rolled onto the ground. The other fired and missed again. Seeing that his friend was now still, that Alessandro was reloading, and that he himself could not re-load faster, he threw down his weapon and struggled over the top of the trench.

Alessandro saw that the man he had shot had stopped moving. The other had not even jerked. They lay immobile in pools of blood. His face tightened as he slung his bloody rifle. Pressing his right hand against the wound, he stumbled back to the Bell Tower.

Light-headed, he pushed into the map room and stood before

the others. The ones who were sitting, stood up. They looked at his bloodied hand covering the wound, and at his devastated eyes.

Even the infantrymen did not make light of it. One guided Alessandro to a cot. Another took the rifle and went to clean the bayonet. This was their métier. It wasn't something with which you were born, you learned it, and it wasn't even that difficult to learn. They used bandage shears to cut open Alessandro's shirt quickly, the way it would be done if he had been going to die, but then they stepped back. "Nothing," an infantryman said.

"It cut a little channel in the top of your shoulder, that's all," Guariglia stated before he dropped an alcohol-soaked rag on what looked like a sabre cut. The alcohol made Alessandro scream at the top of his lungs.

"Here they come!" one of the infantrymen shouted, as a chilling sound rolled through the Bell Tower—the cry of twenty thousand men beginning a charge.

ALONG THE entire length of the line thousands of Austrians and Germans appeared to rise out of the ground, slowly at first as they went over the top, and then faster as they ran toward the river, shielded by ragged banks of smoke. By the thousands and the ten thousands, they shouted. The Italians mounted the firesteps, looked over the tops of their trenches, and fired. Trench mortars on both sides were continually stoked. They could, at random, level a line of attackers as they began to wade the river, or kill the defenders exposed above their dugouts, and they did. The heavy artillery ceased except for a ten-minute barrage against the Bell Tower, which was hit by hundreds of shells.

The cat Serafina, who had suffered before from artillery fire, was crouched in terror in the deepest corner of the communications bunker. Alessandro lay on a cot, bandaged and throbbing.

At first no one could move, but the concussions of the shells became so great that everything shook, and people were knocked around the room like dice in a cup.

Then, as if pushing through waves in stormy surf, shouting things that no one could really hear but that were obscenities of anger and determination, the infantrymen and the River Guard struggled to the firing ports. They were knocked down. They were pinned under parts of the ceiling as it fell, choked with dust, thrown against each other, but some made it to the outer wall. There, they screamed and they cursed, and they took their weapons.

Hardly able to see or hear, blinded by the smoke and choking on the powder, they fired toward the river, sweeping to and fro with the machine guns, their teeth clenched as if they were using swords and pikes. A man at the center was blown inward and made unrecognizable when a shell exploded just outside his gun port. Another man rushed to his position, but could not find a weapon.

As Alessandro got up to replace a man who fell, one of the other bunkers exploded. After a terrible cry, everyone who was left alive began to run, because the firing ports had been closed and the Austrians, who had lost several thousand men in the river, were now at the shattered wire. Alessandro was last out.

Biondo lay dead in the *cortile*. The Guitarist was climbing over the rubble to get away. The machine-gunner was dead and his machine gun at the entrance to the trench smashed apart. Guariglia had been right. The trench was filled in.

As Alessandro struggled through the craters and began to run toward the Italian line, he saw only about a dozen others from the Bell Tower. The cat ran so fast that she disappeared almost immediately, leaping right over the Italian trench that was everyone else's goal, running like a rocket toward the fields of the Veneto.

The heavy artillery had stopped but the trench mortars kept up their barrage. Some of the men fell. No one went back to see if they were alive, for a thousand Austrians had come through the wire and were close behind.

Alessandro reached the trench and vaulted in. The Italians over whose heads he had jumped were working their rifles madly and had hardly even noticed.

The sound of their firing was tremendous, as if the whole world had been taken up in an explosive wind. Alessandro closed his eyes, and when he opened them he saw the Guitarist crouched down right in front of him. He was smiling, so Alessandro automatically smiled back. At least they had come through. Then he looked more closely. The Guitarist was frozen in place, and his eyes were dead.

"Who's left?" Alessandro cried out.

He looked down the trench. Microscopico was firing. Some of the infantry from the Bell Tower now manned a machine gun in clouds of smoke. Others were vaguely recognizable along the line. Alessandro picked up a rifle that had been lying on the ground. He laid it across a sandbag, mounted the fire-step, and coldly began to shoot at the advancing ranks of enemy soldiers. Some had reached the Italian trench and were fighting inside it. Alessandro was in a daze. He reloaded.

THE MOON AND THE BONFIRES

IN SPRING the remnants of the River Guard were recalled to Mestre and recombined. To the surprise of the naval infantrymen, they were now in the army and their unit had no name. Although they would have preferred the privileges of the navy, they were relieved finally to be recognized for what they were, as they had been army infantrymen almost since the beginning, and it was now 1917. They thought that things would be less confusing, but, then, they didn't know that they were soon to go to sea.

For the entire month of March they were kept within the perimeter of a mine assembly area at Mestre. Venice sparkled across the water, a golden vessel that held all the beautiful and gentle things they had lacked for years, but they could neither go beyond the wire nor let their families know where they were. Nor were they told when their isolation would end or why they had been confined. They drilled in the morning, stripped their weapons several times a day, exercised for hours, and traveled three times a week on a special train to a firing range in the dunes, where they sharpened their aim and ruined their hearing from dawn to dusk with rifles, pistols, and machine guns.

Even in spring, Mestre was gray, at least when compared to the Byzantine water lily over the lagoon. Its church bells rang at noon, and train whistles sounded all day and night as contingents of infantry left for the front or returned. Steam engines exhaled like frightened cattle, and the air was filled with the sounds of metal clanging against metal.

Alessandro lay on a straw pallet in an enormous shed once used to store the detonators of the mines that had been placed in an arc around Venice at the beginning of the war. These had been bobbing in the water for years, sometimes drifting loose and floating casually down the Grand Canal, to the horror of the gondoliers.

"You shouldn't go to him again, Alessandro," Guariglia said. He and Alessandro were the only ones left from the naval contingent in the Bell Tower. Microscopico had been killed early that winter in the push to throw the Austrians from the bridgehead they had established in the fall. "You've gone to him every day for a month, and the answer is always the same."

"I've received no word from my family since January," Alessandro said, as if he couldn't distinguish between Guariglia and the lieutenant of whom he had to beg. "So why can't I have three days to take the train to Rome? Just three days."

"They won't even let us go to Venice," Guariglia said, "and you can see Venice through the cracks in the wall."

They were in a room in which 150 men on gray blankets lay staring at the huge wooden beams that held up a roof of terra cotta tiles. The sun came through fractures and pinholes as if its golden lights were playing across a dark sky. Alessandro had noticed when he first arrived that the color that suffused around the openings where the light entered was a milky orange like that of an orange cream-ice that Roman vendors sold in the parks.

"We're better off here than in the Bell Tower," Guariglia said. "It hurts me that I can't see my children, but I pray to come home to them. I'm not wasting any requests in the middle, and neither should you."

"I told my parents to write to Rafi's. All I need are a few hours in Venice."

"If you go over the wall, they'll shoot you."

"They only execute in the line."

"That's not so, Alessandro. On the train down I leaned out the window to talk to a sergeant in the station at Treviso. He said that it's true, they condemn whole units, or one in ten men in a unit, or the first five, and he'd never *been* in the line. It's insane. They want you to know that they might shoot you even if you *don't* disobey them. It can only lead to a revolution."

Alessandro turned his head without lifting it from the pillow. As Guariglia continued to peer into the beams, he said, "On the day we get sentry duty, when everyone else goes to the firing range . . ."

"They're at S now. By the time they get to G, we may be gone."

"Where?"

"Who knows?"

"But if we're here . . ."

"You can't tell if they'll go out that day."

"If they do, I'll go to Venice and return before they get back. What could go wrong?"

"What could go wrong? Even if you did get back before they did, an officer might come in while you were gone."

"Our officers, all of them, always go along. If anything happens, you need only say that I wasn't here. They'll shoot me, not you."

"You don't have enough patience, Alessandro. You're too used to having things the way you want them."

"Guariglia, if the Guitarist had deserted they'd be chasing him now, but he'd still be alive."

"We're safe now. Why push it?"

"To have a day in Venice before I die."

AFTER MANY S's, not a few T's, some R's and a rich crop of B's, C's, and D's, came two F's, and two other G's, Gastaldino and Garzatti, before Giuliani and Guariglia. Alessandro carefully monitored the calendar and the alphabet as April wore on.

For two weeks they ate mainly salad and minestrone without beans, and during this time they went every day from their makeshift barracks to a parade ground where the mines had been stored, to exercise for six hours—at dawn, in the middle of the morning, noon, in the middle of the afternoon, after dinner, and just before bed. The routine never varied. They marched to the parade ground carrying their rifles. Then, with the rifles held in front of them, they ran around the perimeter for fifteen minutes. Their speed was assured and their mutiny avoided by a stratagem invented by the lieutenant Alessandro had petitioned in vain. A sergeant distributed breadsticks to everyone but the last ten to come in, who, if they made a habit of losing, soon got to be so skinny that they began to win. The troops were hungry, but they had beef or chicken on Sundays, and were allowed cheese for breakfast when they went to the firing range.

There, each soldier was given two hundred rounds of rifle ammunition and a hundred for pistol. Although not a single one of them hadn't fired many more cartridges than this in half an hour under attack in the line, it seemed like a terrible waste just for practice, especially since they had been living with their weapons for years (though most had not had pistols), and could bisect a cigarette at fifty meters. Targets were set up in the dunes, and they practiced until bull's-eyes were routine. Armorers were brought from a nearby arsenal. When a rifle was less than perfect it was recalibrated or taken to be rebored. If that didn't work, it was exchanged. The River Guard shot slowly and carefully. Every pattern of fire was called out, every target returned for analysis after twenty-four rounds. They had nothing to eat and only a bottle of water from the time they left the mine assembly area until they returned. Toward the end of the month it was hot in the dunes, and they came back painfully sunburned.

The days passed at the shooting range, running, or in the barracks where the orange light glowed the color of the orange cream-ice one could buy in the Villa Borghese, and when the circumstances were right, Alessandro was able to take his chance. They drew sentry duty on a clear windy day late in April when the River Guard went to the firing range. As the formations filed onto the little munitions train that took them out to the dunes, Alessandro looked through the narrow windows near the ceiling and saw whole mountain ranges of cloud slowly slipping by in a sky that was every color from the softest blue to the hardest dirtiest gray. Though such clouds were capable of great thunder and of harboring whole bales of woolly lightning, as these started their slide down the pearly Adriatic they were too high to do anything but glide.

Alessandro walked into the now empty room where Guariglia, rifle at his shoulder, stood by double doors at the opposite end. Beyond him was the courtyard, with two enormous beech trees flanking an iron gate. The trees were newly green, and when the wind blew past the leaves it sounded almost like autumn.

"Just us," Alessandro said. His words carried easily through the empty barracks. Curly-haired Guariglia, who had taken the liberty of smoking a cigar, smiled.

"How will you walk around in Venice, Alessandro?" he asked. "It has half a million military police, and we have no insignia."

"I'll do it the way Orfeo would do it."

"Who's he?"

"He's responsible for all this."

"For the mine assembly area?"

"No."

"For the war?"

"No."

"For what, then?"

"For everything."

"He's like Saturn or Zeus?"

"He's the font of all chaos, and he lives in Rome."

Guariglia took some puffs on the cigar. "I'd like to meet him."

"Maybe someday you will. He'd get away with it, and so will I."

Alessandro went into the lieutenant's quarters, which were behind a low partition. He took the battalion dispatch bag and threw it over his shoulder.

"So what," said Guariglia. "A battalion courier has to have a pass and insignia just like everyone else."

Alessandro unpinned one of the lieutenant's gold epaulets from a dress tunic that hung on the partition. He attached it to the center of his cap, and the gold braid shone like an electric semaphore.

"You're crazy," Guariglia said.

IN VENICE, Alessandro passed real couriers with dispatch bags and plumes, and neither they nor anyone else looked at him. As he crossed the Grand Canal he greedily began to take in all things not military. His eye seized upon every tendril on every plant, every curve or flute in iron or stone work, the most faded patches of color, women in clothes with sweeping lines, restaurant kitchens going full blast, and children, some of whom he picked up and kissed, for he had not seen a child in more than a year.

He knew Venice. A thousand places came back to him as he walked through the streets. Then he remembered that he was allowed to eat. Although his deepest instincts told him to go to a bakery, he decided to go to the Excelsior.

At eleven the dining room of the Excelsior was deserted but for some English officers having an early lunch. Alessandro went to a table near a large window that overlooked the canal. Crystal and silver on a bright field of slightly rose-colored linen filled his eyes as he put down his leather case and removed his hat.

"You've been at the front," the waiter said.

"Two and a half years."

"You want to eat everything in the world."

Alessandro expressed his agreement.

"Don't. It'll make you sick. Eat well, but eat lightly."

"What should I eat, then?"

"I'll bring it."

"No breadsticks or minestrone."

"Please," the waiter said, his back already turned.

Before the kitchen doors had stopped swinging he came back out with a towel over his arm, carrying three heavy plates and a carafe of wine. One was a bowl of scaldingly hot fish soup, another a dish of tomatoes and arugula, and the third a platter of spaghetti with mussels.

"The portions are small," the waiter said, "but this is only part one."

Alessandro ate, and as he ate he sang and talked to himself. The waiter cleared his table and brought a plate of smoked salmon, a grilled filet mignon, and a portion of *funghi porcini,* along with another carafe of wine and a bottle of sparkling mineral water.

"Things still exist," Alessandro said.

"Yes yes yes," the waiter said. "You know they will be expensive?"

"I have the money."

Next came *vitello al tonno,* a Florentine egg, and some brook trout. When that was dispatched, the waiter brought a pitcher of *cioccolato caldo,* fruit salad, a dish of rich chocolate ice cream, and a hazelnut cake with whipped Venetian icing.

"I'm satisfied," Alessandro said after this.

"But wait," the waiter said, and he brought a snifter of pear brandy and a plate of the strongest, crispest mints Alessandro had ever tasted.

"Where do you get mints like this?" he asked.

"Since the war they've made them with nitroglycerine," the waiter joked.

"They don't taste like nitroglycerine," Alessandro said.

"You've tasted nitroglycerine?"

"After a lot of firing, the air gets so thick with it that you breathe it in and you can taste it for days."

For this meal Alessandro paid four months' salary, and when he emerged from the hotel he went to a bakery and bought a loaf of freshly baked bread. It was only noon, and he decided to take a walk before he went to see Rafi's parents.

In the Piazza San Marco a beautiful young woman with a solid figure, shoulder-length blond hair, and the bluest eyes was holding aloft a small red umbrella and haranguing a group of overweight old ladies, in German. Her bones seemed heavy. She was perfectly proportioned but she seemed to be weighted with iron, so that any gesture, any movement, was like that of a swordsman swinging something lethal. Her arm, thinner than those that Rubens had portrayed but just as voluptuous and thirty times as strong, looked as if it could smash stone columns, and she gesticulated fiercely. As she described the sights, her breasts leapt vividly against her cotton blouse, and her hair flew back and forth each time she turned her head.

Alessandro approached her. She put down the umbrella.

"Excuse me," he said quietly. "You're speaking German."

"Yes, I'm speaking German," she said in unaccented Italian.

"Why?" he asked. "You're Italian, aren't you?"

"I am, but they aren't," she answered, glancing at the old ladies, who were waiting patiently.

"Germans?"

She said yes.

"We're at war with them," he said. "Not far from here, we're killing each other. We're killing their sons and grandsons, and their sons and grandsons are killing us."

"They're women," the guide said. "They came to see the sights of Venice."

Alessandro was stunned.

"They hurt no one, these old women. No one notices them. They're free to come and go."

"Give me your address," Alessandro demanded.

"Why?"

"I want to visit you sometime."

"You're crazy."

"Don't you want me to visit you?"

She assessed him. Then she said, "Yes, I do, but I live in Paris, and we're leaving for Verona this afternoon."

"Someday," he said, "I'll visit you in Paris. I'll make love to you. It happens."

"It does," she said, smiling.

"What does he say? What does he say?" one of the old ladies asked in German.

The guide turned to her and said in correct, excellent, enthusiastic German, "He says he'll visit me in Paris."

The ladies nodded their approval.

Alessandro turned deep red. "After the war," he said.

"Or during the war, if you can. I live in Passage Jean Nicot. Ask for me there, but come before I'm married and come before I'm old."

She leaned forward, took his hand, and kissed him.

The old ladies said "Ahhhhh!" and then the guide lifted her red umbrella, turned her charges toward the Doge's Palace, and led them away, describing what lay ahead.

FOR THE visitor without the map of Venice by heart the city is a maze that defeats human intention, and, like life itself, blocks and shunts those who live it into backwaters, alleys, and quiet places that never were part of any plan. This it does by watery divisions both great and small, and streets that turn so subtly that they seem not to be changing direction even when they are in the process of describing a full circle, which is how Alessandro, trying to reach the Ghetto, found himself in the Accademia.

He had come here often as a student, but now he knew no one, no one knew him, and he felt out of place. The nearly empty galleries were more eloquent in contrasting war and peace than had been his two years in the mountains, where his dream-like state had gone uninterrupted for want of a fragment of his previous life.

He was almost entirely alone in the rich fields of the Accademia, where he removed his hat and walked slowly about, taking in not only the paintings themselves but the building as well. He had lived for too long in the cornerless, ceilingless, overly narrow and horridly low world of trenches and bunkers. Here were height, volume, stirring proportions, and magical details.

At the end of one gallery, in a shaft of sunlight, a man stood before Giorgione's *La Tempesta*. Even in the presence of so great a painting he had a self-important air, and Alessandro could see that he was lost in thought and wanted to be left alone.

Undoubtedly, Alessandro thought, he's on a fellowship, writing an article, trying to advance his career. How did he escape the war? He was not much older than Alessandro himself. As Alessandro approached, his boots striking the floorboards like hammers on a wooden box, the scholar showed an expression of irritated and delicate superiority.

"Move," Alessandro commanded. "You're blocking my view."

The scholar could not speak for his disgust, but he smiled patronizingly. "Sorry."

"It's darker than when I saw it last," Alessandro said.

"The weather?"

"The painting. I haven't seen it for three or four years."

"A painting that has been stable for centuries," the scholar answered, "doesn't darken suddenly in a few years. You merely think it's darker."

"Wrong," said Alessandro.

"Wrong?"

"The painting is darker now. I can see it."

"Then your eye must be extraordinarily sensitive and precise," the scholar said in sarcastic deference.

"It served me when I needed it."

"In shooting?"

"In shooting, assessment, and appraisal."

"Of what?"

"Paintings. Paintings mainly. You know why? Because they're so easily apprehensible. They're present all at once, unlike music, or language, with which you can lie to the common man merely because he may not remember what has just been and cannot know what is coming. Painting is tranquil and appeals directly to heart and soul."

The scholar touched his glasses. "What did you do before the war?" he asked. After all, if Alessandro, too, had been a scholar he would have been justly offended at his treatment, though not otherwise.

"I was a horse trainer."

"A horse trainer?"

"For the hunt. You know, galloping across the countryside and getting thorns in your ass. I've also written four articles on this painting." He rattled off the titles of the articles and the names of the journals in which they had appeared. "I don't remember the dates, but if you're doing a paper on Giorgione you're bound to run into them."

The scholar had already run across the articles and had remembered them.

"But if you do," Alessandro continued, "ignore them. They're all wrong. I know, intelligent criticism cannot be 'wrong,' but I was wrong to submit to the tyranny by which critics of art live, and to follow the road that they follow, because, to maintain their society and vocation, they parse by intellect alone works that are great solely because of the spirit.

"You're visited with penalties if you transgress," he went on, speaking in a kind of storm, "but I'm no longer afraid of censure by my colleagues or of being without the Academy, for I walked out myself and can never return.

"Do you know why?" he asked, stepping closer to the stranger. "The Academy is a mouse house, and to live within it you must be a house mouse. I didn't want to be a house mouse in a mouse house."

"You've suffered in battle," the scholar said. He was not unsympathetic.

"Not as much as others," Alessandro answered, "but, yes, I have, and it has made me both patient and impatient. Though it has broken and razed everything that once stood within me, I've lost nothing. The ceiling is still there, but now blue, with stars."

"I see," the scholar said, pitying Alessandro's inexactitude.

"That doesn't make sense to you, does it," Alessandro asked. "It does not yet make sense to me. I'll be half a century, if I live, trying to understand why it was that, though I was broken, I was not broken.

"And wrong about the painting. Like everyone else, I backed off. I said, 'We'll never know about *La Tempesta,* it's a mystery.' I retreated to the visual elements, the technique, its strange contra-historical power. I thought it was a dream, because it has the lucidity and freedom of a dream, a dream's unburdening, and a dream-like truth."

The scholar agreed. "*I* think it's a dream, a great dream, with—as you put it—the lucidity, freedom, unburdening, and truth of a dream."

"No," Alessandro said. "Though it could be a dream, it isn't. I know now exactly what it is, and I know the source of its power."

"Dare you tell?" the scholar asked, only half sarcastically, hoping that a stricken soldier might have taken from the fire of his affliction something of value that someone else might use in an essay on Giorgione.

"I know exactly what you're thinking," Alessandro said, "but I'll tell you, and you can do as you wish. For all I care, you can be the chief of the Academy. I'll go back to the front. My blood will wash into the Adriatic before the ink on the pages of your fucking article is dry. It doesn't matter. You'll join me sooner than you know in a place with no academies and no illusions, where the truth is the only architecture, the only color, the only sound—where that which we sense merely on occasion, and which takes us up and gives us the rare and beautiful glimpses of the things we truly love, flows in deep rivers and tumbles about like clouds in the sky."

He stepped closer to the painting. Just to be near it seemed to give him satisfaction.

"I believe that Giorgione was painting for a patron, and that he started out according to a pattern customary for his time. Look, you still have the remnants of it—the raised platform with a long view of a river and a town. The bridge reiterates the platform. The river disappears leftward. It's a windowed view: the buildings in the town are framed by nearer masses, to block them, for, at the time, perspective was not entirely out of the woods. On the platform, a woman feeding a baby—all Flemish in inspiration, quite standard.

"But what of the soldier, so tremendously out of place, so distant, so jarring, and yet the master figure of the painting? And what of the approaching storm?"

"He's not a soldier," the scholar said. "He's a shepherd."

"Like hell he's a shepherd. Shepherds have never been as clean-cut and well dressed. If he were a shepherd he'd have a crook, not a staff. Shepherds don't stand like that. And look in his eyes. Have you not seen the eyes of a soldier? Have you not seen a shepherd?

"I'll tell you how this strange coalition came about," Alessandro almost whispered. "Giorgione was going to paint a conventional scene. I'd wager my life that other pastoral figures were intended for the foreground, another nude, perhaps, or a satyr, or who knows? To me, the soldier looks as if he were painted-in late.

"While Giorgione was working on this scene, with the Academy and his patrons in mind, a storm arose. It was a great and unusual storm, as he has depicted it. Lucky for him, because you can't know history unless you can see it as if it were a stupendous thunderstorm that has just cleared. Light and sound speak clearly then, as if to sweep away illusions and lay down the law. The clouds went straight up in mountainous walls of gray and green, the trees bent in apprehension, the lightning was so thick, supple, and young that before it attacked the town it played in the clouds and lit up the world, just as young horses gallop in a field just to feel the wind.

"As the world darkened before him and the wind rose, Giorgione felt his own death and the death of everyone and everything he loved. He understood dissolution. He saw ruin and night. He saw the future of prosperous and proud cities, of the arches, bridges, and upright walls. These broken columns are his vision of the Academy, of rules, and rivalries, and opinion.

"Only in the lightning and in the foreground is the light active. The woman and the soldier steal the light and color from everything that is in ruin. Unclothed and unprotected, with her baby in her arms, she defies the storm unwittingly. Entirely at risk, she shines out. Don't you understand? She's his only hope. After what he's seen, only she and the child can put the world in balance. And yet the soldier is distant, protected, detached. They always say about the soldier that he's detached. That's true, for he's been in the eye of the storm, his heart has been broken, and he doesn't even know it."

THE GONDOLIER who took him to the Ghetto wanted to go in a straight line to avoid the curves of the Grand Canal. He went via narrow and obscure channels, through which he spent much of the time backing out to let oncoming boats pass under bridges so low that he and Alessandro had to run from end to end of the gondola to tilt the bow and stern to allow it to slide underneath. They poled through several flooded buildings in which the gondolier had to light a lantern.

In the last of these, the chamber they negotiated was long and dark, and Alessandro began to yell at the gondolier, accusing him of everything from cretinism to impotence, but the gondolier said, "I know the only straight line in Venice, and nothing you can say will shame or anger me."

Both Signor Foa and his wife were in, having just finished lunch. Alessandro introduced himself. Rafi's father seemed only about half his son's height, but twice as strong. Signora was the tall one, an Austrian Jewess with silver-white hair. Her husband had a heavy gold chain hanging around his bull-like neck, which was hard to call a neck, as it was like the buttress of a bridge.

"What's that?" Alessandro asked, pointing at the chain.

Signor Foa thought Alessandro was pointing at him. "I'm Rafi's father."

"I mean the chain."

"This? This is the chain," he said, pulling the rest of it from under his shirt, "that holds this. Do you know what this is?"

"Of course I know."

"The Shield of David. It says who I am, and the chain makes it easier for them to hang me once they find out."

"With your neck, what would happen if they did?"

"I could probably hang for days," he said.

"It's true," his wife added. "Once, he was caught on a meat conveyor and dragged twenty meters into the air, with a rope around his neck, all the way to the deck of a freighter. It took them half an hour to get him out, and while they were doing it he kept on asking questions about the ship and where it had come from."

"Rafi is slim, like you, Signora," Alessandro said.

"Too bad," said Signor Foa. "He could have been much stronger."

Rafi's mother brought a silver tray of delicate white wafers, which Alessandro would always remember but never again see. "Are these Venetian?" he asked.

"No no," Signora said. "My recipe, from Klagenfurt. We used to call them Turkish something...Turkish tiles, or bricks, I don't remember exactly."

"They're good," Alessandro added, so as to explain why he had already eaten most of them. "Will you make half a ton for Luciana's wedding?"

"Assuming that Rafi will be there," she said, subjugating the issue of assimilation to the question of survival.

"At least you can give the recipe to my mother," Alessandro said.

Signora Foa's eyes darted and she took in a breath, but Alessandro didn't see, for he was bent toward the silver tray. When he straightened in his chair, with half a dozen Turkish wafers in his hands, he saw that the eyes of the hostess were brimming with tears, and when no one could break the silence, he replaced the wafers on the tray.

"Tell me," he said. "Tell me."

"Alessandro..." said Signor Foa, leaning forward.

"Do you have a letter for me?" Alessandro interjected. "I asked them to send my mail here because I wasn't getting it in the north. How is Rafi?"

"Rafi's fine, as far as we know," Signora added anxiously. "He's in the Alpini."

"I know."

"I do have a letter for you, Alessandro," Signor Foa said. "It's from your father. We thought you knew. Alessandro, your mother died in December."

ONE MORNING in the early part of May the River Guard were awakened in their barracks at 3:00 A.M. As they shaved and dressed in the cold night air, they speculated—a raid on the Dalmatian Coast, combat against the Germans in East Africa, taking an island in the Adriatic. One of the more imaginative and least intelligent of them said they would go by submarine up the Danube to seize Vienna. No one, not even the officers, knew where they were bound or why they had neither insignia nor a unit name.

By four they had assembled on the parade ground, under full packs, their rifles on their shoulders, bandoliers and pouches of ammunition hung from pistol belts, bayonets fixed and sheathed. Twenty-one wheeled caissons were interspersed among the ranks. These contained field kitchens, tents, three water-cooled machine guns, signaling equipment, and ammunition.

They were a sharp and elite unit, and had been in the trenches long enough to have been blooded a hundred times. Lean and fit, they were so accustomed to drill that they found it comforting, and took pride in the clipped and powerful sound of their heels snapping to attention.

Their early morning thoughts were stimulated by the confluence of great energy and minds freshly drawn from oblivion. They had no light, nothing against which to measure the difference between wake and sleep, no harsh mid-morning sun to assault their dreams and regulate the beating of their hearts.

After they were called to attention they were counted in the most formal military manner and checked against a list. Then a lieutenant sealed the list, put it in a pouch, and gave it to a mounted divisional courier, who took it and galloped away. The lieutenant produced another list and went through the exercise once again, but this time he called only first names.

"You will notice," he said when he had finished, "that in each platoon only a few men have the same first name. Whoever shares names will decide upon nicknames or some other way to tell one from another.

"From now on, you'll never mention the cities and towns where you lived, you'll forget the last names and home towns of your friends, you'll be known only by your first name, and you'll address your fellow soldiers and officers only by first name or rank. Understood?"

The lieutenant looked up. He was tall and thin, with an aquiline nose, and a mustache that made him look both very old-fashioned and very up-to-date. In civilian life he had been a chemist. His name was Giovanni Valtorta, but no one ever called him anything other than Lieutenant. Two sub-lieutenants acted as if they had understood the reason for the orders, and were embarrassed when the lieutenant responded to the dazed and contemptuous expressions of his men by saying, "Evidently these orders are legitimate, and we're to follow them. Don't ask me why, because I don't know why." He stepped back two paces, surveyed his men, looked about, and said, "You may laugh and curse for one minute."

The soldiers were angry. They hadn't seen their families, and it seemed especially cruel that not only did they have no opportunity to be with their mothers, fathers, sisters, and brothers, and to return, if only for a short time, to their wives and their precious and holy children, but for a month they had had no news, and now they were told to forget their names. As the curses and the laughter died down, someone asked, "What is to become of us?"

This question cleared the air and brought total silence.

"I don't know," the lieutenant answered. "We shall see."

Then he called them to attention, and they snapped to as if the last that was gentle about them was fleeing along their rifles and shining bayonets straight into the dark sky above Mestre.

They went southwest along dirt roads, across railroad tracks, through fields, and past factories for an hour and a half at double time in the dark. As the sky lightened they came to an arm of the lagoon that surrounds Venice. They marched along the edge of this until they stopped at a wooden pier that pointed to the rising sun. Three large steam launches, boilers fired, were lined up to receive them. Usually military units take a long time to load, but the River Guard were so light and so practiced at being together that they were in the boats, caissons and all, in five minutes.

Guariglia turned to the sailor who manned the tiller of the boat in which he and Alessandro sat aft and to the starboard. "Are we going to a battleship?" he asked.

"No," the sailor answered. "You're going to a bucket of shit."

"I don't understand," Guariglia said, thinking that perhaps the sailor merely disliked his ship.

"Neither do I," the sailor said, "and I'm not supposed to talk to you."

The three launches cast off, sidled into the currentless estuary, and moved forward. Though the River Guard didn't know where they were going, at least they didn't have to walk. The land and its tangles were replaced by the blank slate of the waves, but the seaward journey did not take the infantrymen into the clear. By some perversity the sailors directed the launches straight for the silhouetted spires of Venice. They drew closer and closer as the sun pushed through the slots and cuts in the dark mass of the city and blinded them with its pale bright light. Trapped in the glare, Venice looked threatening and enormous, until they came to it and entered the Grand Canal.

Except for Alessandro, no one had been near a city for many months, and with their weary eyes they looted it in its every detail. Young soldiers who hadn't the slightest idea of form (other than in a woman) took in the lines of Venice as if they were architects on their way to being executed. When a waiter in a black dinner jacket and starched apron stepped to the side of the canal and tossed a bucket-full of soapy water into the air, they watched intently the motion of his arms and back. As nearby gondoliers strained forward, the River Guard passed a house at the end of the canal and heard a piano, and as they rode by with their rifles on their shoulders they wished that they could stay.

As quickly as they had entered Venice and steamed through the Grand Canal, they exited. The sun caught San Giorgio Maggiore in a warm flare of orange, ochre, and white, as the hesitant blue dawn over the Adriatic was cleared of all but the most tentative clouds. These had red underbellies, or gold, and were grouped together in long luminous strings like golden willow branches.

The waves picked up as the sun strengthened, and the River Guard headed out to the roads, where many ships lay at anchor. The prows of the launches rose up and down vigorously, sometimes slapping the water into spray that was blown back into the boat.

AS THE hysterical morning bells of Venice rang out six, the three launches looped around a rusty cattle boat that lay between a destroyer and a cruiser. At first the River Guard thought they would board the cruiser, and, then, the destroyer. When they came alongside the cattle boat, they groaned.

"It doesn't even have a name," someone said. "Don't ships always have names?"

"Why should it? We don't."

"What will they write if we get torpedoed?"

"Don't worry. Torpedoes are too expensive to waste. What do they care about a load of cattle, sheep, and goats?"

"But what if they see *us*?"

"That's what I'm talking about."

"You know what I say," Guariglia shouted to all the launches. "I say, I don't have a name, I'm not from anywhere, I have no family, I don't know where I'm going, what I'm doing, or when I'll be back. So you know what I say? I say ... fuck it!"

"I know where we're going," a normally quiet soldier said. "We're going south."

"Perhaps that's because ships don't go on land."

"We're going to conquer Turkey."

"I'd rather fight them than the Germans."

Then they thought back to the War of 1911, and someone said, "I wouldn't."

When they embarked they were in high spirits, hauling caissons over the sides two at a time with hoists that usually lifted terrified horses and cows. The launches cast off, the caissons were stowed below, and the cattle boat began to move. A hatch popped up in the bow and two sailors emerged to winch up the anchor. Soon, they were underway in the wind, gulls maneuvered around them, and whitecaps appeared in the water.

The two sailors, who wore decrepit uniforms without insignia, brought up a large metal container with sides that were fogged and covered with droplets. It was a bucket of vanilla ice cream and strawberries. "This is a gift from the cruiser," they said, "and it's the last of it. We have no refrigeration."

"Where are we going?" they were asked.

"We don't know. The captain doesn't know either. They give him an envelope with the name of the next port, the course, and the speed. When we arrive, he gets another envelope. It's been like that since the beginning of the war."

The lieutenant came down from the bridge. He knew. "First we're sailing for the naval base at Brindisi, where a colonel will embark and tell us what we're going to do."

"Sir?"

"Yes?"

"A colonel?"

"That's what I said."

"For three platoons? Colonels are for brigades."

"Find places to sleep on deck," the lieutenant commanded.

"At sea the dew is impossible," a soldier said. "We'll get soaking wet."

"No. This boat has a shallow draught, because it was built to skim the reefs of out-islands where it transported animals. The captain says we're going to follow the coast. The wind comes off the land at night, and it will be dry. We'll be so close to shore you'll think you're on a train."

After the ice cream, Alessandro and Guariglia settled on the upper deck amidships on the starboard side. They washed their bowls by lowering them over the rails and allowing the sea to batter them clean, and they lay down on the beds they had made of their blankets and packs. They were so comfortable and tired that they slept through intense heat, and only awoke now and then to look at the gulls vibrating on the wind as they held position over the ship.

BY LATE afternoon their uniforms were stiff and white with salt. "I saw a man's ashes once," Guariglia said. "They're grayish white, just like those lines on your shirt."

"That's not so bad," Alessandro stated. "When you realize that everyone is not much different from the stuff that's listed on the sides of bottles of mineral water, death takes on an air of tranquillity."

"Why don't they do it on wine bottles?" Guariglia asked.

"Because there's too much crap in wine, and if the stuff in water takes up the whole side of a bottle, in microscopic print, every liter of wine would have to come with a manual."

"When my brother was a kid," Guariglia said, "he tried to make wine from chicken shit."

"Did it work?"

"Yes and no. He put what he got in a Chianti bottle and took it around to the cafes. No one liked it, but a lot of people bought a glass or two."

"Or *two*?"

"They wanted to be nice to a kid. Most of them were pretty old, anyway."

The soldiers lined up at the water casks and drank deeply of the warm and tainted water that would not have tasted better had it been from a numbing alpine spring. They let it pour over their heads and soak their shirts.

When the sun, still white and yellow, was hovering over the mountaintops, one of the sailors staggered from the hold under a quarter of beef. So many flies were around him that at first they thought he was carrying a huge cluster of grapes.

"Are we supposed to eat that?" someone asked.

"You'll love it," the sailor said. "It's good meat and it's been curing."

"Since before or after the birth of Christ?"

"It's safe. We live on it."

A small circle of men including Alessandro and Guariglia gathered around the sailor as he opened a locker and dragged out a long rope and a steel grappling hook. He pushed the hook through the quarter of beef, attached the rope to a cleat on deck, and threw the beef into the sea. It crashed into the brine and skidded across the surface, turning and bouncing violently on the waves in an enormous amount of froth and foam. The flies disappeared and the meat took on a good color.

As the meat was pulled through the sea the cook used a short bayonet to cut up several sacks of carrots, potatoes, and onions that he threw into a huge cauldron. The cauldron was carried to a hatch cover upon which a barefooted soldier had burned himself earlier in the day. The cook opened the hatch with the receiver on the bayonet. "Main steam pipe," he said, lowering the cauldron into a recess for which it had been designed. "Bring me two buckets of sea water."

They pulled in the beef, which now looked like the meat in the windows of expensive butcher shops on the Via del Corso. The cook set upon it with the bayonet until blood flowed off the deck into the sea, and dumped the pieces into the cauldron to boil with the sea water and vegetables.

While the soldiers washed down the deck, he disappeared, and bobbed up again carrying two enormous straw-covered wine bottles, and a string of garlic that he put on the deck and crushed under his boots. He threw the garlic, a box of ground pepper, two liters of olive oil, and five liters of wine into the boiling brine.

"One hour," he said. "The other bottle is for you, two long drinks each—not too long."

After the bottle was passed around and each soldier had drunk as much as he could, they went to sit on their improvised beds and watch the sun go down over the mountains. Cool and dry, ravenously hungry, lost, perplexed, and safe, they leaned back against their packs and blankets as they listened to the engines and the sea and watched the shore go by.

The beaches were completely deserted, but now and then the River Guard saw a peasant in the fields or an ox cart on the road that paralleled the sea. The perfect rows of olive trees and the net of stone walls looked as if they had been there since the creation. Even fortress-like villages perched on outcroppings of rock seemed empty, until dusk, when their lights went on. At dusk, too, occasional bonfires on the beach told of a military encampment and an army dinner.

"Why couldn't we have done something like that?" Guariglia asked. "I'd like to spend the whole war on the beach, fishing, making fires, never firing a shot."

"That's for the old men of the civil guard," Alessandro answered.

"They must have some real units among them."

"Why?"

"What if the Austrians invaded? Rome is just beyond the mountains."

"How could they invade here?" Alessandro asked. "You know that every single man they've got is up there," he said, pointing toward the Isonzo, "and if they were to move them, we would take Vienna."

Guariglia lit up a cigar. He was upwind of Alessandro, but Alessandro didn't care.

The fields beyond the beaches were low and gold, and they stretched to the mountains. By day, white smoke followed the contours of the land in slowly rising walls drawn like a curtain along the entire length of coast. As the farmers burned their fields for the second crop, in some places the fire was bright enough to be seen in full sunlight, and though a thousand human hands had set and were guiding it, no one could see the men at such a distance, and it seemed out of control. As the sun dropped behind the mountains the smoke grew dark and the flames brighter, until finally the smoke was invisible except when it blocked the stars, and the River Guard could see only the silhouettes of the Apennines, with endless and repetitive chains of smoldering orange flame at their feet. The wind came from ashore and brought them the smell of rich summer grass, and smoke. It brought them back to life.

"I feel like a civilian," Guariglia said, "because it makes me remember. Sometimes I'd get a big order from an estate. I'd work for months and then deliver the stuff myself, and fit the horses in the field, line them up along a fence and harness them one by one. The stable boys would use the opportunity to pull off the ticks and throw them in the fire. I don't think I've ever been happier than when I'm standing in a pasture, quietly harnessing a line of good horses. It's better than working in the shop. They say that God's everywhere, but I think they just say that, because He must prefer the open fields."

"Guariglia," Alessandro said, his eyes fixed on the mountains.
"What?"
"Can you swim?"
Guariglia nodded. "Naturally I can swim."
"Three hundred meters?"
"Three thousand."
"Rome is ninety kilometers beyond those mountains."
"They'd catch us, and they'd shoot us."
"But the mountains are empty, and I know them."

"They wouldn't look for us there, they'd wait until we got home."

"Who said they go looking?"

"Rome will last until after the war."

"We could go to America."

"I thought you wanted to go to Rome?"

"We'd stay in Rome for a year or two."

"Sure."

"Over the side," Alessandro mused, "a swim in the sea, onto the beach in darkness, walking through the fields and across the rings of fire, into the mountains by dawn, and then, in a few days, Rome."

AFTER THEY had eaten, the captain directed a spotlight into the hold. Then he opened the bridge window and threw down a soccer ball that bounced from bulkhead to bulkhead, and, even before it stopped bouncing, two teams had formed, and the River Guard played a triple-fast game with no out-of-bounds and many soldiers bloodying themselves as they hit the walls. "Why don't you play?" Alessandro asked Guariglia, remembering from games in the *cortile* of the Bell Tower that Guariglia was capable of shaming the younger men.

"I don't fancy splitting my head on a steel beam, thank you. When I was a kid and would get hurt playing soccer my mother would beat me with a whisk broom. I remember her chasing me around the kitchen table. I was bigger than her when I was eight, but she'd still chase me.

"I thought she was crazy, beating me for getting hurt, but then I began not to get hurt just so she wouldn't beat me, and it made sense. It became a habit. In the shop my assistants are always cutting themselves. They drive needles and spikes into their hands and thighs as if they were drunk." He proudly pointed at his own chest.

"Not me. Never. I never shed my own blood." Then he leaned back. "Because of a whisk broom."

"My mother left that aspect of my upbringing to my father," Alessandro said, "and he didn't know about whisk brooms."

"What'd he use, a riding crop?"

"He only hit me twice in my life, and one of the times didn't really count, as he had no choice."

"Then who hit you?"

"Nobody. Once, I accidentally knocked some spokes off one of the carriage wheels. So I tried to even up the pattern—with a hatchet. In my quest for symmetry I left my father a carriage resting on four empty hoops."

"He really gave it to you. . . ."

"Just that once. He chased me into the garden. As I went up an apple tree he waited until my behind was at good striking height, and he slapped me like a rug."

"Your mother never hit you with a broom?"

"Never."

"Didn't she love you?"

"I don't know," Alessandro answered, staring at the bonfires.

"How could you not know?"

"I never knew her. She was born in Rome in eighteen sixty-eight, and she died in Rome in nineteen sixteen. I never thought of her as being anyone but my mother. She was just my mother, like a wall of the house—always there, always the same, you didn't have to think about her."

"I didn't know that she died," Guariglia said.

"When I went across to Venice I found out that she died in December. The army said I was beyond reach."

"The bastards," Guariglia said, throwing his cigar into the sea.

"I wonder what she looked like when she was young. We have one picture of her, on my father's desk. She must have been about seventeen, but you really can't see her. The picture is brown, she's as stiff as a board, and her hair is in all kinds of knobby little knots, which was the style then. I wonder what her voice was like. My father knows. He loved her, and he'll carry the memory, but he can carry it only so far."

"Someday the war will be over, Alessandro. Then you'll go home and they won't call you back again. In the next war they'll take some other son of a bitch, and you can sit in a cafe and read in the paper about each offensive."

Alessandro wasn't listening. He was looking at the fires against the mountains. "Guariglia, what happens when you let go, when your strength leaves you and you sink into darkness, when there's nothing that you or anyone else can do, no matter how desperate you are, no matter how you try? Perhaps it's then, when you have neither pride nor power, that you are saved, brought to an unimaginably great reward."

"I don't think so," Guariglia said.

"You don't believe it?"

"No."

"The saints believed it."

"The saints were wrong."

After the soccer game ended and the floodlight was extinguished, the River Guard returned to their makeshift beds, and a full moon came up and hung over the mountains. Half the soldiers slept and half did not. The land was close and lines of fire crept through the darkness up and down the coast. Over the buoyant waves, across the beach, and on the other side of the mountains, was Rome. Perhaps because of the parchment-colored moon, Alessandro was comforted by his passion for the city, as if by the passion of unrequited love.

THEY GLIDED into the protected harbor of Brindisi, steaming between shore batteries on windy promontories, and a dazzling white city that rose up on a hill. Brindisi was so hot and bright that anyone who looked at it too long would go blind, and, apart from Virgil's Column, everything was as square and flat as if it had been hewn from salt. The naval base, which had been built with Africa in mind but now was the jailer of the Hapsburg fleet, was choked with gray. At its edge, however, where the mass of warships thinned, huge flags of brilliant scarlet fluttered above barges laden with explosives.

The River Guard had washed and shaved, and they stood at the rails, peering at the land, their faces red from wind and sun. Only when they had rounded the Gargano and when they pulled into Brindisi Harbor had they smelled the sea rather than the land—the rich wet smell of salt, iodine, and shellfish curing in the sun. Brindisi was where the Adriatic flowed into the Mediterranean, where wind and waves rocked the brine back and forth through the coral.

"Ah! We look good, don't we," said Fabio, a young soldier who was terribly handsome. Everyone liked him, and smiled in his presence. He had a thousand friends and had had a thousand women, and he was happy all the time, but he was afraid to be alone.

"What does that mean?" Guariglia asked. Guariglia was balding and misshapen. The teeth on the right side of his mouth were bigger than those on the left, and his nose looked like the horn of Africa. Fabio had been a waiter in a fancy cafe near Guariglia's harness shop, but they hadn't known one another.

"What does that mean?" Guariglia repeated.

"What?"

"What you just said."

"What did I say?"

"You said, 'Ah! We look good, don't we.'"

Fabio blinked. "I was just wondering if there were any women in Brindisi."

"How could a city not have women?" Alessandro asked.

"I mean *women*," Fabio answered. "I'll go to a cafe. I know which women come to be taken away, and I've never looked better.

In half an hour I'd be in bed with a woman with tits as big as the Matterhorn."

They regarded him with wonder. "What's wrong with you, Fabio?"

"Me? Nothing's wrong with me. I wear a white jacket and shiny shoes. I'm saving for my own automobile. What's wrong with you, Guariglia? You sit around in a filthy apron, pushing heavy needles through pieces of leather. Sometimes four or five women a day want me to sleep with them. You, you're lucky if a horse breaks wind in your face."

"But Fabio," Guariglia said, "you're a feather."

"I'm a feather?"

"An ostrich plume. A man should not be an ostrich plume."

Fabio straightened his hair and tucked-in his shirt. "You're jealous, Guariglia. You're ten years older than me and I've slept with one thousand, four hundred, and sixteen women. How many women have you slept with?"

"You count?" Alessandro asked.

"I have them in a book. How many, Guariglia?"

"Just one, my wife."

"Then I can't even talk to you," Fabio replied triumphantly.

"She loves me," Guariglia said to the waves.

After the cattle boat tied up next to a slender pier on the sea side of the naval base, not far from the red flags, the River Guard disembarked and marched up a rocky hill to an open shed where hammocks were slung from the beams. As they were eating, Fabio started the rumor that they were going to be allowed a few days in Brindisi. Even he believed it, until they were told that they could exercise by running up and down the hill, but that they would leave in the evening, when the colonel arrived.

Alessandro was summoned to a corner of the shed, where the three officers had settled.

"Alessandro, you'll go to tell the colonel that we've arrived. You speak well and I'm sure you'll make a fine impression on him," the lieutenant said.

"You'd better," one of the sub-lieutenants added. "It'll be hell for us to be directly under a colonel. I think you should know why we're sending you, and I'm prepared to be frank."

"I'm prepared to be Alessandro, and I know already."

"You do?"

"You want me to be the lightning rod."

"Only because you're intelligent enough to handle it properly."

"And you're not."

"If one of us goes he'll treat us like corporals. If he arrives and finds us in charge, having sent you, he may treat us like majors. After all, he's used to dealing with majors. Tell him that we're here, and that we're ready. He's at the Hotel Monopol. Naturally, we don't know his name, but how many colonels could be staying in one small hotel?"

"Who shall I say we are?"

"Us."

"Yes, but who are we?"

"We don't know, Alessandro, and even if we did, you know we can't say."

"I can't say we're the River Guard?"

"No. I imagine he'll know who we are, even if we don't."

"And if he doesn't?"

"That's why we thought of you, *Dottore*."

Alessandro rode a donkey-engine to the perimeter of the base. Then he walked into Brindisi, disappearing among the horse butcheries and the cemeteries. Before he went to the Hotel Monopol he bought a kilo of prosciutto in three packages, one for Guariglia and two for himself.

In the Hotel Metropol, which stood across the street from the Hotel Monopol, a desk clerk told Alessandro that the colonel was on the fourth floor, in room 43.

Alessandro labored up long flights of whitewashed stairs, to an open window that gave out on the town and the sea. He stood on a worn Persian carpet that covered the landing, gazing at the brilliant colors. The town had closed for the afternoon, with the exception of the faint sound of motors and engines and an occasional steam whistle in the naval area. To the south were no warships but only empty rooftops, date palms, and sparkling rust-colored headlands projecting into an agitated sea. Alessandro listened to the wind whistling dryly over the sill.

He turned when he heard footsteps, and saw a woman descending from the floor above. Her hair was dyed blond badly enough to look orange, and she was cinched into a Bristol-blue dress that made parts of her appear much smaller than they really were and other parts overflow. She was almost short enough to have been a midget, and her expression was of permanent confusion. When she saw Alessandro she began to sway outlandishly as she came down the steps.

"Where is your mama?" he asked.

"At home," she answered.

"And your papa?"

She seemed not to understand, and looked at him blankly.

"Your papa."

She gave no response.

"Go home!" Alessandro said, as if to a dog that had followed him on a country road, and she ran down the steps.

He found the colonel's room on the fourth floor, straightened his uniform, stood at attention, and knocked sharply. After no response, he knocked again, and he kept on knocking thereafter, until an impatient voice screamed, "Why!"

"Colonel."

"Why!"

"Messenger."

"Goddamn it!" To a private, such irritation in the voice of a colonel was not encouraging. "Wait a minute," the colonel said.

Alessandro remained at attention, listening to muffled conversation within, to shutters slamming, doors opening, and drawers closing. After ten minutes, he stood down. After half an hour, he began to pace. After an hour, he sat on the floor, his legs sticking out into to the hallway and resting on the crimson runner. Another half hour passed, and he took out one of the packages of prosciutto and began to eat.

Then he heard the latches on the door. By the time they were unlocked, Alessandro was on his feet, trying to put the remaining prosciutto back into its package, but it wouldn't go, so, just before the door opened, he tried to eat it even though it was a very large piece. His cheeks ballooned to the breaking point, and a lengthy sheet of it, fat and all, hung down almost to his collar bone. The door opened.

A woman with hat, parasol, and jewelry flitted past Alessandro on the way to the stairs. She looked very married to someone notable in the town.

The colonel was in full uniform, tremendously beribboned, ready to kill. He held out his hand as if a message would land in it. When he saw Alessandro's stuffed cheeks, and the dangling ham, he looked skyward in disgust.

"What is this?" he asked.

Alessandro put his hand to his mouth and spat out a huge ball of saliva-covered prosciutto. He snapped to attention again, holding the prosciutto slightly behind him and out of the way. "Sir!" he said.

"You shut up!" the colonel screamed. He pointed to the dispatch bag that Alessandro had brought for carrying groceries. "Just give me my message and get the hell out of here!"

"Sir, I . . ."

"Shut up!" the colonel screamed. He grabbed the bag, breaking one of the straps and leaving a welt on Alessandro's neck. He ripped it open and pulled out the two packages. For a moment, he held them in his hands. Then he opened one. As the colonel saw the ham, Alessandro thought he was going to be killed. "Unwritten message!" he said as fast as he could.

"Unwritten message?" the colonel repeated, with one eye closed, the other squinting, and his fist clenched around the ham.

"Yes sir!"

"What is the message?" the colonel asked, breathing like someone who is about to die.

"We're here."

"Who's here?"

"We, sir."

"Who is we?"

"My unit, sir."

"What unit, idiot!"

"I can't say."

"You can't say, or you don't know?" the colonel asked. "Who sent you? You have no insignia. Why are you out of uniform?"

"The lieutenants sent me, sir."

"What lieutenants?"

"From the cattle boat."

"I'm going to kill you," the colonel announced, "but first I want to know what you're doing. What's the name of your unit?"

"You should know, even if I don't."

"What is the name of the lieutenant who sent you?"

"He has no name, and *you know it!*"

"What about you, do you have a name?"

"Of course not!" Alessandro screamed.

"Your unit has no name either."

"No."

"You don't wear insignia."

"No."

"Are you in the army?"

"Yes."

"Well what the hell do you want from me?"

"I'm supposed to tell you that we've arrived."

"From where?"

Alessandro thought the colonel was either an idiot or playing games. "I know," he said, "that you know that I don't know and that you do."

"Where are you stationed? Did you escape from a hospital?" The colonel was now almost dejected.

"We're not stationed anywhere. We float. I'm a private, but I warn you, don't play games with me."

The colonel blinked.

"We await your coming."

"For what?"

"To take command."

The colonel was a decorated officer. Alessandro could see from his ribbons that he had been wounded in battle. He stepped into his room, looked back at Alessandro with a hurt expression, and slowly closed the door.

"My prosciutto," Alessandro screamed. "Give me my ham!" When he heard no reply other than the sliding of bolts, he began to kick the door. "My prosciutto! Give me my prosciutto, you bastard! My ham!" A woman passing in the hall clung to the opposite wall and hurried to the landing.

Alessandro charged down the stairs, knocking her into the banister. His teeth were clenched, and by the time he reached the lobby he was trembling. He felt abused and victimized. Switching the mass of half-chewed prosciutto from his left hand to his right, he pitched it as hard as he could at the desk clerk. The clerk ducked, and the ham jangled some keys as it penetrated deep into one of the cubbyholes behind the reception desk. The clerk rose, and held up his arms as if to say, *What?*, and Alessandro went out onto the street.

As soon as he stepped on the pavement he saw a sign across the way that said HOTEL MONOPOL.

UNDERWAY SINCE the previous midnight, beyond the capes of Otranto and Santa Maria di Leuca, they found themselves in the middle of the Ionian Sea, heading south into a space that was purely hot, blue, and empty, and in which no clouds appeared and the water was the same color as the sky. In mid-afternoon the wind stopped, so they had only the breeze they made with their own speed. All the soldiers stripped down to the waist and changed into the campaign shorts they had never worn, other than for swimming, in all the time they had been in the Veneto. Despite the heat they had to wear boots, or their feet would have been burned on the deck.

"We haven't turned since we left Brindisi," Fabio said.

"How do you know?" Alessandro asked. "You can't see any fixed points of reference."

"What are fixed points of reference?"

"Nothing."

"Fuck you. We haven't turned."

"We're heading directly south, to Africa," Guariglia mumbled.

"You know what the Turks do, Guariglia?" asked a steelworker whose name was Ricardo. "I'll tell you what they do."

"I know what they do...."

"They cut you up in a thousand pieces while you're still alive."

Fabio looked devastated.

"What's the matter, Fabio? You'll still be handsome even when you're cut into a thousand pieces. You may even be a thousand times handsomer, and, think, you could sleep with a thousand women at once—if they liked shish kebab."

"Fabio would rather be dead than mutilated, wouldn't you, Fabio?"

"Yes," said Fabio. "To be mutilated is the worst thing. I cannot think of anything worse."

"That's because you're a feather," Guariglia added.

"No, it's because I want to die knowing that I'm whole. What's wrong with that?"

"Don't worry," Alessandro told him. "You may drown."

"You said they wouldn't waste torpedoes on a cattle boat."

"Now we're in the open sea. A submarine can surface, and sink us with its gun."

"How can they get to the gun? When the little guys run from the inside, a hundred and fifty of us would shoot them."

"They can emerge near the gun, which has an armored shield."

It was too hot to read, and the two books that Alessandro had in his duffel were meant to be read not in the sun but in a warm library on a winter night, so he stared at the waves, which moved in flat swells and did not break. The water, though full of light, was translucent. As even and smooth as gelatin, it moved in shallow breathless sighs, and was a deep mesmerizing blue.

In the evening they had bread, cheese, wine, and a lot of water. After they watched the sun go down they assembled in the main hold.

The real colonel had called for the floodlight. It shined over their heads and lit the forward bulkhead as if it were a backdrop in the theater. Highlighted against the rusty orange, the colonel sat down on a canvas chair.

He was a Neapolitan of about fifty. Though they didn't know it, his name was Pietro Insana. He was short, fat, and fatherly. Careful to think before he spoke, he had uncanny authority. Alessandro knew immediately that its source was mainly that he knew the right course of action. He had been a politician, but he spoke gently, and though they imagined that he did not know how to shoot a rifle or throw a grenade, all the power was his.

"Good evening," he said when they were quiet. He could hardly be heard over the engines, and he relaxed in the chair as if he were at home in Naples, on the terrace, listening to his daughter play the violin. His feet did not touch the floor, and sometimes in the pauses and even as he spoke he stared up at the sky, where the stars had begun to appear.

"I'm your colonel and perhaps you won't be surprised that I can't tell you my name," he said.

The soldiers looked at each other and rolled their eyes.

"This is madness, no? You've been instructed not to use your names, you have no insignia, your unit has no title, and here we are, sailing south, perhaps to Africa, you think, you have a colonel for three platoons, and the colonel is not a military man. What next?

"This: not only must you not use one another's last names, you must forget them. You must forget the names of your friends, and you must forget *your own names.*"

This occasioned nervous laughter.

"And that's not all. You!" he asked a soldier in the front row. "Where are you from?"

"Santa Rosa delle Montagne," the soldier said, thinking of the contentment he had left behind.

"No," the colonel said.

"No?" the soldier asked meekly.

"You are from Milano."

"But Colonel," the soldier ventured, "I'm from Santa Rosa delle Montagne. I was born there. My mother and my father both..."

"No," the colonel interrupted, "you are from Milano. From now on, you are all from Milano." He looked away, and added, "Milano is very big."

"Ahhh!" they said, almost to a man.

"Upon pain of death," the colonel affirmed.

"Upon pain of death," a soldier repeated.

"Do you want your families to be murdered?"

To this they responded with rapt attention.

"I think it was a mistake to have brought you together already knowing each other, but the army thought you would be good for the job—naval infantry, only a hundred and fifty left, with nothing to do. Unfortunately for you, you were too few to be used in a conventional sense and too many to disband. In war it's dangerous to be experienced, battle-hardened, and decimated, because you are at once necessary and expendable.

"We wanted to shut you up even before you left Mestre. You may find this hard to believe, but no one knows where you are—neither the army nor the navy. You won't be sending any mail, and you won't be getting it. Not because we want to deprive you of contact with home, but because we don't want any kind of trail, either to you or from you."

He shifted in his chair and looked up at the night sky, which was crossed by a ribbon of smoke. "Why?" he asked, almost like a philosopher. Dancing courtesans could not have held the River Guard's attention better in the long moment during which the colonel composed the answer to his own question.

"The army has had even more desertions from the line than are generally known: tens of thousands, in fact. In most cases the army relies upon the police, the *carabinieri,* or the military police. It's not hard to catch deserters if you know where they are. They seldom resist. If they do, two or three men are enough to deal with it, and that kind of thing is what the police do best.

"But the army has a special problem. Deserters are of many types and strengths, like the sperm that try to reach the egg. Most are weak and frightened, and they're caught before they exit the Veneto. Some get as far as Rome or Milan, and these come in various shades of trouble. The very difficult ones, however, get all the way to Sicily. Sicily is the egg. There they are not content to remain mere deserters. Many of them have gone into the hills and banded together. Not just alone, with the Mafia. Before the war I was a magistrate, and I used to work on this kind of problem. We had begun to make inroads against these people. Half of them had gone to America, and we were beginning to get at their structure, but since the war they have revived, especially the ones deep in the country, because the army doesn't sweep anymore the way it used to: we don't have the manpower for anything but the struggle in the north. We don't know to what degree they maintain contact with their brothers in the cities, but we must assume that they remain loyal to each other and that they have strengthened.

"Several hundred deserters have gone into the hills in half a dozen places, and they now rule the countryside, taking direction from bandits who formerly had only swords and single-shot rifles. The war has brought them repeating rifles, grenades, bayonets, and even machine guns.

"This in itself would not be intolerable, but word has spread in the lines, and the Austrians have begun to supply some of the hill bands with their weapons. They do it by submarine.

"We're going to try to accomplish what the *carabinieri* and the local army garrisons cannot. We're going to break up these groups, forcefully and by surprise. We're going to capture as many of the deserters as we can, and bring them north to court martial.

"You don't want to use your names in Sicily, not if you value your families." He shifted in his chair.

"And you needn't look so disconcerted. They don't know we're coming, they don't know who we are, we'll strike both overland and from the sea, and I promise you that we'll be steaming back this way with our prisoners before the summer is over."

THEY SWUNG wide from the land so as not to be seen. It wasn't that they thought anyone might expect a cattle boat carrying 150 crack soldiers, but they wanted to avoid the land itself, as if the uninhabited mountains were so spirited as to have eyes. They dropped languidly south into the Mediterranean between Sicily and Africa, lost in the blue. Once, they saw a British destroyer steaming on a distant parallel course. They kept it in view for half a day, until it veered away and became a dot, a mirage, and then part of the throbbing memory of whatever it is that makes up the eye—a disturbance in the field of azure, something like a slightly white wake, in the end only an illusion.

When the destroyer disappeared they were alone again on the sea, off the trade routes, away from the war, in utter silence but for the sound of their own engine and the play of the waves. For 360 degrees round they saw not even a single whitecap on the blue water, and the sky was just as empty—neither clouds, nor birds, nor any variation in texture.

Guariglia and Alessandro were at the bow as they pitched gently on a mild swell. "Look at this," Guariglia said. "Nothing but blue. We can't do anything with it. You can't make anything from it."

"It's beyond our reach," Alessandro answered. "It's important and we're not."

"You can't even touch it," Guariglia said, looking out into an infinity of blue. "And yet, if it weren't for my family, I could stay on the sea forever."

"Guariglia, you wouldn't want to be on the sea in storms."

"Even in storms it must be calm under the surface. I don't think I'd mind drowning. I'd have no body, no weight. I'd be just a piece of blue—Guariglia blue."

The captain of the cattle boat knew of a small island with a spring. He had taken the last of its shepherds to the mainland when the war began. Now only a few feral sheep were there, he said, strange creatures that were both savage and terrified, and the wells were overbrimming. They could also get some brushwood to stretch out their coal. You could see the southern part of Sicily from atop this island, and they would approach it from the blind side to the south.

They coasted to a stop, the anchors were thrown overboard, and the sailors lowered two dinghies. When the colonel saw his three platoons silently perched on rails and machinery, scanning the island in the noon light, he gave them permission to go ashore. Those who could swim were over the side as soon as they could get their boots off.

Alessandro jumped from the prow. After a week at sea, he surrendered to it. Wearing only a pair of soot-stained khaki shorts, he longed to float, and it seemed that he flew through the air for hours. His arms were spread in complete abandon, he exhaled, he spun on the wind like a leaf. Then he broke the glassy surface of the sea into fountains of white foam, pulling the air deep down with him until it rebelled and pushed him back up into the wind. The other men hit the water like artillery shells, and as Alessandro dived down, shut his eyes, and did weightless acrobatic turns, he listened to the concussions of soldiers entering the waves as if they were angels plunging into the atmosphere.

Something made them start out all at once, more than a hundred of them, in a race for the narrow crescent of beach. They looked like a school of migrating porpoises. When they pulled themselves from the water they began to scale the hills, and made good time even though barefooted, for the island was covered by clearings with neither thorns nor rocks but only pines that had for millennia shed their needles and softened the ground.

They came to the top of the ridge in an uneven line and stood looking northward to the peaks of Sicily in shimmering heat. The sea was completely empty. The soldiers stared ahead, shielding their eyes with their hands. One word traveled up and down the line, and though it was shouted, it sounded like magic—*Sicilia*.

THEY WENT west and hugged the bone-white coast of Tunisia for several days until, at three in the morning, with the stars blazing and not a single light from the town of San Vito Lo Capo, they glided to shore on the eastern side of the northernmost promontory of Sicily. The cattle boat put on as much speed as it could and then cut its engines to run in silence. It hit the sand, without lights, as if it had been driftwood.

"How will you get off the beach with no power?" Fabio asked one of the sailors.

"The tide is rising and the current is offshore. By dawn we'll be far enough away to light the boilers without awakening anyone in the town," the sailor answered.

Caissons and crates of supplies were lifted over the side with winches and booms while the River Guard disembarked, carrying rifles and full packs, on ropes. They landed in water up to their waists and held their rifles and ammunition in the air as they waded. A group was formed to drag the caissons through the low surf, and the crates went ashore on perilously overladen dinghies.

When the boat was unloaded it rose on the tide just as the sailor had promised, and floated out to sea with neither engines nor lights.

Overlooking the beach between the place where they had come ashore and the town a few kilometers to the north was a group of buildings joined by massive stone walls topped with ramparts. Once a prison, it now was empty. They walked toward it, careful not to make noise, skirting the few darkened houses nearby. At the front gate, signs warned away intruders with the promise of harsh punishment from Rome. A huge lock sealed a steel hasp welded to iron doors. One of the River Guard speculated that they would have to climb the walls and pull up the caissons and crates with ropes.

"That would be too loud," the colonel said, fumbling in his dispatch bag. "I have the key."

As the cats ran out in terror, the River Guard filed into a vast courtyard and the door was shut behind them. They could see nothing in the shadows but shadows. On the sea side of the *cortile* they couldn't hear the surf but they could see mountains looming up inland. On the inland side they couldn't see the mountains but they could hear the sea. The colonel ordered them to bivouac on the inland side. "No fires," he said, "and no noise. Stack your rifles and sleep. I want one sentry at the gate and one on the ramparts. As soon as the sky lightens, close the window in the gate and come down off the ramparts.

"We'll look around then and decide what to do about house-keeping, although I hope we won't be at home very much."

"Sir? We won't?" asked a thin soldier with glasses, who looked like a puppet but who, either because of his rifle, his nerves, or his background as the son of a gunsmith, was one of the best shots in Europe.

"You like to walk, don't you?" the colonel asked.

"I love it, sir," the puppet soldier answered.

They stacked their rifles, laid down their packs, and stretched out. For a brief moment Alessandro looked up at the stars. Though they were not rolling and his eyes did not need to follow them as on the ship, now they were framed by dark walls. He did not think that his mother was wandering among them, though, that they were immutable, unreachable, and incomprehensible led him to allow that he might be wrong.

THEY STAYED in the prison for several weeks. Each man had a cell, where he kept his equipment and submitted to inspection twice daily for making sure that he was packed-up and ready to go—with rations, ammunition, and water arranged in a rucksack that hung on the cell door. No one went near the windows in the daylight hours.

Their routine was much like that in the shed at Mestre, only everything was accomplished in silence. They exercised, ran circles around the *cortile,* cleaned their weapons, and drilled in almost total quiet. Commands were spoken in a whisper. As at Mestre, they ate little. Before the moon came up, and when the moon had disappeared, they were allowed to swim, five at a time, in the gentle surf behind the prison. They went down a rope that was thrown over the seaward wall, and ran into the breaking waves. Here they discovered how strong they had become, and that they could propel themselves through the sea at great speed, not even breathing hard. When they climbed the rope it was as effortless as flying. "The sons of bitches we're going after," Fabio declared, "must have big bellies by now. They probably eat all day and drink wine. When we chase them across the hills, in the heat, carrying weapons and water, who do you think will win?"

"They will," the puppet soldier answered. "They'll hide in the bushes, and when we walk past them they'll pop up and shoot us in the back."

"Not a hundred and fifty of us."

"And what if we're in places with neither bushes nor trees?" Alessandro added.

"What will we eat?"

"I don't know, what we always eat—dates, figs, spaghetti, and dried meat. What do you expect up there," he asked, gesturing toward the steep mountain that loomed over the prison, "restaurants?"

During the night Alessandro lay in his open cell, listening to the sea. At one time he would have longed for that which he remembered, and he would have worked hard to reconstitute the past, fixing in his mind exact memories, colors, sensations, and the changing light of the seasons. At one time he thought that for everything to fall back into place he had merely to escape the army and return, but now he was convinced that though they might buy back the garden, clean out the weeds, restart the fruit trees, plant vegetables, and put in their places new sun chairs, lazy cats, and water in the fountain, it would never be the same. It had been undone, and memory offered little comfort except to those who had not quite understood what they had loved.

As he stared at the rounded ceiling of his cell, Alessandro decided that, should he ever get home and be tempted to rely on them for memory, he would throw away the pictures of his mother and his father. Resurrection, he thought, comes not by plan or effort, and should the past ever come alive, it will be a great surprise, in which images and ritual memory will pale.

One of the lieutenants passed by. "Get up," he said. "We're going into the mountains."

As THEY stood for review in the *cortile,* five men were picked at random to stay behind and guard the machine guns and other heavy equipment. The colonel would also stay behind, but he had given his lieutenants precise instructions. They moved out five at a time, crossed the empty road, and began to climb. They were to assemble at the summit, where they would re-form into smaller groups. It was five o'clock in the morning.

They crossed the road unseen, although the very last of them had to lie flat in the grass as a peasant passed with his donkey. The donkey smelled them and brayed, for which his flanks were slapped as if he were misbehaving. As soon as it was clear, the men rose from the ground, took up their rifles, and ran for the hillside.

It was steep enough that they had to pull themselves up by hand, and the grass was so slippery that they stuck their fingers into the earth, grabbed the edges of rounded boulders set weakly into the dirt, and held on to clumps of weeds that were like horse tails. Cursing and sliding, they reached the rock, which was a pleasure, and they scrambled up it until they found themselves at the summit, a thousand meters above the sea.

While they were waiting for stragglers they looked toward home. With no lights in San Vito Lo Capo, and no moon, only by starlight could they make out the edge of the sea and the sea itself, in occasional faint sparkles, when the waves broke the right way to catch a bright constellation and reflect it toward the mountain.

In Alessandro's group were Guariglia, Fabio, and the puppet soldier, who was a great prize because of his marksmanship. He had been magnificent in training, with near perfect scores. On the line he had been the scourge of the Austrians, as he could hit small, distant, fast moving targets. He could also get off more shots in a short time than anyone might have believed possible.

The senior lieutenant circulated the gastronomic order: six small sips of water, one dried fig, one biscuit. They had learned on the line that many small meals would take them much further than a few big ones. This was a matter of the highest discipline, which they had.

The officers checked their maps. An informer had marked the first camp they were going to raid, and was now on the sea somewhere between Italy and Argentina, where he hoped he might live out his days alive. The best approach was by the Trapani road, but the colonel had been wary. Instead, they were going to come in from the north along a ridge of mountains so deserted and difficult that, save shepherds and goatherds, no one ever set foot there, and they required three days to move into position, outflanking a steep valley that became a cul de sac rather than taking a road that led into it.

"Three days?" Fabio asked. "We're going to walk through this stuff for three days?"

"If you save two days by walking up the valley," Guariglia told him, "you can be buried with scratch-free legs."

"At the zoo in the Villa Borghese, Guariglia, they have a baboon. . . ."

"Yes, I know," Guariglia interrupted. "After the president of the zoo came to my shop, he ran back to name the baboon *Adonis*."

"Take the highest ridge," the lieutenant ordered, "and remember that sound can carry very far along the cliffs. Get to this position before dawn," he continued, indicating a place on the map which corresponded with a peak downrange. "If you don't make it by first light, stay concealed where you are, and the others will wait until you show up at night. Divide your provisions for three days. You can find water here and there just below the line of the ridge. If you encounter anyone, bring him with you."

"What if he's a shepherd or a goatherd?"

"What if he is?"

"His animals will escape."

"He'll find them eventually. No fires, of course. Go."

A moisture-laden breeze from the sea came straight up the hillsides. The soldiers were impressed by the vastness and the wind. Even in the dark they could see the land spreading out and rolling into enormous ranges of mountains. Just as on the sea, the stars were on fire, but now they were sometimes blocked and hidden by looming black shapes days and days away.

THEY LOST themselves on the high ridge for two days as they made their way through the greenery and over mountainsides of blond and yellow grasses, where all seemed safe and life had been made to stand still. They covered a broken front at least a kilometer wide, individually or in groups of two or three. They couldn't see each other unless they strained to pick out their fellow soldiers from the rocks and brush, and from the towns along the sea, and the coastal road, they were invisible as they crossed saddles and valleys, accompanied only by the wind. Were it not for the heavy steel they carried, they might have thought that they had escaped from history itself.

As he made his way across the hills Alessandro asked himself over and over again if it were not right for the deserters to have chosen refuge in God's peace. His only answer, though he strained for others, was yes.

Off Tunisia, Guariglia had said, "Some of these men have left the line not because they were cowards but because they couldn't bear never to see their children again. If that's so, how can we, in good conscience, chase them down?"

"It has nothing to do with conscience," Alessandro had answered. "The colonel wants to fight the Mafia, the generals have to keep their troops from running away, and we have to do as we're told. If we don't hunt, we'll be hunted."

"And what if everyone refuses?"

"The army would disintegrate and the Austrians would be in Rome within a fortnight."

"Is it worth dying to keep them out?"

"Yes."

"Why?"

"Because you'll die anyway, sooner than you think. In addition to the incongruity of Austrians walking through Rome in swords and plumes, they would need us—you and me—to help them conquer France and Greece, and if we didn't want to help, they would chase us down and shoot us.

"In history, Guariglia, will is only an illusion and success does not last. You can only do your best in the short time you have. If you decide to remake the world you'll just end up killing people out of revolutionary impatience and triumphalism."

"So we kill the deserters."

"Yes. If we join them, we'll die with them."

DAWN OF the third day found them on a hilltop, looking across a precipitous valley cluttered with rocky ledges and banks of laurel and juniper. At the head of this valley, on a rise where trees had grown in a line that marked a stream, were half a hundred white tents.

As the sun came up behind them in the clear, binoculars were circulated and the squads of men lying flat on the ridge discovered that in the enemy camp were women, strings of mules, laundry hung out to dry, pits for roasting meat, a platform that looked like a stage, and sentries, of whom at least a dozen lined the dirt track that led up to their camp. A dozen more were around the camp itself. They had diverted the stream for their gardens, and they had a sweeping view of the valley.

"They're Italians," someone said of the men they were supposed to go against, but the morning wind carried away the thought.

When the camp was raised, the west wind carried the smell of freshly baked bread and cake up over the ridge, like water flowing over a stone, where the semi-starved River Guard lay amid rocks and thorns, waiting until noon for six sips of water, a tiny bit of meat, five crackers, and a single piece of dried fruit.

The lieutenants backed the men off the ridge into a forest of scrub where wild boar rested in their dens waiting for the night. Left on the ridge were three observers with binoculars and notebooks. They were spread far apart and instructed to keep low. Alessandro was one of them, a wiser choice than anyone knew, for he had grown up on the Gianicolo with a telescope in his room, periodically looting the city of Rome, the mountains beyond, and the high clouds, of the never-ending particulars and detail accessible only to a trained and patient eye.

When the three thirsty and sunburned soldiers gave their reports that evening it was apparent that they had done some counting, but then Alessandro spoke.

"At least two hundred and fifty men are in the camp," Alessandro began.

"How can you tell?" one of the other soldiers challenged. "They were all moving around, inside and out."

Alessandro looked disgusted. "I took a random sample of tents. I counted how many soldiers were in each one, and then I multiplied, allowing that the leaders would have tents for themselves."

"They were going in and out all the time. We found it impossible to determine how many men were in each one."

"I didn't."

"Why not?"

"I simply remembered who went in and who came out."

"How could you distinguish them?" one of the lieutenants asked.

"By dress, size, coloring, gait, and a thousand other signs."

"And you were able to keep all these things in mind?"

"Yes," Alessandro said. "There were only six men to a tent."

"Go on."

"Of the two hundred and fifty, two-thirds are former soldiers. A third has never been in the military."

"How can you tell!" one of the other two observers burst out jealously.

"For the last time, now," Alessandro said severely, "by the way someone carries himself, the way he sits or moves in a group, by dress, mannerisms, colors, textures, equipment relics, the making of a fire, the tying of a knot . . . For example, when someone who has been in the army for a while is addressed, he becomes slightly stiff, as you are now. The others drop their heads a little. Hill bandits don't shine their boots, they don't stack things in rows. . . . Look," he said, "take it or leave it."

"Go on *Dottore*," Lieutenant Valtorta urged.

"All right. They're nervous, guilty. They may not be expecting us, but they're expecting someone. Their sentries overlook the road and are posted all around the camp. They're in the brush, halfway up the sides of the valley. One was below us about four hundred meters away. He was from Civitavecchia and he was singing '*La Cincindella*.'"

This was too much for the other two. "We saw him," one of them said, "but no one could hear what he was singing. And how could you know he was from Civitavecchia?"

Alessandro glared at them. "I couldn't hear him, but I read his lips and watched him move his shoulders." Insulted, he turned abruptly and walked away.

"Come back," the lieutenant ordered. "Don't pay attention to these idiots. What else?"

Alessandro began again. "They're armed with Mannlichers, and they have plenty of ammunition, but neither mines nor wire. They're organized for the watch, that's all, they have no defensive plan. The half dozen women in the camp are prostitutes from

Palermo. No children. The mules bray continually because of the wild boar moving in the brush. In the late evening and early morning hours the boar crash through the vegetation. No one will notice the sound of our approach unless we knock our rifles against the rocks."

"Who's the leader?"

"I don't know. He may be in a villa in Messina."

"The numerical ratio is not in our favor, and the country is vast and intricate," the lieutenant stated.

"I have one other thing to note, sir. They're short on time-pieces, because the sentries don't trust their relief to keep the time—they don't want to sit on a rock singing '*La Cincindella*' while their replacements are sleeping, or swimming in the stream, hours after they should be at their posts—so they take the watches with them. Each post is a separate system, and no one cooperates, which is, I assume, what happens when you draw entirely from a pool of disciplinary failures. They repeatedly pull the watches from their pockets and look at them toward the end of the shift. Because the relief doesn't know what time it is, the sentries leave their posts and come into camp to get them, which is very stupid, especially if we're waiting on the route back."

That evening the River Guard ate the rest of their food, intending to fight for bread the next morning. The sentries would be captured, or struck in the back of the head with rifle butts, whichever would be quieter, after which the River Guard would enter the camp, cutting the tent stays with their bayonets. Most everyone would be inside, and most everyone would be trapped. As they crawled from the collapsed tents, one by one, their first act would be to look into a rifle barrel.

No one thought the plan would work with so few River Guard and so many deserters. It would be hard to eliminate all of the sentries without noise, not everyone would be inside the tents, and, if even one man escaped, all Sicily would know of the operation.

Guariglia suggested putting a block across the road and stationing men along the ridges, but the lieutenants had already detailed ten men for this, and said that once the prisoners were grouped together a hundred of the River Guard would sweep the valley to flush out stragglers.

During the night they positioned themselves near the sentry posts in a riot of noise that did not betray them, for the boar, much disturbed, ran close to the sentries and even through the camp. The valley came alive with rifle fire. Bullets whined, cutting leaves off at the stem and shattering rocks.

By the end of this, the River Guard had taken position, with fifty of them poised to eliminate the sentries and eighty more ready to rush the camp if anyone managed to sound an alert. During the shooting, shouting, and abandonment of posts as pigs were dragged through the brush by groups of unarmed men, everyone wanted to start the attack, and everyone knew that everyone else wanted to as well, but because they were spread out they had no way to confirm it, and though darkness favored assault it did not favor either taking or holding prisoners, so they waited until dawn, bayonets fixed in case they were charged by the pigs.

"It doesn't matter," the puppet soldier said to Guariglia and Alessandro as they fixed bayonets. "If a boar charges, I'll shoot him. Then I'll scream, 'I killed a pig! I killed a pig!' That's all." Even so, he fixed his bayonet—for the little pigs, who, though not as fearsome as their elders, were very aggressive and somewhat quicker.

Lying in fragrant herbs, they listened to the birds announce the sunrise, and their hearts began to beat fast. At six o'clock it was light, the sun shone hot against the mountains, and the valley was in shadow. The sentries began to walk in. One of them, his rifle slung, stumbled upon a group of ten River Guard, who thrust their bayonets close to his face. He put up his hands, closed his eyes, and held his breath.

The other sentries returned to camp, and long before their replacements stirred, the River Guard had taken up position and were waiting. Everyone was sweating, most were tense, some were terrified. They were used to trenches, wire, mine fields, and artillery. They expected whistles and flares as the signal for an attack. Though war in the line was much more dangerous than what they were doing now, they had become accustomed to it.

Newly aroused sentinels straggled out lazily, unevenly, carelessly. The minutes of their walk to their posts seemed very long, and when most were halfway there, they suddenly stopped. An instant later the River Guard looked up, and everyone cocked his head to listen. The sound of engines came roaring through the valley, echoing off its walls.

The plan collapsed as sentries ran back, unshouldering their weapons, and others came running from the tents. Two bi-planes appeared from beyond the ridge and flew right over Guariglia, who had been trying to wave them back with his hat. Then they cut across the valley, firing their machine guns at the tents.

When they banked to the east and disappeared, they left the camp in complete chaos. Wounded men, panicked sentries, and nude women clutching their clothes fled barefooted, hopping along the thorny ground until they had to sit down. Everyone was screaming. As the planes came back up the valley, guns firing, the River Guard stood up and shook their fists.

The bullets cut into the dirt, knocked down and shredded the tents, and slaughtered the hobbled, braying mules. The deep roar of the engines seemed to reset all the clocks and registers of the world.

Hundreds of half-dressed armed men had spread into the brush. "Who sent those planes? Who sent those planes!" Lieutenant Valtorta screamed over and over until he was hoarse, and then he started to shout, "Form ranks! Form ranks!" but this was impossible, because everyone was spread out in a circle. As they approached for the third time, the planes released their bombs, which ripped down the tents before they detonated, and then made four enormous explosions.

Throughout the battle, the birds sang at a high pitch. If they had done so in ignoring the fighting, it was remarkable, and if they had done so because of the fighting, it was also remarkable. The combat took place in small groups or man to man, as the deserters fought like panicked horses. At first the River Guard were restrained, perhaps because they found it difficult to kill Italians. Only when their natural courtesy had cost some of them their lives did they begin to fight like men who had fought Austrians and Germans with bayonet and mace. They shot their enemy, gutted him alive, and swung the butts of their rifles to smash open his face.

When it ended, the sun was hot and the survivors thought they would die if they could not reach the stream. In many instances, they were right.

THOUGH WHEN he sat on a campaign chair his legs didn't reach the floor, Colonel Pietro Insana was a man of great decisiveness. As soon as the River Guard returned with their wounded and the prisoners, he changed everything.

He raised the flag, put sentries at the gates, and sent men into town for provisions. So many had escaped from the cul de sac that everyone in Sicily now knew of the River Guard, who, rather than be poisoned, stopped buying food almost as soon as they had started, and relied upon their stores and the fish they caught. Now they patrolled the roads and hills, descending in long columns as far as Trapani, going east almost to Palermo, just to show that they were there.

The River Guard had been so secret that hardly anyone knew of their existence, much less that they were in Sicily. The bi-planes had been sent by another branch, in a fatal coincidence, and had returned to the Veneto almost immediately. Their appearance exactly at the moment of attack caused word to spread that the Italian army was going to pacify Sicily with airplanes, machine guns, and artillery. Though no slaughter had been intended, the death of more than a hundred men sent a potent message. In Alpine trenches far to the north, where in the middle of July Italian soldiers still braced their rifles on banks of snow, the mishap in the cul de sac had come to be known as the Monte Sparagio Raid. Everyone who had taken part, it was generally asserted, was doomed, but that was not so. No one knew who was in the force headquartered at Capo San Vito, and no lists were kept anywhere, not even in the Ministry of War in Rome, where the lists had been destroyed.

A warship came to pick up the prisoners. Manacled and in chains, they were ferried in motor launches out to a camouflaged destroyer that lingered offshore, its stacks smoking.

By August the River Guard missed the north with a passion unique to those who have been confined in a stone fortress in Sicily for most of the summer, with long and strenuous hill patrols their prime diversion, and only half a dozen moments of unexpected excitement. In June a bomb had been thrown over the wall. It made a big noise and killed some chickens. Two blonde women appeared inexplicably at the beach behind the north wall and bathed in the nude. Suspecting a trap, the colonel ordered his men off the ramparts, but not before serious injuries had resulted from fights for possession of an insufficient number of binoculars. The women were Scandinavian academics who thought that Italians were sexually repressed, and who thought they were alone. In the confusion of 150 men in thrall to two nude women in the surf, no one noticed at first a tiny voice from below the rampart. A soldier they called *Smungere* was screaming out his customary sermon. "Think of all the trouble and impurity in your life, the sin, the suffering, the filth that can be laid at the door of the minor hose and its associated appendages that swing from us, pushing the devilish parts of our nature toward the impulsive and the disgusting. Thank God," he whined in a high-pitched voice, "for the miracles of modern surgery. A simple, painless, almost danger-free procedure can lead us to a purer life. Tension vanishes. A certain restlessness disappears," he squeaked, "in favor of irreversible serenity." No one even turned around. Whoever had converted him must have been a genius, and now he fished for converts in an empty sea. Soon after the Swedish nudes, another bomb was tossed over the wall. It put some metal in the foot of a boy, who screamed, but then quickly recovered. The bomb-thrower was shot dead as he ran, and left unburied. In morbid compulsion, the River Guard observed the steady decomposition of his body—from a distance. They could smell it at night. They were used to such smells, and it was so hot and the birds were so efficient that within a week the only things left where the body had come to rest were shoe leather, bleached bones, and a black stain. In the middle of July, the French fleet passed far offshore. It looked both fancy and powerful. Alessandro told them that Napoleon was a native speaker of Italian and had never mastered French, and this pleased them tremendously, because they had heard of Napoleon and were eager to claim him. Shortly after the passage of the fleet they caught three enormous tuna that they brushed with oil and roasted on fires of herbs and vines. The beginning of August saw a great meteor shower. At night the River Guard lay on their backs, on the ramparts, and watched the sky disintegrate in tracer-like shots of silver and white. The light was silent and the tracks of the stars were as flirtatious as girls in spring. They shined, they smiled, and they disappeared.

One evening early in September the colonel called them out of their beds and made them stand in formation. "No cheering, no oohs, and no aahs," he said. "We're going back north. I don't know what's planned for us after we return. They wouldn't tell me."

A soldier who generally was silent asked for permission to ask a question. "How do you know these things? No messengers come or go."

"I have a little dog," the colonel replied. "His name is Malatesta. He can speak, he can swim, and he can fly. He is my only link with the outside world, but through him I can know everything and I can make everything known."

Alessandro could not restrain himself. "Sir?" he asked.

"Yes?"

"Have you ever heard of the blessed sap that flows from the cloak of the exalted one, on the eucalyptus throne, in the deep shadow of the whitened airless valley of the moon?"

The colonel ignored his question. "We're leaving tonight," he said. "The cattle boat will be here in an hour. You remember the cattle boat. On our way north we're going on a raid. We'll hit the eastern part of the island, to let them know that we can strike anywhere and at any time. Several bands of deserters are near Catania."

"Are they army?" someone asked.

"Yes. They're not well organized, but they're so strong they collect taxes in Randazzo and Adrano. No one has gone after them, because they operate in the rugged country on and around the volcano, but we'll arrive from nowhere—no planes this time—and break up into small endurance groups. Then we'll track them. They're mountain soldiers, a lot better than you are, but we have the initiative."

"Do we get to go to Catania?"

"Oh yes, you will, but you shouldn't want to. When the operation is finished we'll run the prisoners through the streets. Rome insists that we do so even though we may be shot from the windows."

"Not even time to stop for a sweet?" Fabio asked.

The cattle boat had cut its engines and was floating silently to shore on the steady current that lapped the cape. Though they hadn't seen it, it was moving deftly toward them.

ONCE AGAIN they passed the whitened coasts of Tunisia and drifted so far south that they were cut off from almost everything in the world. As if they were in orbit around the sun of Sicily they fell in a curve through the hot empty spaces, and then ceased their relaxed floating to steam north. The prow of the cattle boat cut through the sea and rolled it into chattering foam that said the same thing over and over before it fell asleep in the waves. They skirted the islands and drifted onto a deserted beach on the south coast a few hours after dark.

They waded ashore, this time taking neither heavy equipment nor supplies but only rifles and packs. Far to the left, a single bonfire burned on a hill blue with darkness.

The lieutenant and the colonel studied a map. They had been landed a kilometer distant from the target, and they would have to ford a river, but it was almost certainly dry at this time of year. After the cattle boat had begun to drift away they crossed the dunes into an immense citrus grove through which they walked in the dark for miles. They had time to eat oranges and to stand in the open spaces between the trees, listening to the birds upwind that had not yet been silenced either by the approach of the River Guard or by the night. It was a pleasant walk, though the rows were not exactly straight and in the dark the soldiers sometimes bumped head-on into tree trunks.

They regrouped at a raised trackbed, far from any village or town, and waited while eating oranges and lying against the gravel bank that supported the rails. A corridor of stars in a moon-whitened sky brightened as far as the eye could see down the track.

"When we get to Catania," Fabio said, "I'm going to go to a cafe and have five cups of cappuccino."

"No you're not, feather," Guariglia told him. "You're going to run through the streets just like the rest of us, pointing your rifle at your prisoners and hoping you don't get shot in the back of the head."

"No," Fabio said. "Cappuccino, five cups."

"You'll be so lean when you get off the volcano," Alessandro said, "if you get off the volcano, that your body won't need or recognize cappuccino. You won't need food or cafes, Fabio. You'll be as hard as steel and no more hungry than a bayonet."

Fabio blinked. "I'm already as hard as steel," he responded. "We all are."

"The mountain soldiers know what they're doing," Alessandro continued, clutching a handful of stones until the softer ones shattered in his fist. "When you get through there, you won't want to go to a cafe."

"What will I want?" Fabio asked.

"You'll drink urine, you'll smash rocks, you'll be a fighter."

"I was in the line for two years," Fabio protested. "I *am* a fighter."

"You never ate dirt."

"That's right," Guariglia said. "You never ate rocks."

"Oh fuck off," Fabio told them, and bit into an orange.

Far down the line, to the west, a light appeared. At first it was just a splinter of white, like a star lost in the orchards, but then it grew and overflowed until it was a bright blinding yellow that moved slowly up the track. The lieutenants ordered everyone except Guariglia into the trees, and they ordered him to stand between the rails and light a cigar.

Though Guariglia was apprehensive, he didn't protest, so great was his love of Cuban tobacco. He stood puffing contentedly, and inquired of the officers, who now were crouched invisibly under an orange bough, "What for?"

"The train was supposed to have been here when we arrived," the colonel whispered, although he had no need to whisper.

"I see," Guariglia said.

"If they see the glow of your cigar, they'll stop."

"That's nice," Guariglia stated, blocking out the stars with a huge cloud of fragrant smoke. "If . . ."

The light approached, slewing back and forth as the engine swayed over small inconsistencies in the otherwise perfectly parallel steel rails. The train crept along as if it were ashamed of being late and running flat into a company of soldiers waiting for it amid the trees.

When it got so close that the petulant and neurotic motion of the rods and cams was audible, and when the steam escaping from half a hundred pre-war gaskets sounded like a menagerie of snakes, Guariglia stepped off the tracks and waved the cigar.

"Don't wave your cigar," he heard the colonel say from the darkness. "We're not beggars. These people are under orders."

Even though the engine was relatively small and pulled only three gondola cars, when it came to Guariglia it seemed like a huge tower of iron.

"I'm supposed to pick up some people," the engineer said. "Where are they?"

"Let me look inside your cars," Guariglia demanded.

"Go ahead."

They were all empty. "Come forward," Guariglia called into the darkness, with undisguised triumph. "No one's on board."

From both sides of the dark orchard the soldiers appeared, and climbed into the cars. In no time they were all in and the officers had entered the cab. After a few minutes the colonel mounted a platform at the rear of the engine. Over the steam, the roar of the fires, and the dripping of water from condensers and leaky tanks, he addressed his men.

"The engineer says he's sorry to be late. His daughter was married today and he couldn't tear himself away from the celebration. Besides, it would have looked suspicious. At least he didn't lie, didn't tell us some filth about track repairs or broken wheels. . . . He says that the volcano is a long way from here, as we know, but he says that he can get us there by daylight, because he assures us that, no matter what his train looks like, it can go very fast."

"Bravo!" some soldiers cried out.

The engineer appeared unbidden on the platform, next to the colonel. "Soldiers," he said, "my train goes very fast. It's dangerous to go at top speed." He smiled at the rows of heavily armed young men. "But this is war."

THEY LAY against the sides of the gondola cars, their rifles leaning with them, sheathed bayonets extending above the steel bulkheads and whistling in the wind. Guariglia had the only seat, on a crate in the first car. He had lit another cigar, and was enjoying it as the wind flew past and occasionally flicked the ashes off the tip, making it flame. Even the last soldier in the last car could smell the smoke, and Guariglia's head was turned up to the stars as if he were on the porch of a summer resort.

Lower down, on Guariglia's right, Alessandro was also looking up at the night sky. He was hungry. They had had nothing for dinner but oranges, and they felt bodiless and giddy. As the train picked up speed it was as if they were high in the air, running with the constellations. Alessandro loved the stars for being unassailable, and believed that each and every one of them was his ally. As if they were jewels that he possessed, and he were a different man altogether, they gave him tremendous satisfaction. Though war might make a soldier inconsequential, a soldier in turn could delight that they would always put war in its place.

The engineer had been telling the truth. To judge from the speed and jostling of the train, he had had two bottles of whiskey and was beating at the throttle with a hammer. Metal things popped and snapped. The cars wanted to separate one from another, and yanked at their couplings if one lurched left and the other right. The wind got stronger and stronger as they left the lowlands and ascended to plains with not a single tree to stop it.

When they came to a grade, they slowed, and everyone was relieved that the engineer had come to his senses, but as they crested the top and started down, they grew dizzy with acceleration. Neither prudence nor restraint, but just gravity, had slowed the train, and the driver had been cursing it until, when it began to throw him forward, he blessed it.

In the middle of the night they broke out at white-hot speed onto a vast plain that could hardly hold the onslaught of the broad sky and its blazing, three-dimensional, phosphorescent cargo. A meteor shower shot through the clear, like tracer bullets, and enhanced the depth of the sky by shining so close to earth. With no lights and no fires, only the animals were up, and in the open. Their masters were barricaded in bedchambers, but they were under a shower of stars, and, even though they were lowly and suffering and mute, the light spoke to them so clearly that even they could understand, promising an end to their burdens, promising them souls, and tongues, and perfected spirits. The soldiers in the gondola cars, under the same stars, racing through the same fields, breathing the same scented air, were included in the pact. They too were promised redemption, love, and a ride out.

THEY WERE dropped in several groups around the base of Aetna. While the officers struggled with their maps, many of the River Guard went to sleep in the fields. "I thought it would be like the mountains around Rome, but it's as big as a province. How do we know where to find them?" Fabio asked Valtorta.

"We don't," the lieutenant answered. "We have a sector to comb. If they're in it, we'll find them. If they're not, we won't. We'll start here, and walk around in zigzags until we get to the top."

"It would take a million years to cover all that ground," Guariglia protested.

"Not if we go individually," Valtorta said, his eyes focused on the clouds at the top of the cone, thirty kilometers distant. He started to load his pack. "You don't fight wars that way, but this isn't exactly a war. With so many individual patrols on the volcano, they won't be able to elude us."

"What if one of us finds a dozen of them," Alessandro asked.

"Shoot them. We'll all close in on the sound of firing."

"You may not arrive for an hour."

The lieutenant dropped loads of ammunition in the side pockets, and cinched them up. "What are you worried about? You have a lot of ammunition and a good rifle. Keep a distance; you'll be all right."

"They'll scatter."

"We'll be closing in. We'll pick them up one by one, or drive them into the clear."

"The smart ones will lie down and wait for us to pass," Guariglia said, "and then escape into the valley."

"I don't think so," Alessandro said. "I think that, like hunted animals, they'll seek the deep forests or they'll run for the heights. The colonel must be a hunter."

"He is," the lieutenant confirmed. "Are you?"

"No, but I used to have a hunt horse. Sometimes we'd chase game, and, when we did, by evening we always found ourselves deep in a forest or high on a hill."

STILL EARLY in the morning, Alessandro and Guariglia, who had left together to proceed to adjoining sections, happened upon a farmhouse surrounded by barns, a mill, and a cistern. Two women were doing laundry at a sluice where the water flowed as plentifully as in the Alps. At the sight of the heavily armed soldiers they froze like deer, but were reassured when Alessandro asked to see the men. "Only my father is here," the younger one said, and then put her hand to her mouth as if she had written her own death sentence.

"Don't worry," Guariglia told her. "All we want is to eat and take a bath."

She ran into the orchard to get her father.

"Why so much water," Alessandro asked the other woman.

"We sell it."

"Will you sell some to us?"

"Why not?"

Within half an hour Alessandro and Guariglia were floating in a huge cistern as the father of one of the girls harangued them about patriotism and the king. He was a veteran of the African wars. He had seen other soldiers walking through the fields, and he suspected that Alessandro and Guariglia were hunting for the deserters on the volcano. Though he insisted that they bathe and eat for free, they refused to answer any of his questions for fear that he was other than what he seemed.

"How do we know," Guariglia whispered, with ice-cold water dripping from his mustache, "that he won't shoot us in the pool, like Euripides?"

"He's been playing with our rifles, Euripides," Alessandro answered, motioning toward the farmer, who was fondling the weapons, "and he hasn't shot us yet, has he? Besides, only old soldiers fool around with rifles that way." Then Alessandro dived for the bottom. In complete darkness, he swam downward until the pressure against his eardrums was unbearable. He turned about and surfaced as fast as he could, releasing from his aching lungs silver bubbles of air that preceded him on the way up, until he broke the surface with a gasp.

"How deep is it?" he asked the owner.

"I don't know," the old man said. "It's part of the mountain. Sometimes it bubbles, but not often. We drink it. We've never had a line long enough to reach the bottom. When I was young, my father brought in a reel with a thousand meters of wire on it. The sinker never hit anything. May I look at the bayonets?"

"Sure," they said, nervously.

He unsheathed the bayonets and watched the light glint off their oiled blades.

"He's a moron," Guariglia said under his breath, treading water.

"I can't argue with that," Alessandro answered.

When they got out they shaved with hot water and put on their newly washed, wet uniforms. Then they went to a loggia where they propped the rifles on their packs and sat down to eat. The women, whose husbands had been in the north for years, and who had been peeking at the two soldiers as they swam, had worked themselves into a frenzy. As if afflicted by a disease of the nerves, they made strange, unmistakable, and yet obscure gestures with their lips, tongues, jaws, eyes, hands, and fingers.

The old man sat at the table with Alessandro and Guariglia, declaiming about the Austrians and the Africans. Slamming his fist down now and then, he failed to notice that his daughter's eyes were glazed, or that his daughter-in-law stood behind him for a few seconds, placed both her hands on her breasts, touched her tongue to her nose, closed her eyes, gyrated her pelvis, and moaned like a wolf.

Alessandro and Guariglia did not know quite what to think. From the way their mouths hung open and their eyes popped, the old man thought they were totally mesmerized by his account of the war in Eritrea, and that he was inspiring them with the will to fight.

The one who moaned like a wolf threw open the kitchen shutters and, still holding on to them so that she could close them if her father turned around, let her blouse drop to her waist. Alessandro and Guariglia cleared their throats, sighed, whistled, and stabbed their veal chops.

"That's right!" the old man shouted. "Those fucking Turks! We knew what to do with them!"

When the meal was just about over, the daughter-in-law turned briefly, stuck a huge Sicilian bread into her dress, and hopped into the kitchen.

"Now what, boys?" the old man asked.

"Maybe we should sleep. We were up all night," Alessandro offered.

"And waste daylight? My God! When I was in the corps, we marched for weeks on end, every night, and fought through each day. Go out there! Get those bastards!"

"If we sleep, we'll be better fighters!" Guariglia begged.

"Bullshit!" the old man shouted, jumping to his feet. "And God bless you!" He brought their rifles and packs. The three of them left together and walked up a hill that led to the volcano. The farmer blessed and congratulated them again, and departed for his fields.

Alessandro and Guariglia walked a short distance and then turned to look back at the house. In the windows of the upper storey, the two women were doing a rather strange dance.

"They're naked," Guariglia stated.

"I can see that."

"Let's go back."

"He's watching."

Guariglia turned. "He's waving. The son of a bitch is waving. He's going to watch us like a dog, until we disappear."

"He's devoted to a cause."

"Wait a minute," Guariglia said. "Who's that?"

From the side of the compound, within their view but just out of the farmer's sight, a soldier with a rifle plodded up to the house. His knocks on the door made the women run from the windows as fast as greyhounds.

"Who is it!" Guariglia shouted.

"You know who it is," Alessandro answered. "Look at him standing there tucking in his shirt and arranging his hair. Who else could it be? Who else *would* it be?"

"I'm going to kill him," Guariglia said.

Then they separated and began to zigzag up the side of Aetna. By now the sun was high, their uniforms were dry, and they were so hot that they craved altitude if only because they knew that the wind on the heights would be cold.

ALESSANDRO'S PACK was too heavy. He had to carry 150 rounds of ammunition, probably far more than he would need, heavy clothing, enough food to last for a few days, and water. This, combined with the weight of boots, belts, clips, leather pouches, rifle, bayonet and sheath, pistol, pistol ammunition, and the many miscellaneous items that had accumulated in his pack and pockets, weighed almost as much as he did.

At four in the afternoon he halted in a clearing of young chestnut trees. Even before summer was over, the leaves were beginning to yellow—not, as elsewhere, from the heat, but from the cold at high altitude. At several thousand meters, the gradually receding forest seemed more appropriate to Northern Europe than to Sicily, and so dark and well watered that it looked like a wood in medieval France, or the Villa Borghese at the beginning of December. In their sweet alarmed chatter, the birds seemed to be saying that they had never before seen a man, although that could not have been true, because the peasants came to Aetna to gather chestnuts. Perhaps the birds had never seen a soldier.

Alessandro dropped his pack and rifle, and without the weight on his shoulders he felt like an angel drawn skyward. He sat down. For many hours he had labored up the mountainside, through forest, scrub, vineyard, field, and over black lava runs that scuffed his boots and bruised his ankles. His uniform had darkened with his own sweat, and the part of the pack that rested against his back was wringing wet.

Twice he had passed Guariglia, though no one else, and they had remarked that they would never find anyone, because with their eyes stinging and their heads bent forward with the weight on their shoulders, they did not have the freedom to observe. "Undoubtedly," Guariglia had said, "they hear us and they see us."

An ice-cold stream in the middle of the clearing was just deep enough to flow over Alessandro as he pushed himself down in the middle of it. The breeze was cool and he knew that the night would be frigid, but he would find Guariglia, hunt for the first time, and they would roast their dinner over a fire.

He emerged from the stream, shook off the water, dressed, and went to sit on his pack. A long way in the distance, the sea was illuminated by the hot afternoon light. Something about the color blue, placid and cool, far away, in a silent dazzling band below the horizon, allowed Alessandro to give up all care and let the moment have its way.

He leaned over, grasped his rifle near the base of the bayonet, and pivoted it around to rest it against the fork of a sapling, ready and within his sight. At sea a ship moved slowly across the strip of blue, the white speck of its wake becoming a thread that eventually disappeared. Alessandro picked up a chestnut and smelled it. It made him think of Rome in autumn, of looking down the Via Condotti from the Piazza Trinità dei Monti at dusk, when the fires began to blaze in restaurants along the Tiber and a darkening orange sky silhouetted the royal palms on the Gianicolo. He regretted not having taken his mother to see the views of Rome that he had come to know as he was growing up. Never would she see them again, and never had they seen them together, because she walked slowly, and he had not had the patience to walk slowly with her.

Suddenly, he was thrown forward as if he had been butted from behind by a bull. He flew over half the clearing and was about to smash headlong into a fallen log when he was turned in the air away from it. Whatever had launched him was clinging to him still, and for its own convenience had rotated him belly up so that he now saw nothing but blue.

As they landed, and as all the air left Alessandro's lungs, he received a tremendous blow to the face. He had no chance to move, no opportunity to respond. In split seconds, he tried to comprehend. Then an enormous, balding, blue-eyed man pulled back, left him, and casually walked over to the rifle. After he took it from the forked sapling and removed the sheath from the bayonet so forcefully that it flew into the air, he twirled around and came at Alessandro.

His own bayonet, with which he himself had killed a man, was moving toward him like a routing hound, but more swiftly and more surely. The man guiding it seemed unperturbed, as if he were about to stick a shovel in a pile of earth before sitting down to have his lunch.

Alessandro watched the oiled silver point and sucked in his breath. He had a choice. He could think, now I'm going to die, and this is the last thing I'm going to see, or he could find himself a tenth of a second to one side of the blade, just having escaped and not knowing quite how.

Though he had no balance or strength, his muscles exploded and he flew to the side. The bayonet went into the soft forest floor and cut a clay-colored gash in the underside of the fallen log.

Alessandro somersaulted backward into the brush and rolled down the hill, his flesh torn by rocks and branches. To encourage gravity, he pushed with his legs and arms whenever he touched anything, windmilling recklessly down the slope until he found himself, breathing like a whore, at the bottom of a little grassy knoll.

He had a clear line of sight all the way up to where he had been, miraculously far away, and he cocked his head to see if he were being pursued. The breeze didn't even move the leaves, and

the balding blond man was disappearing straight up a lava run at
disheartening speed, carrying Alessandro's pack and rifle.

Without thinking, without at first even standing up, Alessandro set out after him.

HE WANTED neither to lose him nor to be observed, so he kept
to the edge of the lava run, among bushes and trees. The cuts on
his face still bled, the black dust that he breathed settled in the
open wounds, and he turned his ankle half a dozen times, but
eventually he got his breath and stopped bleeding.

He had to move quietly because he was so close. The deserter
was in the center of the lava, making his way steadily up, as even in
his pacing as a mountain guide. Alessandro followed him for two
hours, a hundred meters to his right and a few meters behind, and
in all that time the deserter did not look back once, but as the sun
began to set and a shadow covered the east he stopped and scanned
everything below him on the mountain. Alessandro fell flat against
the rocks.

The deserter stood straight and tall, backlit by the sun. As the
evening breeze came up it caught his hair and made it flash wildly,
as if he were wearing a golden helmet. He was standing amid fields
of yellow grasses that still showed a tint of green where the hillocks
rose and the ground was uneven. Beyond him, the sky was empty.
It was getting cold, and Alessandro could clearly see the outline of
his rifle and bayonet slung over the deserter's shoulder, tight
against the side of the pack that had food, water, ammunition, and
warm clothing.

In the dark, Alessandro moved closer. He was downwind and
could hear his quarry, although he himself could not be heard.
Sometimes he caught a glimpse of the man's outline against the
slightly violet sky of early evening, and later he could see him when
he blacked out the stars.

Now and then, Alessandro heard shots from far below. They were so faint that he could not be sure that he had not imagined them. If the wind were cupped in his ear just a little, the sound would vanish, and, compared to the uncertain reports, the footsteps of the deserter were like hammer blows.

At about ten o'clock the deserter halted at the edge of the crater. With nothing to do but think and be cold, Alessandro watched him climb onto a huge boulder and settle at the top like a Biblical ascetic. He's going to rest until dawn, Alessandro thought, because he can't move through the crater at night. Then he's going to go like hell to the northeast and disappear in the direction of Messina, or to a cave where he'll be safe.

Alessandro curled up into a soft clump of grass, gripping his ankles and trying to cover as much of his body as he could with his arms. It wasn't very comfortable, but it was warmer than standing or sitting, and he fell asleep.

He awoke in complete silence at about four o'clock. Not even the wind was fast enough to make any noise, and the mountain air was clear and dense, with the stars and the Milky Way shining through as if they were agitated and angry. A crescent of moon so thin as to look like celestial breakage was suspended just above the sea on its way to the other side of the world.

Alessandro decided to wait until two or three minutes after the deserter had set out, when he was clean, well rested, well fed, and convinced that he was safe, when he was no longer thinking of Alessandro and was sure that he had not been followed. And then Alessandro would strike, when both were euphoric with the high-altitude dawn.

He went ahead to find the path that, before the war, tourists and naturalists had worn into the rim of the crater. No one walking over the mountain could avoid it. Though Alessandro climbed straight for the rim, it took him longer than he expected to get there. Lakes of fire in the crater far below turned over and boiled and were covered in hideous red scales and flakes as if they were the dried skin of a mythical animal. Now and then a line of fire would leap into the air and fall back, leaving an impression temporarily upon the molten lake from which it had sprung. The air that flowed past the rim was sulfurous and unbreathable, and the malevolent lakes had been working through the night for many thousands of years, scouts in a war so great and so deep within the earth that the surface was held in contempt.

Alessandro walked the path until he found a set of boulders on its eastern side. He climbed up to a flat ledge, and went down again to search for a rock that had a sharp and jagged edge and would fit comfortably in his hand. Just as the first rays of weak rose-colored sun struck the spot where the deserter had slept, a small fire appeared, as neat as the light of a lantern.

When the fire went out, Alessandro's terror began. In the detonator shed at Mestre he had had training in unarmed combat, but no exercise could prepare him for what he was about to do. In a candid moment, his instructor had told the troops that they had little chance of prevailing against someone much bigger, no matter what they knew. Alessandro had only half learned the drills, and had half forgotten what he had learned. He remembered the speed and grace with which the deserter had seized the rifle, unsheathed the bayonet, and soundlessly positioned the blade. He remembered with what serenity he had attacked, not even breathing hard. Alessandro tried to master the skating that was going on in his stomach, by staring at the boulder under his feet and remaining still. The rising sun soon outplayed the molten lakes, and though they were in shadow they could not match the smallest part of its blood-colored circle. The higher the sun climbed, the less Alessandro was afraid.

The deserter was coming up the path and Alessandro was shaking, afraid that he would let him pass or that when the moment came to jump he would be so dazed with fear that he would leap either too early or too late.

No longer was Alessandro angry, or at least he didn't think so. All he wanted was to live. Why not let him go, he thought. Just let him pass. That way, I stay alive. Because the son of a bitch stole my rifle and my clothes. When he came at me with my own bayonet he was going to kill me, and for him it was nothing.

He tightened his jaw and clenched his right fist around the rock. Now the sun was blinding as it rose like a balloon past the rim of the volcano.

Alessandro thought of a lion on a rock, waiting for its prey. A lion would be neither afraid nor angry, but as it sailed onto the back of what it was going to kill, it would appear to be angry. It would roar, and rake with its paws. Like the lion of Venice, it would have a mane stiff with sun and dust. Like the lion of Venice, with a sad face that was brutal and wise, it would let God and nature guide it in its fight.

It would have to be that way for Alessandro, because he had no time in which to think further. He heard footsteps at a rapid pace. The deserter appeared. He had no idea that anyone was waiting for him, and he moved ahead like a hiker.

In the second that Alessandro was airborne he lost his fear. He was about to return a favor, and he was flying in like a hawk. As the deserter turned, Alessandro tried to strike him in the face with the rock, but gravity conspired against him and the blow landed to the side.

They both went down, the pack fell away and seemed almost to crumple, and the rifle clattered on the rocks. For a moment neither moved. Alessandro threw a punch and felt his fists lightly touch a row of teeth, but the next thing he knew two boots were pressing against his stomach. They didn't merely kick him, they pushed until he was lifted away and thrown back against the boulder. The rock flew from his hand.

The deserter went straight for the rifle. He put his hands on it and was about to turn when Alessandro ran against him like a ram, butting him off the edge of the trail to a place far below. He had suffered in the fall. Alessandro, on the other hand, was untouched, but the rifle had gone over the edge, too. The deserter slowly picked it up, worked the action, and pointed it toward Alessandro, who pulled himself back from the edge so fast that no shot was fired.

When Alessandro looked out from the rocks he saw the mountain soldier who had tried to drive a bayonet into him limping toward the floor of the crater, with the rifle cradled in his arms, checking the path behind him so frequently that it looked as if he were having trouble making up his mind about what direction to take.

Alessandro undid the pack. The deserter had not known of the pistol, wrapped in its belt, at the bottom of the left inside pocket. Alessandro strapped it on. He drank his water and ate dried meat, biscuits, and fruit as he examined the deserter's belongings—a torn sweater, a French knife with a wooden handle, a socialist political manifesto dated May, 1915, a jar of jam, and a postcard of the Sistine Chapel. The postcard was from a woman named Berta, it said that she was returning to Danzig, and it was addressed to a Gianfranco di Rienzi in a battalion of the Alpini that Alessandro knew to be superb mountaineers who had fought for years in the snow.

Perhaps because Alessandro now knew the deserter's name, that he was a mountaineer, and that he had been in love with Berta and had not been loved back, he had no desire to kill him, or even to capture him, but he could not tolerate the fact that he did not have his rifle. Alessandro wrapped a sweater around his body like a bandolier, drained the last of the water, and set out once again. As he took to the path he drew the pistol to check it and release the safety catch, and as he holstered the gun he felt the inexplicable energy that sometimes comes in the morning to soldiers who have not slept the night before.

BY THE time Alessandro reached the caldera he was very thirsty but he knew that Gianfranco di Rienzi must have been thirstier. The sun was strong and heat rising from the lakes of fire bent the air until it waved back and forth in vertical sheets that looked like water.

Because of hidden pools of magma under a crust that might collapse with a man's weight, Gianfranco now and then hit the ground with the rifle butt in much the same way that a skater stamps his feet to test the ice.

Gianfranco turned, raised the rifle, and fired a shot in Alessandro's direction. As the report echoed amidst the fumes, Alessandro winced and bent on one knee, but the shot had already passed.

The second shot was more considered. Alessandro had time to drop to the ground, and he heard the bullet fly over his head, but he was not in good cover. Gianfranco wasted two more rounds, and managed only to sting Alessandro's face as they shattered the sharp and jagged rocks nearby, and to reduce the ammunition remaining to three rounds.

Alessandro felt strangely unafraid, because Gianfranco di Rienzi now had only three chances, three little bullets. In the Bell Tower and in the trenches thereafter, bullets had been like rainfall. Three bullets in a vast open area simply did not impress him, so he ran forward, leaping the hot seams that crossed from lake to lake and patch to patch, and he forced Gianfranco, at fifty meters, to track him and waste another shot. This one, though, had been very close. Only two remained, and Gianfranco did what Alessandro thought he was going to do. He decided to use the bayonet. He carefully removed the sheath, hung it on his belt, and doubled back at a run.

Alessandro drew the pistol, flung away the belt, and fled into a rock-strewn depression, hiding the pistol in his waist. When Gianfranco appeared at the rim of the depression, shrouded in clouds of sunlit yellow fumes, he would have the option of shooting Alessandro or moving closer to bayonet him. Knowing that Gianfranco would want to preserve his last two cartridges, Alessandro sat on a rock and kept his feet on the ground.

Gianfranco did appear in the sulfur fumes, but he was behind Alessandro. He could have shot him, but they had been living off one another's mistakes for almost a day, and it continued. Gianfranco was greedy for the two cartridges. He started to descend.

When Alessandro heard the clinking of rocks rolling down the slope he rose and turned.

Gianfranco was sure that he had him. "Why did you chase me, you idiot. I took from you what I needed, and twice I let you live. Twice. Couldn't you let *me* live?"

"No."

"Why not?"

"You're a deserter."

"You don't like deserters? You're a monarchist? Stupid!"

"I'm not a monarchist," Alessandro said when they were standing so close that in ten steps Gianfranco would have him on the tip of the bayonet, "I don't like deserters."

"Why not?"

"Guariglia. Guariglia has a wife and children. When you left the line, you son of a bitch, you made it more difficult for him to stay alive."

"Maybe you and Guariglia should have left, too."

"No, because of the other Guariglias and the others like me."

"Perhaps they should desert as well."

"So Austrians would be looking for them, instead of Italians? You know what would happen. The deserters would band together to fight the Austrians, and they would be an army."

"I promise you," Gianfranco said, "that army, too, would have its deserters."

"And *I* promise," Alessandro responded, "that people like me would go out to look for them."

"That's too bad," Gianfranco said, "because we've come to a standstill. We both have interesting arguments, but I have the rifle." He dropped the rifle into bayonet position and came forward. His right hand gripped the neck of the stock, and his trigger finger was pulled out of position.

This gave Alessandro just enough time to move a step back, take hold of the pistol, and withdraw it from his shirt. By the time it was aimed at Gianfranco di Rienzi's head, Alessandro had cocked the hammer. If Gianfranco continued forward or changed the position of his right hand, he would be shot.

"Right through your head," Alessandro shouted, his finger so tight on the trigger that he himself could not be sure he wouldn't fire.

If Gianfranco surrendered, he would live until he was executed. And, yet, he could no longer go forward, so he threw down the rifle, drew back, and bolted, thinking that Alessandro did not have it in him to shoot.

OF THE seven prisoners on the cattle boat, three were wounded. They lay on deck, in chains, under a canvas canopy. Those who weren't wounded wanted the ship to hit a mine, for then they would be unshackled and given a chance in the sea, but the wounded had no hope: they were not strong enough to swim ashore, and in the water they would bleed to death.

Gianfranco di Rienzi was bandaged on the shoulder and on the leg. His expression was blank. Alessandro had watched him as they marched through Catania. His eyes took in everything but returned nothing. He had ridden on a cart with two other prisoners, under a rain-soaked blanket. Catania is flat but gives the impression of being on a hill above the sea. All the shops were shuttered, everything gray. They passed a restaurant where Fabio ducked in and tried to order a cappuccino, and even though he was forced back into the line, he had been inside long enough for the smoky fire to make him smell of lamb and hot oil. The soldiers of the River Guard marched double time, pushing the big two-wheeled cart over the rough cobbles. Rain ran down their faces in streams.

Their uniforms were wet, as were their boots, packs, and everything inside. The rifles were covered with beads of moisture, and the oil that beaded the water turned cloudy as it cooled.

Only now and then did a light appear in a window, or a woman or a child peek through a curtain at the column of soldiers. When rain swept through the streets of Catania the city had neither the architecture nor the custom to cheer itself up, for whereas cities like Salzburg or London had been built for rain, Catania had gambled everything on a blue sea and a flawless sky.

Gianfranco di Rienzi was without expression, but as his gaze jumped from overspilling gutters to water-slickened façades to rain-laden palms dripping in the wind, he studied the city as if he were a mother touching the face of her child for the last time.

They boarded the cattle boat in silence. The prisoners were astounded and depressed to see it, as if they thought they might have been happier had they been brought to the site of their execution in a new destroyer with sanded decks and polished brass fittings, and perhaps they would have been. Given their first view of the cattle boat, so low in the water that it looked like a man whose belt had dropped to his knees, their melancholy made some sense, especially in the fog and the rain. And when the cattle boat cast off and just drifted through the mist the prisoners were thrown into the deepest despair. Engines, lights, and forward motion would have given them reassuring order, and rhythms for their fingers to copy and their hearts to follow. If the modern world were to execute them, it was obliged to keep them busy beforehand, but they found themselves soaking wet, wounded, and floating blindly on a flat gray sea. In one respect it hardly mattered, for the life of a soldier is an introduction to death, and when death comes or is about to come, the soldier is at least partially satisfied.

The weather cleared as they crossed the Gulf of Taranto, and in the middle of the morning, as the sky became blue and the sea sparkled for the first time in days, Alessandro visited his prisoner.

"It was kind of you not to shatter the bone in my leg," Gian-franco di Rienzi said to him. "I'm so grateful that you shot me in the ass."

"I shot you in the rear of the thigh."

"That's the ass."

"I wasn't trying to miss the bone. I wasn't thinking about it one way or another."

"Thank you. I'm sure you'll enjoy my execution."

"Who says you'll be executed? You'll be tried. Maybe you'll do a few years and they'll let you go."

Gianfranco stared at Alessandro, who was kneeling on the deck in front of him. "You think so?" he asked quietly.

"No."

"I don't think so either."

"What about your record?"

"I was a good soldier. I killed a lot of Germans. I also killed a military policeman."

Alessandro lifted his head.

"On the Via Cardano, in Pavia, in front of a hundred people, I shot him in the chest with my service pistol. I knew at that moment that I was dead, which is why I went to the volcano."

"Were you expecting us?"

"For five months."

"We weren't coming for you, we just made a sweep."

"I should have killed you."

"You tried."

Gianfranco smiled. "How did you make that jump? Are you a cockroach? Humans can't jump backward like that."

"Have you ever seen a bayonet coming at you?"

"I have."

"What did you do?"

"I shot."

"I jumped."

"If I could," Gianfranco said as the mist lifted off the sea in glittering silver, "I'd break the shackles and swim to Africa."

"You'd bleed to death in the water."

"I'd take the chance. Cut the chain." The other prisoners stopped talking.

Alessandro clearly would not cut any chain.

"Why not?"

"Then they'd shoot *me*."

"Come with us."

"To Africa? Even if I thought that you wouldn't bleed to death in the sea," Alessandro said, rising to his feet, "I wouldn't cut the shackles, because I want to return to my family."

"The army really has you by the balls," Gianfranco declared.

"The army has always had me by the balls," Alessandro answered. "Since the very first day, and I've always known it, but—you know what?—we were wiped out in the Veneto, and I lived. I was lucky, and I'm going to stretch my luck."

"Look at me," Gianfranco commanded. "Look at me."

Alessandro did as he was told.

"I'm not going to be here very long. I'm almost relieved, but I'm agitated. I see things. I see clearly now." He paused, showing obvious satisfaction. "And you're not going to make it."

WHILE THE cattle boat rounded the headlands of Otranto and turned north, the prisoners on the starboard side saw an apparently limitless sea and did not know that the untouched beaches of southern Italy were merely a few hundred meters away, or that on the port side it was possible to watch the land move by as smoothly as if it had been on rails.

One of the prisoners, an emaciated, pop-eyed, insanely nervous bandsman who had been captured as he was washing his clothes, kept asking to see a priest.

"We have no priest," he was told. "This isn't a battleship."

Then he would ask someone else exactly the same question—"May I see a priest?"

"Why do you want a priest?" Gianfranco asked.

"To help me face death calmly."

"And what if you don't face it calmly?"

"My insides," the bandsman answered, "would go crazy."

"So?"

"I might lose control of my sphincter. I don't like to do that. Do you?"

"I don't know what sphincter you mean, but it doesn't matter, because it would be over in an instant."

The bandsman looked at Gianfranco as if Gianfranco himself were the firing squad.

"And then you'd find out about the other side. If it was nothing, well, what a disappointment, but you wouldn't know it. If it was something, it would be like being shot out of a cannon."

"I've never been shot out of a cannon, but I always wondered what it would be like to be dead," the bandsman said sarcastically.

"You see," Gianfranco told him, "now you'll find out."

"You're not scared?"

"I'm scared to death, but I'm risking that there's another side."

Alessandro and Guariglia had been listening from the narrow deck above. "Why?" Alessandro asked.

Gianfranco looked up. "You, you go fuck yourself," he said. "All my life I've known about the other side, in a thousand ways, but I'm not sure, I'm merely taking the chance. Soon, thanks to you, I'll be in front of a firing squad. When they pull their triggers, I'm going to fly."

Alessandro slipped through the rails and dropped to the prisoners' deck. Guariglia followed on the stairs.

"Is that what happened to the military policeman in Pavia?" Alessandro asked. "Did he exit into a realm of joy? Or was it just over—frozen, finished, dark. I would like to know what it was like for him when your bullet smashed into his chest and stopped his heart. Did the blood backing up and bursting out of him do it? Was that how he was propelled into joy?"

"I hope so," Gianfranco answered, "because if it's true, I'll be just as happy, and if it isn't, I'll be just as still."

"I remain curious," Alessandro insisted. "You said you knew in a thousand ways. Tell me just one."

"I can't tell you. It comes like a spirit."

"I know it comes like a spirit, goddamn you," Alessandro said. "Look over there," he told the prisoners, motioning at the horizon. "All you can see is blue water. To the north, east, and south, an empty horizon. Tell me, what's on the other side?"

"The same thing," a prisoner answered.

"No," Guariglia said. "We follow the coast. Because we have a flat bottom, we can stay in the shallows to evade submarines. From the port side you can see the beach, you can see every shell, you can even smell the trees, and on the other side you can hardly hear anyone talk, because of the sound of the surf. The smoke from fires in the fields smokes your clothes; you see birds darting about; the mountains are close, and in the Gargano they rise very high."

"Bring us over to that side," Gianfranco said.

AFTER THEY came around the Gargano, where the steep mountains and rich forests looked like a paradise, they turned into a steady north wind that made the Adriatic a choppy road. Even after the heights of Aetna, the breeze seemed cool, for it had been born on the glaciers and icy summits of the Alps. Though the sea was like a washboard, and progress upon it was both nauseating and cold, the acerbic smoke from the engines of the cattle boat was slicked back from the funnel like the hair of a pilot in an open cockpit, and it no longer tangled over the decks in crosswinds, tormenting the condemned and their captors alike.

They had an excellent dinner, by army standards—cheese,

tomatoes, red wine, and freshly baked bread. The sight of the land gliding by and slipping off to the south comforted the prisoners as if everything they saw were being added irrevocably to their accounts.

They thought that the hills in the distance and the shadows before them, the feathery lines of fire in the fields, the moon, and the mysterious and beguiling songbirds that rose from thickets and trees, and hovered like black sunlight, would stay with them forever.

The wind swept through the rigging and the iron rails, the surf was as busy as if it were anticipating a miracle, and the mass of dark air above them was at first blank and then brilliant as the light of the stars collided and crossed.

They forgot everything they had ever been told, they shed their opinions, they abandoned their expectations. The River Guard withdrew from them because the prisoners were on their way, soon to leave the world, and had no more need for pity or understanding.

Although Alessandro wanted to know about Berta of the Sistine Chapel postcard, and what Gianfranco di Rienzi had done before the war, he was content to rely upon imagined answers rather than interrupt the peace that descended hour by hour as the cattle boat pushed through the wind.

"Why did you desert?" he had asked Gianfranco as they were still drifting in the Gulf of Taranto.

"I was tired of the army," Gianfranco answered. "I calculated that if I waited it out somewhere until after the war my chances would be as good or better than if I stayed in my brigade. We were advancing. Everyone was dying."

As they approached the abbreviated lights of Pescara, they settled down for the night. Coastal towns were supposed to be darkened in fear of naval bombardment, but they never complied absolutely. The moon was floating over the crest of the hills, throbbing bright.

Soldiers spread out their blankets and packs. Rifles, bayonets, and other implements of war lay in between them, pointing at all angles. The River Guard had become so closely knit and efficient that they could do almost anything without orders. They could make and break camp, line up for an attack, receive an assault, embark upon a ship, scramble down the nets, all with astonishing speed and unspoken coordination. It took less than five minutes for them to bed down, after which they were completely silent.

Alessandro and Guariglia had laid their blankets on top of two adjoining hatches, apart from the sleeping troops, because they had the later guard. Knowing that they would have to wrest themselves from sleep in a few hours' time, they found it difficult to settle, and they took a little walk. On their way forward they passed the prisoners on the deck below. Leaning over the rail unobserved, they bent into the cream-colored moonlight and looked down. Not a single prisoner was asleep. They were all staring at the coast, their eyes flooded with the light reflected from the sea.

"Listen," Guariglia whispered to Alessandro. They heard something over the wind. As the breeze shifted now and then they could hear it better. Someone was chanting.

Moving his lips as his head bobbed up and down like a float on the waves, Gianfranco di Rienzi was repeating one word over and over: *"Gloria, gloria, gloria, gloria . . ."*

"I DON'T like him," Alessandro said to Guariglia as they lay on their blankets, heads propped up on knapsacks.

"Who said you have to like him?"

"With what I've been thinking, I'd better like him."

"Are you crazy?"

"Guariglia, I've killed many men, some of them no doubt a lot better than Gianfranco di Rienzi, but I've never delivered anyone to execution."

"You can't free him. There are two guards, around the clock. Even Fabio would shoot you."

"We have the detail at midnight."

"You're insane. If he escaped on our watch, they'd shoot *us*."

Alessandro smiled.

"He killed a military policeman, Alessandro, and how many times did he try to kill you?"

"Twice."

"Isn't that enough?"

"No, it isn't," Alessandro said.

"You miss it."

"I do." Alessandro rolled over and went to sleep. Guariglia looked after him for a while, and when he was satisfied that Alessandro was sleeping, said his customary prayer, in which he begged God to allow him to see his wife and children one more time.

PAYING NO heed to the desires of the soldiers, the cattle boat moved forward. Whether they were hallucinatory deserters or responsible officers, it took no account of their deepest longings, and it did not credit their deeds. It just moved against the wind as its steady track ordered the many states of feeling to which it was cold.

Alessandro's face was bathed in bright moonlight the color of pearl, with grays, silver, and gold all beaming from it in a flash. The same light also shone on Guariglia, whose half-smiling face rested on a pillow made from a sweater. As Guariglia slept, Alessandro dreamed.

He was on the beach between Ostia and Anzio where he had gone so many times, in all seasons, where he first had learned to swim in the surf, riding on his father's back as they bobbed in the waves.

In the dream he was set down on the sand, close to the water. A hurricane wind was rising, and high clouds covered spots of blue like windblown gauze. Straight down the beach the air had the gray quality of fall, and the moment Alessandro was set down, it began to stir the sea into rising mountains of green and white as smooth and cool as aspic. The breakers were held high in the wind and they curled and revolved in contradictory fonts of air and rocking parabolas of foam.

From Ostia to Anzio the sea was drawn back in a high wall of water. At first Alessandro feared that with the weakening of whatever held back its invisibly buttressed mass, it would collapse and cover the plain of the Tiber. Physics decreed something like falling, and yet the hills of surf, with their own valleys, peaks, and plateaux, confounded his expectations.

When he opened his eyes he saw the tremendous lighted globe of the moon.

"Guariglia," he said, turning over to call to his friend. "Guariglia."

Guariglia awakened.

"What time is it?"

Guariglia looked at his watch. "Eleven-thirty. You woke me up to ask what time it is?"

"Who's guarding now?"

"Fabio and Imperatore."

"Let's relieve them early."

Guariglia looked at Alessandro, and then glanced over the deck to the water and beyond. "Why?" he asked, but he already knew. Rome lay directly across the Apennines.

GUARIGLIA TRADED never knowing what might become of him for the one sweet certainty that would mean his death. Like Alessandro, he decided to go home even if it meant walking across the mountains, even if it were the last thing he would ever do.

Although Alessandro's chances of remaining alive were probably neither better nor worse in the line than in trying to keep ahead of the military police, he was pulled to Rome by what he loved. He thought of the trains rushing out of Tiburtina, their whistles shrieking; of pigeons the color of gray pearls whirling around the high domes, mixing with the pale blue sky; of the Tiber urgently overflowing its banks in heavy rain; of the silent streets and stairs that had learned their unexpected sympathy for mortal man by watching him for generation after generation; and of the thunderstorms that washed the city clean and left it sparkling and steaming in the sun. He wanted to return to his family.

Instead of putting on their boots, he and Guariglia quietly joined the laces, and hung them over their shoulders.

Every infantry unit had heavy wire cutters. With a little extra pressure, these could be made to snap manacles and leg irons. One did not have to be a mechanic to know it. The wire cutters were kept in a wooden crate with the signaling equipment and the battle flags, but when Alessandro and Guariglia reached the crate, they saw that the open latch was swaying with the mild roll of the ship, and the wire cutters had been removed.

They descended to the main deck, moving in a strange and stilted gait because they were not used to walking with their boots off. Someone was standing at the rail where the prisoners had been chained to the deck. They thought it was Fabio, but as they got closer they realized that it was the bandsman. He was staring at the mountains and the shore, his manacles and leg irons cut away from him.

The spot on deck where Gianfranco had been transformed into a not entirely pure beatitude was empty, as were all the others.

"I can't swim," the bandsman stated, as if he were discussing his rejection from a military unit.

"Where are they?" Alessandro asked, though he knew.

The bandsman gestured toward the mountains.

"Where's Fabio?"

"Who's Fabio?"

"The one who was guarding you."

"The waiter?"

"Yes."

"He cut the chains," the bandsman said. "He went over the side with the others."

"All the prisoners?" Guariglia asked.

"Everybody," the bandsman replied.

"What do you mean, *everybody*?"

"Everyone."

"The prisoners."

"Everyone. If you don't believe me, go look. Don't you know what happened? Someone killed your colonel."

"Gianfranco?"

"Fabio cut the chains, the waiter."

"He killed the colonel?"

"I don't know."

They rushed up the companionway, and then recoiled. The colonel was sprawled across the deck, his throat cut. The line of the cut was thick and maroon-colored, and the deck was sticky with blood. They ran to the next deck, where blankets were spread as if invisible men were lying on them.

They returned to the bandsman. "I can't swim," he said, "and they're going to have to shoot somebody. That's why I left in the first place," he added, laughing. "Everyone was being shot, and I didn't want to be. But I've changed my mind. I can't avoid it, can I? I might as well finish it."

"Use a life preserver."

"There aren't any. It doesn't matter, anyway. They'd catch me. I know they'd catch me. You caught me, didn't you?"

As the boat continued ahead, they looked at the bandsman. The cold light accentuated his bird-like features, and they thought that if the world were just, he would be surprised and rewarded, and that merely by moving his arms gently back and forth he would fly like a bird over the mountains and into the moonlight.

"You can swim," Alessandro said to Guariglia yet again. Somehow, solely because of the way that Guariglia looked, Alessandro never believed that he could swim.

Guariglia looked back in disgust. "How do you think I got to that island and back?"

"I wanted to make sure."

"Alessandro," Guariglia asked dryly, "do you think I'm too ugly to know how to swim?"

"That has nothing to do with it."

"As much as it pains me," Guariglia said, "we'd better go separately. The hills are going to be thick with deserters. Wait a few minutes so you'll be carried north a ways."

"We could stay, Guariglia."

"No. They shoot everybody. It's like pulling ticks. They'd question us for an hour and put us up against a wall. Fuck them, fuck all of them. I'm going to my children." He climbed over the rail. "Maybe we'll make it."

Guariglia jumped away from the ship. He hit the water with hardly a sound and disappeared in the waves. When he surfaced he had already turned toward shore and was swimming strongly. The way he moved reminded Alessandro of the way an animal swims in a flooded river that has taken his home.

The bandsman walked to the stern, talking to himself like a patient in a hospital for the terminally ill.

Alessandro stood with his hands on the rail. He had no good way to gauge the time. If he had counted, he would have counted too fast. If he had tried to mark the progress of the moon from peak to peak, he would have been mesmerized for too long. So he simply waited for the boat to come even with a stretch of beach that looked wide and clear.

The sea was no longer like a washboard, for the moon had stroked it into rambling waves that said what the sea was supposed to say in moonlight, and these gave the cattle boat a lovely motion as it slid down their shallow troughs. Alessandro climbed up and sat on the rail.

He looked out. The sea was marbled with foam and drawn into molten hills and valleys that were cool and smooth and flooded with the moon. Soon the moon would be behind the mountains and he would be crossing the rings of fire. He stepped outward into space and felt the lovely light caress him with affection. He hadn't known that anything as cold and clear as moonlight could be so full of promise, and as he fell it seemed to him that his hands clawed a trail of white sparks through the air, but these were the stars.

STELLA MARIS

THE SEA was warm, and the surf was unusually high for the Adriatic at that time of year. The wind coming off the hills, dry, full of smoke, and seemingly driven by the moon, knocked the crests from the waves as if they were as light as snow. In this kind of beautiful water a swimmer might want to drown, and the heart of the temptation was not so much the quality of sensation but the way the water moved, endlessly rocking, endlessly meeting the wind and falling back, endlessly engaged in a conversation wiser than any act of will.

Loosely churning half asleep in the white sound of the waves, Alessandro stopped swimming, but the very moment that his thoughts turned to the possibility of release he was picked up by a whip-like stroke and slapped against the sand as if he were a piece of meat thrown onto a marble slab in a fancy butcher shop.

With the wind knocked out of him, he stood to fight the undertow. Keeping his balance, he emerged on an empty beach, in a warm wind that had dried his clothing by the time he put on his boots and that promised to dry the boots themselves before he crossed the first ring of fire.

The walking was easy. The grain had been harvested and the fields were flat and unplowed, with golden stalks littering the ground in a soft mat that glowed in the moonlight. The olive trees had been pruned, and he moved through them as if on a garden path.

After half an hour he came to the first line of fire. From the cattle boat these lines had looked like luminous golden cables braided across the fields. It had seemed that they could easily have been straddled, though it was possible even from the sea to make out the thick curtain of smoke that rose from sullen flame.

Alessandro was surprised to discover that the fires were taller than a man, and burned in a solid unbroken front for as far as he could see. In the distance, figures in shadow appeared to be tending the slowly moving wall of flame. They held torches, because they were present not to control the fire but merely to spur it on.

The line, though not drawn by a straight-edge, was remarkably even, because the wind was remarkably even. It was so hot and so bright that Alessandro could hardly get close to it.

He wondered if, just the way that one can pass one's finger quickly through a candle flame, he might pass through the fire unscathed. At first he made tentative approaches, with his hands in front of his eyes, but it was too hot to bear, and as the wind pushed the fire at him he had to retreat.

When he looked to see what the farmers were doing he saw that every now and then one of the torches would speed toward the flame and disappear into it, and sometimes the wall would spit out a drop of fire, a torch borne by a man.

Alessandro started to run. He held his breath, jumped at the flame, and in an instant he was on the other side. He felt no pain. His clothes had not caught fire. He had not even felt the heat in the midst of the flame, but only before and after it.

On the other side, a new field stretched toward the mountains. Though the ground was charred and covered with ash, the way was smooth. He would get through a line and raise dust and ashes for half an hour until he approached another, which he would take as he had taken the one before it. Each time he crossed he was encouraged, and each time he crossed he was closer to the dark mountain that he was using as a guide. At first the moon had been directly over it, but now was far to the right. Some of the River Guard, Alessandro guessed, not knowing how to move across open country, would use the moon as their compass and make an oddly curved track.

The last fire-line was in a rocky pasture on the side of the mountain itself. Because the ground was not as even or well tended as the fields on the coastal plain, the line was broken and Alessandro could have crossed in the breaks. Instead, he went for the highest wall of flame, which now he could hardly see, for the sun was coming up behind him and hid the fire even as it showed the smoke. He went through it like a spirit, without closing his eyes. Now only the mountains lay between him and Rome.

IN THE Gran Sasso d'Italia are summits of almost three thousand meters. Compared to the Alps, they are minor, but not for someone who must go among them with neither food nor blankets. Though Alessandro had to cross more roads and rail lines than he had expected, these were empty but for occasional farmers in the far distance, moving so slowly next to an ox or a donkey that Alessandro could not tell if they were coming or going. Once, a train of empty boxcars rattled down a rusty track, pushed by an engine that seemed half dismantled. Alessandro was tempted to jump aboard, for it was heading west, more or less, but he knew that half the soldiers of the River Guard would seize upon this easy way to get home, and that military police watched freight trains with great interest.

He surveyed a few towns from the hillsides above them but never went in for food. Near one little village perched at the top of a rock in a manner that seemed offensively defensive even to a soldier on the run, the bakers had been baking and the smell of hot fresh bread was almost his undoing, but Alessandro kept walking.

He skirted lakes bordered by rocky outcroppings, and passed over boulder-covered hills and through glades in the forest where possibly no one had ever been. His one salvation was the pure water that ran in ice-cold streams from the lakes, for when he was hungry he knelt down and drank until he felt satisfied. Then he would force himself to drink until he was bloated, after which he could walk for several hours without thinking of food. The land he put behind him, the altitude he gained, and the delight of crossing open country brought the kind of rapture he had known on his rides between Rome and Bologna.

As he crossed the Gran Sasso he was nearly overcome by a steadily mounting desire for women. He was as deeply in need of a woman's embrace as an animal is in need of salt. The equation, so long out of balance, cried for restitution. At times he half floated over the mountains, summoning the memory of almost every woman he had ever known, of all the nudes in paintings subject to his precise and vexing recollection, of the poignant and charged encounters on the streets and in parks, theaters, and lecture halls, where one sees the woman for whom one has to have been born, and then feels the deft and overpowering pain of circumstance as it draws her away, because the train must be caught, dinner is at a certain time, or the store that sells a particular kind of kitchen implement will close in half an hour.

On the morning of his third day without food, Alessandro had crossed the Gran Sasso and was sitting on a bed of pine needles above a small lake. The wind rushed through the trees and he was drunk on stream water and staring out over the lake. In this condition, he expected that some beauty would appear from nowhere and take him in her arms. He was not surprised, therefore, to hear soft footsteps behind him, and a jingling that sounded like bracelets. He breathed deeply and shut his eyes, and then a thousand sheep and half a dozen dogs came flooding through the forest, bumping up against the trees to scratch, and nibbling at inedible pine cones.

They soon surrounded Alessandro so that all he could see was wool.

A FERTILE meadow of untouched grass lay on both sides of the stream that fed the lake. It was as big as a small town, and no sheep had been near it for a year. Dogs watched the flock from miniature bluffs upon which they perched like models of the Sphinx, and the shepherds camped on the lakeshore as they waited for the sheep to fatten.

Of the thousand sheep, four hundred were to be driven to Rome for slaughter. The three shepherds had argued for months about the best means to accomplish this. Should two go on the long drive, and leave only one to watch over six hundred sheep? On the other hand, one man could not expect to drive four hundred animals over rough country for sixty kilometers without losing half or more. The only solution was to get someone else.

They didn't know Alessandro, they found his speech hard to understand, and he admitted that he knew nothing about sheep, but he was willing to accompany them to the Mattatoio in Rome. There, after a glass of wine with his companion, and the simulated splitting of shares, Alessandro had only to cross the Tiber and he would be home.

"I don't like the idea," the oldest shepherd said to the other two, speaking across a campfire that blazed higher than a man's waist. It was the middle of September, they would have to leave in a few days, and at two thousand meters light snow sometimes fell at night, only to be burned away by a hot sun the next morning.

"We've been through this a hundred times, Quagliagliarello," said Roberto, a man of Alessandro's age, who was to go with Alessandro to Rome. "We can't do it with only three of us."

"But he's a deserter."

Alessandro's eyes shot back and forth, crossing the flames to follow the point of view.

"So what. He was in for two years. What did you do?"

"We raise sheep for the army."

"We raise sheep because that's our business."

The old shepherd looked about. He hated to argue, because other people were always much faster than he, and confounded everything he said. "We raise sheep because *that's our business,*" he stated.

"That's what I said," argued Roberto.

"Well, it is our business."

"All right, Quagliagliarello. He was in the army for two years. What have you done?"

"I raise sheep because it's my business."

"What's more important, defense of the country or business?"

"You're trying to trap me."

"Answer either way. I don't care."

"Business. Business is more important."

"Then he'll help in our business."

"But he's a deserter."

"So what?"

"What's more important, business or defense of the country?"

"You tell me," the younger one demanded.

"Business!"

"So why do you ask?"

"Because he's a deserter."

"So what?"

"So, what's more important, business or the defense of the country?"

"Business," Roberto answered. "That's what you said."

"That's what I *say.*"

"Yes."

"But he's a deserter."

"So what?"

"So, what's more important . . ." This went on until the fire had burned down sufficiently to require the third shepherd, a mute by the name of Modugno, to throw on more logs.

As soon as they blazed up, Quagliagliarello knitted his brows and turned to Roberto. "I don't like it," he said.

"Why not?" Roberto answered.

"He's a deserter."

Roberto was writing a letter to his sister. He kept on writing even as he argued with Quagliagliarello. "So what," he answered mechanically.

"What's more important?" Quagliagliarello asked.

"Business or the defense of the country?" Roberto continued.

"Business."

"Right."

"But he's a deserter."

"So what," Roberto said, moving on to another page. It was easy to argue with Quagliagliarello, if you had patience, and if you could pronounce his name.

Alessandro crawled into a sheepskin sack and turned away from the fire. They were camped on a small sandbar that jutted into the lake, and as the fire died down he could see the stars without the intrusion of wavy air or flashing smoke. The argument between Roberto and Quagliagliarello had slowed until it sounded like a ritual incantation, and the wind was cold and dry.

WHEN THEY moved through the mountains toward Rome they moved at the pace of the sheep, and the sheep moved at the pace of the clouds, the swaying of trees, and all the other things in nature, except lightning.

The beauty of the lakes, the forest, and the stretches of tranquil blue sky gently took the army out of Alessandro. For weeks he heard nothing but the wind, the bleating of sheep, and the regular overturning and knocking together of the small rocks kicked about by the herd.

Hawks circling on invisible rivers of air never saw fit to swoop down as long as the shepherds flanked the lambs. So attuned to the sound of the wind and its slightest variations was Alessandro that had the hawks descended he would have heard them, and he would have been where they were going to land, ready to use his stick.

The only time Roberto and Alessandro disagreed was once when they came to a small lake, far beyond L'Aquila, where Alessandro had wanted to halt on the eastern side and Roberto brought the sheep around to the western. Though they were too far apart to shout across the water, their dispute was about how to look at the light, for Alessandro wanted to see the world gilded as sunlight flooded over the lake, to feel the heat on his face, to be surrounded by glare, but Roberto wanted to keep his eyes clear as the sun penciled-in every rigid and perfect detail of the hills. He stood watching the gulls on the lake. They were whiter than a glacier. In the stars, clouds, and wind, Alessandro hoped to be able to restore what he had lost, for beyond the disintegration and the glare, by the tenets and faith of the West, were clarity, reconstitution, and love.

The closer they came to Rome the more towns and farms they had to skirt lest the sheep graze in a field yet to be harvested or find diversion in narrow streets. Where they were unable to break out over open country they held by rivers and streams and sometimes passed near a village, all four hundred sheep forging ahead as if they knew where they were going.

One morning, as they looked out from a forest on the crest of a mountain, they saw Rome silently straddling the Tiber, fresh, pale, and without mass. In the eastern light ten thousand roofs flashed like the refractive scales of a fish as its stripes cloud into a dying rainbow when it is pulled from the sea.

They came down past Subiaco, San Vito Romano, and Gallicano nel Lazio, and entered the city from the south. Although sheep were often driven through the center of Rome, two men could not hope to keep a large flock from breaking up in the maze of streets. Alessandro and Roberto marched their animals down the Via Ardeatina until they got to the Aurelian Wall, which they followed west. They stopped to ask a soldier what day it was.

"It's the fifth," the soldier answered from the top of the wall, where he was standing with a rifle slung from his shoulder.

"Of October?"

"Where have you been?"

They didn't bother to answer his question, for they had another of their own. "What day?"

"I told you."

"Not number, day."

"Friday," he said, incredulously.

"I'll have to pay for feed until Monday," Roberto said.

The air was mild and gentle, and the scent of pine needles, wood fires, and hot olive oil vaulted over the wall.

They drove the sheep down the Viale del Campo Boario and turned them inside the wall at the Protestant Cemetery. Circling around Monte Testaccio, upon which many goats were standing, they came to the Mattatoio and drove the sheep through a wide gate. As soon as the animals entered the vast courtyard of ramshackle pens they knew they had been betrayed. Though the slaughter had ended for the day, voices were left that they could hear, and the smell of death made them bleat in terror. Their eyes were wide, as if they could see what was bearing down on them, but the fences were too high to leap and the walls too solid to breach. The hearts of the ewes must have broken for their lambs.

ALESSANDRO FOLLOWED as direct a route as he could through the winding streets of Trastevere. The corners where toughs had been stationed since the time of Caligula were now empty. They were in the army, in prison, dead, or hiding in the hills. Now and then he passed young soldiers with tortured expressions that meant their leave was running out. They glanced at his beard and sheep-skins, at the shepherd's staff, and at his glittering eyes, that said he spent all his time in the open air, and they envied him.

As he climbed the Gianicolo's thousand steps in a dim October sunset he smelled the leaves, felt the cool air above the stones, and was comforted by the special darkness of the steep hill on which he knew every turn, every rock, and every palsied iron rail.

He was half convinced that climbing the Gianicolo, coming up the steps, and rounding the corners was a pendulum in some great clockwork that would set everything right. On an evening like this, his father would be tending the fire, and his mother looking after dinner, in dispute with Luciana over how to set the table or the length of time that something needed to be cooked. The lights would be shining from the windows, and smoke would be rising from the chimneys. The leaves in the garden would be raked, the sidewalks swept. At dusk the house was like a lantern.

As he took the steps one by one, Alessandro prayed with all the gravity and passion that were in him for that which he had once merely taken for granted.

WHEN LUCIANA returned home at a quarter to eleven she opened the front door, stepped inside, and threw the bolt. Then she walked in the dark until she came to the wall by the stairs, where she searched for the light switch. As soon as the light went on, she stood for a moment to listen, and looked about apprehensively, lifting her eyes to the top of the stairs.

Though the house was cold and empty, Alessandro had been sitting in the living room for five hours. He was warm in his sheep-skin clothing, and he had remained in the darkness, hardly moving, staring at the faint shadows on the ceiling. He had called out and gone into every room. It was as he had remembered it, but no one was in, and he had no way of knowing where they had gone.

The fires were out and the ashes cold. No fresh food was in the kitchen. Several cartons of mail were on his bed, including a packet of letters that he had sent from the Bell Tower. Resting on this was a letter from an adjutant's office in Verona. *Famiglia Giuliani: Alessandro Giuliani, 5 Batt. Fant. Arresto, 19th River Guard, is detached for special service and out of communication until later notice. Please have patience for the allotted time.*

Alessandro imagined that everyone was out for dinner and would arrive later in a carriage. His father would take a long time to get out, and then they would come up the walk. Even if the lights of the house did not burst on simultaneously, the fires ignite, and the rooms suddenly smell like fresh flowers, it did not matter, if only they returned.

Perhaps his mother had been desperately ill but had not died after all. He would never believe any report until or unless it came directly from his father or Luciana.

When he entered his parents' room he felt as if he were a child again, driven there by a thunderstorm or the sound of a squirrel scampering across the roof, and he remembered when he lay between his father and mother, taunting ghosts and lightning.

Faint illumination came from the windows facing the city. The bed was curiously stiff and unused, with summer linen, but the paintings had not moved a millimeter and the furniture was positioned exactly where he had last seen it. He held his breath when he opened the clothes cupboards. They were full of familiar bathrobes, suits, dresses, and slippers. His mother's perfume was still strong on her clothes, and his father's jackets had their customary aroma of pipe tobacco.

He approached his father's long desk, which was in order except for one thing, the picture of Alessandro's mother as a young woman. The photograph of a smiling girl at age seventeen, in 1885, was centered on the blotter. In starlight alone, he could not recognize her face, but he could make out the pattern of the background against the subject. Its shape was familiar, like a country on a map. Still, a photograph propped up in the middle of a desk was not the kind of confirmation that would make him lose hope.

As he left the room for the upstairs hall, he stopped short. His head sank, and he turned around. When he reached back for the light switch he had difficulty finding it. Then he found it and the room became so bright that for a second he was not able to look up. His eyes went everywhere but to the desk. He swept them over all the familiar things—over the paintings, across the windows, to the bed, the books—but he had seen from the corner of his eyes exactly what he feared to see, and then he had no reason not to look anymore. The photograph of the smiling young girl was in a new frame. The frame was black.

As Luciana's eyes adjusted to the brightness her brother called to her but she didn't hear. "Luciana," he said, in a subdued voice, so as not to startle her.

She threw her arms in front of her chest. Tightening her fist, she stepped back.

"Rafi?" she asked.

"I'm sorry," Alessandro said, stepping into the light.

SATURDAY MORNINGS on the Gianicolo were as quiet as if time had stopped. Carriages might not pass for an hour or more, and you might not hear boots on the pavement for a day. If it were wet you would be aware not only of the raindrops but of the slower counterpoint of water falling from eaves and the undersides of iron rails after it had clung in rows of heavy teardrops that had marched to the point where they had to let go. And when it was sunny and dry you could smell the pine needles as the sun struck the soft ground underneath symmetrical rows of trees.

Alessandro lay for as long as he could in his own bed. After he opened his eyes and saw the marvelous eastern light on the ceiling and walls of his room, he suffered the kind illusion that nothing had changed. On this cool October day in Rome he thought of riding to the sea, of wandering on horseback through fields and past bonfires of olive branches that had been cut during the harvest, but as the light grew stronger, he remembered.

It was insanely luxurious to have a room in which to sleep in private, to have space and silence, and to be covered in a warm navy-blue silk robe. The paintings and statuary in the hallway, the cool gray light that came from the glass roof above the stairwell, and the very mass of the house, were intensely enjoyable. He ran his hands over the long and ancient cherry-wood desk that was placed against one wall of his room. Among the many things he had not seen in two years was wood with a finish. He thought it strange that, with his father gravely ill in a nearby hospital, his mother dead (Luciana had been astonished that after a year Alessandro had had to ask if it were true), and almost certain death facing him, he could take pleasure from the feel of a smooth desktop or the sound of brass hardware. But why not? When Gianfranco di Rienzi thought he was going to be shot in Venice the next day he concentrated upon the moon, the stars, and the bonfires until he seemed almost to float in the light. No matter that it was madness. Madness was appropriate at the end.

Alessandro knocked on Luciana's door.

"Come in," she said.

Her room was still blue, the furniture coverings still white with blue dots. On the bookcases were rows of schoolbooks, Japanese dolls, and bottles of perfume. "What time is it?" he asked. "I don't have a watch anymore. I never know what time it is."

"It's ten to nine," she said, after leaning to the side of her bed to peer at a delicate woman's watch on her night table.

"How can you tell with a watch that small? You can hardly see the face."

She propped herself up on the pillows. The night before, she had been tired and drawn, with shadows under her eyes and hardly any color in her cheeks. Alessandro had been moved by her appearance, for she was no longer a girl, and she had looked troubled.

She was youthful enough, however, to have recovered her beauty after one night's sleep. Now her cheeks were rosy, her eyes their customary bright blue, and her long blond hair, splayed across the linen, was shining from every shaft.

"You've gained weight," he said.

"I filled out after Mama died, it's true."

Her face, shoulders, and arms seemed entirely different. "You've become very beautiful."

"Oh," she said, as if to say that it didn't matter, because everything was going to waste.

To comfort her, he went into detail. "Your arms aren't skinny anymore," he said. "You have long arms, and they used to make you look like a grasshopper. And your shoulders... They have just enough roundedness and just, precisely, enough angularity..." His voice fell off short when he realized that her arms and shoulders, but for the slight straps of her nightgown, were bare, and that he had overstepped a line that had never before existed.

She, however, for want of company or want of affection, was frighteningly direct. "And here," she said, pressing her breasts to her in a modest gesture, like that of a new mother who is satisfied with nursing. "Suddenly, I'm full here."

"It's true," Alessandro agreed, sharing in her pride enough to banish his apprehension. "Luciana, I came in here to tell you something. Sooner or later, unless I go to America, they're going to catch me. I haven't decided what to do, but I'm not going anywhere until Papa gets well."

"How will you evade them?"

"I have strategies. For one, I'm going to dress like a banker—"

"You never did before," she interrupted.

"Deserters try not to be noticed. They look down and attempt to pass unseen. My best chance lies in doing exactly the opposite. The walk to the hospital is short and we can go through the passage in the wall so they won't see us going in or out of the house. If they come to the house, I'll hide. Only we know about the recess behind the armoire in the guest room."

Luciana pulled off the covers and left the bed. Although she did so matter-of-factly, and immediately pulled on a robe, he saw virtually every part of her as her nightgown rode up or was pulled taut against her. He was disconcerted, especially because she seemed to be aware of her effect on him. "I'll be ready at ten of ten," he said. "I want to be there when they open the doors. He's all right, isn't he?"

"This week," Luciana said, "the doctors have been saying that he's not going to die."

THEY LEFT the garden through a passage in the Aurelian Wall. After they emerged among the tall twisted pines of the Viale della Mura, a passerby would have thought that they had come from the Porta San Pancrazio, for the wall appeared unbreachable. The police might watch the entrance to the house for a decade and never imagine that Alessandro could come and go on a street in what was almost another part of the city.

The Viale della Mura was empty all the way to the Villa Sciarra, where they passed housewives on their way to market, and the vanguard of the old men who came every day to occupy the domino tables. Alessandro was clean-shaven and dressed in his best suit. His hair had grown to civilian length during the weeks in the mountains, and that morning he had washed it with shampoo, something that in the army simply did not exist. He was sunburned, he walked with a slight limp so that people would think he had been wounded and taken out of action, and he had pinned four medals over his breast pocket. These were not the bread-and-butter kind of decoration that soldiers of the line accumulate for serving in an active unit over time, and he had sent them home from the Bell Tower. Most deserters either would not have such decorations or would not think to wear them around the Villa Sciarra on a Saturday.

"I go every morning," Luciana informed him for the second or third time, "and stay from ten or ten-thirty through lunch. Then I come back at five and stay until ten or eleven.

"Sometimes he sleeps, and sometimes he sits up and seems as healthy as he ever was. We play chess, I read to him, and often we say nothing. We stare out the window."

"Then why is he there?"

"He can have terrible pain. We were in the midst of dinner a few days ago—it was quite pleasant. . . ."

"They bring two dinners?"

"If you pay. I eat at a little table next to the window. Suddenly Papa jumped forward as if someone had stuck a knife into him. All the dishes and his full wine glass overturned first onto the bed and then the floor. The sisters heard it and ran in to give him an injection. They made me leave. He's slept for most of the time since, but last night he stayed awake long enough for me to read to him."

"It's his heart?"

"Yes, his heart. They say he needs rest in a hospital."

"How long must he remain?"

Luciana threw up her arms just slightly. The barely perceptible breeze rippled her dress like the waters of a small lake. "They don't know."

"What have you been reading to him?"

"The newspapers. He's interested solely in the war news. He's looking for you. He has me read every report of every action and every unit. Sometimes he's very confused, and he thinks he's found you."

"How?"

"I don't know what his reasons are, but when he feels that you're there, hidden among the numbers and the names, he makes me read it over and over again."

As they walked through the Villa Sciarra, which, though private, was open to the public for much of the day, Luciana took her brother's arm.

He was overwhelmed by sensations so keen and clear that he was able to view with equanimity even the prospect of his own death, for the intense satisfaction he now found in nearly all things seemed to be the compression of many years.

Upon awakening that morning he had moved his arm across the covers. The sound of the linen, barely audible, was a great thing. The feel of gravity, too, was a surprising pleasure, as was the fact that he could extend his arm and bring it back, and that its strength was intact and served by the complicated apparatus of muscles, joints, ligaments, tendons, and bone compounded within his arm like a block and tackle used to raise a plinth.

They stopped for a moment in an open clearing paved with smooth stones. Children were playing at the edges, little boys kicking a soccer ball, and girls trying to propel hoops over stones, which was extremely hard to do.

Luciana was standing next to him, close enough so that now and then he felt her against his thigh through the cloth of his suit and the silk of her dress, which was a restrained but intense blue, with little snow-white boxes in a tight pattern. Her hair was shining in the indirect morning light, as were her sapphire-blue eyes. Because she was his sister, he assumed that he would take only the same kind of delight in her beauty that he had in all the other exquisite details that now loomed so large. The sound of the fountain directly opposite them across the square might have held him for hours. The water was black, cold, and it came from between perpetually wet black stones. Metal-colored goldfish were suspended within it just above the moss-covered bottom of the pool. It was now about to fall much farther and run to join streams that made their way through the city, almost unnoticed, to the Tiber. Each leaf on the path, in orange or brown, wet or dry, seemed to attract Alessandro's eye. He could feel the moisture in the air around plants in the walls that had held more rainwater than those on the flat ground, and now were giving it up in soft and invisible clouds that made almost imperceptibly cool currents on the wind.

"One moment, Luciana," Alessandro said, still holding her arm. "I want to look at the sky."

"Why?" she asked, thinking that, when he said it, he sounded remarkably like their father.

He looked at her to answer, sweeping his eyes across her eyes and then taking in all of the rest of her before he responded with a smile. When he looked up, she, too, bent her neck and narrowed her eyes to adjust to the brighter light from above.

It seemed as if they were staring at an airplane or a balloon, and one of the mothers in the Villa Sciarra shielded her eyes with her hand, almost in a salute, and scanned the sky.

Unlike the brittle blue of the Tyrrhenian that colored it from afar, the sky was pale and soft. Low clouds, slightly dirty, slightly pink, and slightly gold, scudded by on the sea wind with great speed and with hardly a sound.

THE MONUMENTAL hallways of the Hospital of San Martino were filled with soldiers in silent recuperation or soon to die. Every soldier could look up at the light as it tracked across the empty heights of the long galleries in a bright clockwork, streaming through the windows in luminous beams that struck the agitated dust. At the beginning and end of each double row of iron beds was a large table with an enormous arrangement of flowers upon it. Some visitors had already arrived, and they stood near the beds of their sons.

Alessandro and Luciana climbed a broad marble staircase from landing to landing and floor to floor. "Did he have to climb these stairs?" Alessandro asked.

"They carried him on a stretcher," Luciana answered. "They kept it perfectly level as they went up. The man who led bent down as far as he could, and the man who followed lifted his arms in the air as they turned at the landings. Papa seemed embarrassed."

"At one time he could have run these stairs without taking a breath."

"I won't ever be ashamed of being weak," Luciana said with youthful fire.

"Nor will I," her brother answered.

The attorney Giuliani's room was on the top floor in a corner, facing south and east. Four tall windows gave out on the city and the mountains over the treetops in the Villa Sciarra. The door was open, and Alessandro saw his father through a small hallway. The attorney Giuliani was propped up in an iron bed, a tiny figure in a cloud of glacially white sheets and pillows. A crimson blanket was neatly pulled up under an apron of sheets. Dozens of yellow roses filled two vases just beyond his bed, and he stared at them as they were struck by the morning light.

Alessandro was gripped with a momentary terror when he saw how frail his father had become in the two years they had been apart. Though the old man's hair was the same length, it seemed much longer in contrast to his emaciated face and neck. His legs, too, even under the covers, looked emaciated, like sticks, their mass atrophied.

His father now had a beard, an elegant, correct, Roman beard that was white, or at best silver with some dark gray.

Luciana walked straight into the room, approached the bed, and kissed her father. She knew that Alessandro had stopped at the door, and she did nothing to direct her father's attention to him.

"A beautiful dress," her father said in a subdued voice. "And a beautiful color." His hands moved across the covers in almost automatic seeking, the fingers contracting and relaxing, contracting and relaxing, as if they had already embarked on an independent journey.

"Have I seen that dress before?" he asked.

"Of course," Luciana answered defensively, "many times."

"I don't remember it."

"I wore it at the opera."

"What opera?"

"When we went with the judge from Pisa, and his wife, and his ugly son."

"He was a nice boy," the attorney Giuliani said.

"Not to me. He was rude and nasty."

"Because he was hurt."

"Hurt?"

"Yes."

"Who hurt him?" Luciana asked in a flash of temper.

"You did."

"*I* did?"

"The moment he saw you," the attorney Giuliani stated, forgetting that he was tired, "he was deeply hurt because you are so beautiful and he was so ugly. He knew that he had no chance."

"I wouldn't have cared what he looked like," Luciana protested.

"He admired you too much to understand that. He was not a great man, as he would have had to have been to proceed in his infatuation without flagellating himself."

Luciana screwed up her face in disbelief. "Flagellating himself? Papa, are you crazy?"

"I'm not crazy. I remembered how that poor louse suffered through every minute of *Tancredi*."

"*Nabucco.*"

"Whatever it was. He sat there glowing in the dark, red hot, mortified, frustrated, and ashamed. He was undergoing more physical pain then than I know now."

"How can you say that?"

"I remember," her father said. "Why are you wearing that dress now?"

As Luciana smiled, tears came to her eyes. "A surprise," she said.

"What surprise?"

"Papa, look." She gestured at the doorway, at Alessandro.

"Alessandro?" his father asked. "Is that you Alessandro?"

Alessandro closed his eyes.

"Yesterday," his father stated with great difficulty, "a flight of military planes passed over the city. I was able to see them clearly." He held his head high. "I could see the pilots, I could even see their hand signals. A dozen planes were flying in formation."

He paused. "I said to myself, I wonder if they will bring me my son."

ALESSANDRO FOUND himself caught up in the obligatory descriptions in which a visitor goes to the window to tell the patient about the things the patient cannot see. Almost as a rule, they are minor and ephemeral—a flight of ochre-colored steps leading down the hill, the small segment of a bridge otherwise hidden by palms, an undistinguished part of a villa, a brown awning, a horse cart passing through an opening in the Aurelian Wall.

They commented on the food, when it was supposed to arrive, and how it was always late, and they complimented the room itself. The bathroom was small, yes, but, apart from that, the attorney Giuliani's hospital room was a good place in which to recover, it was quiet, and it had high ceilings.

During the first day the hours passed slowly, as they tried to conceal from one another everything but a ritual optimism that only Luciana might have believed, had she not been able to see that her father and brother were as anxious as if they were about to board a ship to a place where they would stay forever, where they would be stripped of possessions and clothing, and where the streets were teeming with people who spoke another language.

They feared that they would be stripped not of their clothes and their possessions, but of their senses and their memories. They feared being so light that the only word that could describe what would happen to them was *ascension.* They feared that soon they would know everything, that they would lie promiscuously in the bodies of men and women and in the mechanics of every thought and every calculation, that they would rest high on individual grains of sand and feel the thunder of their overturning, that they would flow down streams, sit at the bottom of the sea in the dark, and be dashed upon the beach in the waves of cold winter storms.

The rivalries they had sustained, the ambitions they had harbored, the slights they had endured, and the desires that had made their hearts beat faster, now, if not forgotten, seemed minor. And yet the hours passed slowly, because they dared not say what they knew and they talked instead of things so strange and unexpected that Luciana was astounded, and often could do nothing but let her hands come to rest on her lap. The attorney Giuliani saw a cross-section of the sea on the wall of his room. At times he called it a waterfall. He was amazed as he watched it move, and would point to fish leaping inside it, storms, and breaking waves, as if his children could see everything that he could see.

During lunch, her father picked up his glass of wine and held it to the light. "Look how red it is," he said. Luciana's eyes darted to her brother.

"Stairwells are dark and cool at the bottom," the attorney Giuliani said, "and the upper levels expand with the light. You hardly ever pass anyone on the stairs anymore, especially on summer days when you enter, like a hunter, much more alert to every sound than you would be outside in the heat.

"Why are doctors always foreign?" the attorney Giuliani asked.

"What do you mean?" Luciana inquired, alarmed. When her father seemed either to lose control or become irrational she reacted with the impatient anger born of fear.

"My attending physician is Dutch," her father said.

"It must be the war," Alessandro commented.

"I don't think so. When my father died, his doctor—not his regular doctor, but the one with whom he ended up—was Spanish. Imagine, a Spanish doctor. The Spaniards are primitives who fight bulls, but it was a Sunday in August and all our esteemed Italian physicians were asleep in beach chairs. His doctor of fifty years had gone to Capri, and we couldn't reach him." The attorney Giuliani thought for a moment. "I'm not sure he would have come back even had we been able to reach him. The death of an old man isn't anything out of the ordinary. People say, well, he lived eighty years, and he was lucky to have had such a long life. This after the man in question has died in excruciating pain and perhaps with no less fear than if he had been a boy of eighteen—except that it's worse in a way, for by the time a man is old he's seen scores of people fall away, and he *knows*.

"And if a woman who is past fifty dies, no one but her husband and children even blink. When your mother died . . . Your mother was young. I remember her at nineteen, when she felt that she would live forever. When she passed away we didn't really hear from anyone. Isn't that strange. They didn't care.

"As I die I'll be holding her in my arms when she was close to your age now, Luciana, and the two of you, when you were babies. When you were infants I loved you more than you can imagine. In my flight through darkness I'll hold to that image: the four of us— your mother in her early twenties, and you at two and a half, or three.

"And my own father," their father said in a suddenly high and weak voice. "When I see him I will have to be a child myself. It wouldn't do for me to be an old man. Alessandro, can I be a child for the sake of my father, and a father for the sake of my children? Will God grant that?"

"I don't know," Alessandro said.

"How do you know?" his father asked.

Rather than disappoint him, Alessandro improvised. "I don't know for sure," he said, "but I can't imagine that God, who is so adept at linking parents with children, would so cruelly separate them. Perhaps it isn't anywhere near the truth. Perhaps I'm merely self-serving. I don't know, but I believe against all odds in exactly what you say."

"You don't care what anyone else thinks, do you?"

"No, Papa. I never did."

"That can only be because you believe."

"Yes."

"And how does God speak to you?"

"In the language of everything that is beautiful."

Alessandro stared at the sheets as they rested upon his father's legs. A nursing-sister came into the room, rapid and businesslike, wheeling a cart ahead of her. When she opened the door, the curtains leapt out the windows and fluttered as if they wanted to escape.

Though the attorney Giuliani was weak and tired he appeared to be neither sick nor in any danger, and to Alessandro it seemed as if his father had been condemned to a school or a barracks as punishment for being unable to bound up stairs or remember immediately the capital of a protectorate in Arabia. Soon he would return home, and by spring he would be sitting in the ruins of the garden, meditating upon the execution of his son. Despite his frequent mention of death, his children did not believe that his time had come, but when they arrived the next evening, he was sleeping and could not be roused.

"Has this happened before?" Alessandro asked Luciana, who had just come in from the nursing station.

"Yes."

"When does he wake up?"

"Once he woke up after about an hour. Another time he was like this for two days."

"What's the name of the doctor?"

"De Roos. They said he was here this afternoon just after we left."

"Why haven't we seen him?"

"I've seen him. He makes his rounds when the visitors are gone. He told me that, compared to most of his patients, Papa was in good health."

"But Luciana, behind the screens the place is full of soldiers with abdominal wounds, a whole battalion of them. They're dying."

"Why is it so quiet?"

"They don't scream when they die. Death is quiet. It gets its way with hardly a whisper. They've probably been dying here ten or twenty a day."

"Oh God."

"What does the doctor look like?"

"He's your age. He wears a bow tie and smokes little cigars."

When Alessandro found him, De Roos had just gone into a records room. He was the model of politeness and consideration, and Alessandro soon sensed that this was not manner alone.

"What can I do for you?" De Roos asked.

After Alessandro had introduced himself, he said, "Please tell me about my father. Don't hide anything. He may not have time for that, and I don't either: I'm going back to the front."

In his white coat and bow tie, with a small tin box of cigars clearly visible in the side pocket and a stethoscope arched over his neck like a cat that has learned to ride on its owner's shoulders, the doctor was the picture of authority and expertise. His was the latest knowledge. He was fresh. He would neither miss a clue nor make a mistake from habit. His intelligence made him so pleasantly alert that he probably did not have to rely on habit.

"I have more hope for your father than I do for many of my other patients. He might walk out of here."

"Are you doing everything you can?"

"No. We're understaffed. We lack sufficient quantities of the drugs we need. When your father isn't able to get the proper medication, he slips into a coma. If he dies, that's when it'll be."

"What medicine?"

De Roos said a word that, for some reason, Alessandro was unable to take in.

"What is it, again?"

De Roos repeated it slowly, but, seeing that Alessandro was not comprehending, he produced a piece of paper and a fountain pen, and wrote the word so fast that Alessandro could not have fathomed it unless he had already known it. It looked like a tangle of branches in a forest, it was Latin, and the waves and jagged edges of the doctor's pen strokes defeated Alessandro's eyes. Nonetheless, Alessandro folded the paper and carefully put it in his breast pocket.

"The army has it," De Roos said, coughing, and then hitting the tin box with the palm of his right hand as if to punish the tobacco. "They use it to stabilize the heart in surgery, of which more is now being performed than ever in the history of man. We get very little, but I have heard that battalions of soldiers in the mountains scour meadows for the plant from which it is extracted."

A chill went up and down Alessandro's spine. "Can you buy it on the black market?" he asked.

De Roos considered the idea. "Probably not. Most of the demand is satisfied. The army has its own closed system. It's just the old people who can't get enough, and I don't think the black market is attuned to their needs or ours."

"But this is partly a military hospital."

"For soldiers who have been written off. The surgery is done up north. Then they drop them behind the lines to recover or to die. About seventy percent die."

"You'd never know it. The visitors don't seem to know it."

"The visitors always look worried."

"Yes, but they keep up a good front, and they dress very carefully."

"Ah, they do, but near the end that all falls apart."

"Don't you do surgery here, to save the ones who are dying?"

"We drain the wounds, sometimes we clean out a cavity. It's hardly surgery. Anyway, the army doesn't think so, not from the way they ration out supplies."

Alessandro retrieved the little piece of folded paper and held it up. "How much do you need?" he asked.

"As much as anyone would care to give."

"And when will you next examine my father?"

De Roos looked at his watch. "Probably around midnight. It's hard to say exactly. If you'd like I can write a note so you can enter the hospital and be present when I do see him."

"Thank you."

"Around midnight, give or take an hour."

"I have to bring my sister home. Then I'll be back."

De Roos was writing, in the same unfathomable script. "She can be there, too," he said.

"You've noticed her?"

"How might I not have noticed her?" It seemed to Alessandro that the doctor was taking refuge in ambiguity, until De Roos said, "She's insanely beautiful." That was all he said, and he was in perfect control, as if he had simply been making a clinical observation. He folded the second paper and gave it to Alessandro.

"Thank you, thank you so much."

"No," De Roos said. "You mustn't thank me. The relatives of patients thank the physician as if the physician were God. It's no good, and if the patient dies it turns to ash—not just for them, but, as you can imagine, for me. I'll see you later."

Alessandro bounded up the stairs. At least now he had done something to further his father's chances. The two pieces of paper in his pocket seemed to lift him up as if he were attached to a sky-hook. *Sky-hook* was a term that his father sometimes used, the meaning of which Alessandro had never really understood, for, after all, no such thing existed.

LUCIANA WAS asleep in her bed as Alessandro passed furtively through the opening in the wall and ran for the Villa Sciarra. If the *carabinieri* happened upon him at that hour they would demand to see his papers. The gates of Villa Sciarra were closed. He climbed them, dropped in, and moved through the dark with only the sounds of the gravel paths under his feet, the streams, and the fountains, to guide him. Though he could see nothing, he moved ahead, all of his senses sweeping the way in front of him for any sign or signal.

"Good," De Roos said quietly when Alessandro walked into his father's room. The young doctor, who had just arrived, was shaking down a thermometer. "Help me turn your father toward you."

Alessandro saw that his father was awake.

De Roos spoke to him. "Signore, we are going to take your temperature."

The attorney Giuliani, disoriented but wise, nodded and tried to turn in bed. He couldn't. Alessandro took him in his arms and pulled him over. Though his son held him as if they were at the edge of a cliff, the old man had only turned on his pillows so that the doctor could insert the thermometer in his rectum.

"You see, Alessandro, what it all comes to?" he asked, glassy-eyed.

"Papa," Alessandro said. "Forgive me."

"For what?" his father asked, as his head rested on Alessandro's shoulder and Alessandro grasped him forcefully. "For being young when I'm old?"

"Yes."

"I won't forgive you for that." His father took a breath as the thermometer was withdrawn, fell back, and looked at his son. "It's my salvation."

"You have a fever," De Roos said loudly into the attorney Giuliani's right ear, "because you have a cardiac infection. The very weakness of your heart allows the infection to rage, further weakening it, and so on. If we can stabilize the heart, we can reverse the decline."

"Good," the father said, as if he had not understood, as if the doctor were a fool who didn't know what was ahead.

"How do you feel?" Alessandro asked, adopting the same authoritative tone.

His father looked at him half with suspicion and half with amusement. He shrugged his shoulders. "Not all that good," he said, weakly.

"Do you have pain?" De Roos asked.

"No."

"Are you afraid?"

"No."

"Good. Rest, Signore. If all goes well, you'll walk out of here."

"If all goes well," the attorney Giuliani echoed, in the same voice that he would have used to draw attention to a spurious clause in a contract.

De Roos took Alessandro aside and they spoke in the considered manner of young men who are given the task of controlling events that they do not yet comprehend and that they do not yet know are uncontrollable. The attorney Giuliani understood this, and had seen it a dozen times before. He didn't blame them for their efforts. To the contrary, he was seduced by the hope that seemed to come to them so easily. He knew that to guide themselves when they couldn't see, to be firm in the face of the unknowable, and to do what was right when they didn't know what it was, they—even the doctor—had to posture. When he saw that Alessandro was trying to do the impossible, he realized that Alessandro was moved by love.

He understood that Alessandro knew, and yet did not know, that they would soon part forever. Above all, the posturing alerted him. He recognized the tone into which Alessandro had been forced, for, once, a long time before, he had been forced into it himself.

ALESSANDRO DID not visit Orfeo at home, because a poor man with burning ambition can hate his house as much as he hates the many other things that weigh upon him. Instead, he went to the palatial Ministry of War, where Orfeo sat on a raised platform overlooking hundreds of scribes, typists, and sealing-wax clerks who were busy manufacturing the documents that fueled the war.

Orfeo was hunched over an enormous desk, scratching with a plume at an unrolled sheet of vellum weighted casually at its four corners with heavy royal seals. His feet did not even begin to reach the floor, he was dressed like a dandy, and anyone who looked at him could see that he wasn't merely copying the proclamation, but composing it as well, for the features of his unusual face seemed to be dancing in the rapture of creation, and he hummed a song to match the rhythm of his prose.

A minute later, in his private office, where one wall was of heavy vault doors and the other of glass, he kept glancing through the panes at his underscribes, and he spoke to Alessandro in a mad whisper.

"Of course scribes have always cleared up their masters' punctuation, adding a comma here, a hyphen there. And spelling, well, that goes without saying. If you're supposed to copy the word *tintinnabulation,* and it's spelled *tintinnablution,* or if *heinous* is spelled *anus,* as sometimes occurs, what are you supposed to do, leave it?"

Now his voice began to rise, and Alessandro realized that at the end of the interview he would be raving.

"And then come adverbs, wrongly used prepositions, et cetera.

We correct them. We have to. And we hold our masters in no little contempt when they are cripples with the pen.

"Ah, but then where is the great mortal leap! I'll tell you. It's when the exalted one infuses into the body of a scribe sufficient quantities of the sap that flows in the boiling passages of the bony valleys of the moon...." Orfeo suddenly jumped as if a pin had been thrust into him. "And Mars!" he said, apoplectically.

"What?"

"Yes, the mortal leap is a gift of holy gracious sap from the exalted one."

"I don't understand, Orfeo."

"It means I write what I choose!"

"You do?"

"Yes. Yesterday, for example, a battalion of the *bersaglieri* was supposed to have been moved to a new sector on the Isonzo, but I withdrew them to an encampment in the Po Valley, took away their machine guns, and issued them vast amounts of beef."

"Why?"

"Because," Orfeo said, gravely, "when the world ends, the cloak of the exalted one will drag across the Po Valley."

"Christ, Orfeo," Alessandro said.

"That's nothing! You think the king himself has escaped my sap-driven edition? Not a word that comes from him through me is unchanged—subtly, of course, but it's necessary for me to put my stamp on history by jumbling it apart and putting it back together."

"All revolutionaries think that, Orfeo," Alessandro stated, "and they're never as good at putting it back together as they are in jumbling it apart."

"I'm not a revolutionary," Orfeo said. "I'm the conduit, the reservoir, the nozzle of the blessed sap that pounds against the bone-dry valleys of the moon. The sap makes the birds fly. It whistles through their hearts like the spray of a fountain."

"Orfeo."

"When explosives from Factory Thirteen in Pisa are supposed to go to Factory Six in Verona to be stuffed inside artillery shells, I send them to Milan for packing into flares. I run the war the way I see fit, and I've been doing a good job, because I've been blessed by the exalted one, who has directed at my person great quantities of invigorating sap.

"The gracious one has ushered me to this spot because my destiny is to invigorate the armies and liberate the world from common rabbits and scrugs. Though sometimes I want to stop short, to stop everything, and, instead of struggling or fighting, instead of Cumbrinal the Oxitan, and Oxitan the Loxitan, I would look up at the light and ask God to take me up and show me what is great and make it so I don't have to wait anymore. I could fly. My back would not be bent. I would not have a hump. I would be handsome. I would be light. I would be tall." He smiled, and then he placed his finger on the side of his nose. A scribe at one of the many long tables had asked permission to pee, and Orfeo had granted it.

"Orfeo, my father needs this," Alessandro said, unfolding the paper with the name of the drug written on it.

"Who wrote this?" Orfeo asked.

"A doctor."

Orfeo shook his head slowly back and forth. "The world is truly going to the dogs. I'll have a hundred thousand units sent to him tomorrow morning. Why are you always asking for favors?"

"What favors, apart from this?"

"I've been doing you favors all along."

"You have?"

"Who do you think got you in the River Guard; what was it, the Ninth?"

Alessandro was suddenly weakened by rage. He could hardly speak. "You?" he asked.

"Me, the male, the one."

"Why?"

"You were supposed to have been put on the *Euridice,* that's why. I had a bad feeling about it, so I moved you to the River Guard. How many survived the *Euridice*? You see? I was right.

"I'll do you favors, yes, because I owe you a certain amount of respect and gratitude, but gratitude is not immortal. I have to turn from the past to the gracious sap. Quite frankly, Alessandro, I'm running to the end of my tether with doing the Giulianis favors. Now, I'm the important one. I don't quake anymore. I don't have to sit and eat my own sap. I'm the chief scribe. As my powers well through my fingers, I touch the soft open eye of the monster that is eating the century. Cumbrinal the Oxitan. Oxitan the Loxitan. Loxitan the Oxitan. I told you once that I'd ride upon his back. Now I'm his master, the master of worlds. You drove me to it; the so-called 'typewriter' drove me to it.

"Politicians and kings suffer the agony of constraint. Not I, I need merely dip my pen in the holy blessed sap and my orders are followed to the letter, with never any consequences for my person, which is totally anonymous. Ah, but I'm more than that, I'm blessed, I'm omnipotent, I'm baked in sap."

Without even looking at Alessandro, Orfeo strode from his office and mounted the platform. Breathing heavily, he fixed his gaze upon an invisible horizon and declared so that the scribes and clerks would hear, "I am lightning! I am a lion!"

"ORFEO IS completely mad," Alessandro told his sister in a thunderstorm with the rain beating against the windows of his room and the wind rising in gusts that propelled water through crevices that were supposed to have been sealed. "He sits on a platform amidst hundreds of scribes. He's supposed to copy orders and proclamations, but he changes them at will and composes new ones according to whim—always in the proper style and with the proper seals and codes."

"Shouldn't someone be told?" Luciana asked innocently.

"Who's going to tell?"

"One of the scribes."

"Them? They're terrified. They raise their hands even to ask permission to go to the water cabinet."

"How can that be?"

"They're young. If he fires them they go straight into the trenches. He has it all figured out. It's not because he's evil, but because of what he believes to be his mission."

"The holy sap?"

Alessandro nodded.

"Alessandro, you must tell someone."

"Me? It was difficult enough for me to walk into the Ministry of War. If I made an accusation about one of its employees the first thing they'd want to know is who I am. I might as well shoot myself now."

"I'll tell them."

"They won't believe you, and it probably wouldn't make any difference. Tomorrow they're going to deliver the medicine to the hospital. Let things rest for the moment."

"They'll find out. He'll give himself away."

"He's been there for two years, and seems quite comfortable."

As a blast of wind blew ribbons of fog through the garden, Luciana turned her head to listen, and the shape of her long neck came clear. Luciana had become, as De Roos had put it, insanely beautiful. In the first week, Alessandro had done a great deal of looking away. To begin with it was easy and habitual, but then he could do it only by redirecting his attention, or by a deliberate relaxation in which he put all thoughts of her out of his mind. He wanted to touch her, to kiss her, and though his desire for her was so wrong that he likened it to setting off a bomb in the middle of the house, he was unable to banish the image of her delicate hands, her clear blue eyes, her hair the color of white gold.

For the sake of his father, who lay dying in a hospital bed, and for the sake of his mother, who was already gone, he would not succumb to his sister's grace, to her peach-and-rose-colored flesh, and to her frazzled unguarded charm. After he was arrested, they would keep him in a cell, they would bring him one morning to a courtyard to stand him in front of a shattered wall, and he would see his life about to end. He wondered if at that moment he would think of Luciana, and he hoped that he would not.

"We have to sleep," he said, rising, and turning to leave. She seemed almost offended, but as he walked down the dark hallway to his room, her door closed as it always had.

Alessandro sat on his bed, listening to the rain. Without taking his feet from the floor he lay on his side as if he were embracing an invisible presence. He drew his arms closer to him, until they were clasped against his chest and his eyes were filled with tears. And then, in a hopeless whisper, he said, "Papa."

HE WAS awakened by cracks of thunder that threatened to shatter the windows. The rain was driven so hard that it backed up in the gutters and cascaded from the roof in solid curtains of water that turned silver when the lightning flashed. Rain like this emptied the streets and made the city into a lifeless model of itself. The Tiber would already be in flood and the only people outside would be the sentries who stood before palaces and ministries, and even they had little houses made for chocolate soldiers.

Alessandro went to the long table, where he put his face close to the brass carriage clock that Luciana had always taken the trouble to wind, even when he was not there, even when his mother was dying of influenza. When she wound the clocks she walked all alone from room to room with the keys jangling in her hands. He could hear the ticking over the rain, though the rain was so hard that it sounded like gravel being spilled across metal sheets, but he couldn't see the hands. He turned to sight them through the corner of his eye, but it was still too dark. The ticking grew in intensity. He had no idea how long he knelt before the clock, staring at it without seeing, listening to the thunder of the machinery within.

Then a bolt of lightning struck the Gianicolo somewhere close by, and the face of the clock was illuminated so brightly that its image was burned into Alessandro's eyes for minutes. The hour hand held its breath and pointed off to the right halfway between two and three, the minute hand had succumbed to gravity and was resting at one notch before the half hour. Now Alessandro was wide awake, and he pulled on an oilcloth jacket and went downstairs with an insatiable craving to go into the night.

It was raining so hard that the water ran down his neck and soaked his shirt. He entered the garden, which was covered in a shallow pool of water exploding in a hundred thousand places as the rain beat down upon it. At one point he bent over and pressed his palm against the white gravel on the path in the center, as if it were the bed of a stream. Gusts of wet wind lashed at him from all directions as the trees and hedges shuddered under the weight of the rain.

THE NEXT day was sunny, clear, and unusually quiet. Rome sometimes became as dramatically silent as if everyone had left it. You could hear the wind rushing through leaves and reeds just as it did at the seaside, and the sky was a deep, dizzying, oceanic blue. Children were in shady classrooms, clerks wrote their figures in cool shadow, and the tops of the trees glistened in the sun like sequins.

Alessandro and Luciana sat near the window in their father's hospital room, listening to him breathe in his sleep. The sun came in sharply, bathing the blood-red geraniums in a window-box in unworldly fluorescence and drawing a sharp black triangle of shadow on the butter-colored sill. Now and then cool air lifted the curtains inward and dropped them again, as if they were riding on the waves.

In waiting for their father to awaken, they could not talk, but sometimes their eyes met. When nurses looked in they saw two exemplary young people, healthy and strong, dressed like patricians. Their father himself was handsome and imposing, he spoke well, he was engaging, he was obviously a man of great resources. On this cool October day, the Giulianis appeared to be in control.

The nursing-sisters came quickly when the attorney Giuliani called. Nothing was forgotten, every service requested was provided, and De Roos or the other doctors who made their rounds—specialists in infection, the heart, and Röntgenology—had long technical conversations with Alessandro, thus keeping him far better informed than most of the other supplicants who were drawn daily to the hospital.

Alessandro thought that if he paid and demanded close attention he might catch a fault in treatment or stimulate the doctors and nurses to do so, and that if he kept up the privileged bearing that, oddly enough, had begun as a fugitive's method of evading capture, he could provide for his father a small margin that in desperate circumstances might be critical in preserving his life. He had seen it a thousand times in the River Guard: impeccable, careful, meticulous soldiers seemed to survive longer, or at least to be more conspicuous as they survived, though, of course, even they were sometimes instantly disemboweled by a shell that came from the blue.

He kicked Luciana's white stocking. When she looked at him, he held up his finger as if to say, listen. Without the patience her brother had learned in two years' watch for infiltrating enemy soldiers, she went back to her dreaming.

He kicked her again, and pointed down the hill.

She leaned forward. She could just barely hear a noise some-where in the streets that fell to the Tiber.

"That's a horse pulling a caisson."

"How do you know?"

"I've spent two years with the sound."

For the next five minutes Alessandro listened to the clip clop of an army-shod horse and the distinctive squeaking of a caisson. As they came up the hill in the sunshine, he heard them through the red and green of the sunlit geraniums, and he felt the wind that carried the sound.

Guided by a soldier who seemed to be sleepwalking, the horse drew up to the hospital. The soldier looked at the sign on the hospital's wrought-iron gate, and then, with the deep depression of a private who has drawn garrison duty and been doomed to spend the most adventuresome period of his life as an office boy, opened the top of the caisson and took out a large package.

Luciana was by now leaning over the sill, and her hair caught the sun like a flair. "Perhaps Orfeo isn't as mad as we think," she said.

"No," Alessandro corrected. "Orfeo can give the medicine to dying soldiers only because he has taken it from dying soldiers."

"That isn't mad. It's neutral."

"It's by no means neutral, Luciana, it's violent and it's mad."

The attorney Giuliani awoke, breathing as if he were resting after a foot-race. His eyes went first to the blank walls, then to the sunlight, and then to his children. Though awake, he seemed in some ways like a man who is asleep. His breathing was labored and loud, his eyes were glassy, and he hardly moved.

"Did you hear the thunderstorm, Papa?" Luciana asked.

The attorney Giuliani turned to his daughter, waiting for her to explain. His expression showed that he had no memory of a thunderstorm. "I missed it," he said weakly.

"It was tremendous!" she announced with such enthusiasm and buoyancy that Alessandro smiled. "Ten bolts of lightning hit so

426 | A SOLDIER OF THE GREAT WAR

near the house, and in such rapid succession, that I thought I was going to fall down. I had the same feeling of being out of control that you get in a boat that is too small on a sea that is too windy!"

"It's a blind," her father said.

"What's a blind?" Alessandro asked.

"Memory of things like days at the sea, or thunderstorms."

"I love those things," Alessandro said. "You can't imagine how much I love them."

"Alessandro, in memory, things, objects, and sensations merely stand in for the people you love." He had to rest and breathe before he continued. After a while, he said, "If I long for a thunderstorm in Rome sixty years ago, or seventy, for the heavy rain and the disheveled lightning, for the wet trees that were completely free and completely abandoned, it's not because of the rain, or the quiet, or the ticking of the clock in the hallway—all of which I remember—but because of my mother and my father, who held me at the window as we watched the storm."

"Papa," Alessandro said, with assured optimism, "the medicine came this morning, in an ammunition caisson. Orfeo sent it. The hospital didn't have any, but now they can stabilize your heart. Now you'll be able to fight the fever with all your strength, and in a week or ten days we'll bring you home."

"Sandro, what do my eyes look like?"

"They're all right," Alessandro said, though his father's eyes were cloudy and gray.

"You know what happens?"

"When?"

"You betray your parents."

"Papa, you're talking nonsense."

The attorney Giuliani shook his head as if to signify that he agreed, but then he returned to what he had been saying. "When your parents die, Alessandro, you feel that you have betrayed them."

"Why?" Luciana asked.

"Because you come to love your children more. I lost my mother and father to images in photographs and handwriting on letters, and as I abandoned them for you, the saddest thing was that they made no protest.

"Even now that I'm going back to them, I regret above all that I must leave you."

"You're not going back to anybody," Alessandro told him. "We'll solve those problems later."

"Alessandro," his father said, almost cheerfully. "You don't understand. This kind of problem is very special: *it has no solution.*"

LATER IN the morning, De Roos came in holding a hypodermic needle as if it were a dueling pistol. Drops of liquid emerged from the hollow end of the needle and slowly slid down the shaft. The attorney Giuliani was impassive.

"We have it," De Roos announced. "A hundred thousand units. It'll hold us for months, a very great thing. What this does, Signore," he said, vigorously wiping the attorney Giuliani's frail arm with alcohol-soaked gauze, "is to make your heart as even and temperate as the heart of a young horse. Not as strong," he added, plunging the needle in, "but as even and as steady. And if your heart doesn't lag, doesn't race, and doesn't skip beats, you'll see, all will follow onto an even keel." He gripped the attorney Giuliani's hand, squeezed it, and quickly let go. "You have a good chance now, Signore. You have a good chance."

"I hope so," the attorney Giuliani said quietly as De Roos left.

"I'd be very grateful," he told his children, "if I could put this off, but, Alessandro, promise me that when the time comes you'll be with me."

"I'll be there," Alessandro said, "if I'm still alive."

"The house," the attorney Giuliani started to say, as if now he might inquire about the condition of the house that he had been convinced he would never see again, but he was interrupted by the sudden appearance of a group of orderlies and nurses clumsily wheeling-in a bed in which lay an unconscious soldier.

They took no notice of the Giulianis, and moved their patient about as if no one else were in the room. Luciana felt her heart go into check. Alessandro asked if they had the right room.

"This is the room," an orderly said, "and we're going to bring another one."

The attorney Giuliani fell back against his pillows. The dying soldier, whose eyes were closed and whose lips were white, had told him far more about his chances than had the doctor.

"We need the privacy!" Alessandro said to Luciana. "He's grown used to this room. The balance is delicate." As he left, Luciana went to her father to be comforted as well as to comfort.

In the hallways outside, orderlies were running a railroad, and every bed in the hospital seemed to be in transit. Patients from the enormous halls on the first floors were being moved to the small chambers upstairs. On the stairs themselves, the procession of orderlies and nuns transporting men on stretchers looked like something from a religious tableau, for they moved in and out of mitred beams of light alive with flashing dust.

Flattening himself against the railings to let the stretcher-bearers rise, Alessandro made his way downstairs. When he found De Roos, he asked, "What is it?"

"We've been ordered to triple our capacity all at once."

"All at once?"

"By tomorrow afternoon."

"Why?"

"The Germans and the Austrians," De Roos said, "have broken the front on the Isonzo."

"Where?" Alessandro asked.

"Everywhere."

"Everywhere? That's impossible."

"They tell us that a million men are in flight."

Alessandro raced back upstairs, on fire. Perhaps he and Luciana could care for their father at home. Perhaps, in the confusion of a million men in flight, he could rejoin the River Guard, or the army would proclaim an amnesty, reclaim the deserters, and make a final stand against the enemy, who was now in Italy itself.

He felt like a soldier once again. When he met a military messenger on the stairs he urgently asked him where the front had collapsed.

The messenger looked at him with the brotherly look that soldiers have for one another in civilian places, and took note of Alessandro's medals. "At Caporetto," he answered, "but they say the line has folded everywhere. Maybe they can regroup."

As Alessandro climbed the stairs with the nursing-sisters, the orderlies, and the mortally wounded soldiers on stretchers, he was full of schemes. They would take his father home, get him out of the room that was now a ward of the dying, allow him once again some sunlight and tranquillity. He was in his eighth decade, and he deserved privacy and honor. When he was well, Alessandro, with Guariglia and Fabio, would rejoin the 19th River Guard. His father would live, he would be forgiven. The winter would be hard and dangerous, but then spring would come.

He came to his father's room, and his heart went out to Luciana, for three soldiers were there, not a single one conscious, and delicate Luciana, with her elbows on the covers, was trying to shield her father from the presence of death.

Alessandro approached the bed. "Papa, I spoke to De Roos, and I'm going to speak to him again. Perhaps we can take you home, to your own room, with a private nurse."

"Alessandro," his father said. "Don't fear for me."

"I want to take you home."

"You must understand that I'm your father, Alessandro. I'm your father. I came before you, I split the path into this world, and

I'll split the path into the next. It isn't unreasonable, and you mustn't fear, for you will follow in time, and then, it will all come clear."

"I'm going to get De Roos," Alessandro said.

He made his way downstairs again, and brought back the doctor, who thoroughly examined the patient. "You may know something I don't," De Roos said to their father, "but I don't think so. I see no imminent danger. After a few more days, we should start to think about your going home."

The attorney Giuliani lifted his hand slightly, smiled, and fell asleep.

"I'll stay with him," Luciana said to Alessandro. "Go do what you have to do."

As Alessandro set out on what he realized might be his last walk through Rome, the sun was blazing in the cool air and the city was half gold, half blue.

THE TREES on the banks of the Tiber had not lost their leaves, and as the wind coursed through them it rattled their brittle foliage and raised fantastic black clouds, for Rome was occupied by millions of birds, perching on every branch, singing as if to warm the wind, hopping about in mad distraction on rails and cornices. The starlings, warblers, finches, and swallows had come from Northern Europe, the Baltic, and Scandinavia, and were about to cross to Africa, to the deserts and the savannahs, the Congo, and the Cape of Good Hope.

Their journey was so deep and impulsive that even at rest they knew only delirium and drive, and their immediate and explosive rising at any sound or motion was not an indication of fear but rather of the love of flight. When someone below merely clapped his hands, when a truck lurched by, or when the wind itself became anxious or fierce, they rose in a buoyant cloud that hovered over the trees like a ball of hot smoke and then formed into a wing that rallied back and forth until it broke into a hundred thousand anarchic flights and the air was uniformly colored by birds darting on the winds of catastrophe.

The smaller birds rose with a deafening sound. Sometimes their flickering mass was shifted by the wind, like a black balloon, but one by one they returned to their perches, gliding to a landing with the seriousness of new pilots, and then they jumped and chirped in the branches until they took to the air once again.

As the warblers and finches filled the skies, people looked up at the weaving above them and felt their more prosaic burdens lighten. The starlings were a plague, almost like bats, though somewhat smoother as they moved. They were the birds that formed the clouds that held the sunlight and the air, and hovered gently over the swollen Tiber. Though they seemed to float with great ease, Alessandro discovered in watching them that the motion of each one was no less a struggle and no less beautiful for their having been caught up in such a way that their individual paths were hard to trace, for if you followed one, and if you had the patience, if your eyes were quick enough to keep him separate and to stay with him in the dizzying turns, you could see that the way he took the air was a great thing.

But of all the birds resting in the trees along the Tiber at the end of October, none was half the flier, half the sounder, half the whistler, or half the darter of the swallow. The swallows flew in great circles, picking up speed, and rising like leaves in a whirlwind. They ascended in this madness, climbing up and up, until they flew among the higher and thicker clouds, in the soft and rosy walls of which they would disappear and from which they would then suddenly burst in surprise. Though you could barely see them—at those altitudes they were only spots and flecks that vanished as readily as they came into view, as if they were merely the coloration of the air—it was very clear that in the higher altitudes they encountered something of extraordinary beauty and import, which is why they strained so hard to rise and stayed so long.

Coursing from cloud to cloud, in roseate light, they had escaped, they knew the pure and the abstract and were freed from everything save light, force, and proportion. The waves of air high above the clouds were more hypnotic than waves in the sea. The light was a burst of pink and gold, and the color of the sky ran from China blue to the pale white that held the sun.

And yet, though they were taken by the wind, and flew like golden confetti in the clouds, and might have stayed, they descended, they came down, they whistled like rockets as they fell toward the ground. They chose to return, as if they had no choice, and what struck Alessandro above all was the consummate and decisive beauty of their fall. It was not a hopeless fall, for as they shot downward they fought the air, and, ascending momentarily with great strain, they sailed off to left or right, and circled about on the plateau they had marked, before another dizzying drop, another spreading of wings, and another partial ascension.

They seemed to fly faster than the imagination could imagine. They turned with breathtaking force. They made perfect curves. The air sang with their passage.

And when they were finished, these small birds that had been flecks of gold airborne on light and wind in a place from which they need never have returned, they settled gently in the dark spaces among the branches, and here, at the end, they sang a simple and beautiful song.

GUARIGLIA'S SHOP was in a ramshackle building that was part of a ruin. Hanging from heavy wooden beams and cast-iron rods were hundreds of harnesses and bridles. Two dozen saddles were mounted on small logs that projected from the walls.

Guariglia looked different out of uniform, yet neither better nor worse. Although his worn leather apron suggested that he knew his trade (and he did), he did not seem like a man with good prospects. When Alessandro entered the shop, Guariglia was anxious.

He crossed the floor, locked the door, and put up his lunch card. Alessandro noticed that Guariglia, too, wore all his medals. A small chill ran up Alessandro's back when he realized that no doubt every deserter in Italy had decided on the same strategy. Guariglia, too, limped, but he was not pretending: his left leg below the knee was wood.

"What happened?" Alessandro asked.

"A harness-maker doesn't need legs. He only needs his hands."

"Who did this to you?"

As Guariglia walked to the back of the shop, Alessandro saw his children illuminated in the light of a brazier—a boy of about five and a girl of three. They huddled in a corner, with little leather horses in their hands, afraid to move.

"It's all right," Guariglia told them. He took them into his arms one at a time, and then they went to play. Embracing them as if he would never see them again, he had paused as he held them, taken a breath, and briefly closed his eyes.

"How can you live this way?" Alessandro asked as the children resumed galloping their leather horses across fields and forests on the floor.

"I have no choice."

"I don't understand why you submitted to such a thing. It's your leg, for Christ's sake."

"I submitted to nothing," Guariglia said firmly. "Harness-makers must sometimes work with the thickest and most stubborn pieces of leather. Did you ever cut a saddle? A harness-maker knows nothing if he doesn't know how to cut. We have the tools and the practice, and we cut leather, brass, and iron all day long."

"A harness-maker did it? You're lucky you didn't die. Who was it?"

Guariglia smiled half with embarrassment and half with pride. When Alessandro's silence seemed as if it would last forever,

Guariglia broke it. "I did it for them," he said, looking at the children. "It wasn't that difficult when I thought of why I had to do it."

"How did you stay conscious?"

"I willed it. I tied my leg above the knee for a long time. After that the whole thing was numb and there wasn't much blood. I made everything clean, I drank half a bottle of brandy, I bathed it all in alcohol, and I had the right tools. I can't tell you how much it hurt. It took an hour. What an hour. After I cauterized the wound I was near death for a week, but then I recovered."

Alessandro was astonished.

"When I pass military police, they salute! How do you like that? I've never been asked for my papers, not once. At my age, with this," he said, patting the wooden leg, "with the medals… We're moving to the south as soon as we can. I'll use a different name. After the war, when things settle down, we'll come home.

"Alessandro, I killed at least eight of the enemy, that I know of. I served in the line for more than two years. I did my part. They took me away from this one," he said, meaning the girl, "before she was a year old."

"You don't have to justify yourself to me, Guariglia. I gave you the idea."

Guariglia shook his head. "No you didn't. I'd been thinking about it since the first day. I think I gave you the idea."

"The police may simply come and take you away."

"We're leaving soon," Guariglia said. "Until then, I don't have any other place to go. We live upstairs, and I might as well work. It could take months until they get around to us, and, if they just walk in, I'll tell them that I'm my cousin. I'll make something up. They'll see my leg."

"Do you need money?"

"I always need money, but not the way you mean. I'll know when they come, because they'll take Fabio first."

"Why?"

"The alphabet. *Adami* comes before *Guariglia.* He works on the next street over, between here and the piazza, in the cafe on the corner. He doesn't even bother to wear medals, because he's too young, and he knows that trick won't work for him."

"What about America?"

"He doesn't care about anything but laying Englishwomen who come to his cafe."

"He might like American women. They have lots of them in America, although he may not know that."

"It isn't that he's dumb, Alessandro, it's that he's pretty. His face skates over his brain, if you know what I mean. If he's not caught, I won't be. And if they come for him, there's a place underground where I can stay for a few days."

"A catacomb?"

Guariglia nodded.

"That's probably the first place they'd look."

"They're afraid. They go there only when their officers force them to."

"How do you know?"

"I've been there. Alessandro, at least ten thousand deserters are living under the city right now."

"They'll smoke them out. There's no safety in numbers. It's too big a prize to forgo."

"You don't know the catacombs. They have thousands of exits and entrances. The tunnels are endless. More of Rome is underground than above it."

"How do they eat?"

"With their mouths."

"Come on."

"They steal. They slaughter cows and sheep that they get from the fields—the tunnels go far beyond the walls. And they have people who help, like me."

"I'm going back," Alessandro said.

"They'll just shoot you."

"Not now," Alessandro said.

"Because of the collapse?"

"Yes."

"They'll be shooting so many people now," Guariglia said, "they won't have enough bullets."

"No. When they regroup they'll need everyone alive."

"You're crazy," Guariglia told him.

"I don't want them to come for me at my father's bedside. He's sick. It would kill him. I have a strange feeling that, if I tell the truth, I can help keep him alive. So I'm going to tell him that I have to go back, and I will go back."

"As you can see," Guariglia stated, with a trace of bitterness, "even if I agreed with you, I wouldn't be able to do anything about it."

"I know."

"But you're going to take my warning bell, aren't you."

"He may be a little light of mind, but he's more than just your warning bell, and he deserves a chance."

"Some chance."

"That's his decision."

"Naturally it's his decision. And he'll go with you. He's so young and he's so stupid that he'll go with you. They'll take you both and put you up against a wall."

"Maybe."

Guariglia went to his children, who were playing by the brazier. "Look at them," he said. "I know they may not be as beautiful to you as they are to me. . . ."

"They are," Alessandro interrupted.

"No," Guariglia insisted, "they're not beautiful in that way, but to me, Alessandro, they are all that is good and holy. I didn't know God until I saw them. It's funny, as soon as you lose faith, you have children, and life reawakens."

The little girl came up to her father. "Da Da? When are you going to make me another horse?" she asked.

"I'll think of you," Alessandro said as he left. Guariglia locked the door and turned inward.

BY THE time Alessandro reached the cafe, the clouds had disappeared and the sky was as blue as a gem, with no variations, and no white on the horizon. Though the day had become hot and blindingly bright, the inside of the cafe was cool and dark, and the waiters squinted when they looked through the large windows that faced the street. It was quiet. Nevertheless, long banks of expresso machines were steaming like locomotives. They gleamed in highly polished copper, brass, and silver, their tanks full of pressurized boiling water to shunt into armies of cups next to armies of saucers and brigades of shining spoons. The lighted glass cases were packed with cakes and pastries, and on the marble counters, between tubs of sugar and pitchers of milk, were marble salvers that held little wood-piles of buttered bread. The aromas of coffee, pastries, and chocolate fought battles in the air like fighter planes. Everything was polished to a sparkle, the water bubbled, and the waiters, mostly old men, stood in a crooked front along a copper and mahogany bar, waiting to charge forward at their customers.

Eight pairs of eyes kept track of every motion. If someone moved uncomfortably in his chair, a man with a towel over his arm would appear, ready to carry to or from the table anything within reason. The waiters were psychic. They could tell of a bicyclist whether or not he would brake and come in, and exactly what he would order if he did.

When Alessandro stepped into the shade, an old waiter said softly to the man behind the bar, "One hot chocolate, extra dark, very hot, and three breads."

"Tea and two breads," the expresso operator said, and they had a bet.

Fabio stepped forward out of place. From this they knew that he was Fabio's friend, and the bet was off. No matter, in another hour they would be so busy that a man would not be able to hear his own voice.

"Not bad, Alessandro. We made it!" Fabio said, bending over the menu as if he were explaining it to a customer he didn't know.

"Can you sit down?" Alessandro asked.

"You mean in the abstract?"

"I mean now."

"On my coccyx?"

"What?"

"Gluteus maximus? Obturator internus? Pyriformis?"

"What's gotten into you?"

"I'm an intellectual now."

"Why?"

"Women these days like intellectuals, especially the women with big breasts, so I'm an intellectual."

"No kidding."

"Really."

"Can you talk about Plato and Giordano Bruno?"

"Both guys."

"What about Mallarmé?"

"The inventor of the velocipede."

"You're the same."

"No, I'm different."

"How so? And could you bring me a hot chocolate and some bread?"

Fabio called out the order. "You won't believe me. You'll think I'm crazy."

"Not after where we've been."

Fabio knitted his brows and concentrated. Then he broke out in a smile and laughed as if he were laughing at himself. "I'm embarrassed to say."

"Say it."

"Well . . ." He looked at Alessandro in silence as many seconds passed. Both of them felt like idiots. "I want to go back," he said. "It's insane, but I never wanted to leave. I had to, though."

"What happened?"

"I told Guariglia. He works..." Fabio lowered his voice and almost hid behind the menu. "He works just around the corner."

"I came from him."

"He didn't tell you? I cut Gianfranco's chains. Then he took the bolt cutters from me and started to cut the others loose. At that moment, the colonel comes strolling by on the deck above. As soon as he saw it, he ran to get a gun.

"Gianfranco vaulted up to the next deck and followed him. He killed him with the bolt cutter. He tried to cut off his head. And then he jumped right into the water without even looking, like a wild animal. The colonel was a very nice man, and he had a daughter. You see, the army was right. Gianfranco was no good, and he'll probably live forever.

"Anyway, that started it. The more people jumped over, the more those who remained wanted to go too. Even the lieutenants went before I did. No one wanted to be blamed. I figured I'd do better to go home for a while and then get shot than to get shot when we got to Venice, but now I want to go back. I really must be crazy."

"That's what I came here to ask you."

"Guariglia can't go. He cut off his leg."

"I know."

"Let's go today. They might shoot us, but I don't think so."

"I don't think so either, not now."

"And we could just go up to the line and get into a reorganization; they'd never know."

"It's possible."

"Let's go."

"I can't go now," Alessandro said, and he explained. When his father was well enough to go home, then he would go, in about a week or perhaps ten days. Was Fabio willing to wait? Fabio was willing to wait. Among other things, a woman from New Zealand had begun to frequent the cafe.

"New Zealand?"

"Chisel-sharp nose, auburn hair, green eyes, and breasts as big as this." He held the menu at arm's length.

"All right then," Alessandro said. "You work on her, and I'll be back. Hope for the best."

"Naturally," Fabio answered. "Intellectuals always hope for the best. It's called cynicism." Then he brought Alessandro a silver pitcher of chocolate, and some buttered bread. "On the house," he said, and he melted back into the line.

As Alessandro ate he surveyed the spacious half-empty room. Fabio stood in the middle of the group of old waiters, a towel over his arm. He looked exactly in place in his handsome waiter's jacket and cummerbund, and he also looked far out of place, for Alessandro remembered very vividly the young soldier with a rifle slung over his shoulder as naturally as if it had been part of him.

THE NEXT evening, half an hour after Alessandro left for the Hospital of San Martino, four soldiers in battle dress arrived at the house. One entered the garden from the side street and took up a position behind a tree. He put a round in the chamber of his rifle and propped the barrel on a branch, aiming at the back door. While it grew dark he waited as tensely as if the Germans were going to charge through the kitchen. Another soldier was stationed up the street. He would have a clear shot at anyone leaving the house, and he would have so long to shoot that he left his rifle slung over his shoulder and sat on a barrel, dangling his feet as if he were a child.

The other two went to both sides of the front door, drew their pistols, and pulled the bell. After five minutes they knew that no one had gone out the back and they expected one of four possibilities, all of which they had experienced repeatedly. Either the house had been deserted to begin with, the fugitive had escaped by some hidden passage, he was cowering inside, or they would have to kill him in a fight that would range from room to room.

As one soldier kept watch on the windows, his gun pointed up and his finger on the trigger, the other picked the lock. It took twenty minutes, but then the bolt moved back as placidly as if the attorney Giuliani had used his key. They pushed open the door and peered inside. Then they rushed in, breathing hard, their eyes darting into every corner, with both hands on upraised pistols, ready to slew and fire by instinct. This they did throughout the house, never relaxing. Several of their comrades in the same detachment had eased off when most of the houses they had been searching proved empty. In each of the very last rooms—a linen closet in one case and a wine cellar in another—a suicidal deserter had been waiting behind a barricade, armed as if by the army itself.

They didn't holster their weapons even after they had gone through every room in the house and called in the other two soldiers, for they could never be sure their quarry had not eluded them and would not suddenly appear and shoot them in the back. People lost all sense of restraint when cornered in their own houses.

The four of them spread out on the lower floor after the two from outside had gone upstairs to look at Luciana's underwear strewn across her unmade bed. The sight of the rose-colored silk and the smell of perfume made them almost reel with desire. When they spotted a pair of pointed shoes that had been thrown into the corner by the same feminine presence they knew to have rumpled the sheets and dressed within the very space they now occupied, they were good for nothing for at least a minute. Then they rejoined their comrades and set up an ambush for the man they assumed to be her lover.

They refrained from smoking, because they knew that it was possible to tell from a long way off that the air in a house was full of nicotine. They settled quietly in the living room, the reception room, and on the stairs, just out of view. For a few minutes they spoke in normal voices, but their voices quieted in proportion to the time that passed and the likelihood of Alessandro's return.

One of them broke the silence. "Do you think he'll fight?" he asked. "Do the rich ones fight?"

"Usually they don't," came the answer from the top of the stairs. "They don't know that their best chance is right here. They don't understand what's going to happen. They think everything will work out."

They heard a click. "What's that?"

"I took off my safety."

"You had it on? You stupid."

"I thought it was off."

"Shut up!"

"You shut up."

"Just be quiet," someone said, and they were. They waited, half asleep, in their scratchy green uniforms and their leather belts, with their hands on their rifles, or with pistols held across their chests.

"What if he's not here?" the soldier who was sitting in the reception room said in an inappropriately loud voice.

"He's here. Someone reported him."

"What if he went away?"

"Then we lost him," said the voice at the top of the stairs, "but don't worry, they always come home. It's why they leave in the first place."

"I don't like it."

"You could be fighting Germans, you know."

ALESSANDRO KNEW that his father was dying, but at the same time he did not know. As the old man's life proceeded to its conclusion, the signs were unmistakable. Even Luciana was aware of what was happening. Her father was amazed, sometimes frightened, and full of regret, but he was not fooled.

Alessandro, on the other hand, was able to see things that did not exist, and not to see what did. One knows when one is seeing double, but is hard pressed to state which of the two images is real. Alessandro observed his father's increasing frailty, the painful absences in which he seemed to be ahead of himself and in another world, the subtle signs of breathing, tremor, and color, and the involuntary way his father's hand swept across the covers as if searching for something that existed in a different dimension. After years of solidity and sobriety, of wisdom, power, and control, the attorney Giuliani was now forgetful, inappropriately amused, and unaware. He left even his lovely daughter, whom he loved more than anyone or anything in the world, for uncontrolled flights in which it seemed to his children that an angel was leading him on to a place of which he was receiving larger and larger glimpses. He didn't want to go, he was scared, and sad, but the angel was winning him over in preparation for a journey into darkness, light, and infinity.

Alessandro had not known the world for even half a second without his father. Not all parents love their children above all, and often the bond between parent and child is less than their regard for strangers or principles, and only after the death of one does the other know his love, or confuse love yet again with a notion, a principle, or regret, but something had happened between Alessandro and his father early on, perhaps the way the father had embraced his boy, or spoken to him on occasions of great sadness or fear. Perhaps it had been merely love unadorned, apart from touch, reassurance, or admiration, or that in loving his children beyond measure, the attorney Giuliani had elicited their love without measure for him.

Alessandro's struggles and preoccupations centered on hope and will. He could not allow his father to die. He was appropriately scientific and disciplined when conversing with De Roos, or with the specialists who appeared with the regular infrequency of trolley cars in the rain. He was alert, observant, good with his hands when the nursing-sisters needed dexterous aid, and astoundingly strong when the attorney Giuliani had to be lifted. He was a model of decorum with the nuns, and he bent his soul to theirs so that they would be pleased to come to his father's station. He dressed carefully, was always neat, and spent hours trying to think of something the doctors had missed. He knew how to press them subtly on equivocal points, and how to apologize without a word when he had overstepped.

It seemed appropriate that the Italian lines had collapsed, as if the attorney Giuliani and millions of soldiers were fighting the same losing war on entirely different fronts, but they weren't. The wars were different. Alessandro's still allowed for strength and will. It listened to young men and paid heed to chance and desire. His father's was the great war, less a contest than a mystery. It was gossamer, silent, and absolute. No one had been victorious in the war his father was fighting, except by faith and imagination, and of these victories no one could really be sure.

One of the soldiers had died, and his empty bed had yet to be filled. The others were barely alive. Luciana sat rigidly by her father, her face contorted into what reminded Alessandro of the expression of a soldier trying to judge the direction of hostile fire. The attorney Giuliani was sallow and gray, so that everything that was white and silver in him seemed to be bright. He was unconscious yet again, in such a seemingly delicate state that they dared not try to awaken him.

"Where have you been?" Luciana inquired of her brother. Though she had planned to be bitter and angry, she was too tired to be either.

"I went to see a specialist, but he wasn't there. He's at an army hospital in Vicenza."

"What kind of specialist?"

"Heart."

"But we already have one."

"Perhaps this one would have had greater knowledge. Which is worse, a weak son of a bitch who lets you know he's losing the battle, or a strong son of a bitch who makes you think all the way to the end that he's winning? I don't understand how doctors dare to be so arrogant: they lose patients all the time. You'd think they'd be the most humble people in the world, and yet they walk around like generals."

"Why do generals walk around like generals?" Luciana asked. "They lose soldiers all the time. If they were businessmen they'd be bankrupt. Why is it that if you lose souls you're less accountable than if you lose money?"

"I know, Luciana," Alessandro said without looking at her. "I've seen it illustrated." He walked around the bed. "Papa?" he called, though he knew the answer would be raw breathing, now and then inexplicably interrupted by a silence that made them look up with a start even when they had been half asleep. "He's so small now. Look at him. I can't believe it. This is our father. He's as white and silver as a sunbleached reed."

"Don't say that."

"It's true. Look what he's become. I remember when he stood far above me, when his hair was jet black, when he was sunburned and strong."

"Why did he stop rowing?" Luciana asked.

"He didn't have the time. As he grew older, it was difficult for him to lift the boat, and fight currents when the river was running fast. He's so slight now that it's as if he's sublimating."

"What's sublimating?"

"When a solid becomes a gas without melting, like snow in the sunshine. It disappears right before your eyes."

One of the soldiers began to groan in his sleep. It sounded like the end. His teeth rattled like a machine. "Get a nurse," Alessandro ordered, and Luciana ran from the room.

Alessandro knelt down and put his face on his father's pillow. "Papa," he whispered in the old man's ear, "stop all this nonsense, get up, get alive again, stop dying." His father suddenly opened his eyes, which made Alessandro almost jump backward across the room, and when the attorney Giuliani focused on his son, he looked surprisingly well rested and alert.

"Alessandro, where are we?"

"The hospital."

"What hospital?"

"San Martino."

The attorney Giuliani looked around as best he could. "When did I come here?"

"A month ago."

"A month?"

"Yes."

"What for?"

"Your heart."

"I feel as if I'm dreaming, but I'm not, am I."

"You're going to get better. Now we have the medicine that you need. Orfeo got it from the army. Your fever has gone down."

"I didn't know I had a fever."

"How do you feel?"

"I feel as if I have no body. I'm floating, and I don't like it. I'm not drunk, am I?"

"No," Alessandro said.

"I feel light, as if all I am is a pair of eyes—not even eyes, but just a point, from which I can see out. I'm not floating, am I?"

"You're in bed. You have a body." Alessandro squeezed his father's hand. "See?"

"Did they give me drugs?"

"Yes, that's probably it."

"I don't mind floating that much, but tell them to stop."

"I will. I'll tell them."

"Where's your mother?"

Alessandro bowed his head, because his eyes had filled with tears. "She's not here now," he said. "She's asleep. We've all been taking turns at your bedside. Luciana's here, and she'll be back in a minute."

"Luciana," his father said, closing his eyes. When he opened them, he asked, "Where's Luciana?"

"She's here. She went into the hall."

"I thought you were in the army, Alessandro."

"I am. I came home for a while."

"They didn't use to let you."

"I'll have to go back again, soon."

"I thought you were dead."

"Papa, I'm right here."

Luciana came in, followed by a nurse who went to the soldier, pulled a cloth partition around him, and began to do whatever she was going to do, unseen.

"He's awake," Alessandro told Luciana.

Her father called for her, and she kissed him.

"Papa is a little confused, but I told him what happened: that he's getting better, that the fever has subsided, and that he'll be able to come home."

"What time is it?" their father asked.

"It's evening, father, about nine o'clock. We're going to be here until you no longer feel that you're floating."

"You don't have to."

"We want to," Luciana answered.

"Luciana will go home now, so she can get some sleep, and I'll stay with you."

"I'll stay," Luciana volunteered.

"You've been here all day."

"I'll tell you what," she said. "Go home, take a nap, and come back around midnight to relieve me. I don't mind a few extra hours, and if you're going to stay up all night you should get a little sleep. You can walk me home and come right back."

"That makes sense," Alessandro agreed.

"Let me wash my face before you go." She turned to her father. His eyes were half closed, and fluttered as if the eyelids were weightless. "I'll be right back."

When Alessandro was alone with his father he hesitated for a moment, but then he bent down. "Papa, can you hear me?"

"Yes," his father said so weakly that Alessandro asked him again.

"Can you hear me?"

"Yes, I can hear you," the attorney Giuliani said with irritation, which Alessandro loved, because it showed that he had fight in him.

"I want to say..." Alessandro began, and then halted, because he was overwhelmed. "I want you to know... Do you remember, when I was two or three years old, that you read me a book about German rabbits?"

"What rabbits?"

"A children's book about a family of rabbits in a field—how the hunters chased them, their adventures, and so forth?"

The attorney Giuliani nodded his head.

"I used to sit in your lap and lie against your chest. Sometimes I would fall asleep."

"I remember."

"You read it to me when you came home from the office. You'd have a shirt and jacket on, before dinner. I used to put my head against the shirt, and it smelled of pipe tobacco.

"I wanted to say to you... I don't know exactly how to explain it, but these were the best times of my life. I was happier then than I have been ever since. The world was perfect."

Alessandro cried. Tears fell down his cheeks even as he held himself stiffly and with a soldier's discipline. His father extended his hand and gripped Alessandro's hand on the bed.

ON ALL documents, notices, and orders, the vast concrete and stone fortress on a cliff above the sea south of Anzio was called Military Prison Four, or M.P. 4, but never did anyone who had been inside ever call it anything but Stella Maris. It seemed to float above the sea like the plain of stars that on a clear night rides above the waters and the wind. In conversation mysterious and deep, in the crackling, hissing, seemingly inconsequential sounds of the foam, waves, and wind, the stars were talking to the enraptured sea, and, as with many of its greatest secrets, nature entrusted knowledge of this to whoever would not be believed or who could not speak. Staggering volumes of wondrous information were exchanged between the waves and the stars, in traffic so thick, fast, and full as to be beyond understanding, in sounds that rose up in fumes and clouds, in musical dialogues, and in uncountable voices speaking to uncountable lights. The condemned soldiers of Stella Maris, with neither reputation to uphold, nor gain to desire, nor hope to sustain, knew the soul of the sea at night. It was their compensation and their reward.

Alessandro was taken to Stella Maris, a short distance from Rome, in half a dozen conveyances. The army needed four days and the stamps and signatures on half a hundred pieces of paper to get him from his house to a tiny cell overlooking the sea.

He walked the last few miles, in a line of men shackled and chained by the left ankle. The guards counted them now and then as if they did not trust either their own eyes or the constancy of steel. The prisoners had been put in uniform, because the discipline that it reawakened in them made them easier to handle.

They descended to the beach at Anzio and walked toward Stella Maris, which they could see quite clearly in the distance. It was one of those mornings in November when the sun is out so full that it seems like spring or summer, and the only way to know the fall is by the depth and darkness of the shade. The sea was agitated and blue. Breakers pounded the beach, and the wind that had driven them propelled the spray far beyond the crests, so that the soldiers who wore glasses had to peer through encrustations of salt on their lenses. Even without the spray they would have had difficulty, for, despite the wind, the hot sun and its reflection from the sand made them sweat. They walked in the sound of the pounding surf, their olive-colored shirts stained dark, their chains shining.

Though Alessandro was pleased by the waves and the wind that drove them on, every step he took away from Rome was agony. He was next to the sea, walking in the sun, and his father and Luciana were without him in a room on the top floor of the hospital. No doubt the sky was a brilliant blue and the geraniums in the window boxes as red as blood, but the cool sobriety of the streets and squares, the shade trees, and the stones was less than what he had now as he marched to Stella Maris.

Had things been minutely different sometime earlier, the Giulianis might now be together on the beach. They might have arrived with food in a basket, and Alessandro and his father might have gone in the water, proud to be less sensitive to the cold than Signora and Luciana, who would pretend to be disgusted by the fact that the two men were so indelicate as to be able to float in the Tyrrhenian in November.

Alessandro hoped that with Luciana by his father's side the old man would rally, but he feared that, even if they withheld the news until summer, when his father was told that Alessandro had been executed, the shock would kill him. And that would be almost the end of them all. But perhaps he would live beyond his time. Perhaps, if Rafi survived, Luciana would bear a child, and the attorney Giuliani would have a grandchild with golden hair. Perhaps they would name that child Alessandro, or Alessandra.

ALESSANDRO WAS thrown into a narrow cell with a small window that looked over the courtyard where the executions took place. Beyond the courtyard, over a high wall, was the sea. In the window were a pair of iron bars, but no glass. Pervading the air was a smell like that of a much-used kitchen. It had the smooth quality of vanilla cream, of something that was white, and semi-sweet.

The cell's other occupant, permanently chilled by the maritime winds that whistled through the damp prison block, was wrapped in two blankets, like an Indian.

This Indian had wire-rimmed glasses and the face of an intellectual. He looked pained, he sighed, and he threw off one of the blankets. "It's yours," he said.

"I don't want it," Alessandro replied, still hot from his walk in the sun.

"When you cool down, you'll want it, especially at night. Two are hardly enough. Now we'll both freeze."

"What's your name," Alessandro asked after he had introduced himself.

"Ludovico."

"Ludovico what?"

"Just Ludovico."

"Why?" Alessandro asked.

Disgusted, Ludovico replied, "Because I'm a communist."

"Communists don't have last names?"

"When they're in secret organizations they don't. If the army puts together a few more pieces of the puzzle, they'll capture my comrades and shoot them."

"You didn't desert?"

"I did."

"Are you going to be shot for desertion or for being a communist?"

"It's the same thing, but it's too complicated to explain when I'm cold."

"It doesn't matter anyway; I'm not interested."

"I suppose that's because you have faith in the judicial system that will try us."

"Yes. I have faith that we will be found guilty and that we will be shot."

"Your faith will be rewarded."

"Why? It hasn't been for the last few years."

"I think I don't want to talk to you," Ludovico said. "You're neither scientific nor rational." He went to the window, like a sulking child.

Alessandro bumped him out of the way to get a look. The courtyard was about twenty-five meters square, and on the opposite side was a row of ten poles, each slightly shorter than a man. They were splintered and crumbling, as if thousands of linemen had been climbing them for weeks, and the wall behind them was as pockmarked as a squash court. Beyond this was the blue sea. The waves made refractive lines that seemed to hold more than the light, and the whitecaps speckling its windy surface bloomed like flowers. "That's where they shoot people," Alessandro said.

"Fifty a day," Ludovico confirmed. "Under communism, it would never be."

"Of course not."

"It's true."

Alessandro shook his head. "Ludovico Indian," he said gently, but firmly, "since its beginning the world has seen empires, theocracies, slave states, anarchy, feudalism, capitalism, revolutionary states, and everything else you can think of, and no matter what the variation, the bloodstained stakes, guillotines, and killing grounds remain."

"Scientific socialism will make it otherwise."

"Scientific socialism will make the killing scientific and socialistic," Alessandro replied.

"True, it may be necessary, initially, to liquidate opponents of the revolution," Ludovico admitted.

"Yes, I know. The stakes do come in handy. It's why no one ever takes them down."

"You commit a great evil," Ludovico declared, "by abandoning belief in the perfectibility of man in favor of dreams of the heavenly city and of a God that cannot be proved."

"The heavenly city in which I believe, Ludovico, cannot be demonstrated. It is a matter of faith and revelation, not reason. You, however, claim that your heavenly city is demonstrable, and, of course, it isn't."

"In our lifetime."

"You are as short of proof as am I. The difference is that, for you to prove what you attempt to bring about, you'll have to harrow the world. At least my dreams don't rest upon compelling all of humanity to pose for them."

"What the hell are you," Ludovico asked, "a Jesuit?"

"No."

"How do you know about political systems?"

Alessandro sat down on the plank that served as his bed. "I had a wonderful horse," he said.

"That's how you know about political systems?"

"Yes."

"From a horse?"

"Yes. His name was Enrico. When the war broke out they took him for the cavalry. If I know him, he's still alive somewhere, though he's not as young as he used to be. I trained him well. We used to race against trains, and win, and I had a trick that I taught him. That's how I know about political systems.

"We often rode in the Villa Doria Pamphili. Sometimes it's open to the public, sometimes not, but you can't tell that to a horse. Horses are like communists: they don't like the idea of private property, and Enrico would want to run in the Villa Doria even when it was locked.

"On the north side, near the gate, is an iron fence as high as a man, with posts topped by spear points. The entire length of Enrico's belly would have to clear that fence; and his legs, and his awkward equine genitals.

"We did it. We actually did it. Not just once, but all the time."

"Why does that bear upon political systems?"

Alessandro leaned forward. "Because, Ludovico Indian, problems of the intellect, including political questions, are much the same—puzzles and mazes in which you can meander for the rest of your life, that turn you hither and thither until you sometimes get so dizzy and confused that you don't know what's going on.

"The barriers in these mazes are like iron fences with sharpened spikes, and they condemn intellectuals to wander, but if an intellectual can jump those fences he can see how the puzzle is laid out.

"After the fences I took on Enrico, the problems of political systems do not seem intractable."

"You're crazy," Ludovico announced.

Alessandro held his finger in the air. "Ah!" he said, "but at least I'm able to tell you my last name, and at least, when they take *me* out to the stake my dreams may be just beginning, whereas yours, by your own definition, must and will come to a dark end."

"You fool yourself. Your illusions will fall away even before the end. They won't do you any good. You'll see."

Alessandro got up and went to the window. An afternoon mist had settled on the sea almost at the horizon, where it made a sparkling band of blue and white light. "Would you have trusted the horse to carry you over the spikes, time and time again, and not be impaled?" he asked.

Ludovico said no.

"Yes," Alessandro continued. "It was dangerous, irrational, the fence was far too high. Even when I approached the barrier, I myself did not truly believe that he could take me over."

"So why did you do it?"

"I trusted his strength and his goodness more than I believed my weakness and my doubt. It always worked. It was a good lesson."

"If it fails?"

Alessandro smiled. "It fails." He leaned against the wall. "All right, Mr. Indian, what will we talk about tomorrow?"

"The food. All I can say is that I'm glad you're not religious. When the religious ones are put against the wall they begin to slip, fear takes hold of them, and they beg God. They should just be quiet."

"But I am religious."

"Yes, but not the smarmy kind."

"No, not the smarmy kind."

Suddenly, in the middle of the night, Alessandro said, "The difference between a man and a woman has been driven even deeper into my understanding."

"What do you mean?" Ludovico asked from a painful half sleep.

"If you were a woman, even were you a total stranger, we would have been in one another's arms fifteen minutes after the sun set."

"But I'm not a woman."

"I know that, but your sister would be another story."

Ludovico jumped up in one motion, like a fierce dog roused from sleep by a huge kick. "Leave my sister out of it or you'll die before you get downstairs!" he screamed.

"If your sister were condemned to death, you wouldn't care if she took comfort in my arms, would you?"

"I don't know."

"I would hold her very gently. I would press my face against the side of her face and her neck. I would make her warm. It would be innocent, Ludovico. I'd love her, even though I didn't know her. It wouldn't matter if she was pretty or not. That's not the point.

"The difference between men and women," Alessandro went on, "is something that I've enjoyed a great deal. I would almost say that I wish I had enjoyed it more, except that at least half was the feeling that arose from restraint and modesty—and you have to go lightly with those, as I did. And perhaps I did it just right, even if at the time I thought I wasn't bold enough. I don't know, but here, at the end, I see that the most beautiful thing between a man and a woman is not the consummation of their love, but, simply, their regard for one another."

"That may be so, but you probably can't know it until you're condemned to die."

"You're always condemned to die. It's just a matter of timing."

"There's something about having only a week or two left, though, isn't there," Ludovico asked. "It's too bad they don't shoot women here, because then we could have women in our cells and we'd all be warm, happy, and modest."

"They wouldn't have to shoot them. They could just bring them in."

"Good," Ludovico said, smiling as madly as the Cheshire Cat. "Why don't you tell them about it at your trial?"

"I'm not altruistic, like you."

"That's because you're not a communist."

"How old are you, Ludovico?"

"Twenty-two."

"You're forgiven."

"How old are *you*?"

"Twenty-seven."

"It's not your place to forgive me. I'll die a communist."

"I know."

"What do you do, anyway?"

"Why?"

"I think you're probably a social parasite."

"I was about to become a professor of aesthetics."

"Ahhh! See! You don't make anything, you don't do anything. No wonder."

At first, words flew through Alessandro's head like machine-gun bullets clearing the air over the trenches. His education, still intact, was suddenly fired up. Just the names—all the Greeks, of course, and Descartes, Locke, Shaftesbury, Leibniz, Vico, Eberhard, Herder, Schiller, Kant, Rilke, Keats, Schelling, and a hundred others, loaded all the cannon and made them ready to fire. And he was ready to marshal the principles of intuition, analogy, sympathy, historicism, intellectualism, spiritualism, the relation of physics to aesthetics, various schools of theology.... But in the end, he realized, it was all talk, lovely talk, with no power. In the end, beauty was inexplicable, a matter of grace rather than of the intellect, like a song.

"You're right, Ludovico," he said, and it hurt.

For ten minutes the sea wind pumped wet mist through the window, and they shivered.

"Wait until the morning," Ludovico warned, "when they start the executions. It'll shake you up. You'll lose your bearings. I've seen it many times now."

"I saw men die in the line," Alessandro answered.

"It's not the same."

BREAKFAST ARRIVED before dawn, just as the candles in the long corridors between the rows of cells were burning down. Dazed prisoners under the watch of several guards handed out small cups of milk and unequal sections of bread.

"Don't eat too slowly, and don't eat too fast," Ludovico warned.

Alessandro asked why.

"If you eat too slowly, the shooting will start before you're finished, and your stomach will turn. If you eat too fast, your stomach turns when they start to shoot."

"What's the right speed?"

"Follow me," Ludovico commanded. He ate faster than Alessandro had ever seen anyone eat, and, after he finished, the gates to the courtyard were unlocked and pushed open.

A squad of soldiers with good military bearing marched into the execution yard. Their boots were shining, their uniforms pressed, and they looked straight ahead and turned their rifles in the kind of drill accomplished by elite units that never fight.

"They do nothing else," Ludovico said. "It's the same group. They'll never be able to live with what they've done, but they can't mutiny."

At the window, Alessandro saw that their buttons glinted and sparkled even though little light fell on them. "They know better than anyone exactly what would happen to them if they did," he said.

"They should run away."

"Everyone they shoot tried to run away."

Alessandro gripped the bars as the ten men were brought out, accompanied by three priests with open Bibles. A dozen guards stood by. The manacles and chains of the condemned would not be removed until after the execution. Grave-diggers waited on the left, with two-wheeled carts that some of the prisoners eyed painfully.

The priests began to read from the Bibles. Sometimes they would look up into the faces of the men. They were soldiers in uniform, and it was hard to distinguish one from another. Some stood impassively. Some swayed back and forth. One was sobbing, bent over as if he had cramps.

"You smell that?" Ludovico said to Alessandro. "That's shit. They shit in their pants. You will too."

"Like hell I will," Alessandro answered. "I'm not going before God with shit all over me."

"Someone else said that," Ludovico added. "He said it, then he thought about it, and he looked up at me and said, it doesn't matter. God will have me washed clean before I'm brought to Him."

Two officers carrying papers solemnly entered the execution yard. They quietly read each man his sentence, and stepped back. One of them issued a command, and the prisoners were marched along the wall until they were lined up at the stakes. They moved slowly, dragging their feet, shuffling, crying.

Alessandro was mesmerized by the uneven and halting gait of the condemned men. Seventeen or eighteen years ago, their parents had held them up and guided them in their first steps. And now it had come to this. Stumbling, tentative, and afraid, they were walking once again like very young children.

They took their positions in front of the stakes. They didn't need to be tied, because they had nowhere to go and they knew it. One dropped to his knees. The two priests nearest him went to lift him up, but he had lost his courage and two guards moved forward to hook his manacles over a bolt in the post. The posts were not to hold them in place, but to hold them up.

How can they do this? Alessandro asked himself. These men did nothing more than fail to be in a particular place at a particular time. Given another chance, they would fight like Gurkhas, but, then again, if all the soldiers in the line knew that the only penalty for desertion was simply to be returned to the line, the line would evaporate.

Though Alessandro found it nearly impossible to believe that habit, custom, and civilization could be so strong as to compel the ten men below to walk to their deaths, he knew that when civilization, habit, and custom do not exist, executions proceed apace, even if with less formality and less warning.

The priests wore black cassocks dripping with beads that some of the prisoners tried to clutch. They circulated among the men who were going to die, and comforted them as best they could. By the time they withdrew from the line of fire most of the men were staring at the clouds and sky, over which the dawn light was vaulting and could not be turned back.

Half the firing squad knelt down. An officer drew his sword and lifted it. Orders were shouted, but Alessandro was in a fog and could not hear them. The soldiers raised their rifles in unison. As they worked the bolts to place rounds in the chambers the sound echoed from wall to wall. Alessandro had always liked that noise. It had signified protection and preparedness. Even when it had drifted up en masse to the Bell Tower as a thousand Austrian soldiers made ready to attack, it had been comforting and it had dispelled his fear, but now it was the sound of despair.

The soldiers aimed. They were standing far enough away so that it was unlikely that they would place the bullets directly in the hearts of the men facing them, as they were supposed to do—as if they could know exactly where the hearts of these men lay.

"Now it comes!" Ludovico cried out.

The officer lowered his sword.

AFTER ALESSANDRO had witnessed a number of dawn executions he had more detail than he wanted. When the prisoners were led into the courtyard, the sun was touching only the top of the west wall. By the time they had marched along the north wall to the stakes, it had lit the tops of the stakes themselves. And when the priests had left those who were about to die to their last moments, the sun was tracking toward the firing squad and taking up the cream-colored dust in its powerful beam. It looked as if the firing squad were shooting at the advancing light, to keep from their eyes what the prisoners, who were blinking and squinting, had just seen. When the bodies were unshackled and loaded on the carts, the shirts of the men who did this work were quickly blackened with blood.

On cloudy days, when the prisoners had no glare in their eyes, the lack of confusion and the even temper of the light seemed to make them suffer even more. Alessandro was repeatedly enraged at the grave-diggers, who loaded the bodies on the carts with little care. From their lack of respect came the movement, far too free, of loose and relaxed limbs, heads that rolled back, and mouths that fell open. He hated it when a man's arm hung down from the *charrette,* and the fingers, slightly curled, tripped in the dust.

In the afternoons of clear days when the sea was so blue and open that it was too painful to look at, Alessandro stared straight into the glare. He wondered why he hadn't taken any of the many chances he had had to put a little boat on the sea and leave the land behind. Better to die in the waves than between walls. To be pounded to death in the cold surf was preferable to being shot by a row of illiterate marksmen who had not yet picked their teeth clean of the previous night's *scungili*.

Stella Maris had been built to hold four hundred men. It now held eight hundred, and soon it would bulge with twelve hundred souls. The mere ten executions a day were due not to a dearth of candidates but to the necessity of trying them, and to the difficulty of transporting paperwork and documentation to and from Rome. Firing squads in the north were more efficient; it was said that some used machine guns, and the paperwork was nonexistent, but in Rome the populace could not be affronted. They had been spared proximity to the executions, very few of which were carried out in the city itself, the seat of government, where agitation was unwanted. A guard had told Alessandro and Ludovico that if Stella Maris had been close to the bureaucracy the toll would have been sixty a day. That they were alive was due to slow couriers and the fact that officials did not like to be trapped at the seaside in autumn.

Nonetheless, the loss of ten men a day, after two weeks, meant that, for Stella Maris to keep its business-like air, new prisoners had to arrive. Empty cells, like empty rooms in a resort or empty shelves in a store, spoke of failure. When the Italian armies re-grouped in November and held their ground, the prisoners had hoped that the army, relieved of fatal pressure, would show mercy, but at the same time they despaired as they realized that their exe-cutioners would not be overthrown. The passage from hope to de-spair was, as always, more painful than the despair and more powerful than hope itself, but the whipsawing ceased as the days passed and they saw that the Italian victory meant nothing to Stella Maris, that the executions had actually accelerated.

A hundred new men, breathing hard from their walk across the sand, were left in the execution yard for an hour as small groups proceeded to the cells. Though Ludovico did not in principle allow himself pleasure from the misfortunes of others, he could not suppress his amusement at the expressions of the newcomers as they filed in and saw the posts and the pockmarked wall. "You ought to look at their faces, Alessandro," Ludovico said. "I don't know why it's funny, but it is. Their innocence is so offended that you'd think they're all here by mistake. Look at them."

Alessandro studied the new prisoners. Their expressions were familiar and their uniforms black with sweat. It was the army, where everyone looks the same, but in the southwest corner was a soldier who was using a cane and leaning on a friend. Alessandro pressed against the bars. Then someone called to them. They had been given nicknames on the walk by the sea, or perhaps in the holding pens on the road from Rome. The one who limped and the one who helped him were called *Bruto* and *Bello.*

As soon as Alessandro heard the names he remembered Guariglia's children, and the beneficial effects of Stella Maris and the sea, which had begun to spare him from pain and prepare him for death, immediately vanished.

ALESSANDRO CALLED out to Guariglia, but not to Fabio, because he thought he would sound like a bird if he said, "Fabio, Guariglia, Fabio, Guariglia," and that the prisoners would mock him.

The two turned their heads immediately, and walked across the execution yard until they stood directly beneath Alessandro's window. Alessandro and Fabio smiled in embarrassment, while Guariglia, who looked as if he were going to fall apart, tried to keep up a solid front.

"It didn't work," he said, his head tilted up, his hands shielding his eyes from the glare. "The catacombs. I got to them, and I was soon lost in the dark. When the soldiers who were following me turned back, I thought I was safe, but a few hours later a trolley went overhead and the roof caved in. Luckily, the earth was light and dry. I dug my way through and came out a little hole into another tunnel, where I walked for a few minutes, feeling my way in the dark, and then sat down. I was there for an hour or two, spitting out dirt and trying to breathe, when I saw a lantern coming at me. I bolted in the other direction, right into a squad of military police. I knocked a few down when I collided with them, so they beat me with their rifle butts. I thought I was going to die right there, but they wanted to get into the air and the light, so they stopped."

Fabio said, "Three plainclothesmen came into the cafe and sat down. It was only a few days ago. They asked for me. I should have run out the back, but I thought they were going to leave a big tip, so I served them. Can you believe that? They had expresso and the kind of cookies that we called bracket cakes, the ones with the little chocolate ends." He smiled. "They stayed for half an hour, and then arrested me. I was stupid, huh."

"You weren't smart," Alessandro said.

"They had maps of the catacombs," Guariglia told Alessandro. "They sent surveying parties down there and made maps! Only then did they clear the place out. Why don't they fight the fucking war that well?"

"It doesn't matter now."

"They'll shoot us, won't they?" Fabio asked.

"Yes," Alessandro answered from above.

"Against those trees."

Alessandro nodded.

"Oh well," Fabio said.

Guariglia closed his eyes.

"Alessandro," Fabio began with great earnestness. "Do you think they'll have beautiful women in heaven?"

Guariglia cringed.

"Millions of them, but how do you know you're going there?"

Fabio looked intensely pleased. "My mother told me," he answered. "She said, no matter what, I was going to heaven. She promised."

Alessandro shrugged his shoulders.

"How's the food in this prison?" Fabio asked. "Is it decent?"

"Sometimes we get an egg," Ludovico said, coming to the bars.

"What?"

"Sometimes we get an egg."

"Who's that?" Fabio inquired.

"His name is Ludovico Indian. He doesn't have a last name, because he's a communist."

"Adami, Fabio," Fabio volunteered, almost coquettishly, "and this is Guariglia." Guariglia stared at the ground. "He's a real veteran, but he's not so happy now."

An officer entered the yard and ordered the prisoners to form ranks. They were used to such exercises, and in no time at all they formed orderly rows that, though they had neither weapons nor equipment, made them look formidable.

The officer was yet another student-type, with wire glasses, and he addressed the prisoners. "This is M.P. Four, which you'll call Stella Maris. You can't escape, and anyone who tries will be shot on the spot. You get three eggs and two oranges a week, a haircut and a bath every two weeks. Don't complain about the food, it's as good as in any other prison, or better. We maintain military discipline up to the last, even as you come out here to be shot.

"Everybody asks why, so I'll tell you. It's the only thing you've got. You go through all the motions of life knowing that you're going to die, don't you? You go through them anyway. You shave, you play *bocce,* you polish the doorknobs, you make a big deal about growing a mustache. Everybody wastes time. The same goes for Stella Maris. You're still in the army, and you'll maintain military discipline until you die. It'll give you satisfaction. On the other hand, if you don't do it, you'll feel like a jellyfish and you'll suffer too much, and at the very end you'll crap in your pants. You're all going to die, soon. So am I. I'm under sentence, too. On the first of January, I'm the first to go. Follow my example. Watch what I do. Stand straight until the bullets enter your chest. It's the only way. Dismissed! Line up at the gate."

"Who the hell is that?" Alessandro asked Ludovico.

"Didn't you get that speech?"

"No, and I didn't get a bath, either. Is he for real?"

"He killed a colonel, because the colonel was shooting his own men. They sentenced him for the first of January. Usually you go the next morning, but they wanted to give him plenty of time to think about it."

"He's beating them."

"So far."

"What about the bath?"

"Tonight. And a haircut."

"I don't want a haircut."

"Tough. I think they sell the hair, for mattresses."

"That's disgusting."

"No it isn't. Maybe a baby will sleep on the mattress. I like the idea."

THE BARBERS arrived in the afternoon. They were little rotund men, almost all of them bald, who balanced on ammunition boxes and sheared the hair off the heads of the soldiers, who stood for their haircuts after waiting in long lines.

The prisoners were removed from their cells in groups of fifty, in a complicated pattern based on cell blocks and floors. They were assembled in a huge hall where the barbers stood on their ammunition boxes, electric clippers in hand, the cables twisted into a braid that disappeared through a hole knocked into one of the walls.

In groups of five the prisoners were then passed into a terrazzo-floored shower room where miserable common soldiers threw buckets of soapy water at them and sprayed them with cattle-washing hoses borrowed from a slaughterhouse. After they were rinsed they were pushed into a shallow pool of hot water, where they were allowed to stay for a few minutes. When they emerged they filed through long halls and were dried by the wind. At the end of the halls they picked up their damp newly washed uniforms. They called all this the washing machine.

Alessandro and Ludovico were at the ends of two of the lines, and another soldier, Fabio, and Guariglia were at the ends of the others. Everything was rushed, and though they weren't permitted to talk, they did.

They never knew the other soldier's name, and they never saw him again. He was two days from his execution, and very eloquent in his desperation. He was probably a physicist.

"Shit!" he said, which seemed eloquent enough. "Damn! I can't die. I can't die. I have to survive. It'll take forty years to develop my theory. Jesus, I can't die."

"What theory?" Fabio asked.

"Gravity," he said, "I figured out gravity. I know what gravity is, and magnetism, and they're going to shoot me before I can develop the theory. They don't listen. I try to tell them, but they don't listen.

"There's no such thing as gravitational pull. It's a push from an all-pervasive force, but the force moves in straight lines, so it casts a shadow because it can't go around mass. It goes through and it gets absorbed. On the other side, another object is accelerated toward it because of a lack of pressure between the two—because the gravitational rays that would balance it have been weakened or cut off by the intervening mass.

"The perfect radiative body is the perfect absorber of gravitational force, and so everything is pushed to it and doesn't escape, because nothing goes through it to moderate the effect of the pushing on the other side.

"Variations in gravity are simply a function of intervening mass. Mass is a function of molecular resistance to gravity, and what counts is not what everyone takes to be the traditional determinant of mass but, rather, the expanse and force of the atomic and molecular bonds.

"Magnetism is the exclusion of gravitational force from an area between two bodies, so they're pushed together, as if in a vacuum. And electrical energy is the release of the potential from the violation of this condition, convertible at will to the recreation of it.

"It's not particles or waves that fly about the universe but an ether of sorts, and what we perceive experimentally to be movement is the opening and closing of gates. Light is the condition when the gates are open. That's why it doesn't interfere with itself, why the speed of light is uniform no matter what the relative speed of its starting point, why two beams fired head-on do not cancel one another out.

"Christ, I can put it all together. I've thought of a hundred tests for verification. I see light, magnetism, electricity, and gravity in equation, and the theory handily explains inertia. I have a lifetime of experimentation, but I can bring it all together."

He turned to the barber. "You've got to tell them. Please! You've got to tell them. For God's sake, tell them that I can reconcile Newtonian mechanics with the theory of relativity. Tell them to get a physicist here. In an hour I can pass it on to him. Get an officer. Tell an officer."

The barber hadn't the slightest idea what the physicist was talking about. "If *you* thought of it," he said, "someone else must have thought of it already. Don't worry." He pressed the switch on the clippers, and electricity ran through the cord, to power the magnets that spun the shaft that turned the gears that moved the blades that shaved the physicist in preparation for his execution. A blue spark was playing inside the motor, crackling and making ozone.

The barbers cut close to the scalp and drew blood. They had just started, they were already ankle deep in hair, and the sound of the clippers was like the sound of a mechanized bee hive. "It's getting dark, and they're tired," Alessandro told Guariglia. "After all, they've already had a day's work in Rome."

"I hope my children never find out that before they shot me they shaved my head."

"If your children found out, they'd love you even more."

"I miss them. They won't remember me."

"Yes they will."

"No," Guariglia said. "The memory will fade. They're too young."

Alessandro, Ludovico, Fabio, and Guariglia stepped into position by the barbers' ammunition boxes. As the barbers ran the electric shears along their skulls, their hair fell to the floor, matting and entangling with the hair of the soldiers who had preceded them. Then they moved forward, each of them bleeding from small cuts, and removed their clothes.

"How do they get us back our uniforms?" Fabio asked.

"Ever the fashion plate," Alessandro said.

Ludovico told them that a soldier looked at them, judged their size, and reached without looking into one of three bins. "He throws the stuff at you. He doesn't look at it, and he doesn't look at you, since by the time he's going to toss it he's already sizing up the next guy."

"Shut up," said a guard standing off to the side.

"That's tailoring..." Fabio stated.

"Shut up," the guard repeated without passion.

". . . fit for the King of Spain."

The shower room smelled of mold and salt, and was lit by one clear bulb that projected the sharp shadows of its filaments onto the walls. The bodies of the five soldiers were pale, but their faces, necks, and forearms were sunburned. With shaven heads and blood dripping down their shoulders they seemed like animals on the way to slaughter. Alessandro could hardly look at Guariglia's stump. It was rounded, covered with fresh scar tissue, and still inflamed.

The hoses stiffened and the men were hit with shockingly cold blasts of sea water. The first volley pushed Guariglia over and made Alessandro sink to his knees. It knocked the breath out of them, opened their cuts, and, though he tried valiantly to get up, it kept Guariglia on the floor.

"Sea water!" someone exclaimed. It was ice cold and it stung. The two soldiers threw buckets of cold soapy water at them, and they struggled as if they were in the surf.

Then they were hit again with the high-pressure brine. "Christ!" Fabio screamed, and, because he had protested, the soldier with the hose aimed the stream of water at his jaw. It hurled him against a wall. When they were done, Fabio was less steady than Guariglia.

They stumbled through a corridor, went down some steps, and were literally pushed into a pool of warm water.

"What is this?"

"It's a swimming pool," Ludovico said.

"It's too shallow."

They were unable to figure out what it was as they sat in it and listened to the wind coming up from the sea.

"It's a bubble bath," Fabio said, his hand pressed to his jaw. Then, for a few minutes, no one said anything.

"Alessandro, you have money, don't you," Guariglia asked.

"I don't. My father is fairly well off."

"That's what all rich sons say," Ludovico mumbled.

"Compared to me, you're rich," Guariglia continued.

Ludovico had assumed the expression of a pointer in a bird sanctuary, because, for him, wealth was an indisputable sign of evil.

"If you get out of here," Guariglia asked, "will you take care of my children? To help them . . . It will be difficult for their mother."

"I'm not getting out of here, Guariglia. . . .

"Will you write a letter?"

Luciana had many troubles. Their father was permanently incapacitated, and would need care. Alessandro didn't know the state of the Giuliani finances other than that the garden had been sold for the sake of acquiring the land near the Villa Borghese. He didn't know if this land was now worth anything at all, or even if they could afford to carry it. If Rafi were wounded or killed, Luciana would need all the money she could get. And yet, Guariglia was a harness-maker, and he had two small children. Their timidity and innocence had been perhaps the most beautiful thing Alessandro had seen since the war began.

"Are we allowed to write letters?" Alessandro asked Ludovico.

"After the trial you have the whole night to write letters. They give you the paper and pen, and they don't censor."

Alessandro turned to Guariglia. "I will," he said. "We're not rich, but we have some money. I'll ask my father to do it for me, I promise."

Guariglia bent his head until his face almost touched the water.

WHEN THEY left the pool they were just as dizzy and breathless as when they had entered. At the end of the long corridor a soldier threw uniforms at them, and after they dressed they were brought onto a long terrace flanked by battlements. Fabio immediately went to look over the side and reported that anyone who wanted to drop down would not have to go through the trouble of being executed.

Alessandro looked about for chains, ropes, cables, vines, or anything that might be useful in descent. He peered over the side, looking for holds, but the wall was perfectly smooth. They settled into a corner to await the return to cells.

Though it was nearly dark, the sun struck the tops of huge clouds that had skidded in from the sea. They were not the kind of marine clouds that build up like mountains but, rather, like traveling foothills, ragged on the edges, black beneath, and pink and white on top. The sky was the mildest blue anyone had ever seen, and two planets shone just above the horizon.

"Look at the clouds," Alessandro said. "They pass so gently and so quietly, but as if with such resolution. Someone once said they were rafts for souls."

"I would like that," Guariglia said. "I'd prefer to stay nearby and look down, to pass over Rome. It sounds to me a little better than all the stuff about being in the stars, because you wouldn't be able to breathe up there, and it would be either too bright or too dark. In the clouds, on the other hand, ah, that would be nice."

"Yes," Fabio added, innocently. "You would be able to see your children. You could paddle over Rome and check on them now and then."

"I'm going to write a letter to my children and tell them to look for me there," Guariglia said. "Even if it's not true, it's a good way to remember.

"A few days ago, my youngest, who is two and a half, refused to go to bed. She cried so hard she choked for air. My wife said leave her, it's the only thing to do if you don't want to ruin a child.

"But in my daughter's cries I heard that she was hurt. I picked her up and held her. I couldn't help it. I find it almost impossible to be hard with her: I didn't see her for the first two years of her life. It took fifteen minutes for her to stop gasping for air. As soon as she'd stop for a moment, she'd start up again. She was red, her face was swollen, and she pounded my chest with her fists. Because she was so hot—she sleeps in a kind of sack that my wife made for her, which is very warm—I took her up to the roof, and she stopped crying. I don't think she'd ever seen the night sky. There's a war on, I told her, but the sky is still there, the stars are still there.

"She loved them, she really did, and while she held on to my neck and stared up at the sky, half an hour passed. You could almost hear the dark clouds moving overhead. I know that something up there spoke to the soul of my child, so perhaps Alessandro is right. Perhaps the clouds are the rafts of souls."

They watched the clouds slide by in the vanishing light until the terrace filled with soldiers who had finished the ordeal of the bath, and then they marched back to their cells. That night, in addition to bread and water and some sort of vegetable paste, each man was given an orange and a hard-boiled egg. Long after they stopped talking, they listened to the faint sound of the clippers, and when Alessandro awoke at about four all he could hear was the wind coming off the sea.

Now, to dream, he did not have to sleep, but merely to consider, and he would find himself in tranquil scenes where action was so delicate it could cross memory and leave no track. The waking dreams came and went like things swept in and out on the waves. He saw a ship from all angles at once as it moved through air, water, and time. Though no one was visible on board, its stern light was glowing, and as it pushed over the dark ocean the light pulled away along a faint silvery furrow. He knew neither where the ship was headed nor how it would find its way, but the tiny lantern kept moving at an insistent and recognizable speed, until it was just a speck.

Suddenly, darkness became light as hundreds of clear electric bulbs illuminated a children's carnival on the Piazza Navona, in the days before Christmas. The lights and caravans seemed to be a single mass, and the noise of the crowd was a cross between silence, the surf, and the weak high-pitched cries of children playing in the distance.

A blur of coats and hats went by, but Alessandro was too close to make out what it was, or to understand how a group of people could travel by him as fast and evenly as water in a stream. They were hunched over into strange positions, grouped together in bunches, packed into tight spaces, and intent upon their forward course in a circle. He stepped back, amazed to see that a chain of electric lights moved above and with them. Grown men and little children were sitting in tiny cars that moved around a track. Each car was attached to a wooden spar extending from the hub of a wheel, and the whole contraption was spinning at a speed sufficient to dazzle the babies as the fathers pretended they were driving real cars.

Alessandro effortlessly followed one father and his child. The man who bent over his little boy was wearing a brown coat and gray pants, and had no hat. He had taken it off and left it with the child's mother rather than lose it in the December wind. This was Alessandro's father, and his mother was holding the hat, watching from beyond the rails. Gravity and centrifugal force made it difficult for Alessandro to look at them, as if he were on the ride, and not they.

The little boy was dressed in a wool coat and a close-fitting cap with ear flaps. He turned the steering wheel back and forth with no reference whatsoever to the motion of the car, and sometimes excitedly pulled a rope that rang a bell mounted on the hood. Every now and then he would try to squeeze the horn mounted on the steering column, but he wasn't strong enough to make it sound, so his father held his hand and helped him.

Alessandro tried to enter the dream. He watched the attorney Giuliani's silver hair glinting in the electric lights, and for one brief and ecstatic moment his eyes settled somewhere between the man and the boy, and he felt himself trapped in their embrace. He felt the father's pleasure at keeping an arm tightly around his small child, and he felt the child's pleasure at being held. They circled round and round, hoping that the ride would never end.

THOUGH ALESSANDRO had lost track of the days, on a Tuesday, at seven-thirty in the morning, he was removed from his cell and led through so many long cold corridors that he thought he was being shown an underground passage to Rome. Finally he came to a drill hall configured as a courtroom. Sitting at a long desk upon a platform at one end of the room were three colonels. Other than from the fact that the colonel in the center possessed a gavel, not even their own mothers could have told them apart, and each was as tall as a boy of thirteen. Each seemed to be about seventy years old, with a narrow pink face culminating imperfectly in an unimpressive jaw hidden by a goatish beard and a dandyish waxed mustache twisted at each end, like the king's, into opposing points. They wore braided tunics with cylindrical military collars, peaked caps, high boots, swords, and jodhpurs. Because they had painstakingly aped the king, they looked the part of circus ringmasters.

Herded onto benches facing the judges were the captured remnants of the 19th River Guard, in four sets of two: Alessandro and Guariglia, Fabio and the Puppet Soldier, and four others, in unexpected reunion. Though they were not allowed to exchange words, their sheepish smiles and flashing eyes said everything. Some had been captured at work, some at home, some on the street, one on the railroad, and one in a bordello. They assumed that, for the rest of the River Guard, in other prisons in other parts of the country, the scene was being repeated, had already played itself out, or soon would, but no matter what the outcome of the war, no matter what the measures yet to be adopted, they knew that at least a few of their original number would live on into the rest of the century, long after the urgency of the moment had faded, and from this they took some comfort.

Even though they expected nothing from the trial, and knew they were going to die, they thought it was funny to see the three little colonels, with folders stacked in front of them, pitchers of water protected by upturned glasses, and ramrod straight little backs.

The one with the gavel did most of the talking. First he identified each man—all the River Guard except one, a soldier from Milan whom they remembered for being sullen and depressed. For that reason, no one had wanted to know him well, and no one had. They didn't recall his name until the president of the court called it out. "Grigi, Alonzo," he said. Yes, that was his name, that depressing and nasty little son of a bitch, Alonzo Grigi.

"No," Alonzo Grigi stated to everyone's surprise. "I am not Grigi, Alonzo."

"You aren't?"

"No."

"Who are you?"

"I am Modugno, Giancarlo Scarlatti Modugno."

The River Guard were riveted by this claim.

"Do you have identification?" the court president asked.

"Of course I don't."

"Why not?"

"I left it in the bordello."

"What were you doing in a bordello?"

"What do you think I was doing in a bordello?" Grigi asked, to the wild delight of the River Guard. "What does anyone do in a bordello? What do you do? How do you do? How are you? I'm fine, thank you. They wouldn't take me in the army," he said, raising his arms in exasperation.

"Why not?"

"They said I was too stupid. I volunteered, which is why they said I was too stupid. I tried, but they wouldn't take me. It's not my fault. Don't execute me. I'm someone else."

The court president inquired of the rest of the River Guard if they knew this man to be Alonzo Grigi. Of course they all said that he was not Alonzo Grigi, so he was removed from the courtroom and returned to his cell. Now seven of the River Guard remained, each with a triumphant smile on his face.

The judge to the right of the court president reprimanded the defendants. Shaking his head from side to side, he appealed to a soldier's knowledge of hopelessness. "At most he will gain a week."

A clerk was instructed to read the charges: dereliction of duty, desertion of a post in time of war, aiding the enemy, abandonment of prisoners, theft of government property, conspiracy, and murder. As the words tumbled off the clerk's tongue, the River Guard knew that death was coming.

"Usually," the court president stated, "we don't have such a full measure. Do you plead innocent or guilty of these charges?" It was clear to anyone that nothing in the universe could have exonerated the River Guard, who knew that they were guilty of everything except the murder.

Alessandro raised his hand and was given permission to speak. "One of the prisoners, Gianfranco di Rienzi, killed the colonel. None of us had anything to do with that, and when we discovered it, we took to the water."

"Why?" the court president interrupted sharply, and with genuine puzzlement.

"In the line, even before Caporetto, they were shooting people like dogs. We jumped into the sea to gain time."

"But it was not a certainty that you would be shot."

"That may be so, but we had been told that we were going back into the line. Given our rate of attrition, we hadn't much reason to take the chance of being forgiven."

"You're admitting your guilt?"

"Of course," Alessandro said. His temper rose in indignation, and he was supported by the rest of the River Guard. "Do you imagine," he asked, "that after several years of slaughter in the line and in our expedition to Sicily, we are going to quake like cowards in the face of the truth? Do you think that we did what we did from lack of courage? Each of us left knowing full well that we would end up here. We decided to take from you some days and weeks in which to see our families. It was just like going into battle. The feeling was the same. The reasoning was the same.

"I am saying, sir, that the war has made your army brave enough to express its will. We did not desert—we rebelled."

"That's a charge far more serious than even murder."

"And more forgivable."

"Tell me how you can think such an outrageous thought," the court president demanded.

"Our rebellion shows that when we tell you what we are going to tell you, you'll be able to believe us."

"Pray tell what you are going to tell us," asked the judge who had not yet spoken.

"Put us to work."

"Doing what?"

"Fighting the enemy."

"We've tried that," the court president said.

"But you didn't have our consent."

"I was under the impression that we didn't need your consent."

"But you do, you do. You don't need our consent to put us in prison, or to shoot us, but you do need our consent if we are going to fight."

"That's nonsense," the court president stated. "The terms cannot be set from below; nothing could be clearer."

"On the contrary," Alessandro answered. "You've outmaneuvered us, and we offer our consent because you've forced us to it."

"No, you were to have been forced to it originally, by the knowledge that anyone deciding otherwise would be condemned. The method works, it would only unravel were we to make exceptions."

"Now is the one time that you can make exceptions."

"Because of the defeat?"

"The armies are in flight. We are not so unusual now."

"We have a new line, and it seems to be holding," the court president declared.

"We promise you that we'll go back and fight like the devil: eight hardened soldiers."

"Seven."

"Seven, then. Don't waste us. We were never afraid to fight."

The judges conferred. It was not like a civilian court, and they made their decisions quickly. Only Guariglia had any hope for the success of Alessandro's appeal, and even he did not allow his hope to show.

When the judges were finished, the president of the court began his speech by looking down and shaking his head, and, after that, nothing that followed was a surprise.

"In times of great stress the rules of the state come forward as the means of its preservation, and they become ever so much more important, if only because judgment is so hard to make. We fall back on them for the purposes not only of initial faith in their wisdom, but because we are forced to turn to something solid and unchanging. Furthermore, this court is not empowered to make exceptions.

"The only way we might do so would be to find you not guilty, but neither are we free to contradict the facts. We have taken note of your appeal, and we are sympathetic, but now, above all, now, when the nation is threatened, we sharpen our loyalty to the state. Hard rules, in belated emergence, give us confidence and restore our bearings. We take note of the humanity of your appeal, but in war humanity is swept aside. This you already know."

He paused. Perhaps he had a son. He intoned their names, and then he said, "I sentence you to death. The sentence shall be carried out by firing squad, at the customary time, in the execution yard of this prison, one week from today."

Then Fabio asked, "Why a week?" as coolly and with as much detachment as a customer in a bank wanting to know why his funds had not cleared.

The court president did not object to this unceremonious interruption, for the sentence was severe enough to cover any and all offenses, past, present, future, and imagined. His tone was friendly and somehow reassuring. "We need a little extra time for your friend Grigi."

At this, the soldiers of the 19th River Guard, now condemned, began to laugh, and the gavel struck.

THE DAYS before Tuesday passed slowly, but when they were remembered they were the shortest and quickest Alessandro had ever known. Every minute after dawn on Monday was a time of day that he would never see again, and he parted with the rich and familiar hours while the clock moved not in a circle but in a spiral. In near delirium, as the clouds built into white mountains and passed overhead on their way east, he imagined substituting for all the clocks of Europe a more honest machine, a finely threaded spiral of three dimensions, that would signify not only the coming and going of day and night, but that no single day and no single night would ever return.

Ludovico Indian was informed that he would be tried on Thursday with fourteen others of his brigade. The judicial apparatus was now working without pause: thousands of new prisoners were headed for Stella Maris, and the cells had to be cleared.

Ludovico now began what appeared to be a series of desperate calculations. It was as if he felt that in a clarified understanding of the workings of economics he could make himself comfortable with the notion of eternity—but due to the minimal relation of economics and eternity, he was forced to calculate faster and faster, and to no avail.

"Marxism won't carry you into the next world," Alessandro said. And then he asked, "How can you reserve your most sacred beliefs for a descriptive system, and one that is imperfect at that? I can't imagine myself believing in trigonometry or accounting, and yet you guide your soul according to a theory of economics."

"It won't fail me as surely as your system will fail you."

"I don't have a system."

"Theology is a system."

"Not my theology."

"Then what is it?"

"What is it? It's the overwhelming combination of all that I've seen, felt, and cannot explain, that has stayed with me and refused to depart, that drives me again and again to a faith of which I am not sure, that is alluring because it will not stoop to be defined by so inadequate a creature as man. Unlike Marxism, it is ineffable, and it cannot be explained in words."

"Well," said Ludovico, "socialism is effable, which is what I like about it. It's solid. Very little of it is conjecture. It may be limited, but it's honest and down-to-earth and you can prove it. It gives me something I know I can hang on to."

"Why don't you hang on to a toilet?"

"I'd rather hang on to a toilet than believe in a collection of wishful thoughts."

"Then, in that case," Alessandro answered, "all you need do is secure yourself a toilet and you will have solved the mysteries of the universe. It would be easy enough to provide every man with a toilet at his death, or a porcelain amulet, and then the world would be perfect. Husbands would not grieve for their wives or wives for their husbands, children would not suffer the loss of parents, nor parents the loss of children, as long as production were regulated and the workers controlled the economy."

"To tell you the truth, Alessandro," Ludovico said combatively, "I'm not concerned with what happens after life on earth, since I believe that nothing does happen. I'm concerned with what I've been allowed, and screw the end. It only takes a second. Why waste time worrying about it?"

"The answer is simple."

"The Church has a simple and unprovable answer for everything."

"I don't care what the Church says. This is a simple answer that comes from my own heart. I've seen and felt many things that I cannot believe are simply material artifacts. They so clearly transcend all that is earthly that I have no doubt that they can run rings around death."

"What things?"

"Had you been with me, Ludovico, for the last twenty-seven years, I could have shown them to you, one by one. They exist everywhere. They're as simple as a mother embracing her child, they're as simple as music, or the wind. You need only see them in the right way. Perhaps I could not have shown you. The question that comes to me is why would you need to be shown? Why haven't you already seen?"

"What, exactly, are you talking about?"

"I'm talking about love."

"I'm unconvinced."

"I wasn't attempting to convince you. I'm now sufficiently tranquil not to have to convince anyone of anything."

"Will you be tranquil in front of the firing squad?"

"I don't know. We'll see tomorrow. You'll be able to watch from the window." Alessandro winked at Ludovico, to show him that he was undisturbed.

"The way you winked," Ludovico said accusingly, "the way you winked at me was just like a religious fanatic."

"Sorry," Alessandro said. "I'll try to wink like a Marxist."

TOWARD EVENING a new guard opened the cell door. Alessandro's insides tightened. "I have until tomorrow morning," he said.

"You have a visitor," the guard announced.

"No one in Stella Maris has visitors."

"You do."

As Alessandro passed through the long, weakly lit corridors he was overcome with sadness and regret. He was so fatigued that had he simply lain down on the floor and tucked himself up against a wall he might have slept. A visitor, no matter who, would break his equilibrium and leave him in panic.

He was brought into a little room with a window facing the trees and open fields east of the prison. Sitting at a table, her hands clasped, was Luciana. Even in the dark he could see the blue in her eyes.

"Is there a lamp?" he asked.

With the turn of her head over a millimeter of space, and the slight closing of her eyes, she said that no lamp was in the room.

He sat down across from her. "I'm on the other side," Alessandro said, "the side that faces the sea. It's much warmer here, without the wind."

Luciana could think of nothing to say.

"How did you find me?"

"Orfeo."

"I thought Orfeo wasn't going to do the Giulianis any more favors."

"He said this was the last."

"No reprieve."

"He wouldn't do it. He was bitter. What's going to happen?"

"I was tried last week. They're going to execute me tomorrow."

"I came then, Alessandro. They turned me away. They turned away dozens of women—mothers and wives...."

"They shoot the sons and husbands and bury them." Alessandro stood up and went to the window. "I want to look at the trees," he said. "On the sea side, I forgot about trees. I suppose I'll never see one again, just as I'll never swim again, sleep, read, or see a child, an animal, or a field."

"What am I supposed to say?"

As Alessandro surveyed yellowing poplars with leaves that barely glittered in the last light, he asked, "How is Papa?"

Luciana closed her eyes briefly, thinking that she was out of Alessandro's sight, but he had her reflection in the partially open window, just enough in the vanishing light to see the change in her expression.

With discipline that she did not know she possessed, she said, "He's fine." As Alessandro continued to look over the fields, her voice was unwavering, and she held herself straight. "He's been strengthening for the past few weeks, and soon he'll come home. Now he's lucid. He makes no more comments about angels or waterfalls."

"I trust you haven't told him about me," Alessandro said to the reflection.

"No. He thinks you went back to the army, for the battle in the north. He reads the war news just as he used to. I told him that you went to join Rafi's unit, that Orfeo got you in, and that you'd be together. That is, after all, what I begged of Orfeo." She closed her eyes. "I even told Orfeo that I would sleep with him, but he was unmoved."

Still looking out the window, Alessandro winced. "Why did you tell our father these things, when the truth is so different?"

"Would you have wanted me to tell him?"

"Why not? His weak heart?"

"Yes. It would hurt him."

"But it wouldn't kill him. It wouldn't kill him, would it?"

"He should be allowed to live out the rest of his life without that kind of blow," she answered.

Stars were now visible in the sky above the hills, and, as Alessandro took in the last traces of the light, he saw that tears had begun to form in Luciana's eyes.

"You say he no longer speaks in delirium about angels and waterfalls."

"No longer."

"When I was little, before you were born, he told me that birds were angels, that they fall into the sky from above, and that flying through the air is for them like swimming through the sea for us, because the air is so much thicker than the ether. He said that they're sent to watch over us, and to give us reason to lift our eyes to heaven.

"And I asked him, I said, Papa, they die. How can God let His angels die? And he said, that's the saddest thing, that even God must let His angels die.

"I believed him, and then, of course, I disbelieved him, but now it's comforting to think that the birds are there because angels have dropped into the sky, like boys who jump into a river. Think of how exciting it would be. When I see birds flying at great heights, specks wheeling amid the clouds, I like to imagine that they've just come down, and are learning the air in hope of rising, so they can return.

"Luciana, everything rests on you now, and on your children. Even if Rafi doesn't come home, you must have children."

"By whom? The milkman?" she asked with unaccustomed bitterness.

"Even the milkman," was her brother's urgent response, but then he pulled back. "You're very beautiful. You'll have your choice."

He told her about Guariglia's children and asked that she apportion some money for them as long as she was able to do so and for as long as they needed it. She agreed.

"I put these burdens on you, Luciana, not only because I'm going to die tomorrow but also because I have to speak for our mother and father. I've always admired you, ever since you were a baby."

"You have?" she asked, dumbfounded.

"Yes. I thought you were far superior to me."

The guard opened the door and peered in. They were blinded by the electric light that earlier had seemed so dim. "Please finish," he said quietly.

Luciana trembled as she got up, and she was crying.

"I love you, Luciana, as a brother loves a sister."

She had no words.

They stood across the table, looking at one another. "Did you bury our father next to our mother?" he asked.

"Yes."

AT TEN an officer came to ask Alessandro if he wanted to be alone until morning. Alessandro explained apologetically that he would like that very much. Turning to Ludovico, he said, "I'll probably be talking to myself all night anyway, or singing, and it would keep you awake, because, among other things, I can't sing."

They smiled. Ludovico took Alessandro's hand, and gripped his elbow.

"Thank you, Ludovico. I wish you only the best."

Then Ludovico gathered his few possessions. Staring at the floor, and terribly afraid, for he knew that soon he would be in Alessandro's place, he was removed from the cell. The door swung closed, keys turned in the lock, and Alessandro was alone.

Contrary to his expectations, he neither talked to himself nor sang. The night had no words or melodies, but was insanely clear and cold, as if it were already winter.

Never in his life had Alessandro had to squint in starlight, but now the stars were so bright that at times he had to cover his eyes, and when they burned too brilliantly for keeping still, they sometimes shot across the sky in short bursts. Though these quiet illuminations vanished almost as soon as they had started, they lingered in the eye's inexact memory of their luminescent paths. Perhaps had they been stronger and more constant, and hung in a dull white line, Alessandro's heart would not have risen each time he saw them. They were less than little puffs of smoke, their tracks thinner than a hair, the burst of light mainly a matter of memory.

BEFORE DAWN, a key was turned in the lock, and the door swung open. An officer, two soldiers, and a priest were astounded to see Alessandro sleeping soundly. One of the soldiers went in and touched his shoulder. Then he had to shake him.

"Did you sleep last night?" the officer asked.

Alessandro, who seemed perfectly rested and content, said "Yes, I had a very good sleep."

"Your nerves must be like rock," the officer said.

Alessandro threw down his blankets and began to walk. When they stopped him and manacled his hands behind his back he was so strangely undisturbed that they themselves were disturbed.

As they walked, the priest, an old man from a country town, asked Alessandro if he were a believer.

"Yes," Alessandro told him, "but I don't need your job of words to propel me directly into God's hands. If God will have me, it will have to be without an introduction."

WHEN THEY reached the *cortile* the light was just beginning to hide the stars, and the east was pale blue. The eight soldiers of the 19th River Guard were familiar with the part of military life in which men who are gathered before the sunrise speak in whispers, their rifles weighing down upon them, and their bodies shivering. Always, in training and before an attack, the rifles had appeared as dense black silhouettes against inexplicably lucid skies. Even on misty days the air at dawn had seemed clear, and even if one could not see the stars, one could feel them floating overhead.

The twenty soldiers of the firing squad, in crisp uniforms, dazed with sleep, their heavy well oiled rifles slung from their shoulders, made the River Guard feel as if this were just one more dawn in the trenches, when they had had a good chance of staying alive.

Following them were four priests, each reading a different portion of the Bible both mechanically and sincerely. The words of great truths that everyone had heard since birth, when crossed in unintelligible babble, seemed a fitting end, and the archaic Biblical rhythms, spoken like interweaving songs, gave the River Guard courage to add to the courage they had had before. Not a single man of the eight wept or moaned. After years of fighting a cruel enemy in a difficult place, it simply did not occur to them.

The two officers strained to read their orders by starlight and the rim of dawn. Alessandro heard someone in the firing squad talking about a girl, and although he heard neither a description nor her name, he knew from the tone and the intonation of the word *she* that she was young.

Guariglia was shaking. "Stay in control," Alessandro said to his friend in a low whisper. Guariglia took in a breath that was almost a gasp, as if he would no longer be able to restrain himself but wanted Alessandro to know, at least, that he was still there.

"Stay in control," Alessandro repeated. "Your children and your wife must know that you died defiantly. If they know, they'll be proud of you."

"Who'll tell them?" Guariglia asked.

"Someone will tell them," Alessandro answered. "They'll know. Guariglia, my sister came last night. I told her about your children, and I asked her to help them as long as they needed it. She can pass through the world almost as if by magic—they won't throw her in railway cars and put her in irons, or stand her up against a stake and shoot her. She'll be able to take care of your children. It will be as if they are protected by a saint. You see?"

Guariglia's response was to weep, and in so doing he shattered the River Guard's flawless control.

"What they need the most is you," Alessandro said, "but they'll be provided for, and they'll have your love."

Guariglia nodded. "Not only do I love them," he said, "but they really love me. I could be ten times as ugly as I am, and they would love me just as much. When they look at me, they see something beautiful, and, dear God, they are so beautiful themselves."

A third officer entered the *cortile,* and the soldiers of the River Guard were directed toward the stakes.

They felt hollow, empty, and as if they were falling. Alessandro had the sensation that his lower legs were caught in fire and darkness, and that he was walking through thick mud, but with each breath he felt the strength to counter his affliction. As if he were a soldier in the last seconds before battle, his fear joined with a tremendous longing for the clash, and he imagined that the force of the bullets would unleash the furious angels of speed, velocity, and light.

"I don't like it that no one will remember us," Fabio said as they turned left toward the stakes.

"They'll remember *me,*" the Puppet Soldier declared. "They'll remember that I was the best shot in the whole fucking army."

When they reached the posts, they stopped talking, and stood straight. Not a single one of them knelt down. Not a single one asked for a blindfold.

The priests were humming like bees on a summer day. As they withdrew, they said to each man, "Christ be with you." They had pronounced this many times already and they would pronounce it many times more, and yet they were moved.

Taking up position, the firing squad did not unsling their rifles until ordered to do so. They stood at attention while the three officers conferred over their papers. One of the officers lit a match, and they peered down at the documents they were checking. "It's true," said the last officer to enter.

They walked across the *cortile,* approached each man, and said his name. When they got to Alessandro, they said his name twice, and then they made it part of a question. "Are you Alessandro Giuliani?"

"Yes."

"Rome has commuted your sentence."

Without hesitation Alessandro said, "The man next to me has children. I've seen them. They're babies, beautiful babies. He shouldn't die. They won't understand, and they need a father. Please, give him my name, and I'll take his. No one will know."

The senior officer, a major, thought for a moment, and replied. "You can do that kind of thing in the north," he said. "At the front anyone can do anything he wants, but not in Stella Maris. Stella Maris is too close to Rome. We're as powerless as you." He ordered one of the guards to remove Alessandro.

Alessandro refused to go. With his hands and feet bound, he shuffled and dodged, trying to stand his ground.

"Knock him down," the officer commanded, as if he had seen such a thing before.

The soldier raised his rifle and hit Alessandro on the back of the head. Alessandro fell forward into the dirt. They picked him up and dumped him on the ground behind the firing squad.

The priests went forward once again. Alessandro could neither move nor talk, but he could see everything. He wanted to shout to the River Guard that he would remember as long as he lived, and he tried, but the blow had rendered him speechless: He heard the priests in recitation—*Ave maris stella, dei mater alma, atque semper Virgo, felix coeli porta*—and he watched them withdraw.

"Unsling your weapons," one of the officers ordered. "Express rounds. Take aim."

Alessandro was overcome by the sound of the rifles loading, but then all was tranquil, and in the silence before the fusillade he heard Guariglia say, "God keep my children."

A SOLDIER OF THE LINE

A THOUSAND soldiers labored on the cliffs of a chalk-white bowl in the Apennines, cutting marble plinths to mark graves. At the beginning of the war a few hundred military prisoners had been sent to work under a cadre of quarry workers, but time and the course of successive battles had greatly augmented their number. When working in daylight proved insufficient to honor the dead, the quarry detail had been divided into groups and shifts as complex and disorganized as the rock faces they mined, and their industry continued into the night at a fast and even pace, under and above the glare of torches, floodlights, and strings of clear electric bulbs. The engines never were quiet. As one shut down, others took over, supplying current, traction, drive for the cutting blades, cables, and pumps, and steam to polish the plinths until they were whiter than the bones they would memorialize. When the mechanics took one generator out of service and switched over to another, the lights would surge under double power and then fall back to something that was merely steady and bright.

The few accountants and bookkeepers who found themselves laboring alongside revolutionary factory workers and lethargic peasants might have calculated that even had each man turned out one complete stone every day—which was not the case, for each stone had to be cut from the steep cliffs, lowered, re-cut, beveled, polished, and transported—they would have had to labor for many years to mark the graves of their fellow soldiers.

Given the extent of the operation—men crawling like ants upon scaffolding that hung over nothing; the crews sawing, cutting, and driving wedges; and trains moving back and forth carrying what looked like sugar cubes—it was hard to believe, though it was true, that this kind of stone was being cut all over Italy.

Alessandro arrived in the middle of the night. Two sergeants armed with pistols met him at a small station a few kilometers away. "Are you the only one?" they asked.

"Yes," he said.

"We were under the impression that a platoon was on its way."

"You were betrayed," he said.

Because he despised their familiarity, they marched him double time down a moonlit road that threaded between bare rock cliffs, and allowed him none of the customary rests on the uphill portions. Only when they came to the ridge that gave onto the quarry did they let him pause, and this they did not to be kind but to impress him with the otherworldliness of their work.

From the quarry, scepters of light emerged at sharp angles, like mineral crystals, and the thicket from which they came was a fume of light. Sometimes the beams were cranked into different positions as if they were choosing new targets among the stars. Hundreds of men worked below, in a brilliance that made the vast quarry look like a piece of bright moon that had crashed to earth. They appeared to be mining not stone but white light, and when they took the stone in slabs and caused it to float through empty space, tracked by searchlights, hanging on gossamer cables and unseen chains, it was as if they were handling light in cubic measure, cutting and transporting it in dense self-generating quanta from the heart of magical cliffs.

Huge rectilinear masses of white marble glided at all angles past each other in skew paths of descent, suddenly emerging in full blaze from darkness, and then dimming, only to gain strength again upon reaching the steel frames where they would be cut apart in the glare.

The sound of hammers striking rock and steel never ceased. From above they seemed to be the individual ticks and tocks of thousands of clocks that had been freed from telling time and taught to talk. Patterns and cross-patterns emerged in their excited conversation, music extracted from the gossip of the rocks.

Wheels spun hypnotically, illusions among their spokes oscillating back and forth in gleaming counterpoint. Open fires, forges, and white-hot boiler fires were fed by stokers and incensed by bellows. Rows of machines surrounded by tenders and oilers pulled an astonishing web of cables past innumerable pulleys mounted on every dihedral and face. The movement of the cables suggested that the whole scene was steadily rising. Scores of men dragged about clay-colored rubber hoses from which jets of water were ejected onto the cables that slowly cut into the marble. On a wide section of quarry floor a corps of bevelers and polishers worked in an orderly crowd not unlike that in armories where military clerks milled about their desks. In rows of tents beyond, no one was sleeping, for Alessandro had arrived right before the change of shifts, and every row between the tents was occupied by men pulling on their clothes. Camp stoves steamed with vats of broth and pasta. Alessandro could smell coffee, tea, and freshly baked bread. The shift engaged would eat before they slept. The shift that had been sleeping would eat before they were engaged.

"Everyone here eats a lot," one of the sergeants said. "Here you don't just sit on your ass the way they do on the fronts. You work. Each man is like a goddamned engine, and engines need fuel."

Alessandro didn't know what to say, but he did know he was hungry.

"Don't you have any things?" the talkative sergeant asked. Though he had been repulsed he could not cease being proprietary.

"What things?"

"A mess kit, a blanket. You don't have anything, do you."

"No," Alessandro answered as they started him down the path

that shortcutted the vehicle road into the quarry. "They took everything away from me before they were about to shoot me, and they never gave it back."

"What luck. Why didn't they shoot you?" he was asked cheerfully.

"I don't know."

"Don't worry about it. In your two months here you can make the gravestones for the boys who were going to shoot you. We need hammer men. You look like you were pretty strong before you softened up in Stella Maris, and in a couple of weeks you'll be stronger than you've ever been in your life. You're going to be swinging a ten-kilogram hammer sixteen hours a day, and I don't mean like some ass-head clerk. I mean sixteen hours, and you don't steal from us even a minute."

Then they reached the floor, and they were bathed in light and noise.

THE SOLDIERS in the quarry grunted, groaned, and hummed when they consumed their bread and soup. Half were shirtless in the cold night wind. Their muscles, seemingly as dense as steel, pressed against their skin like swellings. Veins and arteries with no place to go stood in isolation between hard muscle and elastic skin, like the vines that strangle oaks.

Alessandro had never seen human beings who looked like this. He had always been strong, especially when he climbed, but these men were three or four times stronger than the strongmen in the circus. Next to them, weightlifters were fat-ladies. The only people to whom they bore resemblance were the ancients who served as models for anatomical sketches and statues. Hundreds of men who had been born ordinary men, some of small stature, some surprised waiters and tailors and other unathletic weaklings, had become as strong as galley slaves. Whatever the process that had turned them to stone, it had also frozen their tongues and given them mythical appetites. A huge dark-haired man next to Alessandro drank hot soup until he sweated in the cold wind, and, as Alessandro watched, he ate four loaves of bread.

"Do you always eat like that?" Alessandro asked.

"Arrrghh!" was the answer he received, followed by a long arm extended as if to cuff him, but the arm was on its way to one of the two loaves that was still on the marble slab beside Alessandro's half-finished soup.

"Go ahead," Alessandro said, but only after the bread-eater had done away with most of it. "Would you like some of this one? I can't eat the whole thing. Here." The bread-eater took it like a trout taking a fly. "For me," Alessandro went on, "it's a great luxury to have so much bread. I was in a line battalion, where we didn't get much to eat. And then, in prison, well, I suppose everyone starves in prison."

The bread-eater's expression seemed to say, talk all you want, but wait until you face what it is that makes me eat five loaves of bread at a sitting. This silent communication was punctuated by one of the hammer men, who broke wind, which elicited the most extraordinary chain reaction from all of them, as if they were a drill team.

Alessandro, who felt that he had nothing to lose, addressed the hammer men. "I don't want to be like you," he said. "I don't want to be a muscle-bound bread-eating jackass who sings in a fart chorus."

"What did you do on the line, kill people?" asked a dark little ape.

"Naturally," Alessandro answered. "What else was I supposed to have done?"

"More work for us," the bread-eater said to his bowl.

"Is this a company of pacifists?" Alessandro asked.

They smiled an astonishing array of toothless, half-toothed, and toothy grins. "Less work," someone said.

"I take it you don't care about the soldiers who are killed, just about the demands they make upon your time?"

"We never see them," the little ape said.

"You should be ashamed," Alessandro told them. "I've seen them. You should be ashamed."

"Tell us that after you've used the hammer."

"I will," Alessandro shot back. "And I won't eat half a dozen loaves of bread at a sitting, either. You become an ape only if you're an ape to start."

"Not all of us are apes," he was told by a soldier who looked, indeed, like the model for the statue of Perseus.

"At least you can talk."

"All of us can talk, but we save our energy."

"I was in the line for two years," Alessandro said, as if to identify and defend himself.

"This is not the line," Perseus said, "but something entirely different. This is a dream."

As ALESSANDRO marched in a line three or four hundred men long on a steep path that led across the shelves and ledges of a cliff, he felt exceptional peace. Rising on a rock face was cause for an inner jubilation that, perhaps because it could not find an exit past the discipline and caution necessary to stay on, spun like the gleaming armature of an electric motor and stabilized the soul of the climber as surely as if it had been a gyroscope. Alessandro had once remarked on this to Rafi, when they were invisible to the world, hidden in the crags of a cliff in the clouds. Not only had Rafi understood, which surprised Alessandro, for Rafi was not partial to metaphysics, but he had responded immediately, telling Alessandro that the real beauty of forward motion was that, to achieve it, something else had to move either around or up and down—like wheels on a train or a cart, or the pistons and propellers of a flying machine, or the screw of a ship, or, in the case of a man walking, his bones, his ligaments, and his heart.

The hammer was ungainly, badly balanced, and heavier than a rifle. It pulled Alessandro off his stride and was hard to carry, and he wondered how he could possibly have the strength to swing it through a sixteen-hour day. And yet for the others it seemed as light as air.

Squads of men veered off to ledges and tables on different levels, but Alessandro, being near the end of the line, went as high as it was possible to go, to a platform of clean rock a hundred meters above the quarry floor. He and a dozen other men were taken to a forest of iron stakes, which served many purposes. They made fissure lines for the eventual separation of the slabs, provided bases and pivots for cables, cranes, and hooks, and, in a fanciful sense, they killed the virginal marble just as harpoons kill a whale before it, too, is cut into slabs.

"Take this one," a sergeant instructed Alessandro, guiding him to a stake that was waist high. "Work on it until you lose so much blood that you faint."

"I beg your pardon?" Alessandro asked.

"Fainting is a pleasure, and, don't worry, we carry you down."

"I don't understand."

"Your hands. The skin will come off your hands."

"Why not use gloves?" Alessandro asked.

"You're better off facing it directly," the sergeant said. "If you use gloves it takes longer, you're more exhausted because you're not yet fit, and you tend to succumb to infections more readily. And a glove will stick to the tissue underneath the skin."

Alessandro found the sergeant's account hard to believe, thinking himself strong enough to drive this and other stakes without much injury to his hands. "It all depends on control of the hammer," he told the sergeant.

"Exactly. The more the shaft moves, the faster you come apart. Grip the shaft hard," he said as he left.

Alessandro looked at the iron stake. The head was partially flattened and exfoliated, but its disintegration had been checked as if the stress of the hammering had hardened it.

He swung the hammer, and when he connected with the stake he heard a lovely metallic ring that joined the fast-moving chorus on the cliff face. The first strokes were pleasant, as were the following dozen or two, even though ten minutes of labor pushed the stake in only a few millimeters.

Because he knew he couldn't rest he started a slow and deliberate stroke that he hoped would protect him. After half an hour the skin of his palms and fingers was pink and blistered. Had he or anyone else been doing this in the garden, he would have gone inside for lemonade.

He stopped. The blisters were not painful, but they covered the inside of his hands. As he was looking at the stake and hoping for the best, the sergeant returned with another sergeant in tow. Now Alessandro became acutely aware of the pistols at their sides.

"Why stop now?" the new sergeant asked.

"Blisters," Alessandro said, knowing their answer and that they would give it with utter dispassion.

"Not a reason for stopping, a blister or two."

"My hands are like water skins."

"The bar has hardly moved."

"All right," Alessandro said. "If it has to be," and he knew it did.

The blisters didn't break until he had struck the stake twenty times or more, and when they did break, the fluid kept the pain from him for another twenty blows.

"Keep on," the sergeant ordered.

When his hands had dried and the handle was hot, each bell-like ring rolled up the loose skin that had been hanging from his palms and tore it so that eventually it all fell to the ground. In fifteen minutes his hands were the color of a rose, and in half an hour they had started to bleed, to exude viscous white fluids, and to crack apart.

The air itself hurt his harrowed fingers and palms. To grip something solid was out of the question, to hold a heavy object, quite insane, to swing a sledgehammer, unimaginable—and yet he did, for he knew that when he had bled enough he would faint and they would carry him down.

He surprised them with how long he kept going, and they had to step back because the blood flew in distorted parabolas that made thickening lines upon the rock floor. At times it appeared to be raining in a dense windblown cloud whose underside had turned red as it passed over a raging fire. The sergeants waited for Alessandro to fall. He didn't fall. Instead, he struck as hard as he could, for he had come to believe that he was holding a piece of the sun in his hands, and that he would use it to cleave the rock as Guariglia had severed his own leg. His muscles tightened and then relaxed, his arms flew out before him as flexibly as elastic bands, and the head of the hammer struck the top of the stake with costly precision. The stake was driven down until it disappeared flush into the floor.

Alessandro's clothes were soaked with sweat and blood, and his eyelashes were stuck to his eyebrows by drops of blood that had blown against his face like raindrops in a squall. He dropped the hammer and turned to the two sergeants. "Is that the procedure?" he asked, and fainted dead away.

THREE DAYS later he awoke on his back in a tent through which both the sunlight and blue sky appeared pale white. Wind-luffed plains of fabric shook the seasoned mahogany-colored poles.

His hands were bandaged in clean gauze that made him feel as if he had been changed into a nursery toy. Beneath the bandages he felt no pain, but only heat. After three days of sleep, he awoke as untroubled as if he had been in a tent on the beach during a seaside holiday.

Perseus came through the tent flaps. "You have only a few minutes," he said.

"No," Alessandro replied. "I have, in one form or another, all of eternity and the rest of time."

"Not before you begin to work you don't."

"How am I supposed to work?" Alessandro asked, holding up his padded hands.

"Your hands will be healed in ten days," Perseus told him, "and then you'll have the hammer all over again, but they let you do it in stages."

"Ten days is not a few minutes, or has Orfeo changed time?"

Perseus was ignorant of Orfeo. "Until you start the hammer again, you'll carry. Then they mix hammering and carrying. Your hands gradually toughen and you end up only hammering."

"What am I going to carry?"

"Steel rods."

"They have cranes," Alessandro protested. "And if they let me do the hammering gradually now, why didn't they to begin with? Did they want to see if I had special skin?"

"No, they wanted to lay you so low that you'd be able to carry rather than hammer."

Shaking his head in disbelief, Alessandro asked, "Why didn't they just assign me to carry?"

"If they had done that, they wouldn't have been able to transfer you to hammering. Now all they have to do is transfer you back. It's easier for them."

"Did you go through the same lunacy?"

"We all did."

"Why didn't you warn me?"

"Had you been anxious, it would have been worse."

"What do they do if you refuse to work?"

"Hit you with a rifle butt."

"And if you still refuse?"

"Shoot you. Do you know how many graves have to be dug?" Perseus asked. "In my estimation we're the most important men in Italy. Cadorna was a fop and a jerk. He'll be forgotten as nothing, and our gravestones will last ten thousand years."

"In the courtyard of my house," Alessandro stated, "are fragments of stone that came from the days of empire. They are devoid of anything but the quality of having lasted. The old laundress washing blouses in a tin tub used to catch my eye a hundred times better. A pine tree bending in the wind, or a bird alighting, would easily overshadow them—and I knew what they meant, because my father had translated them, and he told me. He used to take guests around after dinner, discoursing upon the fragments. I knew it all by heart at a very early age, but the maid walking past them in the corridor, her fat legs like spindle cones, her blue dress wrinkled everywhere except where it had been pressed by the heat of her stupendous ass, was far more gripping."

"Why?"

"Alive," Alessandro said. "I now think of anything alive the way the poor envy the rich."

"That's a long jump from your maid's ass. Obviously, you're educated."

"Like you."

Perseus made a slight bow. "Faculty of Philosophy, Rome, nineteen sixteen—interrupted," he said.

"Bologna, nineteen fifteen," Alessandro answered. "Faculty of Aesthetics. Nipped in the bud."

The smell of hot bread came from underneath the tent walls, and Perseus said that the ovens had just been opened. "You haven't eaten in three days. You'd better strengthen yourself."

"How can I eat," Alessandro answered, pointing his nose to his padded hands.

"Don't be ridiculous, they're perfect for holding a hot loaf of bread. You'll look like a kangaroo, but you'll be able to eat all you want. Now you can pick up a bowl of boiling soup as if you were a Cossack."

"Wait. Before you go," Alessandro said, when Perseus had already turned to exit. "Rome is still beautiful. The proportions are the same, the colors, the light, the shadows."

Perseus turned. "I know," he said. "I was there recently. It's going to be taken care of by women, isn't it. They'll have to be the guardians now that so many of us are dead, and will die." Alessandro nodded. He found the notion pleasing. "It makes sense," Perseus continued, "that we love them, and they will be entrusted with everything beautiful, and then, children."

AFTER HE had eaten several loaves of bread and been the object of friendly ridicule because of his kangaroo paws, Alessandro began to work. They put a pack frame on him and loaded it with iron rods until the tendons at the sides of his knees were so sharply defined they cast shadows. It was almost too much. He had to stagger up even the first steps, and was breathing hard just a little way from the ground, and he had to catch his balance at corners lest his exhaustion and momentum combine to push him over the edge of the unprotected trail.

Bolts and cables were affixed to the rock here and there, but for the most part the trail was an unadorned narrow path with rock projections that knocked against his iron rods and pushed him toward the abyss.

Though every step was painful, he soon found the rhythm of it, got to know the stairs, strengthened, and was able to sustain waking dreams.

As his bandaged hands moved in front of his eyes when he used them for balance and counter-balance, he was tempted to self-pity. Sheathed as he was, he seemed touching even to himself. *Once upon a time in the war they took a good panda bear who was completely alone, and wrapped his fat paws in gauze until he could do no harm. Then they made him carry iron rods up steep stairs until he was ready to drop in exhaustion. They were bad and he was good. He knew the right thing to do, always, and they knew how not to do it, always. This is because the little wood doll with squeaky joints had been put in charge, and dangled his legs from a high seat in the Ministry of War, where he wrote out the orders that had turned everything upside down. The evil little wood doll laughed and rocked back and forth in his seat as the panda carried and carried, but someday the panda would take the bandages off his paws, get on the train to Rome, and smash the wood doll into a thousand pieces.*

Initially, the idea of killing Orfeo had not been delightful. Alessandro had no passion for killing, and he wondered if he could actually bring himself to do the deed—but it had to be done. Quite clearly, Europe had come apart and millions had died not because of the shifting of great historical forces or the accidents of fate or destiny, the several bullets of Sarajevo, colonial competition, or anything else. It was because Orfeo had slipped from his seat in the office of the attorney Giuliani and been carried upon the flood, like a corked bottle full of shit, until he had lodged upon a platform at the Ministry of War, where his feverish hand and only half-innocent imagination had been directing the machinery of nations in homage to the exalted one and the holy blessed sap.

There he sat, with no neck, with the sexual feelings of a chamber pot, his right foot tapping out the rhythm of his hand as his hand sang out orders and decrees in cursive lines and flourishes that looked like vine tendrils or wrought-iron railing. Perhaps if his feet had reached the floor, or if he had had no moles growing on his face like the cairns tourists leave on trails above mountain lakes, or if he had not slicked down his carbon-black hair with ink and olive oil, Europe would not have come to ruin. It didn't matter, he had to be killed, and Alessandro was the one who had to kill him.

Alessandro now knew how to kill. He knew exactly what to

do—plunge a bayonet at a forty-five-degree angle into Orfeo's chest, entering just at the base of the neck. To accomplish this he would have to put his left hand behind Orfeo's head, as if in affection, to hold the little scribe in place.

He went up the stairs under his nearly impossible burden, cleansed and clear-eyed because he knew that the destiny of Europe depended upon his courage and resolution. Thousands, tens of thousands, millions of graves would be filled if he wavered. Lovely young girls in uncountable darkened houses all over the world would be deprived of the men for whom they had been born, and who had been born for them.

Alessandro was not so foolish as to imagine that the instant he killed the inkish thing the war would stop short amid the clatter of discarded rifles and bayonets. Such a great thing as war, like a potter's wheel, would keep on of its own momentum, but when the tiny jewel upon which the wheel found its central bearing was crushed, the wheel would slowly wind down.

He knew that as soon as Orfeo saw him, aged twenty years and heavily scarred, striding down the long aisles between the rows of clerks, he would jump to the floor and disappear like quicksilver. He might even produce a pistol and fire at Alessandro from behind the lectern, his legs jerking at every shot, but it wouldn't matter, Alessandro would take each bullet as if he were an oak or a melon. He might start to bleed and go blind in one eye, or feel warm blood burst inside him like a sack of water, but he would pick up speed, race past snub-nosed clerks still drafting orders, draw the bayonet, and get the dwarf.

From this he derived great satisfaction, even joy, as he labored in the quarry under a rapidly changing winter sky. Once he had determined to do it he felt all his strength returning, for he had discovered how to break up the white ice that covered the blue lake of Europe.

The guards marveled at the way the new man had adapted. He had his breath, his heart was not pounding, and he returned time after time in an even sweat to request another load, which he took up to the heights as if he were a pack animal or a mountaineer with calves as thick and dense as the barrels of small cannon.

THEY STARTED him driving some of the rods he carried, five minutes at a time, then ten, fifteen, and so on, until, three weeks after his panda pads had been removed, his hands were so heavily callused he could calmly hold a hot coal. Eight or ten hours a day walking up steep trails, under seventy kilograms of steel, and six or eight hours swinging a heavy hammer, changed him physically into something he had never been. In the first few days, his softer flesh simply disappeared. With no reserves of fat, he began to eat four loaves of bread at a sitting, as he had predicted he would not.

The heart and lungs of this soldier in his late twenties were shocked and strained almost to collapse, but they soon rebounded. He thought of himself as an engine. To fuel the incredibly dense and powerful musculature, he need a great bellows and a first-class pump, and he had them. He moved up and down the cliffs and swung the hammer like the ancients of whom he had read, like a Phrygian who worked the mines, a prisoner of Knossos, or a Pala-conian slave boy.

After Alessandro had rushed through his meal, he washed in a piped torrent of icy water and ran for the tent, where he spent ten seconds removing his boots, ten loosening his buttons, and five straightening the blankets and making a pillow of his spare clothes. As soon as his head was down he was unconscious, surrounded by a dizzying blackness that rocked him in smooth stressful arcs that compromised with gravity like a pendulum or a swing, and then, for eight hours, he was free.

Even as he slept he knew somehow that this was his good time, that he had best sink into it as deeply as he could, and at reveille, whether at night or in the day, he had great difficulty rising and felt as if he weighed a thousand kilograms, or as if he were coming back from the dead.

Hard labor, deep sleep, simple food, cold water, the lack of possessions, and the presence of the morning stars upon arising gave the quarry soldiers so much strength and energy that they might as well have been the rulers of Europe lost in manic conquests. For hours after dawn they raced up and down the paths and struck at the rods like athletes and knights. By nightfall they would be exhausted, and then the lamps would flash on, and volumes of white light spilling through the dust and spray would energize them again, until only much later would they be ready to drop, anticipating with pleasure sleep that was studded with brilliant dreams.

As much as Alessandro's life was sharply divided into feverish activity and absolute rest, so were his thoughts. He killed Orfeo a hundred times a day, and each time was as elaborate as a bullfight. He would see himself walking up the aisle and drawing the bayonet from its oiled sheath. He went through innumerable mental versions of the speech he would deliver before the lunge, the actual twist of the bayonet, and what he would say when he turned to the newly liberated, frozen clerks.

As he struck the stakes he murdered Orfeo, and when the head of the stakes reached the level of Alessandro's solar plexus, at the level of Orfeo's head, they became Orfeo's head.

At night Orfeo made no appearance whatsoever. Alessandro's dreams were as free of obsession as his waking hours were controlled by it. At night, he melded images until they sang. Their intensity reflected the state into which he had fallen and the world into which he dearly hoped he someday would rise.

In the 19th River Guard it had been said that if a soldier were lucky enough to survive the war he would spend the rest of his life trying to figure it out. Whatever time they had left was taken from them by gas, a bullet, a shell, typhoid, or, if not those, a series of unanswerable questions that would go with them to the grave. Indirectly, Alessandro began to pose these questions in his dreams.

For half the year the Tiber was nothing more than muck and reeds, and seldom was anything but opaque, so the fountains of Rome were for Roman youth something to ponder like a river. Once, having left his house after an adolescent raid upon his father's patience, Alessandro had bested all his previous records and spent seven hours next to a simple round pool in a little park in what was then a new suburban quarter to the south, and if it is true that nothing is ever forgotten, he had the images and coordinates of a hundred million lazy trajectories marked in cascading water and hesitant droplets revolving at the peak of sunlit wavering arcs. If it is true that nothing is ever forgotten, the pictures he could summon of a stream collapsing upon itself in silky alternation from side to side might have been enough to provide the stuff for him to construct in his unconscious the extraordinary plumes of water that he saw in his dreams, and that, within his dreams, for want of a better word, he called fountains.

He probably dreamed what he dreamed for the sake of the well lighted struggle at the top of their arcs. Here, just after the maximum disintegration of the main stream, when the water had burst into a continual and rapturous explosion, individual droplets took to the air. If a nature could have been attributed to them it might have been one of optimism and hopefulness, for when they were driven apart and they shot off on their own they went into a brave and jovial roll, spinning as if to gain altitude.

Despite their hopeful twirls, the masses of droplets fell back and disappeared, but Alessandro had watched too many fountains for too long not to have remembered that some of the droplets escape. At the very top of the plume, in the greatest violence and turmoil, the water is beaten and pulverized into a fine mist, and the air that is pushed out of the way by the upward jet of water propels the mist in its own arc until it slowly begins to sink in diaphanous curtains that oscillate in the breeze. Some droplets are combined and some separated. Those that combine head downward at a faster rate. Those that are further separated continue to hang in suspension, bobbing up and down and glistening in the light.

If the wind is right, some are swept into the sky at high speed. They shrink and disintegrate until they are invisible and can ride the high blue winds that girdle the earth.

Alessandro's dreams took him to the top of the arc, where he watched the explosions of foam, the fight against gravity, and the downward collapse as the waters combined like an army in retreat. Though he could not rise with the mist, he did not deny the fact of its rising, and he watched it with a hopeful eye.

Then the water was transformed from broken foam to an unbroken surface as hard and smooth as ice, and Alessandro was hurled across it with the sun reflecting in the waves below. The engines of a float plane swelled to full power, and the noise was as riveting and dramatic as an endless crash. Alessandro could taste the cold fresh lake water, and the palms of his hands were seared against the hot metal of the engine. The floats that skidded over the surface as they tried to break free were polished rosewood richer than the light in a clearing at sunset. They had the same feel and quality as the rowing shells in which Alessandro had loved to race, but they were heavier and stronger, and they skipped like bobsleds over the speed-hardened surface of the lake.

The engines reached maximum power early on. Their sound never varied, but the plane itself kept accelerating—not because the drive grew more powerful but because of less and less resistance. When it lifted off the chill lake the echo from the mountains virtually disappeared.

"You've failed," said a man who sat between two other men at a table covered in green felt. They were in extraordinarily elaborate robes trimmed with ribbons and decorated with purple bars, red pom-poms, foxes' tails, chains, keys, and ermine. Alessandro wore a black robe, its only decoration his head emerging from the flat collar.

"Me?" Alessandro asked, acutely aware that they had the foxes' tails.

"You, yes, you," replied one of the two who were assistant professors restricted mainly to words of one syllable, even if they had inestimable quantities of polysyllabic magma beneath their tender crusts, waiting for the chance to erupt into professorhood.

"Why? I've tried to see the truth in things."

"But you haven't been clever enough."

"I was clever when I was a child. I could do all kinds of tricks; I could memorize, analyze, and argue until my opponents were paralyzed, but whenever I did these things I felt shame."

"Shame?" the professors asked, angry and amazed.

Alessandro lost himself for a moment in the great hall where bookshelves rose to a vaulted ceiling five storeys high, and stained glass windows at either end made the scholars feel both that they were submerged in a tropical sea and that they would be prepared were scholasticism subsumed in theocracy. He was sharply retrieved by his inquisitor. "Shame? For what?"

"It was easy to be clever, but hard to look into the face of God, who is found not so much by cleverness as by stillness."

"Is that why so many foolish people believe in God?"

"If an idiot sees the sun does it mean that the sun doesn't exist?"

"Why did you embark upon an academic career?"

"My father wanted me to join him in the practice of law, but I saw how greatly he suffered the requirement of being clever. It separated him from his soul, and it didn't get him anything other than a living. He said he spent most of his time scratching in the dust. I thought that, in my career, I would be charged with searching for the truth. I apologize for mistaking the requirements."

"You should have gone into the Church."

"No. The Church brings argument and analysis to the door of heaven itself."

"But you could have lived on a stone pillar in the desert, or entered one of those monasteries where they don't talk to each other."

"Italians don't make good hermits."

"You failed your examinations because you could not exercise the cleverness that would demonstrate that you understood."

"Demonstrate to whom?"

"To us."

"I felt no need to demonstrate to you."

"You knew, then, that you would fail?"

"I had hoped to slip by. My passion is not for analysis, but for description."

"Anyone can describe."

"Anyone can analyze. You, sir, work in a big grocery store with lots of things on the shelf. You arrange and rearrange them, but to describe something so as to approach its essence is like singing. I told you this when I wrote about Oderisi da Gubbio and Franco Bolognese. Oderisi's *'Più ridon ...'* was how Dante drew attention to the humility of the miniaturists, who tried in the simplest, densest strokes to convey the essence of what they saw, and were not interested in discursive interpolations, conceits, or dazzling excursions that proved them to their fellows—although they had to do some of this simply to arouse their patrons."

"Oderisi da Gubbio is no excuse for failing to do what you tendered."

"I thought you might mistake for cleverness my love of beauty."

"That might be clever in France, where they confuse wisdom with appreciation, but not in Bologna, where we are at war with the perfect world that God has decreed. Our passion, no less a thing than yours, is to go underneath, to take apart. In that sense, we who scratch in the dust are desperadoes and outlaws, and our lives are tremendously exciting."

"In the end," Alessandro declared, "your workshop full of parts will prove infinitely less than the whole, and you won't even know what it was you have pulled apart, much less how to reassemble it.

You'll have only your efforts, which will evaporate like warm beer, whereas I will have been looking at the world and rendering it just to know it for what it is, and it is something far more solid and sensible than warm beer."

"You are condemned."

"I would rather be lost in the breakers than on some flimsy platform above the sea."

Then came a volley of rifle fire, which, like the sound of artillery or the central point around which Alessandro's dreams revolved, could not be adequately described or remembered. The sharpness and percussion, like the roar of great engines, were always less when recalled.

Alessandro was standing in a sunlit grove on the side of a hill, half a century after the war. An old man with white hair and white mustaches, he had come to witness a memorial to the combat, the dead, and the peace.

He saw himself from the outside, as is possible in dreams. He was in his seventies, his frame was slight, and he had a marvelous shock of white hair. Gravity had shortened him, and only God knew what accident or slow disability had provided him with the opportunity to carry the gold-handled cane that he grasped in a lean and gnarled hand.

Of all the people assembled at the memorial no one had a better claim to being there than he, an old man on an autumn day, standing in a high collar and a stiff morning-coat, as light as a locust, peering down a long row of white headstones. He strained to see himself and felt pressure against his chest as if he were leaning against a breastwork.

Two old men, one a double amputee, sat on his right, in the uniform of the Great War, their heads bowed. Next to them was a younger man who could not have seen the war but was subdued exactly as if he had: he could only have been a politician or an orphaned son. A table on the grass was covered with a mass of white and deliriously fragrant flowers.

With names, dates, and battles set into them in sharp grooves made by hardened steel, the gravestones stretched in long rows for as far as anyone could see, just the way divisions used to move single file down the roads. But these rows were still and orderly, for everyone had arrived.

The wind that coursed through the pines made their supple branches paint the deep blue sky behind them, and just beyond the first line of markers three riflemen were firing volleys in the air. The same breeze that moved the branches whipped satin flags on staffs bent forward as if in a charge, and carried the small puffs of smoke that emerged from the rifle barrels up and over the heads of the crowd.

While a detachment of young soldiers did their best to imagine, the two old veterans on Alessandro's right had bowed their heads in defeat. Alessandro himself was still wondering after all that time, trying to make sense of memories that never fell into place.

At the front of the crowd were two girls of nine or ten, one wearing a coat and hat of navy-blue wool, the other a more summer-like frock and a hat with flowers marching around the brim. The tops of their heads came up to the elbows of the riflemen. The one in the woolen coat had placed her hands over her ears, and the one with flowers on her hat jumped with each shot, and both were smiling in amazement at the strength of the sound. They must have been a little afraid, and they must have wondered how the men could fire rifles, held so closely to them, without flinching.

ON THE last full day of work before release, when the fires under the machines were welcome for their warmth, it snowed. No one had ever seen the quarry in snow.

As the first flakes descended early in the morning everyone stopped to stare. For a moment all was silent except the engines, and then even they were disengaged as their operators turned toward the sky to feel the tiny snow crystals falling against their faces.

The snow grew heavier throughout the afternoon, until the white marble was covered in white, and chains of airborne ice twisting in whirlwinds danced about the soldiers' legs and swallowed them in freezing clouds.

At night, searchlight beams cutting through the snow made it speed up or slow down as they moved, sometimes until the immense number of particles seemed to be rushing to the ground like crashing airplanes, and sometimes until they appeared to be frozen still, or moving back whence they had come.

Blinded by patterns of light and sound that grew ever more confusing and more intense, the soldiers worked themselves up to a feverish pitch to match the pace of falling snow and racing pistons, and, caught in a thousand rhythms, Alessandro seemed to float. Dozens of slabs rode the aerial trams, flashing in and out of the smoke, light, and snow, crossing and intersecting as hammers and saws rang out against the rock. The music of his own heart and breathing, the dervishes of snow that sometimes blinded and sometimes entertained, the mournful steam whistles, the clatter of engines moving across rickety tracks . . . the weave here was as tight as it could be, tight enough to elevate the bodiless spirits that labored in it until they floated like swimmers. It had a life of its own, but that life was suddenly shattered when lightning struck amid the snow, homing for the iron that had been laboriously driven into high points. For half an hour hundreds of speechless soldiers were shelled by thunder and light that illuminated every snowflake and blinded them as it scourged the marble cliffs with brightness. The thunder rattled the heavy engines and the lightning made the fires beneath them seem dark and cool.

In the intervals of the bombardment the soldiers were blind, but when the lightning struck they saw every great detail as it was forced upon them with merciless clarity, for whatever it was in the world that cast spells also sent storms of sound and light to break them.

THE TRAIN north was stopped in Rome for forty minutes, the doors of its windowless boxcars thrown open, and the men allowed to pour out. Believing that they were on their way back to the Isonzo, most of them dashed for the prostitutes and restaurants conveniently located in and around the railroad station.

"For those of you who wish to visit libraries and museums," a sarcastic young officer had said, "keep in mind that if you are not in the train when it leaves, you will probably be condemned to death."

Few went beyond the confines of the station itself. Those who did dared not venture more than a block or two, where they spent half an hour bouncing up and down on a woman in a bed, or eating a meal, of exaggerated richness, that they might later involuntarily display to their comrades cooped-up in the same swaying boxcar.

But Alessandro ran through Rome as fast as a horse. He hardly ever touched a sidewalk, preferring the street. His papers and his pass were in his left hand, and a bayonet was tucked inside his tunic.

The streets were crowded early in the evening, so Alessandro allowed himself fifteen minutes to get to the Ministry of War. Assuming that he could evade capture, he would need fifteen minutes to get back. Including the difficult and perhaps impossible feat of gaining entry to the ministry and finding Orfeo—if indeed he were there—Alessandro would have ten minutes in which to do the deed.

Had the changing of engines, filling of tanks, and loading of provisions taken another twenty minutes, Alessandro would have run home to see Luciana, but chance had directed him to murder the old scribe.

That evening the wind was coming from the northeast, where battles and winter were in action simultaneously. The city had been ever-so-lightly dusted with snow, and though none had lasted, the chill remained. People wore heavy coats and furs. Many soldiers in all sorts of uniform were walking casually, marching in units, bearing messages, driving carts. No one seemed to notice Alessandro.

As he raced through streets and piazzas and the warrens and alleys that surrounded them like masses of brambles, he smelled chocolate, coffee, and hot milk in expresso bars, and fish frying in olive oil, beef roasting, bread baking. If the doors to a leather shop, a stationer's, or a haberdasher's would happen to open as he flew by, he caught the scent of their wares and remembered the delights of peace. He loved Rome most when the wind was cold and the piazzas were empty. Then, if you listened hard, you could hear the accumulated song of the city, the residue and reflection of whole ages and their destruction. He was going extremely fast, but occasionally he had several seconds' view through ranks of houses, when he saw the Gianicolo, and his own house perched on the hillside like a lifeless projection of rock. He looked for lights and was disoriented because he saw none.

One could not enter the Ministry of War without either a pass or an appointment, and half a dozen efficient sentries monitored the in-going traffic. They checked each pass and detained holders of appointments until receiving telephone clearance. Alessandro approached the enormous building, hoping to find an unwatched opening or a clear space of fence that he could scale. One of the entrances in the back was filled with motorized trucks unloading supplies. Thinking to ride like Ulysses under the belly of a ram, Alessandro walked up a ramp upon which half a dozen provisioners' vehicles were parked. Then he veered toward the loading dock, intending to help in carrying or just to walk past the two lackadaisical sentries. After all, he was in the uniform of the Italian army, and he felt entitled to be there. As he passed a wine truck he noticed that its front wheels were resting against chocks. He removed the chocks.

The truck was overloaded with five-liter Chianti bottles. It rolled silently down the ramp, hit a stone pillar, and overturned in such a way as to fling out the bottles and smash them against a stone wall in a chain of muffled explosions.

No one was able to resist the overturned truck, and as the sentries ran to it, holding their rifles by the throat and swinging the butts like pendula, Alessandro walked past a phalanx of cooks who had gathered to watch the catastrophe. In a minute he was wandering freely in the corridors, just like any other clerk or orderly.

The hall of scribes was dim and half deserted. Only the grayest, palest natural light came from its high windows, and that was rapidly fading. A few gas chandeliers were lit above the long rows between desks, but most of the scribes had turned off their individual electric lamps and gone home. Those that remained were bent into pools of cheerful yellow light in the center of the desks. The scratchings of the remaining pens, the occasional adjustment of a chair, and the quiet breathing were appropriate to an examination hall, and yet here, where the absolute destiny of hundreds of thousands was decided as if this were heaven itself, was none of the terror and urgency of a university examination hall, in which the stakes were almost meaningless. Here the pen scratches sounded like insects chewing leaves or corn, but in the great written examinations of Bologna they had sounded like flames consuming a house.

Orfeo's lamp was lit but he was not at his desk on the raised platform. "Where is Signor Quatta?" Alessandro inquired of a stray scribe.

"The chief is absent from his desk."

"I know that. Where is he?"

"He's in a different post."

"Where?"

"He's not available."

"Excuse me," Alessandro asked, after a moment of reflection. "Would you be so kind as to direct me to the water cabinets?"

"Of course," answered the stray scribe. "Down the center aisle, just outside the main door, to the left."

A pair of pointy black riding shoes was suspended over the floor, heels resting above the porcelain base of a toilet so as to set them at a ninety-degree angle to one another. Before the view was cut off at the top by the stall door, the headline of a newspaper showed, upside down. Smoke rose in a white twisting column, and every now and then a bitter laugh would echo within the marble walls of the latched chamber. Alessandro rattled the door with martial violence.

"What! Occupied!" shouted Orfeo, but Alessandro shook the door so fiercely that the screws began to work out of the marble. "Occupied! Occupied! Occupied!" Orfeo screamed.

Then Alessandro began to kick-in the door.

Orfeo screamed "Wha?" and the pointy shoes hit the ground. When the latch was broken and the door flew open, Orfeo had just finished buckling his belt and was trying to button up his fly.

Alessandro appeared with his bayonet drawn. It glittered with gun oil that oozed down the blood groove.

"Filthy! Filthy!" Orfeo yelled. "It will make an infection."

"Infection will be irrelevant."

"I saved your life."

"You murder others."

"What were they to you? If you had told me, I could have spared them, too. It never even occurred to me."

"You wrote the execution orders?"

"Of course. We have to do everything at a steady pace. If we don't—huh, well—the pile of execution forms in the supplies cabinet looms over the others, and it looks asymmetrical. So, for every transfer, and for every ten requisitions, five discharges, et cetera, et cetera, *toga virilis,* we have to do an execution."

Alessandro stared at Orfeo in disbelief as the time passed dangerously and the water in the toilet pipes hissed like singers in an insane asylum. He remembered how Guariglia had died, and he pushed Orfeo farther back into the stall and closed the door behind them.

"I had to do it! I had to do it! You can't let things get asymmetrical. If you do a job you do it right—*totus porcus, hocus pocus, diplodocus, fari quae sentiat le farceur!*"

"Christ!" Alessandro screamed.

Orfeo had retreated to the toilet, where he stood with one foot in the bowl. "For the love of God, don't kill me in a toilet," he begged.

Breathing hard, Alessandro stepped back, and leaned against the door. "Where would you like to be killed?"

Orfeo cleared his throat. "I would like to be killed . . . in the whitest most boneless valley of the moon, where the blessed sap congeals like alabaster and flows in dough-like strata. I would like to be killed within earshot of the soundless sweep of the blessed one's hot golden robe as it decapitates the breathless atmospheres of the lighter planets and takes the air of day from the unchangeable path of the holy blessed sap." He paused. "I would not like to be killed with a bayonet," he said, smiling.

"No?"

"No, he wouldn't like it."

"Who?"

"The great master of the holy gracious sap, the lord whose foot quashes suns, who directs and interprets through my tense hand the jerky flow of the holy blessed sap. The sap of his outermost capillaries plays havoc with the earth, for the way the sap exits in lines and curves is the scythe of fate. As the holy blessed sap falls in chanting forms, life and death follow. Not even a breaking wave could strike harder than the blessed sap as it quietly dries on parchment and vellum wrenched from the innards of piously dancing sheep."

Alessandro lowered the bayonet and leaned back against the door.

"My scribes admire me," Orfeo replied, still standing in the toilet. "They shine my boots, press my coat, and bring my lunch on a silver tray. When I talk to them about the gracious sap, everybody listens. A symmetry has evolved because the sap will not surrender. The blessed one approaches, throwing veils of sap ahead of him like an American mantis.

"I don't murder anyone. I sit with my sap. No longer do I create orders anew. I gave that up long ago. It was not helping the gracious symmetry of the sap."

"Now you write the orders exactly?"

"Exactly, but for one thing. I transpose numbers. One hundred and seventy-eight sappers to Padua becomes eight hundred and seventy-one. The tenth of May becomes the fifth of November, and so on."

"I'm surprised we haven't lost the war."

"To the contrary," Orfeo said, wagging his finger, "the war goes brilliantly, and I don't even care. My effect on the war is like that of a rainstorm on a sailing race. I'm not after anything but sap. It doesn't make any difference. It's like those cages full of monkey balls. It doesn't matter which one is drawn—except for the monkeys—the effect is the same. What do you want of me? Really! I warned you. I warned everyone.

"You were all too tense and too tall. You thought life was graceful and would continue gracefully, and that you would never hear from people like me, but now the harpsichord sings for my kind—not from our effort, but from the mad turning of the ball.

"Go ahead, kill me. I'll die in ecstasy. I'm standing in the bonewhite valley of the moon. My feet are anchored on flumes. My heart sings in my chest with all the pain of little men, and I have my triumph in sadness, in sorrow, and in sap."

"How can I kill you?" Alessandro asked, as if in despair.

"After all these years, you know how to kill, don't you? You've killed?" Alessandro nodded. "And yet you can't kill me. Why? It's because I'm distasteful. I am. I'm like the rotten little oil fish, covered with spines and slime, that fishermen in small boats quickly throw back.

"When my mother saw my bent legs and oversized head, even she wanted to kill me, but she couldn't, because it was too distasteful. Thus I was left to usher in the sap. I have suffered all my life. I've not had one free moment. I've not been happy a second. It's always the blazings of lightning or the burial dark."

"It hasn't been so easy for me, either," Alessandro said. "Not recently. But I'll die before I'm mad like you."

"That's your choice," Orfeo told him. "Me, as surely as I stand upon this commode, I'll have the power to wait for the gracious sap. I'll wait in fog, rain, or on the mountaintop, but I'll wait, and the blessed sap will come, and do you know what it will do? I'll tell you. It will *fuck* the typewriter."

Alessandro was stunned. Still, he managed to say, "I saw typewriters in the hall of scribes."

"No one said the battle would be easy. They creep upon me like a lapping tick. All day long, tick-tock tick-tock tick-tock, ding! Tick-tock tick-tock tick-tock, ding! Whoever invented that machine...!" His eyes fired in rage.

WHEN THE boxcar was sealed and all but a few were safe within, rolling north to the battlefronts, each soldier told of the pleasures he had enjoyed in Rome. The tales of flesh were so graphic, real, and unabbreviated that some of the soldiers had to sit modestly with their knees up against their chests, or with newspapers on their laps. Complicating their distress, the stories of sex alternated with the litany of the cooking school: "First they brought a single bowl of *zuppa di pesce*. I ate that while my steak was cooking on the grill and the chef mixed the pasta and oil. To my left was a plate of fresh basil and tomatoes. . . ."

By the time Alessandro's turn came, a fire burned in the fire pit and water was boiling for tea. As the night grew colder and the car warmer, he spoke to men half illuminated by flames, but he was also speaking to the darkness behind them. "I haven't eaten," he said, "I didn't enjoy a woman, and I didn't go home. What did I do? I stood in a toilet stall in the Ministry of War and debated within my heart whether or not to kill a little dwarf who combs his hair with ink and olive oil. He was perched on the toilet in front of me, with one foot in the bowl, ranting about what he calls the coming of the blessed sap."

"Did you kill him?" asked a man whose face, like a planet in a candle-lit orrery, was yellow, orange, and black.

"No."

"Why not?"

"Your question speaks to the heart of things. At the moment, and maybe forever, I can't answer it."

Alessandro was happy to drink boiling-hot tea from a big tin cup. The frigid night air whistled outside as the train dashed through tunnels in the Apennines, and the black of night was like a cathedral. His eyes sought its infinitely high ceiling, and although they found nothing he felt as if he were going forward not to some obscure death but to the resurrection of beauty and a meeting with those who had gone before. As the train broke into open country-side, cutting a path through the dense cold air, racing the winter moon, Alessandro felt as content as a child in its mother's arms.

SOMEWHERE PAST Bologna and before Ferrara the train went onto a siding and the doors were opened. The soldiers folded their blankets and jumped down from the boxcar to walk in the sodden fields and breathe the fresh air, as a winter afternoon precociously imitated evening. The sky was dark gray with solid cloud and sporadic rain.

Walking across an inundated field on islands that barely rose from shallow puddles with wind-ruffled tops, Alessandro smelled the air and was reminded of other winters and other dark places, where, after you came in from the cold, the battle was over. The one thing above all others that distinguished army from civilian life was that in the army you lived outside. The wind and the cold came in from under the sides of the tents, through the flaps, and through the cloth itself, both the seams and the weave: a breeze that passes through a tent is remarkably cool and persistent and sometimes strong enough not only to pressure its way in but to go right out again.

A soldier who spends years in the open air gets something about him like a deer. He can hear events in the wind and read the terrain, distinguishing readily between the scent of a pine forest, carried on droplets of rain that have been blown through it horizontally, and the scent of air rising from a field of shoots and stubble soaked in cold water. Hunters returning on November nights are grateful that the skin is flushed, the nose is cold, and the senses as sharp as those of the animals that have been killed. So it is with soldiers in wartime, and much more so, for they live in the wind and cold for years.

Alessandro turned around at a row of impenetrable brambles and went back across the field to the train. Several thousand men had grouped around small fires: now and then sharp gusts of wind sprayed water on them, but the wind was cold and dry enough to take the water up in almost instantaneous transpiration.

A tall soldier with a beard so thick and black that he looked Persian whispered to a man inside the boxcar to bring him a rifle. He had seen a buck come to rest after it had tucked itself into a thicket of its own color. The rifles were chained. "Get an officer," the man in the boxcar whispered back.

With his eyes fixed on the place in the bushes where he thought the buck had stopped, the Persian stumbled along the trackbed until he found an officer. Immediately interested, the officer unlocked a stand of rifles, and the Persian disappeared into the semi-darkness as the officer wondered if he were going to come back.

Ten minutes later a shot cracked across the field, and everyone stared into the dusk. Then the Persian appeared as a dancing black dot that eventually grew arms waving for others to join it. Soon the buck was carried in, its head and horns hanging down, the nose still glistening. The fur, somewhere between the color of a chestnut and the color of dust, hadn't a single blemish other than the bullet hole.

"You have to drain the blood, it takes at least a day," someone offered.

"In peacetime you drain the blood, but now you get a butcher," the Persian responded.

"From where?"

Calls went out for a butcher, and they got two, who eviscerated, skinned, and carved the carcass with bayonets that they stopped several times to hone on sharpening-stones they had been carrying in their pockets. Alessandro imagined that the butchers had taken them from civilian life as he had taken a small volume on Giorgione.

For their labor they were given some cuts of venison, and the rest was left for the soldiers in Alessandro's car, with the Persian in charge of both cooking and rationing. The wood fire was too small and had already burned down, so they took a gas cylinder from the caboose and flared a welding torch into a cooking fire that was as bright as a gold flag in the midday sun.

They made a rack from their ramrods, and swept the flare back and forth as if it were an enormous basting brush. As the sizzling venison was distributed, a train from the north came whistling through the dark and shrieked by them, shaking the earth. As soon as it had passed, they were ordered to re-embark.

Alessandro returned to his blankets with a banquet-sized piece of meat too hot to eat. The fire in the fire box was re-ignited, the doors were slammed shut, and the train began to move. By the time it had clicked across the switch that routed it back onto the main line, paused to pick up the switchman, and started gaining speed, the soldiers were silently devouring their roast, which, though it had been cooked without salt, herbs, or wine, was the best that Alessandro had ever had. He tried not to think of the head and horns upside down on the field, with neither a living thing nearby, nor a light, nor a sound except for the wind whipping occasional sheets of rain through the dark.

THE TRAIN ventured onto every millimeter of railroad track in Italy and crossed into every siding to await with deference the passing of generals in their private cars. After the slaughter of the buck, the soldiers had been in the dark. They went outside to eat and stretch only at night, in cold fields and damp forests through which their fires shone like lights in a jack-o'–lantern.

And then one morning the soldiers grew suddenly still as the heavy latches were lifted and turned. Just before the doors slid apart, a man from Pisa took the opportunity to say, "The air is thin. We're in the mountains."

Alessandro straightened his back and raised his head. The mountains, unpredictable in their power, were the heart of his recollection, and he knew that the Pisano was right. He had known it all along from the way the train took the many grades, from the metallic thunder of bridges over which they had run in the middle of the night, and from the white sound of streams falling and flowing in velocities that could have been imparted only by awesome mountainsides.

When the doors were opened the mountains appeared in massive scale. They seemed to advance upon the car, threatening to break apart its filthy wooden walls. They were blindingly white, in volumes so great and cold that they forced open the eye to admit the glare of day. Fifty kilometers away, ice-covered peaks blazed in the morning sun. Down a valley that seemed to run forever, its floor hidden under deep snow, its sides patchworked with stands of pine and meadows in a dappled coat of green and white with borders as trim as military haircuts, walls of glistening gray rock rose to spectacular heights and ribbons of water and ice fell silently from overhangs and outcrops. Before the water could hit the ground it froze into mist, briefly turned gold in the sunshine, and disappeared on the wind.

Their view of this made the soldiers in the freight car as giddy as glider pilots, and Alessandro was painfully thrown back to his youth. In summer, emerging from a deep forest, he would hold fast in the sudden revelation of a sunlit peak, or watch from above as mist traveled through a valley as if it were possessed of human tenderness. "The valley is tired and sick," his father had said. "Clouds and mist have come to blanket it as it rests." At the age of ten, Alessandro had not known the further meanings of words like *rest* and *peace,* and although now he did, he realized that he would never fully know the mountains in all their guises and enchantments.

The lieutenant who had opened the doors told his company to collect packs and weapons, and form ranks. As the soldiers leapt to the ground their rifles banged against their backs and awakened them with an exact reminder of who they were and what they were doing. The rifle, Alessandro had long known, is the infantryman's tool, franchise, and birthright. Without it he is a creature of indefinite despair—a gazelle without legs, a rhinoceros without a horn. With it, he knows his small place in the universe, and that not a being alive will take him for granted until he is stone dead.

Still primed to run, the compact engine that had pulled the train through alpine dawn exhaled at short intervals. It shuddered and dripped as fragrant pine smoke flew from its stubby chimney, and the soldiers formed ranks, adjusting straps and belts, squaring their rifles, and straightening their backs. Two thousand men, not a single one of whom had eaten breakfast, finally stood at attention in groups of fifty.

Low-ranking officers inspected, cajoled, and firmed them up in preparation for two things. The sun was going to rise over the mountains to the southeast, making brilliant a landscape already packed with light, and a general was due. No one knew which would come first, and only a few understood which was more important.

"Oh Christ," the man next to Alessandro said under his breath.

"What's the matter?" Alessandro asked.

"You can wait all day for generals."

"Still, when they arrive, everyone smiles."

"True," said the soldier, "but why?"

"That's what makes a general," Alessandro stated. "They have the ability to cause any number of miserable sons of bitches to smile like idiots in an insane asylum. Even I myself, and I know all about it, begin to feel like a grateful and adoring dog."

"Yes, yes, it's true. How do they do it?"

"I think it comes from the feudal past," Alessandro answered. "When the lord of the manor met his assembled serfs they were always intoxicated with happiness that they could neither justify, nor explain, nor prolong in his absence."

"What did you do before the war?" asked the other soldier, who spoke like a Milanese.

"I was a sardine," Alessandro said, looking straight ahead. "A blue-and-gold, in the Mediterranean." Alessandro stole a glance at the Milanese, yet another intellectual with an air of deadly seriousness. "I swam about. I ate tiny sea creatures. At night," he added, almost as an afterthought, "I was the managing director of a company that decorated roller coasters."

"The economy is rich and complex, and we have much in common," the Milanese said.

"How is that?"

"I, too, was the managing director of a company that decorated roller coasters, and I worked almost exclusively at night."

"Perhaps it was the same company. Where was it?"

"Where was yours?" the Milanese asked.

"In Rome."

"Mine was in Ostia."

"We had a branch in Ostia."

"Then you must have been our competitor."

"The branch was inactive."

"Ours as well."

"Shut up!" an officer screamed. In an army wracked by mutiny, conversations such as these were nothing more than coded sedition, and if the officer didn't understand the code, all the more reason to stop it.

The Milanese said so softly that only Alessandro could hear, "You should be more exact."

"What do you want from a sardine?"

"Precision. A sardine is a precise kind of fish. Look how many get in one can. They don't fuck around, because they don't have heads. We should be like that."

"We are." Alessandro smiled crookedly at the Milanese, who briefly smiled back. Then, as the ranks grew still, they stared ahead, listening to the occasional exhalations of steam and watching a curtain of light envelop the mountain range ahead of them.

They heard an automobile engine in the distance. Officers began to primp, and some ran to and fro. It was just like the action on stage before the curtain rises on the elephant scene of *Aïda*.

"Dogs," someone said, in reference to their officers, but, still— without orders—the ranks stiffened.

A staff car approached from down the mountainside, winding through a small Alpine village and shifting gears for the last, steep, snow-covered stretch. Alessandro had never seen a car go uphill in snow. This one had chains on the drive wheels, and its tires dug into the compacted road surface, like a cookie cutter.

Though the general was young, he had been in the mountains for years, and he was attentive not to the scenery but to the fresh troops. They stood rigidly, but they still had an air of confusion and dizziness. He, on the other hand, had long ago assimilated the grand scale of the peaks.

Realizing that it would be difficult to speak above the noise of his automobile, he signaled for his driver to stop the engine. Then, apart from the irregular hissing of the locomotive, the only sound was the sound of the wind. As a hawk passed over them, the general let it speak for him, and not until it had disappeared did he begin, by raising his stick to point to the section of blue that the hawk had deserted.

"Did you see that?" he asked, referring to the hawk. "That tells the story. A lot of hawks are still up here. They don't pick at carcasses. They fly above us as if we were unworthy of notice, which, in their world, with its time, is quite true. As impossible as it now seems, the mountains will soon be silent. We and our guns will have come and gone, and the wind and trees will stay forever.

"This white and silver one that flew overhead was going north up the valley. You'd think that I'd sent him, because that's where I'm going to send you." He turned to the north, and, with his arm still extended, turned three-quarters back—an attractive gesture that seemed to say he might understand paradoxes and contradictions.

"That ridge, in the west," he said, pointing to a line, far above the tree line, disappearing into the mass of white summits, "goes all the way to Innsbruck. Between it and its twin to the east, not far north, is the Brennero. Some of you may have passed through the Brennero on the way to Munich or Warsaw. We are going that way too, on our way to Innsbruck, because we haven't any other way to go. If we move through the valley they'll fire down at us, so we have to go straight on, confined to a narrow field of maneuver.

"I myself would prefer to outflank them by way of Norway or the Black Sea, but, not being British, we don't have that option. For us, it's straight up the camel's back and right down his throat. They know we're coming and they've got the route fortified with belt after belt of trenchwork, mine fields, and firing positions.

"These things are a rather intricate piece of art, at least in the Germanic sense. Whenever they have a trench, they've got a number of trenches behind it, like zither strings. If you see wire, it means mines. And it seems they never are content with just one row. They alternate in many layers. After all, they invented the Sacher torte, didn't they?

"You may wonder how I can ask you to die so that we can take apart their layer cake, especially when you and I know that no matter what we do, the mountains will soon be silent. How is it that, if you turn from this meaningless task, I will have you shot?

"It's rather simple. If I turn from this unpleasant task, I, too, will be shot. So it goes all the way to the top, and you know as well as I that the chiefs of the people, if they surrender, are shot by the people they would shoot for surrendering.

"This is a conundrum easily resolved by shooting only the people on the other side, and that's how war goes on and on. Though the whole world may have gone mad, we are going to regain our sanity, gradually and fully, by means of a slow and rewarding fiction. I am asking you to go to Innsbruck. Every meter will be contested, and for every meter, someone will die, but we are going to regain our sanity by vesting in each particle of ground an artificial value. It has been done throughout history with metals and spices. Merchants assess their lives in numbers, and they are almost always saner than those who set out to seek the truth. Like merchants, we will peg our sanity to artificial standards—land taken, and days alive.

"I'm responsible to Rome for capturing ground, and I cannot change that. I'm responsible to you for keeping you alive, and that

I will not change. I do my best to balance the two. We don't practice the same carnage up here as they do lower down. It's the terrain, the thin air, and our relative lack of mass. And the north is not infinity, for the mountains stop, and then you're in Germany. If you survive, you'll be able to remember having been there. You'll recall it fifty years from now, in some quiet place, surrounded by children, not a single one knowing the folly to which you were committed, and all sweetly ready to commit it anew."

He hesitated. "And if you don't ever leave this place . . . Well, the air is magical here, and so is the sudden darkness, and so is the chill. In the daytime, in the light, with the sky changing, nothing is quite as alive. At night or in storms it seems like the tunnel to death. Don't misinterpret me. I want that tunnel so crowded with the braying enemy that no room will be left for us, but, should you not make it back to a table in the piazza, you will have died in the best place for dying the world has ever known. What I mean is, here, you're practically at the gates."

AFTER THREE hours' march they turned off the road into a pine forest heavy with wet snow, the last stand of trees before the meadows that led, eventually, to Innsbruck. In the near distance they could see the Italian fortifications and trenchworks, and, beyond them, the Austrian.

Theirs was only a little crowded corner of the forest. Already settled among the trees were twenty thousand men who appeared to have been there for quite some time: they had elaborate tents, log shacks, and covered galleries around their mess fires. Not a single tree had been cut for firewood or construction, because the trees sheltered them from enemy observation and broke the force of incoming shells.

Alessandro's brigade divided into battalions, companies, and platoons, and pitched tents of sand-colored canvas. They tied the tent stays to trunks and branches, extending them at all angles and elongating them to reach the anchor points. This transformed the densely populated forest, which had been open and free of brush, into a maze of twisting passages formed at random where the spider-work of tent stays did not block the way.

Field kitchens and latrines stood uncomfortably back to back in small clearings. The cooking apparatus for Alessandro's battalion blazed within as the cooks made still more *tortellini in brodo*. The reason that Italy had entered the war, Guariglia had said, was to stimulate the production of *tortellini*. Though the broth might be watery and the *tortellini* full of foreign matter and donkey meat, it would be hot, and, in the mountains, anything hot was a virtue.

Alessandro claimed a space in the corner of a ten-man tent. He didn't want to know anyone, he was too tired, and he knew it wasn't worth the effort, for they would die or disappear just like everyone he had ever met in the army. Though he had fallen in with the Milanese, it was by accident. The Milanese looked much like Alessandro, but Alessandro thought he was a harder case—tougher, older, and more military. Unaware of what he himself had become, Alessandro was wrong. They spoke to one another in mild insults and half-insane prolixity.

As they lined up to get their soup and bread, snow began to fall. Almost first in line, Alessandro and the Milanese, independently, had drunk the soup as fast as they could, put the bread in their pockets, and run for the latrines. Through the hissing snow came an invisible voice from a fetid canvas stall. "It makes sense, of course, that two roller coaster guys should eat as we did and pocket their bread, but even though we shared the same profession in civilian life..."

"Avocation," Alessandro interrupted. "For me, it was just a hobby."

"Naturally," said the Milanese, who, because of the fierce and explosive quality of army food, could speak no further.

After they had washed their mess kits they walked through the snow to the tent, where they found only a young boy who was too sick to eat. They removed wool sweaters from their packs, put them on under their coats, and lay down to sleep. It was not very cold, but when the heat of the broth wore off they began to shiver, and they took out their blankets.

"A beef-ox," the Milanese suddenly declared. "I was a beef-ox."

"What?" the bleary-eyed sick boy asked, turning on his elbow.

"Not a bad way to make a living, if you play your cards right," Alessandro said.

"Not bad at all."

"Tell me," Alessandro asked, "how did you know to get to the head of the line, eat quickly, run for the latrines, and the rest?"

"How do you think?"

"A veteran of the line."

"Just like you."

"What were you doing in the quarry?"

"What were *you* doing?"

"Too serious to say," Alessandro answered, thinking of his father, Fabio, and Guariglia, "and too sad."

"That's where we differ," the Milanese declared. "Me, I was too frivolous."

"In the army? How did you manage it?"

"I'm almost ashamed to say. I left the ranks—I deserted, if you must—because I have an uncontrollable craving."

"For what?"

"I'm ashamed."

"Just say it."

"Office supplies."

Alessandro stared at the Milanese in disbelief only because he knew that he was telling the truth. The sick boy rolled over, sighing as if in a dream, and the Milanese went on with his confession. "War does crazy things. I always liked fine paper and envelopes,

expensive pens, drawers full of little brass clips, labels, ink bottles—
you know. And staple guns. And I've always been partial to port-
folios, folders, and briefcases, and postal scales. These things are...
they're comforting. They're like presents under a Christmas tree.
My desire for them is informed by the same impulse, I believe, that
sculpted the national character of Switzerland. I even like rubber
stamps."

"What about postage stamps?" Alessandro inquired.

"I love postage stamps. Nothing is as reassuring."

"What does your father do?"

"He passed away when I was seven. He had a stationery store,"
the Milanese said. "Why do you ask?"

"No reason," Alessandro said.

The Milanese went on. "Nothing is as reassuring as a good
supply of paper clips. If you have them in little leather boxes, it
makes you feel like Cesare Borgia."

"And you deserted," Alessandro asked, "to buy office supplies?"

"Not to buy them. To be with them. They're going to keep me
alive."

"How?"

"Yes. My desk at home is perfectly stocked. I have the most
complete selection of papers, envelopes, implements, stamps, and
supplies that you can imagine. I have Venetian stationery and Florentine boxes, and enough stamps to last for twenty years—if I
live, if I don't get a disease of the liver, or a stroke, or something
like that. I spent all the money I had, and everything is arranged
just so."

"How is that going to keep you alive?" the sick boy asked. He
no longer seemed so sick.

"My books are dusted, alphabetized, and catalogued. Every
week, my mother winds the clock. Wood is in the stove, ready to
burn. My mail is stacked carefully in a walnut box. The lamps are
well polished."

"But how is that going to keep you alive?"

"As long as it's kept in perfect order," the Milanese said with disarmingly deep concentration, "it gives me a protective aura. It's around me, lock set, like the atoms of a crystal. Bullets won't touch me if my office is tranquil."

"What if your mama comes in and craps up all the stuff?" the boy asked.

The Milanese smiled. "Then I'll die."

Alessandro looked away. "How long were you in the line?"

"A year and a half," the Milanese said.

"It did things to you, you know."

"It may have, but I'm going to live. How long were you in the line?"

"Two years."

"Don't tell me that your mind is completely unaffected."

"Did I say that?"

"You implied it. Where were you?"

"Mostly on the Isonzo. And you?"

"Right here," the Milanese said in a hopeless and resigned way.

"In this wood?"

The Milanese shook his head in the affirmative. Alessandro could just hear his blankets move. "In this wood, in every corner of it, and in the trenches on the hill. I know every one, the Austrian trenches, too. They used to be ours."

"It's not good to come back to the same place."

"I have my aura."

"Does your aura extend a few meters from you? An aura can't be as tight as a silk stocking."

"Oh yes it can. It's tighter than a silk stocking. One thing about an aura is that the man next to you can be blown into tiny particles, and you remain unscathed. Sorry. And there's something else you should be worried about if you have no aura."

"Which is?"

"They haven't passed out ordnance. In the whole brigade we have no machine guns. I haven't seen any mortars, grenades, or flares, and we have only four clips of ammunition for each rifle."

"What could happen between now and tomorrow?" Alessandro asked.

"They could attack."

"But the trenches . . . We're in reserve. You don't think it's likely that the trenches would go tonight, do you?"

"In the mountains the trenchworks are shallow and inadequate, which is why we're here—to be ready to break through if the Austrian line buckles, and to hold the line if our defenses are overrun, giving the strategic reserves behind us time to mobilize. At the western edge of the wood, we're in the most dangerous position. We should have our ordnance now. We should have had it when we came in."

"Has it ever happened?" Alessandro asked. "Have they reached this encampment?"

The Milanese looked at Alessandro with a pitying glance. "It used to happen twice a week."

Then the other men began to stream back into the tent. They shook off the snow and went for their blankets, where they lay shivering in the dim light of the afternoon. As the soldiers slept, brigades of cloud glanced across the hillsides and threaded through the pine wood, mixing with the smoke of the dying fires in the field kitchens. No sentries had been posted in their section, because, although they were close to the enemy, they were hard by thousands of other troops. The snow brushed against the tents and slid off them, and the clouds became so thick that it seemed like night.

AWAKENING AT five in the afternoon, with icy fog rushing by as if it were water from a broken dam, Alessandro felt feverish and sick. Though he hadn't suffered a chill, had had sufficient rest, and was neither wet nor exhausted, he felt, nonetheless, like a typhoid patient. Everything was sore to the point of paralysis, he had no energy, and he was burning hot.

The cure for this was to get up and walk. A cup of tea, some deep breaths, conversation, and perhaps a task to perform, would do it. No one was in the tent. He struggled to put on his boots, fold his blankets, and stagger out the door. As soon as he was in the open air he felt slightly less feverish, but he remained giddy and weak.

In the center of the brigade clearing a huge bonfire burned; in sub-clearings, the battalion kitchens rattled and shook as they built up steam; and as far as the eye could see into the dark wood, the fires were replicated, until those very distant hardly broke through the snowy maze of trees, giving the impression of both hell and a summer night in fields swarming with fireflies. Half the soldiers wore their blankets, which Alessandro knew to be a mistake, because the blankets would get wet and dirty.

The aromatic smoke was difficult to distinguish from the fog except that the fog, which was really low cloud, left moisture that sparkled in the firelight and the smoke left a scent that promised to follow each soldier for the rest of his days. A string of pack mules nearby stamped and brayed. Troops from other brigades wound through the encampment, moving to and from their own tents, the trenches, the headquarters, and the road.

The huge bonfire was surrounded by a Sufic ring of men who slowly turned in circles to warm themselves. Places in this line were hard to find and jealously guarded. Magically held gaps stayed open for the passage of mysteriously chosen acolytes and subalterns who fed the fire with huge pine logs so heavy they had to be carried like the Cross.

Alessandro despaired of finding the Milanese among fifteen hundred men in half darkness and fog, each man in uniform, many hooded in blankets as if in domino, and he went back to the tent to get his cup and bowl.

As he placed his hand on the butt of his rifle to steady it during the strange little curtsy required at tent doors, he heard the deep rumble that he had not heard for almost a year, the familiar and dreadful sound that soon grew shrieking tentacles capped with blasts that lit the dark. Scores of guns were firing simultaneously. He knew the trajectories were streaming in his direction, he felt the blasts in his chest—hollow metallic bursts like the cross between thunder, cymbals, and bombs—and he saw the light darting into the tent as if the purpose of the barrage were to make shadows on army canvas.

Young officers ran swiftly through the wood, darting this way and that way in the twisting corridors. Soon, thin lines of soldiers, some running with straps and pack flaps whipping the air, and boots not completely laced, thudded in all directions on the paths across the snow-covered forest floor.

The officers of Alessandro's brigade were absent for indoctrination at headquarters, and the noncommissioned officers were acutely aware that their men were badly armed. In no way could the soldiers of a freshly constituted brigade be marshaled into fighting units when no one knew his platoon sergeant and no parade ground existed for sorting everything out. As a result, everyone was running every which way, and not a soul knew what to do.

Returning to the tent, the Milanese said, "This is a poor time to have a battle," and rolled himself into his blankets.

"Why?" Alessandro asked. He could no longer see the Milanese, but only hear his slightly muffled voice.

"My mother winds the clock tomorrow, and I don't like to fight if the clock isn't all wound up."

"Don't worry," Alessandro said reflexively. Big flakes of snow began to fall like cinder from a volcano.

"And the guns. I never heard so many guns before."

"On some sections of the Isonzo," Alessandro commented, still on his knees, "they massed thousands of guns."

"Look," the Milanese said, "the Austrians come running through, and they always reach the trees. By the time they get here they're wild-men, and now I have only twenty rounds of ammunition. Everyone has only twenty rounds. You can go through three dozen before the first charge. What are we supposed to do? And I don't like fighting in fog. With the stars there's something more tolerable about it, and in the cold air up here the stars go crazy. They're so bright they jump around like fleas, they burn like magnesium. If you get killed on a night like that you go straight up."

"How many make it to the trees?"

"As many as don't die in the field or on the ridge. They resent the fact that we have this place, sheltered from their artillery. It's so foolish it's crazy. The attack will start in less than an hour. Sleep, and when the guns stop, you'll wake up fresh."

"How can you sleep?"

"I think of a girl I knew in the university. I never had a chance with her, even though I was the one for whom she was made and she was made for me. She married someone else. When I think of her face I can fall asleep, because she's so beautiful and I love her so much that the sadness of losing her pushes me down and away from life."

"What about your stationery?"

"A poor substitute."

Alessandro rolled himself into his blankets and tried to sleep. He wasn't tired, and although the shells flew over them, explosions seemed to bounce the forest floor. Eventually, though, he did sleep, and in a dream he told himself two things. In between the blasts of artillery he said to himself that he was sleeping fitfully and was not well. And he scolded himself over and over, a thousand times, for not being awake, because if he were not awake he might not have enough time when the order came to fix bayonets. He slept this exhausting sleep until the barrage stopped. Then he and the Milanese jumped up as if the silence were an artillery shell exploding in their ears.

"Now we go up to the firing line and waste all our cartridges," the Milanese said.

They groped around the tent, looking for ammunition, but found none. Then they went into the dark among the trees, where they saw that the clouds had been pulled apart in the wind and tossed up to higher altitudes. The stars were revealed steadily in the gaps, making patches of the sky look like ocean liners that suddenly appear on a dark sea.

"It's colder," said Alessandro, "and it's almost dry."

On the ridge, where the trees had been topped by passing shells, a long line of troops lay on the ground, their rifles in front of them. A vast meadow descended to the northeast, dropping off below the trenches. They waited for the ground to change color as the Austrians advanced en masse. The sergeants had caged only a few crates of ammunition from the brigade to the east, and extra rounds were passed out as stintingly as if they had been roast beef or money. One machine-gun squadron had gotten hold of a machine gun, but they had just two boxes of belts.

Someone asked why the trenches didn't extend across the meadow. A stocky sergeant with a pitted face told him that the meadow grew on rock, and that when the snow melted, or in summer in the rain, it became a sluice.

"Where's our artillery?"

"Why waste shells?" was the sarcastic answer from someone down the line.

Further sarcasms were cut short by the appearance of a dark mass at the base of the hill. Not only was it too slow and too uniform to have been the shadow of a cloud, but the moon had not appeared and the stars cut shadows too weak for men to see.

Conversation ceased. The companies in the trenches to the left and right started an enfilade, but an enemy mortar barrage, like a huge wave smashing against a quiet beach, silenced them immediately—their firing ports were aligned in the wrong direction and they could only shoot if they rose above cover. At the same time, the main body of Austrians emerged from forward trenches onto open ground.

A moment after this, the dark shadow at the bottom of the hill snapped into different form as more than five thousand men who had been crawling suddenly began to run.

On the unfortified Italian line rounds were rammed into chambers and bolts locked. The sound was like that of coins rattling in a mechanical sorter. Mixed and informal prayers arose and then were forgotten as the firing began. Sergeants scolded premature ignitions but were soon drowned out by the growing cascade, and at the first flashes from the approaching enemy the whole line opened up until the guns made so much smoke and noise that no one could see or hear. They fired at the enemy where they remembered him to have been, as the pits of their stomachs fell because they knew that he was really much closer.

A gust of wind lifted the smoke. Now the compact mass of attackers was thinning, and began to move in many directions at once. Orders were shouted on the Italian line, and groups of men suddenly jumped up and ran madly to other positions. Alessandro's brigade, with neither formations, nor officers, nor ammunition, was in panic. As the Austrians divided to encircle the hill and come into the tent forest, some of the brigade stayed at the ridge, and others returned to the trees.

Alessandro and the Milanese remained until they had no more ammunition. They had waited until they could sight individual soldiers and fell them with well placed shots, but most of the men in their sector, being inexperienced, had wasted their ammunition in early firing and been unable to hit anything with the few rounds they had held back. The enemy soldiers were very near and coming forward at a run.

As the brigade heard the Austrians breathing and watched them emerge from the smoke they tried to move to either side, but their own lines had curled into flanks and they had to fall back. This they did without hesitation, racing into the trees as if they were game-birds racing out.

Alessandro and the Milanese stayed together even at a run, and they found themselves in the brigade clearing with a thousand terrified soldiers. A few officers who had made it through the mortar barrage on their return from headquarters were screaming assembly orders, but it was hopeless. Then they gave up on making formations. "Fight among the trees! Fight among the trees!" they commanded as the Austrians entered the thicket and started to fire.

"We have no ammunition!" they were answered.

"Fix bayonets! Stay in the trees!" the officers shouted, knowing that to be chased into the open would be the end.

Alessandro and the Milanese fixed bayonets and stood in the pines. Bullets were knocking against the tree trunks like woodpeckers, and severed branches fell as if a hundred foresters were in the air above them pruning the greenery. A third soldier joined them. "What are we supposed to do?" he asked, and when he received no answer, he left.

No time had remained for an answer. Thinking that the Italians were so disciplined as to forgo firing in thick cover, the Austrians ceased fire and charged with bayonets and trench clubs. Even the most inexperienced among the Italians, the little clerks and the young boys who had never been away from home, knew that they now had an even chance.

The Austrians were bigger almost to the man, and wore barbaric cloaks and furs that made the neatly tailored Italians shudder. Alessandro thought that his own uniform, in comparison to the pointed hoods, horned helmets, and sheepskin vests of the enemy, made him seem very weak. As the Austrians ran through the trees, cutting the obstructive tent cords with bayonets and short-swords, and as a line of enemy advanced toward him, cocking their arms if they carried clubs and raising their rifles if they were going to use bayonets, Alessandro realized that the entire Italian army was dressed like waiters. He wanted to laugh and cry at the same time, and, when he found he could do neither, he was angry.

Three men approached. Never in his life would he forget them. The one on the left had no neck, a snapping-turtle's jaw, a mouton cap, and, in his right hand, a long mace with steel spikes mounted on four gleaming brass plates at the head. In his left hand was a small sword. The man in the middle, in fur vest and spiked helmet, was preparing to lunge with a bayonet, and the one on the right had a red beard and was carrying all kinds of leather holsters and sheaths that were strapped onto his coat. He raised his rifle as if to shoot.

The Milanese was nowhere to be seen, and Alessandro had no place to fall back. Although these three were the immediate threat, their companions had fully infiltrated the wood, and everyone was surrounded. Certain that he was going to die, Alessandro watched the red-bearded man slowly draw a bead on his chest.

"You're out of uniform," Alessandro said, thinking that this pointless declaration would be his last, but he was surprised to see the three of them suddenly take their eyes from him. He heard a loud crack and saw the red beard tip back as the rifleman was thrown dead off his feet. The round intended for Alessandro ignited as the dead man's finger closed on the trigger, but the short Mauser was already pointed into the trees.

"I saved a bullet," the Milanese said, stepping from behind a tree. "I don't need it. I've got my aura."

Then the one in the spiked steel helmet and animal-skin vest came running, bayonet gliding ahead. Steel coming toward Alessandro at whatever velocity, as long as it was a blade, allowed him a surge of happiness undoubtedly derived from the many hours of vigorous release and good fellowship of fencing classes that broke day-long immersions in Greek and Latin. He held his ground, firmly parried the blade, and drove it to his left. Not without experience himself, the Austrian accepted the blow and turned his rifle so the butt flew toward Alessandro's jaw.

I don't have a helmet, Alessandro thought in the instant he raised his rifle and met the blow. The weapons slammed together and both men pulled off as fast as they could, rocking their rifles down and forward again, but whereas the Austrian took the direct route and went straight ahead as soon as his blade was aligned, Alessandro took a small step left and, with the bayonet, knocked his opponent's rifle also slightly left. In that restrained gesture, he gained the advantage. The Austrian followed through and missed, and as he was trying to correct his vanishing momentum, Alessandro took a tiny step back, rocked for half a second, and drove the point of the bayonet a hand's depth through the sheepskin and into the man's side.

As the Austrian convulsed, his bayonet cut Alessandro's left forearm cleanly, opening it like a butcher's stroke against a steak, but his force was spent and he could not recover. With the bayonet pointing off to the side, he received Alessandro's full thrust in the solar plexus, and when the point of the knife reached the spine, the whole body shuddered and left the ground in a stiff jump.

Talking to himself, moaning, gasping for air, Alessandro pulled out the blade. When he turned he saw the Milanese backed up against a tree, holding his rifle in front of him to protect himself from the remaining Austrian, who was swinging his mace as if he were a knight. It splintered the wood of the Milanese's rifle, broke off the bolt lever, and made pocks and grooves in the barrel. The Milanese's hands were battered and covered with blood, but he held the rifle even as he collapsed.

As the Austrian hit harder and harder, Alessandro started to run. The mace took off most of the fingers of the Milanese's already bloody left hand. The rifle dropped, the Milanese's head tilted to one side, and the mace, like a machine that could think, came down hard and quick against his face and skull, puncturing it in twenty places and turning half of his head into what looked like ground meat. His cheeks fluttered and air came rattling through his mouth like wind vibrating a reed.

Alessandro clenched his teeth and drove his bayonet at the barbarian in the mouton cap. The barbarian knew how to fight. With his left arm he brought his sword up to deflect Alessandro's bayonet, and with his right hand, and a huge grunt, he swung the mace at the center of the rifle, intending to knock it from Alessandro's hands.

Alessandro's entire body vibrated, and only because he was enraged was he able to hold on. The mace had embedded itself in the wood of the rifle and would not come loose. With every move either man made came a howl or a grunt, as if they had no other way to breathe.

Alessandro pulled hard on his own rifle, jerking the mace from the hands of the Austrian, who now had only a sword, as in a fencing class.

For Alessandro, every move was predictable. In school, the match would have been called and a better opponent found for the Italian. "Education," Alessandro said as he steadily and easily beat the man back. Baring his teeth, as the word demanded, and widening his eyes, he said it ferociously in German: *"Erziehung! Erziehung! Erziehung!"*

He knocked the small sword from his hands and pushed the bayonet into him. The Austrian had jumped backward, but Alessandro had jumped forward, and he heard what sounded like an apple being cut in two. The man had not died, but he was dying. Alessandro turned away from him.

His arm hurt. Clutching the wound to try to stop the flow of blood, he fell on his knees and crawled to the Milanese. The Milanese's mouth was open, his tongue projecting, blood still seeping from within. The side of his head had been transformed into an anatomical drawing. His right eye had been knocked from its socket, and lay between his legs in the snow, and his left arm was upraised, locked in the position he had faithfully held until and after the rifle had fallen from his hand as the fingers had been severed. The Milanese looked like a body that had been left in the trenches for days, but he had been dead for less than two minutes.

Alessandro had never known his name. As he stared at the corpse, he imagined a woman going into a neat little study and carefully winding the clock.

WHEN THEY found Alessandro he was unconscious, but he was kneeling, with his shoulder against the tree, and his mouth open. They went right to him, because he looked like someone who was about to stand up. His pulse was twenty, and the corpsman who closed the wound expected him to die.

The name of the village to which Alessandro was sent to recover had been changed from Gruensee, a pond that reflected emerald meadows, to Vittorio, where the Italian army had gained the momentum it needed to reach villages like this so as to dictate to them their new names.

Three-quarters of the population had fled and half the rest had been put in detention. The fifty empty houses, three small hotels, and two public buildings had become an army hospital. For the first time since he had run through the streets of Rome, from Orfeo's toilet stall in the Ministry of War to the train station, Alessandro saw women—not just the sullen German matrons who had stayed to tend livestock and little children, but a large number of army nurses and volunteers: not only Italian women, but French, English, American, and Scandinavian. They went alone or in small groups, and for wounded soldiers removed from the front they awakened an entirely new sense of the world.

As Alessandro rode into Gruensee on the back of a flatbed truck, the sight of these women assaulted him with more force than had the fleece-jacketed Austrians. Their gentleness, tentativeness, and beauty made him feel as if he were in a vivid dream. Some wore gray uniforms, others gray coats over white uniforms. The mountain light was such that blond hair took on a fine metallic sheen, like white gold, and darker hair came up in full color. Light glancing from faraway snowfields and glaciers filled in the faces of these women as if they were angels.

Just before the truck halted, it passed a dispensary. A young nurse in a white gown was standing at the door, looking out at the mountains. She was slight and blonde, with a beautiful, evenly proportioned face. A starched nurse's cap rested almost invisibly on the back of her head, framing her face with a thin white border, as if it were a Swedish halo. Her standard-issue nurse's gown was closed at the neck by a red-and-white enameled cross that was repeated, in cloth, on a white band around her left arm, and the gown fell away voluminously, belted with a sash of the same wrinkled cotton. Her hands were clasped behind her as she rocked slowly back and forth from heel to toe, with her head tilted toward the mountains. Enveloped by gray light reflected from the snowfields, her eyes were brown with a touch of slate and green. Had they been blue, her golden hair would not have been so warm. She was the most beautiful woman he had ever seen.

AFTER AN orderly moved Alessandro from the hallway of Ambulatory Clinic 2, a nurse took him into an examination room. She had shallow black curls and teeth as white as the ice on the mountains. Her bright eyes were magnified by spectacles that made them sparkle as if they were wet. As she cut his bloody sleeve, her gown fell forward and Alessandro saw her breasts. Even though her body was nearly touching his, he stared at the mountain range that separated Gruensee from the battle beyond. The light was vanishing but the image of the nurse in the afternoon sun did not fade.

Alessandro's tunic was in shreds, and the dressing applied by the nurse with the spectacles was growing heavy with warm blood. He watched as the mountains turned gold and then salmon-colored in light so delicate that it seemed as if it might have been blown out like a candle. Cold rain swept by in the valley below, raiding the fields of Gruensee, and when the mountains shone through they seemed to be floating on movable platforms of cloud.

Alessandro was not surprised at how long he had to wait. In the army, it was said, if you entered a dispensary with an arrow through your heart you would have to wait at least four hours, and, according to a rumor that had swept the ranks after Caporetto, a soldier carrying his own severed head appeared at a field hospital and was told to come back later.

When a doctor finally removed Alessandro's bandage he did so with a roughness that suggested more than just fatigue. Alessandro felt a cold and treacherous pain echoing through him. The cut spiraled gently from just beyond the elbow to just above the wrist, and underlying the pain was a chill lack of feeling, as if the flesh were dead or dying.

"Not a hint of gangrene. The circulation has been impeded, which is the quality you feel that suggests death. Look," the surgeon said, spreading the wound to prepare it for cleaning—and nearly killing the patient. "It's purple. Hardly touched the muscle, except in the center. How did you get it?"

"Bayonet," Alessandro answered, grimacing in pain.

"Whose?" the doctor asked aggressively.

As the accusation came clear, Alessandro felt a surge of contempt. "I didn't know his name, and after I killed him he was dead, so I couldn't ask."

The surgeon dipped a handful of gauze in a jar of alcohol, and slapped it down on the wound. "I'm doing this," he stated, "to clean the wound so you won't die of infection, and because of the way you speak to officers."

Alessandro had no words. He tried to imagine that his arm was not a part of him, and that the son of a bitch who was his doctor was not there.

"Some soldiers wound themselves to get out of the line," the doctor said as he finished bathing the cut. "Because of the way they miss the vital part and yet make convincingly bloody gouges, you'd think that they were surgeons, but they're not as clever as they think, and a third of them die of sepsis.

"Now, this," he continued, examining the wound, "is very neatly done. It looks as if you paid someone."

"I didn't."

"Whether you did or didn't, you'll need a drink while I sew it up. I'll only have to put in twenty or thirty shallow stitches, but some will be in muscle."

"A drink of what?"

"Grappa." The doctor went to a cabinet, poured some grappa from a five-liter can into a laboratory flask, and presented it to Alessandro.

"Is this a lot? Is it enough?" Alessandro asked.

"Here, I'll help you." The doctor took a drink.

"If you finish what's left you won't be able to walk. Put these tablets in your pocket. Later, when you feel sick, take one or two in water. Let them dissolve."

Alessandro acquiesced.

"Drink as much as you can."

Alessandro had long before met his match in wine, of which he had had, at most, a glass a day, always cut with water as if he were ten years old, and he downed the grappa as he held his breath. It burned his throat, but the heat was not entirely unpleasant: his face flushed until it was the color of the red velvet that lines an expensive box at the opera or the public rooms of an Egyptian whorehouse.

"Keep it down," the surgeon ordered. "I'll be back in ten minutes. Don't fall off the chair. Pretend you're on a ship. When I stitch you up you won't know what's happening. Do you feel it?"

"Yes."

"After I finish, a nurse will take you to a room. You'll be able to walk. Do you feel it?"

"Oh yes. A nun?"

"What do you mean, a nun?"

"Take me to a room."

"A nurse, not a nun. We have no nursing-sisters here."

"Which nurse?"

"I don't know."

"Get the one with the beautiful face."

"The beautiful face?"

"The beautiful one."

"To soldiers who come from the line," the surgeon answered, "they're all beautiful."

When Alessandro was alone, he entertained himself with speech. At one point it grew so loud and emotional that a nurse came up to him, put her finger to her lips, and said, "Shhh!" very slowly and with great sympathy.

Comfortably swaying in a little ellipse, Alessandro was convinced that his spirit had left his body and was floating high in the examination room, but he refused to trust the notion that floating free would bring him eternal joy, and kept his eyes open.

The surgeon re-entered, trailed by two orderlies. They approached so rapidly and were so business-like that before Alessandro knew it they had lifted him up and pinned him to a table in the center of the floor. They strapped-in his ankles, his unwounded arm, and only one thigh, because one of the thigh restraints had been snapped or cut. The orderlies held his wrist and his head.

At first none of this seemed like either a threat or an indignity. He didn't have a body, and his spirit, now curiously upside down, observed with detachment.

Then the surgeon began to thread his needles. They were curved, of varying lengths and thicknesses, and they glinted in the light of the kerosene lantern by which he planned to work. Alessandro's spirit said, "Oh no," as the surgeon laid out his skinny arsenal. Like a diver who is about to dive from a height that frightens him, the surgeon looked at the wound for a long time. Then, with his right hand, he picked up the first needle, and, with his left, an alcohol-soaked bandage.

Each time the surgeon pushed one of the steel needles through Alessandro's flesh, Alessandro screamed, and his body locked as rigidly as a cannon breach. The needle found its way forward in three or four pushes per stitch, and at every one Alessandro jerked like one of Galvani's frogs. After the needle emerged, the stitch was tied, and Alessandro shuddered in fear of the next. Some stitches, deeper in muscle, were worse than others. After half an hour the orderlies unstrapped him and moved on to a patient who had been sleeping on a stretcher in the corridor, and soon this next patient's screams were sufficient to awaken all the soldiers who had died in the Alto Adige. Though drunk, Alessandro was lucid. He knew that over the next several weeks his body would respond to the half hour that had just passed, but while the body was still trying to decide what had hit it, he would enjoy his equanimity.

"What about dinner?" Alessandro inquired of the air. When no one answered, he appeared to be mildly annoyed.

Soon the same nurse who had put her finger to her lips and said "Shhhh!" came to take him to the house where he would sleep. Again she said "Shhhh!" He thought that perhaps this was her way of breathing, or that she had emphysema or belonged to a Hindu cult. They had had such things before the war, to teach people how to breathe and how to laugh. But the unstated purpose of each and every one was to outwit death, and trustworthy Hindus who had come to Italy grew rich.

Alessandro was unable to see what the nurse looked like, because she wore a loden cloak with a hood that hid her features. She took him outside into the darkness, which made recognition even more difficult. Though Alessandro tried, all he could tell was that she was tall and thin, almost like a stork.

Every now and then he would turn, nearly falling off his feet, and try to peek beneath the hood.

"Don't try to kiss me," she said. "It's against regulations, and I don't kiss just anybody."

"I want to see your face," he said. "Are you a Hindu?"

"No kisses," was her reply. Apart from that, she talked nonstop, something about hairdressers at mineral spas, and how after the war she was either going to work for one, marry one, be one, or all three, because after the war mineral spas would be crowded with the wounded and the infirm—and their wives.

Just before they got to the chalet where Alessandro was to sleep, he tried again to look at her face. "I don't understand a thing you're saying," he said. "I don't know why, or why hairdressers are why, never having been to one. What are they?"

"Uh uh uh," she answered, steering him into a doorway. "No kisses." And she said it because the nurses, touching men all day, surrounded by them, bathing them, and carrying them, some-times, in private moments, kissed their patients—and allowed their patients to kiss them—deeply. In a place where even plain women were beautiful, it happened all the time.

She and a heavyset young nurse helped Alessandro up two flights of stairs, one broad and one narrow. "Do you have to use the W.C.?" they asked.

"As what?" he wanted to know.

"What do you mean?"

"As a broom, a bayonet, a hat, what?"

Uncomprehendingly, they settled him in.

"No! Open the window," he protested. "I like the air."

They opened it. "You'll need six blankets."

"Two will be fine, if you double one of them."

They put the blankets over him and propped his head on a pillow covered in an ice-cold white case with so much starch in it that at first Alessandro thought it was wood.

Although the room was the size of a closet, it was his alone, it wasn't a cell, and the door wasn't locked. The walls were cedar. It had been a child's room, and the bed was too small, but the pillow made up for it: he hadn't used a pillow, except in his brief stay at home, for almost three years.

Free and alone, with his boots finally off, an arm in a sling, and a fire burning comfortably within him as he lay under the three layers of wool, he breathed the pure air that fell like a river from the glaciers, and he sank back onto the glistening pillow case.

He waited for the moon to tint the clouds ghostly silver, but he suspected that by the time the moon flooded the room with light he would be asleep. He smiled to himself in admiration of the mountains, for although he had been there only two days, connections were forming and dissolving with awesome rapidity, as if every time the sun or the moon were hidden by clouds or revealed by rising mist, a new world had formed. He had seen it before at high altitudes. Time was both compressed and extended. The air coming in the window was laden with messages Alessandro no longer understood. As they broke in their millions like whitecaps on the sea, they shattered the peace of the room and restored it in a rhythm that ebbed and flowed and rocked the wounded soldier to sleep.

WHEN HE awoke he thought that the next morning had arrived, but it was only later in the evening. He smelled dinner cooking, and not only did it repel him, it made no sense, as nowhere that he knew, and certainly never in the army, had anyone heard of beef in the morning.

He had developed a high fever that reminded him, in its intensity, of racing in a single shell. His body was pleasantly burning at an even pace, and his face was as hot as it would have been had he been in the sun for several hours. The steady combustion was such that if nature had had a fire-tender, the fire-tender might have been sitting with his feet up, marveling at the flame.

Alessandro lifted his right hand from the blankets and touched his nose, which, despite the rest of him, was ice cold. If by some miracle he were to die of a superficial wound, to die painlessly in a fever would be best. Mumbling to himself from within his chest in speech that seemed so pleasurable and fast that it was almost like singing, he said, in quiet measured cadences, "Perhaps passing through the gates of death is like passing quietly through the gate in a pasture fence. On the other side, you keep walking, without the need to look back. No shock, no drama, just the lifting of a plank or two in a simple wooden gate in a clearing. Neither pain, nor floods of light, nor great voices, but just the silent crossing of a meadow."

Now it was dark, and not even a hawk could have told a white thread from a black thread. Alessandro tried to turn his head away from the window and toward the door, but his neck was stiff and he could hardly move. He thought this was the first sign of death, and although he was content to die, he wanted to pass with the illusion, at least, of warmth and light.

He must have said so, and clearly, for a woman sitting in the corner behind him, on a chair with a rush seat, answered the question he had not really asked.

"You're not going to die," she said.

He was embarrassed that she had been with him all that time and he had not been aware. "How do you know?" he asked.

"This isn't the building for it."

"It isn't right," Alessandro said, "that you've been listening to me and didn't warn me of your presence."

"I don't usually find it necessary to warn people of my presence, especially if they're unconscious. I didn't know you were awake."

"Neither did I. Didn't you hear me?" he asked.

"I heard someone talking in his sleep, or in delirium. You're delirious now."

"I wouldn't have spoken had I known you were here."

"But I'm too tired to move from this chair merely to save you embarrassment."

"I can't see you," he said with sudden irritation. "I can't turn, and it's dark."

"Why do you need to see me?" she asked.

"Simply to know to whom I am speaking. Why don't you come to the window so that I can see you."

"Because I'm sitting quite comfortably on this chair. I'm warm, I have my coat on. I'm here to make sure that your fever doesn't get the best of you, and to bring you food if you want it, and I have no intention of going to the window so you can see my face. Why do you need to see my face?"

"Why do you have a face? Why do you have a body?"

"For the same reason that everyone else has a face and a body, so that I can carry on in this world."

"Then what's wrong with showing me what it is that enables you to carry on in this world?"

"When soldiers come out of the line, having been without women for months, or a year . . ."

"Or two years."

"They fall in love with the first woman they see. You could be a butter knife, and they'd still fall in love with you. It isn't very flattering, it happens continually, and I'm tired of it. Even the ones who have been blinded, mutilated by shells that have burst in their faces, though they do not dare presume that they will be loved ever again, fall in love with a voice. And what can I give them? Nothing. I'm just a woman. I'm not the end of the war, or the end of your suffering, or some magical, higher being who will undo all that you've seen."

"Are you familiar with Giorgione?" Alessandro asked as he struggled to sit up, and then fell back. "Giorgione painted a painting that flatly contradicts you. It flatly contradicts you. In the painting, a woman quiets the storm and is a soldier's only hope. You may not like the idea, it may be too much for you, but what you deny, and what Giorgione asserts, is true.

"I know that some soldiers come out of the line filled with sex. I've heard men talk like animals, even about their wives. They go home on leave and they fuck their wives until they're raw."

"Until who's raw?" she asked, wondering why she was allowing a man to speak to her in this way.

"Both. It's as if they're seeking blood. It's always until blood, or beyond."

"How do you know?"

"They talk freely. The coarse among them think like mechanics—so many days without sex, a simple arithmetic theory of pressure, water behind a dam, what-you-will. And then they talk about it as if the soldiers staring at them from the mud are more important than the wives they've left at home. They're like cats who drop prey at your feet."

"I wouldn't know."

"I would. There's something to the notion of accumulated desire, and many soldiers sense that they're driven by something less coarse than they think, but who has time to think it out?"

"You do."

"Only because you've forced me to think and talk. If you'd let me see you, talk would be unnecessary."

She made no response. It encouraged him.

"All right, then, I'll have to keep on talking—I like talking to you. When soldiers go home, their first desire, whether they know it or not, is to have children, children being the only antidote for war. In the painting by Giorgione, the woman and her baby are imperturbable, the center of the universe. The soldier may stray, the waters may rise, but the mother and child save the world, again and again."

"What has that to do with me? It's just as I've said. I could be *any* woman."

"Yes. And I, in the trench, shivering, wounded, could be any man. To be reduced so, to what is elemental, is not a dishonor. Never will anyone know you better than he who has known you when everything you have has been stripped away. Never will anyone know you better than when you are as you are now, sitting in a chair, with your coat on, in this cold dark room, hungry and exhausted."

"You can't see me," she said. "You don't know me. We've never seen one another's faces. We may feel a certain affinity because we may have similar backgrounds, and now we're struggling in this place, but after the war it would disappear. For two people on a raft at sea, being rescued changes everything."

"It depends on how long they've been on the raft," he said.

"You don't give up, do you?"

"Not yet."

"You're one of a million soldiers. I speak to a hundred a day. Half of them fall in love with me. It means nothing."

"I ask nothing," Alessandro said.

"You think you've captured me?"

"No."

"Why are you suddenly confident?"

"Confident of what?"

"Detached."

"I'm not detached. I'm only certain that I've touched upon the truth."

"How do you know that I'll come back? It would be very easy for me to trade you to someone else. Besides, we're rotated and transferred just as you are. Tomorrow I could be back in Trento. You might even die."

"Then I'm not in the right building."

"I'm sorry. The fever is a good sign. You're in the right building."

"Why can't I turn? I feel paralyzed."

"When you have a fever and you sleep in one position in the cold air, it can happen."

"If you don't come back," he said, "then you won't come back, which will mean that you aren't the woman I think you are. I was sure that you were. Your voice is beautiful. Still, it doesn't matter if either of you disappears, because the other will remain."

"You're delirious," she told him.

"I am."

"When I return in a few hours, if you're awake, if you're no longer delirious, you need not be embarrassed."

"Love is only embarrassing to those who cannot love. And, besides, I didn't say that I was in love with you. You did."

"Though I haven't seen you, I won't say that you don't attract me, but I think that in a day or two I could forget you. That's what happens up here. You can't know someone in five minutes. You can't fall in love in five minutes."

"Please come back," he said.

THE NEXT morning, the stork-like nurse, the Hindu, came to take Alessandro's temperature, change the dressings, and deliver breakfast. When she attended to the bandages her touch was as gentle and communicative as anything Alessandro had ever known. Whoever married her would have her intelligence, gratitude, and kindness for the rest of his life, and would perhaps know something far more entrancing than romantic love.

"When will you return?" Alessandro asked.

"At lunch."

"What about the evening?"

"I don't have the evening shift."

"Who does?"

The stork shrugged her high shoulders. "Someone else."

"Do you know her?"

"No. The schedules change all the time."

Alessandro pressed no further, but the tall nurse was kind. "I could find out," she volunteered, "and tell you tomorrow, if she doesn't return tonight."

"It won't be necessary," he said. "I was just curious about who would bring dinner."

After she left, Alessandro fell asleep, but he was awakened in the middle of the afternoon by artillery echoing in the mountains, half a day's journey away. It sounded like distant thunder—although it did not roll like thunder, and it did not rest like thunder, and probably never in the history of nature had thunder been so tense, repetitive, and gracelessly timed. Almost sitting up, Alessandro listened for a moment and then sank back into his warm bed. He slept until dusk, when he lay awake, waiting for her to come.

Downstairs in the chalet were a dozen walking wounded in various states of recovery. Soon to return to their units, they played games and talked by the fire. Someone played a zither. It was not likely that an Italian would be playing a zither. Perhaps it was a remaining villager, a wounded Austrian magically absorbed into the Italian ranks, or one of the collaborators who helped the Italians reconnoiter the newly captured territories. Whoever it was, his music had a sad edge. Alessandro wondered how a song could be both sad and cheerful, its counterpoint dancing forward even as it pulled back.

It was because the world had a life of it own. Leave winter alone or watch it to death, it would still gradually turn to summer. Miracles and paradoxes could be explained by the marvelously independent courses of their elements, and perhaps real beauty could be partially understood in that it was not just a combination, but a dissolution; that after the threads were woven and tangled they then untangled and continued on their separate ways; that the trains that pulled into the station in a riveting spectacle as clouds of steam condensed in the midnight air, then left for different destinations and disappeared; that the drama of a striking clock was impossible without the silence that was both its preface and epilogue. Music was a chain forged half of silences and half of sound, love was nothing without longing and loss, and were time not to have at its end the absence of time, and the absence of time not to have been preceded by time, neither would be of any consequence.

In these metaphysics, and in these metaphysics alone, it hardly mattered if she came or not. He closed his eyes and tried to remember what she had looked like in the light that had reflected from the glaciers. Though he had seen her from a distance and only for an instant, he remembered the way her dress cascaded from her shoulders, the red-and-white enameled clasp that had shone out as if in a painting, and the neckline that it had held together, in proportions that were almost perfect. He saw again the light in her face as she stared into the breeze that carried cool air up from the ice fields. When the truck had rounded the corner and she had become suddenly backlit, her hair glowed and her hands were clasped behind her as she rocked on her feet. He had her forever. And she need not have come. But she did.

WHEN THE door opened and shut, and the legs of the rush-bottomed chair scraped against the floor, Alessandro could barely speak.

"What time does the moon rise?" he finally asked, as matter-of-factly as if he had been querying a ticket agent about the arrival of a train.

"I beg your pardon?"

"The moon."

"What about the moon?"

"What time does it rise?"

"I don't know. I don't have a watch. Sometimes I don't even know what day it is, much less when the moon rises."

"I thought you would."

"Are nurses supposed to know when the moon rises?"

"Yes. In Rome, every nurse knows when the moon rises."

"As you can undoubtedly hear," she said, "I'm a Romana, and you know that I'm a nurse. I don't know when the moon will rise, do you?"

"What do you think I am," Alessandro asked, "an *idiot-savant*? The moon is capricious to the point of insanity. It rises and sets all over the place, at different times. You never know what it's going to do. Sometimes it doesn't appear, sometimes it's disguised as a pale crescent, and sometimes it comes out full in the daylight. The sun doesn't shine at night, does it."

"Not in Europe."

"Imagine if, like the moon, the sun did as it pleased. Only an *idiot-savant*, someone intoxicated with logarithms and railroad timetables, would know when the moon rises."

"Do you know?" she asked.

"In about an hour."

"You're an *idiot-savant*."

"I was almost an *idiot-savant*, but I didn't succeed. When I was in middle school I could memorize three hundred words of French in a minute. That's as close as I've come."

"I'm not impressed," she announced.

"Why? How many words of French can you memorize in a minute?"

"All of them."

"All of them?"

"Yes," she answered. "Every single one."

"And how is that?"

"I'm French."

"I don't believe it. You have no accent whatsoever."

"My father was Italian."

"Was?"

"He died on the Isonzo."

"I'm sorry."

"So am I," she said slowly.

"And your mother?"

"She was French. When I was a child, she died of influenza." Alessandro heard a break in her voice, even now. "I became a nurse."

"You've come here because of your father?"

"Yes. At the beginning of the war I was on the Somme. I loved my father very much. He was a Romano, who spoke like a Florentine. He was just like you."

"How do you know what I am?"

"You're an educated man who was born in Rome and will die there," she said.

"You're right. I was born in Rome, and I have been educated almost to death. What was it like on the Somme?" he asked. "No matter how many thousands die here we're always left with the impression that we are only pretending, that the real war is there."

"The real war is there," she confirmed. "When it stops there, it will stop here. If it goes on there, it will go on here. France is the heart of the war. France is always the heart of the war."

"Why?"

"Geography, illusion, or because the French see themselves as the center of the world. The country is so beautiful that when the world is finished with its work it looks to France for what it loves. With everyone's head turned so, it becomes the center. I'm able to say this not because I'm French, but because I'm Italian."

"You think in broad terms."

"At times."

"You're a nurse."

"Yes, I'm a nurse." After a moment's reflection, she challenged him. "Would you be surprised to learn that I have read a book on economics?"

"I suppose I would have to be."

"What about twenty?"

"Twenty?"

"Yes, economics—history, theory, prices, inflation, why not? It's true."

"You can't, being a woman, earn a living as an economist."

"I know."

"I am deeply impressed by a woman who, for no reason other than her own fascination, has read twenty books on economics."

"But I stopped."

"Why?"

"I wanted something more alive. The first book I read after that was a description of the South Pacific. Cerulean blue on every page."

"Let me see you."

"No."

"What if the house were hit by a shell?" he asked.

"*Pouf, au revoir,* goodbye," she said. "Do you think it will be?"

"No."

"Then do you think you should turn around?"

"No."

"Tell me why?"

"Because I'm the only soldier of the thousands you've seen, other than those who are blind, who has fallen in love with you without seeing you."

"And how could that possibly matter?"

"Because you're beautiful."

"Perhaps I am, perhaps I'm not, I really don't know. Don't turn around."

"It's difficult."

"Then perhaps what comes of it will be good."

"I don't know your name."

"I don't think I should tell you. The more time passes when you know neither my name, nor anything else about me, and have not seen me, the better you'll know me. It's your supposition, but I've come to believe it."

"Well that's good."

"But aren't you disappointed that someday you might come to know me, my name, my age, my face."

"I know your age."

"You do? How?"

"By your voice. You're twenty-three."

She was amazed. "And when is my birthday?"

Instead of thinking about it, guessing, or fearing that he might be wrong, Alessandro said, "June," and he was right again. "You were born in Rome, in June. It was when I was four years old, and loved to ride on merry-go-rounds and in pony carts. For several years, at least, we both lived in Rome, completely unaware of one another, though we may have crossed paths a dozen times. Rome was for me an entire universe. Young children see so clearly things of poignant detail, even if they soon learn to forget."

"But not you."

"I hope not."

"You know me by my voice."

"It's no talent of mine, but the lovely way you speak."

"Le refus de la louange est un désir d'être loué deux fois," she said.

"I don't have to translate that," he told her. "Only in France are the wounded required to speak French, and even there the requirement is harsh, because life is difficult enough without having to pronounce it correctly. Did you smile?"

"A little smile."

"Tell me your name."

"No. I resent you. I resent that you can see me without looking at me. I resent that you may have fallen in love with me without having seen me. I resent that you lie here, wounded, and your power darts about the room."

"You won't let me see you," he answered, "but I have seen you. In our conversation you haven't been subordinate. Our powers are exactly equal."

"Yes, but you're wounded!"

"And you're tired. We're exactly equal, to the longest decimal, precisely, and it will always be so. The balance is perfect, and you know it."

"If it's true, it isn't fair," she said.

"Why?"

"Because you're going back in the line." Her gown rustled under her coat as she rose from the chair. And then she left.

Alessandro lay in bed observing the light of the moon as it bleached the window panes and washed the sky with silver. He felt his fever warm the blankets and burn his face. He waited quietly, and was prepared to wait longer.

Half an hour passed, enough time for her to have walked home and walked back. She was all grace, and he might not have heard her on the stairs, especially if each step was taken with hesitation.

Now the moon was fully visible through the open window, perfectly round and bright. Though she had not returned, he put no limit on his waiting, and refused to think of its end or of disappointment. He was prepared to listen for her until his strength failed. The moon crossed the window, and its uncompromising light left in darkness the side of the room it had first lit. The clock in the village struck the quarter hours, the halves, and the hours. The snow-covered streets, bathed in white and glistening with ice, were empty, and sentries at the edge of the village would have slept had it not been for the dazzling moonlight that brought them marvelous waking dreams.

It was not a time for coming and going, but Alessandro heard the door open. She had come back. She spoke haltingly and with great feeling.

"I went to bed, but then I rose and dressed again. I can't stay. My name is Ariane," she said. "Your name, Alessandro, is written on the chart."

THE NEXT day, Ariane came at five-thirty in the afternoon. When Alessandro had glimpsed her standing outside the dispensary, with her left hand shielding her eyes from the sharp light of the glaciers, almost in a salute, she had been thinking that she wanted a man, even if it were someone barely acceptable. It would not be the greatest sin to take a man who was perhaps a little coarse, or not of her social station, or who would leave her later, or philander, or die before he departed the mountains. Souls were floating up at such a great rate that surely God would forgive her for holding one down and keeping him close to her in the warmth of her bed. She wanted a man who had seen the bodies lined up in rows, the tatters, the endless columns of exhausted soldiers walking bitterly from place to place, the corpses sprawled over the wire. She would not know how to talk to a man who hadn't seen these things, as she had, much less lie with him in love, and here every man knew what she knew.

One of the minor casualties of the war had been her expectation of finding someone in circumstances that were more joyful than those of the dispensaries in Gruensee—at a dinner party, a ball, a picnic, the racetrack, or on the terrace of a house at Cap d'Antibes, surrounded by geraniums and bees. She had assumed that love would come under blue skies, perhaps early in June, with a young man of good prospects and family, perhaps of wealth, perhaps as quietly handsome as he was strong. She was uninterested in towering, square-jawed men with huge domineering faces, who were to be bred like horses with horse-like women. She wanted someone to match her in fineness of feature—a man whose virility did not crawl all over him, but who was, instead, meticulous and unassuming.

After months of sleepless nights and exhausting days in the snowbound village of wounded conscripts, she cared no longer for anyone to be sent to her, as if on a breeze, in a lovely time of year. As much as she needed love, she had to refuse it. Hardly a man came through, even those who were married, who was not as desperate for affection as was she, and, each time, the symmetry served to seal her heart. Boys who were mutilated and dying called with their eyes for her love, and that she could not love them was slowly killing her.

She had lingered in Alessandro's room at first merely because she had been cold and tired. Their eyes had yet to meet, their judgment had not been overwhelmed, and the accident that had tested their patience was as if the terrace at Cap d'Antibes had been transported to Gruensee, as if the reticent graces for which she longed had been married hypnotically with the stronger things that drove men to women and women to men, in a place like this, the first refuge from battle.

"It's Ariane," she said as she entered the room.

He had always been impressed by the self-possession of someone who could refer to himself, in this way, by his own name.

"I took over some shifts. I'll be in and out all evening."

Alessandro sat up straighter in bed. He tugged at his linen hospital gown until it was smooth. "If you do things like bring me dinner and take my temperature, the game may be over."

"It's not a game," she said, closing the door behind her. The latch clicked.

She hadn't removed her cape, and her right hand held the gold chain that crossed at the top near the throat. She walked forward to the open window, closed it abruptly, and turned on her heels.

She neither moved nor spoke, and she was the color of a rose. Backlit once again by the darkening evening sky just as she had been at the dispensary, she rocked to and fro almost imperceptibly, not because she was cold, but because the blood was pounding through her so forcefully that it actually caused her to sway.

As Alessandro sat in the bed, and she stood still, he fell so deeply in love with her, so hard, and so fast, that he was able to follow her even in her reticence. After she unclasped the gold chain and put her cape on the sill, she stood before him in the flowing and pleated nurse's gown.

"My father used to say," she said, "that I should look for someone who would be able to sail a boat in heavy seas, who would be a master of his profession, who would love children. And he used to say that I should seek the kind of man who could take me into the private rooms of an expensive jeweler and show me diamonds and emeralds. What he meant by that was not that this person would be rich—I think his image was of an employee—but that he would have to be patient, trustworthy, considerate, and refined."

"I have a temper," Alessandro said.

"Not with me," she answered. "Never with me."

He dipped his head and briefly closed his eyes, as if to signify a vow. "Never."

Not knowing what to say, she asked if he wanted her to bring the dinner.

"Why must we eat so early?"

"For the same reason that you eat early in the line, so people don't have to work too long in the dark."

"I'm not thinking about dinner."

"No?"

"No."

"What are you thinking about?"

"I'm thinking about you," he said. "I've forgotten what it's like to touch a woman, I've forgotten how to do it, but I want more than anything to kiss you, to hold you. Would you forgive me if, at first, I were awkward?"

"Yes."

"Would you forgive me if at first I seemed cold?"

"Yes."

"And for having, at the moment, only one good arm?"

"Oh yes."

Ariane walked forward until she stood by the bed. Her eyes swept down toward her feet, and as she kicked off her shoes, her mouth tightened. Then she straightened her head, and her eyes and Alessandro's met.

SEVERAL HOURS later when Ariane crossed the green to sign the nurses' muster sheet, her face was red and her hair disheveled in a fashion that connoted neither the pressing-down of sleep nor the action of the wind, but something quite different. Her eyes were in rebellion against focus, and she felt as if she were floating through the moonlight. Her commanding officer, a Swede who was able even at fifty to wear her blond hair in a single braid and still look like a young woman, stood up abruptly next to a little table at which she had been writing in a notebook, approached Ariane, and put the heel of her hand on Ariane's forehead. When she saw that the young woman's neck, chest, and shoulders were almost pink and red, and that her hair was tangled, with a lock in front falling until it touched her right eyebrow at the top of its strikingly bold arch, she dropped her hand and stepped back.

"You must be less obvious. You must never appear in public the way you look now," she said in French.

Ariane blushed.

"It's quite apparent that either you have typhus or you have spent the last three hours making love. Ariane, even in France you would cause a stir in this condition, would you not?"

"It would depend upon the reason, Madame."

"Anyway, this is not France. Try to be more discreet. And if you're found out, come to me. I'll say you have a fever, and all will be well."

Ariane smiled in gratitude.

"Ariane."

"Yes?"

"The war has put an end to many things. One cannot expect the forms of the past to prevail, but will you marry this man?"

Ariane tightened her lips and pulled-in the lower one somewhat, as she often did when she dealt with a difficult question. "I hope, Madame, that he will not be killed."

IN THE high mountains, summer and winter are shuffled throughout the year like wild cards, and in the last days of Alessandro's recuperation summer came briefly to the Alto Adige. As the sun shone from dusk to dawn in clear motionless air, the dispassionate colors of winter were enriched, birds sang as if for their lives, and it was so warm and bright that the partially recovered soldiers took to the snowfields, where the air was hot with dazzling reflections.

One morning Alessandro went to the nurses' barracks to wake Ariane, who lay in a bed just behind the partition that divided the sleeping quarters from the dining room and the kitchen.

The other women, who were standing half dressed at ironing boards, holding kettles, or sitting on their cots lacing their boots, froze as Alessandro knelt by Ariane. As he put his left hand under her head, and his right hand on her shoulder, and lifted her gently from sleep, no one moved. They watched as if the world depended upon it, until she modestly pulled the blanket up almost to her chin. Then they resumed what they had been doing.

As Alessandro waited outside, leaning against a stucco wall that had already been warmed by the sunlight, he thought of the women who lived with Ariane in the chalet. He longed for the gentleness in the way they lived, the peace, and the safety. Even their fingers were beautiful—their voices, the way they brushed their hair, the way they laced their boots, leaning down with tresses about to tumble forward but held in check as if by a miracle. They were beautiful even in the way they breathed. A few days before, as Ariane had taken off her dress, Alessandro had watched the rising and falling of her chest, the movement of the rib cage barely perceptible under the skin, and the changes in color that accompanied the steady sound of her breathing. Though neither he nor Ariane knew, she had begun to carry his child.

When she came out, fresh from sleep, Alessandro asked, "Do you think you can walk all the way down to the Adige?"

"I can," she answered. "I'm not sure about you."

"I don't walk on my arm. Anyway, if I have trouble, you can carry me."

THE SLOPE from Gruensee to the Adige was white without imperfection. Alessandro and Ariane skated down and across it for an hour. Falling brought not pain but surprise, for the snow was powdery and dry, and even when they fell they stayed warm. Though the glare hurt the back of their eyes, and they were quickly sunburnt, they felt like the angels who inhabit the cool air above a flume, and who, with nothing to do but sing, give to the water its tranquil and hypnotic sound.

On the riverbank they found a bare concave rock facing south, and stayed there for as long as the sun warmed them, lost in lovemaking in which sometimes Ariane's hair hung over the edge of the rock and was lapped by the ice-cold Adige as it surged and relaxed. The river roared, and on their granite platform it was so hot and bright that they leaned down to cup the cold water in their hands and drink.

"What is the name of the painting?" Ariane asked as if she had suddenly realized that she hadn't remembered.

"It's called *La Tempesta,* and it's in Venice, in the Gallerie dell'Accademia. They say, what could it mean, a woman with a child, disrobed, and the soldier, standing apart from her, disconnected. But I know exactly what to make of it. Today I saw a lovely sight—the nurses lacing their boots, brushing their hair, fastening their earrings. If I were a painter, I would have wanted to paint it. So with Giorgione. He intended to praise elemental things, and to show a soldier on the verge of return. I'm not surprised that scholars and critics don't understand it. Giorgione lived in the time of the plague, and the scholars and critics, for the most part, have had to do without plague or war, which make the simple things one takes for granted shine like gold. What does the painting mean? It means love. It means coming home."

Alessandro had been ordered to a unit of Alpini far to the north of Gruensee. "When the war is over," he said as he held her, full of hope, "we'll marry, we'll live in Rome, and we'll have children."

She cried.

ON THE morning of Alessandro's departure, a squadron of six Austrian bi-planes on a snow-covered field near Innsbruck started their engines. The powerful winds of the high ranges, in updrafts, downdrafts, and cyclones that raced around the peaks, made flying dangerous, but these airplanes were much heavier and more powerful than most of the light craft that daredevils had flown through the mountains before the war, or even the fighter planes that were dispatched to reconnoiter and to harass the Italians in their solid trenchwork and fortifications. Most of the time, in the vastness of the mountains, airplanes were no more threatening than insects. These, however, each carried four hundred kilos of bombs. With twenty-four hundred kilos of high explosive and incendiary, a small group of aircraft, if piloted well, could destroy a railroad train, explode an ammunition depot, cause great harm to a column on the march, or obliterate a river crossing.

Just to fly in the Alps, with no place to land, was an act of daring. Parachuting onto a glacier or the slopes of a mountain was extremely dangerous, but flying in winter winds and storms that were lifted over mountain walls like soldiers going over the top of a trench made parachuting seem safe. When the planes lined up on the field, engines bellowing and snow lifting from the ground in patches that rocketed away on the wind, the pilots cleansed themselves of inhibition, and in the unbearable sound of the motors and the ceaseless vibration they entirely forgot fear and softness.

One by one the planes lumbered forward on the clean snow still violet in the dawn, gunned their engines, and sailed down the runway. The pilots were dressed in leather and fur. They had hot-water bottles that they would jettison as soon as the heat dissipated, vacuum bottles of hot tea, and meat sandwiches. Though they were not to be aloft for long, they wanted to be warm, and the cold air made them hungry.

They left the valley floor and soon were in the mountains, an abstract of ice and rock devoid of greenery and human works. In the shadows below them, the slightly blue-gray ridges woven into desolate ice fields were the color of someone who has frozen to death. They turned west and flew briefly over Switzerland, and then started a broad left-hand bank that would bring them to the Italian lines from the rear, with the morning sun at their backs. As parts of their faces froze in the wind they threw out their used hot-water bottles and joked, with hand signs, of having bombed the glaciers. Below them, the ice was still blue.

By the time the sun, now high enough to bring yellow and gold into the world, had carpeted the snowfields with shadows, they were over Italy, patiently cutting through the air in their broad turn. They opened the tea and sandwiches. So appreciative were they of the heat that they let the tea scald them. It strained through their tea-colored mustaches, and the vapor from the vacuum flasks was instantaneously left behind to hang quietly in frigid sun-filled air several thousand meters above a snowy plateau.

Arising that morning at three, as troops of soldiers often do, a group of Italian lancers had broken camp under dazzling starlight. It had taken them an hour to dress, wash in the thundering black Adige, and kindle the breakfast fires. The river water was so cold that it made the air seem like the morning air in Rome in late spring. Just to breathe the mist that hung above the rapids was to wake a hundred times.

The fires burned quickly and with a lot of crackling. Orange sparks ascended from wave-like sheets of flame that showed the same intense and shadowy glow as footlights. The thousand lancers had their bread and coffee by scores of these fires. They were silent and reflective almost to a man, thinking of their families in recollections brought on by the special grace of early morning. At times like these, they felt as if the war were over, they had won it, and they were about to start home.

By first light the littered camp on the riverbank had been forgotten, its bright fires turned to patches of lukewarm ash. A column of a thousand men and almost two thousand horses, wagons, and caisson-borne machine guns moved slowly northward to the Brennero, with the river always in sight. Now the black water that had slipped away so fast in the starlight was pale blue, or white where it boiled over rocks. Forced between huge boulders in the riverbed, it rose in serpentine arches with silver underbellies. The saddlery and harnesses had long before been worn to soft, dark colors, and could hardly be heard, but the click of metal bits as nervous horses worked their jaws back and forth, the snortings and whinnies, the creak of wagon wheels, the slappings of sabre cases against the horses' flanks, and the high-pitched commands shouted by the officers floated on the sound of the water, and when the column rounded a bend and was hit by a gust of cold wind, the lances and pennants made a whistling noise.

They were marching north on a snow-covered road because a general studying a map in Rome had come across the long narrow fingers of flat ground that rested on the great north-south ridges, and decided that a proper conquest required a regiment of cavalry. Not much room existed for maneuver, but a small cavalry unit, lances down, might exploit a break in the enemy lines and rush across the windblown ground to the next and distant redoubt.

The cavalrymen were not used to the mountains, and their officers were unfamiliar with the terrain. Accustomed to the thick, sweet air of sea-level farms, the horses were agitated and unnerved by the light, the thinness of the atmosphere, and the ways in which sound carried. Cliffs rearing up to dizzying heights were beyond their ken, and they grew skittish as the road began to bend into steep switchbacks.

Shortly before ten in the morning the lancers began to move onto the plateau upon which sat Gruensee. The head of the column halted at a fork in the road. The way right led down toward the valley and up again, and the way left passed through Gruensee to the high plains where the lancers were bound. They had been marching for six hours, and wanted least of all to descend only to climb again, so they went left toward the town.

THE UNIT of Alpini to which Alessandro had been assigned was camped far to the north, under the precipitous walls of the Cima Blanca. Trying to wrest the heights of this massif from the Austrians, it had suffered heavy casualties, and needed men to work machine guns, do guard duty, haul wood, and take care of isolated outposts.

The car that had been sent for Alessandro was so large in comparison with the diminutive platform upon which sat the driver and a tiny freight box, that Alessandro asked about it. He was told that the machine pulled field guns up mountain roads and did not need a large freight box, and that he would ride on the running-board.

He examined the grooved metal wheels, tossed his pack into the box, and, as the motor idled, left to say goodbye to Ariane. He would tell her that he loved her, and take leave as if they were going see one another the next day. He knew what to do, and he would come back.

As he walked across the meadow at Gruensee, his step was light. The sun was brighter and higher, summer would come. Someday he might be an old man sitting by a fountain in Rome, knocking at the rim with his cane to chase away the flies, shielding his eyes from the sun, and waiting for autumn, when the fields burned and the smell of ash covered the countryside and drifted into the city on cool currents of air over the Tiber.

Alessandro saw the column of lancers entering the village, a hundred meters from the dispensary where Ariane was on duty. It was halfway up the street when two doctors ran from one of the houses, their hands at shoulder height, palms out, making a gesture that said, *go back*. Gruensee was a medical refuge in which active formations were forbidden.

The argument with the colonel at the head of the troop was short. He was not about to turn on the narrow road, reverse-march his tired lancers and their mounts, and drop into the valley to reach the whitened meadow that was his goal, when it was visible above the town, like a dancing-platform at a seaside resort, only a few kilometers distant. The column moved forward, lances as high as the upper storeys of the chalets.

Nurses, orderlies, and patients stood at the windows to watch the mass of horses, men, and caissons, and all the metal flashing in the light. Alessandro saw Ariane, her hair shining in the sun, look-ing down from an upper window.

From the air, Gruensee was a spot on the flank of a huge snow-covered hill. Behind it, far to the north, the spires of the Cima Bianca sat like a wall, rose-colored at the base and as white as a flare on top. Beyond the valley of the Adige, and west to Switzerland, other mountains and their glaciers caught the light and cast stark country-sized shadows. The line of aircraft coming up on Gruensee from the south was funneled toward it by the disposition of mountains and the track of the sun.

When the pilots neared Gruensee they saw a black line, centered upon the village, running north to south. At first it looked like a buttonhole with a button in the middle. Then it looked like a mule driver's whip lying on the snow. And finally, when the pilots were close enough to see that it was not a solid strip but something broken and of many parts, and that it moved, they knew that they had found a rich target.

As they pulled up their gloves and tightened their harnesses, their expressions changed. The leader signaled that they would drop into single file and loose their bombs along the line of the enemy column. Then they would bank from the north to strafe east to west and west to east. The sun would be in their eyes on the return run, but the road was outlined between houses and steep meadows, the column trapped on a narrow axis, aim nearly automatic. The squadron leader pulled ahead, twisted, and corrected the twist as he descended, and the others followed in well practiced order. Each pilot lightly touched the bomb levers, to make sure that at the right moment his hand would find them quickly, just as drivers blindly pat their controls before they are needed in a difficult maneuver. Here, the maneuver was precise and dangerous, for if a bomb was released at the wrong moment its shock waves could bring down the plane, and if the levers were not operated symmetrically, the change in weight at a slow bombing speed could flip the plane over and cause it to plow into the ground.

The first to see the aircraft was a young officer who had wheeled his horse around and was about to gallop to the end of the column. His eyes had been directed to the upper windows of the houses, where he had hoped to see the face of a beautiful woman so that he could hold it in his memory as he rode into battle. He saw, instead, black dots in a tight constellation that moved as if it were damped in oil. For a moment, he hesitated. He pulled at the reins of his mount, reversing his prior command. Frustrated and confused, the horse gasped and sidled. The officer narrowed his eyes. Now he was sure, and he shouted.

The colonel turned in the saddle. It was hard to find the formation of planes as they came out of the sun, and he heard them before he saw them. From a distance they sounded like insects. He could hear each one individually and as it combined into the roar that subsumed it.

With his column trapped in the grave of the road, with no place to go and no cover to seek, the colonel told his men to dismount and fire. "Machine-gunners! Machine-gunners!" he shouted, but it was too late.

The order was passed down the line with phenomenal speed. Before the planes were overhead most of the troopers had dismounted and a few had swung their rifles into the air and were working the bolts. The horses panicked and lurched from side to side, forward, and back, rearing up hysterically, breaking wagon shafts, bouncing into the walls of houses that shuddered as if in an earthquake. Some animals stood stock still and whinnied as softly as if they were commenting upon the scene. Others flashed their teeth and showed red eyes as they tore their harnesses and broke from the traces of wagons and carts. Some men who were knocked to the ground laughed because they and their friends looked so foolish.

Alessandro had not understood what was happening. Then he heard the planes, and then, as he stood paralyzed on the snow, he saw them. When the first bombs were dropped, he was running at full speed toward the dispensary.

The planes raced directly above the long column, clearing chimneys by the length of a lance. Their engines were deafening. When they loosed bombs they went to full power and veered alternately left and right, rising in a roar that compounded the concussion of the explosions they left behind.

Horses that were lifted into the air on geysers of dirty blood and smoke somersaulted and landed dead on their backs. Men were blown to pieces, vaporized, or slammed down by shock waves. Others, who had taken shrapnel through their cheeks or their shoulders, staggered blindly away, but many of the wounded pointed their rifles into the air and fired.

Bloody horses ran up on the snowbanks, pumping their haunches in the climb. Some dragged dead troopers still caught in the stirrups. Others limped and panted. As a horse dragging a lance galloped past him, Alessandro saw the second from the last plane release its bombs. They floated through the air and hit the side of the dispensary where he had seen Ariane a moment before. As they went in with a thud, the building collapsed upon itself, and it was halfway down, compressed, puffing out white dust, when they exploded. In the explosion the house expanded to three times its volume, with unidentifiable pieces tumbling in the air above a ball of orange flame that kept the ruin suspended for what seemed like an impossibly long time. Only after everything had collapsed did the fire stop burning in a circle and the flames orient themselves on vertical lines. The house of two and a half storeys had become a pile of rubble a meter high, burning so fiercely that Alessandro had to hold up his hands to shield his eyes from the heat.

The planes came back to strafe. They flew up and down the column, firing machine guns at what remained. Bullets slammed into the ground, into the carcasses of dead horses, and into walls. Only now had the machine-gunners set up and begun to fire.

Alessandro grieved. His punishment was that nothing in the world could touch him. His punishment was that God had put him into battle and preserved him from its dangers.

THE GUN tractor with the short freight box wound through sunlit mountain forests, steep switchbacks, and dark greenery in the valleys of the streams that tumbled to meet the Adige. Just off the road where lines of howitzers and columns of infantry often passed in great drama, trees sang in the wind and rocked to and fro as if nothing were amiss.

Alessandro stood on the right running-board. The wind and sun burned his face, and the sensation of fast gliding only a short distance above the ground was much the same as in a dream of flying, and when they turned on the switchbacks he found himself hanging over the edge of a five-hundred-meter drop with nothing in sight but massive pearly-gray clouds. Peering tensely through his goggles, the driver labored to run his machine safely along the road. Now and then he caught sight of the passenger, who was standing on the running-board and grasping the heavy nickel-plated mirror struts in his fur-lined gloves.

When they came to the forest where the Milanese had died, Alessandro turned to look into the grove of trees. The brigades had moved on and the woods were deserted. The gun tractor drove on a makeshift bridge over the Austrian trenches, and strained to the top of the ridge. Here, except for prairie-like undulations where in summer wild flowers grew sheltered from the wind, the terrain was flat all the way to the Cima Bianca. They moved forward with the pleasing motion of a launch in swollen seas, and at the top of each wave the Cima Bianca glinted in the distance. It sparkled in lines across its lower ridges, and, unlike the spangling of the sun on crystals in rock, or upon a lens of broken water, the flashes moved slowly.

"What's the flashing under the snow line?" Alessandro asked.

The driver turned, almost happily, to talk. "What snow line?" he asked. "The snow is everywhere."

"The glacier line, then," Alessandro answered.

"Muzzle flashes," the driver shouted, his words half blown back into his lungs by the force of the wind. "The Austrians fire their guns straight out, and the shells fall upon our fortifications. The trajectories are the same as if you were firing on level ground, but instead of tilting back the barrel of the gun, the whole earth has been bent."

"I understand," Alessandro said.

"Put it this way. Instead of elevating the guns, the target has been depressed. So the guns point straight out, and way over here we see straight into them. They like to fire at lunchtime. They eat before we do, and for them it's not a big meal, so they try to ruin it for us. The barrage never lasts more than fifteen minutes because they can't afford to waste shells. You know how hard it is to move shells up to those heights?"

Alessandro was hardly listening, but the driver went on. "Then they'll fire one every few minutes just to keep us on edge. They can see us so clearly through their field glasses that they know when we eat, and they aim for the kitchens, but we ordered stove pipe from Bolzano, and now we pipe the smoke away from the cooking fires. The Austrians aim for the smoke, and we eat in peace.

"I'm hungry. Just ahead is a good place to stop. Do you have food?" When Alessandro didn't answer, the driver spoke louder. "Do you have food?"

"Yes. I have a sandwich and a bottle of tea."

The field in which they halted was sheltered from the wind and littered with the dead. After the driver unpacked his lunch and sat on the lee running-board, Alessandro poured tea from his vacuum bottle, held the steaming cup in his hands, and drank. Then he put the cup on the hood of the tractor and replaced his gloves. He walked through a gentle wind into the middle of the field.

Some yellow stubble, like hay, was projecting out of the snow where the grass would have been high in summer. Uniformed corpses, not two weeks down, were scattered alone and in groups. They had been Germans, Austrians, Hungarians, and Italians. Some had died in close combat, but most had been either shot as they ran across the field toward the trenches on each side, or stopped by artillery. They rested unnaturally. Sleeping men would not have been able to hold the positions they held, with necks bent, shoulders hunched forward, and heads pushed into the snow. Even the ones on their backs did not look like they were sleeping, for those who still had faces stared at the sky with open eyes, their mouths fallen into expressions of astonishment.

Here were three hundred fathers, brothers, and sons. Their families had been told only that they were missing. Had the people who loved them known, each of the corpses would have been retrieved, each tenderly bathed, their dirty cheeks kissed, their hands caressed by parents, children, and wives. But they were to lie in the open air and decompose like branches.

THOUGH THE regular army was still stuck on the plain at the base of the Cima Bianca, subject to spiteful bombardment by mountain guns that appeared to be fired point-blank, the Alpini had filtered into the eastern flank and begun a war of high places.

Here, where the air was thin, the ground was treeless, and a single unwary step could easily end one's life, the great nations at war had been stretched to their limits. On level ground and in richer air their vast economies had produced armies of millions, luxuriously supplied, attended by monstrous machines that ran on rails, over the ground, or on the sea. Here it had all been reduced to a few men carrying pieces of wood or packs of ammunition to the heights. A single mortar shell, shot off in a second and almost sure to miss, had been a day's work for the strong man who had carried it up the mountain.

Living-quarters often were cantilevered out from precipices, or hung on heavy chains that had been carried up by teams of mountaineers. Every meter of board, teaspoon of sugar, and drop of kerosene was brought by railroad, truck, mule, and man. Fortifications were hewn into the dolomite by hand, in the cold, in air that caused newly arrived troops to gasp for breath. Though the air may have been thin, the wind was such that outposts were sometimes, literally, blown away. Its effects on marksmanship were ruinous, but that hardly mattered, for the distances were so great that most gunfire was merely to let the enemy know that a height or ridge had been reached or occupied: the war was not so much between the two armies as between each army and the terrain, and the test lay not so much in combating one's opponent as in reaching him.

The eastern face of the Cima Bianca was broken into a mass of cirques and towers, the kind of perspective-and-distance-charged landscape that changed as one moved across it. Cliff faces, rock chimneys, small glaciers, and snowbound plateaux seemed deceptively close or deceptively wide apart, depending upon one's vantage point. Even careful attention to the map did not stop the ground from continual mutation. As soon as you thought you understood the relation of one feature to another, you moved to a new post, and everything looked different. The maps were not entirely accurate, and judgments made by alignment of the map image with actual sightings were apt to be just as wrong as if made by eye alone.

In peacetime the protean characteristics of the mountainscape meant nothing more than that parties of sportsmen lost their way and were forced to extend their food supply to cover a few extra days of walking. Sometimes it meant mountaineers taking the wrong route and losing a member of their party to rockfall or the cold, but these tragedies were few and far between.

In war it was different. Supreme efforts were made to capture one summit or another, and when the battle was over, the soldiers who had pushed forward discovered that they had actually retreated, or that they and their comrades had suffered and died only to lay claim to useless ground far from any strategical point. The battle was slowed by the lethargy that arose from realization that all movements were as if in a dream, for the small groups of men fighting in the cirques and towers were subject not merely to the wishes of Rome or Vienna but to illusions of time, space, and the alpine air.

When Alessandro went to brigade headquarters to receive his posting, he was kept waiting outside a bunker where the major who would decide his fate was deciding the fate of the people who had arrived before him. He sat on a bench, next to his pack, for five or six hours during which the sun shone brilliantly and reflected from the stone wall behind him. He hadn't been as warm since Sicily.

A staff sergeant emerged every half hour to tell Alessandro that he had to wait another half hour. Finally, after ten of these announcements, none of which Alessandro believed, the sergeant was embarrassed enough to want to be friendly. "Would you like to see something?" he asked Alessandro, and started to walk around the corner of the bunker. Alessandro shouldered his pack.

"No, leave that there," the sergeant told him. "It's just up here."

They climbed a ladder to a sandbagged firing position manned by a dullard sentry whom the sun had dyed the color of smoked bacon. Even when the two visitors arrived, he hardly moved.

A mortar stood next to two heavy iron posts within the ring of sandbags. Mounted on one post was an anti-aircraft machine gun, and on the other a pair of binoculars as long as Alessandro was tall. The sergeant removed metal caps from the eyepieces and objectives, and swung the binoculars into position. Then he stepped back and invited Alessandro to take a look. The instrument was aimed at a ridge about three or four kilometers away.

When Alessandro brought his eyes close to the bright glass, he saw as if by magic a group of men on a breastworks. Some were eating, some talking, others scanning the plain below with binoculars and a telescope mounted on a tripod. They wore fur cloaks and snow-white dominoes as if they were a race of monks, and as they walked along the line of their fortifications the wind made their robes dance. With rifles slung across their backs, and their faces hidden in the shadows of pointy hoods, they did not look like an army of the living.

"That's the enemy," the sergeant said as he followed Alessandro's right eye tracking the figures in the distance.

"Why are they so bundled up?" Alessandro asked.

"It's colder up there."

"Are these Germans?"

"Germans, Hungarians, Bulgarians, who knows, but now you can see them up close."

"I beg your pardon?" Alessandro asked.

"The enemy," the sergeant repeated.

"You think they're close?"

"You can see the fingers on their hands."

"Have you ever touched one?" Alessandro inquired.

"Touched one? Of course not. You can't get *that* close."

"I have. Their blood has squirted all over me like a warm shower. I've been tangled up in them. I know how they smell, and I've seen their dental work."

"Are you a dentist?" the dumbfounded sergeant asked.

"No," Alessandro answered. "Are you?"

THE MAJOR was an aristocrat. Alessandro thought he might be the son of a Methuselan connoisseur who lived in a villa threatened by floods. Within the villa were paintings, and books in Latin and Greek that the major had read and absorbed, distancing himself from most of human society even before he had entered it. And now here he was, rich, urbane, and tremendous, in a green Alpini hat with a red feather, doing paperwork in a bunker at two thousand meters.

Like many a veteran of repeated combats, Alessandro was unable to avoid provocation.

"How many dozens of obscure Latin and Greek tomes did you read as the marsh ebbed to and fro, the insects buzzed around the marble mausoleums, and the moths ate your father's tweed hunting jackets?" he asked, after failing to salute.

The major's mouth opened as if he were sucking in cool air to compensate for having scalded his tongue. "What?" he asked, forgetting military etiquette, as had the private who had walked into his office like a general in command of the sector.

Knowing that the major had heard, Alessandro sat down, stared at him, and expanded his thesis.

"You shot skeet with an English shotgun, didn't you. You learned to drink akvavit, and read Apuleius. Your father worried all the time that the foundations of the villa were rotting and that he didn't have the strength to rake up the fallen leaves, which he believed might be poisonous if their essence found admission to the water supply."

"*My* father?"

"White *baffi* and bulging eyes. He wore dressing gowns and wrote with a pen made of ebony and gold. Don't you remember? On the marsh?"

"My father was an engineer," the major said defensively, his voice rising. "We lived in an apartment on the Via Cola di Rienzo. What is this about moths eating his tweed hunting jackets? He had no tweed hunting jackets."

"How am I supposed to know about your father's wardrobe?" Alessandro asked indignantly. "Who was I, his tailor?"

"You said he had tweed hunting jackets."

"I made the best guess available, given the information I had."

"What information?"

"Your face."

"Who are you?" the major asked, amazed. "You didn't even salute. You're sitting in my chair."

"The part of me that lies between the top of my legs and my waist, in the back, that is cleft in two, and rounded, is tired," Alessandro answered.

"Do you realize," the major asked, leaning forward slightly over his desk, "that men have been shot for lesser insubordination?"

"No, I didn't realize, but in Stella Maris I watched them die like flies. Every once in a while," Alessandro went on, clearing his throat, "they try to shoot me, too, but they miss, or I'm pulled out of line. What? It doesn't matter. I have discovered only of late, I have understood only after becoming embittered, that I have immunity, not so much an aura, but comical immunity."

"Comical immunity?"

"Yes. It's a joke. I have *laissez-passer* and I watch as everyone else is blown to bits. It's that bastard, that little dwarf, Orfeo. He did it."

"I beg your pardon?"

"You think Giolitti and the Kaiser made the war? Franz-Josef?"

"No?"

"A dwarf runs everything, from the first shot to the last, the dwarf Orfeo Quatta. If only I had known. Do you know how many unjust, gratuitous, *frivolous* execution orders that little son of a bitch signed? He's thrown whole brigades into the fire. I didn't believe him when I sat next to him copying the Portuguese contract, but he must have been telling the truth.

"He told me that one of my father's scribes, a Torinese named Sanduvo, had discovered a way to make chickens lay seven eggs a day. It had something to do with playing a certain kind of harpsichord rondo while the chickens were massaged with indelible ink. Orfeo planned to steal the method and start a chicken farm, but he was afraid that Sanduvo would kill him if he found out, so Orfeo planned to kill Sanduvo first. Of course, Sanduvo was joking, I think, but that didn't stop Orfeo."

"He killed him?"

"Sanduvo was found in the Tiber, having struck his head and drowned."

"What does this have to do with . . ."

"I should have killed Orfeo even then. It never occurred to me. When he leaned out the window to throw coins at the imaginary African opera singers, I could have pushed him. The world would have been preserved, and everyone I love would be alive today. I would have gone from party to party in Rome, slept, like Fabio, with fourteen hundred foreign women, and rowed on the Tiber. I would have read books and gotten old, and enjoyed eating and drinking. In the fall I would have walked down the Via Cola di Rienzo, in your father's tweed hunting jackets with the moth holes."

As the major hardy knew what to think, he pulled a cigarette from his dull aluminum military cigarette case, offered one to Alessandro to no avail, lit his trench-lighter, and pensively stared at the ceiling of the bunker. Alessandro added, "The bottom of his closet, even though it was a cedar closet, was littered with moth droppings."

"Are you making fun of my *father*?" the major asked.

"I loved your father," Alessandro answered. "He was much like my own father. How could I make fun of him? I only make fun of myself."

"Why?"

"Why? Because, when I love someone, that person disappears."

To the ceiling of the bunker, the major said, "Even the fresh troops they send me now have battle fatigue."

"I don't have battle fatigue," Alessandro snapped. "I was bred and trained for battle. I've been in the line for more than two years. I'm not tired. I'm not afraid. I'm not irrational. To the contrary. I object to the deaths that result not only from battle, but otherwise. If a cleaning woman dies in her bed in Trastevere, a soldier is liquidated by an artillery shell, or an African chieftain succumbs to an infected ostrich-bite, it's all the same, isn't it? Why bother to make distinctions? I doubt very much that God does. To the tourist in the Pinacoteca di Brera the paintings are the same whether he came by train, horseback, or automobile. I'm not fatigued. I merely resent all this dying."

"That's too bad. What are you going to do about it? You can't bring back the dead."

"I know. I've tried."

"Pardon me? You've tried?"

"Oh, I see," Alessandro said. "I suppose you think that's irrational. It is irrational. You can do little with reason except in the material world. Why should I limit myself to reason?"

"Because no one will understand you if you don't."

"To the contrary. Anyway, reason is just as irrational, and those who are rational just as unreasonable as anyone else."

"What?"

"You're a modern type. You are. You accept the theory of evolution, don't you."

"Yes."

"Of course, it's an underpinning of your thought. And the idea of entropy, are you familiar with it?"

"Yes I am," the major said.

"Do you accept it as well?"

"I don't know."

"Most people do. They think that what's true for acute physical processes is probably applicable to cosmology itself."

"What of it!"

"Only this. You believe in entropy, which postulates that all phenomena tend to sink to lower levels of organization and energy, and in evolution, which postulates that the history of life has been just the opposite. People like you credit both theories. It's *de rigueur.* Is that reason rational? I say, fuck off. And all my life I've devoted myself to the task of bringing back the dead, only to discover that it's hopeless."

"What did you do, hold séances? Are you a mystic?"

"I learned to concentrate disparate forces and sensations and make them run together, like music, like a song, into something that has a life of its own. That is a song, is it not, something that seems to have its own life, and goes in its own direction, and pulls you along with it.

"I wasn't trained in music, but I've studied musical theory and I know the Aristotelian requirements, and I am enormously moved by music. I can't play an instrument, except the drums, which anyone can play, and I can't compose."

"Oh," the major interjected, slumped in his chair, almost motionless.

"I'm a critic. I write essays about works of art. It's like being a eunuch in the seraglio, but unrequited love is the sweetest, and I have the proper distance. I can compress the qualities of beauty I've been trained to see, store them up, and bring them out at will, rapid-fire, in the combinations I want.

"Images. Thousands, hundreds of thousands of images. My field was the aesthetics of painting. In homage to that, I keep the images compressed in tiny little squares, like the works of Oderisi da Gubbio or Franco Bolognese, like little postage stamps. Each one glows. It's as if you were looking into a firebox through the peephole or peering into one of those Easter eggs with scenes painted within, or watching a brightly illuminated and distant part of a city through a telescope with sparkling optics. Each frame carries the deep reds, the greens, and the dark blues that Italians never seem to manage as well as the English and the Dutch, though we have almost a lock on every other color. When I run them past my mind's eye, the *Bindo Altoviti, La Tempesta,* the *Uccelli,* and all the others that have been provided to me not only by painters but by the sun as it sets or shines on saffron-colored buildings, the sight of perfectly proportioned squares, the *gallerie,* the *cortili,* I see something that is alive, like a song, and in the songs that rise in my memory like curling columns of smoke, up from the darkness in opera houses, ascending on the heat of the footlights to swirl in the empty space above, I see the faces of the people I love, the faces of my parents, and Guariglia, and Ariane . . . and they almost come alive."

"But they don't."

"No."

"Why?"

"My conceits will never serve to wake the dead. Art has no limit but that. You may come enchantingly close, and you may wither under the power of its lash, but you cannot bring back the dead. It's as if God set loose the powers of art so that man could come so close to His precincts as almost to understand how He works, but in the end He closes the door in your face, and says, leave it to me. It's as if the whole thing were just a lesson. To see the beauty of the world is to put your hands on lines that run uninterrupted through life and through death. Touching them is an act of hope, for perhaps someone on the other side, if there is another side, is touching them, too."

"Who is Ariane?" the major asked.

Alessandro seemed not to hear. He turned to the doorway and looked at the square of blue sky it framed. The major opened a drawer in his desk and pulled out a holstered pistol wrapped in a leather belt. "You're not an officer," he said to Alessandro, "but as long as you are in my command, you may carry a side arm. It's a Colt."

"Why?" Alessandro asked.

"Because of where I'm going to send you. I hope that there you'll think less about art and more about war, so that you may outlast the war and spend the rest of your life thinking about art.

"After you're accustomed to the altitude, after some long marches and descents to the floor of the valley, I'm going to send you to a place where you will be the northernmost Italian soldier in the line, the highest, and the most isolated."

"Why?"

"Because," the major said, "it's what you want. You came in here to ask me for it."

IT WAS remarkable to see the whole world, so wide and so blue, from one place. Straight on, the sky had as much depth and distance as above, and with the clouds below running to the horizon like a white floor, Alessandro believed that he was in the sky rather than under it. For that reason, though not for that reason alone, he felt nearly all the time something akin to the sensation of flying: not vertigo or a feeling of motion, but an aura of lightness, disconnectedness, and quiet. Glacier light arising from blue ice is blinding and cool. When it blends with the light of the sky it commands attention and awe, as if in it the real work of the world is accomplished, and the operations of the richer, warmer light below are of a lesser, fallen order.

Thirty men, including Alessandro, had awakened in the dark at one and assembled on a flat snowfield just beyond their camp. They roped themselves into six parties of five, and checked their equipment. In addition to the rations he would need for the climb, each man carried one day's supply of food, kerosene, and ammunition. Some carried electric lanterns, rope, and extra rings and bolts, in case those on the rock face they would climb needed replacement, and every man had rifle, bayonet, ice axe, slings, alpine hammer, and crampons.

Alessandro had never moved in the mountains so heavily laden. The rifle, especially, was a burden, for with its bayonet, sling, and fifty rounds of ammunition, it weighed five kilograms. Strapped to the soldiers' caps were miner's lamps with thick candles. Because this type of lamp burned with surprising brightness it produced no soot, and its highly polished reflectors stayed clear.

When Alessandro had awakened he was apprehensive of the cold and the wind. Most early mornings in the mountains are cold and wet, as the wind blows moist clouds across the rocks and snowfields. To start a climb in the howling darkness is one of the most unnatural things a human being can do, but the morning that Alessandro climbed to Post o6 was warm and dry. It seemed unbelievable that the sky, twisting and boiling like burning phosphorus, was silent, for its light and motion suggested thunder, explosions, and the sound of the sea. The stars were busy and intent, as if before the moon came up they had to unburden themselves of all they had seen during the daylight hours, when they could not speak. Now they ran riot, and their light made the snowfields breathlessly dim.

The equipment was checked, and gloves removed and replaced dozens of times while ropes were adjusted, buckles tightened, and knots tied. A soldier went from man to man with a small torch, and, as the men bent slightly toward him, lit their lanterns. After the lanterns were lit, each soldier dropped the glass shield, straightened his back, and stamped his crampons into the snow, ready to move forward.

The six lines formed into one, with Alessandro near the end. He watched the lights ahead move onto the glacier as if to match the stars, for not only did every lantern sparkle like a little golden sun, but it made a small circle of yellow light that darted back and forth in front of the man who carried it, oscillating as he moved his head. The procession of lights and circles danced across the snow like a glowing serpent, its many bright segments continually trembling. Soon it came to the fractured part of a small glacier and, without slowing, the soldiers leapt crevasses, landing sometimes so that the only way not to fall back into the abyss was to bring the head of one's ice axe down ahead, and use it to pull oneself aright.

The column assaulted a steep and dusty ridge. It faced south, and the snow had transpired as if to make a trail. Crampons slid on the rocks and were buried in the dust. It was like walking up a sand dune while contending with a slow shower of boulders dislodged by walkers ahead. The rocks rolled negligently into ankles, and now and then a small round rock would glance off its flatter cousins and take to the air in a series of leaps that successfully aspired to the momentum of a military projectile. A scream would emanate from someone ahead, all the lanterns would drop as one, and the rock would whistle by like an artillery shell. Then the lanterns popped up, and the climb would resume.

As the moon rose and set, they marched across glaciers, dusty ridges, and flat pools of pure ice upon which they might have skated. When they stopped to drink and eat they were quickly frozen in the wind, and they would shudder uncontrollably, but when they set out again they soon were hot. The air grew thinner, they panted for breath, and by the time the sun came up they were sitting in groups on a snowy platform more than a thousand meters above their starting point.

Their shirts were stiff with salt, they breathed like the wounded, and they didn't talk. With the sun came a wind so cold and strong that it froze the water in their canteens. Not a cloud was in the sky other than in the white carpet near the horizon, and as the sun rose the wind stopped and the air became tolerably warm. As soon as they ceased shivering, they ate. Those who had forgotten to snuff their candles did so, and they started out again, this time on pure snow that ascended in an incredibly steep hump to a great wall of rock.

They marched upon the slope for several hours, crampons crunching the snow and metal jangling in hypnotic rhythm. With the air so thin and volatile, Alessandro began to smell his own clothes. They had been washed only recently, but cookfires in the headquarters trenches had given them a salty, smoky smell, as sweet as resin, so that here, where trees could never grow, Alessandro had the forest to the point of enchantment.

When the sun was high enough, they stopped on the glaring snow and pushed their ice axes into it to serve as coat racks for their anoraks as they removed sweaters and stuffed them into already bulging packs. Then the anoraks went back on and the soldiers ate biscuits and sipped achingly cold water from their half-iced canteens. As they were about to start off again, five hundred meters from the base of the cliff, Austrian guns opened up below.

First came the flash, then a peal of thunder, and then a shattered chorus of tangled repetitions, each slightly altered in volume and pitch, rambling around the cirque like a thunderstorm. With three or four guns launching a shell a minute, the concussions and echoes were reminiscent of the pounding of a rain-swollen falls.

"It isn't time for the afternoon meal," Alessandro said to the man in front of him. "Why are they firing?"

"They're firing at us."

"At us?"

"Yes, but they can't reach us. The shells land on the glacier to the west, and we can't even see them explode. They picked us up in their telescopes and they don't like that we're so far behind their lines. They don't have us in sight until we round the hump, and by then we're out of range. They can't stand the fact that from the minute they start out we have them in our sights. It especially irritates them because when we built the lookout they sent a company to intercept us, and we destroyed them with our artillery before they crossed the glacier. The shells exploding on the ice were as catastrophic as a bomb in a hall of mirrors. The ice did the killing, and it buried them too."

"Tell me why they bother to fire at us if we're so far out of range."

"They're trying for an avalanche. Fifteen of our soldiers are buried at the base of this ramp, just so."

"And fifteen escaped?"

"No one escaped. At that time Zero-Six was manned for two weeks at a stretch. We changed it to a month to lessen the chances of being caught. Don't worry, we haven't had much snow, and it's been dry. Besides, we're more than three-quarters up the slope, so we've passed most of the danger. The higher we get, the smaller the avalanche and the more likely we are to survive it."

Rocks of all sizes were glancing from the wall. As the supply party got closer, the snow was littered with bigger and bigger stones. It seemed that the Austrians had done the Italian column a favor by jarring loose the rockfall before they arrived.

The foot of a cliff hundreds of meters high and the end of a snow ramp two thousand meters long met in a tiny scalloped edge of ice that, if pressured with the little finger, tumbled into the small crease between the two. That two such masses should touch with inimitable delicacy prompted Alessandro to think of the sea and the shore. As the soldiers rested at the base of the cliff, apprehensive of rockfalls and quieter than usual, Alessandro spoke about the variability of the Atlantic. He had seen pictures of houses in France and Spain safely perched five meters from maximum high tide and two meters above it. Their actual distance from the sea, then, was less than five and a half meters. Calling it six, he divided it into the twelve thousand kilometers that he guessed stretched over the open sea to southern Argentina without a break, and determined that the mass of the sea, in all its unimaginable weight and volume, never expanded more than one part in two million, and, indeed, was more stable than that, for he had failed to consider the immense volume of the ocean, which would make the ratio much more severe. The margins of the sea were as delicate and immobile as the fine border of ice that touched the cliff.

"And what do you conclude from that?" a soldier sitting next to him asked with a note of hostility.

"That the natural world is infinitely more reliable than the world of man," Alessandro said, "and that in our short lives we must have volatility or we will not know motion. With more time, perhaps, we might be more serene, and happier."

"You're crazy."

"Of course. And you?"

"Link up," the officer in command ordered, motioning with his gloved hand to two ropes of men. "Form six pairs. I want the relay done fast, so we can get out of here. The Austrians couldn't make an avalanche, but the afternoon sun can."

Although thirty men had been required to carry the supplies to this point, their packs, which they had begun to repack and combine, would go the remaining five hundred meters by rope, passed from team to team. Only Alessandro would reach the lookout, still invisibly tucked into the cliff face. The others would be spread along the route, belayed on ledges or off bolts on the sheer face, working to hoist the supplies with ropes and pulleys.

Alessandro and the soldier who had told him about the avalanches formed the lead team. The other man looked at Alessandro intently. "Are you sure you know how to do this?"

"I haven't climbed in a number of years. I may be slow at first in shifting the *étriers,* but, as the bolts are already in, I'll manage. I've climbed the west tower of the Cima Bianca three times. On the third time, I led."

The other man was impressed.

Alessandro reached up to the first bolt and clipped fast the *étriers.* Soon, having ascended even more rapidly than they might have expected, the two soldiers were a hundred meters above the snow ramp. The world seemed far distant. Once again, it had been reduced to simple and satisfying elements: when a carabiner was clicked into place around a bolt, all was secure. Moving beyond the last position engendered enough fear to make exceedingly lovely the action of clipping in where it was solid, and during the cycles of fear and relief one found immense satisfaction in upward progression. At the top of the last pitch, a broad ledge upon which they were comfortably belayed to a larger than usual bolt in the rock, Alessandro was brimming with joy, even if only for a moment. His feeling was much like the disproportionate satisfaction that old people can find, regardless of their losses, infirmities, and disappointments, in small things, like sitting under the trees and watching the birds flit from branch to branch, or drinking tea from a china cup with a gold rim.

"It's like the days before the war," he said to his partner on the rope.

The other soldier breathed-in the sweet smell of the rock lichen. "Yes," he answered. "Think how fine it will be when hour after hour passes without the report or threat of a single gun—for years without end. Life will be like a dream."

"And no one will appreciate it," Alessandro said to the vast distances around him.

"Except us, and screw them."

Twenty-five meters overhead, a bearded face looked down in agitated anticipation. Then it darted back into the shelter of the observation post, and two ropes sailed into the air. The looped ends slapped the vertical rock halfway down, jiggling the rest of the way as the lookout slowly dropped them by hand. Soon they jiggled right in front of Alessandro's face.

"Goodbye," the other soldier said. "He'll tell you what's required."

"What's he going to do, hang us?" Alessandro asked, looking at the two nooses that swayed next to him.

"Bilgiri."

"Off belay?"

"He's a good man. I wouldn't worry."

Alessandro unclipped himself from the bolt, untied himself from the rope, and stood up on the ledge, which now, thousands of meters above the valley floor, seemed rather narrow. He put a foot in each loop and took hold of the ropes. When the observer saw this, he disappeared once more, and in an instant Alessandro felt the rope under his left foot begin to rise. He followed it, bending his knee, and then stepped up, putting his weight on it. As soon as the observer had belayed the left rope, he pulled the other one a step beyond it, and, so, shifting his weight from loop to loop as the one was pulled past the other, Alessandro climbed a ladder that was crafted for him at each step. In peacetime he would have been belayed by a rope to his waist. Now he had no such guarantee.

Had he fallen he would have bounced against the cliff in several places one or two hundred meters down and been hurled onto the snow ramp, perhaps close enough to the base of the cliff so as not to slide down it. From his exposed perspective, however, not that it mattered, it looked as if he would land in the upper course of the Talvera, which made a disheveled green-and-white line through the gray rock of the lower valley. The air seemed so thin as to allow a man who fell to hear no whistling and feel no wind.

The minute Alessandro put his hands on the stone sill over which the ropes passed, the observer began to question him. "You're new," he said. "I don't know you. What happened?"

Still standing in the loops, Alessandro answered, "Right. May I come in?"

"Were they overrun? I haven't spoken to them since my batteries ran out five days ago."

"Do you mind?" Alessandro asked, straining his stomach muscles as he climbed in.

"Let me help."

The observer was so awkward and enthusiastic that he pulled in Alessandro head over heels, and they both were caught in a tangle of ropes, hooks, and empty knapsacks. Looking around at the cell carved into the rock, Alessandro immediately asked if he had to sleep in the blankets the observer had used for the past month.

"They have fresh blankets for you, and some surprises, too. It's not bad if you don't mind being alone. We've got seven books now, and they've undoubtedly brought up another. If the war lasts for five more years they'll have sixty-eight books up here, and it'll be the world's highest library."

"What about Potala?" Alessandro asked.

"Who's he?"

"The great monastery in Tibet."

"Fuck him."

Alessandro and the observer worked feverishly to haul up the supplies. As they pulled at the ropes the observer spoke at high speed, explaining the tasks and tricks that Alessandro would have to master. When everything was received, the observer took him around and demonstrated how to open ports, change batteries, and record coordinates. Through a powerful telescope chained to a plate in the ceiling so it would not be inadvertently dropped from the window, he showed Alessandro the latest Austrian dispositions, upon which he had become expert. He explained the dangers and defenses of the observation post, the system of rationing, and the miracle of the telephone that sat upon the table in the center of the floor, its wire traveling straight up to a wooden beam in the ceiling, as if it were in a business office in Rome rather than in a cell in the rock just below the summit of a peak several thousand meters high.

Hundreds of spools of telephone wire had been brought up, carefully spliced and reinforced, and then lowered on the other side of the summit. The line dropped straight down a vertical cliff onto a glacier, and detoured across the snowfields, for if it had been laid on the glacier it would have been ripped apart in the shifting of crevasses. For several kilometers it was buried in the snow, until it emerged at headquarters. In daylight, reports were made every two hours. At night Alessandro would be awakened now and then to listen for bolts driven into the rock below him.

After the observer rappelled down, Alessandro was all alone in a miraculous cabin that had taken three hundred alpinists and artisans four months to requisition from the rock, and on account of which fifteen men lay buried on the glacier and two had died in falls.

THEY HAD hollowed out a chamber seven meters deep, two meters high, and four meters wide. It went lengthwise into the mountain, level and true, and its granite walls were perfectly smooth and dry. Two chimneys passed through the rock for ten meters and were vented under rainproof baffles. The chimney shafts were narrow, but smoke from the lamps and the cookstove were sucked into them in quick swirls that, in the alternate rush and hesitation of their spirals, reminded Alessandro of circus acrobats in candle-lit tents. Alessandro had known since his childhood that the circus was bittersweet, and after he had lit the lamps he watched the smoke twist into the chimneys as he floated in and out of circuses—impoverished Gypsy circuses in coastal Sicilian towns, at odds with the blue surf and the citrus groves; Baltic circuses that were colorful and warm despite the dirty gray clouds that lashed the tents with rain; and Roman circuses, the perfect median, with tents of saffron-colored canvas, and sparkling lights, in balance in every way, just like Rome itself.

One wall was empty, which made the room seem bigger. Upon this wall was a grid in which each occupant had three boxes, running from side to side, for the inscription of his name, the dates of his sojourn, and a comment: "Bottai, Rudolpho: I was the first. Send me a postcard to tell me what you think." "Giammatti, Andrea: Don't talk to yourself, and do not smile inappropriately." "Labrera, Anselmo: Any woman would have been welcome, even if she had had a wart on her nose." "Ceceni, Michele: I warned of the Austrian attack of the 5th." "Agnello, Giuseppe: Killed several enemy trying to take this post. Wounded in shoulder." "Costanza, Benito: Why not talk to yourself? I talk to myself all the time."

Alessandro impulsively wrote his name, the dates of his assignment, and his comment, for he did not want to spend a month trying to distill the wisdom of the ages into one line. The message read, "Though now I am the safest man in Italy, I cannot wait to fly." Let them try to figure that out, he thought, though probably most would assume that he was slated to become a pilot. And perhaps not—not after they had spent a month staring out at the clouds, watching the birds disappear beyond the war to places over the sea or islands within it, where the animals had never heard the crack of a gun.

Another wall was entirely taken up by heavy cedar shelves, which gave off a fragrance that filled the chamber. Upon them, in military order, were the supplies and equipment that had been carried up at such great cost. Most of it had been there already, and Alessandro neatly stacked and lined up what he had brought, so he could ration his inventories as time passed: thirty packets apiece of bread, pasta, jam, sugar, tea, powdered soup, dried fruit, chocolate, and cured beef; a small sack of potatoes and onions; two cans of salmon; a diminutive *panettone;* two one-liter bottles of red wine; a crock of butter; a bunch of carrots; a kilo and a half of cheese; two bars of soap; a box of tooth salts; iodine swabs; bandages; aspirin; tincture of opium; six newly washed woolen blankets; a down pillow; eight rolls of toilet paper; ten grenades; twenty signal or illumination flares; a Mauser 98; five hundred rounds of ammunition in ten boxes of fifty rounds; a bayonet; a first-aid kit; an alpine hammer; two dozen pitons; 150 meters of rope; a box of hooks and nails; pliers; a screwdriver; eight extra dry-cells for the telephone; a wash-basin; two huge bottles into which water from a small cistern passed through a hose connected to a stopcock in the wall; and eight liters of kerosene, for cooking and illumination, along with extra wicks for the lamps, and several boxes of wooden matches.

In the center of the floor was a huge oak table that had been put together in the chamber after the components were taken up by rope. Arrayed upon it were the telephone and a row of four cells to power it; the telescope, with its chain rising to the plate in the ceiling; a pelorus, for establishing bearings; an optical range-finder; a daily log; a codebook; a box of pencils and a penknife for whittling them sharp; a pair of binoculars—even the king did not have better binoculars; and a kerosene lamp with a brightly polished reflector. Between bookends of solid granite were the Bible; *Scaramouche,* by Rafaello Sabbatini; the 1909 edition of Baedeker's *Die Schweiz,* with the subtitle *Oberitalien, Savoyen und Tirol; Orlando Furioso;* the original French edition of *La Chartreuse de Parme;* a Boy Scout manual that had been split in two; a small volume of Dante entitled *Vita Nuova—Rime;* and an extraordinary short English pornographic novella (that Alessandro read even before he unpacked) in which a barely disguised Prince of Wales traveled to Paris to spend time in a warm pool with half a dozen of the world's most beautiful and licentious women, exploring with every part of his anatomy every part of theirs as they did the same for him and among themselves. The end degenerated into such a tangle of beautiful limbs, turgid breasts, and open mouths against the fat barrel of the Prince of Wales and his various appendages, that it made Alessandro think of a belaying pin in a vat of *calamari.*

The outside wall had the large opening through which he had entered, and two narrow rectangular windows on either side. All three were covered by steel shutters hinged at the top. A little window opened in the center of the plate that fit over the entrance, and the plate itself was so heavy that it had to be raised and lowered by cranking a winch. A steel trap-door led to the roof without benefit of a ladder: one had to reach up and pull oneself through. The roof itself, nothing more than a narrow ledge carved into the cliff, gave access to the absolutely vertical cliff face above, which went another hundred meters or so to a summit that was nothing more than a needle the size of a hitching post. This roof platform was the latrine, in which one had to hang out, while grasping two bolts, over a drop of nearly a thousand meters.

Alessandro lit the lamps. A thin line of orange light marked the west, and the lights in the Austrian and Italian trenches sparkled in the darkness into which they had been cast an hour previously.

He folded the knapsacks and stashed them on a shelf, made the bed (a cot under the wall of inscriptions), and got things ready in case the Austrians were bold enough to attack at night, which he thought even more unlikely than that they would attack in the day. Still, he bolted shut the steel doors, cleaned and loaded the Mauser and stood it in the corner, and hung his Colt pistol and the bayonet on pegs next to the bed. The pegs had been neatly placed in holes bored in the granite, which reminded him of the Prince of Wales, and he dreamed that night of wonderfully perfumed women with rosy flesh and intoxicated, licentious stares. But when he awoke in the middle of the night, the memory of their beautiful bodies reminded him so much of Ariane that he was lost in despair.

PERHAPS BECAUSE isolation is the mother of meticulousness, Alessandro kept his aerie sharper and better organized than the bridge of a flagship of the Royal Navy. When the bells churned on the telephone, he was always ready to give his reports, and he read them in precise military language as if he had been doing it all his life. On two occasions in the first ten days he warned Italian outposts of impending air attacks. Because of the high winds, he had been unable to hear the aircraft, though he had seen them with the telescope as they rounded the easternmost peaks of Switzerland. He never would have picked them up individually, but five moving together as one were visible, with the aid of a telescope, even a hundred kilometers away. His warnings were well appreciated, and they suggested to him that if he were able to see Austrian squadrons a hundred kilometers distant in the ice-world, then perhaps someone was able to see him, too. He never relaxed, glancing frequently at the trap-door and listening for bolts driven in the rock below him. A bolt could be inserted both slowly and silently. The party climbing toward him could do it a little at a time, and then retreat until the next night. It was possible as well that the Austrians would make the arduous climb up the other side, undetected, and *abseil* down to his post in utter silence.

The chamber was cold. When the steel shutters were open, as most of the time they had to be, his water froze. The winds were sometimes so high that his ears popped with the change in pressure, and the normally hypnotic whistling of the wind through fissures in the shutter frames became louder than the horn of an express train. He could neither ignore the sound nor do anything until it stopped, and it was occasionally so loud that objects vibrated across the table and things jumped from the pegs on the walls.

During a thunder-and-lightning storm two days after he arrived, the vibrations from the wind were so great that they dumped the hand grenades onto the floor all at once. Alessandro had experienced this nightmare while sitting on a rope chair, wrapped in blankets and drinking a cup of hot water. Suddenly, with the most brittle and terrible sound he had ever heard, the grenades began to bounce across the stone floor. With no place to flee and not enough time to open the shutter and throw them out, he waited for the explosion that would paper the walls with his flesh and paint them the color of his blood. In that moment, he looked at the cup of hot water, thinking it would be the last thing he would ever see, and he felt so many regrets, that the tin cup looked like the saddest thing in the world. The grenades remained intact. From then on, he kept them in a neat row on the floor.

He soon tired of the sexual adventures of the Prince of Wales. After half a dozen readings, the goings on in the Parisian brothel were no more exciting than the daily routine of a hardware store. After three days, he opened the package marked *Surprise: Do not open for three days.* It was a fresh lemon. Perhaps because it had been repeatedly thawed and frozen, it had a strange taste, but he used it to flavor half his supply of salmon and two cups of tea.

He hadn't the energy to read the *Vita Nuova* more than a few lines at a time. These took on a magical quality, and he could see them floating in the dark under the rock ceiling, singing and turning in the air like strange fish in the depths of the sea.

During the day he sat for hours in the rope chair, wrapped in blankets and listening to the slow thunder of his heart. When his pulse dropped below forty and his extremities were numb with cold, he would force himself to move. It was painful to rise from the chair and throw off the blankets, but he would do it, and begin to walk slowly around the room. At first he staggered. Then he would run, and bend. When he felt alive again, he did calisthenics for several hours, working up slowly until he was breathing hard, sweating, hot, flushed, and on fire. In these sessions he reclaimed his physical strength. The altitude, the meager rations, and the hardening of his body exercised his spirit. He stopped reading, but the lines kept on coming, circling in the deep, aglow, a phrase or a word at a time. For example, one word, *"bellezza,"* after rotating like a sparkling pinwheel, stopped and drew back like a woman who brazenly asks to be admired. Then it smiled ghoulishly, pulsed in sickening green light, and exploded into silver shards that vanished into the black. Other words had their own repertoires. Sometimes they met before him in the air, in battle or in seduction.

In the evenings after dinner he watched the flame of the lamp. When the wind howled with great strength, it moved as if the abyss were trying to pull it away. Wind and darkness seemed to say that if only the flame would surrender and be extinguished, leaving behind a trace of white smoke, it would be taken at unimaginable speeds and in unimaginable cold, whistling like a million flutes, high over the mountains of ice, rocketing into the darkness of space in distances that had no limit and for a time without end—

but the flame kept burning, wavering perilously behind a thin shell of brittle glass, and it lit the room, turning everything to gold.

THE AUSTRIANS could neither mass for an attack nor enjoy the open air as long as Alessandro was able to see them from his chamber in the rock and guide shells directly to the entrances of their tunnels and trenches, working away at particular points like a miner until he could open up a bunker or excavate a tunnel, and watch the men scatter after he hit the hollow places. It was natural that they would resent this.

At four in the morning the ringing of the telephone pulled Alessandro from a deep sleep. He rolled out of bed, found the table in the dark, and picked up the receiver.

All kinds of static came over the line. "Yes," he said.

"Alessandro?" queried an unfamiliar voice, bathed in noise.

In the dark, with the blankets heavy on his shoulders as he leaned over the table and clutched the phone, Alessandro could not get his bearings, and he felt as if he were drifting in space. "What?" he answered.

"Is that you?"

"It's the king."

"I wanted to make sure they hadn't gotten to you yet."

"Who?"

"It cleared tonight, about a half an hour ago, and we saw lights above you."

"Above me?"

"Yes. They must have come up the other face."

"At night?" Alessandro asked incredulously.

"We were watching them, but then it clouded over. You might want to prepare yourself."

"Thank you," said Alessandro. "How many?"

"Four."

Alessandro thought for a moment, listening over the wind and the static on the line for footsteps or clinking metal. "Thank you," he said again, and hung up.

As the wind whistled through the cracks between the stone and the iron shutters, he stared up into the dark and saw nothing but the inexplicable flashes that were made in his own eyes.

He lit the lamp, moved a wooden ammunition box near his bed, and put the lamp on it. He placed the *Vita Nuova*, face open, on the floor near the head of the bed. Then he threw off his blankets, tucked in his shirt, buckled his belt, put on his heaviest sweater, and sat down on the floor to lace up his boots. His fingers moved like the parts of a spinning jenny. Never had he worked faster, and then he was up in one motion, leaning over the bed to take the pistol and the bayonet from the wall. As he strapped on the pistol, he felt disturbed because he had never fired it. He used precious seconds to unholster the weapon and swing it open. The six round ends of cartridges in the chambers made a brass-colored circle comforting to behold. Upon this metal his survival would rest, just as it had so often depended upon even smaller pieces of steel driven into the rock.

He threw the empty knapsacks across the room to his bed. Moving with incredible speed, he used the sacks to sculpt a man lying on his side, facing the wall. The legs had to be far lower than the hips and shoulders. He covered this with two of his blankets, and it looked real, but nothing in the chamber, save his own head, was even vaguely spherical. He settled for stuffing some clothes into a sock and arranging the end as if it were the ornamental part of a night cap. He would have found this amusing had he time to be amused.

Then he heard the sharp, high-velocity click of tiny pebbles striking the stone roof and the frame of the trap-door, and he froze. Whoever was coming had dislodged some stones while descending, and he hoped that they had not realized it.

As quickly as he could, his heart beating at twice its normal rate, he rested some heavy timbers against the wall and moved the table, in three parts, from its pedestal, arranging the table top against the timbers like the sides of a lean-to. He used a metal plate, which had been hauled up at great cost and for no apparent reason, to armor the wood. Then he hung all the rope and other loose equipment he could find over the side of this construction, grabbed his first-aid kit and the remaining blanket, and crawled between the lean-to and the wall.

As he was stuffing cotton into his ears he remembered that he had left the trap-door bolted. Cursing quietly, he backed out of the redoubt, leapt to the center of the floor, and silently pulled back the bolt. As he stood, with his neck bent, staring at the bolt, he heard the thump of a boot above him.

Teeth clenched, heart racing, Alessandro pushed quietly into his armored sanctuary. He rammed the cotton firmly into his ears and held it between his teeth. Then he unholstered the pistol and laid it before him, and unsheathed the bayonet. Six shots, he thought, and four men. Either he would be calm and unshaken, or he would find himself flailing in the dark with the bayonet.

They waited for what seemed like hours before they lifted the door, and when they did, they did it ever so slowly. Trying desperately not to breathe audibly, Alessandro watched long crusts of snow fall inward and break apart in the air before making little piles on the floor. He saw a man's face slowly descend partway through the trap. He, too, was breathing quietly. He looked at the lamp and the bed, and then pulled back.

At first, nothing happened. Then, after two heavy metallic clunks, the trap-door was slammed shut. Alessandro grit his teeth and bunched the blanket around his head, holding as much of its bulk as he could near his ears.

He counted. One . . . two . . . three . . . four . . . Even though he had been deliberately slow, he had been counting so fast that the explosions came at twenty. One immediately followed the other. They pushed him against the rock wall and threw the metal plate up to the ceiling, but the table top hardly budged. Alessandro's jaw closed on the cotton, and he received a blow to his solar plexus that stopped his breathing. Despite the cotton, the blankets, and his hands, his ears rang, and the nerves in his eyes gave him a fireworks show.

He threw down the blanket, spat out the cotton, yanked the ear plugs, and picked up the pistol, but his hand was shaking so hard that he had to put the gun down. He wondered if he would be able to stop trembling in time, and tried to talk himself into it as if he were trying to talk a horse out of a gallop. While they were dropping down from the hatch, which had been blown open in the blast, he would have to lie with the pistol before him, hoping that at the last moment his hand would be still and strong enough to grasp it and aim.

Before they came in they shone their miner's lights around the room, and one of them shot the blanket-covered knapsacks five times in rapid succession with a semi-automatic pistol.

The first man dropped down. The minute his feet touched the floor he raised the pistol he had just fired and emptied it into what he thought was Alessandro's head. Still holding the gun in his hand, he looked about, the beam from his light sweeping over the rubble, and then he relaxed. The room was filled with smoke.

With a voice that sounded relieved and triumphant, the first man called the others in. They dropped down one by one, and they spoke with animation, for they thought they had succeeded.

The beams of their lights stopped tentatively at the dead soldier in the bed, and then quickly moved on. One of the raiders discovered the telephone. It was in pieces, but the body was still connected to the wire that fell from the ceiling.

"Look, a telephone. Let's call the Italians on the telephone!"

They gathered around the telephone and turned the crank. They were laughing like little boys, with their lights shining upon the semi-dismembered instrument they were trying to revive, when Alessandro's hand stopped trembling.

He placed it around the pistol. It was uncannily steady, far steadier than it had been before the blast, steadier than it had ever been in pistol practice.

Taking aim at the one who had the empty pistol in his hand, which was not the best tactic, he pulled back the hammer.

When they heard the hammer click they turned to stare. Unable to place the sound in the darkness and smoke, they froze. Even after the first fell dead, the other three were more surprised than indignant, and they hardly moved. Alessandro cocked the hammer again and shot one of them through the heart. As this one collapsed, the other two lurched to opposite sides of the chamber. They were easy targets because they hadn't had time to discard their lights, and Alessandro put two casually aimed shots in the body of the one on his left just as he was drawing a pistol.

Before Alessandro could turn, the last of them had begun to spray the room with bullets. He was so frightened that he fired wildly, sometimes not even in Alessandro's direction. Alessandro dropped to his knees and crawled along the floor behind the bulwark of table tops. The enemy soldier fired at them and bullets splintered through the wood ahead of Alessandro, walking from right to left in a design so even and at a rate so steady that he knew if he were to stand he would have time to get off a shot before the pattern broke. Trembling with fear, he took a breath and stood up straight. He raised his gun and fired two shots at the miner's light. The light went out and the room was suddenly quiet. Now three miner's lights lay on the floor, their beams pointing at strange and unlikely angles, as the smoke slowly cleared. The air smelled of gunpowder and blood. Alessandro reloaded the Colt and listened very closely, because someone was breathing.

THOUGH THE explosion had not wounded him, Alessandro was suddenly taken ill. A pain centered in his forehead and eyes made him bend double, and, as he did so, he retched. He could hardly move, and thought he was going to die of suffocation. As the smoke dissipated, he blacked out.

He awoke an hour after dawn, in air that was pristine and cold. Sunlight came through the cracks and was reflected through the hatch. After a while, he heard the breathing. It was so faint he couldn't be sure he wasn't merely remembering it.

One of the Austrians was still alive. Lying on his back with his arms bowed, he clutched a wound on the right side of his chest. He was tall and strong, his face brutal and pale, with fleshy lips, hooded eyes, and a close-cropped blond beard. He looked like a mountain guide. They had probably all been mountain guides.

"Does it hurt?" Alessandro asked in Italian, too sick to speak in another language even though he had intended to.

The Austrian nodded.

"Are you going to die?"

"Nein," was the answer, the abruptness of which Alessandro associated not with rudeness but with vigor.

Alessandro looked around the room. Three bodies were beginning to stiffen where they lay, and the floor was covered in sheets of frozen blood. As always, the dead were sprawled in positions of shock and regret.

Everything that Alessandro had arranged on tables and shelves was now rubble. Beans and rice littered the floor like hail and gravel, stuck in the congealed blood and piled up in drifts in the corners. Bandoliers of bullets had blown apart, the shelves were splintered, cans of fish had been compacted until some of them leaked oil. Everything was everywhere—the pages of the *Vita Nuova* scattered like leaflets dropped from an airplane, instruments and metal pieces embedded in wood and strangely bent, half the messages on the wall blackened by fire. Alessandro had no idea how he had survived, but he noticed that rounded things—bullets, grenades, round cans, anything with a roll to it—had fared better than objects with corners and flat surfaces. The telephone looked mortally wounded; one of its coils had unsprung and popped out to the side like a horizontal jack-in-the-box. "I'll have to take you back," he said to the survivor.

The Austrian grimaced as if to question Alessandro's ability to do it.

"Don't worry," Alessandro assured him. "A line of heavy bolts goes all the way down. You'll be safe. If you stay here you're sure to die."

Alessandro holstered the pistol, strapped down the hammer, and got the first-aid kit. The bullet had not exited, but appeared to have smashed a rib and come to rest. After cutting bandages for making a splint, and laying them out in front of him, Alessandro cleaned the wound, put a gauze pad over it, and had the Austrian hold it as tightly as he could. He then went looking for a piece of wood.

He found some boards, unwound another roll of gauze, and reached for the scissors. They weren't there. He looked near his right hand, where he thought he had left them. He looked to the left. Giving up, he would tear the gauze, and had lifted his elbows in the symmetrical gesture common to those about to rip bandages or tape. Then he hesitated, but it was already too late.

With all his remaining strength, the wounded soldier brought his right arm up from the ground in a powerful arc and drove the scissors into Alessandro's chest. Alessandro fell back, clutching at the blades embedded in the muscle over his heart and crying out with pain. He was so shocked that he hardly understood as the soldier desperately tried to pull the pistol from its tight holster. Alessandro rolled across the bodies on the floor. He ended up on his side, resting on top of a corpse. The pain in his chest was unbearable, and when he pulled out the scissors he nearly fainted again. His shirt and sweater were covered with blood.

The Austrian soldier was trying to reach him, gasping as he crawled over the bodies of his friends, but he stopped short when he saw the pistol that one of them was holding. It was still loaded. Alessandro shook his head, as if to give him one more chance, but the Austrian didn't believe him, and rushed for the pistol.

Alessandro unstrapped his revolver and jerked it from the holster. This was a race in which he could afford to be careful. He raised the gun and aimed it, and as the other soldier pulled the semi-automatic from the dead man's grip, Alessandro cocked the hammer with his thumb.

Realizing that he was too late, the Austrian laughed, and turned to Alessandro. "I'm thirsty," he said, smiling coyly, as if he were going to live.

WITH THE sound of the last shot still ringing in his ears, Alessandro went to the shutter and pushed it open. The world outside was bright blue, the air cold and clean. "Still alive," he said to himself as he looked out on the great mountain ramps, and then the real work began.

Because he couldn't bind the wound, he had to press against it with his hand. He might have weighted a thick wad of alcohol-soaked gauze, placed it over the cut, and taken to bed, but he had too much to do.

First he threw out the bodies, which in some ways was more difficult than killing the men in the first place. They made no protest as he dragged them to the window, and as he struggled to hoist them to the sill their arms and legs hung like loose brush and their eyes focused on inappropriate targets at inappropriate distances. He tossed them into the air, and they fell like cannon shells. He knew that eventually he would see them on the glacier below, half covered with snow, their limbs broken and skulls smashed, their skin parchment-colored and blue. The last was still warm.

Alessandro closed the hatch and one of the shutters so that the freezing air would cease to blow violently through his shattered quarters. After he went through the rubble, throwing out everything that had been irreparably spoiled, he began to arrange what was left.

Because half the kerosene containers had burst and he would have to make fires, he piled all the splintered and broken wood in a corner. Weapons, ammunition, climbing equipment, tools, clothing, and cooking utensils were sorted, with items needing repair set apart.

He remounted the table upon its trestle, fixed his bed, and reordered the books, most of which had been blown apart at the spine. The *Vita Nuova* took the longest to collect, and some of its pages remained glued to the floor with blood and lymph.

He put the pieces of the telephone back on the table. The wooden box was shattered and much of the metal and green wire inside bent or severed. He thought that he might fix it if he could determine the purpose of each part. He had never seen the inside of a telephone. He would, in effect, have to re-invent it, a test not only of his physics instructors, and of him, but of the design of the telephone itself. He looked forward to the task, though he knew he would have to wait until his strength returned. Meanwhile, he put the pieces in order and arranged his tools in rows nearby.

Then came the matter of food. For ten hours he picked grains of rice off the floor and collected pasta, sugar, and individual tea leaves. He would not eat anything that had been tainted with blood, and was left with less than a third of his rations. Some things— powdered cocoa, for example—were uncollectible, or had risen on the wind. He had kerosene enough for one pot of boiling water and one hour of lamplight each day. Some of his blankets had bullet holes.

He cut slits in his sweaters and shirts so that he could bathe his wound without having to strip in the cold, and he folded blankets and coverings so as to maximize their warmth. With three layers of wool underneath, and six above, he would be warm enough, he hoped, not to shiver or go into shock.

He arranged the elements of a meal, including water in a pot on the stove, a match next to its striking surface, and five teaspoons of sugar in a cup with the tea and a spoon. He had only a dozen squares of chocolate, but he put two next to the tea cup. He ate what was left of a compressed can of sardines, tossed out the remnants, and licked the oil from his fingers. Then he cut himself a piece of cheese, and drank a liter of water. He wasn't thirsty, but he knew he needed the fluid.

Waiting for the water to pass through his system, so that he would not have to get up from a warm bed later on, he dressed in many layers of socks and sweaters and put on a wool hat. Then he went to the window and peed into space, after which he felt temporarily warmer.

When the shutter was closed, thin rays of light pierced the darkness, illuminating enormous amounts of crazed silver dust. Alessandro sat on the bed and doused the wound with alcohol. The bandage scissors had penetrated to the length of a thumbnail. Had he not had a hard sheath of muscle over that part of his chest, the point probably would have reached his heart.

HE SLEPT for three days, and thought it was much longer. When he awoke he could hardly move, and he had become a furnace. The blankets were hot and comfortable, his face cool, and his nose frigid. He fell into dreams and reawakened, his breathing shallow and hot. When he lifted the blankets he got dizzy. He laced his boots with great effort and pain, and before he put on his coat he looked at the wound. Though the entry had closed, and it had been small, the risk of infection remained.

As he was drinking tea he remembered that his sleep had been rich with dreams, but he could recall nothing about them except that it had been as if he were traveling through a gallery in which the colors of the paintings enveloped the onlookers.

He set about repairs, starting with the telephone. The observation post was valuable in the conduct of the war below, and because the enemy knew that the attempt to dislodge him had failed, they had to assume that his messages were getting through. It seemed so from the pattern of their deployments, which had remained static and defensive. He thought he owed them what they expected.

Before he tried to reassemble the telephone he had to deduce its workings and obtain anything extra that he might need to supplement them. First, he manufactured glue. For two days he went without anything hot to eat or drink, and used his fuel to melt bookbindings, which he cooked into a viscous fluid by adding sugar, pasta, and kerosene. In theory, the kerosene would evaporate after the mixture was removed from its airtight container, and the glue would set.

He pulled all the brads from the small ammunition boxes, took apart the wood to use as splints, and hunted for wire small enough in diameter to use in binding components or splicing. This he found, long after giving up, wrapped around the cylindrical objective lens of the telescope, which he had removed in search of glue.

While assembling tools and materials he began to solve the mechanical problems, working his way logically toward the innards from the wire and from the parts that were used in operating the instrument: the mouth and ear pieces, the crank, and the bells. He talked to himself to make sure that he remembered his reasoning, to try to avoid too easy a rationale, and for encouragement. In the end, it was easy. The mouthpiece, now empty, must have been filled with the carbon granules he had painstakingly collected in a cup after the explosions. As a little copper diaphragm moved with the pressure of his voice, they would compress and decompress, carrying more or less current. The current, which must have been very slight, apparently went into a coil—like repeater to be boosted before its trip down the mountain.

His first step was to glue together the vessel that held the granules, and replace them. Then he restored the connections to the repeater, rewound it, and remounted it, using brads, wire, and splints. He followed the same procedure for the earpiece, which was a magnet close to a metal diaphragm, and he rewound the magnetic coils.

This took several days, because the pieces had to be straightened, re-formed, matched, organized, or replaced. When everything was done, the telephone sat on the desk, looking fragile and pathetic. He had neither the time, the materials, nor the strength to pull it apart and try another tack. It had taken almost a week to finish, and he had less than a week before his tour was over. Either it would work or it wouldn't.

He stared at it, afraid to touch it. Then, sure that he had failed, he picked up the handset and turned the crank.

"Hello?" someone said, clearly amazed.

"Can you hear me?" Alessandro asked, more amazed.

"Who is it?"

"Can you hear me?"

"Yes, I can hear you. Who is this?"

"It's me," Alessandro said.

"And who are you?"

"Alessandro. Alessandro Giuliani. I fixed the telephone."

After a long pause, the soldier at the other end said, "We were sure you were dead."

At this instant, Alessandro was electrified, as if lightning had struck the telephone wire or Saint Elmo's fire had filled the room, for part of the dream that he could not recall had come back to him with full force.

Because he had never ridden in an airplane or a balloon, he could not have seen Venice from above, for, unlike so many other Italian cities, Venice has no mountains or hills near enough to afford a view. In his dream, however, he flew over Venice in a wide circle, and was pressed down by the centrifugal force of the turn.

From above, the city was orange, its canals sparkling in the sun-shine, in blue, blue-green, and even in white behind motor launches vaulting forward like hounds. Alessandro could see every detail of the city, every color, and the vertiginous blue above it in which he moved.

The streets were shadowy canyons with floors illuminated now and then by the sunlight that flooded across piazzas, or as they made widening turns in the direction of the sun. The rose-and-orange-colored roofs were hot, bathed in a warm sheen of sunlight. Never had Alessandro seen anything like this scarab-shaped city sitting on water, redolent of beauty and the passage of time. It seemed to be the source of all vitality.

Though a detail of soldiers had to carry wood and build an enormous fire, Alessandro was allowed to take a hot shower that lasted almost an hour. Water from a glacial stream was heated over huge fir logs that crackled like rifle shots. The steam from the shower mixed with the fog and with the resinous smoke from the fire and wafted over trenches and dugouts.

Alessandro shaved and put on a new tunic. Because they had had nothing else to give him, he was now wearing the uniform of the Alpini—nailed boots, white puttees, green wool pants and jacket with scarlet piping and a scarlet collar, and a hat with a feather. These were more splendid, warmer, and far less comfortable than his army clothes. After a dinner of broth and grilled perch, he stepped out into the evening air. The stars were pulsing in lakes in the heavy clouds that sailed below the needles and spires of the cirque.

In a wide depression where several long trenches converged, two dozen infantrymen and a few officers had gathered around a bonfire. They turned slow circles to warm themselves on all sides, and their faces were caught in flickering light that danced with tongues of blackness drawn in from the dark.

Many of them had bristly mustaches and the sunken sparkling eyes of infantrymen of the line. Their coats were crossed by leather straps and bandoliers, their rifles slung on their shoulders with the bayonet pointed up at an angle like the one remaining wing of a wounded angel.

Alessandro moved to the fire and spread his hands. His face glowed in the firelight and his new tunic soon took on the sweet smell of the smoke. The other soldiers glanced at him when he wasn't looking, for the story of what had happened to him had been exaggerated as it passed through the ranks.

The wind whistled as it drove before it wet banks of mist so thick that sometimes the bonfire was hidden, and the ceiling of cloud was just low enough to catch the firelight. When the soldiers were not lost among tattered skeins of fog, they could see far out into the cirque, as if it were a bay of black water.

They had gathered around the fire to get warm before retreating to cold beds. Some slept on wooden shelves in damp bunkers, and those in the front trench slept in the mud, curled up in their blankets, shivering.

At the rear of the cirque a flare rose from the Austrian trenches into a glittering arc, and when its parachute opened, the sparkling became a sun. It pendulated in the wind as it sank, slowly gliding left, away from the rock face against which it cast its light.

The undersides of the clouds reflected its glare as if the sun were about to rise in the dark, and then another flare made a graceful ballistic arc until its parachute opened and rocked it to and fro, and then another. The three sailed gracefully under their reflections in the clouds, burning like altar lamps and casting spectral shadows on the high cliffs until the wind took them around a spire.

Another series of flares was launched, but these were harder to see from the Italian lines, because patches of cloud dulled their light. Two officers stepped into the darkness beyond the fire, raised binoculars, and scanned the rock face. The Austrians had begun to fire upon the mountains themselves. Though rock slides and avalanches followed the concussions, the face of the Schattenhorn, their target, remained smooth and strong.

The Austrians were lighting and attacking a cliff that Alessandro and Rafi had climbed twice. A huge arching fissure went almost all the way up. It had wide ledges, and pockets covered by overhangs, and it was the perfect peak to climb in questionable weather, for it offered shelter from the storms that would tumble over the northeast side. Once, Alessandro and Rafi had watched from within a hollow of the rock as lightning and thunder attacked in blinding flares and deafening concussions and to no avail.

"What is their purpose?" Alessandro asked an officer, who seemed not to mind the lack of etiquette, and answered without lowering his field glasses.

"They're trying to bring rock or ice down on one of our men. We can see him, but because they have to look up at a steeper angle, they can't. They're off by fifty meters. He's going to die anyway."

"Why?" Alessandro asked.

"They hit him in the daylight, killed his companion. He crawled into a hollow on a ledge, and they forgot where he was. Last night he signaled. They saw it, and now they're trying to pick him off. He was up there to establish a position behind them."

"What did he signal?"

"When he pulled back on the ledge to where the Austrians couldn't see his candle, he told us his whole life story. He's wounded, and the other man is dead, still hanging off a belay twenty-five meters below him. He himself was shot in the thigh, and he told us not to come for him, because he would be dead before we got there.

"He knows, anyway, that it's impossible. He's on the fissure where it bends left. The traverse that leads to him is the hardest section of the route. By the time we got to him it would be too late. But it wouldn't matter anyway, because even were he alive he would have to be lowered off route, and even if he made it down he'd be right over the Austrian trenches. He says that he knows exactly where he is, and that no bolts or natural belay points are below him."

"He's lying," Alessandro said. "If he knows where he is, then he's got to know that there's a good line of bolts going all the way down. I know the face of the Schattenhorn. He's right on the line of retreat."

"Why would he lie?"

"Because he thinks that anyone who would come after him would be killed."

"He's right, and the major has forbidden it."

"May I see through the field glasses?"

Visible in the shadows was the familiar crack that rose almost a thousand meters, and by the light of the receding flares Alessandro followed it to the high traverse that he knew, and then to the ledge beyond, where the wounded climber was now in his second night, if he was still alive. "Too bad," Alessandro said. "*I'm* not going to get him."

"The cold will take him if it hasn't already," the officer said. "Last night we asked if he wanted a priest, and he declined. We thought, what kind of last rites could he have in the blinking of candles through the dark, but that wasn't the reason he declined. He started signaling us again after a while, and we could hardly believe it."

"Believe what?" Alessandro asked.

"He wanted a rabbi. Can you imagine, a Jew in the Alpini? He's lost."

As ALESSANDRO made his way in the mist over a vast snowfield, he imagined that the army would not even bother to send him to Stella Maris but would just put him up against a wall and shoot him. It mattered little. Given the circumstances, his state of practice in climbing, and the enemy gunfire, the army would never have the opportunity.

The circle would be closed, except for Luciana, who would remain, and bear children who would be as strong as colts. They would think of the war as a fairy tale or a dream. Alessandro and everyone else would be ghosts—mute images in photographs that people soon did not see even when they were looking at them.

Though he was weighed down by 250 meters of *abseil* rope, and other equipment, he moved fast across the snowfield. He had discarded the Alpini jacket for just a sweater, but his pace kept him warm. In gaps in the mist that whistled past him he saw what he thought to be an Austrian patrol moving slowly across his path, headed down-slope, far enough away to look no bigger than rifle bullets. They would appear for a moment in the clear, and then vanish.

To avoid them he had merely to veer to the right and allow them to continue left, but he was in a hurry and he welcomed the collision. He drew the pistol he had used in the observation post. Without altering his pace, he walked toward them. When they saw him, they stopped. They were confused, because he was alone, heavily burdened, moving fast, and making no attempt to conceal himself, and as he drew closer they saw that he had no rifle.

They thought he might be one of them, or perhaps a mad neutral—an Indonesian or a Peruvian trudging through a war zone on a winter night—and they weren't alarmed, because they were four, with rifles, and he was one, without.

"Hallo! Hallo!" they called. Then, when he didn't answer and he kept coming, they looked at each other, in their fur hoods and embroidered cloaks, and almost as one they decided that they had better shoot him.

The second their bodies made the characteristic motion of unslinging a rifle, a slight displacement of the hip, quickly rectified, Alessandro raised the pistol and began to fire.

They scattered so fast down the hill that by the time he crossed their tracks they were already far away. They threw themselves onto the snow and began shooting in his direction, but he was hidden by clouds, and when the clouds dissipated, his dark silhouette was almost impossible to find against the black sky, for all it did was cut out the stars.

He reached the wall at eleven. Rather than hesitate in the cold he removed the pistol belt, tied a harness around his legs and waist, positioned his equipment, had some chocolate and a sip of water, and put on his gloves, wool-lined deerskin thin and supple enough to give him a feel for the rock. Hoping that the floor and the ledges of the thousand-meter fissure he was about to ascend would be relatively free of snow, he began to climb.

Weeks and months are needed to accustom oneself to climbing. Otherwise, much energy is lost in clinging to the rock, maintaining too sure a hold, trying not to be too stiff, and worrying. After a while a climber warms to the mountains and can accomplish with little effort those things that once took all he had, for height gradually loses its meaning. Standing on the edge of a two-thousand-meter precipice becomes no less comfortable than sitting in a wicker chair on Capri, for it is possible to acquire some of the self-possession that enables mountain goats to stand for hours on a tiny ledge above an abyss.

Alessandro was thrown into this state of mind almost immediately. Though it was cold and the patches of snow over which he had to crawl rustled like glass beads, he was warm. The faster he went, the warmer he got. His face was hot, and the inside of his gloves were wet.

It was dark and he could see very little above him, but he could see just far enough to make his way rapidly on rock that seemed comfortable, solid, and familiar. Only when he had to use his ice axe to cross a patch of hard snow that slid away into the air and was too compacted for step-kicking did he realize that he had not been thinking, and for a moment, as if he were awakening from a dream, he began to re-evaluate his chances and to imagine that he would be able to bring Rafi down. He drove the axe into snow that glowed faintly in starlight, and sank back into the all-encompassing pleasure whence he had come, with no thought or hope, but only movement and daring.

LONG BEFORE the war, Alessandro and Rafi had devised a system of self-belay for solo climbing. Had he been able to take his time he might have used it all the way up, but because he had to reach Rafi as soon as possible and wanted to be as far as he could be above the guns by dawn he would use it only on the most difficult and exposed parts of the route.

The climber would climb unprotected until he felt in need of a belay. He would then drive a pin into the rock and attach to it a specially rigged carabiner with two loops of tape stretching perpendicularly from the center of the gate to the closure, and to the shaft of the carabiner directly opposite. The rope would run between the loop of tape where it fastened to the shaft, and the point where the gate rested against the shaft. Were the climber to fall, the rope would break the lower tape, set the carabiner in the proper position, and allow the gate to close. In the absence of a fall a sharp pull from above would break the same tape, move the rope past the gate, and position the second loop of tape on the eye of the piton so that one more pull would break it and free the carabiner. The second tape would always be properly aligned because the climber's knapsack and ropes, hanging from the carabiner on a short runner, would provide resistance and righting force.

With the breaking of the second tape the gate would close and the climber could retrieve everything but the piton left in the rock. He was limited solely by the number of pitons he could carry, but he could climb only five meters from each belay, because a fall of more than ten meters would either pull out the piton, snap the rope, or break the climber's back.

Alessandro ascended rapidly on wide ledges remarkably free of snow. It was so dark that he could hardly see what was below him, and, robbed of vertiginous detail both by lack of light and by the fog that seemed to keep him always at ground level, he went extremely fast. Before the war, he had called this kind of climbing the unthinking ascent. With the illusion of upward momentum the climber is concerned with nothing but the next hold, and does not need holds as solid as he might were he to rest on them.

Alessandro climbed like this for more than three hundred meters, talking to himself freely, discarding holds as soon as he had them, breathing ferociously, and forgoing rest when he reached a safe gallery or runway along the fissure. Instead, he would race to the end, where he would begin to climb again, still out of breath.

He halted at the beginning of the hardest part of the route, what he and Rafi had called the upside down funnel. Here the fissure stopped sloping to the left and went straight up for fifty meters before it resumed its slanting run. For forty meters of its rise the crack was not too difficult. It was the right size for chimneying and it had thousands of step-like ledges. The first ten meters where the route became vertical, however, were open on the left, and funnel-shaped.

This required perfect placement of hands and feet, great strength, and height. Rafi, who was much taller than Alessandro, had done it in the lead, well belayed, in broad daylight, with neither ice nor snow. Even then, it had been difficult.

After shedding his knapsack and rope, Alessandro took out his hammer and tested a large piton that had already been driven into the rock. Then he set up his self-belay, tied himself in, and turned to the open funnel.

The other side was encrusted with ice. He was sure he would fail. On the other hand, Rafi had led it twice before, and Alessandro had seconded. His arms, stomach, and thighs had ached, but he hadn't fallen.

He began with care and deliberation. The holds were narrow, some were blocked by ice, and he soon reached the point where gravity was pulling him backward, off the side of the funnel. Though he tried to control them, all his muscles were quivering as if he were in a fit. Five more seconds and he would drop off the mountain. If his rope held, he might live, but his ribs would probably be smashed. Even were he uninjured, he might not be able to climb back up, and would hang at the end of the rope until he died.

Two seconds passed. He was about to accept the worst. He looked up. Just beyond his reach above him was the eye of a piton. Someone had done the funnel more mechanically than he and Rafi had done it. The piton was driven straight up. Alessandro had no way of knowing if it would hold—he could hardly even see it— but he had nothing else.

In the last second he took a deep breath to stop the trembling. The price for that was that he could not possibly hold his position. Without a sound, he began to pivot from the rock, with his foothold the fulcrum. He had begun to fall, but he had an instant, a fraction of a second, to convert the fall to a leap, and he did.

He screamed, which relaxed his lungs and gave him more flexibility. His right hand caught the piton. Both his upward momentum and the marginal benefit of grasping the outside of the piton provided just enough time for looping his middle finger through the piton's eye.

For a moment he found himself hanging by a finger. This, of course, could not be prolonged, and he curled his entire body, like an inchworm recoiling upon its invisible thread, to push his legs toward the opposite side of the funnel.

His feet slammed against the rock and dislodged an icicle that fell away without a sound, and he fell back, again hanging by a finger. Once more, he doubled up and thrust out his legs. This time he found a hold below the piton, grasped it with his left hand, and used it to push himself out.

His feet made solid contact with the other side of the funnel. The icicle had formed because it was rooted in the angle of a ledge almost big enough to sit on. Here, Alessandro's nailed boots were solidly jammed.

Not daring to let go of the piton, he nonetheless began to walk up the wall with his left hand. When he found a hold with enough resistance he released his grip on the piton and reached out with his right hand. He used the muscles in his abdomen to raise himself, pushing hard against the wall ahead of him even though it was mostly covered with smooth ice.

Finally, when he was positioned at a forty-five-degree angle, he found a ledge that had a little indentation in it. He grasped it with his right hand, and with his left he found a crack and jammed in three fingers. Then he swung his feet back to the wall he had been holding, and scrambled until they were placed in a knob in the rock, after which he began to go straight up the shaft.

AT DAWN, as the clouds were lifting and illuminated windblown coronas of snow were lashing against the blue, he reached Rafi's partner, who was hanging from the rope and swaying slightly in the wind. Alessandro could see neither his face nor his hands. The only human thing about him was one boot that pointed out into the air. He had covered his head to keep warm, and the hood was dusted with snow.

If Alessandro cut the rope the body would be smashed against the ledges and might disappear in the river that ran adjacent to the base of the cliff. If he didn't, it would hang in the air for months until the rope rotted or was severed as it rubbed against the rock when the corpse moved in the wind. Then, when it hit ledges or the ground, it would break apart. The prospects for recovery, no matter how slight, were better now, and might allow a woman in Padua or Verona to be comforted, or an old man in Milan to end his days in peace. Alessandro unfolded his single-bladed pocket knife and cut the rope in eight strokes. The body fell away with no sound whatsoever. First it had been there, a meter below him, and then it was gone.

By the time he reached Rafi, the light was bright. Rafi was completely still, curled into a fetal position, his back pressed against the rock, his knapsack placed over his side as a makeshift blanket.

Alessandro walked on his knees along the ledge. He bent down next to Rafi, and uncovered his face.

"Rafi," he said, shaking him, but Rafi's eyes stayed shut.

With shaking, frostbitten hands, Alessandro took a tiny flask of grappa from his pack, unscrewed the cap, and brought the neck close to Rafi's lips, thinking that the fire of the grappa might wake him. "Rafi," he pleaded, rubbing his hand against Rafi's cold cheeks.

As the grappa spilled down Rafi's chin, Alessandro shook him in anger. He was sure that he could see Rafi's chest rise and fall. He opened Rafi's jacket and put his hand inside. The heart was still, the skin frozen.

Alessandro was so exhausted that, without tying himself in, he lay down on the ledge and slept. The sun was strong, and he had had to close his eyes to block out the glare. If he had rolled in his sleep, he would have flown.

WHEN HE awoke, the wind had stopped and the sun was beating down on his sunburned face. He turned to Rafi. Alessandro wanted to bring him home, and he thought he could. It was still morning, it was warm, his hands wouldn't freeze, and he had all the rope he would need.

The most difficult part of the thousand-meter *abseil* was prying Rafi's arms away from his sides so a rope could be passed around his chest. The body was stiff. Pulling at the wrists did no good: the leverage stopped at the elbows, which bent, leaving the upper arm unmoved. Alessandro had to use his ice axe to lever out the upper arms. To deal with Rafi's body as if it were a log or a board was terrifying, nauseating, and sad. In novels and in the theater, bodies were treated with delicacy: a gentle touch, a kiss, the featherweight pull of a shroud that then parachuted over the face of the deceased in a nearly imperceptible puff of air. In the ancient literature, corpses were handled more gingerly than newborns, but in one single morning Alessandro had sent one hurtling a thousand meters onto rock and ice, and was prying apart the arms of another with an ice axe. Only God, it seemed, was fit to take care of the dead, to lift them without damaging them, and handle them without disgrace. The soul, Alessandro told himself, fled long ago, and I am merely doing what I have to do.

He apologized as he passed the rope around Rafi and tied it at the back of his shoulder blades, and he apologized for what he was going to have to do. The line of bolts and ledges that they had used for their retreat was twenty meters ahead on the traverse. It was a perfect way down, with bolts set at intervals so that the end of each rappel was a ledge big enough to stand on.

Rafi's body would have to be pulled from where it was and swung like a sandbag to reach the line of descent. This would batter his corpse, and it seemed somehow to be immeasurably cruel. Alessandro put on his pack and climbed toward the line of retreat.

For the first time, the rock was not unpleasantly cold. The fissure was sheltered, and only occasionally did breezes run along its length and jump out again into the abyss. They lifted Alessandro's sweaty hair and cooled his head. He stopped twice, once to put on his hat, and once to take it off, and when he took it off he dropped it. It disappeared from sight only after it had fallen for a full minute.

When he reached the line of retreat, the sun and the angle of the rock allowed the enemy to see him moving far above them, and they wasted no time. Soon, hollow concussions echoed through the cirque, sending down torrents of loosened ice and snow. The Austrians were still using phosphorus shells that had been piled next to the guns the night before, and, when these burst, star-shaped tendrils of white smoke were lifted on the upwelling winds. The Italian side replied with a counter-barrage that failed to deter the Austrians from further shots, and made the mountains ring ever the more.

Under fire, Alessandro grew resolute, and the chest-vibrating concussions awakened him as nothing else could. The bolt at the head of the retreat line was solid. Two hundred meters below, almost out of sight, was a wide ledge. The way to *abseil* two hundred meters was to use a light cord that the Germans, and only the Germans, called a *Reepschnur*. Instead of doubling the *abseil* rope, one used this cord to pull it past the rappel ring on the bolt. The end of the rope was tied in a monkey's fist so it would not pass through the rappel ring, the cord tied around the rope between the monkey's fist and the ring. Pulling the lighter line would pull two hundred meters of the heavier rope through, if the lighter line didn't break with the weight and friction of the first unbalanced tugs. If it did, the only thing to do was to go back up, using prussik slings. Such a task on a two-hundred-meter line would take hours. Alessandro hoped that the cord would hold, but it was even lighter than he normally would have used, as it was all that had been available.

He passed the rope through a rappel ring that he set on the bolt with a runner, and when it was taut he pulled hard to bring Rafi off the ledge. Rafi's traverse seemed to take all the time in the world. The body bounced against the rock face, twirled, and gathered speed. Alessandro leaned back, hanging out over space, to take the upward pull. The weight that passed underneath him, swinging to and fro, was the man Luciana had been going to marry.

The Austrians could not have known what this was, but they fired upon it, and although they didn't reach it, their shells exploded halfway up the wall as if to bar the way.

Alessandro lowered Rafi to the first ledge. He had to do it slowly, and he had to stop every few minutes lest the rappel ring heat so much from the friction that it burn through the rope.

When Rafi reached the ledge Alessandro was unable to maneuver him onto it. The body dangled half on and half off and would move from place to place as the wind pushed the rope and spun him on his delicate pivot. That meant that the rope would have to take the weight both of Rafi and Alessandro, and that it would be stiff and inflexible as it passed through the rappel gate that Alessandro had fashioned of four of his carabiners.

He attached the light cord and tossed it down. It unfurled like a stream of water that dashes off a cliff, in waves that overtook waves ahead of them and then were overtaken. After he set the rappel gate he stepped backward over the drop.

The tension that Rafi put on the rope, which was really three ropes tied together, and the weight of the rope itself, had an effect that Alessandro had not anticipated. Not only did it stiffen, but it was held against the rock, so that he was able to use his feet not just to push off, but to push back and put tension on the rappel gate. He walked slowly down the rock face, toward the shell-bursts beneath him.

When he arrived at the ledge he took Rafi in, untied him, disengaged the rappel gate from the rope, and pulled on the retrieval line. Though he had to pull at first with all his strength, and hang on the light cord, it worked.

He then had to endure two hundred meters of rope cascading down upon him and striking in rapid unavoidable blows. The sensation was like that of being beaten by a crowd of people. The second half of the rope fell beyond the ledge and down the cliff. When the end passed him, Alessandro's relief turned to panic. The rope was heavy, it was falling fast, and he had neglected to belay himself. If it pulled too strongly it would take him with it. If he let go, he would have no rope. He wound the end around his forearm, and waited for the pull.

When it came, it jerked him from where he was sitting, with his back against the wall, into a full standing position. He almost tumbled headlong over the edge, but he pulled up and straightened himself explosively, neutralizing the downward force.

Now he set up quickly. He was moving so fast and he had so little time that he actually kicked Rafi's body over the ledge. He was sweating, the artillery concussions were vastly louder, and the shells broke a hundred meters below him on both sides of the rope. The smell of gunpowder, lignite, and phosphorus rose in moist clouds. Ten thousand bagpipes could not have done more to lift his spirits than the sounds of the instruments that sought his death. He trembled as he set the rappel gate and backed off the edge, and he trembled as he descended toward the bursting shells, but he was not trembling from fear. In firing their cannons at him the enemy had done him a great service, and he floated down between the shell-bursts like a man on fire.

The louder the concussions the greater his satisfaction and the easier it was to drop toward them. His natural instinct, it seemed, was to fight. The cannoneers stopped for a moment as they adjusted their aim, and he went as fast as he could, and as unevenly, to make their problems with elevation triply complex.

The first newly aimed shell came in on the left. When it burst, the concussion deafened him and the rush of air pushed him away from the explosion. He scraped against the cliff and twirled on the rope. As if he were in a close fight, he screamed as he twisted himself to face the wall. They had the elevation just right. All they needed was a tiny adjustment in bearing.

He loosened the rappel gate and dropped twenty meters at a time. His feet and knees pounded against the wall. As his hands slid down the rope, the deerskin gloves were smoking. The rope burned through them and took the skin off his palms. Droplets of blood, like warm water, fell from where he had been an instant before. Shell fragments and rock rained down. To keep up the speed, he pushed out from the wall whenever he slowed, and the carabiners in the rappel gate grew so hot that they made the rope smoke as it ran through them. Despite the shells bursting above him, and the fire in his hands, he reached the second ledge, crashing down in a heap next to Rafi's body, and despite the pain and shock of the fall, the first thing he did was remove the rappel gate from the rope.

For a quarter of an hour he lay on the ledge as the Austrians threw shells against the wall above to bombard him with rock fragments and falling shrapnel. It was already past noon, and actually hot, even though the shadowed crevices all around his resting place were filled with snow and ice.

As soon as he set up his rope and tossed over the cord, they began to fire. As he was lowering Rafi he could see the flashes of the cannon at the bore. With his hands opened up, for every flash of the cannon he had stars of light from pain. When Rafi was down, Alessandro followed, falling more than rappelling. The shells tracked his descent but the gunners could not spin their wheels fast enough to catch him.

As he sailed onto the third ledge he felt as if all his organs had burst inside him and as if his ankles, legs, and arms had been broken, too. Blood issued from his mouth. But he was determined to finish. Every few seconds, he spat to clear his throat. He retrieved the rope and took its blows. Then he set up again, noticing with hardly a thought that one of the shells had blown Rafi's feet off, and that a sticky pool of blood and lymph had oozed from the legs.

"Over you go," he said as he pushed Rafi over, as if he and Rafi would later be able to discuss what had happened, and, perhaps, argue about it. Lowering him, he waited for the artillery, but the

Austrians had seen enough detail through their telescopes to hold their fire as Alessandro struggled to bring himself and his charge to the base.

His hands caused him so much pain that he could think of nothing better than to have them removed when he got down. His clothes were caked in sweat, blood, and dirt, his face blackened, and his hair matted. He moved as if in a daze, and fell through the last twenty meters of rope only semi-conscious.

He finally came to rest against Rafi, who was with him at the end, four or five meters above the river, dangling beneath an overhang. There they slowly turned, cooled by breezes that glanced off the ice-cold water below.

A hundred Austrians in coats, caps, sheepskins, and tunics stared silently at the half-dead, half-living mass dangling a short distance above them. Alessandro's head hung back limply at first, as if he, too, were dead, but then he lifted it, and looked at them. They were standing on the bank of the river, their rifles resting on the ground or slung across their backs.

Alessandro lost control of his bladder, and as he twisted on the rope blood still issued from his mouth. "Can you bury him?" he asked, but they couldn't hear over the white water. They put their hands to their ears, and some leaned forward.

"Can you bury him?" Alessandro asked again. They nodded in affirmation.

He reached into his pocket. The knife was still there. He knew the water would be freezing cold, and just before he cut the rope, he closed his eyes.

THE WINTER PALACE

IN THE first week of June, 1918, Alessandro was awakened every morning at dawn by fierce and unintelligible arguments among Bulgarian soldiers unfit for anything but guarding prisoners of war. These former laborers, peasants, and bandits wore sheepskin vests, baggy pantaloons, and fezzes or gray mouton caps, all entirely inappropriate to the wild heat that blew across the Hungarian plain.

On June the second they had halted on the shore of an opalescent blue lake. The land was so flat that the opposite shore failed to show itself unless you climbed into a tree. Standing in the crux, surrounded by apple or cherry blossoms, you could see the plain beyond the water, and silent sheep-like rolls of cloud smoothly skating over oceans of still-green wheat.

The Bulgarians seemed to have rooster in the blood, and to Alessandro, who knew no Slavic languages, every strange syllable was bliss. Dangerous, promising, and horrible, the tongue of his captors was a thrill that he likened to watching a tiger devour the rope with which one is bound hand and foot. It sounded to him like this: *Blit scaratch mi shpolgah. Trastritch minoya dravitz nazhkoldy aprazhga. Zharga mazhlovny booreetz.*

On arising they punched, kicked, and slapped each other. Some drew knives but, after much screaming, abandoned them in favor of the long whips they used on mules. As they dueled ceremoniously with these whips, standing beyond the range of harm, they spat, they clenched their teeth, and the veins and arteries in their necks and faces bulged like vines on a house in the Cotswolds.

They were distraught because they, even they, who could not read newspapers and were eight hundred miles from the nearest front, knew that their cause was lost, Austria-Hungary doomed, and the world in collapse. And then, they themselves, literally, were lost. They knew they were in Hungary, but were unable to narrow their position down further. Four factions had developed among them, with each certain that their destination lay in a different direction. The more educated knew what south and east were, and asked of the illiterates who wanted to go north or west how Bulgaria could be north or west of Hungary. The north and west factions couldn't understand the concept and simply pointed to the horizon beyond which, they believed more and more each day, Bulgaria lay. Fixed by the perfect balance of four outwardly exploding desires, they remained immobile by the shore of the exquisitely beautiful lake, starving to death in gorgeous summer weather.

Alessandro and several hundred other prisoners—Italian, Russian, Greek, French, English, and Sudanese, some who were tall enough to see over the lake—had been delivered to the custody of the Bulgarians for the purpose of making earthworks on the Bulgarian front opposite the Greeks, French, and English.

At the end of March, the seventy sheepskin-clad Bulgarians and five hundred prisoners had set out from Klagenfurt in a cold rain, on foot, bound for Sofia. The supply train was inadequate and by May the only thing left for the 570 men was to live off the land. They made desperate zigzags into Hungary, driven by neither the compass nor the sun but by the need to reach a field where they had seen a sheep, or a barn where they thought they might find chickens.

The lake had some fish, and the farms along its length were rich. Still, they had very little to eat, because, after several thousand years of rapacious tax collectors and alien armies, the local peasants were expert at hiding food. Starving may be more pleasant in summer than in winter, especially in tremendous heat, when it is possible to pretend that to be thin is to be cold, but it was difficult nonetheless.

Prisoners and guards alike swam in the lake, opening their eyes beneath the surface in the hope of seeing a fish. The Sudanese made round nets and tossed them mightily over the water, where they landed with a hiss, but European fish were too cagey for this technique, although now and then a fish was caught purely by accident, and thrown almost whole into a consummately dilute fish-and-potato stew.

In March and early April, with the column in striking distance of the Italian lines and the Adriatic, escape was popular. The Bulgarians did not try hard to prevent it, but when a prisoner, as often was the case, was returned after a few days' starvation in the cold rain, they grew implacably angry and shot him in the head.

Alessandro had not even thought to try. He was still recovering from his wounds, he had difficulty walking, and was covered with fresh scars that he did not wish to torment by running through the brush or diving onto rocky ground. He wondered what he looked like, for he hadn't seen a mirror for many months. When he asked others to describe him, they would say, "You have a scar that runs from your cheek to your ear." It stopped there. They could not describe his face, especially since they didn't know how he had changed. One of the Sudanese had told him, in English, that he looked like a small animal that had barely escaped a lion after being mauled in its claws, and the scars, the Sudanese said, were pink like the sunset after a dust storm.

Not far from where they camped was a church, where the Bulgarians took groups of prisoners to lie on the cool stone floor. For an hour or so they would rest on their backs, staring at a vault high above them that was tinted red and lost in the darkness, or turning their heads to see the dazzling portraits in stained glass. In these lovely hours not even the Bulgarians spoke, not even the Sudanese, who were Muslims. Instead, they managed, by lying on their backs and moving their eyes, to float about as if they were underwater side by side with luminous saints and infants swaddled in brilliant white.

The saints and children, though fixed in glass, moved as freely as the light that shone through them. That they had in their still-ness the most lively animation made Alessandro take heart. Here he heard Guariglia say, "God protect my children." The memory of his father's hand, grasping his for the last time, made him tighten his fist in imitation. And Ariane floated in a circle of silver as fluid as the nets tossed by the Sudanese.

THE BULGARIANS ate rose petals with goat cheese, onion, olive oil, pepper, and salt. Though it was too early for berries, it was just the right time for roses, which made impenetrable barriers between sun-drenched fields, surrounded every house and barn, and grew without inhibition from the heart of broken stone walls.

The olive oil and cheese were strictly for the Bulgarians, and the captives ate their flowers unseasoned. Such a delicate flower with so subtle a scent has nonetheless a taste stronger than that of escarole, and far less pleasant, and it can make you very sick. Be-cause the prisoners had to eat something, the Bulgarians allowed them to forage away from camp, but if they returned after dark they were shot. Two who were unfortunate enough to have thought that dusk was daylight ended their lives with bitter smiles as the other prisoners watched, and from that time forward few dared return when the sun was not still high in the sky.

Alessandro had wandered to the western side of the lake in search of something to eat. Though he was weak from starvation, he enjoyed walking alone, surrounded by fields, orchards, and blue water. Sometimes he would throw himself down on the grass and sleep for an hour or two to cure the giddiness of hunger.

At noon he was four hours from camp and had not found anything to eat. He lay down, deciding to awaken at two or three so as to make his way back by six or seven, which was perfectly safe because the sun was in the sky until nine, but he slept and dreamed so deeply that he awakened at six. He was so disoriented that he didn't realize what had happened. As sunburnt as if he had been in a desert, he went to the lake. The water lapped against the shore in quick waves no higher than the breadth of a finger. He put his hands on two flat rocks just under the surface, and submerged his head. After drinking his fill, he sat on the shore trying to come fully awake, and realized what he had done.

Even if he ran, and he hadn't the strength to run, he would have no guarantee of getting back to camp before dusk. He would make his way through a thousand kilometers of enemy territory and reach the Serbs, or he would proceed more directly to the Adriatic, either of which would be a remarkable accomplishment. He began to walk toward Italy.

After twenty minutes of walking with the sun in his eyes he came to a wave in the prairie, and at the crest a group of six Bulgarian horsemen appeared.

The leader, a familiar guard, told Alessandro that he was going in the wrong direction.

"Oh," Alessandro said.

"Even if you went in the right direction, you'd get to camp too late," the leader said, pulling a service pistol from his holster and aiming at Alessandro's head.

"If you give me a ride, I'll get to camp on time."

"If I don't, you won't, and I'll have to shoot you."

"That's true, but if you do you won't have to shoot me."

"I'm going to have to shoot you, because I wasn't going to give you a ride."

"You weren't going to shoot me, either, so you'll have to give me a ride."

As they galloped down the road they turned away from the lake, and Alessandro asked why they weren't proceeding directly to camp.

"There may be food in this direction," the horseman shouted over the wind.

"What if we don't get back in time?"

"You know exactly."

"Are you going to take that into consideration?"

"No."

The carbine on the back of the horseman nearly hit Alessandro's face each time the horse took a step. If Alessandro yanked it and slid off the back of the horse, he would take one Bulgarian down and have the rifle for the other five. If he could do it fast enough at an advantageous moment, near cover, he might succeed. Then again, they might get back to camp on time, and cover was scarce.

As he struggled with this question the sun did not slow in its descent, but he never had to decide one way or another, for they veered toward a peasant farm in a grove of small trees off the road.

A young farmer came from his house, took a few steps forward, and greeted them as if he knew that they had come to steal his food.

"Where's your food?" one of the Bulgarians asked straight out.

"Have none."

"You're lying. You're not thin enough not to be lying."

"I'm heavy boned."

"Shoot the bastard," the leader said.

The farmer was shocked. These were friendly troops. He hadn't understood that the leader wasn't serious, but neither had one of the horsemen, who, as the others were laughing, lifted his rifle and shot the farmer through the head.

A woman rushed from inside and bent over her husband. Her screams were not only pathetic but, unfortunately for her, very ugly and frightening. The man who had killed her husband lifted his rifle again. Alessandro felt as if time had stopped, and his distress was immeasurable as the woman was quickly knocked over with two shots.

A child, a little girl of about three, walked quickly through the doorway and started toward her parents.

Alessandro had no time to see what would happen. Perhaps they would shoot the child, and perhaps not, but if Alessandro had not moved before he knew the outcome, he would have been too late. He didn't want to do it, because he was sure that if he did they would kill him, but even as he tried to hold himself in check his hand seized the carbine and he pulled the Bulgarian from the horse, choking him with the sling. The horse reared, the Bulgarian had the wind knocked out of him, and in the confusion Alessandro had time to get a round in the chamber and let off a shot that slammed into the foreleg of a horse.

Trying to control their mounts, the Bulgarians were unable to reach their weapons, and as the horses bucked, went rampant, sidled, and bumped, a shooting gallery appeared before Alessandro.

Slewing the carbine, he fired and knocked one of the Bulgarians forever off his horse. He took a half step forward and fired again, but the chance movement of a horse deprived the bullet of its target.

Two Bulgarians had dismounted and were running toward Alessandro, one with a sword and the other with a bayonet. He dropped one, but as he did he was knocked down by the one he had pulled from the saddle. The swordsman kicked the carbine from his hands, pivoted around, and went for the child.

Alessandro crawled in her direction as he was beaten by rifle butts and the hooves of disturbed horses. Through the chestnut-colored legs and risen dust, he saw the swordsman approach the little girl and raise the sword above his head. The child was impassive. She had dark little eyes, like raisins, and a bowl-shaped hair-cut. Only her eyes moved as the sword was raised, and then it came down, faster than the eye could see.

Alessandro closed his eyes, thinking that they would kill him immediately. He was wrong.

They left him on the ground while they calmed the horses, about whom they were genuinely upset, and attended to their dead and wounded. The wounded man rested against a small tree, apparently not too badly hurt, and the dead man looked like a rolled-up rug.

Two Bulgarians went inside the house and came out with several wooden cages. "What's in the cages?" the wounded man called out, thinking that if the cages held rabbits or chickens the wound would have been worthwhile. The cages held four big rats.

The Bulgarians looted everything they could. They pulled quilts and blankets from a huge pine chest and scattered them in the dust. They took the farmer's clothes and his wife's jewelry. A photograph of the child was tossed to the ground, and landed face down.

As the horses calmed and the Bulgarians stared at the rats, trying to decide whether or not to eat them, Alessandro was told to dig two graves. One was shallow, the other deep.

Many thoughts raced through Alessandro's mind, and when the Bulgarians lowered the pine chest into the earth, he assumed it was going to be a coffin for their friend, but then they buried their friend in the other grave.

Since the Bulgarians evinced no interest in the family they had murdered, and didn't even look their way, Alessandro concluded that they had prepared it for him, but it didn't make sense that the Bulgarian would be buried in raw earth and Alessandro given a coffin.

Then he saw one of his captors coming from the house, with a hammer and a handful of homemade nails. Alessandro looked at the Bulgarians, who were laughing, and he looked at the rats. Then he bolted.

It was almost dark. He tore through some brambles, running as fast as he could. Though he was clearing a path for the Bulgarians, they were going slower, as their reward for getting through the brambles was so much less than his.

Alessandro thought he might escape if the darkness would protect him, and he ran until long after the Bulgarians' few rifle shots had stopped. After an hour he threw himself deep into the brush and stayed absolutely still. He listened all through the night, and he heard only the sound of nightingales and a stream.

AT DUSK the next day, after wandering through the heat-filled plain without having had a single bite to eat, he came to a small hill upon which a profusion of flowers was blooming untouched, uneaten, and in colors as rich as the panels of saints and swaddled infants that he had left to the Bulgarians and Sudanese. As he was eating, he thought he saw a soldier, but the man standing stock still behind a clump of foxglove was dressed in red pants the color of poppies, a royal-blue jacket with white trim, and a golden helmet. He was festooned so with buttons, braids, and colorful bars, and his boots and mustache were so black and so heavily waxed that Alessandro assumed he was either a hallucination or a toy.

"Remarkable thing about foxglove," the hallucination said, in German. "They stay colorful for months after they're cut. It's because they're poison that they last. I had some on my estate and we cut them to make way for a tennis court. Three months later I knocked a ball over the fence, and when I went to get it I saw the foxglove stacked in a huge pile, with gnats buzzing above it in a beam of light, and its colors had not faded."

Alessandro addressed this vision. "Where is your estate?" he asked in faltering German.

"Just outside Vienna."

"I didn't realize," Alessandro said, continuing to graze upon flower petals, "that German was the language of my subconscious."

"German is the language of my subconscious," the hallucination replied.

"Don't you speak Italian?" Alessandro asked, looking up at him.

"Yes, certainly. Would you prefer to speak Italian?"

"It would be easier."

"Much delighted," the hallucination replied in Italian with a heavy German accent.

"Can't you speak without an accent?"

"I'm afraid not, but, then again, your German is not exactly sublime."

"Yes, but you're from my mind, and you should be equipped with perfect Italian."

"Do you imagine that you are imagining me?" the hallucination asked.

"I know for a fact that I'm imagining you."

"That's very interesting. I've never met anyone who believed that he was imagining me as we spoke. From your costume as well, it's clear that you're a lunatic. Am I correct? Where is your asylum? Have you escaped, or do they let you out to eat flowers?"

"Disappear, toy," Alessandro said, dismissively waving his left hand.

"I refuse."

"Vanish!" Alessandro commanded, snapping his fingers. The hallucination smiled and stood fast. Alessandro suddenly straightened and stepped back, admiring a rose bush as tall as he was, with a score of vigorous yellow blooms. "I think everyone in the world misunderstands roses," he said.

"Not you, of course. You eat them."

"Be quiet. It has nothing to do with that. They talk about the thorns and the blooms. Forget about the thorns: only idiots get stuck, anyway. The remarkable thing about roses—luxuriant feminine blooms that attract you with their scent, their softness, and their blush, almost as if they actually were a woman—is not that they come from a bush that has thorns, but that they come from a bush that is so awkward: imbalanced, gangly, and skinny, like a young girl who's terribly clumsy in her adolescence and then becomes the most beautiful woman in the world. It has nothing to do with thorns. On that account, the canons of metaphor, poetic and visual, should be revised."

"What did you do before you became a lunatic?"

Alessandro explained, and went back to eating flowers.

"Then all you are is an escaped Italian prisoner of war who, because he has been starving, is eating roses, and thinks that I am a dream."

"That's right," Alessandro said sarcastically. "That's *all I am.*"

"And if you wander about you'll be returned to the Bulgarians, who will shoot you."

"For sure."

"I'm going to ask you a question," the hallucination said, "and your answer will determine whether you live or die. So many times in life, it gets that simple."

Alessandro looked up at the hallucination, which had come closer, and was uncannily real, even in that its teeth were so imperfectly human.

"You must answer with complete truthfulness, for the truth will be found out quickly whether you do or you don't."

"The truth is the only thing I have left," Alessandro said.

"Can you ride?"

"As well as a cavalryman."

"Then you live. We leave at dawn."

TWO BURLY troopers dressed almost like the hallucination found Alessandro, face in the dirt, his right hand clutching a rose bush. They pulled him up and helped him mount the hill. "You're a lucky wop," one of them said. "You've been saved by Strassnitzky, and you have a great road ahead of you."

From the top of a small rise Alessandro looked down at a grassy cup of ground next to the river that issued from the blue lake. The scene that lay before him in the most extraordinary color was more like something from *Orlando Furioso* than from the war he knew, and like one of the images men have before they go to war and are disillusioned.

In a perfectly straight line, hundreds of chestnut-and-black horses, each an Arabian and all of uniform size, grazed between the river and the camp. A hundred white tents, their canvas stretched tight enough to bounce coins, formed a U, with the open part facing the river. Saddles, rifles, and swords were arranged in constructions that looked like miniature towers, and from the center of each projected a lance with a pennant. Sentries marched stiffly at the perimeter and among the saddlery and weapons, which shone in the light of the setting sun. Water boilers and stoves of chrome and brass were puffing and glinting, their interiors filled with fire.

Between the wagons and the horses were long camp tables set with china, stemware, and cutlery. Sides of venison turned on spits rotating over dunes of red coals, and by the side of an ice-making machine a huge zinc tub was filled with crushed ice and jeroboams of champagne.

Officers and cavalrymen were dressed in the red-and-blue uniforms that Alessandro had disbelieved. Some were not dressed at all, still in the river or trudging toward the beach after their evening swim. Others were reading, writing, playing chess.

Alessandro passed his hand in front of his eyes and closed them. When he reopened them, nothing had changed.

"The First Hussars of the Belvedere," the trooper said, "the emperor's own."

Soon Alessandro found himself in a tub of painfully hot water. After he scrubbed with soap, a barber bent over the wooden rim and shaved him without a nick. The barber cut his hair, Alessandro washed it three times, and he emerged from the tub as if he had been groomed to appear before God.

They fitted him quickly in gray twill pants with blue side stripes, brown riding boots that came up almost to the knee, a navy-blue shirt of Egyptian cotton, a brown leather belt with a brass buckle, and brass spurs. They gave him a pewter comb and directed him to comb his hair and roll up his sleeves.

Alessandro's intelligence, bearing, and self-possession made him stand out not only among the prisoners but among the troopers and their officers as well. "What am I?" he asked.

The barber asked an officer, who replied that he would have to ask Strassnitzky. At dinner, prisoners and auxiliaries sat at the same tables as troopers and officers. Alessandro himself sat at Strassnitzky's table, though Strassnitzky was far away.

The oysters were from a jar rather than the shell, but they were fresh, and Alessandro was too stunned to ask how a cavalry unit in the depths of Hungary had come by iced shellfish in summer. After the oysters came Sevruga caviar with lemon quarters, chopped egg, and diced onion. A subaltern next to Alessandro apologized because they were going to skip the regular fish course. "Don't mention it," Alessandro said.

"Why should I not mention it?"

Alessandro looked at the young officer and said, "It's an expression. It means, *Everything's splendid nonetheless.*"

The subaltern made amends by refilling Alessandro's champagne glass. The main course was venison that had been roasting over the ruby-colored pits of charcoal. With it came an excellent decanted claret, a salad of endive and tomato, and new potatoes roasted in olive oil and paprika. For dessert, Sacher torte and Darjeeling tea.

"Do you eat like this all the time?" Alessandro asked his neighbor.

The subaltern, a Czech, blushed in embarrassment. "Sometimes we eat more simply—consommé, a salad, smoked fish with quail eggs and lemon, and then tea, fruit, and schnapps."

"What about a meal in the field?"

"This is a meal in the field."

"What about battle rations, then?"

The subaltern, who seemed a little bit too fleshy, even if the flesh were generously colored by his well circulating blood, was beginning to dislike the interrogation. His reply was defensive. "In battle we eat just like everyone else: pâté sandwiches, truffle tarts, Turkish apricots, and brandy from a flask."

"When you return to barracks? What then?"

"I'm not answering."

"Oh please."

"In the barracks," the subaltern said, "the chef and the sous-chefs go crazy. They're very happy when they get back to their pastry squeezers, their marble blocks, and their walk-in ice chests. When we're in the barracks, after the privations of the field, we all overdo it—especially when the emperor honors our mess with his presence. You may even meet him."

"What a strange thing."

The troopers didn't linger over dessert, but Alessandro, not knowing what to do, remained at table. A high-ranking officer whose insignia were as mystifying as his accent approached Alessandro. "The field marshal would like to see you."

"Field marshal?" Alessandro answered.

"Count Blasius Strassnitzky. Have you heard of him?"

Alessandro shook his head from side to side.

"Don't worry. The less impressed you are with him, the more he'll like you. He's that way."

Thinking very fast of motives for summoning a new prisoner to the tent of a field marshal, Alessandro decided to bring up the issue before he might be obligated to land himself in front of a firing squad. "This Strassnitzky, he's not, uh . . ."

"Who do you think we are? Greeks?"

STRASSNITZKY WAS sitting on a camp chair in his tent, his tunic off and shirtsleeves rolled up. He was dressed almost exactly like Alessandro but for the fact that his pants were red and his boots black. He sat amid low tables covered with maps, dispatch pads, books, newspapers, magazines, and hardwood cases for telescopes, pens, and the like.

"Do you play chess?" he asked, showing Alessandro to a chair facing him.

"Not well," Alessandro told him. "Should I not salute you?"

"You're not in our army, are you."

"We used to have to salute our Bulgarian guards—they were privates—and you're a field marshal."

"As long as my men are willing to die for me," Strassnitzky said, "as long as they follow my orders with alacrity and do their jobs with the skill I expect of them, I don't stand on ceremony—except where people would misunderstand.

"I'm a field marshal because these are the Emperor's Own Hussars. I would ordinarily be a colonel, but, as no one is allowed to issue a command to the commander of the emperor's own unit but the emperor himself, the colonel becomes a field marshal."

"With a field marshal's privileges?"

"You've had dinner?"

Alessandro smiled.

"The emperor protects his prerogatives by protecting his own."

"Won't his own become terribly overweight?"

"Wait until tomorrow. If you ride hard for twelve hours each day you can eat anything you want and still be as thin as a greyhound."

"How do the wagons keep up?"

"The wagons go straight. We sweep the countryside in zigzags. Whereas the wagons may travel fifteen or twenty kilometers a day, we go no less than seventy-five, and when you throw in all the fighting, you've expended much energy that needs to be replenished."

"When did you last fight?" Alessandro asked.

"Today."

Alessandro's face twisted in disbelief. War had not yet come to the *puszta,* the plains of eastern Hungary. "The Greeks are stuck in Salonika, the Italians in the Veneto, the Russians collapsed, the Serbs thrown into the sea. Whom did you fight?"

Strassnitzky sighed. "Two days ago we engaged a column of enemy partisans: Serbs, Rumanians, Greeks, Bosnians, who the hell knows what, all mounted as *csikosok.* In a battle lasting two hours and stretching over twenty kilometers of plain, we completely wiped them out, with the loss of many of our own men. Today we fought again, and of our remaining six hundred and eighty-four men, we lost forty-three. Now we are six hundred and forty-one."

"Their demeanor and condition are extraordinary after such a battle," Alessandro said.

"Medals all around," Strassnitzky declared. "My men are the very best."

"Sir?" Alessandro suddenly asked. "Where is your other group?"

"What other group?"

"The other three hundred and forty-one. I counted your horses—thirty groups of ten."

"Numbers in war—what is your name?"

"Giuliani, Alessandro."

"Numbers in war, Giuliani, are not like numbers in peace."

"They're not?"

"Surely you know that. How many years of service have you?"

"Three."

Strassnitzky shrugged. "Well, then you know. You must know. War acts upon arithmetic much like a gravitational lens upon light. This is a highly arcane concept that I do not imagine Italians have fully absorbed."

"I am familiar with it," Alessandro declared.

"Come now," Strassnitzky shot back contemptuously. "How can that be?"

"It can be," Alessandro told him, "because I read the paper on the theory of general relativity when I was in the trenches on the Isonzo, in nineteen fifteen. My father sent it to me. It was the last thing that got through. The behavior of light is to aesthetics what physics is to engineering. And, as for the behavior of light, I'm familiar with Eddington's work, because British journals get through to us rather easily. More easily than they get to you, I imagine. They just come in the mail, whereas your spies in London have to stuff them into false-bottomed suitcases or copy them in tiny writing so they can be strapped onto the feet of carrier pigeons."

"You're a physicist?" Strassnitzky asked, like a man who thinks he may have just hit the bull's-eye. "I'm a physicist. Well, I'm not *really* a physicist, but I was trained in physics. I started with ballistics...."

"My work includes as much of physics and cosmology as I can take in," Alessandro said, "but that hardly makes me a physicist."

"Your field is aesthetics?"

"It was."

"Croce?"

"Croce, yes, among others."

"I hadn't imagined that our professions were linked enough for you to be cognizant of what I must know."

"In a sense, they are one and the same. You can't understand science without art, or art without science. Only the idiots in the two disciplines think that they are anything but two different expressions of the same thing." Alessandro leaned forward. "But what about numbers in war? I'm not sure I follow you."

"Let me explain. It's marvelous. Numbers, as you well know, are delicate illusions. You don't have to have Archimedes talking about rabbits and turtles to know that when you start in with negative numbers, as we do with young schoolchildren, you are singing like a Druid. Are you not? Yes, you are.

"So. In war, the terror, the compression of eschatological questions, the abridgement of the laws of man, the lack of sense in it, the confusion, the entropy...All combine to demolish completely the meaning and integrity of numbers. Look at war expenditures. Look at the unbelievable casualty figures on the Western Front, or, for that matter, on the Isonzo. Look at the complete confusion of time. Time, something expressed analogously with numbers, goes entirely awry in battle, as you must know. So it is with numerical abstractions."

"But where," Alessandro asked, "are the other three hundred and forty-one men?"

"Trust me. Some matters are not to be discussed too deeply. This is war, you are an enemy prisoner, and I am a field marshal. You don't expect me to discuss items of military secrecy, do you?"

"I suppose not."

"You may come to understand. Tell me, you are finely educated, but do you have an elegant hand?"

"No."

"You don't? What a pity."

"For me to write a single word is like grasping a set of live electrical poles. My hand and arm want to do anything but what I want them to do, and it hurts. Yet I must write papers and articles almost continually, and I have neither the temperament nor the opportunity to dictate. When I served in my father's law office, God help me, I worked as a scribe. He never knew how difficult it was for me. He thought I was merely careless. I forgive him."

"Why didn't you choose another profession, in which you would not have to suffer?"

"Is it unusual for someone to be mated to what incapacitates him?"

"What about one of those things, what are they called, that print letters as you strike them?"

"Typewriters."

"No, it's another name, a French name, like *rotopisseur.*"

"That's one of those kiosks where you pee."

"Ah, I know, it's called an *engrosseur papyréanne.*"

Alessandro began to worry. Naturally, any kind of enthusiasm, of any sort, about the typewriter was deeply disturbing to him, and he hoped that Strassnitzky would change the subject.

"Can you use one?"

"Surprisingly, in view of my muscle-control difficulties, quite well. My problem comes from grasping. When my fingers can fly freely, they can do just about anything. But the learned journals still look askance at typescripts, so I'm doomed. Of course, that's a petty doom."

"This is why I ask. I need an educated man to be my private secretary until we get to Vienna. There, my personal secretary will rejoin me after he recuperates from a wound he received in Russian roulette."

"How did the bullet miss his brain?"

"That was easy."

"Do you have a typewriter?"

"We have a little machine that the ministry sent out to the staffs of all the field marshals."

"Forgive me, but why not one of your officers? Their German would be more precise, you can trust them more than you can a prisoner, and they would be familiar with addresses and salutations."

"No," Strassnitzky said. "They prefer not to compose the story of their own exploits. They find it embarrassing. My secretary, you see, is a civilian. That's why I thought a prisoner might be a good substitute."

"I'd like to do it," Alessandro said.

"Good. I'll pay you the going rate. Dankwart is very happy with what I provide: he keeps an apartment in town and a chalet near Innsbruck, where he ski-jumps."

"But I'm a prisoner of war."

"The war will soon be over, the empire is finished, and everything has changed. Let us resume our lives with equity and decency."

"That's kind of you," Alessandro said. "And, after Vienna, what will happen to me?"

"At the rate we're making our way north, we should reach Vienna sometime in September. The war may be over by then. If it isn't, it will be over soon. Get the typewriter. Things are changing very rapidly, and they must expect a field marshal's reports to be engrossed. Why else would they have sent the engrosser?"

AFTER ALESSANDRO had taken half an hour to position himself and the machine so that his elbows would be bent at just the right angle, he was ready to take Strassnitzky's dictation.

"I'll put in the unit names and the codes later. Leave appropriate spaces. Ready?"

"Yes."

"0400: We break camp in darkness at Szegy-Maszlow, and proceed northwest, by light of quarter moon, in four columns spaced at two kilometers.

"0600: With full daylight, columns wheel north, breaking into squadrons to sweep a path of fifty kilometers.

"0700: Charger disabled by fall. Broken leg. Shot. Substitute mount obtained from rear echelon encountered on western flank at 0725.

"1200: Break for midday meal.

"1230: Resume northward sweep.

"1315: Sweep-line wheels west, proceeds with all speed fifteen kilometers to group of hills running northeast-southwest. Our maps show that beyond this small rise lies a lake. Patrols sent out during halt to find condition of hills and terrain beyond.

"1337: Front rider, west patrol, returns to report smoke and gunfire at the edge of the lake.

"1340: Re-form into four columns, proceed over hills. Riders sent on point.

"1350: Halt at summit of hills. Gunfire audible, smoke visible, west-northwest near the lake. Await return of patrols.

"1400: Patrols return in a single group, having lost two men. (See casualty reports appended.) A prisoner-of-war group camped by the lake had rebelled after catching its guard unaware. The escort, all Bulgarians, were murdered to the last man, and the prisoners, many of whom were able soldiers of considerable experience, were in possession of at least a hundred rifles and pistols. Though their ammunition was limited, our patrols reported that they had begun to deploy in defensive positions and were aware of us. Perhaps they were clever enough to judge, from the faint sparkle of dust rising high in the air behind the hills, that eight hundred horses were riding toward them. Depending upon the geology of a specific region, it is sometimes possible to hear, through the ground, a large group of cavalry as it approaches. Also, we have seen mirages on the plain for weeks, and, perhaps, in the heat that bent the light, they saw us galloping across the sky."

Alessandro took this down almost without breathing.

"Thinking that the sooner we engaged, the less time the enemy would have to build revetments, firing positions, and barriers, I divided the regiment into eight formations and immediately charged. Orders were simply to overwhelm the enemy camp as quickly as possible with a direct assault from three sides. Troopers were advised to fire low so as to avoid wounding their fellows attacking from a different direction.

"1408: Simultaneous contact with enemy on three sides. Their breastworks were under construction and not too high for our horses to jump. We penetrated the lines by sailing right over them with such speed that we all were in within a minute or two. After a pause in which we and they gathered wits, they climbed to the other side of their breastworks and began to fire.

"Without ground for a running start, our horses would not jump, especially when they saw that those that attempted to do so were stopped.

"At about 1410 I ordered the bugler to sound dismount. In these minutes we suffered most of our casualties. Enemy fire was accurate and well controlled. When one of the enemy would fall, another would pick up his weapon. Thus, the battle was prolonged at surprising intensity.

"At 1500 I ordered Second Battalion to remount. Finding their way through gaps in the defenses, they then encircled the main body of the enemy, who broke by 1530.

"At 1600 we remounted the two other battalions and set out after the stragglers.

"1730: Recovered by shore of the lake. Watered horses. Buried our dead. Forty-three dead, no wounded. The enemy had notched its bullets for maximum impact, and the firing distances were extremely short. Counted five hundred and fourteen enemy dead. Approximately three hundred escaped. One prisoner. (See attached and supplementary reports by adjutant.)

"2000: Made camp on south bank of river exiting from lake as described. Will proceed northwest, 0400 tomorrow."

When Alessandro finished typing, his fingers were shaking.

"I didn't make the war," Strassnitzky said, "and neither did you. Our only responsibility is to get through it as best we can. The empire is finished, and so is Italy. Italy will win, but will collapse inward. I think God made war so that you and I could sit here by this stream, in the lamplight, covered with sweat, amazed that we escaped killing one another.

"Anyway, we ride at 0400 tomorrow, without breakfast. That's why we eat regally in the evening, though some men have difficulty sleeping after a full meal. The vagaries of the digestive tract have no rhyme or reason. Someday, they'll use Röntgengrams to make maps of the stomach."

AT THREE in the morning, under a sky blazing with shoals of stars, the troopers, their prisoners, and the civilian auxiliaries were awakened by a subdued reveille. The sentries were glad that the watch was over and that they were no longer the only ones awake so far in advance of dawn.

By four o'clock, assembled according to squadron and company, they faced Strassnitzky and his officers, whose horses, unlike the less fretful horses of the lower ranks, pranced back and forth. Alessandro was mounted on a mare who compared favorably with Enrico, and the saddlery was as good as any he had ever owned.

Alessandro had seen Italian cavalry on the roads that led to Rome, riding between ranks of tall poplars that sparkled in the wind and sun. Both lancers and swordsmen always had a grave expression, as if they were not entirely sure that they could stay on their horses, and their armament seemed purely ceremonial. Strassnitzky's men, however, were armed more like infantry than cavalry. A hundred were lancers, and every man had a sword, but here their similarity to traditional cavalry ended.

Every trooper had a semi-automatic pistol hanging from his belt. Two pouches for extra magazines were lined up behind it, and a leather bag with half a dozen others was strapped to the saddle. In a scabbard on the left of the saddle, running neatly under the rider's calf, was a rifle, the Mauser 98: it never jammed, it was powerful, and it was accurate. Kangaroo-style on the scabbard was a bayonet. Other leather bags, tightly strapped down, were balanced on the back of the saddle. They held rifle ammunition, wire cutters, a steel helmet, a medical kit, a canteen, and two hand grenades. Every thirtieth man carried in lieu of a rifle and saddle-bags a light machine-gun strapped across a special mount on the back of his saddle and held in balance by a geometric arrangement of straps that could be rapidly disengaged. The large amounts of ammunition for these guns were spread among everyone almost equally. Strassnitzky himself rode with fifty rounds.

Many of the horsemen had knives strapped across their chests, extra bandoliers of ammunition, and trench clubs. Alessandro felt that a thousand or more standard Italian infantry and their armament would be required to match these three hundred men. Each was an expert rider and an experienced soldier. Deeply impressed, Alessandro imagined that he would see within days the fierce Balkan engagements of which he had heard on the Isonzo. These were of mythical proportions, perhaps because, when Italian troops looked toward the east as the sun rose, the mountains had an air of distance not only in space but in time. He was confused, however, about where they might find an enemy, for, as far as he knew, the countryside all around them was entirely peaceful.

Strassnitzky trotted to the unit where Alessandro sat in the saddle nervously awaiting the order to ride. The stars were wheeling in the sky, and a faint band of light was visible on the rim of the hills. Strassnitzky looked at it and stood in his stirrups. As he sat down he turned back to Alessandro. His horse shuddered, made two steps to the rear, and then two to the front. "If you can't ride like a cavalryman, as you assured me," he said quietly, "I'll shoot you."

"You wouldn't be the first Austrian to shoot at me," Alessandro told him.

"I didn't say shoot at you."

"Prepositions are to language what aim is to a gun," Alessandro stated.

"Exactly."

"Where is the enemy?" Alessandro asked, because they were set to move as if into the fiercest battle, and yet were a thousand kilometers from the nearest front.

"The enemy," Strassnitzky said, "is out there."

Strassnitzky guided his horse into the open. He stood in his stirrups once more, so that his voice would carry over the heads of men in the front rows. "Six groups, close spaces, on the road west until dawn. Then we turn north. Ride!"

He spurred his horse and took to the stream. In the water the animal moved like a hobbyhorse, casting off sheets of white. Then he mounted the opposite bank and disappeared over it onto the road. The others followed, churning up the stream. In a few minutes the three hundred horses were galloping at full speed, and they sounded like a thunderstorm lost on the plain.

SOMETIMES THEY passed rows of short trees that enclosed the road like one of the columned galleries in Rome where businessmen and lawyers spent three-hour lunches in the shade. Even before dawn, the cooler air seemed to linger in the space between the two rows of trees. When the sun lit the fields obliquely and put the sides of hills in shadowless light, the smell of grass and dew filled the atmosphere with its promise of contentment. And when the sun was on the troopers' shoulders and their horses cast monstrously elongated shadows, the columns wheeled right and advanced northward at tremendous speed.

The sound of steel-shod hooves compressing the grass was like that of a field being chewed by locusts. The horses breathed steadily and gave the impression that, like airplane engines, they could go for hours without so much as a twitch. They were always able to break through the bushes, jump hedgerows and walls, and wind their way through the trees. They sailed over ditches, marsh, and logs, at full speed, never hesitating, responding to obstructions not by slowing down but by speeding up.

To ride this way is almost as taxing as if the rider were carrying the horse. He shifts his balance so often that all his muscles are in continual flex, his eyes dart, and he thinks so hard as he is propelled along that the time goes as fast as if he were falling from a cliff. When, at midday, they halted in a hot field full of the bleached golden stubble of harvested winter wheat, Alessandro was soaked with sweat and breathing like a wounded stag. For eight hours he had thought nothing save what the physics of plunging forward forced him to think. He had been like an eagle or a hart, with no power of reflection, no time for the future, no time for the past, but only an unbearably rich profusion of motion, color, scent, and sound. He loved it.

They had nothing but warm water from their felt-covered containers, and some miniature peaches as hard as rock. Then they set out again with hardly a pause, into three valleys that, according to the map, converged upon a town called Janostelek. At six in the evening, Alessandro's battalion, the Second, rode into Janostelek after having swept the middle valley, and he found the main square packed with tables and chairs upon which were sitting the men of the other battalions, with Strassnitzky off to the edge at a table with three beautiful and intoxicated strumpets.

Waiters ran back and forth from the restaurants that fronted the square. The braziers in front were going full blast as sweating children turned the cranks while their fathers and mothers basted and cut the meat. Each of two orchestras was playing a different Csardas, one that sounded Turkish and one that sounded right, until Strassnitzky got up from his table and unified them, physically and musically, so they might play the beguiling waltzes of which his capital and his kind were so profoundly fond.

The cavalrymen were fully armed, their shirts white with salt, their faces and hands absolutely filthy. They ate under wisteria and grape vines, and put away anything the waiters could bring. The horses were busy, too, in long even lines facing the square, eating oats and drinking from a trough through which flowed a stream of cold water.

Alessandro watched the stolid forms of the buildings and trees take new life at the behest of the music. Strassnitzky had paid in gold and the town was wide open. Even in the stores, each man was allowed to take more or less what he wanted, and in Janostelek the stores sold newspapers, groceries, hardware, candy, books, in short, all the things soldiers hardly ever see.

Though most of the decent women had been herded indoors, the strumpets were out in full force, even if the town was big enough to field only eight. The three at Strassnitzky's table drank too much, giggled, and stroked his hair in the fascinated and proprietary way in which strumpets stroke and play with hair, as if they have never seen it before.

When Alessandro had provided for his horse, he went to Strassnitzky.

"I think I'll be making my report rather late tonight," Strassnitzky said, "and I think I won't report everything." The strumpets burst into a shower of giggles.

"I watched you ride. I thought that perhaps you would ride like a gentleman or a portillion—at a level that would enable you merely to keep up and stay mounted. And then," he said, "I thought..." He took a long drink of champagne. "I thought, well, this fellow rides like a fox hunter. And then I watched some more, and I realized that you're as good as any of my men. You ride like somebody—like me—who was trained in dressage and the hunt before he was ten, and who, on his own horse, pushed himself to the limit thereafter, with the countryside as his academy."

"My horse was named Enrico," Alessandro said, "and my father bought him for me in England."

"Are you Italian?" one of the strumpets asked. "I have a book in my room over the bakery. It's in Italian. I was never able to read it. Perhaps you can tell me what it says."

"Why don't you?" Strassnitzky asked.

"Come," said the strumpet, abandoning Strassnitzky to her two companions. "I also have a toy steam engine you might like. My brother gave it to me before he joined the army."

"Is your brother alive?" Alessandro asked as they walked through the square.

"Yes. He's a baker and he's always beyond range of the shells. I took his room."

"What about your parents?"

"My mother was a singer. We never knew our father, and she didn't, either. She gave us to our aunt, who gave us to our grandmother, who died, and then our mother didn't want us back— she's still a singer; she goes around from place to place. By that time my brother was old enough to be apprenticed, and I became a housemaid.

"When he left for the army he wanted me to keep his room for him, and, because I'm his sister, I get some money from the state." She looked at Alessandro and smiled. "I'm very free," she said. "I do what I want. What about you?"

"I never do what I want," Alessandro said.

"I don't mean that. I mean about your family."

"Everyone is dead except my sister."

"That makes us close, doesn't it."

"Why?"

"You have only your sister, I have only my brother."

"I don't think that makes us close."

"Then maybe we should try something else."

"You talk like a woman I once knew in Toulon," Alessandro told her. "She was an admiral's daughter, and she looked a lot like you—tall, blonde, sunburnt, perhaps not quite as athletic looking. We happened to be in the same compartment of a train. She said she loved to speak Italian, and as we were speaking, she rather haltingly, she said that something had happened to her brassiere. I thought she was going to excuse herself, but she asked me to fix it."

"That sounds so lovely."

"I couldn't fix it. I didn't even know what was wrong, but the more I tried and the more she struggled, the more everything ripped and came apart, until the brassiere was hanging by a thread. Then she took a deep breath, and broke the thread."

The woman's teeth were partly clenched, and, as she breathed, the taste of champagne welled up from her lungs. Her eyes narrowed and were slightly out of focus. They hurried through the streets to her room above the bakery.

ALESSANDRO MADE his way to Strassnitzky's camp beyond the town. The galleries around the square were empty and the streets were so silent that he could hear several fountains, and a river that had been channeled between stone walls. He crossed this river by one of several small bridges that spanned it, and looked down at the water passing below. In the blackest parts were the brightest reflections of the stars.

The camp of the Hussars lay in a huge field bordered on four sides by tall trees swaying lightly in the wind. The proportions of the field made it seem particularly spacious and tranquil.

Bending down to enter Strassnitzky's tent, where the field marshal was sitting in a camp chair, feet up, staring at the lantern, Alessandro looked deeply contented.

"Mine were more demanding, I fear," Strassnitzky said.

"They were?"

"Maybe you should have taken mine and I yours. They were ravenous, almost violent. Perhaps they think that soldiers require such treatment. They, of all people, should know that certain parts of the body, no matter how exercised, cannot be toughened."

Alessandro sat down at the typewriter and cracked his knuckles to limber them up. "We didn't get past the bakery. The baker gave us fresh bread and tea, and now I won't be able to sleep tonight."

"It doesn't matter," Strassnitzky said. "By the time we finish it will almost be time to set out. Tell me, why are Italians always so unpredictable in regard to women?"

"How do you mean?"

"She wanted you. She was aching. I saw it."

"I didn't want to."

"Why?" Strassnitzky sat up.

"When we were sitting in the bakery, at the marble table where the baker kneads his dough, my desire for her, which had been strong, vanished. Death does not weaken loyalty, it strengthens it."

"Who's dead?" Strassnitzky asked.

"The woman I love."

"I see."

"Only after all opportunity is forsaken does devotion come alive."

"Like Dante and Beatrice."

"Maybe."

"I know how Italians think," Strassnitzky said. He was under no obligation to be polite to his prisoner. "Lose yourself in the spirit world now, and you'll be ready for it when it comes later. Devote yourself to the conditions of eternity, and suffer, but suffer no surprise. You're a Romano, are you not?"

Alessandro nodded.

"Naturally. Rome is a training school for the heavenly city, a jumping-off place. You take earthly pleasures and gracefully translate them to the language of the Divine."

"That's called art," Alessandro said.

"But what if death is only a void?"

"Even if heaven doesn't exist, I will have experienced it beforehand, because I will have created it."

"What about pleasure and light-heartedness?"

"You can be as light-hearted as you want, and still be devoted."

"Like Aquinas and Augustine?"

"They had fun."

"They did, did they."

"Yes," Alessandro replied. "Augustine in particular."

"I think you'll regret that you didn't take that girl upstairs, spread her legs, and ram her as deep as you could get. She would have loved it. You would have loved it."

"I'm sure you're right," Alessandro answered, "but I see a high window that shines through the darkness surrounding it. It's full of light, as if the sun were nearby, and in that window, although I'm not able to look straight at her, is Ariane, just as if she were alive. As time passes, she brightens, and I love her more and more."

"In the end, Dante finds Beatrice."

"Yes," said Alessandro. "He does, one way or another."

"How did she die?"

"Your planes. The building they bombed, that she was in, collapsed. The heat was so intense that nothing remained but ash."

"War is war," Strassnitzky said.

"War is war," Alessandro answered, "and I'll find the pilot."

"How? Surely you didn't see him."

"I saw him. I saw his face, but because of his aviator's goggles and helmet I couldn't really make him out."

"Then you'll never find him."

"Even the most Latin Germans," Alessandro said, looking at Strassnitzky as if through a tunnel, "the most relaxed, and the most humane, keep and preserve meticulous records."

"So?"

"The plane had a number."

"You saw it?"

"I saw it."

Somewhat unnerved by what he felt were Germanic currents in a man whom he had taken to be just an Italian intellectual who ate flowers, Strassnitzky cautiously argued that "the records are secret, part of the War Office. How do you expect to match the number with the man?"

"I haven't the slightest idea," Alessandro said, almost arrogantly, "but God is directly in charge of all things relating to life and death. That I've learned in the war."

"You think God is going to get you the operations records of the Austrian army?"

"I don't know, but if He were, wouldn't you imagine that the first thing He'd do would be to have me conveyed to Vienna?"

STRASSNITZKY WAS capable of great variation. The day after neither he nor most of his men had slept for one second in their brightly illuminated camp outside the town, he galloped them toward a range of mountains that were purple between starlight and dawn, and then blood red, rose, pink, and, finally, as white as chalk, with a mist of light that hung like a curtain from the speckled golden cliffs.

Seeking a place he had known before the war, he led his cavalry columns through oak forests at the base of the hills, trampling a path, jumping logs, passing striped wild boar that watched in horror as three hundred horsemen charitably ignored them.

Then they rose beyond the line of oaks to a region of red-hued rocks, short evergreens, pastures, and marshes, and came to a beautiful lake surrounded by clean granite outcroppings between which were beaches of sand as fine and white as the stuff in an hourglass.

They wanted to stop everywhere, but Strassnitzky led them to the western end of the lake, where the river that fed it came down from the mountains. A great flat tongue of granite, like a river itself, formed a ramp that descended to the water, and the river flowed over it in half a dozen warming streams, circling and idling in pools, cascading into waterfalls, and spreading thin over pans of rock as gray as an elephant's back. The sun heated the water as it flowed over the shallows, so that by the time it regained its depth in a pothole it was oxygenated and pleasantly warm.

Here they spent the day. They stood their weapons and slept on their saddles. They circled in the currents that led into and out of pools in the rock, lay on the shallow warming rushes of water, and jumped with the ten-meter fall that filled the lake, climbing up again on the granite by means of ladder-like holds and resinous pine boughs rooted firmly in the cliff.

They ate nothing, and drank a lot of water. After several hours in which most soldiers slept, Alessandro was summoned by Strassnitzky, who was sitting on a flat rock, staring out over the tops of the pines and smoking a pipe that smelled as sweet as the evergreens. He turned to Alessandro.

"Surprise," he said, gesturing at the little typewriter standing by itself on a boulder nearby, with a sheet of paper already in it waving gently to and fro in the wind. "The engrosser. Bernard, who can do anything with machines, took it apart so he could carry the rolling pin in one of his saddlebags and the dentures and piano keys in the other. What a setting for clerical work! We'll do two days' reports in these pleasant surroundings, maybe three or four."

"How can we do that?" Alessandro asked. "Today isn't even over."

"Matrices," Strassnitzky answered. "Matrices and sets."

Not about to argue, Alessandro put the typewriter on his lap and cracked his knuckles. With the machine so close, he thought, he might injure his elbows.

"Ready with the engrosser?" Strassnitzky asked, shielding his eyes from intense sunlight.

"Yes."

"All right. Here we go. I'm going to dispense with the times and all that, and inform them that I've written long after the fact."

Strassnitzky began to dictate, and Alessandro to type.

"Due to events I will now describe, I write this report upon some reflection, a day after the actions. Leaving camp at the usual hour, we broke into six columns and went west-southwest for about twenty kilometers before turning north, as has been our practice. Because the mountains and their foothills extend into the *puszta,* we were no longer sweeping across flat and boundless ground.

"Eventually, we faced three small valleys that led to a common juncture at the town of Janostelek. Intelligence gathered from the local population led us to believe that the Serbs controlled one or more of the valleys and perhaps the town. The first to encounter the Serbs was Second Battalion, in the center."

Alessandro looked up. "I was riding with Second Battalion," he said.

"So?"

"We didn't encounter any Serbs. We didn't encounter anybody. This is Hungary. The Serbs are in Serbia. The *Hungarians* are in Hungary."

"It's all in the mind," Strassnitzky said, tapping his head and closing his lips to suck on his pipe.

"What's all in the mind?"

"Everything."

"Perhaps you mean First or Third Battalions?"

Strassnitzky thought it over. "All right," he said, "Third Battalion. You know, you're Italian, and I'm Viennese, and here we are in Hungary. So why can't the Bosnians be here, too?"

"You mean the Serbs."

"Yes, the Serbs." He resumed his narrative. "Third Battalion was the first to encounter the Serbs, who were hidden behind trees and on high ledges overlooking the route of travel. The Serbs exercised characteristic discipline and did not open fire until the column was completely enveloped. Our men dismounted without orders and formed assault squads. In close fighting in the trees and on the steep sides of the valley they drove off the enemy, killing eighteen of them. Six men of Third Battalion were killed, nine wounded.

"Meanwhile, Second Battalion, in the center, turned back upon hearing gunfire in the distance, so as to avoid an ambush."

"No it didn't," Alessandro stated.

"Yes it did."

"No it didn't. I was with it all day. We heard no gunfire. We never turned back."

Strassnitzky tapped his pipe upon the rock and emptied the spent tobacco. "All right," he said. "Correction: Third Battalion."

"But you just said that Third Battalion . . ."

"Excuse me, First Battalion."

Alessandro typed, "First Battalion."

Strassnitzky continued. "Upon turning back, First Battalion rode straight into an ambush of mortars and machine guns. The mortars, however, were fired too early, and only one shell burst near the column, giving it appropriate warning and enabling it to halt before coming within machine-gun range. The column was traveling in artillery formation, one long thin line, mainly because it was threading a narrow path through the valley. Thus the shells did little damage, killing one horse and wounding another, and cutting a trooper's binocular straps. The men whose horses had been hit quickly transferred to two remounts, and all rode out of firing distance.

"The Serbs stopped firing and stayed their ground, thinking that the engagement was finished, but First Battalion discovered that the route they were taking led to high ground over the enemy dispositions. A dismount was ordered, and the troopers steadied their rifles in prone firing positions. The Serbs, who had seen them, fired a few mortar shells and machine-gun bursts, but in vain, for our men were out of range. The enemy, however, was in our range, though just so, at about twelve hundred meters. Because we were firing from above we had reasonable expectation of hitting them, especially in view of the concentration and volume of fire. When the Mausers opened up, three of the enemy fell immediately and the rest withdrew from the open, losing one more man.

"Meanwhile, Second Battalion made its way through the center, unburdened," Strassnitzky said, and then he paused, "except by a landslide that was loosed upon it by partisans high above."

"What landslide?" Alessandro asked.

Strassnitzky suddenly grew cross. He turned to Alessandro, his pipe sending up too much smoke, and said, "Look! You just write what I tell you, or you're fired!"

"How can you fire me? I'm a prisoner."

"You're right, I can't fire you, but I can shoot you. Take this down."

Alessandro positioned his fingers on the keys in a sign of acquiescence.

"When the battalions converged on the outskirts of the town we discovered that it had been invested by the enemy, who had set up artillery and machine-gun positions, barbed wire, mine fields, and sandbagged revetments."

Alessandro's eyes darted to and fro as he typed at high speed.

"We are light cavalry, ill-equipped to lay siege to a city. We have no artillery of any kind, and only a few light machine guns. The enemy were relatively few, about a hundred and seventy-five, which was why the ambushes had been little more than harassment, but we hadn't much daylight left for an assault. Their ordnance was impressive, as were their defenses, and the town is half circled by a river in a walled channel, which makes a defender's job very easy. Only the open part of the town was in need of heavy defensive work, and here wire had been laid and machine-gun positions set up.

"As we arrived, shells began to fall around us. We were worried that the ambush parties would try to envelop us from the rear, perhaps with the aid of others unknown to us. The mood among the men was not encouraging, and they were tired and hungry. My officers urged me to bypass the town.

"Not only did I reject that course of action, I refused to order a withdrawal from the bombardment. Something was bothering me.

Though shells were falling, the tubes were out of sight, and our men, even while mounted, were able to suppress the spotters (who were in a church tower) with just a few volleys from their rifles. This was the second incident in a day to confirm the wisdom of cavalry carrying long-barreled rifles.

"As the shells fell around us and our horses stomped in protest, I found what I had been seeking. I ordered a trooper to go on foot and measure the watercourse. It took two to do it, because they had to use a cord. When they returned, I had them lay the cord on the ground. Then I had a fence pulled down and laid along the length of the cord. I wheeled my horse around and brought him back toward the road. Then I turned him and spurred him forward, straight at the fence. He took it with no room to spare, but he took it.

"This energized the men. They knew, as I did, that a five-hundred-meter stretch along the river was defended only by a dozen riflemen who were supposed to pick off whoever might laboriously climb into the watercourse, swim the river, and climb out.

"We formed into two lines and assembled facing the river. The twelve riflemen realized what was going to happen, and they began to fire. Then we charged. I led the first line over, and we went right past the riflemen so as to take the others from behind before they could turn their guns.

"The second wave killed the riflemen, with pistols and swords. Eight of our men died when they were shot or when their horses fell short of the other side and threw them against the wall and they dropped into the river. Seventeen horses, altogether, didn't make the jump, but, of these, six were found later in a field west of the town, their saddles dangling underneath them.

"The battle for the town was quick, ferocious, and costly. The first line broke up in the streets and hit the enemy defenses with no mass, in small groups, and not all at once but over a period of about a minute. The enemy appeared to be defeated not so much by our presence behind him, by our fire, and by our swords and lances, as by his own conviction that he was doomed. In such instances, madmen or drug fiends are better able to fight than ordinary soldiers, for they do not understand the calculus of defeat, and they fight on, sometimes turning the great weight of battle.

"Had only one of the enemy erupted in rage or shown enthusiasm for the fight, the result might have been different, but our horses carried us at great speed against their backs, and when they turned they were trapped by their own barricades. We lost twenty-eight dead, and fifty were wounded. Some of the wounded will die. Of the enemy, sixty-one prisoners are to be delivered to the next labor column we meet on the road. Those who were wounded we have left with the local guards. The rest, more than a hundred, are dead."

"Is that it?" Alessandro asked.

"No," Strassnitzky said, continuing.

"Our ranks are steadily thinning from almost daily contact with strong enemy forces spilling over the mountains to the west. In this regard, our intelligence apparatus has proved invaluable, in that the local population directs us to an enemy who would prefer to avoid a strong opponent."

"Now I understand where your other unit is," Alessandro said. "It's in your head. You draw it down bit by bit in fictional battles until, by the time you return to the Belvedere, you will have sustained enormous casualties—every other man killed—and yet all of you, unscathed, untouched by battle, will ride in as a group. What a system! The war will end, and you'll be a great hero, having marched successfully through the deepest valleys of death."

Strassnitzky pulled his pistol from its elaborate holster. "Prepare to die."

"Look here," Alessandro said. "I told you that the only thing I had left was the truth. And the truth will carry me through death.

I've been prepared to die since I first went into the line. What I've said is true. You can shoot me a thousand times, and the truth will not be altered."

"Is the truth really worth dying?" Strassnitzky asked, pulling back the hammer of the pistol. Alessandro could see that the safety was off. He thought that now his life was going to end, and he felt a sense of tremendous elation and purity.

"It is," he said. "Yes, it is."

Strassnitzky aimed at Alessandro's heart, and pulled the trigger. The hammer clicked, but no shot was fired. Alessandro had remained calm throughout. He was almost getting used to such things. He felt that he was about to be pulled up on lines hanging from above, but that he was supposed to swing through history before his dizzying elevation.

"It's not loaded," Strassnitzky announced. "You did well. In having come to terms with death, you'll have a marvelous life, no matter what happens to you."

"Why isn't it loaded? Are you afraid that you'll shoot yourself as you ride?"

"Of course not. These weapons don't go off accidentally. You have to do five things in a row before they'll fire, and accident can seldom count higher than three—which is a mystery of probability that my intuition tells me is rooted at the very base of physics.

"No, it's never loaded. I'm a pacifist."

"A pacifist!"

"When I was in school," Strassnitzky said, "I went out one morning in my riding clothes and shod in heavy boots, and as I left the last step I came down on a young bird that had been resting at the foot of the stairs, having been savaged by a hawk. My weight on it pushed the air out of its lungs, and when I turned to see what had made that unearthly noise, the bird looked at me in such a way that I knew that even animals have souls. Only a creature with a soul could have had eyes so expressive and so understanding, and I had crushed it as it lay dying. It took a full day to die, and since then I have been what is called a pacifist. The term is inexact and demeaning, for a pacifist has no peace in his soul, and he knows rage as much as anyone else, but he simply will not kill."

"What about defenseless people in your charge? Wouldn't you kill, if you had to, to save them?"

"I would hold them in my arms, and we would go together."

"Forgive me," Alessandro said, "but even though I'm Italian, and religious, and find your principles intriguing, I'd like to turn the conversation to something more practical."

"What?"

"How did a pacifist become a field marshal?"

"If the emperor knew, he would have me shot."

"Naturally. To someone in authority, inconsistency is betrayal, and you are certainly the only field marshal in the world, in history, to live according to the principles of nonviolence. How did you advance?"

"Marriage. I never thought we'd have a real war, no one did. I was an excellent rider, my family is of the high nobility, and we have a great deal of money. It was only natural that I join the Hussars, but the Hussars were a circus troupe. The long and the short of it was parades, beautiful horses, dazzling bayonets, a magnificent laundry, and a corps of tailors. We dressed to kill, but no one in the entire regiment had ever fired a shot in anger. That's what war should be, I think.

"When I wasn't riding in parades I was dancing at royal receptions. In the summer of 'eight I danced with a princess, a favorite of the emperor, and by Christmas we were married. The promotions came rapidly thereafter. When the war started, I was already a colonel, and then the general in command died of compounded gout.

"I was put in charge, made a general, and sent into Serbia, where, by dint of my own ingenuity, we served honorably but did not kill a soul. And that, believe me, is very hard with the Serbs, because they are very ingenious themselves, and they have a passion for martyrdom.

"I've been a field marshal for two years. I have so many medals that when I wear them I look like a window in a junk shop."

"And not a single one earned," Alessandro interjected.

"*Au contraire,*" Strassnitzky shot back. "Every single one. Of my three hundred men who really exist, I have not lost one. We have not deprived a single child of its father, or a mother of her son, or a wife of her husband or brother. We have not burned a single town or trampled a single field. When we encounter starving peasants, we use our considerable resources to feed them. We liberate prisoners, we heal the sick, we do not kill."

"How have you avoided detection? How can you exist without being thrown into battle? I don't understand."

"It was more difficult when I was just a general," Strassnitzky said, staring past the rust-colored trunks of the evergreens at mountains that glowed in the blue air, "but with this field marshal stuff it's very easy. A field marshal normally commands one or more armies. The post is semi-political, and normally I would command an entire front.

"But as I have only three hundred men, it's out of the question. Instead, I go where I want and I do what I want, trying not to step on anyone's toes. If I enter another field marshal's sphere of operations my presence challenges his authority, so it is considered political finesse for me to disappear. Everyone is grateful. In this way, we travel, we go anywhere except where there's a fight, and we fight imaginary battles that no one else can either confirm or deny.

"I created the other three hundred men, requisitioned the money for their training and supply, took three hundred real cavalrymen from the Russian front, sent them home to their families, changed their names slightly, and, *voilà,* my ghost unit, integrated platoon by platoon, man by man, with the one that really exists. In the battles, only they are killed.

"The real soldier might have been Hartmut Dankhauser. He was decommissioned even before we set out, and a Hartmut *Dink*hauser came with us. When Dinkhauser dies, it's published in the paper, but who cares? Do you think that anyone actually keeps track of such things?"

"Entire bureaucracies exist to do just that," Alessandro protested.

"Exactly. A field marshal has his own staff! In an industrial state or a conscript army, if you get control of the paperwork you can do anything. War begins with a declaration on paper, and ends with a paper treaty. Paper also keeps alive the middle. Battles are secondary. They last only a short time, the results are often inconclusive, and they are remembered . . . on paper.

"I might have fought had the Mongols or Turks been at the gates of Vienna, had I not been a pacifist, but now we are all fighting for absolutely nothing. No one knows what he's preserving, and nothing is being preserved. A million men die attacking and defending a piece of ground that was inconsequential before the war and will be inconsequential afterward. When they look back on this age, they will look through the eyes of the defeated. You've seen battlefields littered with the dead, haven't you? Of course you have. The first that I surveyed shattered my faith in everything but love and peace. I looked at it and I thought, it has taken several billion people several thousand years to perfect this and the expresso machine. We are fighting neither for an idea nor for survival. The governments on either side are the same. We enjoyed each other's company before the war, and will do so after.

"True, you attacked us opportunistically in the Südtirol, but after what we had done in the Balkans we more than deserved it. Modern times are too quick for empires, which can form and hold together only in a world of slow pace. The faster things go, the less likely that one can rule many, because stirrings and changes in relative positions will be too frequent. Austria-Hungary cannot fail to dissolve.

"In the Hofburg, they don't want to let go. Why should they? Just like everyone else, they know what will happen if Austria sheds its nationalities, that on the map it will look like a mouse turd. But shrink it will. In view of this, and all the rest, our conduct, the conduct of my unit in this war, is exemplary."

"How, in good conscience," Alessandro asked, "can you ride across the countryside in perfect safety, as if you were on holiday, stopping mainly to swim and eat oysters, while men are crushed and pulverized in the filth of the trenches?"

"Because the object of war is peace, and I have merely thrown out the middle. If everyone did the same, no one would be crushed and pulverized in the filth of the trenches."

"Everyone doesn't have the privilege. You do because you're a field marshal in command of a microscopic unit."

"I realize that," Strassnitzky answered, "and, given such a rare opportunity, of which most men cannot even dream, I would be unforgivably remiss if I failed to seize it, would I not? I exploit it to the full."

Alessandro was amazed. He thought that no one would ever know the war for what it really was, for it was as various as life itself. To depict it merely as combat would be a great mistake. "You didn't destroy the column of prisoners?"

"We gave them a wagon-load of tinned meats and baked goods, but they'll never get to Bulgaria no matter what shape they're in. Tell me something."

"What?"

"Some officers have opera singers whom they've captured. It's quite a coup for me to have an Italian intellectual, especially since, in the Viennese view, anyway, so few exist. But, still, can you sing?"

"No."

"Really?"

"I can't sing any better than most people who can't sing."

"Ah, but you're Italian."

"Therefore I should be able to sing?"

"Yes."

"You're Austrian."

"Yes?"

"Yodel."

Strassnitzky smiled. "Let's do the report for today's battle," he said, "and, if we have time, for tomorrow's."

IN JULY and August, Strassnitzky's column moved furiously from one border of the empire to another. The three hundred heavily armed cavalrymen, on horses the color of chestnut and mahogany, looked their part. When they galloped en masse in a long double or triple row, or in squadrons and groups that broke apart and blended together on the run as smoothly as if they had been on a greased track, they made thunder and dust, and their weapons clattered. They were always headed either toward a battlefront... or away from it, and thus everyone assumed that they were either going to fight or had just finished. Although no one had ever asked at what point they turned around, it was usually when Strassnitzky heard the sound of guns or saw the flash of cannon fire. Then he would call the column to a halt, and listen. Rising in his saddle and pointing away from the sound, he would say "Forward!" and they would turn and ride as hard as they could for at least five hours.

They traveled for two weeks to reach the Russian front, though the fighting there had ceased, and to make sure that the Russians were not up to some sort of trick they patrolled the area for most of August, going for periods of rest and recuperation by the shores of untouched lakes and in mountain pastures where they played soccer and quoits.

The towns and villages of the interior, untouched by the war except for the absence and death of so many of their men, were quiet and summerlike, and they reminded Alessandro of Italy before 1911. In these silent places where nothing ever happened, Strassnitzky's column would arrive at a station to receive provisions from Vienna, and wait ten hours before the station master came down from the mountainside where he had been tending his goats. Trains came through once a week, and after a rainstorm the rails would develop a light coat of rust.

They finally came to rest in a little town somewhere in the mountains of Slovakia, where Strassnitzky stopped writing his reports. "Let them wonder a while before we ride into Vienna," he said. "Let them forget the last battles, so they don't ask too many questions. We'll appear generally weary, and, besides, we're through with fighting. All those who do not exist have now been killed."

Alessandro had nothing to do. They were only four days' ride from the Belvedere, and would requisition no more supplies. The typewriter was stored in one of the wagons, the dispatch cases stacked alongside it. During the first week in September, with the tents pitched in a meadow above a church, the column waited for the war to end and the weather to change.

The weather did change. At night the horses shivered and in the day the sun was brilliant and the air cool. Alessandro swam in the river that ran through the town, and could stay in the water only long enough to reach some boulders in midstream, where he stretched himself out in the sun. For a week he did this every day at lunchtime, because lunch had been abolished.

Strassnitzky had decided that everyone was too fat, and that to return to the capital like well fed geese would stimulate inquiries about the life they had been living. The wagons were sent home, guards were set to watch over the small stockpile of food, and the field marshal declared the death penalty for anyone who supplemented the regimental diet with stores obtained elsewhere. The two meals were entirely uniform. In the morning they had an egg, a cracker, and a bowl of clear beef broth. In the evening they had an egg, a cracker, and a bowl of clear beef broth. On special days they were allowed a carrot.

Everyone ate slowly and went around in a trance. Because of all their riding and swimming they had not been obese to begin with, but Strassnitzky wanted them to look gaunt. He also wanted them to be sunburnt and strong, so he made them do calisthenics and stay in the sun from dawn to dusk. This was not unpleasant, because the shade was cold.

Alessandro's day began at six, as he awakened from hunger. Breakfast was at eight. From eight-thirty until noon he would do calisthenics with the rest of the men. Then, too exhausted to continue, many of them would go down to the river and swim out to the rocks, where they would lie motionless for hours, like lizards. Alessandro's rock was the best positioned and the most comfortable, his because he was the only one capable of getting up onto it. On this rock, above the water but close enough to be nearly overcome by the sound of the flow, Alessandro realized that he had survived the war.

Even without newspapers the men of Strassnitzky's battalions could feel that the war was almost over. Soldiers at the front had the peculiar anxiety that comes only near the very end, and feared that they would be killed a month, a week, an hour, or even a minute before the armistice. When everyone knew that the firing was going to stop on a given day, and that the lag between action and intention was only a matter of bureaucracy and communication, the day before that day was the most difficult.

For Alessandro and the strange formation to which he had been attached, the feeling was different, for they were safe. Civilian life and its pleasures lay close ahead. The weather was changing as it does in every electrifying autumn; soon the air would be cold and the winds would drive the crows from the steppes of Russia to the comparative warmth of Vienna. Everything would begin, from the new school year, to the opera, to new governments, and a new world. The troops would return and they would find new women, who would dress in new clothes, and new children would be born.

Here and there, scholars would begin histories. Somehow, Alessandro would return to Rome, even though he had no one to whom to return. He wondered if, in the exhausted world of the

clear Roman autumn, acquaintances would now be more important than once they had been. Perhaps he would merely start all
over, as if from the beginning.

Strassnitzky disappeared on the seventh and returned on the
tenth. He had gone alone to Prague, where he had discovered that
the war, as he had thought, was close to its end. To be safe, he
would keep his men in the meadow above the church until the first
of October.

They had had a week of frost. At night, until they retreated to
their bedding, they stayed inside the church. It was warmed by a
huge white-and-gold stove in which pine and fir blazed and crackled
like the meeting of two armies. Alessandro could no longer swim
out to the rock: the stream had swollen and it was too cold.

On the twenty-ninth of September they had a meal of roast
chicken, and on the thirtieth they realized that, because the wagons
had already returned, they would not be able to take the tents that
had been standing in the meadow for a month, and on the first of
October they had tea, bread, butter, and jam for breakfast. They
packed up their saddlebags and went into formation at nine in the
morning. Leaving the tents behind, they rode from the meadow
and slowly wound through the town, and when they reached the
main road they galloped. After four days' hard ride during which
they ate little, slept little, and did not shave or change their clothes,
they found themselves on the plains that led to the Danube.

Early in the afternoon, they saw the Kahlenberg. Soon they
could make out the city itself. After all the little towns and mountain villages, it seemed to radiate energy like a fire. The tiled roofs
and black domes shone crisply, and the cavalrymen could see the
long and immense shadows of the great steeples and spires. The
road was full of traffic, which, though grim and sedate, was traffic
nonetheless. Alessandro was excited beyond measure at the prospect
of seeing sunlight on a tea cup, a family in the park, a beautiful girl
walking down a staircase—those things for which all the great
battles had been fought, and against which they paled.

They were so excited by the prospect of peace that they spurred their horses all the way to the Danube.

THE GUARDS of the Hofburg took Alessandro to a whitewashed underground room with a vaulted ceiling. Standing meekly at attention were about a hundred Italian prisoners dressed in pajama-like uniforms that Alessandro associated with the men who walk obsequiously through hotel corridors, obsequiously sweeping crumbs into a brass box that hangs obsequiously from a stick.

The Italians, who were soft, pudgy, and pale, looked as if they had been out of battle since the beginning of time. In contrast, in boots, riding pants, and a leather jacket, Alessandro was like a knight. That he was lean, strong, and deeply sunburnt, added to the differentiation.

"You! You!" a servant in a powdered wig said to him abusively. "You are Italian?"

Alessandro nodded, realizing only then that music was drifting down from above, with the rhythmic patter of feet ceaselessly circling around the top of the vault. The prisoners were massed underneath a ballroom. As Alessandro looked up, he imagined all that was there.

"You don't *look* Italian," the bewigged servant said, in a mocking tone.

Alessandro knew from long experience as a subordinate that he was supposed to smile in a cowardly fashion and attempt to say something demeaning about himself. Instead, he stared through his interrogator all the way to the Italians, who already had taken note of his attitude. They looked anxiously at Alessandro and then at a score of lesser servants standing against the walls, each carrying a knobbed cane that came up to his sternum.

"I am Klodwig," Alessandro was told in hysterical, hyperventilated speech. "I am your director. These," he said, gesturing toward the other bewigged, powdered, golden-jacketed lackeys in white knee socks and patent leather pumps with Dutch buckles, "are my assistants. You will call your superiors *Hoheit*. Do you know German? It means *highness*, but you will also memorize their names, for reference."

"For reference?"

"For reference, *Hoheit!*"

"For reference, *Hoheit!*"

"Should one, for example, tell you to carry soap to another, or report to him in the candle closet."

"I see."

"I see, *Hoheit!*"

"I see, *Hoheit!*" Alessandro said, screaming *Hoheit* at the top of his lungs, so that even in the ballroom it could be heard over the music, and some of the dancers looked down at the floor.

"You needn't exaggerate."

"Nor you."

Klodwig did not hear Alessandro's comment, but the Italians did, and were terrified. They knew his tone exactly, whereas Klodwig was still unaware, and they thought that Alessandro was either a hopeless idiot or a phenomenon.

Klodwig turned to his assistants and made the kind of microscopic bow that someone of royal blood might have made to an ant. "Remember well. If you forget, ask the others." And then he said their names: "Liborius, Mamertus, Markwart, Nepomunk, Nabor, Odo, Onno, Ratbod, Ratward, Pankratius, Hilarius, Knud, Polypark, Gangolf, Kiian, Cacilia, Saturnin, and Cornelts."

At the end of this list, Alessandro said, "You're not serious."

"I beg your pardon?" Klodwig asked, half in shock.

"You must be joking."

"About what?"

"Those are not names."

Every one of the assistants had stepped forward, gripping his cane in anticipation.

"Don't!" one of the Italians said to Alessandro, but as soon as he closed his mouth a white wig jerked, a cane flew through the air, and he slumped to the floor, grasping his stomach.

Klodwig narrowed his eyes and approached Alessandro, a thumb away from his face. "I was going to put you up there!" he shouted, pointing to the ceiling, "because you're so handsome. But not now!" He smiled with what Alessandro took to be unapproachable insanity.

"One way or another," Klodwig said, "you must be obsequious. We require it."

Alessandro blinked.

"Well? Can you be obsequious?"

The Italians had stopped breathing.

"Yes, I can be obsequious," Alessandro said, disappointing his countrymen. "I'm a master of obsequiousness—in the Italian style. Surely, being in charge of so many Italians, you know it, *Hoheit.*"

"No, I don't," Klodwig replied, genuinely curious.

"Would you like to see it?"

Klodwig nodded.

"It goes like this," Alessandro said. He narrowed his eyes as he drew back, and, rocking forward from one foot to the other, he delivered to Klodwig's jaw the hardest, fiercest, most brutal punch he had ever thrown in his life.

As Alessandro hung from manacles chained to a heavy beam and Klodwig whipped him with a leather strap, the orchestra above them played *"An der Schönen, Blauen Donau."* Alessandro had known it since his youth. He had listened to it in mountain huts, and danced to it in embassies.

In the Winter Palace, with the doomed Emperor of Austria-Hungary right over his head, he dangled from chains as he was beaten by a psychotic servant in a powdered wig. Apart from his sister, almost everyone in his life whom he had loved or for whom he had felt affection had died, some before his eyes, consumed in flame, executed, butchered, exploded. As the hundred Italians clad in pajamas would undoubtedly have affirmed, the world had simply come to an end. The strains of *"An der Schönen, Blauen Donau,"* though extremely beautiful, now seemed cruel and funny. Had he been a revolutionary or some other type of cynic he might have hated the officers in white pants and gold braid, and the exquisitely dressed women who were gliding above him, but he felt no hatred for them; he was in a world of his own making.

With each stroke of Klodwig's whip, the room was filled with red and yellow lightning, and when each stroke ended, Alessandro was still the same. Even Klodwig, who had intended to beat him until he was limp, was horrified that in the course of the hour Alessandro had not cried out.

Once, in the middle, Klodwig walked around to see if Alessandro were alive. Alessandro followed him with his eyes, and smiled to himself because he knew that at that moment he was totally in control—in control not of Klodwig, not of the Hofburg, not of the war, and not of the world, but of himself.

For each and every stroke, and for each of the lovely thunderclaps in the delirious music above, Alessandro heard ever-so-faintly another music that underlay it all, beyond which was no other, and that was perfectly appropriate both to the elated dancing in the ballroom and his torment in the cellar, because it tied them together and made them equally inconsequential. He shuddered, his hair stood on end, and electricity shot through his body.

"What?" Klodwig asked, amazed that, despite the blood steaming in the gutters, Alessandro had begun to sing to himself.

CIVILIANS SELDOM understand that soldiers, once impressed into war, will forever take it for the ordinary state of the world, with all else illusion. The former soldier assumes that when time weakens the dream of civilian life and its supports pull away, he will revert to the one state that will always hold his heart. He dreams of war and remembers it in quiet times when he might otherwise devote himself to different things, and he is ruined for the peace. What he has seen is as powerful and mysterious as death itself, and yet he has not died, and he wonders why.

When Alessandro was well enough to work, Klodwig came to him and cried. Klodwig, it seemed, had never beaten anyone who had not screamed, and this, along with the impending close of the war and the great changes afoot in the Winter Palace, had filled him with trembling, powdered-wig-style remorse.

"Tell me what I can do to help you," Klodwig said as he sat down on Alessandro's bed.

"First, sit a little way back."

Klodwig was distraught. "What can I do?" he pleaded.

Alessandro put his hands over his mouth and opened them as if to form a megaphone. "Information," he whispered.

"Information?"

"The name of the pilot of a particular plane that flew in the mountains last winter, and where he is."

"A pilot?"

"I admired his flying. Even though he was the enemy, we cheered him, and I want to tell him so myself. Now that the war is almost over, I want to extend my hand to him."

"Was he handsome?"

"Yes," Alessandro answered, *"very."*

"Then I won't do it!" Klodwig yelled, writhing inside.

"Not that handsome."

"No?"

"No."

"What did he look like?"

"He looked like a Byzantine jug, an amphora."

Klodwig was entranced.

"His ears," Alessandro said, "looked like clay handles, and his face was pockmarked with little red and gold ceramic squares. I never saw his body, just his head, but his eyes were red. The airplane pivoted around his head when he turned or flew upside down—because he was so courageous."

"I won't do it," Klodwig said. "Everything you say about him makes me unhappy."

Alessandro accepted Klodwig's refusal.

"But I came to tell you that, because you are still recuperating, I won't make you lug garbage, scrub pots, or grind manure. Instead, you may bird trays in the hallways."

"What does that mean?"

"Hundreds of the nobility, guests, and staff are in residence. When they ask for something, no matter what the time of day or night, it is served to them on elaborate trays. Sometimes they ring for a footman to take the tray away, but more often than not they exercise their noblesse and leave the trays outside their door. We don't need uniformed footmen to bird the trays. Italian prisoners have done it before. You have to be very quiet, and should you meet your betters you bow slightly, if you are carrying a tray, and cast your eyes to the floor. If you don't have a tray, bow deeply and cast your eyes to the floor. You see, they all fuck each other all the time, and we're supposed to be invisible and not see."

"What is the alternative?"

"Have you ever ground manure?"

"Let's say that at four in the morning one of these people awakens and asks for artichokes and caviar, or a salmon soufflé. The cooks arise and light the fires?"

"The cooks are waiting and the fires lit. All is ready. All is instant. The kitchens are as big as Palermo."

"Remarkable," Alessandro said.

"I have the impression," Klodwig stated, "that the King of Italy may be rather ordinary, or even deprived. He doesn't have these things, does he."

"No," Alessandro said, "but he has a special rubber throne with electric balls, and hats that can resurrect dead ostriches."

"Electric balls?" Klodwig asked, inching closer.

"*Hoheit,* do you know why crows are black?"

"No, I never thought of it."

"They taste lousy, and they're black as a sure sign to predators that they're crows, who will taste lousy."

"Why aren't they yellow?"

"They live in cold climates, and black absorbs heat. They don't need camouflage, so they can take advantage of the way their color soaks up the sunlight."

"Why do you ask me these questions?" Klodwig demanded.

"To remind you, *Hoheit,* not to argue with nature."

The next evening, Alessandro went to work. Winter winds made the city sufficiently icy and gray for the stoves to be lit in the huge salons and immense corridors of the palace. For several hours one of Klodwig's assistants showed him through the halls. He noticed that everyone they passed looked shocked and dejected.

Alessandro attributed the grim mood to the state of the empire and the arrival of winter, but even if it would be gray until spring he could not fathom why some of the women cried as they passed, and some of the men staggered and could hardly walk. He could see their hearts beating against their expertly tailored shirts and vests.

"Why are these people so subdued?" Alessandro asked his guide.

"Don't you know?"

"No."

"Today Austria capitulated. The war is over."

Alessandro stopped. He thought of Guariglia's children. "What a waste," he said. "When will I be free?"

"The Italians have taken hundreds of thousands of prisoners.

The exchange will be part of the treaty, and who knows when that will be? Eventually," the assistant said, "perhaps in the spring. Don't worry, you'll go home."

"To what?"

ALESSANDRO BEGAN his work at ten at night and finished at eight in the morning. In theory, he was supposed to be an unseen night porter padding about the halls in felt-soled shoes, encountering only the after-images of aristocrats darting into each other's rooms, but in starting when he did he trafficked with the inhabitants of the palace when they were most lively and most hopeful. They moved as if they were prancing ahead of a prairie fire, because at ten they were both drunk on brandy and champagne, and elated after half a dozen cups of coffee and chocolate.

This concoction of drugs, and the waltzes that drifted through the courtyards and interiors, were the sources of a delirium appropriate to waiting for the termination of one way of life and the forced beginning of another.

Though Alessandro was supposed to avert his eyes, he did not. He sought the eyes, and, through them, the souls, of everyone he passed. Half the people lurched through the spacious corridors, glancing off the gilded walls after repeated muffled impacts.

They sailed past Alessandro, talking to themselves desperately, or they plodded past, almost in tears, looking down at the floor exactly as he was supposed to have done. The singing, even in the halls, of famous sopranos and baritones, the armies of orchestras and chamber ensembles playing music that had been composed when the empire was vital and ascendant, the fires and candle light, the speaking of French and English among people of purple blood, and the strong sense of a ship that was going down, kept Alessandro on edge throughout the nights.

Though these people spoke in the stilted self-conscious idiom of the court, with each word intended to be a pearl for the jeweler-emperor, at one or two in the morning, when the music had stopped and the gatherings had broken up, Alessandro heard the real concert of empire—men who spoke like women and women who spoke like men, the click of latches, sighs, grunts, farts, shrieks, sobbing, the sound of small whips, arguments so fierce that they might have been between black jaguars in emerald jungles, and the sound, always, of people talking to themselves, alone, for even among the aristocrats, or perhaps especially among them, the war had shattered many families.

They needed the songs of Gypsies and Jews, Sicilian ballads, Moravian laments, music of the heart rising from defeat, but all they had was the music of delirium and ascendancy, which, as soon as it took to the air, dived to the ground and shattered like glass. The prisoners lived in a barracks underground, and the little light that came to them did so through basement windows. Rows of wooden bunk beds covered with thin gray blankets lined the walls and marched down the center of the floor. Two gas lamps illuminated everything under the whitewashed ceiling.

They were overworked, malnourished (part of being Italian is the inability to thrive on potatoes and salt), and mentally ill. Most had been captured in early battles and cut off from news of the war. When they had heard that the war was over and they were the victors, they despaired, for their situation had failed to change, and they thought that they would be dressed in pajamas, and beaten and kissed by the sadistic footmen, for eternity. When Alessandro told them that their release would come in a month or two, they refused to believe him.

Because of the way he spoke, and because his defiance had marked him as a leader, he was sought by socialists and anarchists, who were interested primarily in giving directions and commands, and punishing anyone not sufficiently possessed of their vision—with reluctance, of course (punishment, they thought, was something the world could do without were the world only properly uniform), but with enthusiasm.

They were thwarted primarily by the strong sense of religion among the soldiers in the underground barracks, who believed mystically and prayed openly, and whose memories of home and peace were intertwined with the Church and its sacraments. Propagandizing among the troops, the socialists and anarchists had made the barracks into a war of religion, and among the exhausted prisoners theological debates raged at a languorous pace.

Alessandro was lying on his bed, at eight in the morning, waiting for the day workers to leave so he could sleep, when three prisoners, pleasant but ready for ideological combat, approached him in a deputation. During the discussion that followed, he remained prone, like a hospital patient surrounded by medical students. He was watching a tiny red mite that had been caught in a smooth thumb-sized depression in the side rail of his bed. The mite busied itself in trying to escape, and was constantly assessing its predicament, drawing back to look at the rim of the depression, dashing forward to mount the walls, circling in discouragement. It seemed to be full of conviction, disappointment, and schemes.

"You are educated and brave," the leader of the deputation said to Alessandro.

"I am?" Alessandro asked.

"We are in the midst of an important struggle here," they said, quite unable to make small talk, "and we would like to know if you believe in God."

"Oh Christ," Alessandro said.

"Does that mean you do?"

"Yes," Alessandro answered.

"Can you prove His existence?"

"Not by reason."

"And why not?"

"Reason excludes faith," Alessandro responded, watching the blood-red mite as it made a dash for the rim. "It's deliberately limited. It won't function with the materials of religion. You can come close to proving the existence of God by reason, but you can't do it absolutely. That's because you can't do anything absolutely by reason. That's because reason depends on postulates. Postulates defy proof and yet they are essential to reason. God is a postulate. I don't think God is interested in the verification of His existence, and, therefore, neither am I. Anyway, I have professional reasons to believe. Nature and art pivot faithfully around God. Even dogs know that."

"There are ways to argue with blind faith," said the leader of the deputation. "We can do that later, but, tell me, what is it that you think you'll get from believing?"

"Nothing," Alessandro responded.

"Nothing? Do you really believe, then?"

"I never took my religious instruction seriously," Alessandro told them, "because it was delivered in the language of reason. I asked everyone you can imagine, from the nuns when I was a child, to bishops, philosophers, and theologians later on, why do you speak of God in the language of reason? And they said it was because God has burdened those who believe in Him with the inability to prove His existence except in the language of His enemies, which is a language in which you cannot prove His existence. Why bother? I asked. Their answers showed me that they believe in God no more strongly than you do. Can you see a group of people on a beach in a storm, deafened by the surf, their hair blown back from their foreheads, their eyes tearing, trying to prove the existence of the wind and the sea?

"I want nothing more than what I have, for what I have is enough. I'm grateful for it. I foresee no reward, no eternal life. I expect only to leave further pieces of my heart in one place or another, but I love God nonetheless, with every atom of my being, and will love Him until I fall into black oblivion."

"You're grateful for what you have?" they asked, their lips curling into bitter smiles. The leader said, "You're a piece of shit in a dungeon. You live on potatoes and salt, and you're a servant to the dying scum of a dying world. For this you're grateful?"

Alessandro thought for a moment, and then he said, "Yes."

"Why?"

"I know what I was, what I had, what I lack. I can close my eyes and see faces. Even when I close my eyes, I still see light. And I knew a man in the Alto Adige, a Milanese, who held tight to his rifle even after his fingers had been severed from his hand.

"Isn't it strange?" Alessandro asked them. "I believe in God without any hope, in a God of splendor and terror, and you disbelieve because you want to be reassured, because you want some collective spirit, like God Himself, to know that you behaved yourself and suffered no illusions. You fear, above all, to put your weight on a beam that might break."

"Those illusions, your illusions," the leader told Alessandro, "are your punishment. If you were to free yourself of them you would feel something that you might understand as holiness. You would be relieved of a great burden."

"I would be relieved of the burden of love, and I would arrive at the gates of death with no resolution, no determination, no fight."

"Tell me something," the leader said. "Of what use is resolution at the gates of death?"

"Life is so quick that it's all played out at the gates of death, and the value of resolution is that it quickens life."

"I find that hard to understand."

"Of course you do," Alessandro said. "Of course you do. You can't see light. Light tells you nothing. To you it delivers no message."

"And to you it does?"

"Yes. It does, and I love it."

When they were gone he fell back on his pillowless bed, deeply unhappy, and he tried to think of Rome, to conjure visions of rose-colored buildings and light green palms, of a sun that danced in brassy reflections from rooftop to rooftop, of deep shadows in dense gardens, and the spray of a fountain dancing against a deep blue sky.

He wondered if perhaps by stroking his own forehead and remembering himself as a feverish child, held in his father's arms as his mother slowly passed her hand across his brow, he might find comfort. His father's shirt had smelled of pipe tobacco, and his mother's hands had said to him what he would not have understood had she merely spoken it. The high fever had brought convulsions, they had thought that they were going to lose him, and they had done everything they could do, so they simply held him and stroked his head. The rapidly breathing child could not take his eyes away from the window, for the shutters were closed, but the light was coming through the seams and bursting through the cracks.

As SNOW fell in hallucinatory gray streaks past the old glass of the palace windows, Alessandro sat at the long wooden table where the prisoners took their meals. He and thousands of others were angry and exasperated that they were prisoners of war after hostilities had ceased, and he decided that, come what may, he would leave by Christmas. As the light failed outside, the lanterns grew lustrous and warm, like the color of amber, or the sun in Africa. Alessandro slowly ate his potatoes and salt. Each prisoner had been given half a liter of beer. It helped the potatoes taste like something, and it put everyone in a slightly less terrible mood.

He had positioned himself near the place where the manure grinders sat. As he waited for them to return from the riding school he thought about his escape. A uniform with gold braid and medals, and a Lippizaner, could take him almost anywhere in the capital. He knew the location of the Ministry of War. He could speak passable German, and he could speak it with a Hungarian accent. He would be as officious and impatient as possible, demand the information, and, when he had it, ride straight for the pilot, even if to the empire's farthest border. Most pilots probably would have been demobilized early, and they were likely to live in or near the capital.

Alessandro's conjectures were interrupted by the arrival of the manure grinders. They looked not so much like prisoners as like oppressed workers. They had been grinding Lippizaner manure for nearly four years, and in that period they had been unable to overcome the normal human affection for the familiar.

At first Alessandro focused on the two who were neater and more civilized than their colleague, the third, an unkempt giant with fleshy red lips and bulging eyes, but the ordinary-looking ones were set in their ways and would not hear of trading jobs. What if Klodwig were to discover it, as surely he would? Why would Alessandro want to switch in the first place? Why make trouble when they would soon be free? They would have nothing to do with him.

He turned reluctantly to the giant, in whose bloodshot bulging eyes he could hardly stand to look. "How about you?" he asked.

"What about me?"

"Would you like to change jobs?"

"What for?"

"All you have to do is walk through the corridors and, now and then, pick up some trays. You can eat the leftover chocolate, shrimp, and rolls, and you hear a lot of music."

"What's shrimp?" the giant asked.

"One of the fruits of the sea," Alessandro told him.

The giant stirred in his seat. "What's the catch? Why do you want to leave your job and take mine? Why should I do it? What do you get?"

"I get ... terrible headaches unless I have fresh air and lots of exercise. I don't like to work inside, even in winter. Most people aren't as flawed as I am, and would appreciate the ease of my present position."

"I like my job," the giant said. "We can sleep in the hay, and no one disturbs us."

"You aren't guarded?"

"For three men? Why would they bother?"

"But you could just take a horse and ride away."

"Who knows how to ride a horse?" the giant said. He moved his head from side to side. "What's in it for me? I never heard of shrimp." His eyes sparkled, at least as far as they could be said to sparkle.

Alessandro refrained from questioning him, knowing that whatever was rolling around inside of him was going to come out, just as in the case of a man who counts his coins over and over again and never fails to drop at least one.

"Besides," the giant said, with a corrupt smile, "nothing in your job matches what I have in mine."

"What's that?"

"Klodwig's a faggot. All the footmen are faggots. And a lot of our guys, years without a woman, got to be faggots, too."

"But not you."

"Not me," the giant said with a smile that dropped a few bombs of drool.

"Because you," Alessandro said, "you..."

"What's the matter, can't you say it? Maybe you're a faggot, too. Say it. I *do* it."

"You do what?" Alessandro asked delicately.

"I fuck the horses."

"The male ones also?"

"Of course not. Just the ladies. I get on a stool, close my eyes, and make believe I'm screwing Quagliagliarella, but when I get home I may never screw Quagliagliarella again. I should work in the zoo. Someday I'll intercourse a rhinoceros, or possibly a giraffe."

"What about an elephant?"

"Not elephants. Them and hippopotamuses are not alluring to me. So," the giant said, leaning back. "What can you possibly have up there that's better than what I have here?"

AT NIGHT, as he walked the deserted corridors of the palace, Alessandro had time to take stock of his situation. In the high boxy halls, the ends of which were so distant from one another that he could not see both at once, pitch-black shadows danced with orange firelight from enameled stoves the size of blast furnaces. This was a place where one might summon ghosts.

Between the hours of two and six, he rarely encountered a tray, and was free to sit in any one of the forbidden gilt-and-velour chairs that lined his route. Klodwig would have beaten him had Klodwig found out, but Klodwig and his footmen had a pompous step that gave them away in advance of their arrival, and someone moving was far easier to see than someone sitting still. Alessandro had only to make sure not to drift off to sleep. Once, when he had, he was awakened by a footman screaming *"Schlafen Sie?,"* but the footman had been the attendant of a Polish duchess, and had not even known that Alessandro was a prisoner.

Sometimes Klodwig raced along like a silky bat, hunting sleepy menials, but as he turned corners he gave himself away by the whoosh of air, and in the time it took his eyes to focus, Alessandro would have shifted to his knees on the floor, sweeping crumbs from under the chair in which he had been resting. Klodwig always felt the seat. Thus, as Alessandro swept crumbs, he blew cool air over the upholstery, and it worked.

A week before Christmas, his plans for escape having gone nowhere, Alessandro stood next to one of the huge stoves, at the end of a corridor half a kilometer in length. The stove was a bulging, smooth, snowy-white thing as high as five men, disgustingly encrusted with gold leaf. As the winds Bernoullied across the chimney pipes they made the flames erratic, and shadows flew about the walls and ceiling like mystically quick fleets of immense black birds.

It was four-thirty in the morning. At dinner, Alessandro and the other prisoners had heard an orchestra practicing beyond the dining hall of the footmen. Over and over again, perhaps 150 times, with bassoons, oboes, and piccolos embedded within the brass and strings like songbirds in a hedge, they had played the "Swiss Yodeling Song," and now Alessandro could not get it out of his head. It was the perfect accompaniment to the cold mists and snow racing past the palace windows, for beyond the mist and coal smoke were the high mountains covered with blinding ice, where he had always returned to cast off human confusions.

Swaying slightly to and fro, immeasurably fatigued, the "Yodeling Song" echoing through his soul, he communed with his father. As in life, he told him the news. Though Europe was now at peace, Alessandro was a prisoner of war dressed in a pajama-like costume with red tabs on the cuffs and shoulders. He wandered the halls of the Austrian Imperial Palace from dusk to daylight, picking up trays from which he stole chocolates and shrimp, and sampled the best champagne, warm and flat, from the bottoms of many a bottle.

Other than that, he subsisted on a diet of potatoes and salt. He slept in the day and at night played a continuous game of catch-me-if-you-can with a bat-like footman in a powdered wig.

To escape, Alessandro would have to find some way of appealing to a man whose dream was to copulate with a rhinoceros, steal one of the world's most famous and, needless to say, conspicuous horses, ride through Vienna in a purloined uniform, work his will on the Ministry of War by speaking German in a Hungarian accent, find and kill an unknown airplane pilot, and get to the Alps, the white and fatal vastness of which he would cross on foot, all so that he might return to Rome.

AT SIX in the morning, trying to suppress visions induced by fatigue, and moving slowly to preserve his strength, Alessandro walked past the warm basement kitchens where a thousand things were simmering and baking, cooks were squeezing pastry tubes as if they were wrestling anacondas, and exhausted prisoners were up to their elbows in huge cauldrons scrubbing off caked food in lakes of lukewarm water saturated with soap and muck. They had twelve or fifteen hours to go, and it was not the easiest time of day.

He passed the cold-rooms and the harness shops, the carpenters' studio, the wig salon, and the hall where legions of footmen waited on call and jumped up like jacks-in-the-box when their bells sounded on a huge mahogany board. He passed the armory, where a thousand well oiled rifles and sparkling bayonets waited in symmetrical rows. And just before the cobblestoned turn in the long tunnel that led up to the Spanische Reitschule in one direction and the Winterreitschule in another, he came to the laundry.

Thirty copper cauldrons as big as carriages stood over salamandrine flares of flaming methane that swayed slowly back and forth like bouquets of windblown cotton candy. In boiling seas trapped under copper domes were the dresses, shirts, uniforms, underwear, coats, towels, bed linen, napkins, tablecloths, and tapestries of empire. The laundry advertised that it washed in three shifts and never shut down. A line of footmen and chambermaids, some with baskets and others with small carts, faced a long counter behind which half a dozen laundry clerks received or returned the many different items that passed through the kettles. The clerks disappeared into a dark forest of iron racks, and emerged with arms full of clothing or linen. Alessandro stepped into line and observed the procedure.

Beyond the twenty footmen and maids ahead of him in line were the clerks. Speaking too softly to hear, the maids spoke in laundry code, and shortly thereafter their arms ballooned around sumptuous silk and velvet dresses. The line moved fast, and Alessandro didn't know what to do, until a frail footman put down a colorful uniform spattered with medals and announced that he was leaving it on behalf of Leutnant Fresser. A little old man carried the uniform into the depth and darkness of the racks.

Several minutes later Alessandro confronted a stout woman with strong hands and spectacles. The old man had dipped back into the sea of garments and was nowhere to be seen, so Alessandro said, as casually as he could, "Leutnant Fresser must have his uniform now."

"Is it due this morning?" the woman asked, as if to lay down the law.

"No, it was recently brought in."

"It takes five days to take it apart, clean it, and sew it back together," the woman said, happy to educate a slave in the ways of upper class laundering.

"Leutnant Fresser has been called to the field."

"Just as long as he doesn't blame us for not having finished it," the woman said. She wouldn't move until Alessandro agreed, and he deliberately took his time.

Then she disappeared, and returned with the uniform held like a newborn on display. "Is this it?"

"Yes. There's his medal from the battle of Sborniki Setaslava."

Alessandro hurried away in obsequious steps. Noting that the uniform appeared to be his size, he rolled it up, put it under his arm, returned to the empty barracks, and laid it out under his mattress, where it was safer than the crown jewels of Austria, for who in the world would ever look under the mattress of an Italian prisoner of war?

Alessandro took a drink of water, brushed his teeth, and threw himself down on the bed. Were he to wait a month or two, or perhaps until spring, he would be released. He wanted, however, to exit the Winter Palace not in a gray line of prisoners, but on a white horse. He wanted to ride across the Austrian countryside and over the mountains not in a third-class carriage, but ahead of the remnants of the pursuing Austrian army.

He knew that this was because the war was still in him, and that it would be in him for a long time to come, for soldiers who have been blooded are soldiers forever. They never fit in. Even when they finally settle down, the settling is tenuous, for when they close their eyes they see their comrades who have fallen. That they cannot forget, that they do not forget, that they never allow themselves to heal completely, is their way of expressing their love for friends who have perished. And they will not change, because they have become what they have become to keep the fallen alive.

ON ONE of the upper floors was a long corridor with the typical stove at each end. Because it was reached by spiral stairs and led only to a cul de sac in which were three suites, it was seldom used. The guests who were shunted to these rooms were of relatively low station, knew that they were obliged to stay out of the way, and, being from far provinces, went to bed early. On several occasions Alessandro had had the vast hall to himself from dusk to dawn.

He had brazenly slept upon the carpet and stoked the stoves until they whitened like blast furnaces. The hall was flecked with shadow bursts, and tiny explosions of light went aglimmering from the frosted glass to the angels painted on the panels high above. They winked, their wings fluttered like the wings of hummingbirds, and the sinuous patterns that emerged from the thousands of abrupt beats were like the magical reversals of a rapidly spinning wheel. And the snow, driving at the windows and then disappearing, seemed to have been created for a prisoner hallucinating with melancholy and fatigue.

Alessandro passed the hours drawn to Rome and the south, his neck stiff with the chore of supporting his head, held unnaturally so that his eyes might capture the unseen light of memory. Electricity coursed through him to the extent that, had he been made of metal, he might have given off sparks. In unguarded conversation the sentries on the Isonzo had alluded to such things, to ghosts and visions that came to them just before dawn, the heart beating on the edge, eyes held open as if with an invisible hook.

At about three in the morning, as snowflakes churned outside the windows like an artist's exaggeration of a storm at sea, Alessandro heard a faint sound coming from one of the suites. It grew louder, as if whoever was causing it had lost his initial fear of discovery and was consumed by the music of his own making.

And what music. Alessandro had never heard such sounds. He recognized neither the instruments nor the irresistible scales that seemed to have come from the vast and languid plains of a different world. He thought he was dreaming.

As he approached the sound, he was so tired that he struggled to remember his own name, and could not, as if he had only half awakened from a winter nap. Forbidden to look at his superiors, much less walk into a room unannounced, he turned the latch and stepped in quietly, protected only by recourse to questions and statements such as, "You sent for me to collect the dishes?" or "The chef recommends the salmon pâté."

As soon as he was in the reception room he smelled a peculiar kind of smoke that started all his senses fighting against it for control. He won this fight as he proceeded to the main salon, whence came the music, now loud, all-encompassing, and unbearably hypnotic.

Underneath a cloud of blue haze that remained even though the windows had been thrown open to the extent that wind and snow periodically invaded the room, three musicians sat cross-legged on a Persian rug. They might have been Indians, Turks, or Gypsies, and their instruments had the strange proportions and bulbous shapes that Western instruments had lost long before. The fret board on the stringed apparatus was as tall as the man who was playing it, and its base looked like a gourd. It was a gourd. The drums were clipped and curt. They were like neither thunder nor gunfire, but the quick hoofbeats of goats. Alessandro wondered for whom the musicians were playing. For themselves? For a notable? For a satyr who busied himself behind a screen with a box of Egyptian sexual utensils? As Alessandro cast his eyes around the room, he saw nothing but a huge platform covered by what looked like one of the piles of clothes that had been stripped from the dead after a big battle. He wondered what this would be doing in a suite of guest rooms in the Hofburg, in the custody of Indian musicians who played under a cloud of opium smoke. Perhaps, he thought, it was a religious object, a shrine, such as the *Ka'aba* in Mecca. Or perhaps it was a tent in which a dissolute Austrian noble lay puffing a hookah or molesting a cousin.

Then it moved, shifting from left to right and back again, rising in the center before it settled. Alessandro realized that the point to which it came was the back of someone's head. Thinking that a man or a woman was sitting in a chair within a tent of some sort, he walked around to face the occupant. As he did, a column of bluish white smoke rose from the nostrils.

When he came face to face with the person who had exhaled the smoke, his mouth dropped open. It was a being—the whole thing—seated on a chair that it completely subsumed. The mounds of cloth were merely a few capes that had been thrown over a woman who held the end of a water-pipe in her right hand. Her left hand twitched slightly as it hung in the air, cantilevered by foothills of rolled fat.

In one of his essays on painting, Alessandro had expressed the opinion that a face cannot adequately be described in words, or even in sculpture, that it was a province exclusively of the painters, that the recognition of a face was wholly dependent upon the ineffably expressed variations of light and color for which language had few words and sculpture no shapes. Of the infinite variety of angles and intersections that make a smile, language has no inkling: not only no words, but not even numbers. Alessandro had speculated for ten printed pages on the helplessness of photographs and many paintings, the terrible inadequacy of statuary and death masks, even the inadequacy, in death, of a face itself. Only the great visual artists could describe a face, he had said, and poets would be wise not to try.

In an instant, however, standing before this sirenian creature, he knew that he hadn't gotten it quite right. He now realized, almost in shock, that a face may be described in words, or photographs, or a death mask, with perfect adequacy—if only it is sufficiently hideous. The chin was nonexistent. Her jaw, however, was enormous. The lower part looked like a balcony at the opera and was covered with loose mottled skin and moles from which emerged tufts of coarse black hair. Her whitened gums bled, for her teeth were at war with themselves, lying like crossed swords or splayed bodies, leaning either out of her mouth or in, and trying to bridge by horizontal leaps the enormous gaps between them. They were not admirable even individually, like piano keys or mah-jong blocks, but black or brown and shaped like stumps that had been blown apart by dynamite.

And of her ugliness this was only the beginning. Her lips were so big and fleshy that they looked like the spongy bumpers on harbor tugs, and their slick intestinal pink was relieved only by bleeding cracks and aging scabs. The sides of her porcine nose oscillated with her labored breathing, and her eyes bulged so that Alessandro, horrified, was ready to catch them were they to pop out at him like champagne corks.

And then he shuddered in awe. "I know you," he said, thinking that perhaps he was dreaming.

She replied in a froggy voice from deep in a trance of opium or hashish. "I hide, but many people know me."

"Ich träumte, ich tanzte mit einem Schwan," Alessandro said. "I

dreamed I was dancing with a swan. *Er hatte der wunderbarsten flauschigen Polster an den Füssen.* He had the most wonderful fluffy pillows on his feet. *Und er war auf einem Mondstrahl in mein Zimmer gekommen.* And he came into my room on a moonbeam."

She stirred. She seemed to be struggling with her memories, but perhaps because of the drugs or because she was too moved by the recollection of days when she had been—relatively at least—a sylph, she made no response.

Not knowing what to say, Alessandro tried to make conversation, but he was so stunned that he could only manage, "So, how much do you weigh now?"

A dark cloud passed over her. "Five hundred and sixty kilos."

"But, the spiral stairs . . ."

"Outside the window," she said, "are a beam, a hook, and a pulley," and then she bent her head, although it was not able to bend very far, in shame. "That was you?" she asked.

He nodded.

"I remember," she told him. "And now you're a prisoner, even though the war is over?"

"I think so, yes."

"Not many prisoners end up in the Hofburg."

"Strassnitzky brought me. He had no need for me in the Belvedere."

"Blasius Strassnitzky?"

"Yes."

"Poor Blasius. He would have had no need for you in any case."

"Why?"

"He was killed."

Alessandro briefly closed his eyes. "You must be mistaken."

"No," Lorna said. "The Italians had too many prisoners. The emperor needed more to trade, and to hold the throne he had to show that even though he had delivered the empire into the hands of the enemy he had made a final gesture, done a deed of valor. His final gesture was Strassnitzky. He and nearly all his men were killed in a cavalry charge against a fortified line and machine guns. They took no prisoners, they only sacrificed themselves.

"Blasius was always very funny," she continued. "We played together as children. He seemed so alive, so full of stories and tricks and funny ways to say things. I'm sorry for him, I'm sorry that he perished.

"For him it must have been hard to die. In that respect, we, who began life together, will have ended very differently. For me the world is hardly a pleasure. I smoke opium and hashish so that I may spend my life in dreams—it will be easy to die."

"Of what do you dream?" Alessandro asked, having opened his eyes.

Her face grew almost sunny.

"I dream of when I was a baby. My father and my mother loved me. They carried me in their arms, and they kissed me. They could hardly stop kissing me. Even when I was three and four, they embraced me all the time. If I could have a child, I would love her beyond anything that anyone would be capable of imagining. I would live for her. I have so much love in me, so much. It goes nowhere but to dreams."

"Why haven't you had a child?" Alessandro asked.

"The child would be too ugly," she answered, "and would suffer as I have. Besides, no man has ever held me, much less made love to me. In my dreams, I dream of that, too."

"Would he have to be tender?" Alessandro asked.

"No."

"Would he have to know, as you know, what it is to love and be loved?"

"No," she said. "I could pretend."

Not quite able to believe what he was doing, Alessandro spoke in a voice that startled her. "I know a man who lusts for you."

She wept.

"But *I* have needs," he shouted. "*I* have needs!"

"What needs?" she asked from amidst her tears.

"You are of the royal house. You can get things done."

"What things?" she asked. "What things?"

"You can have someone look into a file, to find out about a war hero."

"Yes yes. I am sure. I am of the royal house."

"Then, Lorna," Alessandro said, "make a pact with your swan."

As DINNER was ending and the prisoners leaving their benches, the giant still sat under the kerosene lamp at the midpoint of one of the tables. Someone was singing the *"Libiamo..."* from *La Traviata,* and singing it so beautifully that the flames in the lamps seemed to dance in joy. Alessandro circled the table. Because he kept his eyes on the giant's huge head, the room appeared to spin around it.

He watched the great Neapolitan face, twice the size of a normal face, and as the background in motion, bathed in golden light, blended with the aria, he thought of the difference between the music of his country and the music of the country in which he was captive. Italian music was bound at all times by the limitations of the human heart, never more exuberant or elated than a heart could be without breaking, or sadder than a heart could be without taking hope. In the music of the North, sadness prolonged joy far less, and in dejection no light appeared against the dark. The extremes were magnificent, but it had not the most human of all attributes, balance.

It appeared that even the giant Neapolitan, a violator of draft animals, was moved by the aria, so Alessandro opened the conversation on a relatively high plane.

"So beautiful, like a sunset over the roofs of Naples."

"What sunset?" the giant asked.

"The one in the west."

"Which one is that?"

"The one that takes place in the evening. In the Bay of Naples, ships flee to all parts of the Mediterranean, disappearing into the darkness, moving slowly and steadily under fading and bobbing lights."

The giant stopped eating and turned to Alessandro, looking him over very carefully. "You're not a priest," he said.

"No, I'm not."

"You don't dress like one."

"That's right."

"So what are you talking about?"

"Music."

"What music?"

"Indian music. Do you like Indian music?"

"I don't know what it is."

"It's music from India."

"India?"

"Yes, a country that has many rhinoceroses."

The giant was skeptical. "How many?"

"As many as you want."

"Who owns them?"

"The Bank of India. All citizens, however, and all visitors, are free to ride them and take care of them, feed them hay, feed them oats . . . bed them down."

"Where is this country?"

"It's far, but not that far. You can get there on a ship. Wouldn't you like to listen to the music? The music comes from the places where rhinos wander in vast numbers. I can arrange for you to hear it. Shall I?"

"I don't know," the giant said. "Am I allowed to?"

"Sometimes," Alessandro said, "we do things that we're not supposed to do, don't we?"

"Yes, we do."

"Good. I'll set everything up. For one night, you'll take my job, and I'll take yours."

"A whole night? I don't want to listen to Indian music for a whole night."

"You will find much more than music where I send you," Alessandro said.

"I will?"

"Yes."

As the giant's eyes sparkled in belief and disbelief, Alessandro thought, never mind her sadness, for she must turn directly to God, who cannot but answer her.

LORNA WAS acquainted with an official of the Ministry of War who might have been her twin. Even though they had beheld one another merely once or twice, two prisoners tortured on the same rack could not have had more mutual empathy or trust. To break the rules for the sake of someone for whom all the rules had been shattered at birth was both pleasurable revenge and the cause of great satisfaction: the pilot's dossier had been copied and compiled, sub rosa and without a trace, in a dozen different departments, and it was carefully bound between gray covers with embossed silver lettering. Alessandro guessed that a high official who requested a report would get something similar, on rag-paper pages that had been through a typewriter that could print red, green, and black.

The formation over Gruensee had been *Kampfstaffel* D3, flying Hansa-Brandenburg D3 aircraft. A neatly typed list matched the pilots with their planes, and in 5X, a number that had settled in Alessandro's memory forever, had been a Major Hans Alfred Andri, whose operational report was appended. He had thoroughly strafed and bombed an enemy mounted column and destroyed several buildings in the village of Gruensee, but had not been thorough enough to mention in his account that every building in

Gruensee had had a red cross on a white background clearly visible on the roof. Perhaps in five or ten years inquiries would arrive in the Austrian Foreign Ministry and this might be discussed.

Andri had flown sixty-three missions, and when the war ended he had returned to 87/1/4 Schellingstrasse, in Munich. Schellingstrasse was not far from the Alte Pinakothek, where Alessandro had first heard the guns.

WHEN ALESSANDRO was awakened at dawn, the day was charged with the energy of a lightning storm in the snow. He could hardly keep his limbs still as he followed the roiling black and gray clouds that tumbled over the city, riding on their first light after having been born on the steppes of Russia. Vast thunderheads accumulated in the east, piling up and growing high. The currents, tumblings, and precipitous falls within gave the staid black and gray masses a sense of movement. The crows that in winter fled Russia for the Austrian plains were circling on high by the thousands, black confetti against the light. Falling and rising at remarkable speed, they stiffened their wings as they sought to stay still in the powerful waves of air.

When Alessandro, and the giant's two companions, reached the stables, they idled until they had idled too long, and then began to work. Everyone had a cart and a grinder, and each took a row of stalls. When they didn't see Alessandro emerge from his row with the grindings, they thought that he was working slowly. Then they saw him staggering down the aisle, a saddle and bridle in his arms.

"What are you doing?" one of them asked. In four years, he had never seen such a thing.

"What does it look like I'm doing?" Alessandro answered.

They followed him into the stall of a Lippizaner and watched him saddle and bridle the horse. "You're not supposed to do that!" they said.

"I know."

"So why are you doing it?"

"Why am I in this place?" Alessandro asked them, turning briefly away from his work. "Why are you? Were you born here? The war is over."

"The sentry will shoot as you exit," one of them said, smiling almost in satisfaction. "You won't get twenty meters."

Finished with the horse, Alessandro took off his shirt, pants, and boots, until he stood before them totally naked. They thought he was crazy, until he unrolled the uniform, and then they said, "Ah!"

After dressing quickly, he faced the two open-mouthed manure grinders. "Stop looking at me as if I were Zeus," he commanded.

"You'll be shot," they cautioned.

"No. I won't be shot. I'm going to shoot them, and then I'll go home. I'll be perfectly safe. I can see the future, and the clouds are lifting."

"You can see the future? How can you see the future?"

"I know enough now about the patterns of the past to see the darkness of the future unraveling before the golden light of time. Behind the clouds is the dawn. How can I possibly know such things? The fact is, I do. So watch out."

They protested that if he escaped they would be shot, so he had to hit them on the back of their heads with a manure shovel. Because they were terrified of combat, something they had never seen, he was forced to chase them around the stall. They thought that being hit by a manure shovel would kill them, as it might have, but Alessandro managed to put them gently to sleep in the hay.

He unhitched the Lippizaner. With the reins and bridle in his left hand and the manure shovel hanging from his right, he walked to the guard booth at the ramp.

The guard came out because he was curious about what he had already perceived to have been an irregularity. "Hold the reins," Alessandro told him. He did so obediently.

"You are German, sir?" he asked as Alessandro walked behind him.

"No," Alessandro said, "Italian," and then whacked him on the head with the shovel. He took the guard's pistol and a wallet stuffed with money, then dragged him into the sentry booth and covered him with a blanket.

The horse was skittish. His limbs were twitching, his strength begging for an outlet.

THROUGH THE open door of the freight car in which Alessandro rode toward Linz and Munich, the moon shone brightly over fields and mountains and seemed to jump from place to place as the train changed its heading. The illusion that the moon was bathed in the glow of the snow-covered ground preceded from the fact that the moon does not generate its own light, and is lit from elsewhere. The soldiers on the train were not able to see the sun, now rising in the Western Hemisphere, but they could see the brilliantly lit snow, and perhaps because their world had been turned upside down they suffered the illusion without protest.

The moon was so close and full that it resembled the Roman moon in August, stunningly light and perfectly round as it rides above the horizon like a float on the waves, bathing the palms of the Tiber, the broken monuments, and the ash-colored fields in the warm light of its youth before it silvers in the cold.

Riding with Alessandro were Germans and Austrians who had been prisoners in the east, Frenchmen trying to get to Paris, thieves, deserters, active units returning to bases and camps, farmers going back to their farms, and fathers coming home to their children. They were dressed in dozens of different uniforms, nonuniforms, military coats without insignia, civilian coats with insignia, and even in blankets stenciled with camp names and directions for putting out fires. They wore helmets with spikes, Italian or British flat helmets, mouton caps, wool socks, and officers' hats, and they carried bundles, packs, and sacks tied with puttee straps and artillery lanyards. After years of painful shaving with hand-held blades, cold water, and no soap, they now had beards in all stages of growth, and they knew that when they returned home in tatters and blankets, with gaunt faces, and eyes that sparkled like stars, they would frighten their families, but that after they bathed and as they gradually put on weight and lost the sparkle in their eyes, their families would slowly understand what they had been through, and would embrace them.

Not everyone had families. Alessandro did not. Still, he found that he lacked certain anxieties, for unlike travelers who are expected he did not have to report home or send telegrams. He could take a side trip to Portugal or Japan and never come back, and no one would miss him. Wherever Luciana was, she could only have heard that he was dead.

As he stared at the moon floating lightly above the mountains he realized that returning homeward all throughout Europe were those who had been given up for lost, who had been mistakenly put on the lists of the fallen, who had disappeared, who had been captured, or left for dead. After all the unexpected reunions, even the families of the dead would take hope, only to be battered by the disappointment of the years that followed.

A hundred thousand miracles lay in wait, and millions of tragedies would have to be relived. Alessandro thought with not a little bitterness of the husbands who would unexpectedly return to their wives, and the fathers who would take their children by surprise as they were playing in the front yard, but when he saw the children freeze, and then run to their fathers' arms, his bitterness left him. The more he imagined the scenes of return, expected or unexpected, the more he wished the best for those who would have such luck, and the more he loved them and their children.

———

LYING AGAINST a mound of straw as he tried to keep the wind from under two blankets that he had bought, Alessandro held the 9mm pistol he had stolen from the sentry, in case someone in the mass of men huddled in the car should dislike Italians or covet what he had left. He tried to think of something to tell the border guards. In the chaos of defeat, the demarcations between Germany and Austria had not faded, and each jealously guarded what remained to it.

The long train had started in Russia where the railway gauges shifted, and was so full of men without papers that Alessandro hoped to be passed over. If he wrote all his answers they might think he was German. Many Germans who had served with the Austrian army had left informally when the end of the war whetted their appetites for home, but Alessandro had no wound on his throat to which he could point, no pink line or star-like scar to explain a lack of speech. Had anyone had any alcohol, he might have feigned intoxication, but he could not get drunk on potato soup. Nor could he successfully pretend feeblemindedness, for then he would be hard put to explain the pistol, the relatively large amount of cash, and the uniform of an imperial officer. The pistol itself was a problem, but were he to hide it he might never see it again, and he needed it.

It was too cold, he was too tired, and the train was now going far too fast for him to jump off. He imagined that if the habits of war persisted he might be arrested and shot as a spy, and it seemed that the war was quite alive. In the absence of one of Orfeo's official documents with a waxen seal as big as a dessert plate, how could anyone really know?

After the previous few years, a border and border guards did not seem insurmountable, and yet he could not get off the train and he was too tired to think of a way to save himself, so he stopped thinking and fell asleep.

When he awoke, the train had halted in the cold winter light that seeps across the mountains at dawn. Even though the doors faced south temporarily and were open upon the advancing sunrise, the air that flowed in was unrelievedly frigid.

As the tips of rifles passed by, Alessandro heard footsteps on the snow, but no one looked inside. He heard the muffled voices of border officials at dawn. The officials were always more awake and assertive than the passengers, but, deep down, they were far more tired.

They were ignoring Alessandro's car. A man had been killed in the one next to it, a bayonet put through his heart because someone had wanted his wool hat, and the body had to be removed.

Then two officials pulled themselves up in a practiced move that left them towering above the men who lay on the straw-covered floor. They had the instinctive cruelty of border guards, but were so puzzled at having lost the war that they found it difficult to be inquisitive. One asked for papers, but left off when a ragged soldier had difficulty unbuckling his knapsack to get them. The other asked if anyone had heard sounds from the next car. He was greeted by silence and the hiss of an idling steam engine. He looked around, judging each face, and when he got to Alessandro he increased his pace, hardly touching him with his gaze. Alessandro, it seemed, looked all right. Besides, at dawn, in the cold, who wanted to step amidst the louse-and-flea-ridden prisoners and common soldiers returning from the east?

He leapt down perfectly and the other guard followed. After a minute or two, another set of officials put their hands against the doors and were about to jump up when someone called to them from out in the field and they changed their minds.

Soon the train was rolling, the sun was up, and Alessandro was sleeping. The blankets were now warm enough, the air was fresh, and they would be in Munich by afternoon. Before he slept, he felt tremendous anxiety about what he was going to do, but the rhythmic pattern of the wheels over the joints in the rails cast him into darkness.

————

MUNICH WAS an enemy city, and a city of art. Snow had fallen heavily the night before, and by early afternoon the winds that had shepherded-in a brittle blue mountain sky attacked vulnerable cornices of snow, blasting them into skittish towers, white whirlpools, and sparkling dervishes formed from sun-catching mist.

The first thing Alessandro saw in Munich was a corpulent beggar, in a restaurant near the station, moving among diners for whom he made silhouette portraits in bread. With two long, narrow, rodentine front upper teeth, he effortlessly sawed the exact profile of anyone who gave him a piece of bread. Alessandro saw him put the finishing touches on a portrait in rye of a woman with a gorgeously pointed nose that seemed to ride far out in front of her face like something floating in the air. The beggar then ate the art and moved on to the next table. Only in Germany, Alessandro thought, could a beggar be fat.

He began to wander, seeking out not the streets that were comfortable and close, but those that, like London's roads, disappeared rifle-straight into a point in the distance. Looking down a long boulevard, he saw trees tossing snow skyward as they were buffeted by the wind. Because of the bright light, he could see ten thousand shining windows and a nearly infinite number of refractions in the detail that the centuries had worked into the stone. The sky was sapphire over Munich and pale white over the Alps as masses of distant snow changed the eye's perception of blue.

Mesmerized by the form and color of peace, he wandered with no object, knowing that eventually he would find a hotel, buy civilian clothes and a newspaper—an Italian newspaper, were one available—and that he would take a bath and pay for extra hot water. Had he not spent four years in war he could not have wandered on the boulevards for many hours in hunger and cold, for cold was something he had learned to endure, and hunger a state he could sustain for weeks. He walked the city, watching the faces of women and children, the old, and others he knew had stayed behind, because they still had antiquated expressions of comfort, as if they would never encounter the blackness or blaze into which Alessandro's fellow soldiers had risen by the million.

When a flight of geese crossed the sky above him, Alessandro thought of Raphael. As the formation intersected the line of the boulevard, the chain of birds locked wing in quick succession to meet a strong gust of wind and, like a kite's tail following an ascending kite, rocketed upward as if they had been launched from a ramp. In the Loggia of Leo X, in the Vatican, Raphael had sent a V formation of geese vaulting into the clouds with their wings locked to take a violent wind. He had accomplished great feats of perspective and bewildered the eye into believing that a solid ceiling was a row of airy windows on the blue, and in these bright windows he had placed birds struggling in the air. In the central panel, in pale desert colors touched with fire, surrounded by winged angels and cherubim, God is giving the tablets of the law to Moses, but the eye is drawn to left and right to be lifted through the lesser panels that show the open sky. On the left are the geese, gripped by the force of the wind, and on the right, in a nearly empty space, an owl and a swallow. The owl is looking down as if he were perched on the roof and peering inside. The swallow is passing from corner to corner at great speed, close to the imaginary window. He is there only for an instant, but the strength of his extended wings, the length of his narrow double tail, and the bullet-like shape of his body cutting through the wind have branded his image permanently upon the glass.

In his youth Raphael had sung with color and painted with the courage of a soldier, but in later works he had abandoned the exquisite for the deep, and painted as if with his eyes open not to the world but to the far greater field in which the world is set—as if he had begun to see new perspective, new color, new gravity, and new light. And it was all framed as a question, for although he sensed what was beyond, he could not, for the first time in his life, trust his extraordinary vision to tell him what lay there. He was able only to feel, but what he had seen and how he had seen it propelled him on into a darkness filled with questions he could not answer and a gratitude he could not explain. The figures in his paintings suddenly are unsure, and they do not understand what is happening. It is as if they are witnessing a miracle, but the miracle is far from over.

ALESSANDRO FOUND himself, as he had hoped, in a hot bath. He was almost free, but memories still tormented him and images appeared in rapid sequence, vanishing before he could comprehend their completed conversation with his spirit. As he bought new clothing, ate in a restaurant, or arranged for a bath in the hotel, they flew at him like birds in a storm, and he could find no release from their exhausting impact, for each, in some way, touched upon the truth. To awaken in this manner after years of war was too much to bear, and to prevent himself from breaking under the strain he tried to take simple inventories: he spoke to himself about what he had done that day, and took note of the minutiae of the bathroom in which he lay in a steaming tub of hot water all the way up to his blessed collar-bone.

The ceiling rose five meters into a narrow box of darkness filled with clouds of steam. The walls were glossy white, and the temperature of the room not much greater than the temperature outside. In a hopeless attempt to do away with the excessive steam from his extravagantly applied hot water, Alessandro had opened the window a crack. Beyond it was the black of night, and through it came a torrent of air so frigid that the collision between it and rising steam sent white clouds violently curling over the top of the water, spilling from the tub and cascading to the floor.

The tank that heated the water was affixed to the wall. A crown of gas flames roared within its steel base as it gurgled, boiled, and whistled like a tea kettle. From a spout that hung over the porcelain rim of the bathtub as if it were a brass elephant's trunk came a thick stream of hot water that plummeted to the floor of the tub and spread out as it rose. The excess spilled into an overflow, with a sound similar to that of water coursing between two boulders that speed it up until it is silver.

Hot, red, and semi-conscious, Alessandro glanced at the chair that held his new clothes: a pair of leather mountaineering boots oiled for waterproofness, a navy-blue flannel shirt, a Chamonix sweater, a gun-metal-colored parka with the hood rolled into the collar, Dachstein mittens, a heavy wool hat, and an angora scarf. In his Eiger sack were half a dozen chocolate bars, half a kilo of dried beef, a kilo of bread, and some fruit leather. He had a water bottle, a compass, a candle lantern, matches, and extra candles. A pair of crampons was strapped to the pack, and on each side, through loops provided for the purpose, were ice axes, one short and one long.

He had bought these things at a mountaineering equipment store that he had visited before the war and that now had neither customers nor maps. They told him that they would have both only after a treaty, because the mountains and foothills were strategic.

In one pocket of Alessandro's parka were a rail ticket to Garmisch-Partenkirchen, and the pistol he had removed from the guard at the Winterreitschule. He hadn't the time to take the extra clips on the soldier's belt, and was therefore limited to ten rounds. One, perhaps two, would have to do for Andri, and with the eight or nine left he would defend himself from the German and Austrian mountain divisions that blocked the way south. He was neither optimistic nor pessimistic of his chances, having learned that in dangerous initiatives, battle, and escape, optimism and pessimism have no place.

Reeling with the sensations of the bath—every so often the dark window would rattle in a gust of wind, or because a train passed on a nearby rail line—he was anything but soldierly. He had had a huge dinner of beef soup, pot roast, potatoes, salad, and beer. He almost fell asleep, and it was difficult to stand up once he had let the water out and gravity back in. In his room, the sheets were cold and white, the air fresh from winter winds that whistled through the cracks. For a moment he lay staring at his clothes and equipment neatly ordered by the bed and illumined in the glare of an electric light. When he turned off the lamp the room was filled with Raphael's colors—the greens and reds that had no name. They came as if to lead him over the walls of the mountains and down into the warmth and glory of Rome.

As ALESSANDRO walked through the streets of Munich early in the morning the snow was softer than it had been the day before, the sun hotter. He had a soldier's gait, and when he knocked at the major's door his breathing was shallow, as if of rarefied air. He squinted, not because of the light but because the muscles of his face were taut.

The door swung open and revealed a tall man in an Edwardian suit covered by a medical jacket with a caduceus embroidered on the sleeve. The jacket was stained in oil paints of many colors, and the smell of turpentine flooded out the door with the heated air of the house.

At first the former major was puzzled by a man that he thought looked like an English mountain climber. Alessandro pushed him inside, closed the door after them, and drew the pistol. Andri dared not speak.

Alessandro motioned him backward into a large room that looked out through French doors into a garden. In this studio filled with paintings was a three-quarters-finished study of men in the trenches, their backs to the viewer, peering over a landscape of shattered trees and burning brush.

"To hell with you," Alessandro said. "I don't care if your paintings are good or not."

Andri understood his situation, but, like Alessandro, he had been a soldier and was unafraid to die. He had the same feeling that he had had each time he pushed his plane into a dive or sharply banked to attack a group of enemy fighters. He smiled half bitterly and said, "I see that the war has done wonders for art criticism. You used to be relatively sheepish, but now you get right to the point. You've come to avenge an action in the air."

"Yes," Alessandro answered.

"Were you a pilot?"

"An infantryman."

"The strafing of the Col di Lana? Your trenches were badly laid out. For us, it was a field day. You had only one anti-aircraft gun, and it stopped firing. I could understand your being here if you were in the Col di Lana."

"It wasn't the Col di Lana."

"The Kleinalpenspitze?"

Alessandro shook his head.

"The Grossen Schonleitschneid? What you call the Dolomiti di Sesto?"

With each wrong guess, Andri felt that he was digging his grave a little deeper, but that it would have been worse to stop.

"In the Brenta?"

"Yes."

"The mounted column at Gruensee."

"Not the mounted column, they were soldiers."

"What, then?" Andri asked, lifting his shoulders.

"The hospital."

"My bombs went astray," Andri said with a tiny bit of indignation, and most convincingly. "The column was hard between the buildings."

"That's your first lie."

"It isn't."

"It is. I was there. I saw it. The column had scattered, nothing was left to bomb; yet you came back. You flew at a cross-angle. The hit was direct."

"That's not so!" Andri insisted.

"But it is so," Alessandro added quietly. "I read the operational report that you wrote."

"How could you have?" Andri asked, shifting from indignation to something that was a combination of panic and irritation. "How did you find me? That's how you found me? You got the report from the Austrian army? Are they insane?"

"Remarkable, isn't it," Alessandro stated rather than asked, "that the masters of the bureaucracy are the masters of the world."

"Things happen in war," Andri said, trying to save his life. "Neither side has a lock on virtue." He despaired. "You've come to kill me."

"I have."

"What a waste. I could paint. I could paint for forty years."

"You're going to die."

"What good will it do?"

"I don't think of it that way. For me it's purely justice—not so much utilitarian, but aesthetic. Consult your texts on symmetry. The good that it will do? Maybe, in another war, you would have bombed another hospital."

"There won't be another war, not in our lifetime."

"Not in yours," Alessandro said, pulling back the hammer. "Many soldiers were in the house you bombed. Some were dying already. Some thought they were out of it and would return to their families. And who took care of them?" For a moment Alessandro was unable to speak. Then he resumed, his voice quivering. "Nurses, a dozen or more." He leaned forward. "Who do you think nurses are? Young girls. After you flew away, the rubble burned so hot that I couldn't face it.

"One of them was . . ." Alessandro was unable to finish. He just stood there.

"Would she have wanted you to do this?" Andri asked.

Now Alessandro seemed to grow calm. After a while, he smiled, and he said, "Why don't you ask her?"

Andri nodded in resignation. "All right. I have no arguments. I thought I'd come through. I've tried to be happy these last months. I suppose it will have to do."

A door burst open on the right, startling Alessandro so much that he pivoted to bring the pistol around, holding it tensely in both hands, but standing across from him was a girl of six or seven. She wore a loden coat, her hair was braided, and she carried a schoolbag.

"You're late getting off," Andri said. "The teacher will be angry."

She remained in the doorway.

"This is Ilse Maria, my daughter. Ilse . . . go."

She refused to move.

Alessandro looked at the child, and then, as he lowered the pistol, he turned to her father and said, "Now you've beaten me twice."

When Alessandro had first stood face to face with Bindo Altoviti he had been so rich in attachments as to be enchanted by the idea of solitude. His home on the Gianicolo had been a fortress against time. Never had he returned to anything but a loving family, he had taken for granted the fraternity of the university, and the world was a garden of exquisite and invulnerable women.

He went again to the room in the Alte Pinakothek. The hand of Bindo Altoviti, resting almost effeminately upon his breastbone, looked like the work not of Raphael but of an assistant. A thousand of Raphael's images raced through Alessandro's memory for comparison—balloon-like war-horses whose expressions were true to those of animals and reflective of those of man; scenes and faces rendered deliberately in the golden light of dusk; cherubim whose expressions were those of older children, because babies would not sit still even for Raphael.

Unlike the new paintings, with their disheveled and hallucinatory colors, each and every one of Raphael's brush strokes, all of his shining planes, the rendering of the air in light—whether bright or subdued, whether of morning sky or evening star—was disciplined with an iron hand. Here were no stratagems or conceits, nothing centrifugal, nothing wild, nothing without the rich harmony that seemed to be the world itself as seen in heavenly recollection. The one weight that aligned all the elements, and reconciled every contradiction and variation, was the burden of mortality.

In tireless variety, the painter's subjects reflected what seemed to Alessandro to be their conviction that they had alighted upon the earth only momentarily after emerging from a storm of souls. The sapphire blues and windless skies were a place of shelter, a refuge from great and overwhelming battles, a placid heaven that passed too quickly for most to know and was neglected in favor of the crudely imagined paradise that had been plagiarized from its elements. The world is a quiet place, Alessandro thought, its images forever fixed. They do not vanish. They can be remembered, and they can be foreseen. Nothing and no one are lost. That was the promise and meaning of the painting, and the source of Bindo Altoviti's equanimity. Perhaps, someday, Alessandro would see things as placidly as the young Florentine, but now he would have to be forgiven his restlessness, for he was about to walk from Germany to Italy, over the mountains, in winter, and that was a task not of contemplation but of luck and drive.

THE TRAIN to Garmisch-Partenkirchen was nearly empty, and Alessandro was alone in a second-class compartment. The door and windows facing east were gradually turned southward, and, as the train rocked, Alessandro slept with the sun shining on his face, and his left hand hanging limply over the edge of his seat.

In the early afternoon he was awakened by the sound of the train passing slowly across a steel bridge. Far below, a river dashed over ice-sheathed boulders as big as houses, and mist filled the gorge like an aurora, rising and falling in thick arches that buckled, twisted, and sometimes collapsed. Not much faster than a man could walk, the train moved up a steep grade, over trestles and through tunnels. The air was pristine and fresh, and, despite the stench of the soft coal that fueled the engine, it smelled of evergreens and mountain laurel. Just to the south lay Austria.

Alessandro would have to weave through German, Austrian, and Italian armies, border guards, militia, police, and districts where strangers were both detested and unknown. He thought to turn himself over to the Swiss. Though he wasn't familiar with their policy on escaped post-war prisoners he guessed that they would give him something to eat, make him fill out forms, and hand him over to an Italian consul, who would kiss him on both cheeks and put him on a train to Rome. The mountains to the west, however, looked far higher than those to the south, he would have less daylight the longer he stayed on the train, and, because the area to the west was a natural road to Switzerland, it might be more closely guarded.

He opened the door, descended the steps, leaned out, and jumped into the snow. He hit the ground at a run and stayed up for a moment or two, his boots churning below him, but then he lost his balance and rolled into a drift. The train passed by, clacking steadily as it disappeared around a bend of newly cut pines that looked as thick as rabbit fur.

Alessandro brushed the snow off his clothes. Though the air was cold in the shade, in the sun the day was springlike and the snowmelt shone in blue and gold. Wet ice crusts revealed patches of grass in which wild flowers would not have been unexpected. With four or five hours of daylight and an hour of dusk remaining, Alessandro set out at an even pace, expecting to walk and climb by moonlight.

The first section of country he crossed was the kind of steep, treed hillside that one sees from trains, and that, despite its proximity to a railway track, is wild and alluring. He had half a dozen hills like this to cross before he came to the high meadows that led to the snowfields and glaciers. In the forests the snow was neither as windblown nor as packed as in open meadows and on the mountainsides.

He moved amid the trees, listening to the wind roar in their upper branches and looking through a fragrant tangle to lakes of blue sky. As he walked upward, slowly warming and slowly gaining the balance and footing that he would need for the mountains, he heard the concussions of artillery. Though the sound was an artifact of memory, it echoed off the trees and its more powerful bursts cracked along the granite outcroppings like a snapping cable.

He was comforted by this sound. In summoning it he could remember simultaneously not only his ideals, friendships, and loves, but how they were shattered. In the sound of artillery, he heard the profession of his faith, and it gave him strength to take the hillsides with a purpose, as if, beyond the mountains, where he could not see, someone was waiting.

HE CROSSED six ridges, each higher than the one preceding it, before he came to the point where he would not see trees until he was in Italy, and when he cleared the forest he was confronted by a world of glaciated mountains. In the dusk they were a dusty-rose color and the distance to them appeared so vast that he thought it would take a month to reach them, but it was only a trick of light and shadow, and they were neither as far nor as high as they seemed to be.

Here and there in the snow-covered pastures were hay-filled cabins where he could find shelter from the wind. He sought the one farthest from any farmhouse or village and closest to the great glacier upon which he would soon be walking. Several hours after dusk he stopped at the end of the meadows, in a place where the glacier was so close that he could feel the rivers of cold air that flowed from it and carried its sounds—the muffled sound of a locked wheel skidding on a steel rail, thunder-like cracks, a barely perceptible rumble, as if from a giant piece of furniture being pulled slowly across a rough floor.

He found a hut and went inside, where he burrowed into the hay and curled up like a sleeping dog. Though he was hot from his exertions he knew that in half an hour he would be freezing. He wanted to fall deeply asleep while he was warm, so that he might glide unconsciously through the cold that would follow. The minute he was awakened he would have to set out, moonlight or not, for the only weapon he had against the cold was to move. The moments before sleep were like summer.

He awoke at midnight, shivering so violently that he found it difficult to get to his feet. He buttoned his clothes tight, bloused his pants in his socks, put on every item of wool he could find, and burst out the door, almost falling down the slope that descended to the tongue of the glacier. The moon was down, his head throbbed, and his fingers were too stiff for him to have opened his food even had he been warm enough to try to eat.

He had to use both ice axes. The crampons were not necessary, and he would never have been able to strap them on anyway. After struggling up a short fractured ice wall by pulling himself forward with his arms, he was on the glacier. It rose gradually toward a line of mountains that then shot straight into the air like the spray of a wave exploding through a sinkhole. With luck he would have a moon or a sky clear enough to let the starlight through, and with more than luck he would reach the peaks by daylight.

The sky was almost entirely clear, and he was able to see, even if not comfortably. At summer's end, rivers of melted snow had cut new crevasses into the glacier, sometimes receding just before the cut would have opened to the sky. A perfectly flat stretch of snow only a few centimeters thick might delicately span a chasm twenty storeys deep. Alessandro had never liked walking on glaciers, even in a roped party of three or four: it was too much like walking over a mine field. Now he had no rope, no companions, no light, not even a worn path to trust more than a featureless plain.

At first he went around even the smallest crevasses. Then he began to jump them, and those he was willing to jump increased in number and width until, by the time the moon rose and lit the white expanse in which he was lost, he was running to get his starts and sailing over deep crevasses that at their narrowest convergence were more than a meter in width.

He landed on cornices and projections that sometimes lasted only long enough to take his last step and would then drop away. The cool light of the moon had not prevailed against the darkness of the crevasses, which looked like rivers of black oil.

Soon his fast progress took hold of him entirely. The risk and exertion elated him. He felt ennobled and invulnerable. As graceful as a gazelle, he flew over crevasses, and, when he hit the other side, he ran because he felt too strong not to run.

Long before first light, he took a small crevasse no more than the width of a newspaper. Four or five meters beyond it was a wide canyon for which he needed momentum, so he lengthened his stride and jumped far and high, landing hard on a flat and flawless section of snow. The pieces of snow that filled the air around him as he fell were very thin: he would have gone through even had he tried to tiptoe across.

He felt neither fear nor disappointment, and time stood still. He had a sense of great and overwhelming joy. As he was falling, snow and ice crystals blew past his face, and for a long moment he was purged entirely of regret, guilt, sorrow, expectation, and ambition.

Something wrenched him from fearless perfection and limitless joy to sorrow and determination, and he turned the long ice axe until it was perpendicular to the narrowing walls of the crevasse and both tip and head began to bounce off the ice and scrape channels into it deeper and deeper. Holding on to the shaft of the axe was like being at the end of a rope playing off a pulley and gradually slowing.

He fell slowly enough to hope that he would not be crushed on a jagged floor of ice, but when he hit he discovered that the bottom of the crevasse was soft snow. He landed on one knee, with the other leg bent and the ice axe across it. He was amazed to be entirely intact, unhurt, and happy.

Just before a January dawn at the top of Europe, kilometers from the nearest light, in a snowfield on a glacier as vast as a great city, Alessandro Giuliani knelt in the snow inside a forty-meter crevasse, in absolute and total darkness. With his blood ringing in his ears and his heart pounding, he began to laugh—because he had instantly assumed the exact pose of Sir Walter Raleigh, someone of whom he had not thought for even a tenth of a second since he was nine years old.

THE SUN was rising in the clear, and by the time Alessandro pulled himself out it was lighting the eastern faces of the mountains with the great shadow-breaking glare that follows the weak and tentative light of dawn. By mid-morning he was off the glacier, climbing a steep couloir of ice that would take him as high as he had ever been. The sun was hot and his face was quickly burned. He had neglected to eat, but lack of sustenance seemed only to lighten him as he rose into the thinning air.

Realizing that his energy was flowing from him too fast, he tried to moderate the climb, to breathe more slowly, and to move with less urgency, but he couldn't. He was drawn ahead by a longing he could not explain, and carried upward by great sources of strength he had not known he possessed. He had no belay, and would have fallen five hundred meters had he lost his hold.

At the top of the couloir the wind blew with such ferocity that Alessandro had to squint to see. The way down on the south side was not nearly as steep as the way up, and he would be able to walk. Moving a few steps beyond the ridge, he surveyed what lay ahead. To the left was Innsbruck, a tiny patch of white, terra cotta, and blue, in the valley that led to the Brenner Pass. Along its sides lay the great military camps that Alessandro had seen from the train years before. Were they full, their occupants now would be battle-hardened soldiers rather than fresh recruits. He descended into a populated Austrian valley that he had decided to cross in the light.

On the valley floor he stopped to eat by a river that had swollen and receded so as to leave a dry snowless bank as warm as spring. He passed people on the road and greeted them with the Tyrolean *"Scut!"* and a gesture of his hand, which made them think that alpinists had returned to their region. Only once did he see a patrol of mounted dragoons. Fifty of them suddenly passed him on a bend in the road. They came from nowhere and thundered past him as he smiled in embarrassment. Perhaps it was below the dignity of fifty mounted dragoons to question a man, in climbing knickers, walking on a mountain road in the middle of the afternoon, or perhaps they simply did not care, but as they passed they increased their speed. Alessandro learned yet again that the joy of escape is better than the joy of merely being free.

At the foot of the Stubaital he was more than halfway to Italy. He decided to climb even if he would have to climb in the dark, but the moon that night was so bright that it hardly mattered, and by the next morning he found himself in the northern highlands of the Pan di Zucchero, one mountain from the Italian lines. In a swirling fog that lay thick on the ground under a sky so cold and blue that it compressed the mists and punished them in whirl-winds of senseless velocity, Alessandro, dripping wet and freezing cold, finished the rest of his provisions, discarded his pack, and prepared to make the final push.

He knew the Pan di Zucchero on the other side, where a long ramp would take him down past the Italian lines, on gradually descending snowfields that, though they might blind him with reflected sun, would never see him falter or fall.

THE SUN burned off the fog, which rose, broke, and disappeared like smoke. It lit the eastern face of the Pan with the kind of early morning light that had urged Alessandro on for two days running. By now he was exhausted, and some of his fingers were beginning to show the black of frostbite. His face was burned and blistering, and a rough beard three days in the making was coated with rime.

Had the weather been worse, and it could have been a hundred times worse, he would have died, but the sun was warm and the sky was the color that encourages mountain walkers to venture into places from which they sometimes do not return.

Climbing huge couloirs was by now second nature. After an exercise or two on a vertiginous face it seems only natural to struggle along tiny finger cracks a thousand meters above anything, or to make one's way up an inhospitable ice wall. Each step is an art, and as time goes on, the steps are surer and almost automatic. Anxiety vanishes in favor of affection for the height and pride in sure footing, which is how the mountain goat thinks all his life.

Halfway up a massive wall that led to the ridge over which he had to pass before he could descend, Alessandro began to feel weak and dizzy. He wanted to rest, but, of course, he could not rest. He dared not even slow down.

Breathing in short gasps that made him more comfortable and served as a metronome by which to time the placements of the axes, he turned now and then to spit. After an hour he thought he saw red algae on the snow. As he got closer to the ridge line, he stopped thinking about it, until a patch of perfectly clean snow was filled with red spots just after he spat in its direction.

Fifty meters over his head the ridge line was exploding in air-borne crescents of snow, whipped by a storm of rising ice crystals and bathed in light from a hidden source: the sun, invisible on the other side of the ridge. Snow rocketed up in rivers that bent into the wind and spread into tides of mist and sparkling haze. At the ridge line, everything moved, everything was bright, and every-thing was alive.

But Alessandro was still. For a moment, now and then, he slept, and then pulled himself awake. The sleep was more than merely comfortable. It was black, and warm, and all-encompassing.

Then he awoke, by force of will, and pushed ahead another twenty meters. He knew that were he unable to go on he would have peace. Once again, he slept, and as the sleep grew soft, warm, and forgiving, he began to fall, but now he awoke as if a bolt of lightning had flashed within him, and his fatigue turned to anger and action.

His axes moved so wildly he could hardly see. Though his sun-glasses were covered with blood and ice, he couldn't spare the time or energy to rip them from his face. When he looked up he dis-covered that the comets of snow, the dazzling spray, and the singing of the wind in the sun were right above him. Just over the top, he knew, the wind was flowing up a white ramp many kilo-meters in length, and the gossamer rivers of snow that it pushed before it leapt here into the blue. Ahead was an easy descent that would put him behind the Italian line by dusk. Were he to find the strength for the final two meters, the war would be over. He would look out and beyond, and there, in miraculously clear air, would be the dark blue mass of the Po Valley, a thin line beyond the snow-capped Dolomites. There, in terrain less severe, the rivers ran and the trees swayed in warm winds. Two meters below the rim, he was overcome by a surge of affection for the golden autumn in Rome. There lay his future and his past, all that had been lost, and all that he might piece together. He looked calmly at the driven snow against the cold blue sky, and with the last his heart could offer, he climbed directly into it.

LA TEMPESTA

THE ADRIATIC is shallow and confined. Its storms are fierce in the air and fierce in the light, but on the sea itself the waves break before they come to resemble the movable mountains of the ocean, and the surface flashes with curling whitecaps until it looks like a sheepskin in the moonlight. The action of the Atlantic when it is angry is a wild assault on earth and sky: of the Adriatic, a disciplined self-lashing, a convulsion as quick and bright as the sticks of butter-colored lightning that dance over the sea like stilts.

Almost all of it lies between long mountain ranges, where storms collect after they have forced the passes like flash floods bursting over weirs. There they rise, purple, gray, and black, into an angry wall that the setting sun paints in tranquil gold.

As one of these low gray walls became visible to the east, almost like a distant fog-bank, hardly anyone noticed and those who did gave it no thought. Children built castles and pools in the sand; old people read day-old newspapers from Rome or Milan; and young girls barely in adolescence walked rigidly along the beach, delighting that men of various ages paid heed to their swan-like limbs and soft golden hair.

Only Alessandro Giuliani, immobile in a cloth beach chair, tracked the oncoming storm. Though he tried, he was unable to read a day-old copy of *Corriere della Sera,* and though the sun was bright and hot in the African or Sicilian style, gentle gusts of cool September wind riffled the pages of the newspaper. When the clouds were so high and near that the older people began to stir because, unlike their grandchildren, they would not be able to dash quickly through the dunes to the hotel, Alessandro folded the *Corriere della Sera* and put it under his thigh to protect it from the large drops of rain that had begun to arrive in the vanguard of the storm.

The wind tangled the ribbons on the children's gondolier's hats, old people labored across the dunes, and mothers and fathers called their sons and daughters. Then lightning struck the sea far away in a silent explosion of light, and the beach became a scene of panic. Babies were lifted into the air as if the lightning were slithering along the sand. Umbrellas were collapsed. Towels whipped free in the wind.

The beach porters were skinny boys with huge wet eyes. In uniforms that made them look like organ-grinders' monkeys, they desperately and breathlessly gathered beach chairs and umbrellas and ran across the dunes. One of these boys, who had huge black eyebrows that threatened to bridge his macaque-like nose, approached Alessandro.

"You have to go in," he said. "I have to take your chair."

Alessandro kept his face to the storm.

"Signore?"

Deliberately playing with time that was running out quickly and dangerously, Alessandro turned slowly to the young macaque and widened his eyes as if to say, *What?*

The macaque flashed two rows of incredibly white teeth. "Signore!" he shouted, and pointed, with a thumb extended from a clenched fist, at the storm behind him.

"Yes?"

"You have to go inside because of the lightning!"

As Alessandro's eyes filled with the distant webs of enraged light, the corners of his mouth showed a barely perceptible smile. At this, the frightened macaque exploded forward like a racehorse leaving the gate, and crossed the dunes just ahead of a heavy rain. He took shelter under the verandah of the hotel, where guests who were in robes and carrying baskets stood behind walls of glass to watch the storm, and as he and his friends stacked chairs and umbrellas under the light of an electric bulb, he told them about Alessandro, who was going to be turned into a cinder and blown into the clouds.

On the verandah itself, everyone could see Alessandro sitting still in the rain, his head visible just above the beach chair, his hair blowing wildly in the wind.

Lightning the color of white gold danced awkwardly on the broken surface of the sea and flashed against the dark skeins of cloud from which it had come, cascading over itself in shallow angles and bent limbs. Thundercracks colliding in midair flattened the water into spoon-like silver depressions and rattled the glass windows of the hotel.

"He'll be killed," said a woman on the part of the porch farthest away from the windows. "What's he doing?"

"He's doing what we're doing," an old man answered, "but more so. He seems to have lost the habit of safety."

"Or maybe he never had it!" the woman exclaimed with joyful intolerance as she turned to go inside.

No, the old man thought. It's something that, eventually, you learn to do without.

Lightning struck so close to Alessandro that it pushed him against the beach chair and bent its wooden legs like bows. Blinded, he waited for the next bolt to release him from the reeling darkness, for the logic of the lightning and its approach over the sea was like the logic of a swelling crescendo in music. He was sure it would rush him with perfect accuracy, sure of the greater and greater light and geometrically increasing shock, sure that the walking barrage would end with him, and content that it would.

But it didn't. It lacked volition after all, and did not descend with a kind and quick stroke that would take him where the heart could not be broken. It left him on a beach that the rain had made the color of municipal concrete, staring at the ten minutes of robin's-egg blue hanging in the air over Istria. A cold and tranquil rain came after the lightning, and lasted until dark. Only then did Alessandro rise and turn to the hotel, which sat on the dunes and glowed with artificial light like a ship gliding across the horizon on a warm summer night.

As OFTEN happens after September storms, the weather became cool and clear. On the beach, children wore sweaters. Ships moving placidly up and down the distant aisles of the sea were as sharply etched as diagrams, not that the sea itself was calm, for it still had a fresh, agitated, windy quality, and it rocked and churned in waves as imperfect as slabs of raw glass.

Into this sea Alessandro plunged for his daily exercise. He was the only one to swim out to deep water, for which he was held half in awe and half in contempt. It didn't matter to him, for as soon as he cleared the shallows and found himself suspended at a giddy height over the sea floor, darting ahead and slipping through the swells that hid him from those who watched onshore, he was happy. The farther from the beach he swam, the more serene he felt, and in the midst of waves that had never touched shore or lapped against a ship, he would flip over onto his back and float, his gaze fixed on enormous white clouds. Several kilometers out, he floated, turned, and sounded, swimming straight down, eyes open. When he was as deep as he could get, he would relax completely, splay his limbs, and let the currents under the surface tumble him in dark emerald light for as long as he could go without breath. Then, raking the brine, he would swim desperately for the surface and break through a silver roof into clear air and stinging spray.

He liked to swim back at an angle, reaching shore far enough away from where he started so that by the time he returned to his chair he was dry and in full possession of himself. Reaccustomed to gravity and light, his vision cleared, he would open the newspaper, lean back, give up, fold the paper, and sink into dream-laden sleep.

"I'm speaking quietly so that if you're asleep you won't wake up and I'll go away, but if you're not asleep then perhaps you'll tell me whether or not you're sleeping," someone said to Alessandro, who kept his eyes closed, pretending not to have heard.

"You know, I have a telephone in my office now. When I call someone or they call me, the conversation starts with 'Did I wake you?' even at two in the afternoon. And even if you use the apparatus at four o'clock in the morning and ask them, they'll say, no, you didn't wake them. Why are people ashamed of sleep?

"I think the telephone should stop at midnight, like the buses, but I suppose its value also encompasses emergencies. I must admit, though, that I don't like it. I don't like what it does to people. If I call a client, his secretary will say something like 'Signor Ubaldi is in conference.' 'So?' I say, and she says, 'Let me take your name.' I always reply, 'Ah! We can honeymoon in the Sudan!' But they never get it. That's what the telephone does to people."

Alessandro opened his eyes and saw, standing before him on the windy beach, a middle-aged man in a thick white robe. He was balding, stocky, embarrassed, and sunburnt to the color of molasses, with a patina of volcanic red that said he had a lot of blood in him and that it circulated with great vigor. He also spoke with great vigor, with the ease of movement and solidarity of engagement without which a Turkish wrestler would not be able to practice his craft or tolerate his life. And yet, underlying all this, as the color of his blood lay under his dark sunburn, was both delicacy and reticence.

"My wife asks if you would like to have a cold drink and a canapè with us. My son watches you swim. I told him of the danger, and he thinks you are a hero."

"That's very kind of you," Alessandro replied. Before he could add that he was neither hungry nor thirsty, and wanted just to rest, the wrestler said, *"Magnifico!"* and turned on his heels.

The son was a miniature of the father, with more hair on his head and less on his body; the wife a lovely woman of extreme and endearing tininess. Alessandro immediately and alarmingly wanted to draw her to him and kiss her beautiful diminutive face. She came up only to his sternum, and her hands were so small and delicate that she reminded him of the sweet and innocent mice in children's books. At once he saw that the wrestler was perfect for her, a devoted and tender protector. And at once he saw that the little boy was special, that with such a husky father and delicate mother, he, continually translating between divergent qualities, was poised to become wise, even if, at only nine, he looked like a Turkish wrestler. Alessandro liked them. They were so imperfect and so admirable that he could not help liking them, and he was not sorry that he had been drawn their way.

"Momigliano, Arturo," the wrestler said, introducing himself in the formal manner, last name first.

"Giuliani, Alessandro," Alessandro returned, bowing slightly.

"My wife, Attilia, and my son, Raffaello."

Alessandro thought of Rafi, another Raffaello with a Jewish name. "A friend of mine was named Raffaello—Raffaello Foa," Alessandro told the boy.

The wrestler was slightly startled. "Everyone knows the Foas," he said. "Who is his father?"

Alessandro told him.

"I don't recognize him. What does he do?"

"He's a butcher, in Venice."

"I know only the Foas of Rome and Florence. They're all accountants and rabbis. And the one who was your friend, Raffaello, what does he do now?"

"He was killed in the war."

"I'm sorry. I hope he did not suffer."

"He suffered greatly."

"Do you know for sure? Word of mouth is unreliable, and you can't always assume the worst."

"I can still feel his weight," Alessandro said, "and his blood."

Attilia looked at Alessandro in a way that made him feel another surge of affection, amplified because it was clear that she held herself in low regard, perhaps because she was so small. Alessandro let his infatuation for her become respect for her husband, although he could only guess that Arturo merited it.

"Well, listen," Arturo said. "He must have been related to the Foas that I know. I'll ask when I see them. I know them because I'm an accountant, too—an unsuccessful accountant."

"Unsuccessful?"

"Yes. That's why we're here," Arturo said, "at this not exactly glorious hotel, in the off-season, instead of on Capri in August. Of course, I don't mean to imply that everyone here is unsuccessful, but I am."

"I think you're probably right. I myself am as poor as a swallow, at the moment," Alessandro said—not like someone dreaming that someday he would be wealthy, but with certainty. "And I work in a lowly, boring occupation. I'm a gardener's helper. Not even a gardener, but the helper."

"For someone so well spoken, and such a courageous swimmer . . . I never would have guessed, but what I do is worse," Arturo asserted.

"Why is a strong and enthusiastic man like you an unsuccessful accountant? Are you stupid?"

"Unfortunately, no."

"Then why don't you have factories and fleets of ships? You have the air of a disgruntled magnate. Though you seem disgruntled, you seem like a magnate nonetheless."

"I was born to stand outside myself," said Arturo.

Alessandro settled into a chair, and Raffaello brought him a glass of lemonade, holding it as if, were he to spill it, the world would explode. Attilia passed Alessandro a plate of cheese, celery, and breadsticks. For a moment, Alessandro forgot that he had lost everything and everyone.

"It has always seemed to me," Arturo said, "that, except in art, except for someone like Beethoven or Chateaubriand"—Alessandro's eyes widened—"men of great ambition and great success go through life in a frictionless way, as if they were always riding the waves but never in them. I have found that failure is a brake on time."

"That's just an excuse, Arturo," Attilia said, but in a kindly, loving way suggesting that she was not sure, and didn't care if it were. Arturo, meanwhile, was lost in his impending declarations.

"I cannot be a successful accountant for a number of reasons. First, I am absolutely honest. I take great pleasure in sacrificing my own interests so as to be entirely honorable. Isn't that terrible?"

"Yes," said Alessandro, Attilia, and Raffaello, quietly and simultaneously.

"And then," Arturo continued, his words coming pacifically from the turtle-like jaw under his centurion's face and sparkling black eyes, "most accountants like games, and to them their work is a game. I have always detested games. I never saw them as anything but a waste of time. For me, accountancy is a chore. I suffer when I work, which allows me beautiful visions."

"What kind of visions?" Alessandro asked.

"Religious and poetic."

"You mean, when you add your columns, you have ecstasies?"

Arturo bent his head. "I cannot abide numbers. They drive me insane in the same way that forced labor made mystics of galley slaves."

"It did?"

"Haven't you read *Digenis Akritas Calypsis*?"

"Do you mean *Digenis Akritas,* the first Byzantine novel?"

"No, *Digenis Akritas Calypsis,*" Arturo said. "The first Byzantine novel was *Melissa,* wasn't it?"

"I should have known," Alessandro told him.

"*Digenis Akritas* followed soon after. Or perhaps I've reversed the order."

"No matter."

"The other reason I'm unsuccessful as an accountant is that I love rounded, even numbers. I do my accounting as a matter of aesthetics.

"For example, were you my client and you had, let's say, seventy-three thousand four hundred lire in war bonds, sixty-nine thousand two hundred and thirty-two lire in a savings account, and you collected rents of ten thousand three hundred and fifty lire each month, I would juggle things around so that you might have a hundred-thousand in war bonds, fifty thousand in your savings account, ten thousand in your checking account, and you collected ten thousand a month in rent, but your tenant paid for the gas.

"I'd arrange for your interest to be transferred into a separate collection account, and in the event of an odd balance I'd cash it out and buy you something perfectly symmetrical—like a glass ball.

"I present my clients with the records of their finances in beautiful leather notebooks, in groups of balanced sets, with figures and typefaces in a maximally congruent grid. The client's financial system comprises vessels of constant volume that, when they overflow, overflow into other vessels of constant volume. Uneven excesses go immediately into everyday expenses. I even arrange for crisp new banknotes to be delivered to my clients in beautifully proportioned maroon-and-gold envelopes, in amounts of a thousand, two thousand, four, five, and ten thousand lire.

"I negotiate contracts, sales prices, and fees to be payable in large, round, whole numbers. That's because ragged trails of non-zeros remind me of an infestation of insects, or not having taken a bath for a long time," Arturo said, his eyes gleaming with the azure of the sky, his fists clenched as he held forth. "I arrange for the services to be billed in even increments, and if I make a mistake, even at the bottom of a page of calculations, I don't cross it out, I don't erase it, I throw the page away and start over. To me, a poorly formed letter or number is a mistake."

"And yet," Alessandro said, "your dress and grooming are not pristine."

"I don't care what I look like, I care about what's outside me, which is why I'm unsuccessful. I go to too much trouble in a world where success flows to those who rapaciously avoid trouble, but I can't help it. It bothers me to be slovenly and asymmetrical. Perhaps," he said, blushing, but not so much as Attilia, "that is why I was so taken with my wife, and remain so, for she is a glory of graceful proportion.

"But it is also why we come in the off-season, second class, and why we live in an apartment with no view, in the Via Catalana."

"On the second floor," Raffaello interjected.

"On the second floor."

"It's big," Attilia told her husband.

"Yes," he replied, "but it has no terrace, no view, and it's too close to the street."

"It's near the synagogue."

"Far from my office."

"You love to walk."

"Not when it's raining."

"Most of the time, it doesn't rain."

"Most of the time, I don't walk."

"You mean it rains when you walk?"

"You must confine your judgment of the frequency of the rain to the appropriate times in question. Otherwise you are statistically cavalier."

"I don't understand, Arturo. All I know is that we are well provided for and Raffaello stands on a pillar of granite—you."

Arturo looked at the sand, and then, uneasy with the compliment, turned to Alessandro with an expression that seemed to say, what about you? Now it's your turn to tell us something about yourself, to balance my confession.

"I'm a gardener's helper. That's simple enough. After I tell them, no one ever asks exactly what I do, or why."

"I ask," Arturo said. "I ask. I am most interested."

Before he began, Alessandro leaned back in his chair and looked at the sky as if to take refreshment from the light. "When I came back from the war I had lost everything, but I was grateful nonetheless to be alive. Despite what I had seen, despite the destruction of all I had once taken for granted, despite the wounds I had sustained and my memory of men, far better than me, who were obliterated, I was overwhelmed with gratitude, inexorable, intoxicating gratitude.

"After being demobilized, I took a train from Verona to Rome. I knew that, for the first time, when I arrived in Rome neither my mother, my father, nor anyone else would be waiting for me. It was winter. It would be cold and gray. The train was filled with former soldiers just like me.

"It was a military train, an express that did not stop in stations, and it seemed to go faster and faster, rocking gently to and fro, gaining momentum, sprinting across the fields and through the brakes where startled birds rose like air-driven smoke.

"I looked out the window, and though occasionally I could see myself reflected in the glass I saw the countryside racing by, ancient towns and buildings in all their patience, and the wind pressing down the reeds in its never-ending argument with the land.

"Perhaps it was because certain thoughts and memories could not leave me that the landscape erupted in a vision the likes of which I have not had since. It was gray and dead, littered with rotting straw and stubble, and half buried in patches of snow. The trees were black, soaked through the bark, and stripped of their leaves, and the clouds and sky looked like the waves of smoke that curl over a burning city.

"This was what lay before me, and what I believed to be there, and what I wanted to see. It was not what I saw."

"What did you see?" Attilia asked.

"God help me, but I saw early summer. An explosion of light green floated airily in the trees. Fuses and buds rent the ground and split the branches, and where I didn't see green I saw yellow and blue. The colors were deep, the forms exquisite. The rich summer that I imagined, or remembered, had broken from time and defeated winter.

"Before the war, if I had seen something as startling and beautiful as what I saw on the train that day...but no more. Never again. For the first time, I had looked upon victory from the place of defeat, and because the victory was not my own, and I was apart from it, I felt it all the more. It was God's victory, the victory of the continuation of the world. It would bring me nothing, swell my fortunes not a bit. It was bitter, and I would always be outside, but never have I felt a deeper pleasure, never have I been more satisfied, for even if hardly anything was left of *me*, the world was full. And I was not the only one. A thousand men were on the train for seven hours, and in that time I do not believe a single word was spoken.

"Were you in the army?" Alessandro asked Arturo.

Arturo bowed slightly and blinked. When he bobbed up he said, "I was an armorer in Trento."

"Then you know how lucky you are to have come home to your son."

Arturo crooked his right arm around Raffaello's neck and pulled the boy to him. "Of course I know," he said. "He was a baby when I left, and I thought he might have to grow up without me."

"Papa! Papa!" Raffaello squealed in embarrassment as Arturo kissed him.

"Why didn't you give yourself to the Church?" Arturo asked Alessandro. "With such feelings you might have entered the Church in just the way that men are supposed to devote themselves to God, not as young boys who learn by rote that which a man cannot learn until he is broken."

"I didn't have the temperament. I knew as well that I couldn't go back to what I had done before the war, at least not for a while, at least not as an acolyte."

"What did you do?"

"I was a minor academic. I wrote essays on music and painting because I wanted to listen to music and look at paintings, and because I had to make a living. It was torture. I was too young to approach a work of art with anything but vigor and joy. Now I am able to write contemplative essays. The war is responsible for that, although war itself has no aesthetic. Lives that would be brought together to make a graceful end are abruptly truncated. Characters do not reappear where, by the dictates of a peaceful aesthetic, they should, for they have been killed. The balance between men and women is destroyed. Time loses its fullness. Tranquillity doesn't exist. The lack of an aesthetic empowers the extremes, and they depict war inaccurately, either glorifying it or glorifying its horror, whereas it is somewhere between pure horror and pure glory, with touches of both.

"I can now write contemplative essays, but I don't, because I don't want to."

"You're a gardener's helper."

"Yes. Many practical matters absorbed my attention upon my return to Rome. It's complicated, but it comes down to the fact that I have no money. Except for a few pleasures that they foolishly deny themselves, I live like a monk.

"I work in half a dozen gardens on the Gianicolo, including that of the house in which I grew up. My father sold the garden to the people who lived across from us. My sister thought I was dead, and while I was a prisoner in Austria she sold the house and left for America.

"Things can be redeemed. The people who bought the house

then bought back the garden. Now house and garden are united once again, and three children are growing up in it as their own.

"Once, it was mine, and I was happy there. I see my father, my mother, and my sister again and again as I work. The old gardeners have disappeared, and no one knows that at one time it was my house. I have to be careful not to be too proprietary, but sometimes I tell the new owners, with a certainty they cannot understand, where something will be even if it is buried, or what used to be in a particular place, even if it is gone.

"I'm lucky to have something that I love. Though the garden is no longer mine, it's beautiful nonetheless, and I remember. To see the shoots emerge from the earth; to see the pine boughs, which I keep in clean trim, wave against the blue sky; and to see the children of the house as they grow with the tender illusion that this is theirs, is a cause of great satisfaction."

"Will it be forever?" Arturo asked.

"No. For me, even that place will not always be green, but now it's just what I need. I'm content."

"You'll get married and have children," Attilia said. "You'll see. Everything will change. Time will bring you grace, even more than the garden."

NOT TOO long after their meeting on the beach, Alessandro and the Family Momigliano found themselves at table together in the hotel dining room. It was one of those days in fall when summer returns in every respect except one, the strength of the light. Such a day has the quality of a very old man who possesses every faculty and undiminished vigor, and is doomed merely by the passage of time. Though it was hot, the light was dying.

But declining light is the crowning glory of the seaside and a dream-like reward for the exertions of summer. In summer, the waves toil, but when the air is hot and the light is autumnal, the waves are masters of silent elision: they do not break so much as whisper.

Alessandro dipped a spoon into a bowl of chicken broth and gnocchi almost as golden as the light outdoors. "It's good, this soup," he said. "They don't oversalt it. The reason people oversalt chicken soup is so that they can pretend to be eating something that is virtually nothing, but the truth of virtually nothing is worth infinitely more than a lie that makes almost nothing into a lot of something."

"What about bread and butter?" Arturo asked. "Do you put butter on bread?"

"Not since nineteen fifteen."

"In the army? We had butter most of the time."

"We had lard, so I learned to eat bread plain."

On the verandah was a cast-iron table supporting a phonograph. The base of the phonograph was made of rose-colored mahogany, the hardware shiny nickel plate, and the horn a flowerlike shape of ivory, ebony, and amber. During lunch a boy of sixteen or seventeen too overstimulated to eat with his family went onto the verandah and played the second movement of Beethoven's Seventh Symphony over and over again.

The sound had a frail quality that matched the dying light. Alessandro was thinking about the similarity, and about the ability of frailty to become strength, when he heard a huge clatter and then the phonograph needle sliding across the cylinder like a sabre cutting through tendons.

Alessandro left the table, with Arturo following him in urgent little steps. On the verandah, the boy who had been playing the phonograph, eyes full of tears, was glowering at six local toughs who were on the verandah, the rail, and the ground, all in the pose of leaving, and ready to bolt, clutching sticks and frozen still for the purpose of taunting whoever might show up. When only Alessandro and Arturo appeared, the latter holding a napkin, the six hoodlums moved back a little into the hotel.

As soon as Alessandro saw this, he realized that a complex ritual would follow in which, by voice, wit, movement, and control of fear, either he and Arturo, or the six boys would be vanquished, but he wanted no part of the game.

"Who did this?" he asked. At the sound of his voice they tapped the sticks.

"We don't listen to German music in Italy." They were nearly indistinguishable, and their faces said that they were sorry they had missed the war, and they were going to take it out on as many people as they could torment.

"We don't, do we? And why not?" Alessandro asked. Arturo laughed.

"Because Austrians kill Italians!" one of them stated with deliberate outrage.

"And what would you know about that?" Alessandro asked. "Besides, Italians listen to Italian music, and Italians kill Italians, as you will now see."

"Correct," Arturo shouted. Then Arturo and Alessandro lunged for the six boys, who fanned into a half circle and closed in with sticks and fists, some kicking, and, for the first ten seconds, no one breathing.

Alessandro took a blow on his upraised arm, his ear, and his head. The boy who landed it expected Alessandro to retreat, but Alessandro grasped his shoulders and used his own head as an anvil into which he pulled the boy's face.

Three were upon Arturo, kicking him in the ribs and beating him about the head with sticks, but his arms were upraised, and he broke free, chasing one of the assailants, with the others still upon him, until he caught him and began to rip flesh with his teeth. The boy screamed with such terror that they all broke off and spilled over the railing, at which point Alessandro and Arturo immediately vaulted after them. When they caught them, they punched their necks and kicked them in the back. Then, rather than killing them, which they might have, they allowed them to escape.

Alessandro felt rivulets of warm blood running down his neck.

His clothes were torn and bloody, and he limped. Arturo was in much the same condition.

As they stood on the sand, with the sound of the waves and the smell of the sea all around them, Arturo turned to Alessandro. "You see," he said, breathing hard and happily. "You're alive. You have fight in you. You'll have fight in you till you die."

"But I don't want to." Alessandro replied.

"Why not?"

"Real power is with those who are forever still, and I want to join them."

"Good God. Why?"

"Because I love them."

"You mean like Hamlet jumping into the grave?"

"Yes."

"You can't do that!" Arturo screamed. "This is the twentieth century. And, besides, he jumped out."

"He climbed out."

"All right, he climbed out. Better that your soul should be on fire. It is on fire, and when you give it air it will flare like the sun. Even I . . . My soul is on fire. . . . I, an accountant!"

THAT NIGHT a storm came in from the sea and made the air a three-dimensional battlefield of angry lightning bolts, and thunder that carried on the wind and rattled the hotel as if it were shaking it by the shoulders.

From a rush chair on his balcony Alessandro watched the sea pitch and heave like a cat fighting on its back. Each time the lightning flashed it revealed a massive struggle in the dark, with the surface of the sea as littered and disorganized as a plain where two armies have fought for days.

In the noise of the wind, words came incoherently, and he heard music that sounded as if it were coming from the phonograph on the verandah. In the last movement of the Third Brandenburg, sawing in incomparable glory, came a kind of thump thump thump that Alessandro could not place, and that swelled until it thundered over the forward race of the music like guns echoing in the mountains.

When he was young, he thought, he could bring himself into God's presence by grasping the sharp nettle of beauty, but now he didn't dare.

The whole sky ignited in a painful flash. Another soon followed, and he knew that it would be minutes before he would be able to make out the dim outlines of the sea and beach. Though he was sitting up, he felt as if he were flat on his back, or upside down, twirling in space. Though the pounding sound, much like the beat of a kettle drum, was timed to the insistent tempo of the strings, it overrode them. Whenever it weakened, it took strength again and grew more and more intense, until the whole world seemed to be shaking.

Alessandro strained to identify it. His face contorted in an effort to hear better not its volume but the characteristics of sound within the volume. It was as if he saw clearly an army as it approached, but wanted to know what elements it comprised.

Then, all at once, for no reason that he could name, he realized that the sound that seemed to ride far above the thunder, keeping pace, never faltering, was the beating of a heart, and it said to him, despite all he knew and despite all he had come to believe, that he had not yet lost Ariane.

THE NEXT morning, in a thick gray fog, dozens of people pacing unhappily in the halls and public rooms of the hotel made it seem like a mental institution. Gliding nervously over ruby-colored Persian carpets, Alessandro looked the part of an inmate. He hadn't shaved, and had slept only an hour or two, spending enormous energy in dreams.

When Arturo came to get him for lunch he thought Alessandro was ill. "Didn't you sleep last night?" Arturo asked as they raced toward the dining room, almost knocking over old people with canes.

"I slept like an eel. Hurry."

"Why hurry? We'll only have to sit at the table longer before they bring the lunch."

"If we hurry, then maybe they'll hurry."

"What does it matter? Even if the fog does lift, it won't do so until the middle of the afternoon. Where are you off to?"

"I don't know," Alessandro replied. "I think I'm going to leave."

Before Attilia and Raffaello came in from a walk in the fog-shrouded pines, Alessandro played with his silverware, tapping the china and his water glass, balancing and spinning the knife, and twanging it in his ear even though it made no sound.

Arturo tried to engage Alessandro in practical matters. "What did you mean when you said that you were as poor as a swallow, but only temporarily? Do you live on rice and lottery tickets?"

"I don't buy lottery tickets," Alessandro replied vacantly. "All my luck kept me alive in the war. Nothing is left for numbers. In ten years, nine now, I'll have an income. It's complicated."

"I'm an accountant."

Alessandro shrugged his shoulders. "My father had a modest estate: bank accounts, some investments, a house on the Gianicolo, and an interest in the building that housed his law offices. He also owned land at the top of the Via Veneto.

"Three times, the army listed me as either missing or killed in action, all after I was supposed to have been executed for desertion. My sister inherited everything, liquidated it all except the land, and moved to America.

"She left what we had in trust with my father's law firm, and, for good or ill, they invested the whole thing, including an immense amount of borrowed money, in the construction of three buildings—a hotel, offices, shops, apartments—on the land. All the income is channeled into repayment of the loans. Depending upon the rents, which will depend upon the development of the city and the economy in general, that should be in eight to ten years.

"At that time I'll be entitled to half the income, as I own half the principal."

Alessandro threw his knife onto the tablecloth. "By that time I'll be forty years old and will have spent the previous fifteen years of my life in combat and working in kitchens, quarries, and gardens."

"But all that time, you've been thinking."

"Thinking, yes, I've been thinking."

"Better to have a font of money in middle age than when you're young. Middle age is the time when you'll need it and appreciate it."

"I'll never appreciate it. I've been trained out of it. I don't want money. I want much more. I want what rarely happens. I want what people are afraid even to imagine."

"Like what?"

"Resurrection, redemption, love."

"Forgive me, Alessandro. I'm not as educated as you, but I am older, and my experience tells me that you may have to be content with less—with the exception of love."

At that moment Attilia and Raffaello entered the dining room, having returned from the beach, their hair sparkling with droplets of water that had been combed from the fog. Sputtering with resentment and discontent, a waiter ladled soup from a large white tureen.

"Signora," Alessandro said to Attilia, addressing her formally, as if to balance his disheveled appearance and gaunt expression, "do you know about dreams? My mother was a master of dreams."

Attilia answered, "For such things your education is appropriate and mine non-existent."

"My education once enabled me to fly like a bird, but what happens to a bird with a broken wing?"

"Then tell me."

"I slept only an hour or two last night, but the dream lasted for weeks and months. I was with my family in a storm. It was sleeting and very cold, and the wind almost pushed us over. We struggled through darkness. We were dying. I was at times the father, and at times the son. When I was the son I worried about my parents and did not want them to die. When I was the father, I was nearly insane with not being able to get my children to safety.

"I also saw the family from without, and at times I was the baby sister, the mother, even the wind. I thought that the child in her mother's arms was dead. Delirious and trembling, we fell by the side of the road, but lying on the ground was no warmer than standing or trying to move forward.

"Then everything went black, with no sound. I don't know how much time passed, but when we awoke it was still snowing, and we were covered with snow. We saw a huge house with lights in all the windows and fires burning within, and we managed to get to our knees. 'Surely they'll help us,' my father said, and sent me to knock on the door.

"It opened when I knocked, but no one was there. Though I called out, there was no answer. Still, we went into the hall.

"The house was beautifully lit, and pale shadows danced on the ceilings. We went to a room where a fire was burning in the fireplace as if it had been made fifteen minutes before. It was so warm that we took off our coats. The kitchen overflowed with every delicacy you could imagine, wrapped as if it had come from the most expensive stores on the Via Condotti. Shawls of soft wool were laid across the couches and chairs, books were stacked on the tables, and children's games were piled in the corner, all brand new.

"'They must have gone out,' my father said, 'perhaps to get their guests. We should wait for them in the hall.' And we did. As the fires burned down, we slept through the night, on the carpet in the hall, and no one came.

"All the time I was waiting for the owners of the marvelous house to return, I saw my parents and my sister only through the corner of my eye. We gradually took possession. We ate, we built up the fires, we read, and, eventually, we slept in the beds.

"At first we were very careful to return everything to its exact position. We sat rather stiffly on the couches so that if the owners came back we could get up and quickly fix the pillows before we apologized and explained, but soon we grew more comfortable, we started to put things down in different places, and we locked the door.

"Living there was wonderful. My father and mother were in love. They joked. My sister and I played happily. And then we looked at each other. We saw that our faces were ashen, entirely drained of all the hot and imperfect colors that show life. And when we realized that we had died, the dream dissolved in the most intense terror I have ever experienced—and I was a soldier of the line, or a prisoner, for almost four years."

"Most dreams are not so straightforward," Attilia said. "What is to interpret? Is it not clear to you? It's so obvious. Don't you know? You still love."

WHEN ALESSANDRO left the hotel he felt as if he were deserting the owners at the time of their deepest need. They, however, which is to say the owner's daughter, who was at the desk when Alessandro departed, had no need of his patronage. The summer had been busy and profitable. Usually the place was deserted by this time, and, in fact, they looked forward to the quiet of winter.

But Alessandro burned with guilt. The girl at the desk could not understand why he praised the hotel, which was, at best, threadbare, as if it were one of the Swiss lake palaces. As he described the establishment, insisting that she not refund to him a full week's charges, her eyes widened. She could feel the cool waters of the deep lake parting cold and smooth on either side of the noiseless launch that brought the guests. The sunny glade of firs where it stood was cool enough for the wearing of elaborate and elegant clothing in perfect comfort. And the service of which he spoke could only have been rendered by a corps of ex-cardinals and impoverished noblemen, not by the few oversexed macaques her father caught, day in and day out, peeping through the keyholes.

"I'm so sorry," Alessandro told her.

"That's all right," she answered. "We'll look forward to seeing you next year."

"I had planned to stay another week, but I received an urgent summons." At this, he seemed to sink where he was standing, and the lie pushed the blood into his face with such ferocity that the desk clerk forgot everything else and watched him blaze from crimson to purple.

"Yes," she said. "Perfectly understandable. We'll refund the unused balance. It's our policy."

"No!" he screamed, with an air of madness that pumped even more hot blood into his face. The veins in his forehead stood out so starkly that the desk clerk thought she was witnessing a stroke. And then he left.

She had offered to arrange for a carriage to take him to the station, but he had only a knapsack and had declared that he would walk, and he went ten kilometers in the morning fog that came off the Adriatic. He heard voices in the fog. He could not explain how melancholy he was, not even to himself, and he could not identify the voices, like the chorus at the opera, which now, on account of too many rifle shots and shell bursts, was hard for him to hear, and disappeared as if into the sound of surf, or rain falling heavily on a lake.

Though he could see only a little way ahead, Alessandro thought the road was beautiful. It was a narrow, sandy track between lovely trees that spread their branches as they pleased in the sun and the wind.

Though he knew it was not true, he felt that in Rome someone would be waiting for him. Perhaps it was because the magic of cities is that they provide the illusion of love and family even for those with neither. Lights, the business of the streets, the very buildings close together, the interminable variety and depth, serve to draw lonely people in, and no matter what they know, they still feel in their heart of hearts that someone is waiting to embrace them in perfect love and trust.

Though Ariane was not listed anywhere, either as killed or missing, or even as having served, he had gone from city to city, looking for her, and she had left not a trace. The cities had been desolate, their warmth and comfort an illusion, but whenever his train slowed in the suburbs and began to crawl between the foundries, junk yards, and garages that were the railway's escorts into the heart of the town, he took hope, and, as if he were a salesman, his energy flared as he buckled the straps on his luggage and prepared to take to the fast-moving streets.

He finished his walk to the station at ten in the morning. It was a Saturday, represented on the rail schedule by two short columns. The train for Ancona and Rome would depart at 11:32, the train for Bologna and Milan at 1:45 P.M., and the train for Ravenna and Venice at 10:27.

He wanted to sit in the buffet and read the paper while he had tea and a *cornetto,* but the newspaper stand and the ticket office were closed. The town, though visible on the hillside, was far away, and a sullen woman who manned the buffet alone was not interested in making tea or explaining why she had no *cornetti.*

He settled for tomato soup, breadsticks, and no newspaper. "No one travels on Saturday morning?" he asked as he paid for the soup.

"Who's here? It's not summer. Everyone sleeps."

Alessandro took a table in front of open doors that faced the empty track. Fog rolled into the buffet where once the summer tourists had gone to escape the heat. The woman disappeared, and Alessandro was now the only person in the station. With his knapsack on a chair, like a traveling companion, the breadsticks in his left hand like a sheaf of wheat, and his foot tapping the marble floor, he ate the soup and listened to the ticking of the clock.

It was an enormously loud railroad-clock. The ticks and the tocks flooded the station. Alessandro looked at it at 10:26. The ticking thundered as he watched the palsied second hand jerk around the face until the minute hand jumped to 10:27. He rested the spoon in the soup and touched his pack. As the second hand continued in its mantis-like race, Alessandro heard a locomotive.

A train pulled in. It hissed, sighed, and gave off sparks. Men jumped down. Doors opened. Doors shut. Though this was the train to Venice, Alessandro stood up, took the pack, and went onto the platform.

A conductor was there, looking at his watch, his hand up, ready to signal the engineer with a whistle and a downward chop. When he saw Alessandro he said, "Let's go!"

BEYOND RAVENNA, in a marsh that stretched to a fully circular horizon, the train rocketed from the fog into a dome of bright blue in which every color was concentrated and luminous, whether of the grasses, the shimmering silver channels between them, or the fat sheepish clouds overhead.

The seats near the windows now had little plaques reserving them for men who had been mutilated in the war. The difference between the mutilated and the merely wounded being that the wounded might recover, Alessandro was not sure where he was allowed to sit. Surely if he were in a window seat and a man without a leg or an arm were to come along he would have to give up the seat, but what if the man without a leg or an arm were satisfied and proud? What if he were a criminal? Would Alessandro have to move then? Would he have to strip to engage in a war of scars, or did scars automatically lose to missing limbs, or metal plates in the back of the head? And how did they compare with glass eyes? Did the reservation apply to the blind? Why would the blind need the window side, except perhaps for the better air and the feeling of the afternoon sun on their faces?

At first Alessandro tried to believe that he had boarded the train to Venice because he had a week of vacation remaining, and suddenly a conveniently empty train was ready to take him to a Venice without tourists, in a season that could be either misty or inimitably golden. This, had he believed it, would have been a lie vainly suppressing a dream.

He was not extending his vacation. He cared little for vacations. In the army, he had had no vacations, and before that, as an essay writer and a student of paintings, he had not needed them. He was going to Venice because, after many years of falling, he thought he had the scent of rising.

"Where's your ticket?" a conductor asked. "I've inquired three times now. Are you deaf?"

Alessandro jumped back in surprise, which startled the conductor and made him do precisely the same thing.

"My ticket?"

"Your ticket. This is a train, and you need a ticket."

"For where?"

"Where do you want to go?"

"Venice. I don't have a ticket. I'll have to buy one."

"How many years were you in?" the conductor asked.

Alessandro thought for a moment. "About four."

When the conductor left, Alessandro stuffed the ticket into his pocket and returned to his position at the window, like a soldier who mounts the fire-step and feels his heart beating faster because he has come to the edge. The sea curved to the northeast, where Venice lay, and the train leaned gently to the right as it accelerated in that promising direction.

HE ARRIVED in Venice late enough in the afternoon so that by the time he had wandered from the station to the Ponte dell'Accademia, dusk had softened the sky. The moon had risen, gigantic and full, as if to collide with the domes of Santa Maria della Salute, but it cleared them and it floated in the luminous air as weightless as a song.

Liners lay at anchor in the Canale di San Marco, strung with chains of lights that made them look like whitened cities or illuminated mountains of snow. Languorous traffic on the canal broke the silver carpet that the moon had laid down, and rolled across it in barely audible swells. People had begun to filter through the streets to the squares, where they sat at tables outdoors, in sweaters. The weather was perfect, the air clear, and the city empty.

Alessandro found a *pensione* near the bridge and left his pack in the middle of a bed that the proprietress told him she used for five soldiers or eight Dutch tourists at a time. It was so big, she said, that she also used it for drunks, because once they were in the middle it was nearly impossible for them to fall out.

He went back into the open air, to a cafe in a garden behind a wrought-iron fence. Though not hungry, he had begun to feel ill, and he forced himself to eat so as to gain strength for what might come.

The meal he ordered was simple: *pesce al vino bianco,* bread, a salad, and mineral water. When the waiter brought the bread Alessandro felt weak and feverish. By the time he had paid the check, his heart was throbbing in his chest, he panted, sweated, and sharp pains ran through his body, leaving no place untouched.

Walking back to the *pensione* was so difficult that he despaired when he thought he had taken a wrong turn and would have to retrace his steps. The proprietress was not in. He found his room, locked the door, and crawled onto the huge bed.

He had opened the window, and the moon, now as cold and white as the moon in winter, flooded in so brightly that it hurt his eyes. Everything hurt his eyes. He dared not moan, fearing that if he were heard he would be forced into a clinic, so he breathed in pain but made no sound. Instead, he spoke with his hands, flailing in the air or clenching his fists, and discovered that such a language was perfectly adequate for the purpose, and perhaps even superior. Moving felt better than screaming, even if the proprietress would think, from the rocking of the bed, that he had brought a woman home, and would attempt the next morning to charge him for two.

Whatever was coursing through his body, whether food poisoning, an infection acquired from one of the invalids at the resort, or something else, was fast, relentless, and growing in its power. After a few hours, the moon had worked its way from the room and had begun to spray the buildings across the canal with fusillades of cold light.

The notion of dying alone on a bed that had held eight Dutchmen at a time infuriated and saddened him. All the years at high speed on the backs of dangerous horses, all the years clinging to precipices and ledges above the clouds, and all the bayonets, artillery shells, and machine-gun bullets that had been marvelously rerouted around him, were to be overshadowed by a microbe that felled him in a cheap hotel. The woman would find him in the morning, not a soul would show up for his burial, and he would be interred far from his parents, in a nameless grave in the wet and rotten soil of an island in the lagoon.

He had no fight left. He held his knapsack and bent his head into it as if it were someone he loved. He touched a leather strap on the pack as if it were the warm and delicate hand of Ariane, and he stared at the moonlight whitening the palisade of stone across the canal. Vaguely, softly, in the distance, a woman with a clear and loving voice sang a beautiful aria in the sound of which Alessandro thought he was going to die.

WHO WAS this that arrived half an hour before closing and slowly took the stairs, ignoring all the paintings? Every guard in every museum in the world gets a nervous stomach when such people enter his precincts, for these unshaven glassy-eyed men are the ones who pull knives from their jackets and destroy works close to the soul of man. They are the ones who use ball-peen hammers to knock the noses off marble Madonnas. They attack paintings because in every great painting they see the somber flash of God, they see themselves as the truth would have it, and they see all that enrages them for the lack of it.

A museum guard who resembled, at best, a type of French railway guard of very slight stature, slicked-down black hair, poor health, and too much to drink, followed Alessandro across the highly polished floor with a gait so apprehensive and full of fear that he sounded like a prancing dog with untrimmed nails.

Alessandro wheeled around and glowered at him. "Are you positioning yourself to bite my behind!" he shouted.

The guard's mouth tightened, and he screwed up all his courage. "This is a museum," he said.

"I know it's a museum," Alessandro replied.

"That's all I want to say."

Alessandro turned away and walked through the wide portals from room to room, until he was in the presence of Giorgione's painting.

"That is *La Tempesta*," the guard said, having stuck right by him.

"I see," Alessandro said.

"It's very beautiful, and no one knows what it means."

"What do you think it means?" Alessandro asked.

"I think it's going to rain and that guy is wondering why she's going to take a bath."

"Probably that's it."

"They say no one will ever know."

"It was to have been the story of my life," Alessandro said with the kind of affection that one devotes to defeat that has come so close to victory as to be able to kiss it. "I was a soldier, the world was battered in a storm, and she was under a canopy of light, untouched, the baby in her arms."

"Were you in the fighting? Then it could be you," the guard said, suddenly of the opinion that Alessandro was not a slasher but, instead, one of the many unhappy soldiers who filled the streets of the cities, their hearts and minds lost in memories of the war. "You find a woman, you get married, *binga, binga, binga, binga,* you got a baby."

"It's not that simple."

"Why?"

"Just believe me."

"All right, I believe you."

Alessandro could feel the high wind coming and hear the rattle of the leaves in the trees as they shuddered and swayed. As the rain approached, the light seemed both tranquil and doomed. The soldier was serene because he had been through many a storm, and the woman was serene because she had at her breast the reason for all history and the agent of its indefatigable energy. Between them floated a bolt of lightning that joined and consecrated them.

"Sometimes," the guard said, "people come in here and stare at this painting for a long time, and they cry."

After a silence in which something seemed to have been building very rapidly, Alessandro asked, "Who? Soldiers?"

"Well, no, not soldiers."

Without changing the position of his feet, Alessandro made a quarter turn toward the guard. "Who?"

"All kinds of people."

"Yes?"

"What do you want me to do, name them?" the guard asked.

"Tell me about them."

"Why?"

"I'm one of them, am I not? I want to know."

"It's almost time to close."

"Will you be here tomorrow?"

"I'll be here, but I won't be able to tell you anything then that I can't tell you now."

"So tell me now."

"Oh! What do you want me to do? Describe them?"

"Yes. Describe them."

"All right. There was a gentleman, about ten years older than you . . ."

"Go on to the next one."

"I didn't say anything!"

"I'm not interested in him. Go on."

The guard looked at Alessandro with an expression that said he was returning to his initial assessment of Alessandro's mental condition. "There was another guy," he began.

"I'm not interested in him either."

"This is crazy," the guard said.

"Keep on."

"I suppose you're not interested in the old lady . . ."

"No."

". . . who lost her husband."

"No."

"Or the woman . . . who came in . . . with a baby." Alessandro did not interrupt. In the habit of being interrupted, the guard echoed his last words. "With a baby." After a long silence, he said, "And stood in front of the painting, and cried."

Assaulted by electricity rising along his spine and traveling out upon the path of his limbs, Alessandro quietly asked, "When was this?"

"A while ago. Sometime in the spring. It was still raining and rather cold. I wore wool and ate soup for lunch because it was so cold."

"If you remember that," Alessandro stated cautiously, "perhaps you have an extraordinary memory for details."

"Not extraordinary," the guard said proudly, "but, you know, you stand here all day looking at paintings, and, unless you're an idiot, you learn to notice things. You remember."

"What was she like?" Alessandro asked.

"She was very pretty."

"What color was her hair?"

"Blond, but she was an Italian."

"How do you know?"

"Because," the guard said, rightfully proud to have remembered, "she spoke Italian. She also spoke to the baby in French. She was well educated, and those kind of people speak French to their babies."

"The color of her eyes?"

"I don't remember. I never remember the color of people's eyes."

"What was she wearing?"

"That I wouldn't know either, but my wife could tell you. She remembers clothing from forty years ago."

"Your wife saw her?"

"No no, I mean if she had seen her."

"And you saw her only once?"

"Once that I know of. That doesn't mean she wasn't here more than once."

"What else do you know about her?"

"Nothing. The baby was well behaved. It didn't cry."

"What else?"

"Nothing. That's all."

"Think!"

"I can't."

"Close your eyes."

"I shouldn't close my eyes."

"Why not?"

"All right, if you go over there," the guard said, pointing to the center of the floor.

Alessandro walked obediently to the center. "Closing! Closing! Closing!" the guards were calling out as Alessandro's guard closed his eyes. Alessandro prayed faster than he knew what he was praying for.

"I do!" the guard said, with his eyes still closed.

"You do what?"

He opened his eyes. "I do remember something. One more thing. She carried the child on her hip, in a sash. Baby carriages are not very practical in Venice. And when you walk around with a kid, you have to carry stuff for it. So she carried all the things she needed in a canvas bag, the kind they give to tourists who go out to the Lido for a day. They put their lunch, and a book, and their bathing costumes in these bags. You see them in the summer."

"And what does that tell me?"

"They have the name of the hotel on the bag," the guard said, and smiled.

"And you remember."

"Yes I do. You know why? I'll tell you why. It's a small hotel near the Campo San Margherita. I know because I used to live close by and I passed it every day on my way to work. It was the Hotel Magenta. That's what it said on the bag—*Magenta*. I knew there was something."

"Closing! Closing!" the other guards called in high voices that echoed through the galleries.

Alessandro's guard looked at his watch. "Really," he said, "it's time to go home now. Say goodbye to the painting, because it's time to go home."

ALESSANDRO LEANED against a wrought-iron fence tangled in the soft spirals of young vines. Across the street was the Hotel Magenta, now, in spite of the early fall weather, almost empty. A clerk in a fair imitation of a British admiral's uniform appeared and disappeared from behind the desk with the regularity of a metronome. Alessandro watched him noiselessly bob among the bright lamps and polished brass. The hotel, though small and not well known, was elegant. The only hint of the color magenta was a sash-like magenta line that fell across the upper left-hand corner of a menu posted in a lighted glass case on the fence opposite Alessandro.

He planned to stay in the hotel rather than merely interrogate the staff, who would not remember anything unless they were in exactly the right frame of mind, but he was unsure of what exactly to ask, or why he would be asking. Many women had babies and spoke French. What did it have to do with him? But what if he had been wrong from the start, and the woman he had seen on an upper floor of the clinic had not been Ariane but someone who closely resembled her, or if, in the instant he had looked up at the attacking airplanes, time had elongated, as it does in battle, and, before the building was destroyed, she had simply walked out the back?

The child? The child could be his. Why hadn't she looked for him? The question was easy to answer in light of how many times he had been reported dead.

Like the clerk he watched, he bobbed between one thing and another. Hope would flare and he would shudder with the strong emotion appropriate to the presence or the imagination of miracles, but then his head would sink, and he would draw in a very different breath than the one that preceded it, weary and full of inexplicable friction, when he believed that he was deluding himself.

It would be safer, less painful, and even cheaper to go back to Rome. If he slowly began to work, and gradually took up the life of a bourgeois, teaching and writing until the money came through, time might make of him a different man.

He knew, however, that time only stripped and revealed, and he had never approached an important question in any way but to ask everything. As he stood in the darkening street, he recognized a pattern in his life. He had learned very quickly, not merely by devoted study but by some natural sympathy, to enter so fully into a painting or a song that he could cross into a world of harrowing beauty and there receive, as he floated on air, the deep, absolute, and instant confirmation of hopes and desires that in normal life are a matter only of speculation and debate.

That was all changed, however, and quickly, during the war. Sometimes after an exploding shell, blood and limbs rained down upon soldiers who were too shocked to move, and who stood as if they had been caught in a sudden downpour, and at such moments Alessandro had been ashamed of the life that had taught him to trust and hope.

The debate between his alternating states of belief would not be resolved until he was unable to report the result, and, like darkness and light, his conviction lingered neither at dusk nor at dawn. Why should it have? The answer lay not in compromise, but in one thing or the other.

"I've been walking in the Brenta," he told the clerk. "I need a good dinner, a room with a bath, and a laundry."

The clerk quoted the price of a room. It was excessive.

"Does it have a balcony?"

"No. The one above it has, and an extra-large bath. It is, however, nearly twice the price."

"Give it to me," Alessandro commanded, rapidly writing his name on the registration card. He tipped the astonished clerk with a week of his own salary.

"Here," Alessandro said when they reached the room, and handed over to the stunned young man yet another week's salary.

At dinner he was especially lavish, but he did not ask a single question. He hoped that in the morning, when word of his largesse had spread, not a soul in the hotel would be hesitant to provide him the answer to any question he might pose.

He tried not to, but that night, in a room with a balcony, in the Hotel Magenta, in a bed made with thick white sheets that had been carefully pressed and were cold to the touch, he lay thinking of Ariane as if she were alive.

AT BREAKFAST Alessandro had two waiters, and the chef leaned from the kitchen to behold him. He passed more money around, as if he were not wealthy, but mad. Each time he put a banknote into someone's hand he thought of it not as the pair of shoes, fountain pen, or two years' subscription he would have to do without, but as an inconsequential sum that he was placing on a wager of unprecedented returns, even if he doubted it would go his way. You cannot by force of will undo events, he told himself. You cannot by assaulting the wage structure of a small hotel hope to resurrect the dead. And you do not make miracles by getting on the wrong train.

As he lingered over breakfast he thought back to the many times he had seen the dead jumping off a trolley or walking briskly up a street. He had recognized their faces, their clothing, their gaits, and even after they had objected that he was looking at them as if they had risen from the tomb, he still thought he saw them, and he felt the same way that shepherdesses feel when, on their rocky fragrant hillsides, they see the Virgin.

His father had appeared, in the uniform of a major, in the trenches beside him, and though he hadn't known his son, it was he. Others, too, came back, at least momentarily, perhaps only because he wanted them to. Shrouds are very light. When they are stretched over a corpse the air in the room can move them just enough for someone devastated by grief to think that the person for whom he grieves is breathing and alive. Call the nurses. Call the doctors. Something astonishing has happened. He's alive. You only thought that he was dead. Even when the shroud is pulled back, the chest seems gently to rise and fall. Some have waited a long time for the person who is breathing to wake, in minutes more dramatic than the fall of empires.

"Can you help me in regard to a woman who stayed here earlier this year?" Alessandro asked the clerk, who had returned to his post.

"Of course. What was her name?"

Alessandro told him. "She had a child with her."

The clerk scanned his register, leafing rapidly through the pages. "No," he said, "no such person from the beginning of the year until now."

"Do you have an indication of any woman with a child? Is your register configured to show . . ."

"Yes," the clerk said, rotating the register on its pivot. "It would say, *and child,* or, *occupied by* so and so, *son,* or *daughter,* for older children."

Alessandro spent half an hour with the register. He even looked for Ariane under his own name, in case she had taken it. He found nothing. Only in two instances had women stayed alone with children. They were English. Perhaps they were war widows, or they were going to join their husbands in the East. In fall and winter the British often went through Venice because the Adriatic was better protected from storms than the Tyrrhenian.

"Are you certain that everyone stopping here would be registered in this book?"

"It's the law," the clerk said.

Alessandro tipped him yet again, and went back to his room. He started to fall asleep, but before he could dream he jumped from the bed and ran from the room. The long airy corridor was carpeted in red and gold. Down this path he sprinted until he got to the stairs. Then he sprinted some more, shuttling through the halls as he tried to catch the maid.

On the third floor he saw a cart from which brooms were up-ended like gathered daffodils, and he lost his breath as if he had discovered the Chariot of Ur. "I forgot to tip you!" he shouted at an older woman, who clutched at her heart in fear. He peeled banknotes desperately from a stack, and, as if he were bribing an executioner, he refused to stop.

When the woman had received a month of her wages she thanked him so much that he couldn't get in a single word. He put his finger to his lips, and said "Signora!" And when she was quiet, she was interrogated. She may even have feared that he would take the money back, even though she had put it in a pocket and buttoned the flap, but she couldn't tell him what he wanted to know. She was distressed when she told him of the two Englishwomen and their children, for they spoke neither Italian nor French, one woman had a boy of about eight, and, the other, two adolescent girls.

"Anyone else? A baby, a little baby? A mother with blond hair."

"No," said the maid. "I'm so sorry. No."

Alessandro opened the windows wide in his room, and the sea air, filtered by several ranks of buildings and the tops of trees, blew in from the Adriatic. At first the rim of sea over the tree-tops was blue, but as the afternoon wore on, it turned to pearl gray flecked with painful sunlight. The air was cool and clear when Alessandro fell asleep under a thick duvet. Whenever he slept during the day, he burned as if he had a fever. At dusk, sea and sky were indistin-guishably blue-green. He thought he was in a dream, and had to splash water on his face six times before he was confident that he would be awake enough to order dinner.

Perhaps because a ship had docked, or a tour had booked the hotel, the dining room was full to capacity, with at least a hundred people, and it had the noisy, hot, beehive-like quality of an eating establishment running at full throttle. The sounds of metal striking china, china on china, and metal against metal never stopped. Nei-ther did the swinging door to the kitchen cease weaving back and forth for an instant, like a valve in the heart.

Though they tried, the waiters were unable to be as attentive as they would have liked. Alessandro got his soup, his bread, his beef-steak, and his salad, and then, only when he asked, a bottle of min-eral water. He ate quietly, observing the women in new-style hats, and, at one table, a family of five, who said nothing as they ate and then rose from their chairs and left in different directions.

He would leave in the morning. He had enough money for a third-class ticket to Rome.

IN ROME the grass grows even in January and crops come in, al-beit slowly, in December and February. Unrestrained by cold and rain, a brilliant day can flare into a remnant of the golden autumn. Gardeners prune and cut. They trim hedges, rake leaves, chase away cats, and, if the weather is dry, they make bonfires of branches and stalks. White smoke rises all over the city. Because the grass and trees are not dessicated, as in August, the gardeners never fear to walk away from these fires when it is time to go home, and the fires, or what is left of them, glow in the night like jack-o'-lanterns, hissing at their abandonment.

When the other gardeners did go home, Alessandro knelt and held his hands out to the ash and embers. He would listen to the wind as it whistled through the Aurelian Wall, the orchards, and the pines that sounded like the surf. When he stayed his extra hour or two in the dark no one saw him, because everyone was inside, where the lights were bright.

Often, he had dinner in the railroad workers' cafeteria, where he was taken for a railroad worker. Even though it was open to all, people who didn't look the part were uncomfortable there. Alessandro didn't like to eat at home, not even breakfast. When you go to bed alone and arise alone, the sound of even a teaspoon in a china cup, very early in the morning, can be as graceless as the sound of a freight train slithering diagonally through a railyard, deliberately slow, scraping every switch.

One night in December he came late, for cold chicken, soup, a hard-boiled egg, and salad. He hadn't read the newspaper and didn't feel qualified to join the continual debates about communism, Leninism, socialism, capitalism, fascism, and syndicalism. The debaters, anyway, were the people he had encountered all his life who thought that art should be detached, and politics the seat of passion and emotion. Though Alessandro was well versed in political theory and could go quickly to the heart of nearly any intellectual question, he told those who tried to talk to him about theory or revolution that he wasn't qualified to discuss it, that he preferred to cut and burn branches. He preferred to see a little cupped flower that had just burst through the ground on a short stem, he told them, than to talk about remaking the world. "I am a simple man," he would say.

But, as he was eating, he had no choice but to listen to some fascists who had come down from Milan. One of them, a real bullet-head, was magnetic, showing both incredible pettiness and a form of distorted grandeur. Many of the railroad workers stopped eating as he spoke, and if a railroad worker stopped eating, it meant that something was happening. Alessandro feared that the fascists would flirt with the Left, that, rather than destroy one another, they would combine, but he could not see it happening for at least five or ten years—the country was too exhausted. Surely the bullet-head, who was as ridiculous as he was compelling, would go nowhere.

Alessandro generally arrived home late. His room was so austere that it was good only for sleep, but in the morning the world started anew. He was always out in the air early, before anyone but bakers and newspaper deliverers, because the air and the sky kept him alive, and he knew it.

One night when he came home he lit the lamp and adjusted the wick until the light was as brassy as the sun in southern India, and his jacket was already half off when he saw that a letter had been slipped under the door. He pulled the jacket back on, and stared at the envelope.

He never received letters. His financial business, such as it was, was handled by his father's old firm. He was going to transfer some of it to Arturo if things worked out, but for now he used the law firm's address for everything of that nature, and he received no other type of mail, because he no longer knew anyone.

He had written to Ariane, and his first letter to her had begun with the thought that her death had made his letters to her soliloquies. Of course, he did not mail the letters, and had he mailed them he would not have been able to address them, and had he hallucinated an address, they would not have reached it, and had they reached it, they would not have been answered.

He stooped to pick up the envelope, and returned to the lamp. The letter was from Venice, on the stationery of the Hotel Magenta. He went quickly through a salutation and four or five lines of awkward formalities in an unpracticed hand. Then he read very carefully.

I have not written until now because my sister's daughter Gisella was confirmed in December and I had to make something for her, I work in wood. I made an ocean liner with little electric lights that shine through the port holes, she keeps it in her room and looks at it before she goes to sleep.

Maria told me you asked her about some people. Others said the same. They described them to me. I am a waiter and I was not working when you were here. Last spring a mother and a child, a boy of about two, ate in the restaurant several times. I probably would not have remembered except that I love children especially, and this baby was very beautiful, as was his mother, and he had a boat, a sailboat made from wood, so I noticed because ever since I was in the navy in Libya, or off Libya, I don't know, I have been making boats out of wood.

It was the kind of racing schooner that children try to sail in fountains but they're not rigged right for real sailing. Make sure there's a long pole around so you can retrieve it! Well I thought you would want to know. They were here. Even though they weren't guests of the hotel I gave the mother a bag for carrying the boat—a picnic sack that we have in the kitchen, the boat fit just right. I had wanted to get it back but when I saw how perfect it fit I said keep it and she did. She is a Romana. She told me that her husband was killed in the war but that she could not get assistance and lives with her cousin or a sister or some such.

The boy sails his boat in the Villa Borghese. I held him and kissed him. The mother was moved, and it reminded me of my own son when he was small. I think they came twice, they never came back, if I see them I will tell them about you. We have put a check next to your name in the register in case we forget.

Sincerely yours,
Roberto Genzano

Throughout the winter of 1920–21, Alessandro went to the fountain in the Villa Borghese, where in summer children tried to sail boats in no breeze and watched as they were becalmed out of reach. But for the coin-sized leaves that chased around it in gusts of winter wind, the fountain was empty. In the spring, a man like Alessandro, someone who had been outside for much of the winter and knew the feeling of cold, wind, rain, and darkness, would spend an hour or two cleaning out the basin. He would polish the grayling spigots, clear the drains, and turn the valve that would open the pipes to a sparkling flow of water. The water would spill out and splash upon the floor, slicking it down, and then rise to a depth of a few centimeters. While no one watched, the stream would flow steadily until the basin was full, a perfectly round lake of fresh water that was never still, where dogs could drink, old men could dip their handkerchiefs before tying them around their heads, and children could sail their boats.

Sometimes at dusk Alessandro returned to the fountain and for half an hour or more turned what was gray into blue. In the silence and the chill, he fired up the sun, leafed the trees, and populated the park with children and their mothers.

On the walk from the Gianicolo to the Villa Borghese his dreams became more and more exquisite. Each time he crossed the city he grew happy thinking about what might await him. He never believed that it was not a delusion, that it had not arisen from his love, his loneliness, and every canvas he had ever seen of the Virgin and Child. Perhaps it had arisen from the Giorgione itself, and he had begun to live the painting.

Throughout the winter, as he worked, he imagined a world so perfect and just that sometimes he forgot it was not real. "Have you taken up religion?" one of the gardeners asked as they dug the foundation for a cold-frame.

"No. Why do you ask?" Alessandro replied.

"The way you talk to yourself, and the way you smile at cats and birds. Only priests and crazy people smile at cats. You talk to someone."

Alessandro kept on digging. "And what if I had?"

"What?"

"What if I had taken up religion?"

"Nothing. Nothing's wrong with that," the gardener said, leaning forward and brushing the dirt off his hands. "But what religion?"

"What religion do you think?"

"Buddhism?"

"Buddhism! Why Buddhism?"

"Don't they worship cats?"

Alessandro laughed. "Not cats, frogs."

"Frogs, you worship frogs?"

"The frog god," Alessandro said, still digging, "lives in foundation drains. If you see him, if you just catch sight of his foot, he makes you vomit uncontrollably for sixty-eight hours."

"Why?"

"He likes to be alone."

"Why does he like to be alone?"

"He needs time," Alessandro said, straightening up and addressing the gardener directly.

"You're fooling," the other gardener said. "There's no frog."

"Before you disbelieve me," Alessandro said, "ask yourself how I knew where all the pipes were buried."

"How *did* you know?"

In March he quit.

EVEN THOUGH he no longer worked in the gardens of the Gianicolo, he summoned them in memory and he knew every tree bending in the wind, every shoot, every rustling leaf, the scent of the grass, the color of the sky, the dusk, the dawn, and the rain. Most of all he remembered the hot and glowing fires that he and the others made from branches that had lain in dead heaps, splintered and wet, black with rain, and yet they had burned, and the heat that came from the heart of the wood fought the winter nights well.

He began to groom himself for Ariane as if he were courting her. He took a job as a night clerk in a telegraph office, translating short paragraphs into and from half a dozen languages. The wires were busy almost all the time, singing across mountain ranges and seas, with messages of the deepest import, birthday telegrams, and orders for wing collars.

He rented an apartment that was far more respectable than the one he abandoned. It was small, but it overlooked a garden, and Alessandro put real furniture in it. He had begun to build a new library. That Luciana had sold his books was a blow akin to yet another death. Now, at least, the new books sometimes made him feel that not everything had changed.

He wore a white suit when the weather gave him the slightest excuse, not the bright white of Mexico or India, but a much warmer color, almost cream, that made his face glow. His face had changed. His eyes were deeper, and he had a slowness of expression. One could see that his thoughts were drifting like fast clouds.

He was happy that even after the many years that had passed since he had first quit civilian life he could still be frivolous enough to harbor an affectation—a cane that rounded out the suit and tapped like a horse against the cobbles.

When he went to the Villa Borghese at the end of April he looked like a man who was much older. He took a bench in the sun, near the fountain, and he watched, his cane resting beside him, a book or newspaper on his lap, his hair blowing in the wind like untended grass.

April was too cold. Though he sat for hours listening to the graceful unburdening of the fountain—and of this he never tired—no one came. That is, no one came to sail a boat. Every night, Alessandro would go home, and in the space between his arrival and the time when he had to leave for work he would sit in dejection, his head bent. He breathed as slowly as someone who has sustained a wound, and then the image of Ariane filled him with happiness and warmth, as if he were holding her, and the next day he would have the strength to go again to the Villa Borghese.

Sometimes he slept in the sun for an hour or two, for he never had enough sleep, and he feared that they had come and gone while he had been sleeping. The first two weeks in May were unusually cold, and then it was hot.

People came out in large numbers. Alessandro carefully watched the boats becalmed in the fountain and the children who stood at the edge. In the third week of May, he abandoned the newspaper and concentrated upon the children. He found tremendous satisfaction in observing their faces. When he saw a father cradling a child in his arms, the father admiring the child, the child floating, Alessandro felt neither envy nor distance.

The end of the month was complicated by rain, and for several days Alessandro failed to awaken in time to go to the Villa Borghese except late in the afternoon. He thought that June would be better, and that if he were to have asked a statistician to determine when children were most likely to sail their boats in fountains, or, if not that, when their mothers were most apt to take them walking in the park, the answer would be always June. Among other things, June is the month when children first recognize summer and when their mothers are positive of its arrival. It is the month of vacations and the influx of tourists, and when the sun attains its full glory but not its greatest heat.

Perhaps the woman, whether or not she was Ariane, had been ill. Perhaps the child had been ill. Perhaps they had moved, or were visiting, or had lost interest in the park, or had been there just when he was not. And perhaps he had seen them many times, the mother and child who had been in Venice, and they were strangers.

———

AT THE end of June, Alessandro abandoned his customary bench and moved to the south side of the fountain. Many more people used the south path because the trees were thicker on the north and their shadows were like a barrier. On the south side the sun did not strike Alessandro properly. It seemed to aim for his right eye and the right side of his neck. If for hours these relatively unexposed parts of him were in direct light, he would get a sunburn.

He could not, however, bring himself to move. He told himself that it wouldn't matter, and he didn't move. Riveted to the bench, he remembered the stories he had heard of the soldiers of the line who had seen angels—whole battalions of them. The angels flew above the no-man's-lands between the trenches, and, as they flew, the souls of the bodies that lay upon the artillery-turned soil decomposing into paste rose to join them. Only the battered formations reported angels, and only in the course of difficult battles. No dissenters challenged their accounts. Nothing is as beautiful as an angel, the soldiers said. They moved in massive numbers ten or twenty meters above the ground. They looked ahead undisturbed, giving off light in pulses that made the landscape glow, beautiful insubstantial beings who had themselves seen God. The souls, too, were visible as they ascended, and the luminous host could be seen from a great distance away as it moved in the vast and terrible spaces along the line. Many of the soldiers assumed that the world would end the night they saw the angels, and, for some, it did.

Not only had he abandoned his customary place, but he was unable to read the paper. He would start a column and follow it to the end, remembering nothing. Was it so much to ask that, several years before, Ariane might have walked out of a building before it collapsed? Would that demand the reordering of the universe? The contradiction of physics? It would not, and yet it would be a miracle, still, unimpeachable even by divisions, whole armies, of skeptics.

And yet it was far too much to ask, if only because he wanted it so much, and he stopped asking. As the afternoon grew hot, he began to dry up, and he felt the future on its way. Nothing would come of his beliefs or desires.

He folded his newspaper and was about to stand. In the corner of his eye he saw a white flash from the east side of the fountain as the narrow triangle of a racing schooner darted for its motionless station near the center, where only the water would slowly push it to the edge, not the wind and not its sail.

The child who had launched it was a boy of about three, whose hair was pure gold in the sun. His eyes were brown, he wore blue shorts and a white cotton shirt, and he had the face of a child who carries a great burden.

Alessandro looked beyond him at three women sitting on a bench. Two were talking. The third was sewing, and it was she who had her eyes on the little boy with the boat.

Ariane was nowhere to be seen. Alessandro stood up and began to walk in the direction of the Tiber, but after he had gone a few steps he turned to go the other way, because he had decided that he wanted to pass by the construction on the top of the Via Veneto, to see the changes in the land for the sake of which his father had sold the garden.

The last time he had walked by, iron beams had begun to rise from the foundation, and he wanted to see how high they had risen.

As he rounded the fountain he looked again at the child. The boy looked directly at Alessandro, and pointed to his boat. He wanted Alessandro to get it for him with the cane.

"It's too short," Alessandro said, "and the water is too deep."

The child refused to accept that Alessandro could not help him. He pointed again.

Alessandro stepped toward him. He was going to bend forward slightly and explain, but the words caught in his chest, and he stopped abruptly. Just beyond the boy, hidden from Alessandro's sight until he had moved closer, was a worn canvas bag with loops for handles.

The side facing him was blank. He grasped the bag by the loops. At this the woman on the bench stood up and walked toward them. As Alessandro turned the bag, almost as if in slow motion, he saw letters on the other side, in self-referential color— *Magenta.*

"What's your name?" Alessandro asked the child.

"Paolo."

"And your last name?"

Before he could answer, the child looked up. The woman had arrived. Though she was not Ariane, she, too, had blue eyes, and Alessandro tried to check his reckless conclusion that she might be the cousin.

"Good afternoon," she said, in a careful but challenging voice.

Alessandro could hardly breathe. "Are you his mother?"

"No," she said, as if she meant, *What of it?*

He trembled. "Is his mother's name Ariane?"

"Yes," the woman answered, relaxing. "Do you know her?"

LA RONDINE

ALESSANDRO GIULIANI and Nicolò Sambucca had walked for two days and two nights on the way to Monte Prato. The road they took and the shortcuts they made over ridges and through defiles of whitened rock kept them on the crest of the Apennines, on the line of the westernmost ridge. As they walked in daylight or under the stars, they felt as if they were scrambling along the top of a wall so high that the towns of Italy, glittering below them in the warm summer air, were places in a children's book or a fairy tale. Even the sea, a band of navy blue at night or turquoise at noon, was the unmistakable creation of a compassionate illustrator, and fit tightly within the intarsia of fields and sky polished by a weightless fume of silver light.

They were exhausted, and walked with great difficulty, but the open country, the silence, and the altitude enabled them to imagine themselves proceeding without effort, as if they were rising and falling, driven by the wind, across the smooth swells of a ribboned and color-banded sea. After their encounter with the returning farmers they had neither seen nor heard a single soul. The route had been sufficiently remote to render towns and villages silent and motionless but for the blinking of a light or the slow-paced climb of a pillar of coal smoke into an azure infinity that quickly erased it.

They had had hours of leaden movements and pounding hearts, and hours of flight, but in memory it all seemed the same, for the line they had made was mainly behind them now, and they hadn't far to go. Nicolò had walked long past the fork in the road where he was to have turned toward Sant' Angelo, and before dawn he and Alessandro had halted on a hill that overlooked Monte Prato.

The road curved left and then back to the village by way of rocky shelves in the hills, but if you were to descend to the floor of the valley, cross the river, and go up again, you would come to the church and the piazza directly, after passing rows of olive trees, and stone walls, and through fields in which sheaves of silver-blond hay stood like dispersed infantrymen.

"Aren't you going to take the road?" Nicolò asked.

"No."

"You'll have to go all the way down and then climb up."

"Isn't that what I've been doing?"

"But you're here. Why risk your heart when you've made the journey? You complained that it was skipping."

"I didn't complain."

"You said it was skipping."

"It was."

"The road is easy," Nicolò said.

Alessandro snapped his head in an almost leonine gesture of impatience. "The sun won't rise for two hours. I'll rest here."

"How do you feel?" Nicolò asked, fearful and solicitous.

Alessandro sat down on a smooth rock that jutted from a wave in the hill, and leaned back until his head rested on soft grass. "I remember from my own youth," he said, addressing the sky as much as the boy beside him, "the reason for such a question. You think that an old fellow like me has lakes of blood pressing against dams of paper, don't you. If I take a step the wrong way, or choke a little on my food, or hear that Octavian prevailed at Actium . . . bang! The dam bursts, everything inside ruptures, I'm dead."

"I didn't mean that, Signore."

"You must have. Compared to you, I'm a wishbone. I remember the way I was."

"You're not so delicate, not after what you've been through."

"But I am, Nicolò. I am, and it's a mercy. My body will no longer force me to put up with what I once had to put up with. If something is too much of a shock, too unpleasant, or too painful, God will come as quickly as a nurse on call. The drier and thinner the bone, the more easily it snaps."

"How can that be good?"

"You'd be surprised."

"I never want to die. I'll fight to the end and go with a real struggle."

"I know, I know," Alessandro said kindly. "You can hardly feel time, and yet you are jealous of it more than you will ever be again."

"But you said so many times that when you had nothing left, strength came from nowhere; it flooded into you, and it surprised you."

"It did," Alessandro confirmed. "It still does, but it, like me, grows quieter and quieter."

"Signore!" Nicolò said, in protest of age and mortality.

"You asked me how I felt."

"Yes."

"I feel fine."

"You do?"

"Yes."

"Your heart?"

"Well, my heart doesn't feel so fine, but so what."

"What does it feel like?"

Alessandro turned his head to Nicolò, who was sitting with his right foot and calf tucked under the thigh, the way that girls sat, Alessandro remembered, when they picked berries. "It feels like a man is inside it pushing against the walls with his hands and feet. And my arm feels the same way."

"Is it serious?"

"It isn't comical."

"Do you need a doctor?"

Alessandro laughed. The vigor of his laughter surprised Nicolò. "What's funny?"

"What I need is not to have a doctor. When you die, doctors hang around for weeks, and the poor miserable people you leave behind have to sell all the furniture to pay them, even though ... what did they do? You pay them for their tact when they keep the bare truth from you about the person who's dying.

"The money is unimportant. What hurts is the false hope, in which you are as much at fault as they."

"If someone paid my father to fix his clothesline poles," Nicolò stated, "and both of them fell down, my father would give the money back."

"But?" Alessandro asked.

"But what?"

"But?"

"I didn't say *but.*"

"You should have."

"I should have."

"Keep on."

"But ... but ... but I don't know, but what! But people! People are different."

"Yes. Go on, go on."

"They're not clotheslines. They're complicated. They don't live forever. Even clotheslines could fall, in an earthquake, and it wouldn't be my father's fault, and he'd keep the money."

"Yes!" Alessandro said, in a clipped fashion with a lot of aspiration. "You know something, Nicolò?"

"What?" the boy asked, smiling like a lamb.

"You're thinking, and, two days ago, you weren't."

Nicolò allowed for the possibility. Had it not been the black of night, Alessandro would have seen his face light up.

"Thinking, asking questions, figuring things out, you see, is like a ball. When it starts to roll downhill—even if it starts very slowly—it never stops. Do you understand?"

"No."

"Yes you do."

"Not exactly."

"Of course you do. You're just so pleased with yourself that you want me to describe it so you can enjoy it. I won't. The pleasure should be without expert advice, like your first orgasm."

"What's an orgasm?"

Alessandro sighed.

"Come on," Nicolò said. "I'm not like you. I don't have a lot of money. I can't even afford a bicycle, much less an orgasm."

"My God," Alessandro said, his eyes darting upward.

"An orgasm is a car, isn't it?"

"You mean, like a ... *Hispano-Suiza*?"

"Is that what it is?"

"No," Alessandro said, his voice falling, "it's a type of Japanese lantern."

"We don't need any orgasms, we have light bulbs," Nicolò said.

"But soon you will be willing to trade all your light bulbs for one orgasm."

"That's what you think," Nicolò said indignantly. "Light bulbs are expensive. I wouldn't trade a single one for an orgasm."

"That's what you think."

"You're sure of a lot of things, aren't you. According to you, I'm going to be the president of F.A.I." He waited for Alessandro to deny it. "I'll live in a big house and have a lot of leather books...."

"Leather-bound."

"Leather-bound. I'll sail my yacht to Switzerland for the summer."

"From where?"

"From Capri."

After a pause, Alessandro said, "I was going to mock you, but the Rhone extends to Geneva, and bursts from Lac Leman full blown. Who knows?"

"Why not just sail directly on the ocean?" Nicolò asked.

"You can't. Switzerland doesn't have a seacoast, but, as I was saying, the Lake of Neuchâtel empties into Lac Leman. Perhaps you could go farther. It's the kind of thing one proposes to a geographical magazine, and they never accept."

"Rich guys."

"Yes. Rich guys propose to geographical magazines. Poor guys don't know where to begin, and they don't have yachts. The difference between classes of men is that the vast majority remember youth as their glory, and the tiniest fraction, in escaping a life of drudgery and increasing difficulty, finds something even better."

"Maybe God will make me rich someday."

"Possibly."

"God didn't make me rich to start. I don't believe in Him anyway. My sister does."

"If you don't believe in Him, how can He make you rich?"

"So what if He doesn't."

"I don't think He will. You may make yourself rich. He doesn't care."

"He doesn't?"

"No. Of that I am sure."

"Why?"

"Money is one of the few things that He Himself didn't invent. He invented birds, stars, volcanoes, the soul, beams of light—but not money."

"You believe in God, don't you."

"Yes."

"How can you? What did He ever do for you?"

"That's not the point, what He did or didn't do for me. In fact, He did a great deal, but for some He's done a lot less than nothing.

Besides, one doesn't believe in God or disbelieve in Him. It isn't an argument.

"Though I used to argue it," the old man said, "even with myself, when I was younger. His existence is not a question of argument but of apprehension. Either you apprehend God, or you do not."

"Do you?"

"Yes, very strongly, but, at times, not. The older I get, and the more I see how life is arranged and with what certainty and predictability we move from stage to stage, the more I believe in God, the more I feel His presence, the more I am stunned by the power of His works. And yet, the older I become and the more I see of suffering and death, the less approachable is God, and the more it appears that He does not exist. Being very clever, He has beaten life into a great question that breaks the living and is answered only in death. I am so much less sure than when I was young. Sometimes I believe, and sometimes not."

"What accounts for the difference?"

"My strength, the clarity of my vision, the brokenness of my heart—only these.

"Ariane left me a letter. Apart from the signs on the street, that I read as I rode home, hers were the first words I saw after she died. It was as if she were speaking to me, and she said, 'As long as you have life and breath, believe. Believe for those who cannot. Believe even if you have stopped believing. Believe for the sake of the dead, for love, to keep your heart beating, believe. Never give up, never despair, let no mystery confound you into the conclusion that mystery cannot be yours.'"

"With all due respect, Signore, you'll have to convince me," Nicolò challenged, thinking, awakening, ready for ten hours of disputation.

"No I won't, not me," Alessandro said. "I've stayed up enough nights over long-dead dinner tables, ironing my blood sugar until it was flat. I don't have to convince you. The world will present to you the evidence, and the choice will be yours. It will rest entirely on how clearly you can see out from the tangle of your physical body and your prideful intellect."

"I have an intellect?"

"I didn't say that."

"What's an intellect?"

Alessandro shifted position and snorted to get more delicious night air. "It's a thing you have in your brain. It remembers other things and lets you shuffle them around so you can figure them out."

"Oh."

"You've got one, but you've got to exercise it so it'll get bigger."

"The people who've got these intellects, they're smart, aren't they?"

"Not as smart as they think."

"They're not?"

"No. They don't know it, but the intellect is the attribute easiest to develop, and if it grows out of proportion to the rest of them they think they're smart—but they're not any smarter than a telephone book. A fact of humanity throughout history is the desirability, the necessity, of balance among the intellect, the spirit, and the flesh."

"Flesh, what flesh?"

"Mortification of the flesh."

Nicolò drew back almost imperceptibly.

"What do you think we just did?" Alessandro asked. "This walk, for days and nights in the open air, without sleep, under sun, moon, and stars, is mortification of the flesh. Like thundering music, it agitates the spirit until it rises. In Islam the Sufis and Dervishes use drugs to accomplish this. We're Christians, we don't. We launch our souls from the cannons of art and discipline, and on any one night, hovering over the chimney tops of Europe, halfway to the stars, there are armies of brightly spinning spirits that have risen like fireworks, tethered to the souls of those men and women who, by reflection, mortification, and devotion, effortlessly outdazzle kings."

"Yeah, but you don't... you don't take walks like this every day," Nicolò said, "and if everyone did, the whole world would be crazy, wouldn't it? Everybody walking around the mountains in the middle of the night, Christ!"

"Tell me," the old man said, slyly. "You don't think there are other ways?"

"Like what?"

"Then you do."

"I didn't say that."

"Yes you did."

"All right, what are they?"

"What time do you get up in the morning?" Alessandro asked.

"Me?"

"Who else is here?"

"Seven-thirty. Why?"

"So you can get to work?"

Nicolò nodded.

"And on days when you don't work?"

"Nine, ten, whatever."

"You get up at seven-thirty because you have to."

"Yes."

"I'm retired. I don't have to get up at any time. If I want, I can sleep all morning. What time do you think I get up?"

"How should I know?"

"Guess."

"I told you, I don't know."

"That's what guessing is for, when you don't know. I knew you didn't know—how could you know? That's why I asked you to guess."

"Nine-thirty?"

"No. Five."

"Five?"

"I'm at my desk by five-thirty."

"You must be crazy."

"You're a great runner," Alessandro said. "I saw you run after the bus for kilometers and kilometers. How many times a week do you exercise to exhaustion?"

"When we have a soccer game. You? You can't exercise to exhaustion. You'd die."

"Four times. I row. I row until I have visions. I drink lemonade. I hear music. I hear music, Nicolò, even though no one is playing it. Do you?"

"No. Sometimes I don't hear it even when someone *is* playing it."

"Do you sleep in a bed?"

"Of course I sleep in a bed. Who doesn't sleep in a bed?"

Alessandro smiled.

"You don't sleep in a bed? Where do you sleep?"

"The floor."

"The floor, you sleep on the floor? Why?"

The old man looked at the boy and said, with the air of someone who is telling a great secret, "Because the floor is hard and cold."

"I don't believe this," Nicolò said to an imaginary third party.

"What time do you think your sister's nuns get up in the morning?"

Nicolò shrugged his shoulders.

"Ask her."

"Christ," Nicolò said. "I don't want to be a nun."

"I'm not asking you to be a nun," Alessandro told him. "I'm not asking you to do anything. I'm just telling you that the intellect is of no use unless it's disciplined by the mortification of the flesh, so that it may serve the soul. That's all. The intellect thinks.

The body dances. And the spirit sings. A song, a simple song. When love and memory are overwhelming, and the soul, though crushed, takes flight, it does so in a simple song."

"How do you know this?"

"I've heard it."

"What does it say?"

"It says, at the very end, in the last distillation of all you know, that you have only one thing left, one thing that might travel, though God only knows how."

"What am I supposed to do with that?" Nicolò asked. "You're always talking about stuff like that. Give me a more concrete example."

"A thing?"

"Yes, a thing."

"It has nothing to do with *things*."

"I don't care, just give me a thing, one thing."

"All right," Alessandro said, looking over the moonlit village and across the silvered hillsides and newly clipped fields. "Here's a tiny example, one of millions, microscopic, but it may qualify as a thing, I think.

"I have a desk calendar, a leather book that lies open at my right elbow. It's a thing. Now that I'm old, it's always empty, but I buy a new one every year—from habit, and because when I do have an appointment it stands out nobly on the blank pages, like an icebound ship at the North Pole.

"It has a red ribbon for marking one's place, and for almost fifty years that ribbon sat in the crease as straight as a plumb line. Just recently, I went to answer the telephone with my right hand as I was keeping a book open with my left. I wasn't looking, and I swept the ribbon across the page, with half a twist, at a forty-five-degree angle.

"After I had finished with the telephone call, and after I put down the book, I noticed the ribbon. It had a life of its own, beyond my habits, my intentions, my notions of order, my ideas, and my practices. The little angled ribbon stood out on the page like a banner in the wind, like a pillar of fire."

"So what does that mean."

"Somehow, it tells me that I'm not alone. And even if it doesn't tell me that, I want to believe it, because, over time, it hurts very much to be alone, although you get so that you can hardly tolerate anything else. When you're alone you can long so hard for something like an embrace that you mine it from the air. You find it in meanings that you might not otherwise grasp, for which it is helpful to arise early in the morning, when the mind is clear and the heart is gentle."

"That's not good enough."

"You think not?"

"No."

"Why?"

"It was all intellect."

"Aha!" Alessandro Giuliani said. "And what did it lack?"

"It lacked, you know... Give me another."

"Another example?"

"Yes."

"Are you familiar with the *'Madre, non dormi...'* from *Il Trovatore*?"

"No."

"When you get home, seek it out. It begins with a nine-bar harmonic progression from D-flat major through A major and back to D-flat."

"And what is that?"

"A bunch of tones."

"And?"

"And, my son had a top. If you pumped it up it would spin and generate precisely the sequence from the *'Madre, non dormi...'* How it dropped and went up again I don't know. Perhaps, as it slowed, an internal gate fell back and opened a new passage for a higher register. I don't know how it did it, but it did. It was designed with a mysterious and enchanting brilliance.

"The sequence of notes at the beginning of the song is one of the saddest and most beautiful things I have ever known. Listening to its melancholy, lucid progression has the effect of stopping time. It made the faces of the children infinitely touching, infinitely beautiful, and infinitely sad. When I used to listen to it with Paolo, it transported me to the point where we would separate forever, which I thought would be when I died.

"That simple progression had a power far out of proportion to its elements, for it came close to the elemental truth in which hope, remembrance, and love are joined. After a lifetime of thinking a great deal about the question of beauty—it was my job, just as you make propellers—I have found nothing that illuminates or conveys it save another beauty. No better gloss upon a painting than a song, no better gloss upon a song than its lyric. And in the end, perhaps nothing is as beautiful as a song, perhaps because nothing can be as sad.

"I realized both too early and too late—a long time ago, and yet when I was old enough to have this tremor in my hand—that what I had been seeking in a thousand beauties was one, and that I had had it, and might never have it better, sitting on the floor in Paolo's nursery, helping him push his top.

"I asked myself, why do I love, and what is the power of beauty, and I understood that each and every instance of beauty is a promise and example, in miniature, of life that can end in balance, with symmetry, purpose, and hope—even if without explanation. Beauty has no explanation, but its right perfection elicits love. I wondered if my life would be the same, if at the end the elements would come together just enough to give rise to a simple melody as powerful as the one in Paolo's metal top, a song that, even if it did not explain the desperate and painful past, would make it worthy of love.

"Of course, I still don't know. God help me to have a moment of his saddest beauty in which I do.

"Perhaps I am wandering. Perhaps that was my intent. No matter. I can wander, because my notion of what it is to come to rest is clear and unencumbered, and I may yet find it.

"The top, you see, that my little boy, at the age of three, twirled round and round, played a beautiful song—a song that, from time to time, I still hear. What is the song? The song is love."

AFTER THEY had been still for a while, watching the trees sway in wind that crept across the blackened hills as slowly as if it were blind, Nicolò sat up and pointed.

"What's that!" he asked in the manner of a sailor who sees a sea-monster.

"What's what?" Alessandro answered, in the manner of an old soldier who will never forget the electricity of an imminent attack.

"Up there."

Alessandro turned his head. "The Perseids," he said.

"The what?"

"The Perseids, a meteor shower that comes in August. This must be the first day. I didn't see them last night, and last night we were on a high, open ridge where the stars were visible down to where they're dimmed by the mists above the sea."

"Give me your glasses," Nicolò said.

When he had put them on, he stared at the sky, looking both contemplative and sharp. Alessandro saw in the way the boy held his head, in the smoothness of his face, and the freshness of his movements, not the image of himself at that age, because it was so long ago that he had almost forgotten, but the image of his son.

"Where do they come from?" Nicolò asked. "Look! Thousands of them. Like burning magnesium."

"They drift around in the Solar System," Alessandro told him, "and at this time each year they and the earth collide. They come from the direction of Perseus, and when they strike our air, it lights and burns them. The flashes you see are their last and their brightest. You can look at them all night, imagining that each tiny flash is a man going down, and you won't see the casualties of even a few divisions."

"They're beautiful," Nicolò said. "They must be so hot, and yet all we can see is a streak of cool light."

"One of the categories of beauty," Alessandro said not so much to Nicolò as to an unseen audience of his peers, "that Aristotle and Croce inexplicably neglect, is the beauty of that which is lost. How intensely, and with such great loyalty, do we take to heart a life that has no chance of revision."

"Where do they fall?" Nicolò asked.

"Most of them simply burn in the air," Alessandro replied, thinking of angels cast furiously through pale and endless light. "Of those that do reach the earth's surface, two-thirds, I suppose, nip into the sea, and the other third sinks into forests or skids across savannahs and steppes."

"Do they ever fall in Italy?"

"I'm sure some have fallen in Italy. Probably you can see them in science museums."

"On cities?"

"I don't know. Why? Are you worried? Do you think you should wear a helmet?"

"No, I'd just like to see one after it landed. It really wouldn't know what was going on, would it? Out there in space for a billion years, going at a million kilometers an hour, with no air, no sound, and nothing but the planets moving by. And then, boom! It comes to rest on the floor of a butcher shop in Trastevere, with a bunch of old ladies and a cat backed up against the wall and screaming because it exploded the meat case!

"I'd feel really sad that after a billion years whistling around space it ended up on a tray of pork chops, but I'd like to touch it to see what it felt like after all that time in the fresh air. *La Madonna!* I hope it wouldn't bite me!"

"Wait in the butcher shop," Alessandro told him.

"I don't know. I'd rather hang around at work. I miss making propellers."

"But you're not allowed even to touch them."

"I miss thinking about making them. Someday I'll make them. Why do those meteoroids radiate out like that?"

"Meteor*ites*. They don't. They just look like they do. They're really parallel and straight, like railroad tracks, which also appear to radiate from a central point."

Nicolò returned the glasses. "When I get back to Rome," he said, "I'll get some for myself. I've only been gone for two days, and just to think of going back makes me all excited."

"Rome is like that. It always has been. The city itself is like a family, like girlfriends, lovers, children. I can't tell you exactly why, but it unfolds before you with the grace of water streaming from a fountain. I think that of Rome because for so many years I was either a child, a lover, a father, or a friend, in Rome, and it echoes and echoes, and I'll hear it until I die."

"What happened? When the woman said, 'Yes, do you know her?' Was it Ariane?"

Alessandro hesitated, closed his eyes, and smiled. "Yes. And the child by the fountain was my son. I didn't want to frighten him, so I didn't say anything. I reined in my emotions. I didn't pick him up. I bent down and looked at his face—remarkable. How beautiful. How round. Like a chipmunk! His little legs were as fat as sausages. His fingers were so delicate and diminutive that the fingernails were like the smallest, whitest kernels of corn, the pale sweet ones near the end.

"I said, 'Look, your boat is becalmed, and it's drawn by the currents to the center of the pool. We've got to get a stick.'

"A street sweeper was not far away. I ran to him and gave him some money, a wad of bills, I think, because I hardly knew what I was doing, and I took a rake from his cart and ran back to the fountain, where I leaned over the water and gently pulled in the sailboat, the sails of which swelled in the breeze.

"I knew I could not explain to the woman, the cousin whom Ariane had never mentioned, either who I was or what had happened. I contented myself in playing with Paolo as she read the newspaper. It was more than forty years ago, but I remember it so well. We sailed the boat rapidly all along the perimeter, because that was where the sails could pick up the wind.

"He kept on getting stones in his shoes, and each time he did, I would take off the shoe and dump out the stone. 'What is your mama's name?' I asked. He said, 'Mama!' And when I asked him his father's name, he just looked at me.

"'Is Ariane home?' I asked the cousin as she was getting ready to leave. 'She should be,' the cousin answered, 'by the time we get back.'

"'May I walk with you?'

"'Of course.' The cousin wondered who I was, but she said nothing, and as we walked through the Villa Borghese, and then through the streets, I began to think that I was suffering a cruel delusion, and that, when I saw the boy's mother, I would not recognize her.

"They lived on the ground floor, and on the doorpost was a highly polished oval plaque with the house number. The cousin rang the bell so Ariane would come out. Were I an undesirable, they could turn me away at the door. Or perhaps the cousin was thinking that Ariane might be in the bath.

"She *was* in the bath, and when she appeared to me, after so long, her hair was undone and she was wrapped in a towel.

"The door opened. It was very strange. All the time that I had been looking for her she had no hint that I might still have been alive. When I was nowhere to be found after the air attack she thought I had been killed with the hundreds who died on the street that ran through the village, many of whom were mangled beyond recognition.

"The survivors were brought to Trento, and then Verona, and in the confusion I was listed as killed. When I got back to Rome I discovered that the Italian army considered me dead—in Gruensee, in the observation post, and on the Cima Bianca. That I was reported killed three times seemed not to affect their trust in the reports except to strengthen it. Being the army, they must have thought that anyone who was killed three times was most certainly deader than if he had been killed only once.

"I never altered my status. I was worried about having deserted, and in the years immediately following the war, no one—no former soldier, anyway—was sure that we would not be mobilized again, for whatever reason.

"Ariane was indeed the woman I saw just before the house was bombed, but my conception of time was wrong. She had run down two flights of stairs, and was rushing out to meet me, but stretchers were blocking the hallway that led to the front, so she turned to go out the back. She heard the bomb smash through the roof. She said it sounded like a basket being broken up before it's thrown away. It pierced the ceilings of the third, second, and first floors. She remembered that this sounded like cards being shuffled.

"It exploded in the front room, and the impact pushed the interior walls, in one piece, against the outside walls of the building, which then collapsed upon itself. At the instant of detonation Ariane was at the open door, and the air compressing inside blew her ten meters from the house. She landed on the grass, where she lay paralyzed and hardly able to breathe. Everyone else inside had been crushed, burned, obliterated.

"And then, suddenly, in Rome, on a calm day in June, she was standing in front of me, in a towel. I held her. . . . I wouldn't let go. It must have been an hour. She couldn't speak, because every time she tried to say something, she wept. The towel slipped and she was naked in my arms. Though the cousin was amazed, Paolo, our son, held tightly to his mother's neck, because of her tears, and paid no heed to the scandalous circumstances.

"She cried. Within her crying, sometimes, she laughed, but not much, and the baby cried and stroked her head, and I, I was overcome, but though I was overcome I thought back upon the painting, and my God, Ariane was naked with a child in her arms, and I had found her, and I could not believe it, but it was true, it was certainly true, and if you ask me how or why it happened I can't tell you, but life and death have a rhythm, an alternating rhythm, and you never know what to expect, as it is in God's hands, and I was waiting for a thunderstorm, for the sky to darken, for lightning, and wind. We were as stunned as the people in the Bible upon whom miracles are showered, and even though the thunderstorm did not come until the next night, each and every lightning flash, and each and every thundercrack, was a triumph."

"THEN IT all came out all right," Nicolò said. "It was all resolved."

Alessandro looked at him sharply, as if, despite Nicolò's well meaning remark, he was offended.

"Of course it wasn't resolved," Alessandro said. "You've been listening to me. How can you think that?"

"You said . . . you said you found her, like in the painting. It was perfect: the woman, the child, you had survived the war, you had waited, and you found her. You don't think that's coming out all right?"

"If it had all stopped then and there," Alessandro told him, "but it doesn't stop, it never stops. And what about all the others: Fabio, Guariglia, the Guitarist, the two *Milanese,* Rafi? I told you. Look up at the Perseids. You can see them flashing many times a second. They reach the end of their long and silent journeys almost more quickly than you can note, but if you watch them for hours you will not see the casualties of even one group of divisions.

"Each of the flashes is like the life of a man. We're too weak to feel the full import of such a loss, and so we continue on, or we reduce it to an abstraction, a principle. It would take more than anyone could give to understand the life of one other person—we cannot understand even our own lives—and more energy and compassion than is humanly possible to commemorate even a single life that ends in such a death.

"You cannot know anything but the smallest part of the love, regret, excitement, and melancholy of one of those quick flashes. And two? And three? At two you have entered the realm of abstraction, and are by necessity thinking and talking in abstractions."

"How do you mean, abstractions?"

"I mean, think of a glass of wine that you spend half an hour drinking as it gets dark in the evening, and then think of ten liters of wine, and ten thousand liters. If you can't drink them, they are an abstraction. People throw around abstractions very carelessly because they don't have to live them, and then the abstractions take over their lives."

"So they do live them," Nicolò said.

"No, they don't. They live their lives as dictated by their notions, which is usually something very much different, monstrously different. You don't know what I mean, do you."

"I don't."

"You know the people who are against war, on principle?"

"I'm against war, on principle," Nicolò said indignantly, "although I'd like to fight in one."

"You can't be against it in principle if you can't know it in principle, and you can't know it in principle. You can know only its smallest part, which is enough."

"So why can't I be against it in principle?"

"If you claim to know war in principle you're only pretending, and if you can only pretend to know it you can only pretend to be against it. Many people just like to show that they're thinking the right thoughts. And as the 'right' thoughts change like the wind, so do they."

"So what are you supposed to do?"

"All you have to know is the story of one of the flashes. That's enough. That's more powerful than any principle. And, look, the worst of it only brings to you early and suddenly what would come slowly and late—so don't exaggerate. I've comforted myself with that thought, which is not very comforting, almost all my life.

"The problem with war, as I have seen it, is not so much that it makes misery and grief—all of which would tend to come anyway, in time. The sin is in the abruptness, in the abridgement of those stages that otherwise might be joined so brilliantly to make a life.

"Infants are left without fathers or mothers. Fathers and mothers die with the unbearable knowledge that their children are alone in the world. The love of a man and a woman is neither consummated nor allowed to flare and fade. Generations end, families cease to exist. The line, the story, stops for some, and that, I think, is the worst of it. When your children die before you no recovery exists except perhaps in the inexplicable grace of God, in events that no one has reported, in a place from which no one has ever returned.

"And in war, as I have known it, the children die and their parents are left to grieve."

"Not Guariglia's children."

"No. He perished, but they were saved."

"What happened to them?"

"When I got back, the harness shop was still there, but with another harness-maker—he had two legs—and his family. They had bought the stock and trade from Guariglia's widow.

"I asked where she had taken the children, and the harness-maker told me, 'To get work in the north.' What city? Milano? Torino? Genova? He didn't know. What kind of work? That he knew. Any kind of work, she had told him, whatever it might be."

"Just like my father and mother, the same thing," Nicolò said. "We got off in Rome because there was a guy on the train platform who gave my father a job in a restaurant. My mother left the train with the babies, and my father passed me and the suitcases to them and the restaurant guy. My father had to jump from the train while it was moving. We got some money back on the tickets, and my father worked in the kitchen of this guy's restaurant. Everything was by chance, nothing by plan. Did you find them? How could you have found them?"

"I put microscopic advertisements in the back of newspapers. In those days, the newspapers were full of such things. I couldn't afford more than a line or two: *Signora Guariglia, Rome Harness Shop, Contact Alessandro Giuliani,* and my address. I ran them twice in the first year, twice in the second, then once a year, now and then, far less than the appeals I had published for Ariane, who never saw them."

"But did Guariglia's wife?"

"Oh yes, *she* did. She was in Milano, where she saw the very first one. She clipped it and put it in her sewing box."

"Why?"

"Why? You want me to explain to you what goes on in the mind of a Roman harness-maker's widow? I asked her, years later, when finally she got in touch with me. Suddenly, she sent me a Christmas card. She said she didn't know why, it wasn't that she was busy, or afraid that I was a bill collector, but she thought something like that belonged in her sewing box, where she could think about it. She had let it age, you see.

"She came to see me, with all her children, in nineteen twenty-five. She was married to a foundry worker, and they had enough money, so I started a savings account for the children. I put it in a

Milan bank, and every year I added to it. I would take the children to the bank and make the deposit in the office for trust accounts—a more and more sizable deposit as time went on—and then we'd go to a restaurant where, for an hour and a half, I would tell them about their father.

"The foundry worker was not very comfortable with this, but the swelling trust account, in a blue-and-gold portfolio, eased his nerves. The mother loved Guariglia but she wasn't able to tell the children very much about him. She had always been in a subservient position; he had had to work all the time; and she was the kind of woman who kept yellowed newspaper clippings in a sewing box.

"But I told them. Every year it was the same. I told them about how brave he was in the line, in the Bell Tower. I told them about the other world we saw together in Sicily; and how their father did well in a combat that might have occurred in the Middle Ages. I told them about the cattle boat, and of how he cut off his own leg in an effort to stay alive—for them.

"It took some time, as you can imagine. By the end of the meal—it was more than an hour and a half—the restaurant would be empty except for me and the children, and the waiters leaned against the banquettes, linen towels still over their arms, napping, but facing the street in case a customer would interrupt them. . . . By the end of the meal, I had told them about Stella Maris. I always cried when I told them how their father had said, in a clear voice, *God protect my children,* and they would cry, too. Even when they were older, I would embrace them—in the middle of the god-damned restaurant—but it was all right, because by that time no one else was there and the waiters were too sleepy to notice.

"They were so young when he died that they might have forgotten him, but I think his picture and the story I told every year had their effect—because, as it turns out, they loved him above all others.

"One of the girls said to me, 'At first I loved him like a saint, but then, when I got to know him better as I got older and I could imagine him better, it wasn't like a saint. Saints make you heave with emotion, and then you forget them. I began to miss my father all the time. I would look up and realize that I had been thinking of him, that I wanted him to be there. You never really want a saint to be there, do you?'

"His children grew up the way he would have wanted them to. And when they had children of their own, I released the trust, and I saw them no more. Now it is their father I think of, from time to time. Perhaps had he not been so physically ugly I would not have loved him so much, and perhaps even his children would not have loved him as they did. He was a good man. He was a man who really broke your heart."

A BIRD had begun to sing in a smooth slow warble that came before the first hint of dawn and yet long after the night songs had ceased. Alessandro would have been content merely to listen, but Nicolò was impatient, and pressed for more. "What about Fabio?" he asked.

"What about him? I watched him die. They put his body on a wooden cart and sent it, the perfectly formed face and entrancing blue eyes, the flesh that women loved to touch with their fingers and their mouths, to hold, to run their limbs against it so they could feel perfect and loved and like something light that was made of silk, something that could float on the wind, and they knew it, I am sure, tumbling into the grave.

"The grave-diggers had many men to bury, and they didn't lay them out gently. They tossed them in, hunched up, with limbs tangled and hands an unnatural distance from the body, to be caught and pressed in the earth as if in amber."

"Did you try to see his family?"

"No. No. I hadn't the strength to seek out any but Guariglia's family. I had my own life, my own troubles. Fabio undoubtedly had someone, but God's gift to him was himself. He spent everything up front, and, given what happened, perhaps he was right. When he was gone, he was gone. We loved him because he was, in his vain way, so wonderfully stupid. When I think of him, I always smile, which I am sure is what he would have wanted."

"What about Orfeo?"

"Do you want me to tie up every loose end in my life for you?"

"I just want to know. You told me about these people. You said it never ends: I want to know what happened."

Alessandro was still. Then he raised his hand, as if to say, *Wait.* He had long been sitting up on the ledge, having risen from a position of rest, and when he hesitated Nicolò thought that he was going to lie back and rest again, but, instead, he spoke.

"Look," Alessandro said, "let's not fool around. I'm going to die today, this morning. The walk was too great a strain on my heart. While I try to rest, it struggles on in exhaustion, and I can't control it. It thunders inside me, and seems arrhythmic. Within my chest are hollow spaces like bubbles of air. I can neither calm it down nor stop the pain."

"I'll run to the village to get an ambulance," Nicolò said, his body tensing as he began to stand. Alessandro could see that Nicolò was eager to run.

"I don't want an ambulance. I want you to sit down and shut up."

"But Signore, an ambulance could take you to a hospital. They could help you."

"I don't want to die in a hospital."

"You wouldn't! You'd live!"

Alessandro closed one eye. "I don't want to be alive in a hospital, either."

"You'd rather die outside? On the ground?"

"I've always loved being outside, on the ground. The ground has been my salvation. Sitting here under the stars makes me feel as if I have a place, as if I'm doing right, as if this is where I was intended to be. So you just shut up, please, and let me continue."

Nicolò sank back, half in dejection.

"I'm going to die today, I think, so I can tell you. I never told anyone: neither my wife nor my son. I never told a priest. I had planned to confess it, but every time I thought of it I smiled, so I didn't think I'd get very far in the confessional. They don't like it when you laugh at your sins, and I always do, goddamn me, though it's what has kept me alive. Maybe I shouldn't tell you. Who said I'll die today?"

"You did."

"Who knows? What if I don't?"

"I won't tell anybody."

"And if you did?"

"So what?"

"My idea of a graceful retirement does not encompass six or seven years of hearings and depositions."

"You told me everything else," Nicolò said, sounding injured.

"I haven't scratched the surface."

"There's a statute of limitations."

"How do you know about that?"

"Where I come from is different from where you come from."

"Swear not to tell."

"I swear."

"People say things, and then they lapse, but, between your oath and my health, I think I can tell you. I murdered him."

"Orfeo?"

"Orfeo."

"I don't believe you."

"But you want to hear the story anyway."

"Yes."

"EVEN NOW, at seventy-four years of age, I can't get the war out of my blood. It was too strong a thing—never had anything been like it. I dream of the war more than I dream of the present or of my youth. It is the essential condition to which I always return and refer. Should I slip, it is where I will fall; should I weaken, it is where I will rest.

"All the churches in the world, with their candles flickering in the cool air, and all the masses and all the fugues can't do it justice. My haunting and repetitive dreams receded only after twenty years, and only because my time was over and my son went to take my place at the front.

"What is war, that rolls through history and is more terrible than death, but in whose folds life is vitally compressed more than in the most glorious peace?

"I have never seen anything more riveting than a mountain division, roped in a thousand teams, moving at night, each man with his light, like strings of paper lanterns floating up a glacier half obscured by clouds in a lake of black. It was a whole city of men, moving silently upon the enemy at three in the morning in a place that had hardly felt a footstep since the world began. I remember them rising, their lights swaying, the ice faintly illuminated by the lantern beams from the candles and mirrors on their helmets. The south face of the ice-clad mountain glittered as they walked across it.

"And the cavalry, whether Austrian or our own... Even the coarsest men were moved by the sight of a thousand riders trotting into line. When the line wheeled on a point and began to charge, hearts stopped in amazement, and the clock of the world was started as if for the first time. Did you ever see a merchant snap an abacus back to zero? As a cavalry charge gains momentum, all registers return to the starting point, and life begins anew.

"I dreamed of these things. I could not rid my mind of them. They had their own life, their own logic. War cannot be explained in the terms of the world we know, but as it moves through all we know, it does so with impunity and surprise.

"In the years immediately following the Armistice, I and millions of others were still caught up in the battles just finished. The war had ended, but not for us, not at least for those foolish enough to struggle in making some sense of it—of whom I was certainly one. I now attribute my vain desire to my education, which had instilled in me the splendid and reckless belief that everything can be explained.

"The way I saw it, then, and to some extent still see it, is that war is a separate world to which some are born, and some are not. Guariglia, for example, was not."

"And what about you?"

"I was born to be a soldier," Alessandro said, "but love pulled me back. It made what could have been an effortless passage sometimes unbearably difficult. I understood my reticence, and I banished it in time to save my life. It came, and it went. Luck brought it to me at the right times, and luck allowed me to cast it aside when it would have killed me.

"Some had no ambivalence whatsoever. Any soldier of the line can spot them immediately, the ones born for war. I certainly could, since they and I had sprung from the same root.

"My son was given to me full blown, whole, as if from nothing, the most beautiful child I had ever seen, my own. At first I despaired that he should live as I had, and then, eventually, I was resigned to it, as I had to be, for he never came back. He is the reason that I exhaust myself with all these questions, and cannot die in peace. He and the others are the reason I have vainly fought for an opening into another world. I cannot trade that unlikely chance for happiness in this life, because I remember too well those who have fallen. I keep myself on edge—though, all these years, I have done it indirectly, and saved immediate recollection for the very last, both to honor it and to preserve it forever."

"I don't understand."

"You don't have to. Just listen to the story.

"Orfeo—that little Italian ballroom dog, that bent and extraordinary creature, had hardly been born for war, but he had gone over to the camp of those who were. He gave up his sanity so his obsessions could flow within him without resistance and elevate him to a plane of tremendous power, power that, only because he was comical, appeared accidental. It wasn't. I knew him well enough to have seen his madness fuse irrevocably with the spirit of war.

"I was desperate to protect my son. And I myself was still a little mad. I regretted that I hadn't killed Orfeo in the toilet stall. He was the one who assigned Rafi to the Cima Bianca. He was the one who assigned me. He assigned us all. The evil was not in the steel, but in the paper, and that little son of a bitch knew it and gave in completely."

"So what did you do?"

"I killed him."

"You killed him?"

"To protect my son, and other sons, and other babies. To protect all the babies in Italy."

"But it didn't."

"I was unable to see into the future."

"How did you do it?"

"Although I had killed men in trenches and redoubts and among the trees, I had never killed in cold blood. The difference is stupendous. It is nearly impossible for a sane person to drive a bayonet through the chest of another human being if he is defenseless and still. In bayonet training throughout the world, the soldier who wields the bayoneted rifle is ordered to scream as he drives the blade through. Civilians assume that the cry is meant to terrify an opponent, but it isn't. It's meant to allow you to bridge your natural reluctance to push a long blade into a living human being, and to cover the horrible sound of steel cutting into flesh and bone. As dreadful as is the task, should your enemy be coming at you, you accomplish it so readily and remorselessly that, how can I describe it? It seems no more difficult or disturbing than, say, lighting a match.

"I knew I could never kill Orfeo in cold blood. I would have to provoke him, but I could not imagine how."

"You could call him names."

"He *was* names. It would only have flattered him."

"You could push him, poke him. That would make him angry."

"It would have made him go limp."

"You could challenge him to a duel."

"He was a half-blind, fat, old midget with palsies and ticks. He would have laughed."

"Then how did you do it?"

"You won't believe me."

"Yes I will," Nicolò protested.

"No you won't, but it's true.

"First, I had to find him. I went to the enormous room in the Ministry of War where Orfeo had been seated on a platform above the other scribes. It was empty save for regimental flags hanging from the walls, and the platform was gone.

"A fat little guy in an office down a hall saw me and kept calling out, 'You! You!' and waving for me to come to him. 'I saw you in there looking amazed,' he said. 'You must have been here when the war was run from that room.' I nodded. 'Now it's a marching hall for new recruits who have to wait to go to training camp. Who the hell would join the army now that the war's over?'

" 'The smart ones,' I said.

" 'It's a little like *coitus interruptus,* isn't it?'

" 'Some people can't help it if they're young,' I told him."

"What's *coitus interruptus*?" Nicolò asked.

"*Coitus* is having sex," Alessandro said, "and *interruptus* is when, suddenly, you're not."

Nicolò laughed out loud. "Why would anyone want to *interruptus*?"

"Why do you think?"

"I don't know. It sounds really stupid to me. Why stop if you've started? Why start if you're going to stop? I thought that in sex it was a gradual stop, like a duck landing in a pond."

"Yes, but can you think of a reason why you would stop at a certain point?"

"No."

"Think hard."

"A holiday?"

Alessandro scowled.

"I don't know! What do you want from me? I'd die to have sex. All right. Some people stop in the middle. Boom! That's their problem. I don't even want to talk to them. Get them out of here. It's as stupid as joining the army after the war."

"What about babies?"

"What about them?"

"Having them."

"Having them *what?*" Nicolò asked in exasperation.

"Having them be born."

"What about them?"

"Maybe that's a good reason to stop immediately."

"So you'll have a baby?"

"No, idiot! So you won't!"

"I don't understand."

Alessandro sat up straight. "How is it you think babies are born?"

"Something the mother and father do before sex, some sort of cloth or herb or hard-boiled egg that the father puts in the mother or something, with a rubber bulb and a glass dish."

"No," Alessandro said. "That's not quite it."

"No?"

"No. You just have to have sex—if you're married, fifty times; if you're not married, once."

"You're kidding!"

"I'm not kidding."

"I thought it was something additional."

"Nothing additional."

"That's good to know," Nicolò said, "because, you know, I might have—you know."

"You see how insane the world is, Nicolò? No matter that it is unbearably beautiful. How would I have guessed that during my last hours I would sit on a rock in the starlight, in mountain laurel, explaining sexual hygiene to an apprentice in a propeller factory."

"Well now I know."

"Good."

"But what about Orfeo?"

"What about Orfeo? The fat guy kept talking. 'Remember the hundreds of men who sat at desks in there?' he asked. I said I did. 'Every order and communiqué of the war went through them, and if you promise not to tell, I'll let you in on something that will really amaze you.'

" 'What?' I asked, pretending ignorance.

" 'Not a single order or communiqué ever left the way it came in. If the dispatch said *Advance twenty kilometers, wheel right until enemy is engaged, and hold position on flank as main attack is developed from the south,* it might go out reading, *Advance fifteen kilometers, wheel left, and move position according to necessity as feints are developed from the east.*

" 'Or a naval order. The coordinates would be reversed, ship types changed. I swear to God, Italian ships were sent to Polynesia, and, somehow, Japanese ships ended up in the Mediterranean. Do you know how many men were shot who weren't supposed to have been shot? How many weren't shot who were supposed to have been? I don't know how the army ate. Every gram of army cinnamon was shipped one day to an anti-aircraft battery in Treviso. That's all they had to eat for the whole war—twenty-two and a half tons of cinnamon, and no one else had even a sprinkle. An infantry battalion on the French border kept on getting boxcars and boxcars full of pipe tobacco, and there was a cruiser, I swear, that for several years received nothing but anchovy paste.'

"I told the fat guy that what he described sounded to me like a fair description of what life had been like in the army, and I asked him why, if he knew about it then, he didn't try to stop it.

"He said that he had tried, that he had gone to generals and civilian officials and told them, but that they had said, 'So what? We're winning.'

"We did win, Nicolò, but we lost at least seven hundred thousand killed, and many times that number were wounded. Commissions were formed to determine the number of casualties, but because the record keeping had been so chaotic they couldn't agree even to the nearest hundred thousand. No one knows how many died. Maybe a hundred thousand or two hundred thousand fell in between the cracks, disappeared. The loss of a single man should have stopped the world.

"I asked him why it was that the orders were changed, and he replied, 'A dwarf, a little bat-like thing whose name was Orfeo Quatta. He sat on a dais in the middle of the floor. He was the chief scribe. To his clerks he was Caesar Augustus.'

"'Wasn't he removable?'

"The little fat guy smiled. 'In his safe he had the seals, the forms for patents, commissions, proclamations, declarations, and decrees. He set up a government within the government—by moving the decimal points in appropriations and salaries, sending his speechless enemies to tiny towns in Calabria, and rewarding sycophants with sinecures.

"'He had fits of madness and megalomania upon the dais, as the scribes, their heads bent in terror, pretended not to hear.'

"I talked to the little fat guy for a long time. He told me that everyone wanted to kill Orfeo, that it was a common fantasy. 'But no one killed him,' he said, 'just the way you never get to caress the most beautiful woman in the world.'

" 'The most beautiful woman in the world always finds a lover, doesn't she?' I asked. Of course, he had to say yes. Then I said, 'Someone there is, always, who does manage to touch her.'

" 'Yes.'

" 'Then,' I said, 'someone must have killed Orfeo. Or someone will.'

" 'No,' he said, 'no one ever did.'

" 'How was he removed?'

" 'The war ended. It was just like letting the water out of a tub.'

" 'Where did he go?'

"The next morning, I went there, too. He lived in a cave dug into the base of the Testaccio."

"What's the Testaccio?" Nicolò asked.

"You know where the pyramid is?"

"Yeah, in Egypt."

"No. I mean the one in Rome."

"There's a pyramid in Rome?"

"Did you ever go to Ostia?"

"Yeah."

"How?"

"On the train."

"You didn't see the pyramid across the street from the train station?"

"That thing?"

Alessandro bobbed his head extra hard, so Nicolò would see his answer even in the dark. "What did you think it was?"

"I thought they were building something and hadn't put on the other side."

"No. It's a pyramid. Just down the street, beyond the Protestant Cemetery, is a big hill called the Testaccio. It's made of broken amphorae that were used as ballast on ships that docked in the Tiber. They knew they would dam the river if they kept dropping the pieces into it, so they made a mound. The district is also home to the Mattatoio, and to those who are so poor that they cannot even sit on the street in other parts of the city, lest other people be unsettled in their vanity and dreams of rank. You and I and everyone else are a snap of a finger away from the derelicts with sparkling eyes and blackened skin who stumble forward knowing that they'll be gone in a week or two. The only difference now between me and them is that I'm clean and I can talk."

"You're not so clean anymore, Signore. You're covered with dust, and your eyes are like the eyes of a wolf."

Alessandro smiled. "Like a wolf?"

"Like a wolf."

"All right, I'm not clean, my heart is failing, and I'm lying on the ground, but I can talk. I'm talking, am I not, with some speed?"

"You're windmilling," Nicolò said.

"Good," Alessandro returned. "That can't be unpleasant to you, considering your profession."

"Tell me about Orfeo before you die," Nicolò said, playing a part.

"I won't die until it's hot."

"How do you know?"

"Because I want to, and I will."

"If you hadn't told me about your heart, I would never know."

"I want to."

"Why?"

"I'm ready."

"You're tired of living?"

"I was tired of the world a long time ago, and I'm running half in another realm right now. It isn't unpleasant; it isn't dark. Quite to the contrary, it's a land of light, and soon I'll have to ask you if I'm floating."

"Do you want me to stay with you?"

"No. When it gets light, go back on the road and go visit your sister. Is she pretty?"

"A little bit."

"I wish I could have met her, but she wouldn't have understood. She probably would have been distrustful, or at least shy."

"I don't think so. She used to be a whore."

"What could be more shy than a whore in a convent?"

"She had to do it, but only for six months. A tower buckled when my father was on top fastening the lines. He was unconscious for a month, and he couldn't walk for a long time after that. He never knew. She told him she worked in a cafeteria, and she changed her clothes in the hotel. As soon as he got a job making bricks, she stopped. I shouldn't have told you—she'd kill me—but you told me about Orfeo."

"Let me finish, then, so we'll be even.

"Why did he live in a cave in the Testaccio? I don't know. You would think he would have been smart enough to have ordered a billion lire into a secret bank account in Switzerland, and retire there—like every Italian who does something like that—surrounded by bodyguards, Doberman pinschers, and women with huge breasts.

"But no, he lived in a tiny room hewn from a mountain of potsherds. He used to talk about the whitened bones in the valleys of the moon. Perhaps he thought he was living in a mountain of bones, and that the exalted one was going to go there to pick him up. Well, the exalted one did.

"He had two windows and a door at the front of the cave, and the windows had garish yellow-and-purple curtains: irises and daffodils. I never notice things like shoes and curtains, I see right past them, but these were magnetic. As I stood at the gate of the little garden in the front of his house, I saw him peeping from behind those hideous curtains.

"He didn't know I was watching him, and he thought that I didn't know that he was watching me. His expression was one of deep concentration and concern, like that of an animal, used to running free, that suddenly discovers it is trapped.

"I could see only a quarter of his face at a time, but he moved around enough so that eventually I saw every part. His black hair was slicked down, and he looked nimble and well pressed. He was old, but he was the kind of man who can do a backward somersault until he's ninety. I thought that, with fascism, we were certain to have another war, and, thus, I had an overwhelming desire to get rid of him.

"I waited for several months, and I grew a beard. Ariane was polite, but she preferred me without it. Paolo was amazed and amused. I promised to shave before the autumn. Under an assumed name, I joined a swimming club near the Tiber. It was a horrible club, always crowded and chaotic, especially when the students of a nearby *liceo* were released. A pool designed for seven lane-swimmers would suddenly be burdened with a hundred screaming adolescents. The changing-rooms were so tumultuous that no adult in his right mind would go near them. Good. Part of my plan.

"I went to look at the hovel next to Orfeo's; it was empty. An old woman sitting inside another hovel told me that if I wanted to rent it I should talk to the owner of an expresso bar near the Mattatoio.

"It was a bar for the slaughterhouse workers, and I reeled from the smell as I walked to the counter. The waiter there went to get his boss.

"'I'm a clerk in a rubber factory,' I told the boss, 'and I work the night shift. My mother had an accident getting out of a boat in Ancona, which is where we live, so she can't clean fish anymore, and I have to support her.'

"'What has that got to do with me?' he asked.

"'I took a day job typing orders for a furniture company. They do a lot of business in Greece, and since my father was born in Greece, he speaks Greek, and I know some Greek, and although my typewriter doesn't type Greek, I write things in Greek underneath what I type.'

" 'Why are you telling me this!' he screamed. He thought I was a maniac. He looked like Mussolini. I think he cultivated it.

" 'My landlady in Trastevere likes to sleep in the daytime,' I said. Then I paused. I was going to make him remember me forever. 'She says I can't type in my room. I took a table into the street, but it was too crowded to work there.'

"He was going crazy. Then I closed it. 'I need a place. Your rooms in the Testaccio are perfect. It's quiet there all day.'

" 'Ah!' he said. 'But you'd leave quickly.' He sounded disappointed. 'There are a lot of lunatics there.'

" 'Are they dangerous?'

" 'Who knows? It's not for normal people.'

" 'My poor mother,' I said. 'The furniture company compensates me generously because they don't have to provide me with an office. Because of that, I can pay you well.'

"When I told him how much, which was three times the best he could hope for, he ran to get the key. As the barb in the hook, I paid him for several months in advance.

" 'I hope your mother feels better,' he said, in a tone that proved that even someone who looked like Mussolini could be ingratiating.

"I intended to make it so the police would not even look for the murderer, or at least not very hard, but, if they did, they would be looking for a bearded single man, of Greek extraction, who lived in Trastevere, was a clerk in a rubber factory, and whose mother had recently had an accident in a boat in Ancona."

"What about fingerprints?"

"I didn't plan to leave any. Besides, my fingerprints weren't on record, and even had they been, I wasn't a suspect, so they wouldn't have thought to compare them. At that time, anyway, the police were still used to the Bertillon system, and slow to use the new techniques.

"For a month I approached the swimming pool via the Ponte Sublicio, from Trastevere, where I stopped at a coffee bar and talked endlessly about typing furniture orders. Every time I came in, the bartender's heart sank. Once, on the way home, I bought a hammer and a crowbar, telling the ironmonger that I was going to make repairs on a place in the Testaccio that I had rented to type up furniture orders, and all the rest."

"You got away with it, didn't you."

"Yes, I did," Alessandro answered, "in more ways than one, because, although I killed him, I didn't have to go as far as I had intended. He jumped the gun. He did it for me."

"He did?"

"Yes."

"He committed suicide?"

"No. I'll tell you.

"I had intended to set up a table and a typewriter—that I bought, naturally, in Trastevere—in the ragged patch of garden in front of the hovel that I had taken. I knew that Orfeo would not be able to tolerate the sound of the keys clicking, and the leads striking what he called *the infernal rubber roll.* In the middle of the day, a few people were working in their gardens, scavenging, or sitting about like heliotropes. They were to have been the witnesses when Orfeo lost control and attacked me with my own renovation tools, which would be conveniently nearby when the agitated rhino broke through the decrepit fence between his plot and mine.

"I was going to let him wound me. Everyone would see my blood before his, and, of course, he would be completely berserk, whereas I would be only amazed.

"But you can't engineer things like that. They happen in their own way, and so did this.

"I arrived at about ten-thirty. The sun was high, and three or four idle people had their eyes fixed upon my every move. I couldn't see Orfeo, but I heard him talking to himself, which I took as a favorable sign.

"Within minutes of my first key-stroke he charged out the

door, as enraged as a blast furnace. The eyes, mouth, hands, feet, and arms were moving without a plan, but the legs carried the fuming, bubbling barrel out into the street and into my yard.

"He didn't recognize me. It was probably because of my beard and the smoked glasses I wore, an unusually shaped pair of a type that I had never worn until that day and have not worn since.

"'Will you please! Please! Stop that disgusting noise!' he shouted in a manner at once so obsequious and so violent that it was new to me, and I could not help but liken it, on the spot, to burning oil. 'Everyone knows that certain practices,' he said, 'and certain machines, infernal machines, have no place in residential areas. Will you please! The typewriter was brought from Egypt, and it has ruined more fine people than you can imagine. My colleagues have vanished into its maw. Stop it, or I'll kill you.'

"I stopped, he left, and, as he was gliding over the threshold I struck again, tapping out a monotone tattoo. He began to smash things inside his house, and people came out to the street to see what was happening.

"Orfeo was bellowing, laughing, screaming—all with a self-imploding tension that told me an attack was imminent. I had to exert tremendous discipline to continue typing a list of different-sized dowels and corner clamps, but I kept at it.

"Orfeo staggered out his front door, and, just as I had thought, burst through the fence. He stood before me, twitching in compressed rage. I saw that he had something in his hand, and I was alarmed because I thought it was a gun. Crazy, angry, strange people don't shoot straight, but at that range I had no reason for overconfidence.

"It wasn't a gun, it was a grenade. Grenades have always made me very nervous, and I immediately stood up. I suppose you've never thrown one?"

Nicolò shook his head.

"You never get used to it, no matter how many times you've

done it. When you pull the pin it really perks you up, and when you toss the grenade and you hear the warning detonation, your spine feels like a Van de Graaff generator.

"That's what it feels like when *you* throw it. The ambiance is more intense when someone throws one *at* you. You have to count the seconds—and you never do it accurately—from the first pop, if you're lucky enough to have heard it. Then you have to figure out if you're going to try to toss it back, seek cover, or just hit the ground and roll up into a ball.

"Someone with experience will hold the grenade in his hand after it's primed and let it live half its life before he throws it. On the Isonzo, the Germans would delay it long enough so that it would explode in the air above the target.

"Orfeo pulled the pin, and I began to think that perhaps I was not so clever after all. In the corner of my eye I could see that my witnesses were frozen in place, with their mouths hanging open.

"I backed off. Orfeo strutted forward, his face moving in a hundred independent directions, an abysmal recitation coming from his lips. He was not after me, but the typewriter.

"His eyes narrowed as he approached it. He cursed, spit, and trembled, and, with a primeval growl, he slammed the grenade into the cradle. I heard the first detonation, as the handle was released. He had probably never thrown a grenade, and had kept his fingers around the lever merely by chance. When it popped, he thought it had exploded, and he reflexively pulled back his arm.

"His sleeve caught on the part with which you advance the roller and return the carriage. He was wearing a black wool jacket with a threadbare open weave, and the chrome bar went right through it.

"As Orfeo backed up, the typewriter flew off the table and smashed him in the knees. He screamed. He kicked the typewriter and swatted it with his free hand. 'Let go of me! Release me!' But the grenade was inextricably lodged in the typewriter, and the typewriter held tight to Orfeo.

"When he realized that the machine was going to do more than merely bang him in the knees, and that he could not let go, and that it was only a matter of seconds until his flesh and the many thousand pieces of the typewriter would mesh and intermingle in the final cocktail of his existence, he smiled and he began to laugh.

"His last words were spoken as if he had finally discovered what he had been seeking all his life. You know what he said? He said, *'Moles dash in the wind!'*

"I fell to the ground behind a pile of amphora handles. Another second passed, and I heard a tremendous explosion. Orfeo and the typewriter rained down upon the Testaccio in a way that I had seen a hundred times in the trenches, and I thought to myself, good, now a little bit of war has come home to the paper pusher.

"Though I had once regarded him with affection, I felt no regret. I had been hardened and crazed, and in that way I was able to pass on some of what I'd seen, instead of taking the blow alone. It's a kind of sacrilege, in modern times, that the walls be breached between the common soldier and the bureaucrats and clerks who send him to his death. You aren't supposed to make the connection, and they, the clerks, are supposed to be immune.

"But you take a soldier, and you blood him, and no one is safe, not even the generals. I thought that what was good enough for Fabio and Guariglia would also be good for Orfeo, and I made sure of it.

"I went to the swimming pool, and in a crowd of several hundred shouting adolescents I shaved off my beard at a sink in a cubicle half hidden in the steam. No one noticed.

"I swam a hundred laps, and changed into a white suit. I put my other clothes in a paper bag, and threw them in the trash. On my way home through the Aventino, I passed the police on several occasions. They didn't even look my way. I was numb. I had done it. I had actually killed a bureaucrat.

"Ariane told me that I seemed somewhat shaken, but I said that it was merely that, having shaved, I felt strange. A day in the sun, I said, and I would no longer look like a peeled apple.

"And Paolo—he was happy to have his father again. In my foolishness, whenever I glanced at him I felt elation, because I had imagined that I had cleared his future of war.

"As the years slowly passed and I realized that I had been suffering an illusion, I felt some regret about Orfeo, but when I felt regret about Orfeo it was not difficult for me to shift my remorse, and to remember those who had gone before him."

"THE SUN is about to rise," Alessandro said.

Nicolò turned his head, like an owl, to the west.

"In my experience," Alessandro told him, "it has always risen in the east, which is that way." As he pointed east his arm seemed so straight and still that Nicolò would not have been surprised had a banner suddenly unfurled along its length. "Of course, I'm willing to be open minded. Why not? I'll check the south and the north. You watch the west."

"I know the sun comes up in the east," Nicolò said, "where the moss is. I just didn't know where the east was, that's all."

"Is."

"Is what?"

"The east is. It never ceases to be the east."

"How do you know it's there?" Nicolò asked.

"We've been walking from north to south. At every step the east was to our left and the west to the right. I felt it without letup, and each time I turned from the north-south axis I felt the pressure, and the card would swing."

"You're a compass?"

"One of the great joys in my life has been knowing where I've been, where I am, where I'm going, and in which direction I face. We get our idea of angels from the birds, and they are masters of direction not by accident but because they have a high perspective. The world is less confusing when seen from above, and at the great speed at which they fly and turn, gravity and magnetism are exaggerated. Birds can feel the inertia of direction."

"How do you know about birds?" Nicolò asked, for it was hardly the first time that Alessandro had referred to them.

"I spent a long time watching them when I myself was so broken that I felt no sense of human superiority."

"Do you now?"

"How could I feel superior to something like a swallow, that rises so fast and falls with such abandon again and again, learning quickly and simply what life demands, and staying aloft despite what it knows."

"Did you watch them with a telescope? Did you have a guidebook, like an Englishman?"

"No. They came close. I didn't need a telescope. And I wasn't interested in collecting sightings. Quite frankly, I was uninterested in what you can know of them from books. I admired the extraordinary qualities that are obvious and apparent—that they are able to wheel in the blue and float among the clouds, and yet they always choose to return to earth, to nests of straw on spattered beams under the eaves of barns and churches; that, despite what they have seen, they are silent, except for singing; that though they are the emblem of freedom they have families; that they possess unimaginable power and endurance, and yet they sleep serenely and are, for the most part, as gentle as saints.

"I watched them on terraces and rooftops, in woodsheds, in forests and fields, on ledges like these, from the railings of ships, and from cliffs above the sea. When my son was little, we spent years outside—in the mountains, on the plain that surrounds Rome, in the fields, and floating down rivers. What a life we had. I would have considered it impossible. Most people, free to do almost exactly as they wish, would never understand the way we lived."

"That's what I mean," Nicolò said. "How did you get the time? My father, we never see him except Sundays. He's always worried. The only thing he's interested in about birds is how they taste."

"After the war," Alessandro said, noticing that the east was a shade lighter than black, and, therefore, that the sun was climbing high in the sky over India and would soon light the Mediterranean, "as you might imagine, nurses and armed guards were not in short supply. Europe had more nurses than the rest of the world combined. You looked at a woman . . . she was a nurse.

"And an entire generation of boys had grown up with the rifle and bayonet the tools of their craft. For them nothing seemed quite as real as the trenches, so they didn't throw themselves into the traditional occupations with much fervor. They believed that peace was a dream, and they found it difficult to invest in an illusion. Some stayed in the army, or re-enlisted after a year or two on the outside. Some were bank guards. Because there weren't any jobs that we wanted to do, we ended up with the jobs that no one else wanted."

"You were a gardener."

"For a few years. Then I did something that, had they known of it, would have amazed most of my students of the past two decades."

"What?"

"For ten years, I was a wood-splitter in a lumber mill near the Tiburtina Station. I did it because I could set my own hours, and work as little or as much as I wanted."

"*I* wouldn't split wood," Nicolò said.

"Why not?"

"It's the bottom."

"I was content. I rose at five and was at work by six. Usually I'd split from seven in the morning until twelve. It was five hours of swinging steel, five hours of hand-eye coordination, and five hours' reverie. My hands smelled of deerskin and the sweet lichen on the bark, and I got home at one, by which time Ariane had been at work since ten and Paolo had stayed for three hours with Ariane's cousin, Bettina.

"We'd have lunch, just Paolo and me, and set out at one-thirty, when everyone else was sleeping, and we'd walk. Sometimes we'd take a trolley and spend four hours coming back on foot. Sometimes we'd rush off, our lunches in a pack, and take an early train to the beach.

"We did this nearly every day, and at five-thirty we'd be at the door of the hospital to meet Ariane. We'd eat on our terrace as we watched the lights of Rome ignite gently by the thousand, and the birds and bats swooping in the dusk, outlined against the sunset."

"How much money did you make?" Nicolò asked.

"You'd be surprised. Between the two of us we made enough to satisfy our modest needs, and our greatest expense was that we lived in a nice place, a run-down villa on the side of a hill, with walls deepened and darkened by age, not a single sharp corner, and steps with parabolic centers from centuries of footfalls on the stone. It was quiet there. Standing in its peaceful, ill-tended, and forgotten garden, it was a sanctuary that had survived a thousand years of war. The saffron-colored walls, softened by time, were a great shield for memory and tranquillity.

"We ate simply, we were healthy, and we were uninterested in those things that should be called possessions not because they are possessed but because they possess. Those ten years were the happiest of my life save the first ten, the years in which I had neither position nor success, and no one took notice of me. Those were the years of the parent holding the child in his arms, lifting him high in the air, and pulling him close. As I held my own son, when he was a baby, God was right there."

"So why did you quit?"

"Quit what?"

"The wood-splitting."

"Past forty, I found it increasingly difficult to do that kind of work. I tired more easily. Injuries took far longer to heal. I needed much more rest. After Paolo started school we could no longer walk together every day. The three of us would go out on weekends, and we could go great distances. I think people thought we were tourists from Northern Europe—me, a blonde woman, and a light-haired child, all with knapsacks. Since when do Italians carry knapsacks? During a vacation one summer we took the Via Appia (where we could find it) from Rome to Brindisi, improvising along the way for eating and sleeping.

"I carried a Mauser the whole distance, not because I hunted, but because on the mountain tracks of Southern Italy there were bandits. Now it appears to me to have been reckless, but at the time I had no doubt that, were we confronted, I would prevail. I knew where to sleep at night, how to watch in the day, and what to do should action have been necessary. The countryside was wide open and mountainous, so I felt at home, even with bandits."

"You don't have to tell me," Nicolò declared admiringly. "You were a real killer."

Alessandro smarted. "Yes," he answered, exhausted by implications that he no longer wanted to consider, "I was. I'm not proud of it, but I'm not ashamed, either."

"You know," Nicolò said, "it bothers me. Someone like you, who could do anything he wanted, and you chop wood, which is what people like me are forced to do. Why did you choose it?"

"You would have no right to be bothered unless I complained. I loved it."

"That's because when you stopped you were a professor again, and then what do you do, you read books and you talk about them. Okay, *I* couldn't do it, but, if I could, I wouldn't call it work."

"It's sad," Alessandro said, "that people in different walks of life should think that no one works but they, that no one has difficulties but they. Most of these professors who you think don't work, don't think you work either. To them, what you do is worthless, and they believe that people like you are less than idiots."

"It isn't work if you don't get tired."

"But you do get tired. Your neck gets tired, and, for some people, the neck is important, because it holds up the head.

"At the time, I had no way to be a professor or even to teach in a subsidiary position. The universities were in lock-step with fascism. Real intellectual independence simply wasn't tolerated. I had an appointment here or there, but I didn't stay. At first I simply could not stand the conformism and the cowardice, and then, with the results predetermined, I came up against the loyalty oaths and the informers. I would have left anyway. After having gone through the war, I couldn't understand my colleagues' willingness to quibble and take offense over the meaning of a passage, or to live, die, and divide for their idiotic theories and schools. And nearly everything they said seemed to be in contradiction to the truth of what I'd seen.

"And yet if you ask me what that was, I can't tell you. I can tell you only that it overwhelmed me, that all the hard and wonderful things of the world are nothing more than a frame for a spirit, like fire and light, that is the endless roiling of love and grace. I can tell you only that beauty cannot be expressed or explained in a theory or an idea, that it moves by its own law, that it is God's way of comforting His broken children.

"Such a point of view does not lend itself to the lecture hall. No. I returned to the university only after the Second World War, and, even then, not having been in the resistance, I had political difficulties."

"Why weren't you in the resistance?"

"I was tired. And you have to have a certain temperament. You have to be fixed on the point. You need what politicians have, which is the absence of a sense of mortality. It comes, like a drug, from adoration and deference. Revolutionaries get it from dreams. They say that nothing is apolitical, that politics, the bedrock of life, is something from which you cannot depart. I say, fuck them.

"I was interested in birds. Are birds political? And I thought the finest thing in my life was being with my son when he was a baby. People used to look at us when we went around in the daytime, and wonder what a man was doing taking care of a child, but every word that came from him, every expression, every smile, even his tears, were worth a million times an honorable profession.

"I wrote my books then. They were not seditious in a political sense, being apolitical, though in some places being apolitical is the most extreme political statement you can make. Even Mussolini didn't find them seditious, despite my admiration for Croce. Still, I had to publish abroad, because the books were not written in the spirit of fascism and did not make obeisance to the themes and principles according to which one was deemed, or not deemed, acceptable. Salvemini helped me to publish in America, and I was able to make a small living. After the war, the books returned to Italy like a migration of birds. People said, 'Where has he been?' I said, 'I've always been here, where have you been?'

"In the Thirties we began to receive income from the real estate on the Via Veneto, my father's gift to us, although, as it turns out, Luciana didn't need it. She married a man who just got richer and richer—it's like that in America, because they fight their wars at a distance, so, as a nation, they can keep what they make. She ceded her interest to us. For her, it was pin money.

"I went to see her in nineteen fifty-five, a year after Ariane died. She lives on a big farm north of New York, and they grow champion sheep there. The sheep had so much wool that they could hardly move, and her sons used to roll them down the hill. Because they had been rolled down the hill since they were lambs, they didn't mind. You see, that's the difference between us and Americans. Our soil is too rocky to roll sheep downhill, but even if it weren't, do you think we would?"

Nicolò moved his head slowly from left to right.

"Of course not. It was very nice. It was sweet, in a way. It was funny. But it's not in my blood."

"Tell me about America."

"What's to tell? We went to a movie in a car, the museums are well lit, the Italians are really Sicilians, you can't get good coffee, and the newspapers have pictures of women in brassieres."

"Did your sister become an American?"

"Yes. She had been there a long time, and she spoke English almost without an accent, I think. It was easy for her to fit in because she's blonde and blue-eyed and they really like that. When I saw her, on the pier, in July of nineteen fifty-five, I cried. I didn't mean to. Her husband and sons were there, and Americans are not as emotional as we are.

"I love my sister. I love her for many reasons, not the least of which is that she is the only link I have with my parents, my childhood—all those things that disappear. After forty years she was still beautiful, and she looked exactly like my mother. For an instant, I thought she *was* my mother, and because we were in a huge pier shed and beams of light pierced the blackness, the din, and the dust, I thought for a second, for less than a second, that I had come full circle. The last time I had seen Luciana, I had been under sentence of death in Stella Maris. So, we cried, and though we did not mention Rafi, then or later, I knew that she was crying for him."

"Do her sons look like you?"

"No, they look like their father. They fought in the Pacific. One was a fighter pilot, the other an infantryman. They told me they were sorry never to have met their cousin, my son, and they were not merely being polite, for they had been soldiers, and they knew."

"THE HEART of it," the old man said, "is my memory of this boy, his mother, the men who were killed in the war, and my own parents. That is the problem I cannot resolve, the question I cannot answer, the hope I cannot relinquish, and the risk I must take. I have not forgotten them. May I tell you what, what it is..."

"Yes," Nicolò replied. "I'll stay with you."

"When it's light," Alessandro said, resolutely, "you'll go."

Nicolò shrugged in acceptance. To him, the old man seemed lost, and though he suspected that parting from him might seem difficult and unnatural, he knew that, when it was light, he would.

"Someday, Nicolò, when you get the chance, go to Venice to look at *La Tempesta*. Imagine then that, by the grace of God, the soldier would lose his detachment, and that, by the grace of God, the storm from which he had emerged would pass, and that by the grace of God the child in the woman's arms was his.

"In Giorgione's painting you find very little red. The dominant colors are green and gold: green, of course, being the color of nature, and gold the divine and tranquil color of which, like perfection, so little exists. The painters of Giorgione's time, by and large, spoke in these terms. Red was the instrument with which they portrayed mortality; green, nature; gold, God. With notable exceptions scattered from painter to painter and school to school, you will find this born out subtly and simply.

"You may not even have thought of red as anything more than just a color for decoration, but red is a most precious sign when you're at the bedside of someone you've just lost, for they haven't a trace of it. And red is the color of real love between a man and a woman. Its absence from the flesh in the act of love is far more profound than any protestation or vow. Indeed, in a marriage ceremony, red on a bride's cheek is her real vow, the rest useless and profane.

"I think that had Giorgione painted a sequel to *La Tempesta,* in which the soldier moves to the woman and child, he would have reddened them and made parts of the landscape reverberate in crimson. All the gold and green, the lightning, the reflected sunlight, and the cool colors of the storm, make for a dream-like air. It's like floating in the clear summer shallows of the Aegean, or the separation of the body from its sensations prior to the separation of the senses from the soul before the soul's ascension. That is the natural course, and, upon it, Giorgione, and Raphael, and the others, predicated their work. In Dante, too, the colors are refined with the soul until, at the last, one has risen through lighter and lighter blues, silvers, and golds, and what is left is merely white with a silver glare, far too bright to see or comprehend."

"What of it? What of it?" Nicolò asked, thinking that the old man was ranting, and would not be able to bring his talk of colors into focus.

"What if you didn't *want* to go in that direction?" Alessandro asked with frightening urgency, so that the hair on Nicolò's arms and on the back of his neck stood up.

"I still don't understand."

"What if, after having come into the presence of God, in voiceless perfection, in the perpetual stillness that is yoked to perpetual movement, you asked nonetheless to be released, to go back, to descend, to go down, to revert. What if you chose, rather than silver and gold, and white that is too bright to comprehend, the lively pulse of red?

"I have felt that perfection. I have had a glimpse of the light. I have a notion, perhaps more than a notion, of eternity in its flawless and unwanting balance. Compared to it, the brightest moments are but darkness; and singing, like silence. What great sin do I commit, therefore, if I hold that it is insufficient?

"For when I put my arms around her, Ariane was red. Her cheeks and the top of her chest blazed like a burn, or rouge, and the color spread to her breasts and her shoulders and was only dilute once it had cooled by running, like a viscous waterfall, down the length of her back.

"The baby followed his mother in this flash of her coloring like a chameleon following the light. She averted her eyes. She would not look up. Her lips trembled as if in prayer or concentration.

"What if that moment had lasted? What metaphysical rapture could equal it for its substance, its frailty, and its beauty? Haven't we been taught that it's better to live in a simple house overlooking a garden or the sea than to reside in a palace of great proportion?"

"What are you *saying,* Signore?" Nicolò asked.

"I'm saying that now I know exactly what I want, and that though I doubt it fits the scheme of things, I'll chance it nevertheless."

"What happened when you had a baby without being married?" Nicolò asked, returning, as always, to the practical, and pulling Alessandro with him.

"*She* had the baby. I wasn't there."

"You know what I mean."

"Did I mention the priest in the Bell Tower?"

"No."

"In the Bell Tower, on the Isonzo, he would come to say mass, only it wasn't always on a Sunday, it was whenever he wasn't someplace else and the incoming artillery fire was light enough for him to hop through the communications trench.

"The priest was named Father Michele. He was my age. He had an unusual way of speaking, and everything he said seemed to have been questioned and examined just before it left him, as if he had a little inspection box in his head and each sentence underwent a merciless examination there in respect to its truth and its effect.

"His expressions matched his manner of speaking. He had a big nose, deeply set eyes, wire-rimmed spectacles, and a mouth that was almost crooked and had gotten that way, I imagine, as he carefully pronounced each of his carefully chosen words.

"A lot of soldiers interpreted his hesitancy as weakness. At first, I did, too, but, then, watching him, I realized that it was not weakness that made him think carefully and speak haltingly, but integrity. The need to assert puts us in the habit of assertion: he refused that habit, and spoke as if everything were new and untried.

"One day—I don't even remember in what season or what the

weather was like, for in the Bell Tower you sometimes saw nothing but a round circle of sky above the courtyard, and blue does not always tell you very much—he had come to say mass, and was pinned down because the Austrians had concentrated their guns on our sector and we had incoming fire around the clock.

"No one was hurt until the following dawn. A soldier from Otranto...I didn't really know him. He was seventeen or eighteen." Alessandro stopped, and turned directly to Nicolò. "He looked like *you*. He was young, and he had little to say, and when he spoke he always talked about his parents. His father was a stone mason, and the son revered him as if he were the Pope. Other soldiers made fun of him for it, which hurt him deeply. And his mother, well, you can imagine what he felt about his mother. And he still needed her.

"I hardly knew him. At dawn he went into the courtyard to hang out his socks. Everyone would dash out for a moment or two for that kind of thing. It was a chance you took.

"A forty-five-millimeter shell came in from nowhere. They were so small you didn't hear them until you couldn't do anything about it. It hit the ground at his feet and blew him against the wall, tearing off his right leg and opening a scoop-shaped tunnel into his body. There was blood all over him, organs hanging out.... We had seen it too many times not to know that he was gone.

"He stayed alive for ten minutes. He was conscious, and felt no pain, because he was too far along to feel pain, but he knew he was dying and he felt the holy terror as he slipped away.

"Father Michele went to him, for this was the job, after all, that Father Michele had chosen. He had a bunch of memorized things that he could say, things that had been tested over centuries, and that worked, and that were expected. He was supposed to administer last rites so that he could save the boy's soul.

"I've told you, though, that he took everything for what it was, and judged everything anew. He didn't do what he was supposed to have done. We watched from the doorway, with the door ajar.

"He had gathered the boy in his arms, and he was bathed in his blood, but he held him the way you would hold a baby, and he cried, and he talked to him until he died.

"'I can't see,' the boy said. 'I can't see.' That was the only time that Father Michele quoted the Bible to him. He said, 'Like...a swallow...mine eyes fail with looking upward.' The soldier was dying quickly. His soul was halfway to another place.

"The priest said, 'Where you are going there is no fear and there is no dying. Your mother and your father will be there. They'll hold you like a baby. They'll stroke your head, and you'll sleep in their arms, in bliss.'

"'I wish it would be so,' the boy said.

"'It will be so,' Father Michele answered, and he repeated it again and again, 'It will be so, it will be so,' until the boy died.

"Afterward, when he was clean, I approached Father Michele and asked if he believed what he had said. 'No,' he told me, 'but I was praying to God to make it that way.'

"'Aren't you supposed to shut up and expect certain things—blackness if you're an atheist; overwhelming light if you believe?'

"'I suppose one is,' he answered, 'but I took the risk of telling God to His face that He had faltered in the design, that the boy who died today was not in need of splendor, but only of his mother and father. Perhaps I'm a heretic, but I'll deal with that after the war.'

"I found him. It was easy. The Church always seems to know where its priests are, even when they're traveling. He remembered me. His hair had turned almost all gray, but he still had his kindly, hesitant manner.

"I told him the truth, exactly what had happened.

"'The child was conceived out of wedlock,' he said, 'but the child's father was supposed to have been killed in the war. If you marry the mother now, you can adopt him. Then we will "discover" that he is not merely your adopted son, but your natural-born son. So, he *was* your son, he *is* your son, he *will be* your son, you will have married his mother, you will have returned from the dead,' he said, counting on his fingers. 'What more can you want? Five out of six. I have no more fingers on this hand.'

"'I don't want him to suffer illegitimacy,' I said.

"'He won't.'

"'Why?'

"'I'll take care of it.'

"'How?'

"'I don't know, but I will.'

"And he did."

"How?" Nicolò asked.

"He argued for a dispensation, and he got it. The Church made many an exception during the war, and after. The whole world was shattered and I suppose the Pope was trying to put it back together."

"So you married her."

"Of course I married her. Remember what I told you about red on the bride's cheek? I was speaking from experience. She wore a very simple wedding dress; we could afford nothing more. The ring was so thin that it looked like wire. She had no other jewelry, but her hair crowned her face, and through the front of the dress you could see the top of her chest, which was always so beautiful, especially when she blushed. Underneath the satin lace, it looked like a bed of roses.

"Just to think about her makes me happy. When I die, no one will think about her ever again, which is why I've been holding on. On the other hand, if they've all gone somewhere, should I not be delighted to join them, even if it means nothing except to be extinguished? At least I'll have the knowledge, as I slip into the dark, that I'm following, and that I have been loyal in my affections."

"Did you sleep with her?" Nicolò asked.

Alessandro looked at him in disbelief. "Of course I slept with her! She was my wife! I was married to her for thirty-three years!"

"What was it like?"

"You must really be desperate," Alessandro said.

"No," Nicolò protested unconvincingly.

"I should shoot you for asking such a question."

"You have a gun?"

"No, I don't have a gun, but surely you don't expect me to tell you about a private matter like that."

"Why not? You loved her. You said she was beautiful. You talked all around it. Why not?"

Alessandro thought. "All right," he said. "Why not? It's all up-welling to the surface anyway, and if I don't tell you it will vanish with me, into the air, like smoke, whereas, if I tell you, it won't. Perhaps she would be pleased.

"When I was young, I was a good rower, I rode horses, I climbed, I fenced, I was as fit as a leopard. Once, in Bologna, I had an affair with a woman who worked in the library. We lived in the same building, so I would nod to her when I passed the acquisitions desk, or when I met her at the door in the hallway. I won't tell you her name."

"She must be seventy years old!"

"That's not the end of the world. She's probably closer to eighty. She has a memory, don't you think? Anyway, I never associated her with sex or physical desire, although she was pretty enough, and I suppose no one else did, either. I never saw her with another person, and she was always very busy, and always modestly dressed, even in summer. You could hardly tell she was a woman.

"One night in July I was coming down from the roof, where I had gone to sleep because it was so hot in my rooms. At about four in the morning, ash and cinders had begun to rain down on me, probably from a blacksmith's shop where they were trying to get their work done and fires out before midday.

"As I lurched down the stairs, dressed only in rowing shorts, carrying a cotton blanket and a sheet, her door opened about a finger-length. I stopped to peer into the darkness, and as I did, the door swung open fully, revealing this woman, with her hair down, her glasses off, her face flushed, and her eyes narrowed."

Nicolò's eyes were dancing like glowworms.

"Maybe I shouldn't tell you this," Alessandro said.

"Oh come on!" Nicolò almost screamed.

"It's just by way of illustration. I'm not going to be lewd, not on the day I die."

"Illustrate! Illustrate!" the boy said.

"She was wearing a cotton thing—I never know what to call women's clothing—that had no sleeves, and came up only to just under her arms and down to the top of her thighs. It was supposed to be held up with a string, but the string was untied and its two ends were between her breasts. The only thing that kept the garment from sliding to the floor was the fact that her nipples were stiff and erect."

"What did you do?" Nicolò asked, hardly able to breathe.

"What did I do?" Alessandro echoed contemptuously. "That's the stupidest question I ever heard in my life. I threw myself upon her and she devoured me with every part of her body that could move or be moved. Though it was extraordinarily pleasurable, I felt like a downed wildebeest set upon by a pride of lions. She was everywhere at once. Every touch, at first only for her, and then for me, put out ten aggravating fires but started fifteen more. She may have worked in the library but she loosed everything upon me in pitchers-full, with moaning, hyperventilation, finger sucking, and all that.

"Every night for a month. Then I went to the mountains, and when I returned she was gone. I never saw her again.

"I tell you this only by way of illustration."

"Of course. Was it like that with Ariane?"

"No. The library woman, whom I have always remembered as a *succubus...*"

"What the hell is that?" Nicolò asked.

"It's Latin. Look it up. She had me stand on her bed one evening, naked. Then she walked around the bed, with her eyes riveted on me, and she exploded again.

"I could be regarded that way only by a woman slightly akilter in the heat of July, but her adoration opened channels in me, and in her, that were—how shall I say it—quite wide and quite deep.

"I adored Ariane with the same excitement, but with much greater conviction. Of course, we lived in special circumstances. We thought we had lost one another, and when we found that we had not, we were able to be entirely free. I think it takes some terrible or great event to fuse two people together without inhibition. Without heat or shock, it can't be done. I believe that's why sexual love, which needn't be, is so intensely intertwined with sin.

"When Ariane—the woman whom I have loved nearly all my life—and I made love, we reversed the common expectation. Usually, you see, there's a lot of motion over a very short time, but we hardly moved at all, and it went on for hours. We held together, amazed, locked like cats. And though we would hardly move, we would sweat, flesh to flesh, and our engagement was so tight, stiff, and exhausting that it was hallucinatory.

"She had beautiful, perfectly shaped, glacially white teeth, and when they were wet with saliva they glistened, and I thought of them as the gate to her soul. I kissed them, and I kissed them, and I kissed them. I loved her."

"I've never touched a woman," Nicolò said, in deep despair.

"You will. It'll take you years to learn what to do—not because it's a matter of technique, but precisely because it isn't. It's a matter of deep understanding, and of love. Nowadays, people have a problem with sex, I think. Popular culture is obsessed with it. It has become almost a sickness. It never was when I was a boy, and when I was in my prime.

"Everyone seems to have forgotten that sexual love exists for two purposes," he said, "to unite a man and a woman, and, therefore, to make babies. If you don't understand this, your pleasure will be merely superficial."

"That's what the Pope says!" Nicolò stated with the urgency of a pheasant leaping from cover. "That's *exactly* what the Pope says."

"And he's right, though how he knows is anyone's guess. Why do you think priests are celibate? Yes, yes. To devote themselves to God, but what does that mean? It means that they don't have to choose between God and family. It means that, at the end, they're free to go to glory and beams of light and all that—because, you see, if they had a wife and children, all the ecstasy and beams of light would not be enough."

"You're really an old guy, aren't you?"

"I am. You, on the other hand, are modern. You are at the very top of the hill of history, looking back and down. You see old people like me in outlandish clothes, moving stiffly and stupidly, and you, you can do immortal cartwheels. I remember that. I remember the pleasure that came purely from the enjoyment of moving my limbs—like an electric current, a happy electric current."

"Yeah."

"But what will you look like to the generations that will supersede you? For one, they won't be able to tell the difference between you and me. We'll be the same, we, who are so modern, the culmination of all human graces, we, who wear glass crystals in frames resting in front of our eyes, whose teeth are inlaid with gold and silver, whose skin is painted with pictures of beasts and ships, who wear coats of animal skin and fleece, and walk about with our feet wrapped in the scraped hide of cows; we, who blow ourselves up with grenades and bombs, and carry lit tubes of burning leaves so that we may inhale the smoke, who imbibe with rapture the juice of rotted fruit, and then vomit on the street, and who lovingly eat live molluscs, raw meat, and old goat's milk riddled with mold."

"You're just jealous."

"Maybe."

"I never met a guy who agrees with the Pope about sex."

"Not a hundred percent."

"How many?"

"Seventy-five."

"You believe seventy-five things?"

Realizing that Nicolò had no understanding of percentages, Alessandro said, "Yes, I do."

"You expect me to believe them, too."

"I don't care. It's up to you. I have my own problems."

"But usually old guys like you want everyone else to believe what they do—and watch out if you don't."

"The dumb ones, the ones who have burnt out."

"What about priests?"

"It's their job, like making propellers, or cleaning steeples. A job always conquers your reticence. And the best ones, like Father Michele, never seem to care about how you think—although they really do, but they leave it to you."

"So you don't care what I do?"

Alessandro threw his hands up. "I hope the best for you. You'll have to make a thousand correct decisions and weather ten thousand mistakes, but I won't be there. I wasn't there even for my son."

"He was your only son?"

"Yes."

THE SUN cleared the eastern ridges of the Apennines, having pushed a crescent of itself over the inflamed hills as if to begin its white barrage from a firing slit. Alessandro squinted at it, having saved his eyes all his life to see now that its surface was like a pocket in the waves under a high wind, swirling in contradiction and counterpoint within an arc as luminous and clear as crystal. It ascended in perfect containment, its detonations noiseless, its fires compressed, and it floated over the mountains, flooding them with light.

"I realize only now that I have been cold," Alessandro said as the sun's heat warmed him. "Have you ever wondered what the stars would be like up close?" he asked Nicolò. "They would be like this," he said, shielding his eyes, finally, with his hand. "As you reached them and you sailed by, they would flare and burn, their gases in tumult like the pool under the piston of Niagara.

"The sun is what starts Rome in the morning. The sun pushes the buses out of their garages, unfurls the sails of boats, and opens the office doors. It puts all those little cars on the highways, their engines yammering like uncontrollable bowels. I hate cars, I've always hated cars. They're ugly. They're ugly, anyway, compared to a horse, which is beautiful. They make the air wavy and dirty with their exhausts, and now the whole city rumbles when once it was silent enough for the wind to be heard in the trees."

"You sound like Orfeo," Nicolò told him.

"No. I've adjusted to the way things are, but I've never forgotten the way they were. He, the little maniac, never adjusted to the way things were, but he forgot entirely the way they had been. He was foolish not to have fallen in love with the typewriter. Someday, the typewriter will be obsolete, antique. He should have known that.

"When I was a boy, most of the country around Rome was good for hunting. You could ride to the sea through forests and fields, and never see a road. The fields were deep green, and, where ditches cut through them, or a riverbank was exposed, the red was very rich.

"Two months ago, in June, I took an afternoon walk and continued on into the night."

"Oh! You do that?"

Alessandro smiled. "I guess I do. At four in the morning I crossed the new ring road they're cutting around Rome. Men were working under banks of electric lights. As their machines roared, they seemed possessed, like squadrons of infantry pressed beyond endurance, running on will and fear. They clenched their teeth as they attacked a hill. They blasted and cut, and before they got down to the chalk that filled the air with dust and smoke they had to cross-section a clay bank. There, as the machines whined, I saw the same color red that I had known when the land now a highway was a long alley of pheasants in golden brush.

"If you cut into a limb of the modern world, the blood is the same. I had seen that on the Isonzo, but the lesson was late in coming."

"But what about your son?"

"When I was in training, before I knew what it was going to be like, even though I had read of the carnage in France—you simply cannot understand until you face it yourself—they marched us to a theater in Lucca, half a day from camp...."

"Signore..."

"We thought the march was a field exercise or part of our physical training. They never tell you anything. They're like God. You learn to live in mystery and anger.

"We carried half packs and bayoneted rifles. I don't recall the organization of the training cadres, but we were about two thousand men. Rain threatened all morning, and now and then a huge dusty drop would smack you in the face, but the sky didn't break until after we got to the theater.

"Half of us marched in, and the other half was drawn up into ranks out front. The theater had just been remodeled, and the architects wanted to test the acoustics. For this they needed bodies, and the military analogy must have struck them, as indeed it should have.

"As soon as we had taken our seats we had our first view of war—an argument of epic proportion between the stage manager and architects on one side, and our major on the other. The civilians were unhappy that their test, for which they had positioned all kinds of meters and cones to measure and absorb the sound, would be biased by the forest of bayonets that shot upward from the seats.

"Two acoustics idiots made the mistake of attacking and insulting the major in front of half his men. He could not possibly back down. 'Unsheathe bayonets!' he screamed out to us. The sheaths came off, truly, in a flash. The noise was chilling, and the smell of gun oil immediately filled the air.

"I remember the expression of the two idiots. They, like everyone else in the world, hadn't realized what they were up against, and they also didn't know that our major was having fun. 'First and Second Battalions, *Fanteria,* stand.' We stood, in unison. In unison, the seats sprang back. 'Ready!' he barked. Our rifles were raised to our shoulders. 'Aim!' he shouted.

"We aimed at the two acoustics idiots. We hadn't loaded, but they didn't know anything. The major looked at them and said, 'Please be so kind as to present the full body of your concessions and apologies,' and when they had, the major ordered us to remove the bayonets.

"With peace restored, they began to test. The theater grew dark, the curtain lifted, and though the stage was empty, the lights, in all their marvelous and exciting colors, rose into an expectant glow, and into the circle they made came a young woman. A murmur arose among the thousand recruits. Most audiences at the opera are not armed, and they have not been deprived of femininity for months on end. She was as nervous as a candle in hell, but then the orchestra began to play, and she sang.

"A huge *Ah!* came from the soldiers—I myself said it—when we realized that she was singing the *'Addio del passato'* from *La Traviata,* a song about a woman who looks back upon a past that has vanished, and begs God for His mercy.

"She sang beautifully, or perhaps she didn't, but it was the most beautiful singing I had ever heard. She looked out upon us, and I think that she, too, was moved. Then it began to rain. We could hear the wind and the rain on the roof high above, and occasional thunder, like artillery, echoing among the hills of Lucca.

"In the storm, her singing grew more and more beautiful. At

every second repetition, a company would leave, and another would come in from the outside. Those who had been standing in the rain were so cold that they trembled. The ones who left had an air of hopelessness. It touched her. It must have.

"And then she had to rest, and they brought out a tenor, who sang the 'Parigi.' That was inimitably beautiful, and we, who were as hard as rock and inured to simulations of despair, sat in the darkness and cried. The two singers knew that many of us would soon be killed, and their singing came from the heart. I still hear it. I can summon it. I still hear the rain on the roof. Oh, at times you could hardly hear the rain, but it was there."

"Signore," Nicolò said. "Before I go, if I go . . ."

"In a great aria," Alessandro went on, as if he had not heard Nicolò, and perhaps he had not, "purity and perfection of form are joined to the commanding frailty of a human soul, and when those elements are knit, an arresting battle follows. Once, on the Cima Rossa, I saw an eagle dive at great speed into a group of birds that had been circling around the mountain. The eagle was in command of the forces that can put you in thrall enough for you to forget and relinquish life; the birds were the life that, despite its weakness and vulnerability, or perhaps because of it, rose above the perfections arrayed against it. Watching the eagle destroy the pack of birds, I hardly breathed. To one who lived with violence and death, it was especially poignant to see them assailed, but I had the sense that the meaning of it did not stop there, that of this battle something would come other than suffering. I still suspect it, I still sense it, I still want it, and still I have not seen it. But, think, if darkness did not exist, how would you know light? You wouldn't."

"Your son," Nicolò interrupted.

Alessandro drew himself up and tilted his head back so as to see a sky that was now too full of early morning light to be blue. Then he dropped his head upon his bent fingers and bent wrist, and pressed his forehead so hard that it whitened. His slow and deliberate breathing sounded like the contented breathing of deep sleep.

He opened his left eye, just his left eye, and looked at Nicolò askance. He lifted his head. The white mark began to redden to the color of the red ring around it. For the first time that Nicolò could remember, Alessandro looked bitter, twisted, and angry.

"My son was killed in Libya in nineteen forty-two," Alessandro said, "when he was twenty-three years of age."

"How was he killed?"

"I don't know. He was a machine-gunner, and at first he was listed as missing. In view of my own experiences and the conduct of the war, I knew that he might have been captured.

"The British tore our divisions to pieces. Had it not been for the Afrika Korps it would have been over very quickly, but with the Germans stiffening us we had the opportunity to lose many more men. The Germans kill and die for principles of order. To them, these have more force and appeal than life itself. Such frenzies completely puzzle us, and we don't know what to do when faced with them. It was in the desert, in nineteen forty-two, and I don't know how he was killed.

"We didn't admit that he was dead, until several years after the war, when all the prisoners had come home: even those, the ones with the whitened lips, from Russia. We didn't admit it until we went to the battlefield itself. A British officer took us through the mines. He said that no one was recognizable, and that we would find only bones that had been picked clean and scattered in fights between vultures and dogs. We said we wanted to go anyway. We wanted to see. He had been our only child.

"Anyone who might have seen what had happened to Paolo had most likely been killed himself, and the men in his company—they moved across the sand in companies—who were left to tell the tale of the battle in which he was killed, hadn't been anywhere near him.

"The battlefield was what you would expect: sand, metal, and bones. They brought the bones home, eventually, and buried them all together. We had touched some, in looking for identification tags. Ariane held her fingers to her breast for days thereafter, thinking that she might have touched our son. On the way in, the half-track in which we were riding drove over something that a few years before had been a man. The officer was kind: he apologized again and again, and we passed across the rocky ground without even blinking. All the time, I was unable to rid myself of the thought that this was the last place my son had ever seen, and, because the battle had been at night, the passionless landscape, with nothing soft, and nothing green, had been lit only by flashes and reflections in the smoke. I was familiar with the sounds and patterns of light that he had seen, and so was Ariane, even if only from a distance.

"She and I understood after the First War, certainly, that life is a series of intervals, each complected differently. We had known that our happiness would end, but we had not thought that it would be totally destroyed, as if in vengeance."

"Was he drafted, or did he volunteer?" Nicolò asked, for he was approaching military age himself.

"He was called up. As early as thirty-seven I wanted him to go to America and stay with Luciana, and he almost did. We had a hundred arguments that lasted half the night. I marshaled everything I knew, but though he had little from direct experience, he could argue as well as I could, or better, and in the end I was unable to convince him. I could not adequately convert the arguments of experience into arguments of principle, and he, lacking experience, didn't understand the only language with which I could have convinced him. Besides, he knew about me. I had tried, as every sensible father does, to keep these things from him, but he found out by indirection. He had my example to follow, and my example consistently undercut my words.

"I had thought that, despite everything else, I had at least survived the war, but I hadn't. Death was in me, like a seed, and after a time it blossomed even more cruelly than for Guariglia.

"I remember the arguments. I sat down. He paced. He wouldn't tire even at two in the morning. He gesticulated with his hands, and spoke brilliantly. He was an anti-fascist, and he thought he would have less authority and appeal after the war, no matter what the outcome, had he not suffered through it with the rest of his generation. He was right, of course, but I maintained that the risk wasn't worth it. He maintained that it was. All life is risk, he said, and how could I argue with that except to impeach the word *all?*

"I told him, one by one, of those I knew who had taken the risk and lost. I was very specific, as I have been with you, and it moved him. He was a good boy, selfless and idealistic, as one is at that age. He was so touched by what I told him that, goddamn it, he wanted to honor them by putting himself in the same place, by sharing their risk and, should it come to him, their fate. And he did.

"I loved him from the first moment I saw him, at the edge of the fountain in the Villa Borghese, to the last, when we embraced at the door, and he turned to walk down the street, a duffle bag carried effortlessly on his shoulder. I know he wanted me to think he was carrying it effortlessly. I had done exactly the same for my own father.

"But there was a difference. Before he crossed over to North Africa he discovered that his wife was pregnant. Had he been able to attend the birth of his child, to spend a few days holding her, caring for her, he would not have gone had the choice been his. All his idealism would have withered in the face of the baby's raw cry, but he didn't know. . . ."

Alessandro turned to Nicolò. "Which do you think I prefer, to live and keep all these memories alive, even though they're a poor substitute for life itself, or to die and chance that perhaps, in some way that I cannot fathom, by some miracle, unlikely though it may be, I'll join them?"

"To live," Nicolò said. He had once sold things on the street, and he could weigh a simple proposition.

"I've agreed during all these years, for that is precisely what I've done, but with death on its way, even if not today, or tomorrow, or this year, the choice is not really mine, and I'm awakening to the fact that I may not have chosen well. Perhaps my judgment is too much clouded by fear and too little enlivened by faith and trust.

"All my life I've seen life and death in alternation, with one springing up after the other, and both arising when you least expect them. If no reason exists to believe that life will assert itself after death, how can you explain its original and inexplicable assertion?"

"Me?"

"Yes, you. You came to life. It was no more logical or explicable than if, after you die, you find yet another surprise that is illogical and inexplicable."

"You think so?" Nicolò asked, hoping that Alessandro was actually figuring it out, and would be able to answer his own question right in front of him, right there, for, after all, Alessandro was old, and Nicolò thought he could see over the rim.

"I don't know, but I think it is appropriate for me to decide how to die: not to take control that I will immediately relinquish, but to unify my life, to give it an artful shape, to affirm at the last that everything is not merely haphazard, to honor what I believe, and, perhaps for one last time, even should it mean nothing, to express my love.

"Nicolò, as much as I have enjoyed walking with you on the road to Monte Prato, as much as your vitality bled into me and rattled awake the part of my soul that was going to sleep, that is something I can do only alone. I'm tired, and the sun is rising."

"You want me to leave?" Nicolò asked.

Alessandro slowly shook his head from side to side.

"Then I'll stay."

"No."

"Why not?"

Alessandro smiled.

"All right, I'll leave," Nicolò said. He didn't want to leave, not so much because he thought that Alessandro might need him, but rather because he could not imagine that he would be happy on the road by himself, apart not merely from the old man but from the old man's story, although that he could carry with him. Nonetheless, he wanted it to continue. Though he knew that before he understood Alessandro's life he would have to live much more of his own, he knew as well that Alessandro had done something marvelous: he had kept his love alive despite everything that had happened, and this was something from which Nicolò did not want to tear himself away.

He imagined himself back on the road, retracing some of their steps and then veering off on his own. Though it would be in the heat of the day, it would be cold and quiet. "What will happen?" he asked.

"To whom?"

"To you. To me."

"That's simple," Alessandro said. "I'll die and you'll grow up. You aren't deterred by anything I've told you, are you?"

"No."

"I thought not. You undoubtedly long for the pain of the world with the same intensity that you desire to love a woman."

Nicolò made a gesture of pleasurable agreement. It was true.

"As it unfolds, you may not be so unambivalent, but you're right to want it with a passion. If you didn't now, you'd never last through it."

"I don't quite understand," Nicolò said.

"You will. I think you're awakening as much as I am. I think that when you made up your mind to catch the bus, even though it wanted to leave you behind, you lit a number of fuses that are sparkling on their way."

"Signore, this may seem funny, but I want to do something for all the people in the time of which you spoke. I want to very much, but I can't, can I."

"But you can. It's simple. You can do something just, and that is to remember them. Remember them. To think of them in their flesh, not as abstractions. To make no generalizations of war or peace that override their souls. To draw no lessons of history on their behalf. Their history is over. Remember them, just remember them—in their millions—for they were not history, they were only men, women, and children. Recall them, if you can, with affection, and recall them, if you can, with love. That is all you need to do in regard to them, and all they ask."

As Nicolò gathered his few things in preparation for leaving, he was overcome by emotion. Even at his age, working in the propeller factory, now and then, he cried, and his father took him in his arms, like a little boy. He was surprised by how quickly it happened, and how natural it seemed, and that his father was always inexplicably grateful when it did happen. So he was unable, though he tried, to avoid it. He held back his tears as long as he could, and then, when he could no longer, he no longer did.

Alessandro looked at him with understanding. "Nicolò," he said. "You're a good boy, you're a very good boy. I would like to take you in my arms the way I used to hold my son, but I can't. That's for your father to do. And, as for me, it's something that I knew, many years ago, I could never do again."

"I understand, Signore. I understand," Nicolò said, drawing his hand across his face, slowly recovering, until he stood up, and breathed a sigh in relief, and cleared his throat. The storm that had passed over him was very quick, and now he felt calm.

"Is it that I just leave you here?" he asked.

"Don't worry about me," Alessandro told him. "Don't worry."

"All right," Nicolò answered, swinging up Alessandro's briefcase by its straps.

"That's mine, but you can have it if you want."

Nicolò said, "I forgot," and put it down.

Alessandro struggled to rise.

"Don't get up, don't get up," Nicolò said.

"It's all right," Alessandro told him. "I'm going to leave this place and start down the hill, where there's more sun." He rose with great difficulty, and then he stood, swaying back and forth just enough for Nicolò to see.

Nicolò stepped toward him, and they embraced. "Don't lose your way," Alessandro said.

WHAT REMAINED to him was the simplest thing in the world. Though he struggled at every step as he pushed through the brush to the open, Alessandro felt a wave of contentment, for at last he was approaching the gate about which he had wondered and speculated all his life, and what had once been speculation was becoming, miraculously, an aria, and he was buoyed by resonant singing. He assumed that it had come purely from memory, and he was shaken by the fullness and clarity of the sound. He had always found in singing a momentary escape from the burdens of mortality, and now he was not surprised, as he prepared to rise or fall, perhaps to be gathered in upon streams of sparkling velocity, to hear intersecting voices so lilting, resonant, and beautiful that upon them all the difficult past was effortlessly lifted like a boat in a lock.

Even were it not the simple and beautiful song he had wished for all his life, it was beautiful, and to this music he pushed through the pine and laurel, breaking so many dry branches that he sounded like a fire crackling in the brush. A man who had once risen thousands of meters on vertical cliffs as smooth as building-stone struggled to descend on ledges and steps no higher than his knee. The air was filled with the scent of the fragrant leaves and needles that he crushed: the fumes rose and fell in currents that swept over the hillside in many confusing directions.

When Alessandro broke into the clear, he was breathing as if he had been in a race, and his breathing went perfectly well with the little explosions he felt in his heart, the not entirely unpleasant soft and hollow pounding, and the astonishing moments, followed by an ecstatic weightless feeling, when the heart seemed actually to have stopped.

Holding his cane by the middle and the top, like a canoe paddle, he sat down. His fingers were blanched because he was not getting enough oxygen, but he hardly needed to look at his fingers to know that this was so. He was so weary that things came, thoughts arose, and images appeared, in torrents, in whirlwinds that tore the air of memory as if it were the rattling foliage on the hillside. And he thought, let me rest a moment from my dying, so that I may see where I am.

He was on a hillside. It was as simple as that. He might find himself there at evening, rested and still alive, waving his cane to get the attention of a farmer who would help him back to the road. And it was possible, too, that his heart would recover and he would be able to continue on down the hill, and back up again.

Once, in the Alto Adige, he had descended into the Valley of the Talvera, dropping in less than half a day from the high snow-covered ridges to the banks of the river itself, which, though it ran cold from the glacial streams that poured into it, ran through a sward of dense greenery that might have clutched the banks of the River Po. The heat had made the soldiers strip off their jackets and wool shirts, and they sweated under their packs as if it had been summer. The sun shone, the road was dusty, and they went down on the palms of their hands on flat boulders in ice-cold water and drank from the river. On the hillside in the Apennines, Alessandro remembered the sound of their rifles clattering against the rock, and the sound of the river rushing by as if it were falling without friction into an abyss. The only thing that could be heard as it decompressed over the edge was a hiss.

In the Valley of the Talvera, ruined stone houses and overgrown gardens were the refuge of men and women who looked at the passing soldiers with hollow eyes. Here the sun shone only at midday. Hardly anyone ever came, for the bridges were far away, and to descend to the riverside at this point it was necessary to break through brush that had grown freely since the beginning of time. Who were they, then? They seemed to have had no language. The men were haggard, unshaven, and hungry. They made the soldiers nervous about passing through, for the soldiers shined their boots, polished their buckles, and washed their faces in the snow, which was all part of keeping oneself proud and keeping oneself alive.

Had they been deserters they wouldn't have come out to look at the marching column. Had they been farmers, they would have had a different air, and they would have had farms. It remained a mystery, and after the column found a half-doomed bridge and crossed on broken beams and hanging ropes that swayed over the rapids, Alessandro and the others made their way up to the clear air and sunshine, away from the river that had fallen as if into the underworld.

This valley in the Apennines was entirely different. It was broad at the bottom, and where once a river might have been were fields of grain. At higher levels were grape vines on aged trellises, and higher still, on the saddle of the hill, near the village, olive groves. All of it was arranged in clearings and closes by serpentine runs of brush and low trees that filled creases and ravines in which hundreds of thousands of swallows had taken refuge. The dawn had awakened them, and the sound of their singing filled the valley— this was the base material that Alessandro's long memory had refined into song—but they hadn't yet lifted from their perches and roosts, they hadn't yet risen on the tide of daylight that was soon to sweep through morning.

Perhaps he could go down the hill slowly, cross the fields, and then climb up again, timing his steps, as his father had done, so long before, in ascending to his office. If he reached the village they would say that, like many an old man who lives in memory and must grapple with the present, he had lost his way and had wandered aimlessly in the hills. Perhaps he had no reason anymore for falling or rising, and would do better on the hillside—if not at the crest, then at least high enough to view the beautiful things that are so elusive up close.

He didn't need to gather his thoughts: they were gathering as if in a storm, like leaves, or birds, driven forward on the wind. Though the pace was rapid and the images and memories flashed by like all the notes from the many instruments and many voices that flow into the ocean of an opera, he felt the elements conjoin, for they were beginning to flow together in one stream.

He closed his eyes and saw the Isarco and the Adige after the spring snowmelt, glittering with little onward-rushing waves, descending strongly with the theme and purpose of a single force. Though the waters were brought in on long stretches of silver river and white cascades that flew in all directions, they combined in a beautiful downward run that would take them to the sea.

In an astonishingly short time, for reasons he couldn't discern but could feel, he was washed clean of the petty shame and embarrassments of a lifetime. He smiled when he saw himself, shortly after the March on Rome, in his darkened study, pistol in hand, ready to defend against intruders that he was sure he had heard. Before he could turn on a light, a tremendous thud came from his right, on high. He fired three tight well placed shots, each from a different position as he sidestepped to remove himself from the tell-tale flash at the tip of the barrel. After the ringing in his ears subsided he listened for breathing or the flow of blood. When he'd brought light to the room, Ariane arrived with Paolo sobbing in her arms, and the police were rushing fearfully to the scene. The sound of intruders had been a row of books that had fallen, and Alessandro had brought his military skills to bear in the execution of a textbook of physics. The first shot had struck the binding and flipped the book face out, and the subsequent two had bolted it to the wall. The police made him tell the tale twenty times over, and didn't believe that he had shot so well in the dark, but he had done much more accurate shooting in places that were far darker.

His heart rose in remembrance of the childish enthusiasms he'd had as a small boy—the songs he was not afraid to sing in the presence of adults he hardly knew, the way he had skipped and danced on the street, unselfconsciously—for these brought him to his own child. Even as he had watched him, with great love, as he had done the same, Alessandro had not been able to leave his own discomfort behind, but now his shame dropped away. He remembered when, once, from pure happiness, he had danced on the street in front of his house. A passing adult had called out, "Look at that crazy kid!" and for years Alessandro had flushed in embarrassment at the thought of these words and the laughter that had followed them. But now he was able to cleanse himself of shame and embarrassment because he realized that shame and embarrassment are the result of being thrown back upon oneself, alone, and that they are tests of grace and forgiveness, the stripping away of pride, and the momentary death of vanity, like a clearing in dense woods, or the eye of a storm.

Gone were the embarrassments, and in their place was love; love for the children, including himself, who had skipped like lambs; love for all who were awkward; and love for all who had failed. The stream flowed on, gathering strength, dancing through landscapes and falling through towns; all on its way to the sea.

As much as scenes from his own life, he remembered the paintings to which he had been devoted. To imagine them in their full color, mixed and flowing, the one into the other, was a great gift, for they had taught him how to see. Like music, they touched inexplicably upon the truth; and they were worn and faded with the beauty of trial and age. The painters had painted landscapes, battles, miracles, and the human form. In battle even the expressions of horses were worthy of note. The tense, receptive, otherworldly faces of the soldiers were as real as if the presence of death had washed the canvasses with the glaze of truth. And Raphael, never tiring of angels and infants, painted miracles because his painting was in itself a miracle, and so text followed subject with the levity and grace of the wind.

The aesthetic of the West was bound with the principles of religion, and its religion was bound to the principles of aesthetic. Color, miracle, and song were beautifully intertwined, strong enough, always, to ride out the sins of politics and war, a thread that could not be severed, a standard that could not be thrown down. Alessandro had devoted himself to this above all—even in battle, even in Stella Maris, even in the dark wood where he had left the Milanese—because it was where the truth lay, it was strong and bright, and yet its greatest monuments were constructed for the sake of human sorrow. And finally, and at the end, he had devoted himself to it, to what avail he could not know, because it was so beautiful he could not tear himself away.

All the time that he was thinking these things he was seated on the ground in the bright sunshine, his cane on his lap, his white hair moving in the wind. The ground cover was fragrant and dry, almost as parched and blond as the hills in Sicily. And all the time that he was thinking these things he felt a great warmth and sadness. Just by imagining, without moving his arms, without any pretense of solidity, he felt as if he were holding his wife and his son.

It was mid-morning, and his heart was full, when the swallows rose. They left the trees in a buoyant mass that floated upward like a cloud. They were so great in number, so fast and agile in turning, swooping, and gliding, that it looked as if the sky had burst into black flame, and they brought extraordinary depth and volume to the empty air, transforming its character almost as if it had been suddenly solidified.

A born soldier, Alessandro saw in the corner of his eye something that elicited an ancient response. He turned to concentrate upon the intrusion of a hunter who moved through the olive groves, descending slowly from the right, into the valley that the swallows had filled and from which they had begun to rise to greater and greater heights.

Alessandro turned again to the swallows. Though the sun backlighted them into hallucinatory streaks of silver, he neglected to shield his eyes, and he watched them fill the sky. As the hunter approached the base of the cloud, he made no effort to go quietly or to conceal himself.

Alessandro followed the paths of single swallows in steep arcs rocketing upward or in descent. How quick they were to turn when turning was in order, or to roll and dart through groups of birds fired at them, as if from a cannon, in an exploding star. This they did of their own volition, and they did it again and again.

For Alessandro they were the unification of risk and hope. It is hard to track them in violent winds high in the blue where they seem to disappear into the color itself, but as long as they take their great chances in the air, as long as they swoop in flights that bring them close to death, you cannot tell if, having risen, they will plummet, or, having plummeted, they will rise.

The swallows that were speeding alone in the blue would be far out of range of the gun, but when they dropped down again, the hunter would be there.

These were the birds that Alessandro had seen all his life, nesting in eaves and on ledges, the simple inhabitants of barns and steeples, the ones who tended their young and filled the morning air with swiftness for generation upon generation. He imagined their hearts beating hard as they flew, and he imagined them at rest.

He knew what was going to happen. They would be slaughtered in mid-air, in mid-flight. Their lives would end in a flash. It did not move him, at first, for he had seen far worse, and he was preparing to follow them that very morning. He thought that he would not feel for them, that, being one of them, as it were, he would follow them, without sympathy, to death, the way soldiers do when they are all facing the same fate. But it was not so, for Alessandro burned with the images of those he loved. He threw aside all the great things he knew, he threw aside the ineffable beauties, and the principles of light, and he burned with their memory.

The hunter reached position, and lifted his gun. Two shots rang out in quick succession, and birds began to rain from the air, tumbling and turning as they fell on surprised and broken wing. He reloaded and fired again and again.

The shots punched holes in the sky where dozens of swallows were taken in mid-flight, in groups, in pairs, in whole families that fell. The hunter's aim was true, but, even as they fell, others rose, and continued to rise.

Alessandro did not imagine that he had a choice, for as he watched the slaughter he was moved beyond endurance. He remembered when his infant son had cried for a reason that Alessandro had long forgotten. He had held nothing back. All his heart had been in his cry, and then he had had peace. How beautiful be was when his face was filled with tears.

To the sight of the swallows dying in mid air, Alessandro was finally able to add his own benediction. "Dear God, I beg of you only one thing. Let me join the ones I love. Carry me to them, unite me with them, let me see them, let me touch them." And then it all ran together, like a song.